Michel, Michel

A NOVEL BY

ROBERT LEWIS

Simon and Schuster

NEW YORK

To Piri, my Catholic wife and collaborator

PART ONE

Easter Week–September 1948

1

I T WAS STILL DARK, but from the look of the sky Michel could tell
it was time to get up. Pé was asleep, breathing softly in his bed
across the room. The Nursery was very quiet, but it would not be
long before the alarm went off in Manon's room, and the steps
creaked as Manon went downstairs to let in the earliest mothers and
put on the coffee. She had promised to wake him up when she came
with the tray for Maman Rose. But he needed more time than that.

The housetops across the street were black against the gray sky.
Beyond them was Touville, beyond Touville was France, then the
world, the stars and God. But all that was so big that Michel could
not imagine it to himself. Could God see him now? Yes, even in the
dark. But God Himself was invisible. It was a very great responsibility to know that God was looking at you always, and somehow reassuring too. Through the window Michel stared out at the dark street,
with its pool of light under the lamppost. The glass was very cold.
He breathed against it, and in the mist that formed he traced a cross
with his finger. Holy Thursday, he thought. Excitement rose in him
to think that he was seven, and would have his communion at last.

There was a chill in the air. He dressed quickly, shivering, and
went out, closing the door quietly behind him. The night light on the
stair wall was lit, but it was murky in the corridor. He went downstairs, groped his way into Maman Rose's office, and lit the floor
lamp. Yellow light flooded the rug and his valise lying open with his
things neatly folded in it. His new black suit with the white satin
armband hung on the coat rack. He stroked the satin with his finger-
tips, marveling at how soft and rich it felt.

He knew where Maman Rose kept her official stationery. He
opened the desk drawer and took out a sheet of paper and an envelope. Both had the same words printed on them: CRÈCHE MU-

NICIPALE, PLACE ST. LAZARE, 8, TOUVILLE L'ABBAYE, COTE-DES-ALPES, FRANCE. The paper also had her name on it, off to one side: *Mlle Odette Rose, Directrice.* He hoped Maman Rose would not mind; she flew into a temper when people touched her things. But this was different.

Kneeling on Maman Rose's chair, and squinting in the dim light that reached the top of the desk, he wrote, "Dear Vati, I am going away for retreat. It is for three days, until Easter Sunday." He did not have to think; he had composed the message in his mind during the night, and he only had to write it down. But he took his time, forming each letter carefully. He wanted his father to be proud of him.

By now the sky had lightened, and the Nursery began to stir. Manon came downstairs and stopped at the office door, saying, "Michel? What on earth—?"

"It's me," he said, without looking up. Manon shrugged and went to the rear. Door bolts shot back. Someone was already waiting; Michel heard a little girl's voice, whimpering, and a woman's voice, scolding. Water ran from the kitchen faucet.

"St. Joseph's is not far," Michel wrote. "It is gray with white shutters and there are big trees around it. Please come for me there. If you stand by the gate, I can see you from the front door."

The smell of coffee came to the office. A nurse came out of the gloom and stood in the doorway. It was Mlle Pasquier, wearing a cloak over her white uniform.

"What are you doing up so early?"

"Retreat," Michel explained reluctantly.

Mlle Pasquier grinned at him. "Lots of sins on your conscience?" she said, and went toward the front door, where someone was knocking. Michel stared after her. She was a freethinker, Father Périer had said, she was contaminated by the century. Michel had often watched her, wondering if she knew about hell. The chain bolt of the front door fell with a clank and the lock snapped back. Manon went up the stairs carrying a tray.

Michel bent over the paper again. "I will leave this letter with Pé. He will watch for you. He is a little boy like me." He stopped and studied what he had just written, troubled. Suppose his father came while he was away at retreat, and saw Pé. Wouldn't he think—? No, no, they would tell him. But just to be sure, he made the last period into a comma and added, "but he has black hair."

A little girl came to the door and stood looking at him. Ignoring her, he wrote, "I remember you, Vati. I love you. I will look out the front door. Michel Benedek."

There was a bustle in the hall. Other nurses had come in, and two mothers with their children.

"Stop sniffing. Use your handkerchief."

"They do it on purpose."

It was light now. Michel sealed the envelope, put it in his pocket and went to get his breakfast.

He had a few minutes before they came to take him to St. Joseph's. He stood by the fence, staring through the iron rods at the corner the street made with Place St. Lazare, off to his left. He was nervous and a little frightened at the prospect of leaving home, yet eager to go. All the boys in his form had been looking forward to this moment for months. Two boys had got sick with the excitement and had to be withdrawn. Communion was terribly important. In a little while he would be going. But he had to give his father a last chance.

He let his mind dwell on the memory. In it he is in a dark, smoky place, and he is crying. His father is kneeling beside him, holding him, crying too, and saying, "Michel, Michel." Just the two of them, crying but together.

Then Michel tried to see his father wandering about the world, being a doctor. This was hard to do, because Michel had trouble imagining places like Rome and Istanbul and New York, which were just names to him. But the city didn't matter very much. What counted was being able to see his father in his mind.

When he felt it was time, he made his father close his doctor's bag with a snap and say, "And now, my boy Michel!"

Now his father was looking for him. He was on a train, heading for Touville. Hurry, train! Michel wanted to cry. He had to shut out everything else, and wish. He grasped the iron rods with his hands, and his breath began to come fast. The fence, the street, the ground he was standing on began to slip away from him. He gripped with all his strength, his teeth clenched.

He is standing on a hill, watching the train pass, seeing his father's face at a window. He is in the station at Touville, watching the train pull in. His father gets off. Michel's heart begins to pound. He is here, he is really here! Now his father is entering a taxi. The taxi is moving through the streets, toward the Nursery. "Michel!" his father calls. Michel is almost suffocating. He wants to answer, but cannot. The taxi approaches Place St. Lazare. "Now!" he gasps. "Now, now . . ."

The gate creaked. Michel started and swung around. It was a mother, leading her boy by the hand. She glanced at Michel as she went by, and Michel, drawing a deep, shuddering breath, released his grip on the fence and turned away.

After a while he fished in his pocket for a handkerchief and wiped the sweat from his face. The vision was gone. Inside him there was nothing but a dull ache.

Pé came from the Nursery, wiping his mouth with the back of his hand, and stood beside Michel on the little bare spot where no grass grew. Then he yawned and said, "He's not coming. The nurses said that if he's not back by now—"

Michel turned away. He had heard this many times before. The conversation Pé had overheard had taken place long ago.

"And they said it was a shame, and they shouldn't let you come down here. They said it was cruel. They said—"

"Have you got the letter?" Michel interrupted.

Pé dug in his jacket pocket and pulled out the envelope, rolled and squashed flat.

"Look at that!" Michel said, suddenly angry. "You got it dirty! I should have given it to Manon. I ought to—"

Pé backed away, watching him. "It is not," he said. "It's only folded. He can read it all right. He won't come anyway. If you give it to Manon she'll tell Maman Rose, and if *she* ever finds out you took her special paper . . ."

"I *had* to. So he would know he came to the right place."

Pé licked the envelope and wiped it on his sleeve. "There, it's clean. And you don't have to worry. I won't squeal on you. Even if I did, she wouldn't get mad. Not at you. You're her pet."

"I am not. She loves us all the same."

"That's what she *says,*" Pé said, "but you're the one she's always hugging and kissing. And she sent you to that rich boys' private school, and *I* have to go to the public school. And every time she sees me she thinks I'm up to something—"

"Well, you *are,*" Michel said.

Pé thought that over. "I guess so," he said.

"Besides," Michel said, "you wouldn't like the Jesuits. Do you want to be a priest?"

"Me?" Pé said, rolling his eyes. "Me, a priest? And walk around wearing skirts, like a—? You must be out of your mind. I wouldn't be a priest for a thousand million—"

"Well, then," Michel said.

Pé scratched his head. "Yeah," he said. "Who wants to go to that lousy school? But I wish you went to my school, you could help me with my homework."

The mother who had entered the gate a few minutes before stood on the steps of the Nursery fussing over her boy. She smoothed his hair, settled his cap, and gave him a hug. Then she came down the walk to the gate. Michel and Pé watched her go by.

"My mother used to hug me like that," Pé said.

Michel looked at Pé and then looked away. It made him uncomfortable when his friend talked about his mother. Everybody at the Nursery knew the story, and agreed that it was a disgrace and a shame. Pé's mother didn't want him. She had brought him to the Nursery and told Maman Rose that she was going off with an American soldier. And she said, right in front of Pé, "It's either the street or the Nursery, because I'm going." That was why Pé was so bad, Maman Rose said. He cried at night, and wet his bed, and did mean things, because he couldn't get over it. Michel was very sorry for Pé, especially when Pé pretended that his mother was coming back for him.

"Michel!" Maman Rose was on the steps, calling him.

He went up the walk. Pé followed, whispering, "Say, Michel, suppose she won't let you go? Suppose your father came, and Maman Rose said no, you couldn't go with him?"

Michel stopped. Such an idea had never occurred to him. "She would *have* to!" he said. "He's my father, isn't he?"

"But suppose she won't? You know how she gets sometimes."

Maman Rose made motions to him. He went up the steps, putting out of his mind what Pé had said, but disturbed by it just the same. Maman Rose's face was sad; looking at her, Michel felt his throat tighten and tears start to his eyes. He was going away! He was leaving the Nursery and his Maman Rose. For three whole days and nights! It seemed like an enormous stretch of time. The next instant he was in her arms, and she was murmuring, "My little boy!" He began to blubber.

Maman Rose was also very moved. Her voice was unsteady as she gave him his instructions. He was to pray for all at the Nursery, and a special one for the intention of Father Périer. He was not to forget to brush his teeth. His cough syrup was in one of his slippers, wrapped in a handkerchief. At the slightest sign of a cold . . . If there was difficulty about anything, he was to ask the priests' permission to call home. He knew the telephone number.

He kissed her soft cheek, and turned to go. Félicité followed him with the valise. Pé was wandering about the garden, kicking at the new grass. He waved, and Michel waved back.

The morning was sweet and fresh. Sunlight lay splashed on Place St. Lazare, where the trees were covered with tiny pale green leaves. Michel trotted along at the maid's side, taking three steps to her one. He hoped that Pé would keep watch, as he had promised. Looking ahead to what lay before him, he felt his face glowing.

The boys stood up as Father Roche entered the classroom and walked to the podium. Father Roche bowed his head and said a short prayer. Then he said, "Please be seated." The boys were all very solemn, and nobody whispered. Michel sat very straight. This was the rector himself.

Father Roche was silent a long time, looking at them. Then he began to speak, very slowly. "Dear children," he said, "you have come here to withdraw from the world for a short time, so that you may prepare yourselves for one of the most important moments of your lives. You are young, but you are not so young that you cannot realize the meaning of the step you are about to take. You are about to confirm to God the choice you have already made through your baptism. You are going to commune directly with Him. You are about to become men, with a man's responsibility before the Lord. In later years you will look back to the moment that is now before you, and your hearts will swell with joy to remember this Easter Sunday at St. Joseph's. Many, many years have gone by since I first communed with God, but I have not forgotten, and believe I never will, what I felt in that supreme instant of my childhood. Only last week His Excellency Monseigneur Rebenty said to me, 'Father Roche, I am eighty years old, and in looking back on my long life, I can say that in all those years I have never known a moment of purer, more soul-shaking happiness than that of my first communion.' And do you know what else that venerable, holy man said to me? That he had cried. Yes, dear children, when your bishop was a little boy like you, so long ago, tears of joy poured from his eyes as he kneeled at his first communion. And it was then that he knew he had a vocation."

The room was still. Father Roche clasped his hands. "All year we have prepared for this day. Now there remains only the last step, the days and nights of silence, obedience, humility of soul, meditation. You will put yourselves in God's hands, so that He may ready your souls to be worthy of approaching Him."

His scalp prickling, Michel took a deep breath. It had begun.

Prayers. A sermon. Meditation. Readings from St. Luke and St. Paul. A walk in the cloister . . .

Michel walked with the other boys in the arcade around the quadrangle. As he walked, his mind repeated the rector's words: "Veil of illusion." They seemed to echo in his head. What was the matter with him? He felt very strange, as though these words had touched off something within him, that had gone on growing and swelling until it was ready to burst. Everything seemed bigger and brighter somehow. Full of light. Holy.

It began when Father Roche was talking about the souls in heaven. You could pray to them, he had said. They could see you and hear you, and intercede for you with God. They were up there in the sky, looking down, and—

He knew this, but today for the first time it seemed real to him. The roof went *swoosh!* and there was a wind, or he imagined it, and there were thousands of eyes looking down at him. It was like being naked. Michel shrank into his seat, not daring to look up.

Then Father Roche began talking about reality, and struck the podium with his fist, and all the boys jumped. Did they think *that* was reality? Did they? They were not to confuse reality with materiality. "Blow up the world with atom bombs!" Father Roche cried. "Shatter it into a cloud of dust floating through space! Have you altered reality? Not by a particle! What is reality? Reality is the Word, the eternal kingdom of the spirit, the abode of God. What you see before you, what shortsighted men take to be real, is only a veil of illusion."

That night it was a long time before Michel could fall asleep. And yet he was tired, it had been a long day. When he kneeled for prayers, it was all he could do to lift his head up afterwards. But his mind wouldn't stop. He thought of everything Father Roche had said, and tried to understand it. Reality. God is love. Veil of illusion. And, Why must there be a hell? He shivered, remembering how the rector had cried "Forever!" and the boys' scared faces. His thoughts went round and round, and when he did drop off it was with the feeling that something wonderful and strange was about to happen.

Black Friday. Tenebrae. It was especially holy to stand in the position of Christ on the cross. No bells today. Instead, there were the noisemakers that you spun in circles with their wooden clatter. They were a symbol. A symbol was something that meant something else.

" 'And Pilate again spoke to them, desiring to release Jesus. But they cried again, saying: Crucify him, crucify him. And he said to them the third time: Why, what evil hath this man done? I find no cause of death in him. I will chastise him therefore, and let him go. But they were instant with loud voices, requiring that he might be crucified; and their voices prevailed. And Pilate gave sentence that it should be as they required.' "

Father Roche closed the book. His face was sad. In all the history of man, he said, nothing more terrible than this had ever happened. Could they imagine the awful punishment that lay for all eternity before those who had done it?

Each time he heard the story, Michel was filled with horror. The wicked, wicked Jews! Children of Satan, Father Périer called them. At the Nursery, before he got sick, Father Périer had often talked about it, and waved his hands and recited, "Daughters of Jerusalem, weep not over me; but weep for yourselves, and for your children!" The Jews crucified the Son of God. God was very angry. He burned down their city, drove them out into the desert, and sent Hitler to destroy them. Hitler was bad, Father Périer said, but he had done that one good thing.

Michel was sorry for God, and for what He suffered over His little boy.

Discipline was very strict. But Michel had been watching his chances, and decided that it might be possible during the ten o'clock recess. On Saturday morning, while the boys were crowding into the lavatory, and the priests were talking, Michel slipped away and walked down the corridor that led to the front entrance. No one stopped him. The door was locked, but he could see just as well from the window. He looked out into the street, and saw there was no one there. No one who could be his father. He was not surprised. At the moment of pushing aside the blind he had said to himself, "My father is dead."

His legs suddenly felt weak under him. He sank onto the bench that stood beneath the window and stared down at the flagstone floor. But he had known it all along! As he sat, overwhelmed, his life at the Nursery rose up before him, and he saw himself as though he were another boy, watching and understanding what he had refused to understand before. The strange silences that sometimes fell when he entered rooms where grownups were, and the blank faces that turned to him. The working mothers who left their children and hurried away, and the pitying look that entered their eyes as they passed him. Maman Rose watching him from the office window as he waited by the fence for his father, and the fierce embraces she gave him when he came in. Pé pointing to the dead cat in the gutter, swollen, obscene, its mouth full of flies, and saying, "Your father is like that." He had shouted at Pé, and they had all but had a fight. But why had he become so angry? Wasn't it because he had had the same thought himself and pushed it hurriedly out of his mind?

He had always known his father was dead. If he weren't dead, he would have come for him long ago.

Then why had he continued to wait by the fence? And written the letter that he had left with Pé? Was he crazy?

Walking in a daze, Michel joined the other boys. The priests saw him come, demanded to know where he had been, threatened to report him. Such a thing had never happened before. Michel was too heartsick to care.

But as the day wore on, Michel found a strange excitement building up within him. It was like getting hit in the head, and seeing the whole world go round, and then you shake yourself and everything swims back into place again—but now things are different. Now you've begun to understand things you hadn't understood before, and you can think about them without hurting and turning away. Like death. He hadn't *let* himself think about it before, because if death was like with the cat in the gutter it made no sense, and that was the end of his hopes for his father. And so he had gone on waiting. He knew, but he hadn't understood. Cats didn't have souls, and men did. *That* was it, *that* made all the difference. It meant—he felt himself grow pale as the thought finally stood clear before him—

it meant he had found his father. His father was in heaven, looking down at him. Loving him. Smiling at him for having grown up at last.

The idea left him lightheaded with joy. He sensed that his life had changed. He felt secure and protected. During the rest of the day his thoughts were turned upwards. At odd moments he addressed brief prayers to his father. It was almost like having a real conversation with him.

By bedtime another idea had come to him. He lay on his cot in the dark dormitory, examining this new thing, watching it grow slowly until it was hammering at him and he couldn't think of anything else. Was it possible? he wondered. Had it ever happened before? He tried to remember what he had been taught, but the only example that occurred to him was Jesus Himself, and it frightened him just to think of it. At the same time it filled him with longing. He began to sweat, from being undecided. In the end he didn't dare. When he thought of the distance, it made him dizzy. Suppose he fell?

He started, and found himself sitting up in bed, listening. He must have fallen asleep. Had he been dreaming? No, there it was again, a bell tolling far away. It came from across the river. Now another bell joined in, closer, and then another. Soon there were dozens of bells, and the ringing had become waves of sound. All Touville was echoing to it. Midnight. Easter Sunday. Christ had risen, and the whole world was rejoicing. And Michel knew suddenly that he couldn't put it off. He had to do it. It didn't matter what happened to him afterwards.

The door to the prefect's cubicle was shut and there was no light behind it. The boys slept without stirring. Michel's excitement was like a pain in the chest. He slid to the floor and sank to his knees.

"Vati," he whispered. "Can you see me?"

He knew it wouldn't happen at once. It was like holding on to the fence, wishing. You gripped hard and didn't let your mind think of anything else, because if you could make yourself see it, maybe it would happen. It hadn't worked then because his father wasn't on earth at all. But heaven had to be easier. His father was there, and would help him. God the Father. God his father. This was the secret, Michel knew it now. The two were the same. The voice that said to him, "Michel, Michel" was the same that had said, "Thou art my beloved son: in thee I am well pleased." God the Father was *his* father. His father was God the Father. And that meant he could go to Him, since everything was possible to God.

His eyes were shut tight. He clasped his hands together with all his force. He began to shiver. Vati, help me! It was beginning. Was he floating? He didn't feel anything any more, only that terrible sweetness that was gathering inside him, and that—

His body jerked as though an electric current had passed through it, and he opened his eyes, staring wildly about him. He was on his cot, there was a hand on his shoulder, and the prefect's face was bending over him. What had happened? His head hurt and he could hardly breathe. Had he fallen? "Are you all right, boy?" the prefect whispered. "I found you on the floor." Michel stared up, then turned his head aside. The prefect tucked the blanket firmly under him and went away.

Where had he been? It wasn't a dream, he had been somewhere. And he had seen—what? He didn't know. Something that had left light under his eyelids, like looking at the sun and seeing everything on fire afterwards. And behind this burning thing a—a *form* had begun to stir and take shape, and it was this that he had to reach, because it just *had* to be . . . But he couldn't remember, the images faded and disappeared as he groped after them. All that remained to him was the happiness of having come so close. So close, that if he had been able to stretch out his hand . . .

The organ was playing softly. But when the procession entered the side door, the music stopped and started again with a crash, and the choir joined in. The loudness made Michel's heart jump. It was hard to walk slowly, as they had rehearsed, and to keep his eyes fixed on his folded hands. He stole a look before lowering his eyes again. The chapel was filled with people. Some stood at the sides and back. All were turned toward the side entrance, watching the boys come in. Maman Rose must be there. But he was not supposed to look. He walked, taking small steps. The procession turned down the center aisle. It stopped by the empty benches, and the boys waited. There was the signal. Michel genuflected and slid to his place. The altar was filled with rows of long candles that had flames like moving pencils. And under them were hundreds and hundreds of white flowers, like a carpet. It was very beautiful.

The choir stopped on a high note. Bishop Rebenty appeared beyond the rail. Mass began.

Michel shivered, he felt feverish, but his skin was cold. He was going to try again. But this time it was different. He had been wrong the night before, he had tried too much. After he had thought it over, he had been left more frightened than before. Suppose he had been able to take that last step? And not been able to get back? Sending your soul to heaven and leaving your body behind was like dying. He didn't want to die. It would be easier for his father to come to him. Communion meant communicate, Father Roche had said. And so it was the best time.

The slowness was like a dream. It took ages for the altar boys to cross and return again. They wore white stoles. The bishop's surplice was white too, but with gold threads. The candles were like a wall of fire. Michel stared at them and waited. At length the bishop turned to the congregation.

"Dear brothers in Christ . . ."

It was a long sermon. In the beginning Michel tried to listen. His first communion! he told himself. But the words fell on his ears and ran into each other and faded away. He had better prepare himself for what was coming. He thought of everything he had ever done that he shouldn't have, and in his heart prayed for forgiveness. He wanted to be pure, so pure that God would be willing to—

He was startled when the bell rang out. The bishop was before the altar, raising the cup. He had been daydreaming, the sermon had ended long ago. The moment had stolen up on him, while he was thinking and praying. The bell rang twice more in the silence. Michel was suddenly terribly afraid. First everything was slow, and now it was fast and he wasn't ready. What would God look like? Would He speak? In a moment the bishop would be coming forward with the cup. The palms of Michel's hands were wet. He wiped them on his trousers. Not yet, he prayed. But already the first boys were moving out. Michel's stomach turned over as he slid to the aisle and moved in line toward the railing. There was a rustling sound behind him.

He was on his knees. An old man with a wrinkled face was bending forward, and a hand with a ring on it was moving toward his mouth, and he swallowed, and there were tears streaming down his cheeks. The bishop gave him a queer look and moved on. Inside himself Michel said, Vati!

Then he wasn't afraid any more, and it was all right, and his heart was filled with love.

But no voice answered him. He listened, he waited. On the altar nothing stirred but the candle flames. Everything was as before.

"Now!" he breathed. Now! His eyes darted over the altar and the crucifix beyond. There had to be *something!* The others had risen. He was the only one left. He felt eyes on the back of his neck. With a last despairing look he got up and walked up the aisle.

The mass continued. After the congregation had left, the boys stayed behind to pray. Then they formed a line and filed out to the courtyard as the organ played.

The parents were waiting in the sunshine. They broke up the line, snatching at their boys to embrace them. There was Maman Rose hurrying toward him, crying and laughing at the same time. Renée, smiling, came behind her. But he didn't come! he wanted to protest. Mme Barshowanski saying, "The little angel!" Didn't they understand? Nothing had happened, nothing at all! They were all there, hugging him, kissing him, touching him, shaking his hand. Manon, M. Béjart, Léah, Jean, Pé. Even Cook Annette and Félicité, on the edge of the crowd.

After that there was breakfast in the refectory. The parents talked loudly and laughed a great deal. They all spoke at once, leaning across the tables to hear better. When the meal was over, all stood up as Bishop Rebenty and Father Roche walked out. But the bishop stopped by Michel and gave him his ring to kiss. "This is the boy who cried," he said to Father Roche, who patted Michel on the head.

The collar of his elegant black suit was wet. Michel brushed it with his hand. How cold his tears had become!

2

MICHEL SAT on the stairs with Pé. He had taken off his communion suit for his nap, but now, for the party, he had put it on again, after brushing it carefully. The collar had dried. Pé wore his new suit. Both sat stiffly, watching through the banister those in the reception hall, where the tables had been set up. No one had taken places yet, although Mme Quertsch and Mlle Camélia had turned two chairs with their backs to the large table, and were sitting in them talking while they waited. They would all wait a bit more, Maman Rose said, because it was a long way from Sep for the old one. She said that to Annette, who had come from the kitchen and stood in the passageway looking glum because of the soufflé. And so all waited. At any moment Father Fonsac would appear, and they would take their places under the gay streamers that Mme Barshowanski had hung from the chandelier. The white ones were for purity and the green ones for hope. Maman Rose was lighting the candles, shielding each with her hand until it caught. She laughed with pleasure, holding her head high. She wore the new chartreuse gown that the sewing ladies had exclaimed over when it came from the shop last week, draping it against the light and praising the stitching. Not everybody could get away with that color, they said, but with her hair and her eyes! She looked like a queen, Michel thought.

Mlle Camélia nudged Mme Quertsch, watching Maman Rose, and said in a teasing voice, "Have you won the lottery, Odette?"

"I have, I have," Maman Rose said happily.

Mme Barshowanski and M. Béjart were chatting in the doorway to Maman Rose's office. Across the room, standing by the mantel, M. Joseph was pointing out something on a map to Jean. All looked up, and then turned to smile at Michel.

Maman Rose meant him. He was the lottery. Embarrassed by

their attention, Michel forced himself to smile back, and looked away. He did not feel well. There was a strange heaviness in his limbs, and his eyes were hot and gravelly. It was the crying. He had cried last night, and at the communion this morning; and in his bed later on, when he was supposed to be resting up for the party, he had lain awake listening to the subdued noises from below, while tired, burning tears he could not control welled slowly in his eyes. What had he done wrong? Or failed to do? He kept asking himself that. But when they summoned him, he washed his face with cold water, dressed, and went downstairs. It was his communion party, and he would not think of that other just now.

But you couldn't tell your mind what to think. The guests, on arriving, had made a big fuss over him; called him "communion boy"; lifted him in the air, patted him on the back, put gifts into his hand. Maman Rose had hugged him tight and whispered, "You're all mine now!" and Mme Barshowanski had put the back of her hand to her mouth and turned away, overcome. He should have been proud and moved to be the center of so much attention. Yet he was not. It was all so different from what he had expected. Everything was different, even the faces with which he was so familiar. It was as though he had been away for a long time. He had suffered their embraces, murmured something in reply, and made his escape to the stairs, from where he could observe without being in the midst of things. And inside his mind the word "orphan" took shape and would not go away.

He was an orphan. He had never accepted it before. Ever since he had learned the meaning of the word, he had thought of Pé and Léah as orphans. And Manon, because even though Manon was sixteen and grown up for her age, she had lost her parents as a little girl and had been raised by the Temple Dames, before coming to the Nursery. But he was different, because his father was coming back. Now he knew. His father was dead. Nothing Michel could do would bring him back. He could not go to his father, nor his father come to him. What was he to do now?

Sitting on the stair, he watched through the banister. Maman Rose was gay, she went from one to another of the guests, talking and laughing. She had been that way all morning, ever since the communion. They had walked home from St. Joseph's, forming a little procession that attracted the attention of the passersby in the street; and Maman Rose had stopped to exchange pleasantries with some of them. "My son," she had said, referring to Michel; and her pride in him had been like a radiance in her face.

He was not her son. He knew that. But he also knew of the love that made her use that word; her hunger, so like his own. They were all her "sons" and "daughters," Michel, Pé, Léah, Manon, Renée, Jean, and the others who had grown up and gone. She called them that, but they were not. Maman Rose was unmarried and had no children. And so she took in homeless children and said they were hers. She often joked about it to her friends. She said they were her hobby. Other people collected china or stamps, she collected children. And she said she was the mother of the whole world. But it was not a joke. Feeding and clothing children, and sending them to school, and taking care of them when they were sick was not a joke, especially if you were poor. Michel knew how hard Maman Rose worked to maintain her "family"; the arguments with tradespeople, the putting off of bills, the jealous watch of pantry and linen closet, the mending and making do. He had often wondered what would have happened to him if Maman Rose had not been there to take him in. He had intended to tell his father to be very kind to her. And while he had always known he was going to leave when his father came for him, he would of course come to visit his Maman Rose often, and bring her gifts, and take care of her when she was old.

But that was over now, at least the going-away part. It was like waking up. His dream was gone, and had left a big, aching hollow inside him. Maman Rose was all he had in the world now, and he would be with her always. And so he watched her from the stairs, loving her, conscious of her every movement, seeing her with new eyes.

Below, by the office door, Mme Barshowanski was complaining to M. Béjart. She spoke in indignation, swinging her pince-nez glasses on their black tape. The way the franc was these days! She had had to let her maid go. Her Maxim had been a good eater, she said, but compared to that one! It was worse in Paris than in Touville, she supposed it was because things had to pass through so many hands. M. Béjart listened gravely, fingering the gold chain that hung heavy against his waistcoat, nodding now and then. How distinguished he was! He was a good godfather to have, everybody said, the way things were. The war! they said. The war had ruined France. Michel had seen for himself the shattered house on the way to St. Joseph's, with its wallpaper still hanging in ragged strips from the yellowing plaster. And so it was good to have M. Béjart as godfather. But Michel knew it was not true about the diamond tooth. Annette had said that to Marie the washerwoman in front of Félicité as a tease because Félicité was not very bright. When M. Béjart came for the baptism, Michel and Pé had taken turns watching because M. Béjart was old and serious, but once he laughed and Pé had got a look and told Michel it was not true.

"Oh, my Maxim!" Pé whispered in a whining voice in Michel's ear. Turning, Michel saw that Pé's face was screwed up as if something were pinching his nose. He nudged Pé sharply.

"Ah, she gives me a pain in the neck," Pé whispered in disgust. "Her and her Maxim. Say, Michel, do you remember him?"

Michel hesitated, then nodded. It was not quite true, but when Mme Barshowanski came from Paris, Maman Rose told him to say he remembered her husband, because she would surely ask him, and he was to say yes, he was the man who hid in the cellar. And when Maman Rose said that, Michel did remember vaguely something about a man in the cellar, as though he had dreamed it, or it had belonged to his former world. And so it was almost true.

"I wish she'd go back to Paris," Pé said. "She makes everybody nervous. Annette said that if she puts her foot in her kitchen once more . . ."

"She'll be leaving soon. She just came down for my baptism."

"I know. I had one once, when I was a baby. But I don't remember. Say, Michel, what was the salt for?"

"Well," Michel began. But he wasn't sure. "It's part of it," he said. "You give up the devil and all his works, and the priest puts salt in your mouth. And he baptizes you with the holy water."

"I asked Maman Rose," Pé said, "and she said my mother had it done when I was a baby. I wish I could remember. I don't even know who my godmother is. But I wouldn't want *her*."

Mme Barshowanski had turned and caught Michel's eye. "Little prince!" she exclaimed fondly. Michel and Pé smiled back.

"I've got two," Michel said. "Madame Immermann is my other godmother. But she's in America."

"That's where my mother is," Pé said, turning serious eyes on him.

"I know."

Renée came down the stairs, winking at him as he and Pé moved their knees to let her pass. She had put on the tight blue dress she had copied from *Vogue* magazine, and looked very sophisticated and lovely. She wore her hair short, it was the latest fashion. The wink meant the secret Michel shared with Renée. It was really her secret, but he shared it by promising not to tell. He winked back, remembering the church that Sunday, on whose steps he had waited, cold and bored, while Renée whispered and giggled with her young man. He had been surprised when she said that to Maman Rose about a long sermon. But Michel had promised. Not saying anything was not a lie.

"My, what a grand young lady!" Mme Barshowanski exclaimed, as Renée stepped down. Renée gave a little curtsy, and smiling at the two seated women joined M. Joseph and Jean. They paid no attention to her; M. Joseph's heavy pockmarked face was earnest as he explained something, his finger pointing at the map.

"Politics! The saints preserve us!" Renée cried in dismay.

"Oh, go away," Jean said.

Renée turned away with a little tinkling laugh.

"What do you think, Alain?" Maman Rose said, approaching M. Béjart. "Shall we begin?"

M. Béjart took out his watch.

"When I'm big," Pé said, "I'm going to America to look for her. You'll come with me, won't you, Michel? We'll look for her together. If that soldier tries to stop me, I'll hurt him. And I'll help you look for your father."

He had known Pé was going to say that. How many times had they sworn friendship and made those plans together! He had always agreed, more out of pity than anything else. It was clear to everyone but Pé himself that his mother didn't want him. Now he suddenly saw himself with Pé's eyes, and knew that Pé had never believed in his father either. Michel felt too wretched to answer. He stared down at his black pumps until Pé sighed and looked away.

Maman Rose was at the banister beside him. "Michel, run upstairs and look in on Father Périer, to see if he wants anything. Tell him I'll send Manon up in a little while. Where is she? Manon?"

"Yes, Mademoiselle Rose?" Manon said, coming from the passageway.

"Get a cushion for Léah's chair. And her ribbon's come undone. Hurry now, Michel. What's the matter?" she added, as he stared at her.

"Nothing," he murmured in confusion. In that moment his heart had gone out to her in love. But she had understood; she always understood. She smiled, kissed her fingers and, reaching through the railing, touched them to his cheek.

Michel went up the stairs, glad to be doing something. At each step the unfamiliar long trouser leg rubbed his uplifted knee. M. Béjart always gave a tug at the knees of his trousers before he sat down. It was for that. There was so much he had to learn before he was a man. At the church in Sep, M. Béjart had said, "In we get, old man." But it would be ages before that was so.

The door to Jean's room was ajar. This was where they had put Father Périer when he was taken sick, now that Jean was working at Chambéry. And when Jean came to visit, like now, he took Manon's room, and Manon doubled up with Léah. Michel rapped gently before pushing the door open. The bed was by the window. Sunlight flecked the open curtain and made bright spangles on the coverlet. Father Périer was reclined against propped-up pillows. He turned his head listlessly as Michel entered. He was freshly shaven, his skin was like gray wax. An acrid sick odor filled the room.

Michel approached the bed, trying to put from his mind the image of that spidery tube that had once been taped to the priest's cheek and into his nose, that time the two men brought the heavy metal cylinder with the clocklike dial. Coming down the stairs again, one of the men had said, "Good-bye, mother!" and the other had given a low whistle. And Michel's heart had sunk as he thought, He's going to die. But Father Périer was better, and the head nurse had removed the tube, unsticking the tape with little dabs of ether.

He repeated Maman Rose's message. Father Périer examined him strangely as he spoke. He did not seem to be listening. Michel began again.

"I don't need anything," Father Périer said.

His voice sounded weak and faraway. It was the same voice that had told those wonderful stories from the Bible, but now it came with an effort, as though there were pain behind it. How Michel had looked forward to those evenings with Father Périer! Those long winter evenings, when the day children and their mothers had gone, and so had the nurses and the help, and the Nursery became their private home again; and in Maman Rose's sitting room he and Léah and Pé sat on the rug, listening, while Maman Rose rocked gently, and Renée lay curled on the sofa and Jean sat brooding at her feet, his legs stretched out, his hands in his pockets; and Father Périer, his voice richly strong then, told one story after another, until the flames in the fireplace had become only an ashen glow and the little ormulu clock broke the spell and it was time for bed. Now that was all gone, and if you peered in the door the nurses shooed you away. And even if, rarely, they let you in for a little while, it was not the same as before, it was as though Father Périer scarcely realized you were there. Like this morning, when he came from St. Joseph's in his disappointment, and the old priest made a vague gesture that was meant as a blessing, and turned away, closing his eyes.

For a moment Michel was tempted to blurt out his attempt of the night before, and that of the morning, and to ask what he had done wrong. But great as his urge was, he knew it was not the time. Downstairs they were about to begin, Maman Rose had told him to hurry. Besides, the old man's face was set in an unpleasant grimace.

"Does it hurt?" Michel asked timidly.

"Here," Father Périer said, giving him a queer sidelong look. He tapped his forehead, saying, "Here, here. The other is nothing. But you wouldn't know about that yet."

Was that bitterness in his voice? On a sudden impulse Michel said, "I'll stay with you, if you want."

The priest turned his head and stared at Michel. His hand came up and touched Michel's cheek wonderingly. "Now that's kind of you, Michel. That's truly kind. But you go to your party. Thank you for offering."

But as Michel turned away, the hand, which had dropped, rose again and rested on his arm. Father Périer looked at him for so long that Michel began to feel uncomfortable. Then those sick eyes blinked mistily, and a crooked, tender smile tugged at his lips. "Michel," he said. "Little Michel. We shall not often meet again, in this world. Remember me, pray for me, my boy. I've done the best I could for you. Some day you may know how much that was. And you will thank me for it. And now, run along to your party. I'll be thinking of you. Go now," he added, seeing that Michel did not move.

Michel went slowly to the door. There he heard a whisper, as though the priest had said softly, "If God had wanted . . ." Father Périer was leaning on his elbow, staring after him. The dark hollows under his eyes were wet. Michel stood for a moment looking back, then went out.

Shaken, he went down the stairs, wondering whether Father

Périer had really said that, or he had imagined it.

Father Fonsac had just come in; he stood in the vestibule, while behind him Félicité, grinning with excitement, was shutting the door. And then Maman Rose saw him and cried out, "Here he is now!" The others turned, and Maman Rose came forward scolding, "You wicked old man, we were going to begin without you."

Father Fonsac, contrite, his hand at his chest in the attitude of *mea culpa,* was sorry, truly he was, but something had come up, and he had hoped that they *would* begin without him. Yes, an emergency. Yes, of all days! Michel joined Pé at the foot of the stairs, and received a pinch on the cheek from the old priest.

"He doesn't want anything," Michel whispered, plucking Maman Rose by the sleeve. "But he's got a headache."

"Oh," Maman Rose said, frowning. "This is my brother Joseph," she said to the priest.

Father Fonsac was delighted to meet him. Fancy that, he had known Miss Odette so many years, and had never met her brother. Joseph, was it not? M. Joseph Rose? Ah! M. Joseph ducked his heavy shoulders in an awkward bow, and said it was his pleasure.

"And now, for goodness' sake, let us sit down," Maman Rose said.

Michel sat at the small table against the wall. With him were Pé and Léah, and Manon to keep order. They ate, listening to the conversation at the other table, the long oaken one that had been set up crosswise and covered with Maman Rose's choice linen tablecloth. Maman Rose and M. Béjart sat at the ends, facing each other, and the others in between on both sides of the table, according to the place cards Mme Barshowanski had set up. Paris frills, Maman Rose had said, but Mme Barshowanski had insisted, and painted flowers in watercolor on them herself, and they were very elegant.

They ate hungrily, praising the soufflé. Annette was a good cook, they said. But oh dear, rationing! Mlle Camélia said. She didn't know how Odette managed. At her own nursery—the one on Rue Charente, she told Father Fonsac, who nodded and said, "Splendid!" —at her own nursery, she could hardly make ends meet. How much longer would it last?

M. Béjart said softly, "About as long as the Fourth Republic."

"Now, Alain," Maman Rose said, and M. Béjart held up the bottle and asked if he could give anyone wine, and Michel saw M. Joseph's head lift up and the angry expression that came to his face.

"Don't you want yours?" Pé asked. Michel looked down at the mound of spongy yellow and shook his head.

"Not like that!" Manon said, as Pé reached over greedily with his spoon. She interchanged their plates.

"I ate all mine," Léah boasted.

Félicité removed the dishes. Father Fonsac sent his compliments to the cook. All began to talk at once.

"That was a day!" Mme Barshowanski cried. "I dare say Odette won't forget it in a hurry. Nor will you," she said to Mme Quertsch, who made a wry face and shook her head. "And those two nuns from the Temple, who thought they had stepped into a madhouse. I can still see their faces."

Maman Rose laughed. "Sister Marie and Sister Blanche. They're still talking about it. They ask after Michel, and then they cross themselves."

"Oh, I'm weak!" Mme Barshowanski yelped, bubbling with laughter. "There they were just inside the door, with the Boche across the street, and me in a faint on the floor, and Michel yelling for his Vati, and Odette screaming, It's Father Périer! It's Father Périer! and those two innocents shifting their feet, pale as death and ready to bolt, but not daring to go because of that big ox on the steps with his carbine watching the entrance!"

"Yelling for his what?" Father Fonsac asked, puzzled.

"Yes, yes, never mind that," Maman Rose said, glancing at Michel.

M. Joseph wanted to know when was this, and Mme Barshowanski looked surprised and said, "Oh, I thought—" and got red in the face.

"It was during the war," Maman Rose said quickly. "Louise, I declare, the way you tell a story!"

There was a silence, while M. Joseph took a sip of wine and set his glass carefully on the table. "I see," he said. "Yes. I'd like to hear about it."

It was he who had yelled for his Vati, Michel knew that. He had heard this story many times.

"Well," Mme Barshowanski said, looking around the table, "it was in February 1944, that dreadful winter, and Maxim and I were in hiding here at the Nursery, and one night Maxim woke me up in the dark and said they were making a raid across the street."

Michel knew that part by heart: how the soldiers dragged the little man out of the house, and drove off with him, leaving a guard in front of the door; and how Maman Rose put on her nurse's uniform and went over there to get the man's valuables before the Fritz came back for their search; and how she got past the guard with her piece of paper. Michel and Pé had discussed it many times. They took the man away because he was a Jew, and Maman Rose was very brave to do what she did, because if the Fritz had realized what she was up to instead of visiting the sick as she said, they'd have been very angry at her. But M. Joseph did not know that story. Was that when he was in prison?

Mme Barshowanski had come to the part about the paper. "It was just beginning to get light. I was watching from the upstairs window, and I saw Odette talking to the guard, and him shaking his head. And so she took out this folded paper and put it in his hand, and he looked at it and scratched his ear, and Odette just walked in, and he let her."

"I see," M. Joseph said. "And what was that paper?"

Maman Rose chuckled, and Mme Barshowanski slapped the table and exclaimed that that was the beauty of it, it was just a paper Odette had snatched up from her desk with stamps and seals on it, but since the guard didn't know French—!

"Ha!" M. Joseph said, sitting up straight.

"Wasn't that nerve?" Mlle Camélia demanded proudly.

Maman Rose said that when she thought of it today! She had done it on impulse, and that was what carried her through. It was a question of feeding her children. They were literally starving, and she was desperate. That poor little man wasn't coming back, and rather than let the Boche get their hands on his things . . . But when it was over, and she was walking around the block to enter the Nursery by the playground gate, her legs suddenly went weak, and in the kitchen she had to sit down. And then Louise came running down the stairs.

"I was hysterical," Mme Barshowanski confessed frankly. "I had seen the whole thing, and I was never so scared in my born days. I fainted and slid down in a heap, and Maxim got excited and began to slap me and holler for water, and while he was carrying on, there was a rap at the door. What did Maxim think but that the Germans had found out and were coming for us, and he jumped up ready to run for the cellar. But he wouldn't leave me, God rest his soul, and he tried to sling me to his shoulder."

"It was the nuns," Maman Rose said to her brother. "Mother Veronica had sent them from the Temple to explain that Madame Quertsch was coming with Michel. Sister Marie and Sister Blanche. But when they got to the door of the Nursery, they saw the guard across the street watching them, and got worried. They didn't dare go away, and so they rapped and came in without waiting, and saw a man in the hall wrestling with the body of a woman on the floor. And before I could explain it to them there was another knock on the door, and in *she* walks," nodding at Mme Quertsch, "carrying Michel, and then *he* begins to scream. You can imagine—"

"But wait," Mme Barshowanski cried. "In the midst of all that excitement, I came to, and what do I see? Maxim on his knees beside me bawling like a baby, a strange boy crying, and those two nuns huddled by the door, taking in everything with eyes as big as I don't know what. And *that* was the moment that a priest came in without knocking, and Odette saw him and yelled, 'It's Father Périer!' as if the world had come to an end, and those two nuns looked as though—"

Father Fonsac leaned toward Maman Rose and asked a question in a low voice.

"An old friend of mine," Maman Rose said softly. "He used to have a parish here in the city. I hadn't seen him for years."

Pé leaned over and whispered to Manon, who put her finger to her lips and frowned. But Pé couldn't wait, and he hitched his chair closer to Michel's and whispered, "What did Pétain do?"

Michel whispered back that he had been sent to prison. The boys at St. Joseph's had talked about that, and one of the older boys told them that it was because the old traitor had sold France like a barrel of fish. Michel did not understand that. But he knew about the prison. He hoped that would satisfy Pé; he didn't feel like talking.

M. Joseph's face was blotchy red. "Let me tell you, sir," he said to M. Béjart, "that you're wasting your time. You say Laval was scum, and there I agree with you. I don't defend Laval. But Pétain was another of the same feather. We lived through those years. The record is there for all to see."

"Do you think character changes then?" M. Béjart asked coolly. "The hero of Verdun is the traitor of Vichy?"

"Gentlemen," Father Fonsac said.

"Come now, Joseph," Maman Rose said. "That's enough."

"Let him stop then," M. Joseph said with a rude gesture.

M. Béjart said that time would tell.

"Character!" M. Joseph said in scorn. "He was a fascist at Verdun as well as at Vichy. But it took the shame of France to bring him to power and show what he was. That was proved at the trial."

"And a pretty spectacle that was, too!" M. Béjart retorted. "Oh, it was most enlightening to see that proud old lion set upon by a pack of snarling dogs. Because if people would face the truth, they would see that our shame, as you put it, was not 1940 but the entire period between the wars, with its trade unions and Popular Front and the rabble-rouser Blum, and the destruction of the principles of authority and religion. And when a man comes along, a patriot whose loyalty to France had been proved beyond doubt for over half a century, and says, Let us forget our differences in this national disaster, and work together for the common good, with order and under God, then—"

"Under Hitler, you mean," M. Joseph snorted.

M. Béjart asked M. Joseph to use his reason. Was it Pétain who brought Hitler to France? Wasn't it rather the weakness of our country that attracted that vulture? And who was responsible for that weakness? The so-called liberals, the pacifists, those who—

"Are they going to fight?" Pé whispered to Michel.

"Sh!" Manon said, shaking Pé's arm.

"Let us enjoy our dinner," Maman Rose said. "All that's over and done with."

"Who's talking about that?" M. Joseph demanded. "I'm talking about collaboration."

Jean said, "Yes, that's the point," and colored under Maman Rose's reproachful stare.

M. Béjart was amused. "Ah, youth!" he said, nodding at Jean. "How quick it is to judge! France's greatest general, who could have given lessons in strategy to the Corsican upstart Napoleon, let alone the ranting corporal of the Munich beer halls. Are you going to teach him the double game? Do you suppose he didn't know what he was doing? Give a little here, take a little there, reassure them, catch them off guard. But stand fast, all the same. The lesson of Verdun. We were too close to it to see it. But when history gives its verdict—"

M. Joseph struck the table with his fist, and shoved his chair back from the table, saying violently, "If you ask me, he gave everything and took damned little. And do you know why? Because that famous double game of his was a fraud. Else why did he surround himself in that spa of his with Hitler's bootlickers, who would spit in their mothers' faces for a smile from their Führer? A double game? With Doriot? Darnand? de Brinon? And the militia, the riffraff of our country, to cut out the hearts of their fellow Frenchmen? And the workers he sent to Germany? He gave and he gave, because deep down he believed in the same things Hitler did. And that's why he kept our fleet bottled up, and that's why he went after the Jews."

M. Béjart, who had raised his eyebrows at M. Joseph's movement, suggested that there was no need for M. Joseph to excite himself, they were simply having a friendly chat. He hoped they could have an honest difference of opinion without becoming upset over it. Mme Barshowanski said warmly that that was so, and Mme Quertsch, looking frightened, agreed with her. Maman Rose said that this was Michel's communion party, and hadn't they had enough trouble living through those days without talking about them now? M. Joseph muttered that it was very well, but that he had suffered at the hands of Vichy, with their spies and informers, and their courts that were more crooked than those they sentenced to years of prison. He rebelled against hearing Pétain praised. But he was willing to drop the subject. Pé whispered that if they were not going to fight, he wished they would bring in the cake, he was still hungry.

"Can't you be *quiet?*" Manon said.

"As for the Jews," M. Béjart said, seeing that M. Joseph had calmed down and had pulled his chair to the table again, "I have nothing against them, God knows, and certainly never condoned the Nazis' extermination camps. Although probably the press has greatly exaggerated the matter. But what was to be done with those who were Jews first and Frenchmen afterward?" He turned to Mme Barshowanski and said earnestly, "I've known many who were fine, decent citizens, like any Christian. And I honor them, as I honored your late husband. But it's a matter of record that the shortages and high prices during the Occupation were caused by hoarders who scoured the countryside and bought up the farmers' stocks to lay away for themselves. Most of them were Jews. And I know this from personal experience. At one time, the summer of 1943 it was, eggs suddenly disappeared. You couldn't find one in all Touville. Until then you could usually get some in the black market, if you were willing to pay five francs apiece. Everybody said it was the Germans, but in my opinion the Germans, bad as they were, were blamed for a good many things that were not their fault."

M. Béjart's pale blue eyes challenged those at the table. "I couldn't believe that the hens had stopped laying. But if not, where were the eggs? I went out into the country to see for myself. I spoke to a number of farmers. Everywhere it was the same story, nobody had any eggs. I offered one man as high as ten francs. He laughed at me. He said that only that morning he had sold all his eggs to a rich Jew who came all the way from Lyons, in a motorcar flying the Vichy flag, mind you. The nerve of the man! And at seventeen francs apiece! Seventeen francs! The farmer himself couldn't get over it. 'They're the boys with the money,' he said, 'and the rest of the world can look out for themselves.' And there you have it in a nutshell. They stick by each other, that's part of their religion. Now, I ask you," he said, turning to M. Joseph, "what was to be done with them?"

Father Fonsac observed mildly that Judaism was not really a religion. Many years ago, as a young man not yet in holy orders, he had boarded with an elderly couple in Bordeaux. This was in the Jewish quarter of the city, but in his innocence he had not known that, nor that his host himself was one of them. A very fine person, nonetheless, very hospitable.

"One evening the old gentleman offered me tea in his kitchen," Father Fonsac said. "One thing led to another, and in the conversation he admitted he was a Jew. Well, I wish you could have heard him sneer at the practices he was supposed to follow! All those dietary laws, and prayer shawls, and the things they tie around their wrists and foreheads! Do you know what they do?" Father Fonsac asked, turning to Maman Rose. "They nail prayers to their door. Like the Chinese, with their prayer wheels. How can you take something like that seriously? The old gentleman himself said it was all nonsense, the Jews themselves don't believe in it. No offense meant, madame," he said across the table to Mme Barshowanski, who sniffed angrily and said there were Jews and Jews, and no woman had ever had a finer, more loyal husband. And Maman Rose choked over her glass of wine, and said that *that* was true, and she didn't know whether it was the Jew or the Russian in him, but it certainly wasn't French, and all began to laugh, even M. Joseph, and leaned back in their chairs, and suddenly were friendly again.

It was all very queer, Michel thought. Could Mme Barshowanski's Maxim have been a Jew? But she had gone to school with the nuns of the Sacred Heart. No, no, she could not have done such a thing. Oh no, he thought, observing her with troubled eyes.

"I think," M. Béjart said cheerfully, touching his glass with a fork so that it made a tinkling sound, and standing up, "I think it is time for a speech."

Several at the table clapped their hands, and after acknowledging the applause with a tiny bow, M. Béjart became very serious. He said he was an old man who had seen his country come very close to annihilation, and his heart had bled for her. But even in the darkest hours he had never lost his faith that France would pull through. It was his sincere conviction that France would always pull through, for a world without France was unthinkable.

"We have our faults," M. Béjart said. "And who has not? We are a shrewd people, but our very shrewdness in hard times becomes cynicism, our common sense becomes mistrust. We forget the lessons of history, and we forget the principles that have made us great. Nonetheless, at the very core of the Frenchman there is something tough and indestructible that in the final test will save him and our country. That core is faith, fear of God, a conscience that knows instinctively the right thing to do, a heart that is willing and eager to do it. France will never have to worry about her future so long as she is capable of creating the ordinary citizen in this mold."

How beautifully M. Béjart spoke! All listened with respect. "You are wondering where this preamble is leading," M. Béjart said, fingering his chain and gazing down at the table, "and I will tell you without more ado. Sitting in this pleasant company this afternoon, and looking into your faces, I was overcome by emotion. I thought of our beloved country, and the hard years we have all been through, and two realizations came to me. The first is that we have in our little gathering the finest example of the kind of citizen I am talking about, an example of the deathless Latin spirit that no barbarism from abroad, be it German or otherwise, will ever be able to destroy. I am speaking of a woman whose heart is as big as France herself, whose character is the rock on which our country's future is founded."

Pé muttered, "The cake, the cake!"

"Pé!" Manon said.

"And my second realization is that every one of us here owes her an immense debt of gratitude for what she has done for us. In some cases it is life itself that she has given us. I ask each of you to look deep within your heart, and answer whether this is not so. I think there is no better time to acknowledge that debt than the present moment, while we are all gathered at her board. And so, ladies and gentlemen," M. Béjart concluded, lifting his glass, "I propose a toast! A toast to Odette Rose!"

Mme Barshowanski struggled to her feet, crying out, "I owe her my life, and I don't care who knows it!" and Jean exclaimed, "A toast to Maman!" and everybody got up holding out his glass and laughing. Michel stood up too. There was a great commotion that made Michel's heart swell with pride. Maman Rose was protesting that it wasn't fair, she hadn't dreamed of anything like this; her face had turned pink, and she looked very girlish, crying out, "No, no," and laughing at the same time. Mme Barshowanski, frankly weeping, was leaning across the table chinking glasses with all. And then someone let out a startled "Oh!" and they all swung around and there was a stranger in the vestibule door, a tall, gaunt man wearing a coat and holding a hat in his hand, and looking as surprised and disconcerted as everybody else.

Félicité was behind him, and she stammered, "He wants to see Mademoiselle Rose."

Maman Rose had started to get up and was holding out her glass to be filled. There was still some laughter in her face as she put down the glass and said, "Yes, what is it?"

The man said he was sorry to interrupt the festivity, and that he would come back another time. If Mlle Rose would be kind enough to tell him when it would be convenient for her to allow him to call . . . Michel thought him very strange, with that high, furrowed forehead, those hollow cheeks and heavy-lidded eyes. Apparently Maman Rose did too, for she took him in from head to toe before stepping forward to say,

"What about?"

The man hesitated, then said his name was Louis Konrad, and that he wanted to speak to her about the child Michel Benedek. But since she had company—

"Another one!" Maman Rose cried in a harsh voice. She had suddenly become very pale. Michel looked from her to the intruder in astonishment. What did this M. Konrad want of him? And what was

Maman Rose so angry about? M. Konrad seemed taken aback. He was about to say something when Maman Rose said, "My God, and on Easter Sunday, too. Don't you know it's Easter Sunday?"

M. Konrad said yes, he knew, but it was important. However, he was willing—

Maman Rose interrupted with a strange, inarticulate sound. "Once and for all," she said grimly. "Once and for all, then. Come to my office."

She stalked past him, and with a slight bow to those at the table, M. Konrad followed.

M. Béjart fingered his chain and remarked that they might just as well sit down. They did so, and looked at each other and at Michel. Father Fonsac cleared his throat, and asked if anybody there knew the gentleman. Nobody did. Father Fonsac then said he thought he had noted a slight accent in the voice, and M. Béjart nodded significantly, and said, "Oh, yes." Léah whispered something to Manon, who said, "He's just a man, dear."

Suddenly Maman Rose's voice came to them from behind the closed door of her office. It seemed very angry, and Michel looked at the door in apprehension. As he watched, the door opened, and M. Konrad came out looking distressed, and Maman Rose after him, crying, "Cowards! Cowards!"

M. Konrad turned around and opened his mouth, but Maman Rose did not let him speak. "I'm sick of it, I tell you! Why don't you Jews let me alone? Where were you all when there was danger? You ran like a lot of mice, and the devil take the hindmost! And then she sends you around, when it's all over! Well, you can tell that aunt of his that the boy is mine and I'm going to keep him! Tell her that if she bothers me again, I'll take her to court! Now get out of here, and never let me see your face again!"

M. Konrad was staring at her in disbelief. Above his coat collar his neck swelled and turned red. Maman Rose stamped her foot and cried, "Get out! Get out!"

With a start he clapped his hat on his head and glanced at the others, and said, "I thought I would be talking to a sane woman."

Maman Rose drew in her breath and stepped forward. Michel had never seen her so angry.

"Don't excite yourself," M. Konrad said. "I'm going. You are all witnesses," he said to those at the table. "I think I've been civil enough."

M. Béjart said in a cold voice, "I think you had better go." M. Joseph stood up.

M. Konrad looked from one to the other. He said to Maman Rose, "I warn you this is not the end of the matter. There is still justice in France."

He was already in the vestibule when Maman Rose called after him, "I've had him baptized Catholic, if that gives you any pleasure."

M. Konrad's gaunt face appeared again in the doorway. "You *what?*" he said.

"Baptized! If you know what that is."

"You took a Jewish child and *baptized* him?"

"Tell *that* to that aunt of his!" Maman Rose cried triumphantly.

M. Konrad stared at her for a long time. A thin white ridge moved in his jaw. He said slowly, "Dr. Benedek was a Jew. His wife was a Jew. Their child is circumcised. You didn't have the right, mademoiselle. Do you realize what you've done?"

Maman Rose flung up her arms as if he had struck her. M. Joseph stepped forward with his head lowered, and there was the clatter of a chair as Jean stood up, and Mme Barshowanski screamed, and M. Konrad stabbed his finger out at M. Joseph and said with his lips drawn back like an animal, "Stay where you are!" He looked enormous standing there with his long arm outstretched. M. Joseph stopped short, and Jean, coming around the table, bumped up against him and stopped too. Léah began to cry.

M. Konrad's face was pale and ugly as he looked at Maman Rose and said in a low voice, "You stupid, vicious woman. How did you dare?" Then he turned and walked out the door, leaving it open behind him. Maman Rose gave a strangled cry and shouted that he had insulted her, and ran to the door and screamed after him, "Jew bastard!", and then she slammed the door.

3

❧

MONSIEUR BÉJART lingered in the doorway over his good-bye. She had been quite right to become angry, he said; but the man was gone now, and would probably never show his face again.

Mlle Rose said bitterly, "He spoiled Michel's communion party."

"It was a splendid party," M. Béjart assured her. Gallantly he raised her hand to his lips. "Perfectly splendid." Bowing, he turned to the door, calling out a farewell to Mme Barshowanski, who sat stiffly at the table, her back to them.

If they had at least had the cake, Mlle Rose thought, turning and looking at the table, where the candle flames flickered in a circle over the pink frosting. Like a crown. Like a halo. Everything had gone so beautifully up to that moment. But once that man had appeared, the spirit was gone. For one thing, little Léah had become so frightened that she had to be taken up to her room and given a sedative. And then Michel, dreadfully pale, had slipped upstairs as well. She would have gone after him, except that Mme Quertsch had given the signal for departure by muttering that it was late, after which there was a general movement toward the door. Well, she would go to him now.

She had started up the stairs when Manon appeared on the landing. Léah was all right, she reported. Jean and Renée were with her, telling her stories. And Michel was asleep.

"Asleep?" she said in surprise. A great weight was lifted from her mind. If Michel was asleep, he could not be too preoccupied by what he had heard. You could never tell with children; perhaps he had known all along. She herself had put off telling him, knowing what it would do to his illusions about his father. She had blamed herself for it often. But it was easier said than done to speak the words that would break a child's heart. Someone in the Nursery had not been so careful. Perhaps it was all for the best though.

Almost cheerful again, she went down the stairs and blew out the candles on the cake. How Michel had jumped and clapped his hands last week, after the baptism, when she told him about the communion party, and the cake with seven candles! At that moment it had been borne in on her how much of a child he was, in spite of his unnaturally serious ways. Misfortune, she thought. Sorrow. It was these that aged you, made children grow up more quickly than their years. Michel had already had enough of these to last him a lifetime. Thank God she had been there when he needed her!

Louise was still sitting at the table. She said suddenly, "My Maxim was not a coward!"

Staring at her friend's stricken face, the napkin twisted in her fingers, Mlle Rose was filled with contrition. "My God, Louise," she said, "you know I didn't mean a thing like that. Not Maxim."

"Well, he wasn't," Louise insisted, dabbing at her tremulous lower lip with the napkin. "And I don't mind telling you there was a bit too much talk about it today. And in your house, too, Odette! And so I've been thinking, I've outworn my welcome, I'd better go back to Paris. The sooner the better. Tonight."

"Louise," Mlle Rose began, approaching her.

"That Monsieur Béjart!" Louise cried angrily. "I've always thought of him as such a gentleman. On and on he went, until I wanted to slap him. The Jews this and the Jews that! Does he think they don't have to eat? So a Jew bought some eggs! And Monsieur Béjart, what was *he* doing there? He was looking for eggs himself, wasn't he? Only he wasn't quick enough. Whose fault is that? But very well, I said to myself, Odette's not responsible for what Monsieur Béjart says. I won't spoil the party. And then that man showed up, and you—" She faltered, looking reproachfully sideways out of hurt eyes misty with tears.

Annette, coming from the kitchen bearing a tray, stopped in the passageway and looked from one to the other.

"But I didn't mean Maxim," Mlle Rose said, putting her arm around her friend's shoulders. "You ought to know that. Come into the office," she urged. "I'd never forgive myself if you went away thinking—"

"You never used to talk like that," Louise said, frankly weeping, as she let herself be led away.

"You've been in Paris," Mlle Rose said somberly, shutting the door behind her. "You don't know what's been going on here. Come, Louise, sit down, and we'll have a talk. Like old times. Remember? You there, and I here." She pushed the two soft leather armchairs together. "Jews!" she said, as they took their places. "Before the war, I didn't even know what a Jew was. They didn't go to our church, that was all. They were like anybody else, good and bad. When you and Maxim came here—"

"I know," Louise said in a choked voice. "That's what surprised me when you—"

"They made me mad," she said. "You remember the night Michel came. Right in this very room it was. He couldn't drop off to sleep and was sweating with fever, on that freezing night. All that screaming! I sat in this chair, holding him in my arms wrapped in a blanket, and I said to you I couldn't understand it. That face of his! Like a little piece of heaven. If he were mine, I said, nothing on this earth could have separated him from me. Not while I had nails on my fingers and teeth in my mouth. Suicide was too easy. The mother, anyway. Leaving him adrift like that for anybody's mercy."

"I remember," Louise said. "But—"

"Wait, that's not it. Because if the father had come back, I'd have given Michel to him. It would have broken my heart, but I'd have done it. And told him to hold on to him better the next time. But that aunt! She ran off to Australia, and when it was all over, she wrote me a little thank-you note, as if she'd been to tea, and I could just send him to her where she was. In Australia. With the Japanese sinking ships right and left in the Pacific. No thank you, I thought, if you want him so much you can come for him. And that's what I told the Red Cross when she sent them around. You don't see her budging from there, I told them, but he can cross the world by himself. He's only four, I said, and if I don't lie down beside him at bedtime, he's afraid to close his eyes. Tell her that and see what she says. That's when I wrote to you that I had decided to set up a Council, and have myself made guardian."

Louise had wiped her eyes and was listening quietly. Mlle Rose pressed her fingers to her temples. She was feeling a bit dizzy. It wasn't the wine, she had little enough of that. That man, with his fisheyes and his message from that woman. Like getting kicked in the belly. And then her emotional outburst. But she couldn't have Louise angry at her, not over this.

"You don't know," she went on. "You'd have gotten mad too.

· 42 ·

About a year after I wrote you, the aunt showed up here. It was the last thing in the world I expected, since I hadn't heard anything from her in some time. She walked in here with another woman, an interpreter, and said she wanted to see Michel. Ah! I thought that would surprise you. The things that woman's done! Well, I thought, she's come for him after all. Now what am I going to do? You can imagine, in that moment I could have sunk through the floor. I hadn't realized myself how much Michel had come to mean to me. Dr. Peyrefitte was telling me the other day about a woman patient of his who had adopted a little girl. One day she described her birth pains to him. She was serious, he said. She had convinced herself that she had given birth to her." She laughed, putting her hand on Louise's arm. "I wasn't that bad, but when I understood that the woman was Michel's aunt, it was as though something had been ripped out of me. Like giving birth. I won't pretend with you, Louise. I prepared to put up the battle of my life. Not Michel, I thought. Not now. If she had come before! But now it wasn't fair."

"When was this?" Louise asked. "I mean, how long was it that you—"

"Three years," she said firmly. "Or almost. My God, in three years a child becomes part of your flesh. And a boy like Michel! Suffering inside himself, hungry for love. I was his Maman Rose. He used to put his arms around my neck and rub noses with me, and I'd say, 'Who am I?' And he'd say, 'Maman Rose.' 'And who are you?' 'Your little boy,' he'd say. He needed that. And to tell you the truth, I did too. You can't tell what it does to you. But wait!" she went on. "Let me tell you what happened. There wasn't any battle at all. She couldn't take the boy, she said, she had just come to see him, on her way home."

"What!" Louise exclaimed.

"I couldn't believe my ears," Mlle Rose said. "It seems that her husband had died, and she had decided to return to Austria. She was a poor widow, she said, she had no job and didn't know how she was going to live herself. She couldn't take on the responsibility of a child. She just wanted to see him, to see whether he looked like her brother Karl. The boy's father. Well! I thought. If that's all! And I sent for Michel, and let them have a good cry together. And when she was ready to leave, I asked again whether I could keep him. It still hadn't sunk in. My good fortune, I mean. And she said I had done so well by him so far, and he seemed to have a genuine affection for me, and so on, but she couldn't tell how the other aunt felt about it, and she would probably—"

"There are *two* aunts?" Louise said, open-mouthed.

She nodded. "In London. The one named Lindner went to Australia, and the other, Benedek, went to London. This one was the Lindner woman, and as far as she was concerned I could keep him. It was the first I had heard of the other aunt, and I said so, meaning that if in all that time she hadn't got in touch with me, it was pretty clear that she wasn't interested. And she understood it that way, I'm sure. But between us, I didn't much care whether she did or not, not at that stage. And I thought, Well, he's mine."

Louise looked bewildered. "But, Odette, if she said you could keep him—"

"But let me tell you!" she said. "That's why I exploded just now. You never saw such a changeable creature in your life. She didn't stay in Austria. More than a year later I got another letter from her. She was in Palestine, and now she wanted Michel. Like a doll, or something. Here, hold my doll for me. No, give it back. And if the letter were all! Do you know that the prime minister wrote to me? Georges Bidault himself. Wouldn't I be kind to the poor aunt and return the boy? Some influence she has, that poor aunt! And oh yes, the bishop. She got after him too. Bishop Rebenty, here in Touville. The one who said mass at the communion this morning. He called me in and questioned me about it. It seems that the archbishop of Westminster in England wrote him asking about Michel. It's a wonder she didn't go to the Pope. Yes, Your Excellency, I said, I've got the boy, and I'm going to keep him. And I told him the whole story. Well, he said, that's different, you just let me handle this. He was just as indignant as I was. Do you know what he said? When I bent down to kiss his ring, he said that it was the aunt who ought to be kissing *my* hand."

"Oh, Odette!" Louise exclaimed, much moved. "Please forgive me, I didn't know."

She patted Louise's arm. "All this time it was bottled up in me. And today, when this Konrad person showed up, I just couldn't hold back any more. It was really too much. God knows I'm not an anti-Semite. And you know it too, Louise. When the Resistance decorated me, it was for that. For helping the Jews. You know that. But I don't take back anything I said, except that I meant only certain ones. Not because they ran; I'd have run too. But I wouldn't have thrown Michel to the wolves to be able to run faster. And if I had, I wouldn't have the nerve to come pussyfooting around afterwards, with that self-righteous, suffering look and that snooty attitude of What have you done with our boy? One thing or the other, not both. And not at my expense. The only thing I'm sorry for is that it was now, during the party. And that your feelings were hurt."

"Oh, not any more," Louise assured her. "I mean, now that I know. I should have realized that you had your reasons. What I don't understand"—she continued frowning—"is how the man *dared.*"

It was not until Mlle Rose started up the stairs that she realized how tired she was. It had been a long day, full of emotion. Well, she could rest now. She was glad she had had her chat with Louise. The rancor had gone from her spirit and left her filled with tenderness. She wanted to be with Michel. It didn't matter if he was still napping; she would sit beside his bed for what was left of daylight and do a bit of mending. Had he taken off his communion suit before lying down? Probably. He was tidy, not like that scamp Pé. Tomorrow she would iron it with care, through a damp cloth, and hang it away for special occasions. Marie was all right with the rough work, but couldn't be trusted with a fine piece of cloth like that. She would touch up the satin armband too and put it away in camphor for a long wait in her closet. Twenty-five years? Thirty? Until Michel's son was the age Michel was now. If he didn't become a priest, as Father Périer wanted. And Mother Veronica. Secretly she hoped he would not; the thought of holding another Michel in her arms to cheer her last years filled her with tingling anticipation. This time there would be no question as to whose he was. These days it was nothing for a woman to live to seventy, and beyond. She would be retired then, perhaps with a little house in the country, surrounded by grandchildren. That would be worth everything.

Michel's door was closed. She hesitated before it, then went to her room to get her needle kit.

Why had she been ashamed to tell the truth to Louise? Dr. Peyrefitte's patient didn't exist; it was she herself who had had that strange delusion of having given birth. But in a dream. Anything could happen in a dream. That was nothing to be ashamed of.

Anyway, that was only the animal part of it. That didn't matter if the rest was lacking. Pé's mother, for example. Take him, I'm off.

Like that strange American bird she had read about, that left its eggs in other birds' nests and went about its business. As for Michel's mother, she wasn't anything like that, of course, but the results were the same. Death was a luxury she couldn't afford, not with a young son. Sometimes the other part was harder, the hour-by-hour struggle with necessity. A woman made her child twice, the first time with her body, and the second with her heart and mind and soul. With tender care. And tears.

Tears! She had had her share of those.

She had moved to the window and was staring with unseeing eyes at the street. It was here she had stood, she remembered, a little over eighteen years ago, looking out at the snow on the rooftops across the way and listening to the silence of the great empty building that surrounded her. She had just been made directress of the Nursery and moved into the quarters on the second floor that were hers by right. During the daytime the Nursery was a great hive of activity, resounding with the voices, the laughter, the weeping of children in the playground, or the games room, or the dining hall; the bustling about of the nurses and the hired help; the aura of human lives about her, which she breathed in with peculiar satisfaction, knowing she had found her niche and that it was in this atmosphere that she wanted to live. But at dusk the working mothers trooped in and took their children away, the nurses and the help went home; and the Nursery became a great empty barn of a building, its vacant rooms yawning desolately in the darkness one after the other as she wandered through them. One night she had stood by this window and felt her solitude hovering over her like a menace. It was then that she understood what was lacking. She needed children—not borrowed children dropped in the morning and picked up at night, but children of her own, who would live with her, who would be hers, and would fill the second floor that was her private domain. She knew she would never marry, not after Henri. Very well, then, there were enough homeless children in the world who needed her as she needed them. How to go about finding them?

That had been the easiest part of it. Musing now by the window, her needle kit forgotten in her hand, she smiled to remember how her career as foster mother had begun—not with one child, or even two, but with five. Five little orphans, at one swoop! Only a few days after her decision she had read in the paper the details of an accident at a street corner: a young married couple killed by a car whose driver was having an epileptic fit. Their five children would probably become wards of the state, the reporter wrote, since no next of kin could be found willing to take them in. A half-hour later she was at the address given in the newspaper. A dingy room filled with whispering neighbors and curiosity seekers, staring at the two draped coffins. In the corner, a little boy standing with his arm around the shoulders of his even smaller sister. Jean and Renée. They had stood somewhat apart from the three older boys, as if even in their grief they shared something alien to the others. Her heart had gone out at once to that forlorn pair, so tiny, so stricken, so close to each other. It was these two that she wanted. In the end she had had to take them all, since the authorities would not hear of separating them.

Five! They had filled her Nursery for her! And when, after years had gone by, the three oldest boys, Léon, Guy, and Arthur, had grown up and gone, others had taken their places. Manon. Pé. Léah. Michel. She had not sought these out, they had come to her, cast up like driftwood at her door. Wasn't she the Orphan Lady of Place St. Lazare? What better place to leave a homeless or an unwanted child?

It had not been easy. She had been alone. Everything she owned she had had to fight for twice as hard as anybody else. It had hardened her, but it had taught her resourcefulness. More. It had taught her where the real values of life lay. In the goods of this world she was poor. It had all been cast upon the waters. And yet there was no one richer than she. She had her children. Friends. Her sense of fulfillment. If only there were no Konrads about, to threaten her happiness!

She would know how to keep it, though, she assured herself grimly. Justice! the man had said. The clock had stood still for him, it seemed, and for the aunt as well. It's all over now, let's go back to where we were. Put the tree back into the seed. Michel was no longer the child who had been brought to her, and she wasn't the same either. Something had flowered since then and would keep on growing. *That* was justice, and the only justice that counted.

She shook her head, to rid herself of the feeling of oppression that had come over her, and went to the hall. Opening Michel's door softly, she peered in. He lay on his bed by the window, his arm over his face. He still wore his communion suit, but had taken off his shoes. She entered, walking on tiptoe, and rummaged among his socks in the bureau drawer. Then, noiselessly lifting his desk chair, she set it beside the bed and sat down. Michel did not stir. Nonetheless, letting her eyes linger caressingly on him, she realized with a start that he was not asleep. She could tell; she could always tell.

"Michel?" she said softly.

He gave no sign that he had heard. There was no doubt about it, though. He could fool Manon, but not her. She was sorry now that she had let herself be put off by Manon the first time she had wanted to go to Michel. The explanation with Louise could have waited. No doubt he had been awake all that time, and needing comforting. Why was he pretending? He knew it was she, must have heard her shut her door across the hall. Frowning, she stared at him. Was he so hurt, then? But at what? It was not like him to sulk over a trivial thing like a cake, he was too reasonable for that. Yet if it were fright over the threat posed by that ugly Konrad, he should be clinging to her, rather than this. Was he thinking of his father? Had he understood the import of her exchange with Konrad? If so, her heart grieved for him. It was something he had to face, sooner or later. But not alone; he still had her, she would not let herself be repulsed. Dropping to her knees beside the bed, she put her arm under his shoulders, burying her face alongside his before she realized that his cheek was wet, and much too hot. Fever! she thought in alarm, struggling upright and lifting his arm to see his face. His eyes were open, as she had expected, but so red-rimmed and despairing that his name died on her lips.

4

❦

MONSIEUR LOUIS KONRAD strode toward the river. He took long steps, driven by a fury inside, his head lowered, his face grim. The things that woman had called him! Hannah's letter had prepared him to meet resistance, but he had not expected anything like the violence he had encountered. Jew bastard! He had not been spared even that.

His light topcoat flapping in the spring breeze, he walked along a narrow cobbled street, past worn stone steps and unshuttered windows. A woman coming toward him hesitated, then edged aside to let him pass. Two little girls wearing white gloves and little flowered bonnets, sitting on a doorsill, stopped their chatting as he went by, and stared after him.

Even the children. A death's-head they would not forget in a hurry.

He followed the curving street until it came to an end at the quay. Beyond the parapet the river Char gleamed dully in the afternoon sunlight. He stood at the stone wall, his hands spread on the rough surface, staring down at the water. Easter Sunday. Baptized Catholic. And ye shall observe the feast of unleavened bread; for in this selfsame day have I brought your armies out of the land of Egypt; therefore shall ye observe this day in your generations by an ordinance forever.

There will never be an end, he thought. History's little ironies. A fever in the blood that nothing can change.

He turned and walked along the parapet, picturing Mlle Rose as she had run shouting after him to slam the door, her mouth open, her face flushed and swollen with anger, her hair flying. Perhaps a bit drunk as well. There was no point in arguing with her, a madwoman like that. Well, now he knew. Yes, now he had tried, and he knew.

It was quiet along the quay. Konrad walked past block after block of low stone cottages, with their peaked slate roofs and ancient casements. A few windows were open, and here and there a seated figure gazed out, enjoying the fading sunlight. In happier times he had often walked here to tranquilize his spirit, after the bustle of the modern city, with the abruptly peaceful air of old Touville, that narrow strip of medieval houses that hugged the riverbank, mellowed by time. But now he scarcely glanced at the houses as he passed. He followed the curving parapet until the rocky hill on the other side of the river sloped suddenly and disappeared, and a calm valley vista, faintly tinged with green, opened up to his sight. Far away, over the checkered farmlands and the earth-colored barns, a ring of mountains lifted white peaks to the sky.

The last time he had stood on this spot, in 1943, there had been a file of short-nosed German trucks crawling along that valley road, and the guard before the sentry box at the foot of the bridge had watched him until he thought it best to move away. The trucks were gone now, that hated uniform had disappeared from the land, and there was only a faint discoloration on the sidewalk where the sentry box had stood. Konrad's eye followed the bridge across the river, and the road that went from it up the slope of the low hill to the right. There at the top was a cluster of white houses, shining in the sun. How peaceful it looked now! Puy-le-Duc, the refuge, the new Canaan, land of the stranger—Puy-le-Duc, the deathtrap.

Perhaps at the very moment he had looked up at Puy-le-Duc, almost five years before, thinking of Rina and Judas, so full of despair that if it had been given to him to annihilate the world with one word, he would have uttered that word—perhaps at that moment Dr. Benedek, in one of those white houses on the hill, was looking at his Lili and his Michel, broken with the same despair. No one would ever know what that man went through, helpless in that warren, watching the strings pull tighter and tighter, waiting night after night for the screech of brakes in the street, the summons at the door. He was a doctor, he lived by his practice—illegal under the Nuremberg laws—he had ventured forth into the city to win his bread. What must have been in his heart, when in the evening, after a day of shameful dodgings and subterfuges, he crossed the bridge and stared with dread up at Puy-le-Duc, lifted his eyes unto the hill whence no help came, and his imagination presented to him, in sickening detail, a splintered door, an empty crib, silence?

Six million, Konrad thought, standing by the bridge. Oh, not him! Not Konrad, nor his wife Rina, nor their son Judas; for then, that hopeless November, looking at the valley with its convoy, and under the suspicious eyes of the sentry, he had made up his mind at last, and he had hurried home, thrown together whatever he could carry on his back, and had fled with his wife and child to the south. Six million Benedeks, Lilis, boys like Michel. Take one Karl Benedek, brought forth into the world a squealing infant; comfort him; clothe him; feed him; watch him grow, repository of love, hope for the world; send him forth to school; teach him; train him in righteousness; give him the fading youth of his parents; send him to the university; until he steps forth a man, a doctor, product of civilization. Then hound him, drive him from his country, from Vienna to Switzerland, to the Spanish border, back to France, until he takes his last refuge on a hilltop that must have seemed the end of the world; and then gather him in with merciless hands, put him behind barbed wire until the flesh has melted from his bones, and his bones are cast into a shallow lime-filled ditch. That's one. God of Abraham, Isaac, and Jacob, that's only one. How many more to arrive at six million?

Six million, Konrad thought, gazing at Puy-le-Duc. One and one and one and one and one and one and one. How many was that? Seven. Five million, nine hundred ninety-nine thousand, nine hundred and ninety-three to go. One and one and one—each one a life, an irreplaceable universe. One and one and one and one and one, the shame of the world. Don't you know it's Easter Sunday? Yes, let me make merry at your board while you count up to six million, one life at a time.

In spite of the cool breeze that came to him from across the river, there were drops of perspiration on Konrad's face. He passed his hand over his gaunt brow. It would never stop, it was in the bone. That Rose woman, for example. She had taken in a Jewish child, at great risk to herself. She had saved him, at heaven knows what sacrifices. One had to be fair, she had set her own life at stake for his. Yet when he came for him, sent by the child's family, she had called him Jew bastard, and it was the "Jew" and not the other she had meant as the greater insult. A roomful of people, including a priest, who had sided with her, who had shared her sentiments, had perhaps seen nothing incongruous in the situation. France, home of liberty, equality, fraternity. There was still justice in France, he had said. He had said it, and now he would see if it were true.

It occurred to him that there had been children at the party as well, and that one of them in all likelihood was Michel. He had been so disconcerted by his reception, however, that his consciousness had registered nothing more than a small table set apart, the presence of children, a girl with a ribbon in her hair. As for the others— too bad he had not looked at them carefully!

All right, he said to himself. The Benedeks had died, he in a concentration camp, she by her own hand; they had disappeared from reality, to form characterless integers in a sum of horror that froze the imagination. But their boy still lived, and could yet be saved, in spite of all the Roses in the world. We will see, he thought, whether the civilized world, after it has permitted the parents to be killed, will let their child be kept from his family. We will see whether a willful woman can defy the law of the land. He would not rest until he had righted this injustice, if it took his fortune, his peace of mind, his life.

That night, after the supper dishes had been cleared away and Judas had been sent to bed, Konrad sat at his desk and reread two letters. The first one was only a few lines long. Postmarked "Harad, Israel, March 18, 1948," and written in German, it asked if the recipient was the Louis Konrad who had been a schoolmate of the sender in Gonobitz, Austria, many years ago. If so, another communication of great importance would follow. It was signed "Isaac Lindner."

The other letter from Harad, also written in German, but in a different hand, filled six pages, closely written on both sides. It was signed "Hannah Benedek Lindner." Frau Lindner thanked Herr Konrad for his prompt reply to her husband's inquiry, and apologized for disturbing him with a family problem. But she had no one else to turn to. It was a question of her brother's child, now living in an orphanage in Touville, in the care of a certain Mlle Odette Rose. She, Hannah Lindner, had been trying ever since the end of the war to get possession of her nephew, but Mlle Rose had systematically thwarted every effort on her part to do so. Could Herr Konrad possibly help her?

"Our family was from Vienna," Frau Lindner wrote. "I am the oldest of the children, and the only survivor. Our mother died in

1930, and Papa, a railway employee, after being forced to retire from government employment at the time of the Anschluss, became ill and was taken to a hospital. There he disappeared; we were never able to discover any trace of him. Albert, the youngest, was a photographer. In October 1938 his shop was smashed, and he was taken to the concentration camp at Dachau. He returned home several months later; they had released him with a warning to leave the country. He refused to go. He was arrested again. His wife Mitzi received his ashes in an urn. She went to England, stayed there throughout the war, and is now back in Vienna.

"Karl was the pride of the family. A brilliant medical student, he had only recently completed his internship, opened a medical practice and married, when the Germans marched into Austria. My husband Itzik and I had already decided to go to Australia with our two children, and begged Karl and Lili to come with us. Karl refused. He would go to Switzerland, he said, and from there make his way to a country of advanced medical standards, so as to do research. There was no persuading him, and we went our separate ways.

"During our trip to Australia we lost our older boy Hans. He died of typhus in Trieste, and is buried there. He was a lovely boy, eleven years old, intelligent, full of ideals. He died bewildered, not understanding what was happening in the world about him. Perhaps God has explained it to him. I could not.

"In Australia we received several letters from Karl. He had stayed only a short while in Switzerland and then crossed France to Spain, where he was refused entry. He stayed in France, first at Lyons, then in Touville. Perhaps you knew him there. From Touville he wrote to various acquaintances in England, the United States, Argentina. Always the story was the same, always there were difficulties about his medical diploma, his right to practice medicine. In the end he changed his mind about Australia. He wrote to the Medical Association in Sydney, and asked me to speak to various doctors on his behalf. I did so, but was turned away with vague answers. In spite of all my persuasion, the matter dragged on until the war broke out and it was too late.

"The last letter I received from Karl was dated September 1942 and was sent from No. 1-Bis, Rue du Marché, Puy-le-Duc, Touville l'Abbaye, Côte-des-Alpes, France. He wrote that after the occupation of France he had been interned and then released. A child, Michel, had been born on April 14, 1941. Karl had tried again to get through to Spain, and again was turned back. He begged me, if anything happened to him and Lili, to take care of his child. This I have sworn to do."

The letter went on to describe the various steps Frau Lindner had taken after the liberation of France to discover what had happened to Karl and his family. From the mayor of Puy-le-Duc she learned that Karl had been arrested on a street in Touville on February 14, 1944, and sent to the concentration camp at Drancy, where he was not found among the survivors at the entry of the American troops. The mayor could tell her nothing about Lili, but Michel was safe at the Municipal Nursery of Touville, with Mlle Rose. The mayor mentioned a certain Mme Lise Immermann, Michel's godmother, who could give her more detailed information.

Frau Lindner wrote to both Mlle Rose and Mme Immermann. Mlle Rose did not answer, but Mme Immermann confirmed the mayor's information, and added that Lili had also been arrested, but had taken poison and had died en route to Gestapo headquarters.

"You may imagine how I felt to receive this terrible news," Frau Lindner wrote. "I resolved then that I would bring Michel to me in Australia, in fulfillment of my brother's wish. He would be all the more precious to me as the last bearer of the Benedek name, and to fill the place in my heart left by my poor little Hans. I wrote letter after letter to Mlle Rose. She did not answer. Following legal advice, I wrote to the procureur in Touville, to the Foreign Ministry in Paris via the Free French agent in Sydney, to the Red Cross, to many others. Finally, on November 12, 1945, Mlle Rose answered, saying that Michel was still too young to undertake the journey to Australia.

"Since then I have heard nothing from her, and all my efforts to move the authorities have proved in vain. Mlle Rose has turned a deaf ear to my pleadings and to all official pressures. She told the Red Cross that she 'categorically refused' to give up the boy. She told the same thing to Mitzi, Albert's widow, who stopped off at Touville on her way back to Vienna.

"If only I could go to France! I would see if that heartless woman would defy me to my face, and refuse me my brother's child! But I cannot go. Froschl, my other boy (his real name is Franz), is sickly;

he too had typhus in Trieste, and has never been well since. He needs my constant care, and I am afraid, so afraid— He is sixteen now. We did not want to leave Australia because of his health, but he wanted so much to go. 'I will be better in Israel, Mutterl,' he used to say. And so we came here to Harad, and Froschl has taken to his bed, and it is a pity to see his face. Itzik can do nothing for him, he must be out all day and often at night with his veterinary work. My heart is torn in two, for my own poor angel and my brother's boy, and all my dead.

"If you are the same 'guter Louis' that Itzik has praised so often to me, take pity on a mother who wants nothing but children to love. Go to this woman and ask for Karl's child. You will see from her face what she wants. Is it, as with me, the love of a child? Tell her of us and our losses, and Karl's wish. Is it money? Tell her how much, and I will get it somehow. You will know, your own heart will tell you."

Konrad picked up his pen and stared a long time at the blank sheet of paper he had placed before him. Then, choosing his words carefully, he set down a brief, factual account of his visit to the Nursery.

"You suggest," he wrote, "that I tell her of your losses and Karl's wish for Michel. I never got the chance. She ordered me out, in the grossest terms imaginable, as soon as I opened my mouth. Pity will do nothing there, nor, I think, will money, for she left no room for negotiation. I therefore do not know what she wants, unless it be the boy himself.

"If you wish me to pursue this matter further on your behalf, I am willing to do so, but I must have the authority to act. What you must do is to procure for me a full power of attorney, duly notarized, to act in your name in all matters pertaining to your nephew. Also, write me a complete account of every step you have taken so far to gain possession of the boy, the name and address of every person you have been in contact with in this connection, and summaries of the information they supplied you with. With this as basis I will begin an investigation, and when I know what I am up against, I will have recourse to the law. I am convinced that this is the only language Mlle Rose understands."

Konrad put down his pen and read what he had written. There it was, clear and to the point. And meaningless. It did not touch the problem. Seizing the pen again, he wrote:

"Dear Itzik, dear Hannah, my heart is so full, I could weep for shame and anger. Against myself, against you, against every Jew in the world who let this thing happen to his people. How easy it was to think, This is a momentary madness, this will pass, the immediate problem is to survive. And because each thought only of today and not beyond, because each was for himself, they hunted us down, each in his hideaway, and destroyed us like vermin. I too was guilty, I had a wife and child. I kept quiet, I watched and waited. Waited for what? For the civilized world to cry out in horror and come to our defense. The world eventually turned against Germany, not in our defense, but for its own survival, and by that time six million of us had died.

"It is only now that I have begun to take it in, now that the conflict is over and I see how little difference it has made to all but us. At this moment, all France is shaken by the revelation of a massacre that took place at a nearby village in the spring of 1944, in which the Germans herded the entire population—387 men, women, and children—into a barn and set fire to it. Here people talk of nothing else, their faces full of rage and pity. These were fellow Frenchmen. But do not talk to them of six million Jews. The figure is too big, it is not decent, it cannot be grasped. Besides, is this not part of Jewish destiny? Now that Hitler is dead, the score is evened. What counts is that order be restored, and the future be provided for. This is not what they say, but what lies beneath what they do say.

"I do not blame them as much as I blame myself. Why should they have risked their lives for those who did not defend themselves? When that new messiah of hatred first raised his voice to proclaim anti-Semitism as his dogma, the nearest Jew within earshot should have struck him down like the mad dog he was. I, you, anyone, the closest—and not only Hitler, but anyone else who thought the Jew fair game, from the SS officer to the meanest village idiot.

"But no, I ran with the others, and hid out on a farm near Toulon with my wife and little boy. The farmer, a decent person, fed us in return for whatever labor we could do. At night we slept in the barn.

I will not tell you what we went through, it is of little importance now. We survived. My boy is ten now, to him I am a hero—I saved him and his mother, when so many died. But I am ashamed to look into his eyes. What will he think of me when he is a man? If he does not despise me, I will despise him.

"I am haunted, obsessed. At night voices cry out to me, and I have dreams that leave me trembling. Why should this have happened to us? Why? This is what I used to ask myself. Not any more. Now I know the answer. It happened to us not only now but throughout the history of our people, because we let it happen. There is no other answer. All the other reasons are nonsense, invented as a justification. Ask a man why he kicks a cringing, broken-spirited dog, and he will tell you it is because the dog is dirty, or barks, or is in his way. It is a lie, he kicks it because the dog expects it and will slink off guiltily with its tail between its legs. But no one kicks a dog who shows his teeth.

"It is too late to save the six million who died. We have paid this staggering price to learn our lesson. If we have not learned it yet, then we deserve whatever happens to us. Not six million and one. Not one more Jew. It is no longer the Jew against Hitler, it is the Jew against the world. I will fight, with every weapon in my grasp, against any person or power that harms a Jew, physically or otherwise. I cannot restore to you your brother Karl or his wife Lili—but I can and will restore their son. I have made a vow, and I will keep it, no matter what the cost."

5

IT WAS THE NIGHTS he dreaded most. That was when the fever came, and the bad dreams. He had tried staying awake, but it was terrifying to lie there in the dark, thinking those thoughts, so tiny in the hugeness of the world. Besides, hard as he tried, his exhausted body sank imperceptibly into nothingness, and his fears, freed from his will, swelled out and became a horror in which he was trapped.

The nothingness, that was the horror. Sometimes he stood on a bare, lost pinnacle, enveloped by an impenetrable mist, holding his breath and listening to the stillness of a universe without life. Sometimes he walked with silent feet across wastelands of sculptured rock, stretching away into a receding horizon, where all was shrouded and hushed and gray, and there was nobody to see him, nobody in whose eye to be movement, in whose mind to be a thought, nobody, nobody at all. His skin crawled with fear at the awfulness of his solitude. It was different from any solitude he had known, it was palpable, it enclosed him like steel, it stretched away endlessly into space. To be the only spark of life in all that emptiness, to feel crushed and smothered by it, to feel it encasing his ribs and pressing his heart into nothingness as well, to try to hold back that aching weight by a scream caught in the throat—that was too much to bear, his tortured nerves leaped and throbbed within him, and he awoke to find his face burning, his body drenched in sweat, and the bedclothes tangled beneath him. Vati! he said to himself, like a talisman, a shield, an anchor to cling to. And then he remembered, and his heart shriveled like a dead thing. He had no Vati any more, and no God, and nothing would ever make sense again unless he could put the pieces of his shattered universe back together again.

Night after night he lay between sleep and wakefulness, fearing both. If the nightmares awoke him, his mind began working on his problem, wrestling with it, searching for scraps of memory from the past that might help him explain the mystery. His father was a Jew. This was always the starting point, for it was this that had fallen like a thunderbolt into his little world and left it a shambles. It explained so many things, yet raised new questions horrifying in their implications. He knew now, for instance, why his father was dead. The Nazis took Jews away and killed them, as they had the man across the street. This had happened long ago, when he was too little to remember, that was why he did not remember his father's face, only the voice saying, Michel, Michel. That was when his father left him with Mme Quertsch to take to Maman Rose, and those sobs were because his father was sorry to leave him and also because he did not want to go off to be killed. All the time he had waited by the fence looking at Place St. Lazare had been in vain, there had never been the slightest chance his father would come to him, because he was dead from the very first. All the times he had asked about his father, only to be put off with vague answers—the silences, the reticences, the blank expressions as he entered rooms, the looks of pity—all this was clear now; they were ashamed for him, they didn't want him to know, they hoped he would forget the father who was a Jew. That time in M. Béjart's car on the way to Sep, when he had asked why he had not been baptized as a baby, like Pé and all the boys at St. Joseph's, Maman Rose said it was the war. No, it was because his father was a Jew, and Jews didn't baptize because they were not Christians. And his prayers to God the Father, his attempt to penetrate the veil of the other world, to call his father down to him by the force of his love and his will, all that was a mockery, because Jews went to hell.

The Jews had crucified Christ and they were damned to hell. They were doubly damned, because they weren't baptized and didn't go to church and nailed prayers to the door. His father was a Jew, and was damned with the others. He tried not to picture it, but Father Roche's description of hell was too recent and too vivid, and in spite of himself he saw his father burning like a coal in a sheet of flame, begging to be allowed to die again, only it was forever and ever. Around the fires the demons laughed and mocked his screams. And Michel wanted to scream too, he wanted to cry out that it was his Vati they were doing that to, that what they were hurting so dreadfully was all the sweetness and love that his heart remembered and hungered for, to let him go, and he would never ask for anything again, and they could have him in place of his father. But this too stuck in his throat, this was what happened to Jews, and it was God's justice that could never be questioned.

He had never questioned it before, it had all seemed so fitting and proper. There were the good and the evil, the good were those who loved God the Father, and the others were those who had turned from His ways. Nothing was too bad for these, and he had thrilled with righteous indignation to hear the rector explain the awful punishments awaiting them. He loved God, and it did not touch him. Nor his father—wasn't his father goodness itself?

But his father was a Jew. He said that to himself, and his mind looked at it, and tried to go around it, but always it was there, like a huge stone blocking the path. It meant that everything he had dreamed was not so, and God the Father didn't make sense. It wasn't his father there beyond the clouds. Everything had come to pieces in his mind. God the Father, he said to himself. What did it mean? How could part of Him be in heaven, and another part in hell? If the Jews crucified Christ, and Christ was God, and His father was God and also a Jew, had God crucified Himself? And would He send Himself to hell for it? That couldn't be, something was wrong somewhere. He went over his reasoning again and again, in despair because he knew so little, sure that there was another way of looking at it that would set all to rights again, but unable to find it. But he had to find it. He had to, because everything that he had been taught put his father in hell, and he couldn't bear it. If Christ was God and a Jew, no, that wasn't it, if his father was a Jew, and God the Father was in heaven and sent His Only-Begotten Son to be crucified—

His father was a Jew. Jew, he said. Jew. Jew. If you said it over and over, it became a meaningless sound on the tongue. How harshly it struck the ear! What was a Jew? Children of Satan, Father Périer had said. Then Satan was a Jew too. Did he become one after the rebellion in heaven, or was he one while he was still Lucifer, the greatest of the angels? Dark, sweating faces gloating over Christ on the cross, shrieking, Crucify! Crucify! Could his father have done that? What made a man a Jew? Were you born one, or did you have to study for it, like a doctor? Was there something that made you one, the way baptism made you a Christian? Why did they do it, if they knew they would be damned? Perhaps they *wanted* to go to hell, to be with their father. No, no, that wasn't possible, no one would want to roast in a fire. Besides, why would Satan do that to them, if they were his children? If the Jews were children of Satan, and Christ was a Jew, then—no, there was a horrible contradiction there, if only he could find the loose end that would unravel it. If a man deliberately chose to be a Jew, it must be that he didn't know he would be damned. And yet, it was so clear—Jesus Himself told them, and that was what priests were for, and even Félicité, who never went to school because her head was full of mashed potatoes Annette said, knew, and he was only seven and he knew. It must be something else. Maybe they had to stay one because God didn't want them and there was nothing they could do about it. If so, his father had never had a chance, he had lived out his life knowing that when he died he would go to hell, and he could be as good as he wanted and it would make no difference, and maybe he had cried for that too when he said good-bye. His poor Vati! And then he remembered something the prefect had said, that you weren't supposed to feel sorry for them since that meant you were criticizing God. Prayer couldn't help them either, prayer was for those in purgatory. Besides, to whom would he pray?

Was he a Jew too? That M. Konrad had said so. He said, You took a Jewish child and baptized him. If so, you were born one, he had certainly never done anything to make him one. Yes, but they had baptized *him,* Mother Veronica had insisted on it, and Father Périer too. Then God *would* accept one, and he was more confused than ever. Did baptism wash the Jew in you away? To know that, you would have to know what it was that made you one, and see if that changed after the baptism. He had noticed no difference in himself, but of course he hadn't known and might have missed it. Well, but if it *did* wash it away, all of them would do it and there would be no such thing as a Jew, and since that hadn't happened, then . . . And if it didn't, then he was damned too, and it was unfair because he loved Jesus with all his heart, and would not crucify Him for anything.

But that didn't make sense either. Would they have let someone who was to be damned into St. Joseph's, which was a Catholic school where priests were the teachers, not like the public school that Pé went to? At St. Joseph's they taught you how to get to heaven. Why had Mother Veronica spoken to Father Roche for him, to let him go there without paying like the other boys, who came from rich families while Maman Rose was poor? And bought him the expensive communion suit? And said that he would be a priest when he grew up? A Jew who was going to hell couldn't be a priest and say mass and talk to God.

Maybe there were two kinds of Jews, the kind that crucify and those who were like everybody else. Maybe it was like the Trinity that was three in one, and you couldn't understand it but had to take it on faith. Or better yet, like transubstantiation, that made flesh out of bread, and it was really flesh even though it still looked like bread, and Father Roche said that it was God's mystery and no mortal could understand how God did things. Then when Father Périer blamed them for the crucifixion and the Nazis took them away and Maman Rose called them those dreadful names, that was the other kind, like M. Konrad, while he and his father were safe, and his father could be in heaven after all. And then it occurred to him that it was his father the Nazis had taken away, and not M. Konrad, and his heart, which had begun to glow with a little ray of hope, sank again and he was back in the same misery.

The nights passed with agonizing slowness as he wrestled with these thoughts, or yielded himself helplessly to the fearful solitude of his dreams. Only toward morning, when a wan gray light began to filter into his room, did he find some refreshment in sleep. When he awoke, the Nursery was bustling with activity, the children's voices could be heard in the playground, and he had a fleeting moment of security and happiness until reality crashed in on him, and his weary mind took up its intolerable burden again.

Maman Rose and Dr. Peyrefitte, and the others as well, were worried and puzzled by his illness. They couldn't understand it. It was the fever, they said. He had those nightmares because he had fever. But what caused the fever they didn't know. Dr. Peyrefitte shook his gray beard and muttered that he had never seen anything like it. Michel felt sorry for all the trouble he was causing them, and for Maman Rose's face, which was tired all the time and had dark circles like bruises under the eyes. He didn't want to be sick. He couldn't help it if he couldn't hold things in his stomach, and there was that hollowness within him, and he got dizzy if he tried to sit up. Often, at night, when he heard breathing by the open door and knew that Maman Rose had left her rocking chair by Father Périer's bed to look in on him, he lay still so that she would think he was asleep and would not be worried about him. And when they changed his pajamas, and Maman Rose exclaimed over how thin he was, and he saw the despair in her eyes, he longed to hurl himself into her arms, to tell her what he was thinking, to reassure her and be reassured.

But he couldn't tell her, not even when she pleaded with him. She sat by his bed and talked to him and asked him questions that played over his hurt without really touching it. What she said seemed remote somehow, as if she were speaking to a third person while he listened and thought of something else. Was it that M. Konrad? she asked. Had that dreadful man frightened her little baby lamb? Was he afraid M. Konrad would take him away from his Maman Rose? That was a silly thing to be afraid of, because his Maman Rose loved him and would never let anyone take him away. If that M. Konrad ever showed his face in the Nursery again, she would have him arrested. There now, didn't he feel better? He forced himself to listen to her, and if she insisted he said yes; but that wasn't it. It wasn't M. Konrad he was afraid of, but what M. Konrad had said. That he couldn't tell her. She had kept from him the knowledge that his father was a Jew, she was ashamed of it, and that time on the way to Sep she had told him the first thing that came to her head so that he would stop asking questions, the way grownups did when children pestered them. She would do the same thing now, tell him anything so as to still his fears and make him well. He was too big now to be reassured with baby answers, he was a man now who had had his communion and wanted to know the truth.

It was not Maman Rose he would talk to, but Father Périer. He reached this decision after a horrible night, during which he had thrashed about as if he were drowning, and sleep, when it came, was more like unconsciousness than rest. He couldn't go on like this, his mind no longer reasoned but went in circles, and God, the devil, Jew, fire, his father, were only words that led nowhere. True, Father Périer had been taken bad again, and the tube had been put back into his nose, and Mme Bordat and Maman Rose took turns at his bedside, and anyone who came upstairs walked on tiptoe; but in time he would be better, and he could go ask him his question. Father Périer was a priest and couldn't lie. And then he would know, and whatever the answer was he would have to accept it, and build his life on it. Because he had reached the end of his powers, and the truth was further away than before.

Maman Rose and Renée were quarreling. Their voices rose faintly from below, fretful and shrill. Michel turned his head on the pillow to listen. He could not make out their words, only their bickering tone. Then the voices were silent, and he heard footsteps hurrying up the stairs.

"You little sneak!" Renée exclaimed, appearing in the doorway. "You went and told! I'll pay you back, see if I don't." Renée's cheeks were wet, and her blond hair was tossed and straggling.

Michel sat up, but Renée was gone. A moment later a door slammed in the corridor, and Father Périer's querulous voice called weakly, "Madame Bordat!"

He lay back again, bewildered. Why had Renée called him that name? He had not told anyone their secret, not even Pé. Early that morning, when Pé sat by his bed and told him what they were saying about Renée in the kitchen, he had kept silent because a promise was a promise. Had Renée told Annette herself? Then she should not be angry at him now.

Pé came in, his eyes big with excitement. "Maman Rose slapped her. And Renée was crying and said it was like a prison here and she's going to run away."

Michel was aghast. Pé came to the bed and said breathlessly, "You should have heard them. They were yelling at each other, and Madame Bordat came downstairs real mad and said she wouldn't be responsible for Father Périer with all that noise, and Maman Rose told her she was going to have a doctor examine Renée and Renée kept saying it wasn't true and crying and Maman Rose said she sneaked around corners like a little whore, and Renée spit on the floor and said he wasn't a priest anyway, and that's when Maman Rose slapped her."

Was Renée sick? And what did she mean about a priest? Did she mean her young man? Renée had told him that day that he was an engineering student and would be very rich some day, and she was going to marry him, but not to tell. And so he was not a priest, and anyway they didn't marry, that was part of being a priest. Maman Rose must have slapped her for spitting on the floor. That was a dreadful thing to do.

"Say, Michel," Pé said, sitting down on the edge of the bed, "what's a whore?"

He didn't know. He supposed it was something not nice. Pé thought the same. "It made her spit. And Madame Bordat told Mademoiselle Pasquier to get the children out of there. They were all standing around scared. Renée must have done something awful."

Michel hoped Renée would not run away. Maman Rose had cried when Jean got his job in Chambéry, and said that Renée must never leave her, she was the only one left now. Michel had never seen the older brothers, but he knew their names: Arthur, Léon, and Guy. Arthur was the sailor, and he came back once with a parrot tattooed on his chest that he showed to Annette, but the others never came back and after that one time Arthur didn't either, and Maman Rose said they were ungrateful. She said that ingratitude was the worst of all sins. She said that Jean was going too, like the others, because he was a man, but that Renée was her baby. And when Renée laughed and said, A baby of twenty, Maman Rose said that didn't make any difference, she was the youngest and would always be her baby. Now Renée would go too, and was angry at him besides. He wanted to go to her, to explain that he hadn't told, but he was not allowed out of bed, and anyway she had slammed the door.

"Maman Rose was real mad," Pé said. "She slapped her hard. I bet it hurt. Say, Michel, I don't bother you, do I?"

Michel shook his head.

"Maman Rose told me not to bother you, because you're sick. There's nothing to do around here. When I came back from school, Annette chased me out of the kitchen. I wasn't doing anything. Everybody's mad. And every time I come upstairs, Madame Bordat comes out of Father Périer's room and looks at me. Say, Michel, are you scared of that Monsieur Konrad? Maman Rose told Manon it was your nerves, and you were scared Monsieur Konrad would take you away."

From the hall came Mme Bordat's voice calling down the stairs in soft urgency, "Mademoiselle Rose!"

Pé poked him on the arm. "Say, you don't think he's your father, do you?"

"Oh, no!" Michel was shocked. "My father is—" He turned his head away. He had forgotten for a moment. "Go away," he said into his pillow.

"Don't be mad," Pé protested. After a while he sighed. "Well, they'll chase me away from here pretty soon anyway. I'm going to ask Annette about that word." He slipped off the bed and went to the door.

Michel began to cry. He couldn't help it. He cried silently, feeling the hot tears run down his cheeks and soak into the pillow. He was so tired of being sick, and of thinking such big thoughts and not knowing the answers. After a while he stopped, and noticed the bustling in the hall. Something was going on. He wiped his cheeks and sat up, as Pé came in again. Pé came to the bed and whispered, "They sent Manon for Dr. Peyrefitte. And Father Périer is making funny noises and says he wants a priest. Maman Rose is downstairs telephoning and crying."

Rapid footsteps came from the hall and stairs. A door shut. "And *hurry!*" Mme Bordat's voice snapped.

Nearby a voice was whimpering, "Ah, ah, ah."

He couldn't wait any longer. It seemed to him ages that he had been lying tense in the darkness, watching through the window the lights in the houses across the street as they winked out one by one, listening to those in the Nursery settling down for the night. Now all was still; no one walked in the street any more, and the murmur of cars passing through Place St. Lazare had faded away. It must be well after midnight. The Nursery lay wrapped in sleep, Touville slept in its cradle of mountains, the world slept.

Michel sat up in bed. He felt weak, but his brain was extraordinarily clear. He eased himself to the floor. It was cold to his bare feet, and he shivered, steadying himself against the bed. Pé was asleep, his face turned to the wall. Pé had taken a long time to drop off; once Michel had heard stifled sobs, as though from under a pillow. A great wave of pity came over him. There was so much sorrow in the world. Why did God permit one's loved ones to be taken away? Love hurt more than any other kind of pain. It seemed to Michel that love was like a monster, it was enough for it to come into existence for it to destroy the one who had inspired it. That was what had happened to Pé, that was what had happened to him with his father, and what was happening to Father Périer. Because Father Périer was dying, that was clear. Those animal-like moans he had heard no longer sounded like the person he knew, as though something ominous and alien had taken over that sick body for its own purposes. Dr. Peyrefitte had told Maman Rose that afternoon that he didn't know how the poor old man held on, that there was no life left in him. And they had sent for a priest, a young one that Pé had never seen before, who went in there with the holy oils, and came out soon after pale and angry, saying, "He must not die here." Pé came and told Michel that, and that Maman Rose was angry too and answered, "Where then? He can't be moved." The priest went away muttering that he

·66·

was going to the bishop. Michel wondered about that, but it wasn't important, what mattered was that Father Périer was going to die, and of a sudden Michel realized how much the old priest meant to him.

How strange and light he felt! He moved toward the door as though it were only his will and not his body in motion. What would he do if Maman Rose were there? She would scold him and send him back to bed, and his chance would be gone. He had to take that risk. Father Périer's door was ajar. He eased it open a little more and peered in. The room was dark, but a faint light from the street touched up the closed curtains of the window. Against it he could distinguish the dark bulk of the bed, and the rocking chair at its foot. It was empty, Maman Rose had gone to bed. Something white and round was staring at him from the black corner behind the bed, and he was disconcerted until he remembered the oxygen cylinder and the dial perched on top. Moving noiselessly, he slipped into the room and approached the bed.

Father Périer was lying on his back with the blanket pulled up to his chest, a hand vaguely white at his side. Was he breathing? Or was it his own breath that Michel heard? He moved closer, until he could see the priest's peaked, ghostly profile, and the skin like dirty paper traced by a thin, black line.

Incredulous, Michel stared at him. Could this be Father Périer? Could a week have made so much difference? His face seemed to have caved in, the bones showed through the flesh. Michel felt death in the air, brooding over those sunken eyes and seamed, parted lips. So this was what it was like, that evil presence, already pressing down, greedy for its prey! Michel wanted to drive it away, he wanted to cry out, Don't die! But he felt powerless before the mystery of what he saw.

Poor Father Périer! Poor, poor man! It was almost as though it were his father lying there under that monstrous, invisible burden. With a pang Michel thought of the many times he had run to greet the priest, and how loving had been the kind old man's caresses. How often had Michel sat beside him during the hours of catechism and felt Father Périer's hand rest on his head in a benediction that stilled for that moment the ache that otherwise never left him! Now he was losing Father Périer too, as he had lost his Vati. It was unfair to do this to him twice.

Michel's heart gave a sudden leap. The priest's eyes had opened, and he had turned his head in a convulsive movement that sent the oxygen tube slithering down the pillow, while his hand rose abruptly, shaking, before his face.

"No, no," Father Périer whispered hoarsely, fixing great staring eyes on him in dread.

Michel stood congealed in fright. Who did Father Périer think he was? He managed to stammer, "It's Michel."

Father Périer stared at him for a long time. At length he sighed, moving his head wearily and closing his eyes. Michel let his breath out and waited. Had Father Périer fallen asleep again? It was very tiring to stand, and he let himself sink quietly to the carpet beside the bed. The priest's hand lay on the blanket at the level of Michel's eyes; every now and then the fingers twitched a little. He looked at them, and thought how dreadful it must be to be old and sick. Had his father been like that? Had anyone sat by his bed? Perhaps he too had lifted his head to peer into the darkness, looking for his Michel and wondering why he did not come. The pain of that thought made him wince. Until now he had always thought of how much he missed his father, but his father must have missed him too. But how could he go to him, little as he was? He was not even three when he came to the Nursery, Maman Rose said. Where would he look? Sitting there in the dark, he was filled with a sense of his own helplessness, as though he were living his nightmare again. If he were God, how different things would be! He would not have let Adam eat the apple, and then death would not have come into the world, and you could always be with those you loved. He and his Vati and Father Périer and Maman Rose would all live together, and no one would get sick or die, and little boys could sleep at night and jump out of bed happy in the morning. And then it would not be necessary for God to send His Only-Begotten Son to redeem the world, and nobody would crucify Him, and so there would be no Jews and his father would be a Catholic like everybody else. Why hadn't God let well enough alone? He would ask Father Périer that, along with his other question.

"Mother of God!" Father Périer said with a gasp, sitting up and peering about him in bewilderment. Michel scrambled to his feet.

"What is it?" Father Périer said.

"It's me," he whispered. "It's Michel, Father."

"What is it?" Father Périer said again, groping at his chest.

Fearfully Michel repeated his name. At the sound the priest turned his head toward him. His eyes were wide and full of pain.

Michel stepped closer, and Father Périer with a little choking sound clutched his hand and put it to his chest. Through the clammy skin matted with whitish hair Michel could feel a horrible flutter, like a bird beating its wings against a cage.

"Ah!" Father Périer grunted, doubling forward against Michel's shoulder.

Under the old man's weight Michel felt his knees buckling beneath him. He braced himself, panting. If he fell, Father Périer would fall too. Should he call Maman Rose? He could not hold out much longer. Fortunately, just when it seemed impossible to bear up any more, the priest gave a sigh and lay back on his pillow. Faint and dizzy, Michel leaned against the bed and caught his breath. Father Périer was muttering something, his head rolling from side to side. Michel thought he heard the word "hills." He leaned over the pillow, whispering brokenly, "Father Périer, don't die. Don't leave me alone."

"Forgive," the priest said, opening his eyes. Words struggled in his throat. "No time," he got out at last.

"Father Périer."

The priest's eyes had begun to glaze. But as Michel watched, the film cleared away. "It's Michel," Father Périer said distinctly. "Your face. God sent to take. Glad."

It was his last chance. Feeling a terrible hollow in the pit of his stomach, his eyes filled with tears, Michel said, "Is my father in hell? Father Périer, is my father in hell?"

"Michel?" the priest whispered urgently, straining his head upwards. "Forgive. Tell me God forgive. Can't see. Hurry. I'm afraid. I—"

"Is my—" Michel began again, but stopped at the rattling sound. Father Périer's head dropped, and a hiss of air touched Michel's face. Slowly the head sank sideways and was still.

Michel uttered a little cry, backing away. He moved until he was brought up by the wall beside the door. The door swung wide open and Maman Rose hurried in, her eyes fixed on the bed. "Henri?" she said as she crossed the room.

Maman Rose had not yet seen him; her back to him, she was bending over the bed. She uttered an exclamation and began to sob. He was dead, then, he was really dead! Michel had a wild desire to scream and run, but was rooted to the floor. Why was Maman Rose pulling up the blanket? When she stepped back, he saw that the white patch that was the priest's face had disappeared. It was like a release. Holding his breath, his eyes fixed on Maman Rose's back, under the accusing eye of the dial in the corner, Michel slipped out the door.

In an instant he was in his bed, the covers pulled up to his chin, trembling with emotion. Father Périer was dead! He had seen him die! He had seen the light fade from his face and something dark and fearful take possession of it. This was death, then, that long exhalation like a bicycle tire going flat, that tired collapse. That sound must have been the soul leaving the body. Michel's skin prickled as he remembered that it had touched his face in passing. It seemed to him that he could still feel it against his cheek.

He lay in the dark, listening to the stillness in the Nursery, wondering what would happen now. What did people do when someone died? Would Maman Rose wake everybody up? At the same time his mind went over the details of his visit to the dead man's room. Why had Father Périer been so startled at the sight of him? He had not meant to do that, he had only wanted— A chill went through him as a horrible thought entered his mind. Father Périer had been asleep, and only after he saw Michel had he had his attack. Could Michel's visit have been responsible for—?

The moment he thought it, he wiped it from his mind. It was impossible. He must never think such a thing again.

Lying there, staring into the dark, Michel was suddenly overwhelmed by a sense of loss so acute that it was like a physical shock. It had come to him that Father Périer was gone. What was lying on the bed covered with the blanket was no longer Father Périer. The soul had gone to heaven, leaving that motionless envelope behind; and soon they would bury that, they would dig a hole in the ground and hide it, and there would be nothing left, and it would be as if Father Périer had never lived. Gone! he said to himself. How could that be? How could someone just stop being? He would wake up mornings and summon up his world; there would be Maman Rose, and Pé, and Renée, and all the rest, even the poor half-witted Félicité—but where Father Périer had been would be a gap, an absence, an emptiness. Michel's heart was filled with sorrow and bitterness. How unfair it was! How difficult it was to go on, when those one loved stopped being! Was this all that was left of a man's life? Nothing but the memory and love he left in the hearts of those who stayed behind? Michel felt that he had made a great discovery; for a moment it seemed that he had touched on a great secret that had been hidden behind a veil and that was part of being grown up. He would bear Father Périer in his heart, alongside his father. It would be like giving them a continued existence, it would be like having them again. How stupid he had been to suppose that he could call his father down to him through the altar! Death lay in between, that monstrous presence that lay now on Father Périer's body in Jean's room, under the gray blanket. Yes, but if death took the body, it could not touch his love. His Vati and Father Périer would always exist, so long as he remembered them. And when he thought of them, they would think of him too, they would look down from heaven and smile tenderly, and he would smile back inside himself, and it would be—

But how could he have forgotten? Father Périer had not answered his question! He had let his sorrow over the old man's death blind him to his great problem. What was left for him now? What was he to do? If his father was a Jew, and the Jews had crucified— Oh God, not that, not that again! Anything but that! Rather than that he would ask Maman Rose. He couldn't choose any more. Where Father Périer had been was only a great absence. When Maman Rose came to tell him that Father Périer was dead, he would tell her that he knew, that he had entered the sick man's room to ask him a question, and had seen him die. She would scold him for having got out of bed and disturbing the invalid; but then she would ask, What question? and then it could come out, he would tell her what had been tormenting him all these days and nights since Easter Sunday, that made him sick and gave him the fever. She would tell him the truth, she would have to! He would throw himself into her arms and hold her tight, and she would see how important it was to him, and she would tell him the truth. And then he would know what to do.

Michel would have prayed if he had dared. Instead, closing his eyes and clasping his hands, he timidly addressed himself to the spirit of Father Périer, asking him to intercede for him, to clear up his doubts, so that he could be at peace and happy again.

Michel awoke with a start. It was cold and dark. Pé slept peacefully, his face to the wall. What had awakened him? Then he heard the sound again: a dull thud coming from below, the creak of the stair. A door opened. Pushing aside the curtain, he looked into the front garden, pale and empty under the moon. As he watched, two dark figures moved down the walk to the gate, holding between them by the handles something long and heavy covered by a gray blanket; they staggered under the weight, throwing a grotesque shadow to the ground. The man in front turned in opening the gate, and Michel saw M. Joseph's pockmarked face. A small closed delivery truck stood in the street. Hastily the men shoved in their burden and drove off, the gears clashing loudly in the stillness of the night.

In the morning sunlight Maman Rose's face looked tired under the make-up. Michel sat up, his confession trembling on his lips. But she hardly looked at him.

"Father Périer's gone home," she announced gaily. "Isn't that good news? He felt better and went home. Say good-bye to Michel, he told me. Tell him I'll visit again soon. And now, as soon as you're better, everything will be just as it was before. Manon is coming along with your breakfast. You must eat everything and grow strong."

Stunned, Michel watched Maman Rose's back as she went out the door.

6

ITTING IN HIS high-ceilinged office, his fair, handsome head outlined against the far window, Dr. Lévy said, "It was in 1939.
He came here to ask me to help him find a place with a doctor
specializing in radiology. I knew what he meant, of course, and I
liked him—he was young, eager, had done special work in Vienna.
But I just couldn't use him. My practice is almost entirely consult-
ant, and anyway we don't have the custom here in France that you
find in other parts of the world, of having two or more doctors in the
same office. I did what I could. I spoke to several doctors about him,
sent some general practice his way, brought him into contact with a
pharmacist who would fill his prescriptions."

That would be Arnauld, Konrad thought. The light from the window gave Dr. Lévy a strange, uncertain aureole. Konrad pushed his
chair sideways. That was better. He let his eyes rest on the doctor's
calm face and listened.

"But things were pretty hard for him. There were maybe a half-
dozen refugee doctors like him, who in the beginning could hardly
speak the language, with German or Austrian diplomas that were
valueless in France. They couldn't practice openly, and so they made
their living among the refugees, who paid very little or not at all.
Benedek wrote his prescriptions without a signature, and the pharmacist—Arnauld is his name—would get other doctors to sign them
afterwards. I signed a number of them myself. But there were some
who didn't like it and grumbled. Still, he got by. At the start it was
only a question of practicing without proper authority, and people
winked at it. Things were tougher under Vichy and the Italians, and
of course under the Germans it was as much as your life was worth.
He kept pretty much out of sight, avoided the main streets and
known check points, carried his instruments in a paper bag—he had

an especially fine set he'd brought from Vienna—and so forth. You know. But he wouldn't go, and it was just a question of time."

A paper bag. Something stirred in Konrad's memory. A brown manila paper bag, tied with yellow twine, on a bedspread. Judas' face, burning with fever. The strange doctor, crouched in a chair, his head almost touching his knees. The trembling hand that held the cup. Dr. Lévy was looking at him with a question in his eyes.

"In February or March of 1943," Konrad said, "my boy was suddenly taken ill. Dr. Villeul couldn't come, I don't remember why. I tried to reach you, but you had already gone underground. Villeul's secretary promised to get me someone. He showed up toward evening, carrying his instruments in a paper bag. In his middle thirties, I would say, medium height, dark hair, deep-sunken eyes. We spoke in German. He was from Vienna, he said. He wouldn't write a prescription, said he would have the medicine sent by messenger. It was bitter cold outside; I had a fire going in the boy's room, and told him to stay and warm up. He looked all in, and blue with the cold. But he wouldn't stay, seemed nervous and in a hurry. Rina gave him some coffee, such as it was. I asked him his name. Wait a minute." Konrad stared at the polished parquet floor. "Dr. Weiss," he said finally.

Dr. Lévy nodded. "That was Karl Benedek. Weiss was his wife's name. Lili Weiss Benedek. He used several names. He didn't know you, you see. You can check with Villeul if you want, not that it matters. He was always in a hurry, poor chap. Incidentally, he was a Zionist, did you know? Back in Vienna, I mean, before he came here. We often talked about it. In fact, it was he who aroused my interest in the movement. I hadn't thought much about it either way before. It took the war to make me realize. Like so many of us."

"Yes," Konrad said. "Like so many of us. But now we know."

Dr. Lévy studied his face, but said nothing.

So he had known him after all! He had written Hannah that he had not. Karl Benedek had come to his home, examined his son, sat in his chair. Already, before the Germans had begun their wholesale arrests and daily roundups, the man's nerves were shot, he wouldn't even stay to get warm. Did he have another call? Was he afraid to stay too long in one place? Or were his thoughts in Puy-le-Duc, with his Lili, his Michel? Dr. Weiss. He didn't know you, you see. Another Austrian, another Jew. I am Joseph, your brother, whom you sold into Egypt. But he didn't know you. Another year of it, trudging about with his paper bag. The boy was born on April fourteenth,

1941, Hannah had written; not even two at the time. Helpless, a stone in his belly. And the noose tighter and tighter. Judas at least was five. The difference between life and death.

Konrad asked, "How did they get him? The sister says you wrote to her about it."

Dr. Lévy made a wry face and stood up. "I hated to write that letter," he said, walking to the window. He stared out at Place Chapelle, partially blocked by the church that showed its back to him. "You can almost see it from here," he said, pointing. "It's just a little way up the square, by the café. It was an afternoon in February 1944, and he was on his way to the pharmacy. Incidentally, you ought to go over there and talk to Arnauld, it's on the other side of the square, in that maze of little streets. Benedek used to come round to it from behind, he avoided Place Chapelle like the plague. So did I, for that matter. But that day, God knows why, he came right through, and was challenged by two Vichy men. Arnauld's messenger boy saw it and ran to tell him at the pharmacy. He said he saw them walking off with him, and that the doctor was smiling."

"Smiling!" Konrad said with a stare.

"For the previous several months," Dr. Lévy said without turning around, "I had been hiding out in Arnauld's mother's house, in the cellar. Arnauld came running to me like a madman, with tears running down his cheeks. He thought the world of Benedek, you know. There was nothing we could do about him, of course, but his wife and boy were up there at Puy-le-Duc, and we had to get them out. Benedek had hidden the boy in the country, but we didn't know that. We decided to bring them to the cellar for the time being, until we could find a safer spot. I got on the phone and got through to one of my contacts, Sister Josephine of the Temple Dames, and she got on her bicycle and went up to Puy-le-Duc in a hurry. She reached Lili before the Gestapo did, but Lili wouldn't go. I've never been able to figure out quite what happened. Something must have snapped in her. According to the nun, Lili leaned against the door and looked at her the whole time she was talking. Didn't move, didn't say a word, just looked."

"The boy wasn't there," Konrad said.

"I've often wondered if that wasn't it. Because then she'd have gone, to save him, if not herself. As it was, she must have just given up. Sister Josephine couldn't get her to go. Said she had the impression that the woman just didn't hear what she was saying. I've talked to the Benedeks' landlord, who told me that when the Gestapo did come and made him unlock the door, Lili was rocking in a chair, waiting for them. They took her downstairs, and she collapsed on the sidewalk. Cyanide, very probably."

The man of science, calm, objective. And I will bless her, and give thee a son also of her; yea, I will bless her, and she shall be a mother of nations; kings of people shall be of her. But that joker upstairs hadn't said anything about cyanide. What did she die of? Cyanide, very probably. Next case.

No, no, it wasn't like that at all. Had he lost all sense of proportion? Lévy had tried to save her, which was more than he, Konrad, had done. He had run, while Lévy had smuggled his wife and daughters off to Switzerland and had stayed in Touville, hiding like a rat in cellars, working with the Resistance with that same calm that now rubbed Konrad the wrong way. And Arnauld too, the Gentile with tears running down his face for the Jew Benedek. And a nun, who had pleaded and pleaded.

Konrad rubbed his eyebrow with a long, splay finger and looked at Dr. Lévy with no expression. Dr. Lévy had turned and walked back to his desk. Lowering himself into his chair, he said carefully, "You know, I saw Benedek, two or three weeks before he was arrested. I was surprised. I thought he had cleared out by then. I urged him to go, told him I could arrange a place for him up in the hills. He wouldn't, said he was tired of running." He repeated softly, "Tired of running."

The mouse in the bathroom. He had shut the door, rolled up a newspaper, and struck at the little creature as it darted into corners, giving little bounds and squeals. It couldn't get out, there was no place to hide on the white-tiled floor. He had been almost stirred to pity when the tiny thing ran to his feet and stopped there, quivering, waiting for the blow. But he had struck anyway. Also thou shalt lie down, and none shall make thee afraid. The hand had trembled, and coffee had spilled over into the saucer. February or March, a whole year before. At what point had he—?

"He fainted in my house," Konrad said. "And all I could do for him was to give him a cup of coffee."

"He was a fool!" Dr. Lévy said violently, turning suddenly in his chair. "In God's name, who wasn't tired then? And with a wife and child!" He got up and poured himself a glass of water from a pitcher on a stand. He sipped the water, staring at the wall. He said, "There was nothing you could do."

The clock on the wall whirred gently and gave a chime. Konrad got up to go. Dr. Lévy said, "And the boy?" Konrad made a gesture and said simply, "I'm going to get him." Dr. Lévy said, "Watch out for Mademoiselle Rose. She has powerful friends. I've seen her often at city hall."

"Oh?" Konrad said.

"Didn't you know? How do you think she got to be directress of the Nursery? She was just another nurse there, when His Honor the mayor took a sudden interest in working mothers. In no time at all there was a new directress. It caused quite a stir, and a few people wrote hot letters to the newspapers. You hadn't heard about it?"

"No. But I suppose that's the kind of thing I'll have to find out."

Dr. Lévy regarded him oddly, then smiled, pushed him on the shoulder and said, "You're a strange duck, Konrad, do you know that?"

"I suppose I am."

"Nose around a bit, talk to people. If there's any way I can help, let me know."

"I'll remember that."

"I mean it."

"All right," Konrad said.

"You know something?" Arnauld demanded, pivoting awkwardly on his stool and thrusting his flushed, loose-jowled face close to Konrad's. "Benedek was a doctor. A real doctor. He knew his medicine, by Christ! I've seen all kinds, but that one was born to it. You've talked to Lévy, Lévy brought him here. Sure, I'll fill his prescriptions, I said. What the hell do I care about their laws? He's a doctor, isn't he? A chap down on his luck. There's one of them that used to come in here—not any more—and he said to me, I won't sign, you ought to know it's against the law. Never heard of it, I said to him. A refugee, he says. You won't starve, I told him. By Christ, I did, and he got mad. I see him now and then, but he doesn't come in here any more. Don't talk to me about doctors!

"A man like Benedek, living from hand to mouth! The finest gentleman that ever trod God's green earth, never complained, never talked about himself. He used to sit out front, waiting to see what would turn up. Worried about getting me into trouble, can you imagine? Don't you fret, I told him. I'm a Jew, he told me once. Never heard of it, I said. That's the only time I heard him laugh."

They were sitting in the prescription room. Hardly had Konrad entered the pharmacy and mentioned the name Benedek to the big, sandy-haired man with the staring blue eyes than Arnauld came hurrying out from behind the glass-topped counter to shake his hand and usher him into the sanctum behind the swinging doors. Konrad had liked him at once.

"The sister wants the boy?" Arnauld said. "You know, I've wondered about that. She wrote to me, oh, two three years ago, about the doctor. What could I say? I mean, how can you write a thing like that? So I answered something, and she wrote to me again, to thank me. To thank me, can you imagine? A man like that! But about the boy, I heard he was still here, at that home in Place St. Lazare, and I thought, Doesn't she want him? I couldn't understand it, but it was none of my business. The handsomest boy you ever saw. Benedek brought him here once, couldn't have been more than two at the time. A little bit of a thing. My cashier went wild about him. That hair! she said. He had golden curls. She couldn't get over it, said it was wasted on a boy, and what she wouldn't give, and so on. Skin like milk, big gray eyes. Grabbed his father's pants, wouldn't let go. Afraid his Vati would get away from him. That's what he called him, Vati. You should have seen how Benedek looked at him! Ate him up with his eyes. I've seen doting fathers. Of course, it must have been the boy—" Arnauld stopped and stared down at the floor. Konrad waited.

"Christ!" Arnauld said wearily, getting up from his stool. He opened a drawer and took out a plain brown bottle and two small glasses. He filled the glasses with an amber fluid and handed one to Konrad without looking at him, saying absently, "During the Occupation we helped people get away. Did Lévy tell you about that? We had a chain going, headed by a priest operating out of Lyons. Here in Touville it was Lévy and I, and some others. This was our operating base, here in the pharmacy. It was natural, you see, people coming and going all the time, a back entrance, a telephone, a messenger boy, and so on. It's no secret now, it was in the papers, and we all got decorated after it was over. We got people false papers, and put them in villages and farms, mostly in mountain areas. For children we had a different system, some we passed out to families, and some we got over to Switzerland. You know the Temple Dames? The convent school out there past the barracks, on the highway? The kids would be brought there at certain times and be taken out on picnics in the school bus. It was the damnedest thing you ever heard of for nerve. They'd go right through town, a bus full of children and two or three priests, singing and waving at the Germans, out for a day in the country. The priests weren't priests at all, they were Resistance agents in disguise, and they took the kids up to a village on the border, and in the evening they'd hike them over the mountain through the woods to the other side, where someone would be waiting. It wasn't until near the end that the Germans caught on, and by that time we'd got hundreds of them out."

Arnauld tossed off the contents of his glass in one motion. Licking his lips, he said, "I wasn't supposed to do any recruiting, but one day I couldn't stand it any longer, I called Benedek in here and talked to him. No details, of course, it was too dangerous, but I told him I could get him out, him one place, his wife another, and the kid to Switzerland. Switzerland! he says. How? Never you mind, I said. Over the hills and far away. You leave it to us. And I told him, mentioning no names or places. What! he says. Climb mountains in the snow, at night? Why, he's a baby, he says, he's only two. No, no, we'll stay here. And there was no budging him. Later, Lévy talked to him too, but nothing doing. And so, you see—" Arnauld made a gesture of helplessness, took out a handkerchief and blew his nose noisily.

Yes, he saw. He saw himself in the barn near Toulon, on an icy cloudless night in which the stars shone with a peculiar brilliance, as if mocking the war-torn world. He saw himself lifting the lantern over Judas' face, rosy with the cold, as he slept huddled against his mother under the stiff, greasy horse blanket. And he saw the child's eyes open, the look of wonderment that gave way to recognition and trust, the small hand that moved to touch his cheek, gently, falteringly, before Judas' eyes closed and he slept again, reassured. He had crouched by the sleeping pair all night, his coat over his back, watching through the window until the stars paled, and in the dawn he thought, We have lived another day, we are still together.

Konrad still had the glass in his hand. He put it down and rose to his feet. Arnauld followed him into the pharmacy. "Look," he said, pointing. "That's where Benedek used to sit, on that chair. Right there, waiting. If you knew how many times I've looked up, expecting to see him there still!"

"Sit down, sit down," Rabbi Notarius said with shy warmth, indicating the leather armchair beside his desk. Konrad sank into it, doubling his long shanks sideways. Notarius sat down in his swivel chair and put on his skullcap. Konrad noted the self-conscious movement with irony: the smoothly shaven, boyishly earnest face, the neat gray business suit, the manicured nails, the gleaming shoes, all proclaimed the rising young professional. But no, said the stern skullcap. As always, whenever his path crossed Notarius', Konrad thought of Rabbi Schmul of Gonobitz. The black kaftan whose seams were rotted with age. The sallow flabby face with the mean eyes. The beard stained with tobacco. The gnarled finger with the thimble for rapping heads. Bonk! Say it again, stupid! Bonk! Why are you looking out the window? God is here, in the book. That was a rabbi, the old goat.

God. God who died in Gonobitz. The old ache in his heart. The stump in the clearing behind the house of death. The gangling young man staring, dry-eyed, at the sky. The pale beech saplings, silent mourners for a stone-bruised heart.

"You won't believe this," Konrad said with a thin smile. "For years, as a boy, I thought of becoming a rabbi. Konrad the atheist, who gives you so much trouble at the meetings."

"Why shouldn't I believe it?" Notarius countered, proffering a pack of cigarettes. Konrad lifted his hand in refusal, and the rabbi took one and lit it. Blowing out a stream of smoke, he said, "I've never thought of you as an atheist. There are no atheists."

"Ah?" Konrad said.

"There are no atheists," Notarius repeated. "At most, those who turn away from God. But even those believe that what they are turning away from exists. Like Baudelaire. Shaking his fist at God, and praying to the devil. Do you call that an atheist?"

Konrad let his eyes wander to the well-filled bookshelves that lined the study. Notarius made a deprecating gesture, smiling.

"Better Baudelaire than Job," Konrad retorted. "The Lord hath taken away, blessed be the name of the Lord. Six million Jews. I find it hard to be grateful."

Notarius regarded him steadily, the color rising to his cheeks. "God's ways are not our ways."

Konrad shrugged. The same old wisdom, served up by a man fifteen years his junior. Well, he had asked for it. God's ways are not— Oh, but they are, my friend, they are. And that's why— Drop it.

"At the meeting the other night," he said abruptly, "when the question of displaced children came up, it occurred to me that you might be able to help in the case of a Jewish orphan here in Touville who's being kept from his family. The name is Benedek, Michel Benedek. Maybe you know about it?"

"Benedek? Why, yes. Let me see." Notarius coughed, and dropped his cigarette in the ash tray with a grimace. "I've been told not to smoke," he said, coughing and pulling open his desk drawer. "Benedek? I've got the list here. There are so many. But I remember, a Mademoiselle Rose, wasn't it?"

"That's it."

"Yes, here it is." Notarius put down a sheaf of clipped sheets and pointed to the top page. "See? Michel Benedek, born April fourteenth, 1941, orphan, etc., etc."

Konrad leaned forward, noted the entry, and then studied the heading. It read "Jewish Children's Aid Society. Displaced Jewish Children in the Côte-des-Alpes Department, December 1946."

"There's a line through the boy's name," Konrad said.

"Yes, I made a report to the Consistory in Paris. It's part of their program, you know. Over a year ago. I went to the Municipal Nursery, to talk to Mademoiselle Rose about it. And she said—"

"Oh?" Konrad said, raising his eyebrows. "Mademoiselle Rose received you?"

"And why shouldn't she receive me?" Notarius asked, puzzled. "As a matter of fact, she couldn't have been more cooperative. She brought me the boy to see, and told me the whole story. What's so strange about it? But here," he added, sitting up straight and staring, "what do you mean, kept from his family? If the aunt doesn't want him?"

Konrad stared back. "The aunt doesn't *what?* What are you talking about?"

"You mean she does? At this late date?" Notarius' surprise gave way to indignation. "Oh, really, now!"

"Late date?" Konrad repeated. "See here, I don't understand this at all. What makes you think the aunt doesn't want him? Did Mademoiselle Rose tell you that?"

"It's a shame," Notarius said with feeling, nodding. "Her own brother's child! And so she's had a change of heart? Do you know her?"

Konrad sighed, and leaned back in the armchair. "We keep going in circles. Let's start from the beginning. Suppose you tell me just what it was Mademoiselle Rose told you. When did you see her?"

"Within a few days of getting the list. December 1946. I telephoned the Nursery for an appointment and went over there. I don't know why it surprises you, but she received me most cordially. A woman of about forty, matronly, soft-spoken—"

"I've met the lady," Konrad said dryly. "Go on."

"Oh? Well, she took me into her office and explained the whole background to me. How the father entrusted the boy to her before he was deported—"

"No," Konrad said. "It didn't happen quite that way. Benedek turned the boy over to a certain Madame Quertsch here in the city, a Catholic woman who had connections with a religious day nursery up at Gade. St. Vincent de Paul's. The boy was there when Benedek was arrested. The nuns wouldn't keep him, and so Madame Quertsch took him to the Temple Dames here in town. They wouldn't take him either, and sent the woman to Mademoiselle Rose. I've talked to Madame Quertsch. I doubt that Mademoiselle Rose even knew the father."

"Oh?" Notarius said, frowning. "Well, I may have misunderstood, of course. It's been quite a while. But you seem to know a lot about the case. I gather that you have a particular interest? No relation, is it?"

Konrad shook his head. "I'll tell you about that. But go on."

"Let me see. Mademoiselle Rose took the boy in and kept him hidden until the Liberation. Then she set about trying to locate the boy's family. But the months went by, a year, two years, and no sign of anybody, until—"

"A lie!" Konrad said harshly. "The Liberation was in August 1944. What's this about a year, two years? The aunt wrote to Mademoiselle Rose within a few months, as soon as the mails were running and she found out where the boy was."

"Mademoiselle Rose said nothing about any such letter."

"Not *a* letter. Letters. Parcels of food and clothing. Petitions to the authorities. Here," Konrad said, fishing an envelope from his pocket and placing it on the desk blotter. "This will explain it to you better than I can. If you can make out the old German script."

The rabbi put on a pair of heavy horn-rimmed glasses and slid the thin, folded sheets out of the envelope. He glanced at the opening lines, then turned the pages over to read the signature. "Yes," he said. "Hannah Benedek Lindner. That was the name." He began to read, his brows knit in concentration. Konrad waited, watching the growing trouble in the other's face. Once Notarius' expression changed to abrupt incredulity, and he uttered an exclamation. Finally, he let the letter fall to the desk and removed his glasses. "This is very strange," he said, shaking his head. "Very strange, indeed. The two stories couldn't be more contradictory. And yet Mademoiselle Rose was so positive. She said that it wasn't until a month or so before my visit that she found out that there *were* any relatives, and that was when Madame Lindner came to the Nursery."

"Who?" Konrad demanded, startled.

"Madame Lindner. She came to see Mademoiselle Rose, but she wouldn't take the boy. Said she was a poor widow, and that she couldn't take care of him. And now," Notarius pursued, tapping the letter significantly, "it seems she's not a widow after all."

Konrad had risen to his feet and was glaring down at the rabbi. "Madame Lindner never visited the Nursery," he snapped. "How could she, if she's never come to France?"

"She doesn't *say* she's been here, but of course she has."

"Look!" Konrad said, seizing the letter and ruffling through the pages. He quoted, " 'If only I could go to France!' Does that sound like—?"

"But she must mean, If only I could go to France *again*. At least, that's the way I understood it. Apparently she's changed her mind. As for all her efforts to get the boy, and that letter she says she received from Mademoiselle Rose in November 1945—"

"Ah, yes!" Konrad said. "Explain that to me."

"I can't," Notarius said patiently, "unless she means 1946."

The two men stared at each other. Konrad, who had leaned over the desk to quote the letter and had remained in that position, straightened up and stepped back. With an effort at self-control, he said, "That woman told you a pack of lies, and now you don't let yourself be convinced by the truth. If ever I heard a true word from the heart, it's in that letter. She said November 1945, and that's what she meant. In due time, I'll have a copy of Mademoiselle Rose's letter and can show it to you. It's been two weeks since I got Madame Lindner's letter, and in that time I've been making inquiries. And I find that every piece of information I've got so far substantiates what Madame Lindner says. Unless, of course," he suggested sarcastically, "you think I'm lying too."

"Here, wait a minute," Notarius protested angrily. "I didn't accuse anyone of lying. *You're* the one who's been making accusations. You said that Mademoiselle Rose—"

"I did, and I'm going to prove it. Mademoiselle Rose claims that she didn't know of the aunt's existence until the autumn of 1946, while Madame Lindner claims that she was in contact with the woman as early as the beginning of 1945, almost two years before. Is that right? Very well. In her letter Hannah Lindner mentions that she went to the Red Cross for help. I went to the Red Cross Chapter here in Touville, and talked to the president, Monsieur Fleury. He showed me his file. In May 1945 Madame Lindner took out a permit allowing her nephew to enter Australia in her charge. There's a copy in the Benedek folder. The boy was to be conducted by a Red Cross field worker to Le Havre, and from there to London, where his other aunt was staying at the time. Madame Mitzi Benedek, she's mentioned in the letter you just read. In June 1945 Mitzi signed a commitment charge in London, witnessed by the French ambassador, that she would receive and care for the boy, and put him on board the first available mercy ship leaving London and docking at Australia. You know those ships, sponsored by the Jewish Overseas Relief Agency."

"I ought to," Notarius muttered. "I put dozens of children on them."

"There was one leaving London in August," Konrad went on. "It was all arranged. But when the field worker went to the Nursery, Mademoiselle Rose refused to give her the boy. Fleury himself went to see her, he told me, and Mademoiselle Rose gave him the same answer. A categorical refusal, just as Madame Lindner writes. Fleury had to drop the matter, since he had no authority to take the boy by force. It's all in the dossier, and Fleury will let you see it, just as he let me. This was in the summer of 1945. Now tell me that the Rose woman didn't know of the aunt's existence until more than a year later!"

Notarius said nothing. Seeing his thoughtful expression, Konrad demanded, "Do you want more proof? I told you I saw Madame Quertsch, who took the boy to the Nursery. The mayor of Puy-le-Duc gave me her name. Madame Lindner wrote to her, although she doesn't mention it in her letter. In fact, she wrote her several letters. Madame Quertsch showed me one, dated July 1945. In it Madame Lindner complains that Mademoiselle Rose has not answered any of her letters, and begs Madame Quertsch to visit the Nursery to find out why. And to send her news of Michel. I asked Madame Quertsch if she had done so, and she said she had, and that Mademoiselle Rose admitted having received Hannah's letters, but wouldn't discuss it with her. Now will you believe that the woman lied to you?"

"All right," Notarius said, throwing up his hands. "I never said she didn't. All I said was that the stories were contradictory, and I didn't know which to believe. It seems I've been had. And I suppose that if she lied about trying to locate the family, then she also lied about the aunt's visit to the Nursery. Although," he added ruefully, rubbing his chin, "you never heard anything so convincing in your life. Why, the woman had tears in her eyes. I mean, when she told me how she was forced to the conclusion that there was no family left, that the Nazis had got them all. She must have been laughing at me the whole time. And I swallowed it all, like a—" He gave an annoyed laugh.

"And," Konrad said without mercy, "you went home and drew a line through the boy's name. And reported to the Consistory that the boy was well off where he was."

"Don't rub it in," Notarius said uncomfortably. "How was I to know? Even now I find it hard to believe that it was all an act. I tell you, the story came out with a rush, as though she were so full of it she couldn't keep it back. Indignation, tears, worry, the whole gamut. She was furious at the aunt because, as she put it, the woman didn't show the slightest interest in Michel, but instead demanded to know what valuables her brother had left and where they were. Oh, I know," Notarius exclaimed, as Konrad made an abrupt gesture, "it sounds pretty crude now, but if you had seen her reliving it, you'd have believed her too. Patted him on the head like a puppy dog! she said. Her own brother's child! She said, A widow! Well, I'm an old maid, with no one to help me either, but I fed him when I had to take it out of my own mouth!"

Konrad clapped his hand to his forehead. "A widow! Of course, that's it. The brother's widow. Mitzi Benedek, do you remember? She stopped off here on her way to Vienna. Madame Lindner says so in the letter."

Notarius stared down at the letter on his desk. "That's right, she does," he said slowly. "The other aunt. Then it wasn't an act after all."

"Of course it was!" Konrad said, putting his hands behind his back and beginning to pace up and down. "Don't you see? Mitzi Benedek came to see Mademoiselle Rose, not to get the child for herself, but to urge her to give Michel to the doctor's sister. Mademoiselle Rose refused categorically, just as she had to Fleury. It's in the letter. But when you appeared a short time later, she converted one aunt into the other. She told you it was Madame Lindner who had showed up. Why? Because it was Madame Lindner who had been pestering her and was putting all the pressure on her. Let everybody believe that Madame Lindner had her chance but refused. Now it's too late, and nobody will take her claims seriously. You, for instance. Your first reaction was 'At this late date?' "

"I suppose you're right," the rabbi conceded. "But why? I mean, why should she go to such lengths—?"

Konrad shrugged. "I wish I knew. Maybe she loves him. Maybe she's a religious fanatic. Do you know she's had him baptized?"

Incredulously, with the trace of a stammer, Notarius said, "But how could she? The boy's a minor. She would have to get—"

"I'm telling you what she told me," Konrad retorted. "And called me a Jew bastard into the bargain. No more acting. Cards on the table. You could have heard her screaming from here. What was it you said?" He quoted bitterly, " 'Matronly. Soft-spoken.' "

"She called you that?" Notarius said, marveling. "Mademoiselle Rose? I don't understand it, you must have provoked her. I tell you, with me—"

"One!" Konrad said aggressively, facing him and thrusting out a finger, "I didn't provoke her. I couldn't have said less, and more politely. All I had a chance to say was that I wanted to talk to her about the child Michel Benedek at some future time, whenever it was convenient for her. Two, let's say she was provoked anyway, without reason, because she didn't like my face. When she started yelling, *I* was annoyed, but I didn't call her a Catholic bitch. From as early as I remember, 'Jew bastard' has worn a groove in my brain. I don't intend to put up with it any longer. I'm going to make those words turn to poison in her mouth. And if every one of us did the same, people would stop putting them together."

"Well," Notarius said.

"All right. That's that. The question is now, What are we going to do about it?"

"Maybe you ought to sit down."

There was an edge to the rabbi's tone that made Konrad look at him sharply. Notarius' face was flushed and hard; he held his head averted. Konrad realized now that toward the end of his peroration he had raised his voice.

"I'm sorry," he said with an awkward gesture. "This means more to me than you might think. But that's no reason for me to shout at you."

"Konrad," Notarius said, drawing a deep breath and facing him, "it's about time someone told you some truths about yourself. Ever since I've known you, you've had a chip on your shoulder. Do you hate the whole world? You come to the Zionist meetings as though you were dealing with your enemies, and yet we have the same ideals you do. You came to talk to me about the Benedek boy, but the first thing you did when you walked in here was to sneer at everything I stand for by proclaiming you were an atheist. Damn it, man, I'm a rabbi, and a Jew like you. And maybe I'm younger than you, but I'm not a boy, to be scolded. All right, Mademoiselle Rose deceived me, but *I* didn't take the boy away from his family. And I didn't kill six million Jews either."

Konrad felt his face go pale. So unexpected was the rabbi's on-slaught that his first reaction was astonishment, to be followed by anger. What was Notarius talking about? He, hate the whole world? Who had accused the man of anything? At the same time, the more rational part of his mind was reviewing the stages of his conversation with the rabbi and acknowledging the truth of the criticism. His own sense of fairness made him recognize the inner contempt that had urged him to begin his request with an attack. He had despised Rabbi Schmul for his narrowness, his meanness, his musty smell, his belonging to a world that was dead and past. But Notarius, who was so different in every respect? Was it his youth? His complacency? Was not his antagonism to the man prompted precisely by the fact that Notarius *was* so different from the one of Gonobitz, who was a rabbi, whatever else he was? Who could make sense of such a twisted way of thinking? And who was he, Konrad, to judge others?

He had gone his way like the rest. At Notarius' age he was setting up his business, thinking of getting married, smugly convinced that he was doing his share by participating in long arguments about the class struggle. And if now, in his forties, he had given way to fury over the injustice done the Benedek child, and made of it a symbol for everything he hated, had he the right to expect all to be moved by the same rage, at a contemptuous word from him?

"I owe you an apology," he said. "And an explanation. First of all, I'll sit down." He settled deliberately in the armchair, gathering his knees in his hands. "When I came in here a while ago, I remarked that when I was a boy I had the idea of becoming a rabbi. Let me tell you about that. It was in Gonobitz, a village in Austria near the Hungarian border, that you've probably never heard of. I was raised in a pious home where all the observances were followed, and from my childhood my mother's dream was to give a man to God. I shared that dream. By the time I was sixteen, however, a new interest had entered my life—chemistry—and I was wavering between the two as a career. God or science. I still believed in God, you see. This was in 1918, the war was coming to an end, and I had hopes of going abroad to study, although I was still undecided what my study would be. There was great unrest in Austria, our troops were being driven back on all fronts, there were famines and pogroms.

"One night a platoon of mounted Uhlans rode through Gonobitz shouting, Death to Jews! From their voices it was clear they were drunk. We locked our door and put out the lights. A stone came flying through the window and struck my mother in the chest. It was nothing, she said, only a bruise. But that night she died in her bed. A stone, flung aimlessly by a drunken soldier, who went on his way with no idea of what he had done. And for that a woman died, a woman who praised God in the morning and thanked God at night. I went out of the house and sat in the woods and thought, You I will not serve."

Notarius had turned and was listening intently.

"That was thirty years ago," Konrad went on, gazing down at his hands. "I left Gonobitz, I went to Berlin, to Geneva, to France. I did not forget my mother, but I had convinced myself that it was an accident. The soldier never intended to kill a woman, merely to register a general protest by throwing a stone. But here in Touville I watched the rise of Hitler. This was no accident, but deliberate, premeditated mass murder. My old anger returned, but I was powerless, or so I thought. I ran, I hid, and when it was over I managed to convince myself that the death of six million had been the result of a national hysteria provoked by a madman. It was still possible to live in this world, since the madman was dead. But I joined the Zionist movement and watched and waited. And I learned that the madman was not dead, that a bit of him lives in everyone touched by his poison, even in his enemies, even—incredible as it may seem—in many of our own people. And I decided, this thing must be fought, wherever it is found, to whatever degree.

"You're right, Notarius, I have a chip on my shoulder, I've become sour and suspicious and irritable. I see a Gentile woman who takes advantage of the Nazi murders to steal a Jewish child from his family, and I get angry. The Jew is still fair game, you see. If we protest, we are Jew bastards. Ah, here we have it, you say. This whole pathetic speech is a cover-up for his hurt feelings, it all comes down to the personal insult. You're wrong, my friend. It's the stone against my mother again, the general protest in the heat of anger or drink. Call a name, throw a stone. And then we have Hitler again."

With a forced laugh he concluded, "And that's why I'm impossible to get along with and quarrel with my friends. I ask you to pardon me."

"Oh," Notarius said gruffly, spreading his hands, "forget what I said. I suppose I was annoyed because the woman made a fool of me. But remember, the rest of us have been through it too, and we all feel the same way. You're angry and you want to fight. Well, so do I. But there are ways and ways of fighting."

Seeing that Konrad was listening quietly, Notarius said with a smile, "When you were talking about Mademoiselle Rose, there came to my mind an occasion when I too was called a Jew bastard. It was in Paris, I was a schoolboy, and one Saturday I was on my way to the synagogue when I met a classmate of mine I had always considered a little roughneck. He was going to church, he said, it was what he called an obligation day. He suggested that I accompany him, and afterward he would go with me to the synagogue. I wasn't sure I'd be allowed into the church, and I didn't know how our congregation would react to the *goy* in their midst, but I was filled with a spirit of daring and said yes.

"When we arrived at the church the service was over, and people were pouring out. My friend shrugged and said it didn't matter, and we entered the church. I sat on a bench, while he bought a candle, put it on a table behind a railing, lit it, knelt down and began to pray. After a while I noticed that he put his finger in the candle flame, and then snatched it out and continued praying. He did it several times. I was impressed. I had never been in a church before, and wondered what was the meaning of this strange ritual of fire. When we came out, I asked him, and he said, Oh, it was only to see how long he could keep his finger in the flame without getting burned.''

What was he getting at? Konrad wondered. He let a smile come to his lips, and waited.

"I began to laugh," Notarius said, glancing at Konrad, "and he got angry. He called me a Jew bastard, we quarreled, and he knocked me down. Blood was pouring from my lip. Look what you've done! I said to him. The blood frightened him, he gave me his handkerchief, we patched up the quarrel and went to the synagogue. There he watched without a word, and when we came out the only thing he asked me was, Where are the pictures? I explained to him the prohibition against graven images. You see, he said to me, I didn't laugh.

"It was a hard lesson, but it served me right. I took the boy home with me, he invited me to his, and we became good friends. In school he became my defender against those who picked on me because I was a Jew. I saw him often until his family moved to Calais."

"I wondered where you were going," Konrad said. "That's what one would call a parable, I suppose. Brotherhood through understanding. The fault is as much ours as theirs. Respect them and they will respect us."

"Well, yes," Notarius said earnestly, "though you're oversimplifying, of course. The world accuses us of being moneygrubbers, misers, loud-mouthed, heaven knows what else. Let them know us and they'll see that there is no difference that matters. Let them have their religion, let us have ours—anti-Semitism doesn't come from religious grounds anyway. Education is the answer."

"If that were so," Konrad said slowly, "if it were a question of education and—although you don't say the word—assimilation, you'd think that in the thousands of years the Jews have been knocking around the world, we'd have taught the Gentiles by now that we're no different from them. If we haven't done so, it's because we *are* different. Perhaps there's no fundamental reason why we should be, but we are."

Notarius shook his head. "Look at me. I'm a Jew, I'm even a

rabbi, but I'm as French as the next one."

"Well, I'm not," Konrad returned. "Oh, I'm a naturalized citizen, and I'm French, but with a difference. It doesn't matter if I speak the same language, and dress as they do, and eat the same food, and vote in the same elections, there's a hard core here inside that separates me from the rest. And I find now that I want it that way. What made me a Jew after I gave up my religion? In one word, blood. The blood of my mother. The six million who died. The cost has been too high for me to give it up. I couldn't if I wanted to, I'm not the same person I would have been without it. No, I'll remain just what I am, the Jew who doesn't want to be anything else, the one who's different. I'm a Zionist, I'll help build the new homeland all I can, for those who want to go there. But I won't go myself. I'll stay here, and walk with my head high, and I'll fight back. And if I give the rest of you a bad name, I'm sorry, but that's the way it's got to be."

"Here," the rabbi protested, "you talk as though I'm not a Jew too."

"You want to belong, to be French."

"But why must one exclude the other?"

"Because the world says it does. Ask Mademoiselle Rose how French you are. She'll give you the same answer she gave me."

"Oh, come now," Notarius said in anger, "what kind of argument is that?"

"We don't seem to be getting anywhere," Konrad remarked wearily.

"We certainly aren't."

Konrad took in the rabbi's boyish face and its set look. "Well," he said at length, "let's forget it. We're each entitled to our opinions. But there still remains the question of the boy. What's to be done there?"

Since Notarius made no answer, he repeated the question. The rabbi shrugged. "If the aunt could come to Touville."

"Well, she hasn't, and apparently she can't. But I've constituted myself her agent, and as soon as a power of attorney comes through, I can act in her name."

"To do what, may I ask?"

Konrad regarded him with raised eyebrows. "Why, to threaten her with legal action, of course. And to take her to court, if necessary. The case is as clear as it can be. The evidence is overwhelming. You yourself, for example, could testify as to the shameless lie she told.

Madame Quertsch. The Red Cross, and all the others. Once it's proved that Madame Lindner—"

"Let me understand this," Notarius said in an unsteady voice. "You would take Mademoiselle Rose to court? After she saved the boy's life?"

"I don't deny that she saved his life. But what rights does that give her? Madame Quertsch kept saying the same thing. Suppose you saved a child from drowning, I said to her, would he belong to you?"

"But she has feelings, damn it all," Notarius said. "All you can see is that she told me a lie and yelled at you. But did you ever ask yourself why? She loves that boy. All right, the boy's not hers, he has a family. But you don't have to drag her through the courts. Let Madame Lindner come to Touville, let her go and talk to the woman, explain, persuade. She'll give him up, it's just a question of—"

"And what do you think my intentions were when I went there? She threw me out, I tell you. How can you negotiate with someone who calls you a Jew bastard?"

"Look, Konrad, you're annoyed, you don't see this thing in its larger implications. Don't you see what kind of a scandal it would make? You know what the Consistory is up against. You heard my report, there are five to six thousand misplaced Jewish children scattered throughout the country, a lot of them in Gentile families that don't want to give them up. Would you take them all to court?"

"Yes!" Konrad said harshly, getting to his feet. "I would take them all to court. Every one that wouldn't give up the child to his rightful family. Every last one of them."

"I see," the rabbi said in a voice trembling with anger, "you want scandal then. You want the world to accuse us of being ungrateful. You want to set off another wave of anti-Semitism. As if we hadn't had enough already!"

Konrad glared down at him. " 'Now Caiaphas was he,' " he quoted, " 'which gave counsel to the Jews, that it was expedient that one man should die for the people.' "

Notarius threw up his hands, crying, "Oh, the man is impossible!"

"I take it," Konrad said, "that you won't help?" Notarius put the list in the drawer and slammed it shut. Then he pushed Mme Lindner's letter away from him, to the edge of the desk.

Konrad put it in his pocket. "All right, I'm glad I talked to you anyway. It's been instructive." He strode to the door. "That friend of yours," he said, turning around. "The boy in Paris, the one who split your lip. How much more he'd have respected you if you had split his instead!"

7

꙰

M OVING BACKWARDS, and arching his body with the force of his
efforts, M. Joseph dragged Father Périer along the ground.
He seemed possessed by a frenzy, bucking, heaving, giving tremendous tugs with his head. Michel marveled at his strength. Inch by
inch Father Périer slid toward the opening. In a moment M. Joseph
would see that it was blocked. What would he do then? Michel
placed a straw on the ground behind him. M. Joseph backed up on
it. But tug as he might, he could not get Father Périer's body over it.
M. Joseph was baffled; he ran up and down the straw, raced around
the body, then began to pull it around the shorter end. In the meanwhile M. Konrad had broken away, and was scurrying for cover.
Michel checked his flight with his finger. M. Konrad investigated it
cautiously, then scampered in the other direction. By placing his finger on this side and that, Michel steered him toward the church. But
M. Konrad would not enter, sensing a trap. Several times Michel got
him to the gap in the stones, only to see him dart in panic under the
stone itself. M. Konrad just would not go to church. Michel let him
escape into the grass.

The other ants were milling in confusion around the straw thrust
into the opening of their burrow. Outraged, they ran in circles,
touching their feelers together, then returning to the straw. To them
he must have seemed like some supernatural power, like God. God
out of some inexplicable whim had shoved this huge shaft, this tree
trunk, into the entrance to their home, cutting them off from their
eggs and their food stores. It was a national calamity, as their agita-
tion proclaimed. They returned to the straw again and again, as if
astonished to find it still there. Why did God not take it away? How
could He do this to them? How cruel to separate fathers from their
children!

The ant that Michel called M. Joseph backed around the end of the obstacle, dragging the dead insect. A crew of fellow workers ran to help him. Michel removed the straw from the opening, waited until Father Périer was at the point of disappearing within the burrow, then flicked the corpse away. With the straw he pushed the tiny inert thing into the center of the three stones that were the church, and buried the whole under a handful of earth.

He was sitting on a rock in a meadow tip-tilted against the sky. Behind him, scattered across the yellowing grass, a half-dozen cows grazed peacefully. The meadow was skirted by a dirt road, beyond which was the château, a tall, weatherworn stone house set against an abrupt rocky bank of dark fir trees. Michel sat facing the other way, where the meadow dropped off into a steep, bushy slope plunging down the mountainside, broken by rises and outcroppings of stone, to Sep in the valley. From where he sat Michel could see the church spire and the red rooftops of the village. They would all be in church now. At that moment, perhaps, Father Fonsac was elevating the host. Had he noticed that Michel was not there? What would Manon tell him this time? The first Sunday he had had a cold. The next Sunday it was raining, and only Manon had gone. But this morning he had not given any excuse; he had simply disappeared into the woodshed alongside the chicken run and had waited behind the pile of moldy logs until the footsteps and the cries of "Michel! Michel!" had stopped, and he knew that Manon, Pé and Léah had gone without him. Then he had emerged from his hiding place, faced the scolding of the dour-faced Mme Thérèse, and crossed the road to the meadow, where he lay on his back in the grass, staring up at the sky.

His heart was full of rebellion. It was too much to expect him to go to church, as if nothing had happened. To expect him to pass over the worn stone steps and through the splintering, bolt-studded door, and to see before him the cracked marble font at which he had been baptized, and over it the cross on which Christ agonized. To say to himself, My father did that. To kneel and pray, and wonder if he had the right. To ask himself, Why? until he broke out into a sweat, and Manon, looking at him queerly, whispered to him to use his handkerchief. And then to face Father Fonsac in the sacristy afterward, and respond to his questions, all the while longing and not daring to blurt out what was inside him. They could not demand that of him, not until he had solved his problem and knew what it all meant.

Would he ever know? He asked himself that, gazing down into the valley. In the months since his communion party, when M. Konrad had destroyed his little world, he had begun to wonder whether any answer could put it together again. Suppose Father Périer had answered his question, and had said, Yes, your father is in hell. Could he accept that? His father had loved him, that was the only thing he did not doubt. Could he sleep nights, knowing what was happening down below, where the fires were? And suppose instead Father Périer had patted him pityingly on the head and said, Why, my dear boy, of course not! What ever put that idea in your head? Didn't you know that . . . Could he accept that either? What! You could spit on the Son of God, nail Him to a cross and mock Him as He died, and that was all right, it was forgiven you, and you went to heaven anyway? Did that make sense?

Well, but suppose it was all a dreadful mistake, and he was not the boy M. Konrad meant. He had considered that too; in his attempt to escape from his unbearable dilemma, he had allowed himself to daydream until the drama took shape in his mind with all the reality of life. There is a knock on the door, and M. Konrad enters, apologetic, holding his hat meekly in his hand. I have just discovered the truth, he mutters. There has been a dreadful mistake. There are two Michels. It is the other one whose father was a Jew. A thousand pardons, mademoiselle. Maman Rose is friendly, smiling. She gives M. Konrad a glass of vermouth, and shakes his hand as he takes his leave. How lovely that would be! With what adoration he would kneel before the crucifix again, except that—yes, and the other Michel? Somewhere in the world a little boy like him would be crying and asking himself the same questions, and that was no fairer than if he were the one.

Something was wrong with a world in which little boys were made to cry, and Michel had begun to suspect that it was not merely because he didn't understand it. Could God have wanted it that way? God was all-powerful, He could do anything He wanted. Things could be completely different with a single nod of His head. Then whatever happened was because God chose it to happen. God had warned Adam against eating the apple, and then had allowed him to be tempted into doing it. God had sent His Only-Begotten Son to the Jews, and then had let them crucify Him. What kind of way of doing things was that? Michel did not want to criticize God; he knew that was wrong; but he knew also, just as certainly, that it was wrong to take a boy's father and let the Nazis get him, and send his soul to hell. If God had done that— He was afraid to draw his conclusions. He would wait. Being born, and living, and dying were long. He would watch and wait, and he would learn wisdom, and it could not be but that somewhere in that grown-up tangle of things that were almost true, or partly true, or true according to the way you looked at them, he would find something that was always, completely true. Like what he felt for his father. Like love that couldn't be hurt no matter what you did to it.

Far below, amid the fields lying outside the village, the sun glinted leadenly on a ribbon of water. That was the brook that dashed down the steep slope behind the château, so icy to the touch when you waded in it, and turned the mossy wheels of the mills of Sep. Miles away it emptied into the Char and passed Touville. The Char emptied into the Rhone, and the Rhone into the sea. How big the world was! And how everlasting! It had always been like that, even before he was born. That's what eternal was. It was here when you weren't. Once his father had looked at this river, and it was there. Now he, Michel, was looking at it; it was still there, although his father wasn't. Michel considered this gravely, wondering. How could it be there if he wasn't there to see it?

On a bend in the road below, visible between two gently swelling hills, three figures appeared. He recognized Manon, Pé, and Léah. Mass was over, then; they had paid their respects to the old priest and were returning home. Manon would be cross and demand an explanation. What would he tell her? That Renée hadn't gone either? She would answer that that didn't excuse him, and that Renée ought to have gone too. Michel sighed. He had a little while yet. It was a long climb up the dirt road, which wound in and out of the slopes. They would appear and be swallowed up by the hills several times before they reached the edge of the meadow where he was.

Maman Rose had been right, his stay at Sep had been good for him. He had been so thin and pale when he arrived that the old caretaker had raised her gnarled hands and called upon the Virgin. He had filled out a bit, and the July sun had tanned him, and although he still had dreams, he was sleeping better. There was still a little left of July, and then all of August. He would grow strong again here at Sep, and then be able to confront his problem with renewed energy. He sat idly in the sun, letting his mind think what it would, watching the ants, until Manon and the children appeared at the bend below the house. They looked hot and dusty, as if they had been running. Léah's little pink hat was awry, and she seemed at the point of tears. They hurried to the house without seeing him. A moment later, however, Manon's slender figure stepped out on the porch. She called out to him sharply.

"Hurry!" she cried, waving her arm.

Michel got up reluctantly and crossed the meadow. Manon was pale. "Come in here!" she said, seizing him by the shoulder. "Monsieur Konrad is in the village."

At first he did not understand. He had expected to be scolded. M. Konrad was in the village. Well, what then? But Renée now came hurrying from upstairs, summoned by Mme Thérèse, and her face was so alarmed that a horrible suspicion shot through him, and he looked in apprehension from one to the other.

"Yes, it was," Manon insisted to Renée. "I'd know him anywhere. He was standing in the street, looking at the church."

"I saw him first," Léah said. "Didn't I, Manon? And I got scared."

"Yes, and Pé saw him too," Manon said.

Pé nodded vigorously. He too seemed frightened; his eyes were big and solemn.

"Did he recognize you?" Renée demanded.

Manon wasn't sure, but Pé claimed that M. Konrad had looked at them "kind of funny."

"Oh dear!" Renée said.

They all looked at Michel. No one said it, but he understood. M. Konrad had come looking for him. Somehow he had found out that Michel was at Sep and had come to take him away. With a sinking feeling Michel remembered that during his convalescence at the Nursery he had not been allowed into the front garden, but was told to stay in the playground, whose gate was kept locked. And that Maman Rose had decided to send him to Sep early that summer, instead of waiting for August, because "it was safer," she said. Preoccupied with his problem, he had not given these precautions much thought.

What was to be done? Mme Thérèse thrust herself forward. "That Jew!" she said contemptuously. She was not afraid. She was over sixty, she said, and had yet to see the living thing, man or beast, that she feared. Before now, twice during her lifetime, it had been the Germans. Now it was Jews, it seemed. Let him come. She would meet him at the door and tell him to be off.

"And quickly too!"

Looking at the old caretaker's bent, frail figure, and remembering the long, sinewy arm that M. Konrad had flung out toward M. Joseph, Michel was not convinced. Apparently Manon was not either, for she suggested calling the police.

"We ought to telephone Maman Rose," Renée said. "She'll tell us what to do."

The telephone was in the village. Renée and Manon looked thoughtfully at each other.

"I'll go," Mme Thérèse said, after a long pause. "He doesn't know me." She took off her apron and began to change her slippers for shoes. Manon described M. Konrad to her. He was tall and thin and was wearing a city suit, with a white shirt and a tie.

"You'll know him if you see him. He has funny eyes. Like a snake."

Before setting off, Mme Thérèse went out to the woodshed and returned carrying a pitchfork, which she placed beside the door without a word. Going out, she said briefly, "Lock the door."

Manon took Léah upstairs to wash her and change her dress. Renée followed them, after warning the boys not to go outside.

"Where were you?" Pé demanded in an aggrieved tone. "We looked all over for you."

Michel gestured vaguely out back.

"Manon was mad. She said she was going to tell Maman Rose. And then she thought Monsieur Konrad must have got you. She was real scared. We came up here so fast that Léah kept falling down. Say, Michel, what does he want you for, anyway? Where would he take you?"

"I don't know."

It was true, he had not thought about it. "She sent you, didn't she?" Maman Rose had said. And something about an aunt. An aunt was your father's sister. Or your mother's sister. He supposed it was the latter, since his mother was so much vaguer in his mind and there was more room for mystery. His mother was only what he had had before Maman Rose. She might very well have had a sister. Maybe it was that woman who once came to the Nursery, whom he remembered as "the kind lady with the toys." She had said she was his aunt. She had no face; she had brought him toys, and cried over him, and been kind, and that was all that had remained with him. Had she sent M. Konrad, as Maman Rose said? Because, otherwise, why would M. Konrad care? Michel was nothing to him. She did not come herself because she knew Maman Rose would not give him up, and so she sent M. Konrad, who was a man and could take him by force. But where? Where was the aunt? A chill came over Michel, as he tried to visualize himself in a strange place, away from Maman Rose and the Nursery, which was his home.

In a little while Renée came down. She had changed her blue jeans for a dress and brushed her hair. Her face was animated. "We'll have to wait," she announced gaily. The boys looked at her, puzzled.

"Oh, Michel!" she said, catching his eye.

He did not understand. He shrugged and went with Pé to look at the pitchfork. It was heavy, with wicked, gleaming prongs. Renée told them not to touch it, they could hurt themselves. Manon came downstairs with Léah. They sat down to wait.

A cart was coming up the road. They heard the strident sound of the wheels and the oxbells before the cart came around the bend. Then it approached the house, and from the window they saw the man walking alongside the oxen, and Mme Thérèse beginning to clamber down before the cart had stopped. Manon unbolted the door for her. The old woman burst in, her hair damp with sweat, her face hot with the sun. They were to barricade the house! Under no circumstances were they to let anyone in! Mlle Rose herself was coming to take them all away! And she had seen that Konrad!

"He was in the sacristy," she said, sinking with a grimace into a chair. "Get me some water, somebody. Mother of God, how ugly he is!"

They crowded around her, asking questions. Fanning herself with her hand, breathing hard, she said, Yes, she had got through to the Nursery. Mlle Rose herself answered the phone. What did she say? She was stunned. She called the man a— Never mind. She particularly wanted to know if Konrad was alone. Ah! Manon had brought water. Mme Thérèse gulped it thirstily.

"When I saw him, he was alone," Manon said.

"I saw him first," Léah said.

"Well, I wasn't sure, but I said I thought he was." Mme Thérèse patted her cheek with the empty glass. "And she says to me, Hang up. What? I say. Hang up, she says, and wait by the phone. I'll call you back. And sure enough, not five minutes later, the phone rings and Mademoiselle Rose says, I'm coming up there in Monsieur Béjart's car. Tell Father Fonsac, let him send a man up to the house. Better two than one, she says. Lock up the doors and wait. And if you let him get the boy, she says, don't be there when I arrive. Don't you worry, I tell her, he won't get him. And so I went over to the church and looked in the sacristy, and there's the man himself, talking to Father Fonsac as calm as you please! The look of him, with his head like a skull! Well, I say to myself, it's no good, and I got out of there without being seen. Old Simon brought me up in his cart."

"What was he doing in the sacristy?" Renée wondered.

Michel was asking himself the same question. Was M. Konrad inquiring about him? Surely Father Fonsac would not tell him? But a priest couldn't lie.

Manon said, "Oh!" and looked faint. Imagine that she had not seen M. Konrad in the street, she said. She would have taken the children to the sacristy to greet the priest, as Mlle Rose had instructed her to do every Sunday after mass. That man would have cornered them there. Fortunately, she had forgotten all about the priest in her hurry to return.

Renée asked Mme Thérèse why she hadn't asked Simon to stay with them. "And do you think I didn't?" Mme Thérèse replied in scorn. That peasant brute! Oh, he would come, and with his shotgun, too. Just as soon as he had milked his cows. Go reason with a farmer!

Manon had already begun to close the shutters. The others ran to help her, while Mme Thérèse, groaning with relief, took off her shoes. It became very hot inside. They decided to go upstairs. It would be cooler, and they had to pack their things. Pé could stand by the front window to watch the road.

On the landing Renée gave Michel a big hug. "Oh, Michel," she whispered happily. "We're going home!"

Michel suddenly understood. Renée had not wanted to come to Sep. She had locked herself in her room and sulked when Maman Rose told her she would go with the others, and no nonsense! Because her Jules was coming home from Paris for his vacation, and she had looked forward to it the whole year. Poor Renée! Her face had been so sad on the bus; and during the entire three weeks she had hardly stirred out of the house, sitting on the porch listlessly rocking, or listening to the phonograph in her room. She wouldn't even go to church, in spite of Mme Thérèse's fussing and muttering. Sometimes, during the long summer twilights, Michel sat in her room with her, while she talked about her Jules. She was sorry she had called Michel a sneak. She knew now he hadn't told. Some busybody had called Maman Rose on the telephone and told her a lot of lies. She hadn't done anything wrong. But Maman Rose refused to understand, she was selfish and didn't want Renée to marry, ever. She was to be an old maid and take care of Maman Rose in her old age. Renée was very bitter about that, and said she would not put up with it. In five months she would be twenty-one, and then Maman Rose would see! At twenty-one a girl didn't need anybody's consent. Anyway, Maman Rose was not her mother. Michel was aghast at some of the things she said. She put her hands on her hips, like Maman Rose, and said, "Eighteen years of my life!" And she rolled her eyes and curled her lip and said, "Gratitude!" and "This is the thanks I get!" and things of that sort. And even a remark about "that priest of hers." But Michel knew that sometimes people get carried away and say more than they mean. He was sorry for her, and for her Jules, whom he imagined waiting outside the church, as he himself had waited by the gate. But now they were going home, and Renée was happy again. What a strange thing love was!

Father Fonsac was at the door to the presbytery behind the church, talking to a woman wearing black. He glanced up as the car came to a stop and gave a surprised smile of recognition. M. Konrad was nowhere in sight. Michel, huddled on the back seat of the car with Renée, Manon, and Pé, was greatly relieved. All the way down to Sep Michel had been worried that the man would still be there, and there would be another painful scene like the one in the Nursery. Maman Rose was in a dangerous mood. She talked little, and in a low voice. M. Konrad was "that Jew Communist" and "that kidnaper"; she refused to name him, as if the name were hateful to her. She insisted on stopping by the church; she wanted to know what he had been up to at the sacristy. So much the worse if he were still there! She sat up front with Léah and M. Béjart. Seeing the line of her jaw, Michel hoped fervently that M. Konrad was gone.

Father Fonsac came to the car and greeted them, peering through the open windows. "My dear lady! What a coincidence! Why, only a couple of hours ago—"

"Is he gone?" Maman Rose said abruptly. "Yes, I know he was

here," she added, as the priest stared, taken aback.

"Why, as to that," he said, looking from her to M. Béjart, "he's gone, yes. It was only a short while. Though how you knew . . . But won't you come in?"

Maman Rose made their excuses. They were on their way back to Touville, and they were all hot and tired. Besides, Jean was coming in from Chambéry, and would find nobody at the Nursery. What had that kidnaper wanted with him?

The good priest was astonished. Shading his eyes against the sun with his hand, and squinting to see Maman Rose's face, he said that surely that wasn't so? Kidnaper! No, no, she must be joking. Maman Rose replied that she wasn't joking, and appealed to M. Béjart.

M. Béjart's silvery head wagged solemnly from side to side. "My dear Father Fonsac," he said in his soft, precise voice, "this isn't my idea of a pleasure trip. We came up here in a hurry to take the boy home, as soon as we learned the man was here. He's an Israeli agent, I'm afraid. Mademoiselle Rose has been checking up on him for weeks. There's no telling what he may do."

"Dear, dear, dear," Father Fonsac said. "Who would have thought such a thing? I found the man quite reasonable. Except when he— Yes. But to take the child by force! There was not the slightest hint of it. It was just a question of Michel's baptism. He said—"

"His baptism!" Maman Rose said.

"Why, yes. At least," Father Fonsac said cautiously, "that's what he said. He asked if the boy had been baptized in this church. And when I said yes, he wanted to see the register. But since I did it myself! I said. Nevertheless, he insisted—politely, I must say—and I thought, Oh, very well. You understand," he said to Maman Rose. "There was no reason—"

"And that was all he wanted?" M. Béjart asked.

"Well, we talked for a bit afterward. The strange thing is that he didn't seem to recognize me, although I knew perfectly well who he was, of course. He seemed perturbed at the date. Just before Easter! he said. He said it several times. Why, yes, I told him, in time for his communion at St. Joseph's, you see. He couldn't have his communion until he'd been baptized. By what authority had I done it, he wanted to know. In fact, he gave me a bit of a lecture. Didn't I have to have the consent of the family? Was such a baptism valid? What did canon law have to say about it? He actually brought up the question of canon law," Father Fonsac said, amused. "Oh, yes, and had I consulted the bishop? My dear sir, I said to him, there's no such thing as an invalid baptism. And I baptized so many Jewish children during the war, I really don't see that one more matters."

During this recital Michel saw M. Béjart and Maman Rose exchange a swift glance. Now Maman Rose said, "St. Joseph's! You mentioned St. Joseph's?"

Father Fonsac's jaw dropped. He was afraid he had, he said. It had slipped out somehow during the course of the conversation. Michel wondered why this was important. He gathered that it was from the look on Maman Rose's face, and the way M. Béjart shook his head. The old priest was apologetic. The man had taken him in completely. Even now he found it hard to believe. An agent! And did they dare—? M. Konrad had said he was acting on behalf of the aunt.

Maman Rose sniffed in scorn, and M. Béjart said yes, they had believed that themselves in the beginning. But apparently the aunt was a blind for bigger things. Their good friend Mlle Rose had taken the trouble to have the man investigated. "You noticed his accent?" M. Béjart asked. "He's an Austrian. And a Jew, of course. But he came here long before Hitler, in 1926, to be exact. Hand-picked by the Kremlin. The man's a Communist, with scientific training. He came to Touville and set up as a manufacturing chemist, with what money nobody knows. Oh, nothing big, nothing to attract attention. And there he is during the 1930s, right on the spot when Léon Blum came to power, with Stalin pulling the strings behind the Popular Front. A naturalized French citizen, boring from within. Look at the lengths they go to! But Pétain put a stop to all that, and the man disappeared. Then after the war he shows up again. Where had he been? How had he escaped being picked up? Again, nobody knows. He sets up his business again and becomes active in another big game. This time it's Zionism and Palestine, except that now they call it Israel, it seems. The great homeland for the chosen people! Only they need young blood to scratch some crops out of their exhausted soil, because the Jews who answered the call of the new state were old and sick, tradesmen, intellectuals, who never touched a hoe in anger. That's where our friend Konrad comes in, the perfect man for the job. Round up children, they tell him, so much per head. There are lots of Jewish children in France, saved by the good French Catholics at the risk of their necks. Tell them any story you want, they're stupid, they'll swallow it. Appeal to their hearts! If they won't give them up, take them by force. Only send us children for our *kibbutzim.*"

Father Fonsac's eyes had been widening during this speech. Now he asked M. Béjart to repeat the last word. He hadn't quite—

"Kibbutzim," M. Béjart said, tightening his lips with distaste. "Collective farms. On the Russian model. Or, to give it its true name, slave labor. And that's the sort of dirty deal our government is permitting to happen on French soil."

"Yes," Maman Rose said, leaning forward to speak past Léah and M. Béjart, "why didn't the aunt claim the boy while she was in Australia? Why did she wait until she got to Israel? They put a bug in her ear, that's why. But they reckoned without me. I won't give him up. That kidnaper is in for a surprise. Come, Alain, we'd best be getting on," she added, leaning back in her seat.

They took their leave of Father Fonsac, who waved his hand at them as the car moved away. Looking back through the rear window, Michel saw the old priest gazing after them with a dazed expression on his pale, gentle face.

"A fine man," Maman Rose said. "But—"

"Yes," M. Béjart said indulgently, "a bit naïve. It's the cloth. They lose contact with the world."

"I wonder why he was checking up on the baptism."

"I've been wondering the same thing. Unless it was a blind."

Renée asked why shouldn't Father Fonsac have mentioned St. Joseph's. She didn't see anything so wrong in that. M. Béjart asked her to suppose that one fine day, after school had started again, M. Konrad were to station himself in a quiet spot on the Boulevard Haussmann, say in the shelter of the bombed-out house near the intersection of the Lyons highway. He might have a car parked nearby, with an accomplice in it. Along comes Félicité, taking Michel to school. What was to prevent said M. Konrad from stepping out, and—?

"I see," Renée said, with a little shiver.

Michel stared at the back of M. Béjart's head. Only a few hours ago he had been sitting peacefully in the meadow in front of the château, concerned about the scolding he was going to get for not having gone to church. Now, suddenly, the matter was forgotten, and he was a hunted creature in danger of his life. He had listened intently during the brief discussion alongside the presbytery, and noted how Father Fonsac had first been overwhelmed and then convinced by what M. Béjart said. It must be true, then. However incredible it seemed, M. Konrad was after him. He was an agent. Michel was not quite sure what an agent was, but it had an ominous ring. M. Béjart's remarks had been full of such mysterious words, which belonged to the adult world so far beyond his comprehension. That strange word that even the priest had to ask about. Collective farm. Zionism. Kremlin. But he knew what a slave was, that was when they put a chain around your neck, and you pushed a wheel around and around a well to draw up buckets of water, while a man wearing a sheet stood behind you with a whip to keep you from stopping. He had seen that picture in a book, and under the words "A Greek Slave." So that was what M. Konrad wanted him for! Why him? What had he done? And where was Palestine? It all seemed scarcely real, and yet Maman Rose had come running with M. Béjart when Mme Thérèse telephoned her, and told them to lock the doors and windows until she arrived, and the pitchfork by the door had been real enough. Michel was filled with uneasiness. He would have liked to ask questions, but the others were silent, staring out the windows and thinking their own thoughts.

The car had left the village and entered the open plain beyond. The road cut through green fields, drowsy under the sun. It was hot, although they were going fast, and the air whipped through the car. Renée kept dabbing at her face with her handkerchief. All were moist and uncomfortable. They passed through a village. The road began to climb upwards, skirting a long low hill covered with forest. Suddenly the road became steep, and gorges opened below them, with bare gray rock showing through the trees. It became perceptibly cooler. After a while M. Béjart pulled off the road into a niche scooped out of the hillside and stopped the car. "There!" he said, pointing through the window.

Far off, over the nearby hills, like a cloud against the horizon, towered a white peak whose outlines were hardly distinguishable in the afternoon haze.

"Mont Blanc!" Renée breathed in Michel's ear.

For a long time no one spoke. Then M. Béjart, half turning in his seat, his finger upraised, said with emotion, "Children, you must never forget you are French!"

It was a solemn moment. Michel felt moved, and he could see the others did too. They gazed at the white mountain in silence. At length M. Béjart let out the clutch, and the car returned to the road. His eyes fixed ahead of him, his face grave, M. Béjart began to speak. There had once been a very wise Roman patriot, he said, whose name was Cicero. He had written about what it meant to love one's country. A man loved his wife, Cicero said, and his children, his relatives, his friends. But the greatest love of all was for one's country, because it included all the others. Some day the children would realize the wisdom of what that great Roman had written. The man who did not love his country was a monster. And the most monstrous of all was the Frenchman who did not love France. Because France was the most beautiful land on the face of the globe. France had everything, she had fertile soil, broad rivers, snow-capped peaks, lush valleys, every range of temperate climate, magnificent coasts on two seas. But these were only the physical things. There was something about France that no other nation had, and this he could not describe without using the word "soul." France had a soul, she had God's seal on her; it was in the very air one breathed, it set France apart from the rest. Other peoples abandoned their native place and went off to America, and gave up their citizenship for a mess of pottage. But not the Frenchman! Those who went came back disillusioned, having realized the privilege God had granted them in allowing them to be born in France.

M. Béjart had begun calmly enough, but now his voice rose and he spoke with fervor. "We are living today in a world in which the fundamental values have been lost sight of. We are told we must relegate our love of country to a secondary rank, and instead bow down and worship a supra-national machine called the United Nations. The United Nations is to take the place of God, it is to create and suppress nations by decree. I tell you this," M. Béjart said emphatically. "If the United Nations gave half of France to Spain, and the other half to Germany, that is, wiped France off the map, France would still exist. And by the same token, the United Nations can take land away from the Arabs, and call it Israel, but they cannot make it a nation. Israel is a name on a map, but as a nation it does not exist."

They were perhaps still too young to understand this, M. Béjart went on. But it would come with the years, and they would know what a shameful thing the United Nations had just perpetrated. Yes, it was less than a year ago, last December in fact, that the United Nations Assembly, meeting in New York, the very center of American Jewish pressures, had voted to establish the so-called State of Israel. The legitimate protests of the Arabs had been disregarded. But they would soon learn! The Arabs were a true nation, united by thousands of years of common sufferings, their roots in the soil going back to the beginning of time. They would sweep the upstart state into the sea.

"And that's the country they want to send you to," M. Béjart said over his shoulder, addressing Michel directly. "To be chained to a plow. To be shot by the Arabs. You and thousands like you. To give you a rifle and send you up against fighting men, so as to fill their ranks and make Monsieur Konrad rich. Do you want to go? What do you say, Michel, eh? Does that appeal to you?"

"No, sir," Michel said, swallowing hard.

Maman Rose said something in a low voice.

"Well, he's got to know," M. Béjart said. "But don't be frightened, my boy. We won't let them get you."

Léah wriggled up on the front seat and said, "You won't go, will you, Michel?" Michel shook his head. "He won't go," Léah said to Maman Rose.

Pé said, "I'm not a Jew."

"Pé!" Manon said.

Maman Rose turned and cuffed Pé alongside the head. Pé squawked and fell back on the seat. "Let me hear that once more," Maman Rose said grimly, "and you'll get worse!"

Renée had looked around, startled. She shook Michel by the arm in a friendly fashion. Then she looked out the window again with dreamy eyes.

As the car pulled up before the Nursery, Maman Rose, who had been speaking softly to M. Béjart, suddenly stiffened and stared at the entrance. Félicité was there, standing in the doorway, peering nervously at the street.

"Mademoiselle," Félicité shrieked, running down the walk. Her iron-gray hair was flying as though she had been plucking it with both hands, and her leathery face was streaked and wet. Then Félicité's head was at the window, and she was babbling, "Jean! Mademoiselle Rose, it's Jean! He fell!"

"Dear God!" Maman Rose said under her breath, flinging open the door and shoving Félicité back. "What is it? What's happened?"

She hurried up the walk, with Félicité at her side gesticulating and crying out, "It wasn't my fault!"

"Come quickly," M. Béjart muttered, getting out of the car. "If it's not one thing—"

As they were entering the gate, a scream came from the second floor of the Nursery. For a moment they all stared up, then they were running into the building and up the stairs to Jean's room, where Dr. Peyrefitte stopped them at the door. Michel could not see because M. Béjart and Renée were in the doorway in front of him. But then Renée, with a choked sob, ran in and fell to her knees beside the bed. And Michel saw that Maman Rose was also on her knees, and that a figure was lying on the bed that had to be Jean, but it was hard to tell because the head was swathed in rolls of white bandage, with an ominous red patch on one side. Pé was pushing from behind, grunting, "Let me see!" Michel made place for him.

"No children!" Dr. Peyrefitte said savagely. "Downstairs, all of you!" He turned to Félicité. "You! Get them out of here!"

Michel suffered himself to be shooed away with Pé and Léah. Félicité, taking them downstairs, was moaning and wringing her hands. In the hall below Michel and Pé questioned her. The poor half-witted creature was incoherent. She was obsessed with the idea that she would be blamed for the accident, and kept repeating that it was not her fault. So confused was her tale that it was a long time before Michel understood what had happened. Jean had come home in the early afternoon and found nobody but Félicité in the Nursery. Bored and restless, he went out to the playground, where he had some months before rigged up an iron tube supported by the wall on one side and a pole on the other. Félicité looked out once and saw him chinning himself. She did not know when he fell. Looking out perhaps an hour later, she saw him lying on the ground, motionless. The iron tube had been wrenched loose from the pole and was lying across his body. Someone said, He's dead! She looked around to see who had spoken, but saw nobody. She became frightened and ran to Dr. Peyrefitte's house.

Manon appeared halfway down the stairs and told them to be quiet. Looking up past her, Michel saw Maman Rose being led along the corridor by Dr. Peyrefitte, who was supporting her under the arm and talking in a low voice. Maman Rose's face was like a stone mask.

Behind the shiny black hearse smothered in flowers the cortege came walking slowly. First came the hearse, moving at a crawl, then Maman Rose walking alone, erect, her eyes fixed on the casket. Michel was behind her, with Renée. The others followed, Manon with Pé and Léah, M. Béjart with Mme Quertsch, M. Joseph with Mlle Camélia, and after them a long double line of people. Everybody from the Nursery was there, as well as some of the working mothers. A number of those present were unknown to Michel. He was surprised that there were so many. Had they all known and loved Jean? Or had they come out of respect for Maman Rose, who had been directress of the Nursery for many years, and was well known in Touville? Their faces were sad. How young he was! they had repeated, gathered in the front garden of the Nursery, waiting for the coffin to be brought out.

Renée's eyes were red and her face was swollen. She had not slept last night, but had sat up with Maman Rose beside the bed where Jean's body lay. Renée was very blond, with baby skin and corn-silk hair; whenever she cried, her face looked ravaged. She walked with her head down. Was she thinking of the vow she had made? Or had it all been a dream? Michel was not sure. He had been asleep last night when Renée shook him and whispered that Maman Rose wanted to see him. He did not remember how he went down the hall. Did he walk, or did Renée carry him? The first thing that had penetrated his sleepiness was Jean's face, dreadfully sharp and still in the light of the candles set in slender bronze holders at the corners of the bed. Then he and Maman Rose and Renée were kneeling on the floor, with their arms around each other, and the two women were sobbing, and Maman Rose was exclaiming brokenly that they were her children, the only ones left to her now; and Renée, in a frenzy of emotion, was stammering that she would never marry, but would stay with Maman Rose always, to be her daughter and take care of her when she was old. And she swore to it by her dead brother, because Maman Rose had always been so good to him and given him a home. Michel's heart had overflowed with love for both of them, and he too had cried.

Had it really happened? True, the scene was vivid in his memory; but then, so were his nightmares, which were not real.

The procession entered Place St. Lazare. Lifting his head, Michel saw the tower of the church on the far side, rising above the trees. St. Lazare. His church. Michel's thoughts were troubled. What was he to do? He would have to enter with the others, anything else was out of the question. It was not an ordinary mass. It was for Jean.

St. Lazare. Was this the Lazarus who rose from the dead? He did not know, he had never thought about it before. The square was St. Lazare, and so was the church. They had always been there. You went to mass there on Sundays because it was close, and this was its parish. But it was months since he had gone. April, May, June, July. The communion was the last time, because of his illness. And his excuses. But today he would have to, for Jean. He would have to kneel and pray. To whom?

In the square the passersby stopped and stared, their faces suddenly grave. The men who wore hats removed them. They gazed at the mourners, trying to guess who had died.

The hearse stopped before the church. What would happen now? The driver and his companion, both short, balding men with professionally serious faces, got out and came to Maman Rose. They spoke softly and deferentially. Maman Rose nodded, hardly listening. M. Béjart and M. Joseph came forward, followed by two men Michel did not know. They stood behind the hearse, waiting. The driver began to push aside the flowers on the coffin. Michel understood, they were to carry the coffin into the church.

At that moment a limousine pulled up at the corner.

"The mayor!" someone said.

All turned their heads and watched as a tall, portly man dressed in black stepped out the door that the uniformed chauffeur held open. Michel recognized Mayor Crisenoy's close-cropped, grizzled head, the round, heavy face, the old-fashioned silver-rimmed glasses. He was not smiling now, as he did in the Nursery during his inspections.

The mayor approached, taking Maman Rose's hands in his and patting them. "Mademoiselle," he murmured in compassion.

"Oh, Your Honor!" Maman Rose said, deeply moved. "Thank you for coming."

"Dear friend," the mayor demurred. "As if I—" He shook hands briefly with the men gathered to receive the coffin. "If you will allow me," he said, nodding to where the driver was removing the flowers.

"Certainly, sir," M. Béjart said quickly, making room.

The long black box slid forward, then, hoisted by six pairs of arms, moved slowly toward the steps. It was heavy. The mayor stumbled, recovered himself, went on. Maman Rose followed, holding a crumpled handkerchief to her lips, and all the others came after. Seeing M. Joseph straining at the handle, Michel was reminded of the night Father Périer had died. What had M. Joseph done with the body? He had often wondered about that.

At the entrance, between the columns, stood a glistening metal contraption with rubber-tired wheels. The six men placed the coffin on it, and straightened up with a deep breath. The driver shook hands with the mayor, bowed, and pushed the coffin down the aisle toward the altar, where, in the dimness, Michel could see Father Danchois waiting, censer in hand.

By now a small crowd had gathered before the church. Some followed the mourners up the steps and entered. The others began to disperse.

He would have to go in now. His heart beating painfully, he moved down the aisle with Renée to the forward pews, where he genuflected and took his place on the worn oaken bench. The mass began. Michel knelt with the others, but did not say the responses. He could not, the words died on his lips. He felt his face go pale. Would the others notice? He stared down at the floor.

It was a turning point in his life. He knew it, and he was not ready. He had wanted to wait. In the meadow at Sep he had achieved a kind of equilibrium within himself, with his decision to hold off judgment until he had grown and learned wisdom. But life would not let you wait. Life hurried you along, demanding decisions you were not prepared to make. Even if God let you take your time, people did not. You either went to church and prayed like everybody else, or people whispered about you as they did about Mlle Pasquier, who was contaminated by the century. In his case it would be worse, because he was only a little boy, who could not stand up to the grownups who ruled his world. He saw himself being questioned by Maman Rose; summoned up before Father Roche, who would stare at him in horror; taken to Mother Veronica, who had done so much for him, and whose angelic face would show a disappointment he could not bear to imagine. He would read their thoughts in their eyes: This is the boy who was taken in with such love; the boy that Father Périer had taught, that the priests at St. Joseph's praised for his piety and good behavior, that everybody said was to be a priest himself! But how could he say, Thy will be done, to a God who condemned fathers to hell for something He Himself had permitted?

This was it, then. It could no longer be avoided. He had to face God with his rebellion and demand an answer. Humbly. With love. But no longer to be put off. There was no one else to turn to.

He wanted to cry out, Dear God, give me a sign. One I can understand. Not through anybody, but from You alone to me. Don't make me choose between You and my father.

His eyes were closed. He waited for a voice to speak to him. But there was nothing. There was only a coldness inside. His own words, unspoken, lay heavy within him, as though they had been unheard. He remembered his dream of walking endlessly in an empty landscape, alone in the universe. He was shivering, and there was a cold trickle down his back. At his side Renée was crying softly.

If God gave him a sign, how would he know? God might speak to him, but might just as well choose some other way. A burning bush. A dove. How would he interpret such a thing? There must be no doubts; it would have to be something decided in advance. Lifting his head, Michel gazed at the altar, and then beyond and above it, at the painting of the crucifixion on the wall. It showed Jesus on the cross; that poor, tormented head hung sideways, the eyes swooning upwards toward a dim ray of light in the gathering clouds. The light touched His face and the cruel thorns that sent streaks of blood down the gaunt, bearded cheeks. The face was a somber yellow and was the only part of the painting that could be distinguished clearly from where Michel sat; all the rest was in dull blacks and browns. Michel fixed his eyes on the Saviour's face. A daring thought shaped itself in his mind. God could do it if He wanted to. God could do anything. A simple yes or no, that was all he was asking for.

It was a challenge, and Michel knew it. But he had to have the answer. His scalp prickling, aghast at his own temerity, expecting to be blasted by lightning, he stared at the pale oval in the dark painting, and said soundlessly, "Is my father in hell? Shake your head."

Father Danchois came forward, his moonface solemn, his hand bearing the censer uplifted. He dashed holy water over the casket, punctuating each movement with a prayer. Michel heard his words through a kind of haze; he did not swerve his attention from the canvas.

The head did not move.

Either way would be an answer. Up and down, or sideways. Michel hoped fervently it would be sideways. But even if it were the other way, he wanted to see it. Because anything was better than not knowing. If it were sideways, that would be enough happiness to last him the rest of his life. He would clutch it to him like a precious thing, he would go his way radiant with joy, he would study hard and become a priest and spend his life helping others to achieve the same kind of happiness. God had taken Father Périer, and Jean; He would take Father Fonsac, Maman Rose, M. Béjart, all of them. Eventually God would take him, Michel—and he would go with thanks in his heart, and there, at long last, after so much pain, he would see his Vati again.

And if it were up and down? What then? Could he bear it? Yes, it would be just bearable, because it would mean that God had had compassion on his suffering, and had worked a miracle, like in the Bible, so that he might have an answer to his question. It would mean that God was doing things out of the goodness of His heart, and it *had* to be good because what God did was good. He wouldn't understand, but the sign itself would be the evidence that God had heard him. That there was Someone there.

His heart gave a great leap as he formulated this dreadful thought. Of course God was there. If it was inconceivable for God to condemn his father to hell, it was sheer madness to suppose that there was no one there at all. That would mean that his nightmare was the reality of things, and in that case it would be better not to have been born at all. No, no, God was there, and could do anything. He who had turned back the sea and raised Lazarus from the dead could easily make a painted figure move. Just the head. No one else need see it but Michel. It wasn't so much to ask. Just a thought, a wink, a flick of God's little finger. Just this, and he would never doubt again. Either way. Dear God, take my soul. I offer it to You in love. One sign my Vati is not in hell. I am watching, I won't miss it no matter how tiny it is.

Concentrating with all his might, Michel stared at the head on the canvas.

It did not move.

Dear Christ, You who died for our sins, ask Your Vati to be good to mine. Let me take Your place on the cross, only let my Vati go.

Renée had taken his hand. He resisted, not understanding, staring at her wildly.

"What's the matter with you?" she whispered in alarm.

The ceremony was over. People had stood up and were moving slowly toward the door. Father Danchois was murmuring something to Maman Rose, who said, "Thank you. Thank you." He would have to leave. There had been no sign. Nothing at all. The pale face was fixed, immobile, unchanging in its eternal frozen agony. God could have done it, but had not. He had found Michel unworthy, then; He had scorned the soul Michel had offered. What was he to do now? Whom could he turn to, if God Himself had chosen not to answer?

Michel let himself be led away by the hand. At the aisle he did not genuflect.

As he moved toward the door he saw Jules standing beyond one of the inner columns. Renée must have seen him too, she walked quickly, her face flushed and lowered. Jules watched her go. He seemed surprised.

Jules's face was one of the images that remained with him of that afternoon. Christ's face, set in a sickly yellow grimace. That, and a gaping pit in the ground, into which a darkly gleaming casket was slowly lowered on flat, heavy tapes, down, down, out of sight. A rooster crowing, incongruously, in a barn beyond the cemetery wall. Mayor Crisenoy supporting Maman Rose under her arm. Maman Rose saying bitterly to Mlle Camélia, "He killed my boy!" And a wound in his heart, a maddening sense of futility, of helplessness; the festering realization that he had been passed over unheard, and there was no one else to turn to.

8

❀

R AISE THE WINDOW a little more," Rina said. "He looks warm."
Bending down over the couch, she tucked Judas' pajama top
into the trouser band. Konrad silently lifted the window as far as it
would go, and came to look at his son. He contemplated the ruffled
black hair against the pillow, the soft boyish face, the hand lying
open and relaxed. He put his arm around his wife's shoulder and
squeezed hard.

"Oh, Louis," Rina whispered. "To think—"

"Yes," he said harshly.

Both were silent a long time. They were safe. The horror had
passed. In the morning Judas would awaken in the same bed he had
gone to sleep in and would come out yawning sleepily to get his
breakfast. He would go out and play, and you knew he would come
back again. To look for a ball. To read a book. To complain there
was nothing to do. He would be perspired and dirty, hungry, laughing, noisy. He would be alive. The barn at Toulon was a strange
memory, an adventure, nothing more. Children, Konrad thought,
looking at his son. That was where they had you. You didn't mind so
much for yourself; you had lived and had your chance. But these
soft, innocent, helpless creatures—he got sick inside when he
thought of it.

Every night, during the ritual of looking at their sleeping boy,
Konrad thought of it, and told himself it was over now, they were
safe. Judas could live. And every night the same wave of bitter
thankfulness swept over him.

After a while Rina lifted her head from his shoulder and said,
"Come, I'll make you some coffee."

Her voice was placid, but he knew she had been thinking the same
thoughts and was thankful too. They had that right, he thought, fol-

lowing her into the kitchen. But to be counted among the few who had escaped, was that not a kind of shame? To be alive, when so many had died? They lay in stillness in their various graves, their very silence a reproach. How quickly the world had forgotten them! Had they forgotten the living? He hoped so. If not—the thought was unbearable.

Rina served the coffee and sat down at the table. Nursing his cup in his bony paw, Konrad was aware of her scrutiny. He knew that look. How deeply are you involved? it asked. Please take care of yourself. But do what you think best, I am with you.

"A strange woman," Rina mused. "I don't understand her."

"What is there to understand?" Konrad demanded. "She has the boy and intends to keep him. She must be made to give him up."

"She must love him very much."

He shrugged.

"If I went to see her?" Rina suggested timidly. "Maybe another woman, a mother . . ."

"I won't have you insulted," Konrad said. "You don't know her, she's capable of anything. Force is the only thing she understands. We're doing the right thing. If the procureur can't scare her with his inquiry, then we'll take her to court, and there's an end to it."

"Well," Rina remarked, "I hope it's over quickly. You've lost enough time from the shop as it is. And it will cost a fortune, I'm sure."

"We'll manage. Just leave it all to me."

"All right, Louis," Rina said submissively.

In the upper right-hand corner of the page Louis Konrad wrote, "August 13, 1948," and paused to gather his thoughts. It would be a long letter, he decided. There was much to say, and it would reassure the Lindners to have a full report.

"Dear Hannah and Itzik," he wrote, "I have reached a point in the conduct of your nephew's case at which I am obliged to wait while the law takes its course. In the meanwhile, it is well to bring you up to date about what I have been doing, and to encourage you about the eventual outcome. Yes, without wanting to raise your hopes unduly, I must say that I have every expectation that Michel will be turned over to you soon, for the law clearly backs our position, and Mlle Rose will be forced to bow to the decision of the court (if the case gets that far), whether she likes it or not.

"I will not bore you with all the legal details, nor am I sure I could explain them with any accuracy; but Maître Paul, my *avoué,* assures me that French law is unusually explicit in establishing the supremacy of the family as the indivisible social unit, and that the weight of all precedent is on our side. Barring certain exceptional circumstances, which do not exist here, orphaned children automatically pass to the custody of the next of kin. We might have envisaged difficulties if the various members of the family could not agree on which of them was to get the child; but fortunately there is no such dispute. Mitzi, whom I have contacted by letter in Vienna, writes that Michel should unquestionably go to you, since she is the boy's aunt by marriage only, and cannot care for him properly. (She gives an interesting account of her visit to Mlle Rose, of which more later.) The only other relative is Eva Weiss, Lili's sister, who has not been heard from since she went to China before the war. What's more, we have Karl's last letter to you, asking you to take care of his son if anything happened to him and Lili. Your position is therefore unassailable. Against this Mlle Rose can claim only that she should be allowed to keep Michel because in the four years or so that she has had him no relative came forward to claim him (believe it or not, this is what she has been saying); and all we have to do is to produce in court the letter she wrote you in November 1945 to destroy her case completely.

"But I am getting ahead of myself. You know from my previous acknowledgment that I received your power of attorney. Armed with this, and the various supporting documents you sent me, I engaged the services of Maître Barthélemy Paul, a distinguished lawyer of Touville, who is also a member of the city council, a key figure in the Socialist party (the Touville city administration is Socialist), and, most important, a prominent Catholic layman who enjoys the confidence of the bishop. For personal reasons (I'll come back to this), he was hesitant to take the case, and asked me why I came to *him.* Because, aside from everything else, you're a Catholic, I told him, and the boy's been baptized. He jumped in his chair and said it wasn't possible, that canon law provided that Jewish children couldn't be baptized without the consent of their parents, that such a baptism wasn't valid. He wanted to know the name of the priest who had done it, said he would have him up before the bishop. I was very glad to see his reaction, which confirmed my opinion that he was the man we needed. Frankly, while such a baptism is of course meaningless, it is intolerable that it was done at all; and I have been somewhat annoyed that the people I have spoken to have taken it so calmly. It was this that decided Maître Paul to take the case, if I could establish that the boy had actually been baptized and it was not merely another lie on the part of Mlle Rose.

"I made discreet inquiries in various churches in the neighborhood of the Municipal Nursery, and found that no child named Michel Benedek had been baptized in any of them. It was Mme Quertsch who gave me the clue. I went to her and asked her outright where the baptism had taken place. The poor woman was greatly embarrassed. You will have formed your opinion of her from her letters to you. I find her to be a good, quiet, mousy person who once did a charitable deed with the best of motives, and now finds herself overwhelmed by the consequences. She took the boy, she says, because she would have been unable to face her God if she did not. It never occurred to her that Mlle Rose would do more than shelter the boy until he could be returned to his family. When pressed, she admits that it is wrong of Mlle Rose to do what she is doing, but does not dare remonstrate with her over the matter, and simply hopes piously that all will turn out for the best. Caught between Mlle Rose and us, I am sure she wishes she had never got involved at all. However, when I insisted, she did tell me that the baptism had taken place at Sep, a mountain village some twenty miles southeast of Touville, and begged me not to let anyone—she did not have to tell me whom she meant—know she had told me.

"Since Sep is tiny and has only one church, it was an easy matter to verify the fact. Michel was baptized there only a week before I went to see Mlle Rose at your request. It's in the church register, and the old priest, one Fonsac, confirmed it to me himself. I wish you could have heard his explanation. The old gentleman simply saw nothing wrong with baptizing a Jewish child without the consent of his family. His attitude was, Why not? When I explained to him why not, he peered at me as though I had made a joke in bad taste. As if a heathen rite like circumcision had any meaning! He didn't say it, but it was clear that was what he was thinking. Whereas—this he did say—the boy had to be baptized before he could have his communion. Surely I could see that? Anyway, what difference did it make, he had baptized so many Jewish children during the war, why did one more matter?

"His politely patronizing air, his smug arrogance masked as humility, his absolute conviction, beyond the reach of doubt, that he was in the only tenable spiritual position, were most infuriating. For consider what he believed he was doing: He believed that by sprinkling the child with water and saying a prayer he was wiping away the covenant engraved in his flesh by the boy's own father, the only person entitled to choose for him until he was of an age to choose for himself, and who did so at a time when one's life might depend on the choice. This that meddling old fool of a priest dared to take on himself without consulting anybody, even against the rules of his own church, at the mere request of Mlle Rose. Why not? His was the only way to get to God. Why would that disturb anybody? I brought up canon law. 'My dear sir,' he said to me as if I were a child, 'don't talk to me about canon law.' And that was that, he wouldn't discuss it. *He* was the priest.

"There was nothing to be done with him. A man like that, so unable to see himself, so completely without perspective, so accustomed to a single, fixed idea, may be a good Catholic, but he is not even a Christian. I saw in him a symbol of the Church he represents, which has become one of the great enemies of the world today, not because it believes that it is the only way to get to God—all religions are based on this supposition, whether they admit it or not—but because, starting with this belief, it has through insolence of power in time come to think of itself as God on earth.

"I returned to Touville, where Maître Paul, basing himself on your documents, drew up the *requête* to the procureur. This is the normal procedure, and one that Mlle Rose will be unable to avoid, as she has all your other steps. The procureur is chief administrative official of the Parquet, that is, the legal agency in each district that represents the Ministry of Justice, and as such is both empowered and obliged to weigh and prosecute charges against violators of the Codes. Mlle Rose will be summoned and questioned, under pain of arrest. If this show of force will not frighten her into giving up the boy, the next step is a court action, which can have only one outcome. Maître Paul is convinced of this. Incidentally, I dissuaded him from going to the bishop to complain against the priest Fonsac. If such complaints had been made years ago, they might have done some good; but at this stage, I see little effect other than to raise the religious question, which I want to avoid. To put it more plainly, I do not want to stress the issue of a *Jewish* family against a *Catholic* woman, which might have undesirable repercussions in court and prejudice our case (this is the only reason that restrains me). It is enough to raise the issue of family vs. self-appointed 'guardian.' Maître Paul reluctantly gave in on this, but only until the boy is in your hands, reserving the right then to make a fuss.

"We submitted the *requête* this morning. Unfortunately, it is August, which means that everything in France marches on one foot only. In September, when vacation time is over, we can expect some action. Although Maître Paul tells me that these things proceed slowly, and warns me against possible tricks by Mlle Rose, I am confident that in a short time your dearest wish will be granted.

"In the course of my inquiries I unearthed some information about the charming lady who has your nephew. It seems that she is a fantastic mixture of opposite qualities. On the one hand, she collects stray people the way others collect coins or stamps. Years ago, before the war, she adopted five brothers and sisters whose parents had died in an accident. During the Occupation she took in a number of children, and allowed a Jewish couple to hide out in the Nursery as well. I am told that even now there are several homeless people in her care, and that she provides for them out of her own resources. Those who know her—I am thinking primarily of Mme Quertsch, but there have been others as well—say she is generosity itself and has a strongly developed maternal instinct. This is Mme Quertsch's explanation of why Mlle Rose will not give up the boy.

"On the other hand, it would appear that other aspects of the lady's character are not so admirable. Her love life, for instance, is the subject of common gossip, which links half a dozen names with hers. Except in one case, however, I have paid little attention to this, knowing how exaggerated such things become in the public eye. The relationship I am talking about is that of Mlle Rose with the mayor of Touville. Yes, gossip has put the two together, and apparently with some reason. She seems to have attracted his attention years ago as a nurse in the Municipal Nursery, and persuaded him to retire the old directress at the minimum retirement age and give the place to her. The appointment created quite a stir in local circles. Dozens of letters were written to the newspapers, claiming that the old directress was in full possession of her faculties, and might have been allowed to remain at her post for five years more, as the city charter provides; and that Mlle Rose had an ordinary nurse's diploma, and not the special one required for the job. I have seen those letters myself, at the city library. Some are quite violent and go so far as to attack Mlle Rose not only for professional incompetence but for moral unfitness and scandalous behavior. I'm told that Mlle Rose entered a number of libel suits in reply. In spite of these protests, the mayor stuck to his guns, overrode opposition in the city council, and kept her in her place.

"You will see why I repeat such gossip, which is personally distasteful to me, when I explain its connection with our affair. I went to Maître Paul weeks ago, having weighed his qualities and decided he was the man we needed. It never occurred to me that he might hesitate to take the case. I'm afraid I'm somewhat naïve in such matters, never until now having had any dealings with the processes of the law. I saw only that an injustice had been done and had to be righted, and I supposed that every decent person would feel the same way. Maître Paul, however, seemed uncomfortable to hear my story; he asked me many questions; his attitude was discouraging; and he would not commit himself about accepting the case. I was at a loss to understand his hesitation. I thought perhaps I had unwittingly stumbled into another anti-Semite, and was beginning to get angry, until the question of the baptism came up and I saw how mistaken I was. As a matter of fact, it was the religious issue that decided him. His doubts at first were for other reasons. Since then he has let drop several hints, and today we had a frank discussion in which everything was made clear. Maître Paul belongs to the same party as the mayor, they are old political associates; and I, knowing the gossip about Crisenoy (this is the name of the mayor) and his 'protégée,' was being idiotically unworldly in asking the lawyer to risk political suicide on behalf of a little Jewish boy whose existence he was not even aware of until that moment. I imagine that almost any other lawyer in the same position would have shown me the door. Fortunately, sometimes innocence is rewarded. Maître Paul is a man of principle, and a Catholic whose eyes are not blinded to the rights of others to believe as they please. Not only did he take the case, he will not accept a fee for it. For him it is a test case, he says. He has long been concerned about reports of such ill-advised baptisms and the resentments they create against his Church.

"To return to Mlle Rose, there are other interesting sides to her nature. She is apparently a woman of great courage (she would have to be to protect Jews during the Occupation) and a great brawler. Her many legal suits would convince me of this last, even if I did not have personal experience of it on the occasion of my visit to the Nursery. She also seems to be quite an actress and quite a liar. I have written you already about how she completely took in Rabbi Notarius of our city with a concocted story that she acted out like a tragedy queen. Mitzi writes from Vienna that when she called on Mlle Rose in the autumn of 1946 she was flabbergasted at the way the woman came out with the most glaring contradictions and maintained them with a dramatic force that showed she probably believed her own lies. For example, she was astonished to learn from Mitzi of your existence and that you had written to her, and said she had never heard from you. She wished she *had* been contacted by the boy's relatives, it broke her heart to think that the poor orphan had no family at all, he was a big expense to her, etc., etc. And then, a little later in the same conversation, she showed great scorn for the clothing parcels you had sent the boy, because the garments were of lumpy gray wool, whereas *she* dressed the boy in silk. And this without the slightest sign of recognition that *both* stories could not be true. It was useless, Mitzi said, to try to pin her down on anything like that, the woman sidled off into another topic without answering.

"Mitzi has a different version of Mlle Rose's motives than Mme Quertsch. Mitzi feels that it is not love that moves her, but acquisitiveness—or perhaps a mixture of the two. She sizes up Mlle Rose as a person who is willing to *give* away almost anything, but will fight to her dying breath to keep anything from being *taken* from her. Michel is *hers;* she earned the right to him by saving his life. If she had learned of your existence before you learned of hers, and could win your tearful gratitude by offering him to you, she might have done so. But it was enough for you to ask her for him to make her negative and stubborn. Perhaps psychologists are familiar with such patterns of behavior, but I confess that they are beyond my understanding.

"Another theory has been called to my attention. When Mitzi came to Touville, she went first to the Jewish Children's Welfare Society, to get an interpreter to accompany her to the Nursery. This was a Mlle Poulenc, a young Jewish woman of Alsatian origin, who speaks French and German. I went to see Mlle Poulenc. As soon as I had identified myself and explained the purpose of my inquiry, she threw up her hands and called Mlle Rose a pirate and blood profiteer. She described the visit in much the same terms as Mitzi, but more strongly, and then told me about something Mitzi had not mentioned in her letters. It seems that several times during their discussion, which lasted a long time and got quite heated, Mlle Rose brought up the name Jerome Benedek, and insisted that the person must be a relative of Michel's because of the similarity and rareness of the name. She did not know the man personally, but had heard of him; he lived in Paris. Mitzi replied that the family name was not unusual in Austria, and that for all she knew there was no relationship. The name struck a familiar chord in Mlle Poulenc's memory, as well it might, and she checked up on it later. She learned that Jerome Benedek is a wealthy Paris financier well known in banking circles, and her conclusion is that Mlle Rose saved the boy with an eye to what she could collect for him later, and is waiting for the right bid to be made.

"How much truth there may be to this interpretation I of course cannot tell. If Jerome Benedek is related to your family, and Mitzi was not aware of it, it would be well for you to let me know. Not that I would be in favor of any transaction of the kind suggested, even if the man were willing; it would be a most repugnant business at best, and while I agree that Mlle Rose should be repaid her expenses in caring for Michel, I feel that anything more than that would be unworthy both of her and of us. No—we will proceed along the lines indicated by Maître Paul, and if Mlle Rose did plan that cynical blood profit, the legal action will be the awakening she deserves.

"I must say, however, that Mlle Poulenc's interpretation does not convince me. I do not pretend to understand the strange, contradictory woman that is Mlle Rose, but I do not see money as her motive. If that were so, why would she throw me out without a chance to say a word, when for all she knew it might have been Jerome Benedek who sent me?

"In a way, these are idle speculations. It matters very little *why* Mlle Rose may have adopted the position she has, since our procedure and the outcome must remain the same. But you are doubtless curious about the person in whose hands fate has placed your brother's child; and as for me, I confess I am fascinated by the enigma of the woman. I simply cannot understand her. At times I have the feeling that the people who tell me about her are talking about someone else, so little does what they say conform to what I already know about her. Not the least puzzling feature about her is her anti-Semitism, in view of all she did for Jews during the Occupation.

Perhaps it is another example of *'Alle Juden stinken, nur der kleine Fritz allein.'* There may be much truth in what Mitzi says about acquisitiveness—*her* Jews are sacred, to hell with the rest.

"But let me touch on other things. The first is the state of your inquiry at the Foreign Ministry in Paris. In examining the copies of your correspondence, I saw little evidence of any definite steps that office may have taken on your behalf. They were sympathetic, they assured you that everything possible was being done—but not one word of a specific action taken. I wrote to the Quai d'Orsay, enclosing a photostatic copy of my power of attorney, and asking what disposition had been made of your appeal. I received a prompt reply from an undersecretary, a M. Henri Rousselot, stating that the case had been turned over to the Ministry of Population because of the 'question of nationality.' This puzzled me, and at the same time that I wrote to the Ministry of Population, I replied to M. Rousselot's letter, saying that it was a matter of public record that the child Michel Benedek had been born at Puy-le-Duc on April 14, 1941, and asking—not quite so bluntly, of course—what that had to do with the issue. Again M. Rousselot answered promptly, and this time more fully. He said he was not familiar with the case personally, since it had been handled by the foreign minister himself, M. Georges Bidault (who was then prime minister as well); but from a perusal of the documents, he understood the following: M. Bidault had written to Mlle Odette Rose to inform her that the boy's aunt was claiming him, and to outline the steps of the transfer to Australia. Mlle Rose had replied that she saw no reason why the Foreign Ministry should interest itself in Michel Benedek, since he was not a foreign national; he had been born in France, and his father, the late Dr. Karl Benedek, had stated explicitly, on various occasions, that he was grateful to France for having taken him in, and *his son was to remain in France and become a French citizen.* In view of this reply, M. Bidault had had no recourse but to transmit the case to the Ministry of Population for appropriate action.

"You may imagine my feelings to discover how Mlle Rose used this monstrous lie to thwart the ends of justice. And to the prime minister himself! That her statement is a lie I have no doubt, since Karl wrote you that he wanted *you* to have Michel in case of disaster. Truly, the woman is incredible!

"And so the Foreign Ministry simply washed its hands of the matter, without verifying Mlle Rose's statements and without even the grace of informing you of the transfer of jurisdiction!

"Only a few days ago I received a reply from the Ministry of Population. They write, without any explanation whatsoever, that the dossier of the orphan Michel Benedek has been forwarded to the Ministry of Veterans and War Casualties, 'for appropriate action.'

"I am at a complete loss to understand what the Ministry of Veterans and War Casualties has to do with this matter. But I will write to them, not because I think it will do any good, but so as to leave no stone unturned.

"Something positive has come out of this frustrating correspondence, however; Rousselot's second letter is an additional proof, if one is needed, that by 1946 Mlle Rose was aware that Michel's aunt and uncle in Australia had laid official claim to him. Let her lie *that* away if she can!

"Let me add this: since learning of Mlle Rose's statement to the prime minister, I have asked those who best knew your brother here in Touville whether they had ever heard such a declaration from his lips. They were unanimous in saying no. The pharmacist Arnauld added, 'After Vichy accepted the Nuremberg laws?' (Incidentally, your brother's closest friends in Touville seem to have been M. and Mme Jules Immermann, who were Michel's sponsors at the circumcision. I have been unable to speak to them, however, since they are in America. They are expected back by the new year. I will call on them, simply to make their acquaintance and talk about Karl, since by then our case will no doubt have been settled.)

"Another matter has preoccupied me, but this, after consultation with Maître Paul, I have decided to do nothing about. You write that you made an appeal to the procureur here in Touville, and received no acknowledgment or reply. Maître Paul points out that this might be the result of a number of causes—the civil chaos immediately following the Liberation, the fact that your appeal came from abroad and would have had to be handled by correspondence, or simply your failure to follow prescribed legal forms—but now that you have an agent resident here, and an *avoué* to present the matter in the proper way, the Parquet simply *cannot ignore your claim and must apply the law*. To have presented myself at the Parquet to confront the procureur, as I thought of doing, would have been to invite irritation and nothing more.

"One more thing, and I will bring this long letter to a close. I went to Puy-le-Duc to see your brother's last home. I hardly know myself why I wanted to do this. It was a morbid wish, since it could have no bearing on our cause. Perhaps the best way to explain it is to say that your brother Karl and his family have become more real to me than one would imagine from my brief meeting with him. At first I saw in him—please forgive me for this—more a symbol of what my people and I have suffered than a man, a human being, a person in his own right. To take up arms on his behalf was to afford an outlet for my own bitterness, to strike back in a single case for the six million who have died. But gradually the man Karl has begun to replace the case Benedek in my concern. A personality has slowly taken shape in my mind. I feel that I know him now, I sense his presence here in Touville, in our streets, in my own home. Sometimes I imagine I am he, and try to turn the clock back to those dreadful years and look upon the Touville he saw. I am filled with shame, with a reproach beyond words—how he must have loathed all that appeared to him, the uniforms, the slavery of a nation, the dangerous streets, the apathy of the faces, the closed doors and closed hearts! I go to the bridge over the river Char, and look up at Puy-le-Duc, and I see your brother walking down the hill road, his eyes wary, already sick with fear for what he might find at his return. And my thoughts follow his, and I wonder what that home was like. And I must go up there to see.

"A tall, narrow building at the corner of a tiny cobblestoned plaza. A café on the *rez-de-chaussée*. Three flights of rickety wooden stairs, a musty odor. On the fourth and top floor, a single room, in what must have been designed as a pigeon loft—icy in winter, stifling in summer. The room is let now, to a commission merchant from Marseilles. It is M. Houdy, the landlord, who tells me this. It was he who had to unlock the door when they came for Lili. Houdy is upset, apologetic—what could he do? There were two men in uniform, another in plainclothes. They said to unlock the door, he had to obey. He opens it for me now, the merchant is out and would not mind. The room is dark, with a single window looking out over Touville, the bridge and the hill beyond. A couch, a table, two chairs, a rocking chair by the window, a curtained alcove that is the kitchen. The furnishings are the same, Houdy tells me. He would have liked to board up the window and nail down the door; but times are hard. I do not speak, I hardly listen. It is as I expected—a room like any other. But it is real. I will bear these walls, this rough-grained wooden floor, the cotton-print curtain, with me when I go. And the rocking chair where Lili sat, waiting. These mute witnesses to the reality of their wretched lives are themselves charged with a sadness beyond tears. There is nothing I can say. I nod to Houdy and go out. I have seen where they lived, my obsession has that much more to feed on.

"Yes, dear friends, it is an obsession, and I should be ashamed for revealing it to you, and opening again the wound that has caused you so much sorrow. But strangely enough—I will make this last confession, and there's an end—I feel it is the safeguard of my own sanity. If I told you my dreams, you would shudder for me. I have focused all my emotional festerings on Karl Benedek. In him I see all that has been done to us. But in one man it is compassable. Karl Benedek is real, it is better to see him gazing at me in reproach from the hill road than six million—"

Louis Konrad laid down his pen and stared at the paper. There was perspiration on his forehead. What had happened to him there at the end? He had been carried away and said more than he intended. He read the letter, frowning. No, no, this would never do. With an abrupt motion he tore up the last two pages. Taking a fresh sheet he wrote, "to invite irritation and nothing more," finishing off the sentence from the previous page. Then, briefly, he wrote that Rina and Judas were well, and that they joined him in sending best wishes to Froschl for a speedy recovery, and signed his name. He put out the light, looked in at Judas, and went to bed.

9

❦

IN THE MORNING of a day early in September, Mlle Odette Rose
left the Nursery and hailed a taxi in Place St. Lazare.

"The *mairie*," she said, sinking back in her seat. She might have
walked, she reflected, it was not so far. But Mathieu had told her
nine o'clock, it was ten of, and Mlle Merlin would allow her little
enough time with her chief before she began pushing buzzers and
transmitting "urgent" telephone calls, anything to get her out of
there. Really, Mathieu ought to do something about the woman,
with her ridiculous old-maid jealousies. As if they were holding
hands in there or something! So many problems! Renée. Michel. That
Konrad. It was always like that, one misfortune seemed to bring
another. She had not had a minute's peace since that man showed up
at the Nursery that Easter Sunday. First he had frightened Michel
sick. Then there was that business at Sep, that showed he hadn't
given up and was out to get the boy by hook or crook. He had killed
Jean, as surely as if he had wrenched the bar loose himself. And now
it was the *requête* to the procureur.

Last night Lespinasse had showed her the document, and the
power of attorney the aunt had sent from Palestine. The power of
attorney was a photostatic copy and was attached to the *requête*
itself. "It's legal," Lespinasse had assured her, as she wondered over
the strange squiggly letters in the notarial seal. Hebrew, she guessed
it was. But the stamp of the French consulate at Tel Aviv was clear
enough. The procureur had seen it and accepted it, that was the
point. She had leafed through Konrad's complaint, noted the arguments, and said, "How much time do I have?" Lespinasse had
shrugged; he would do all he could, but this wasn't like the last time,
the man was right here in Touville and would follow it up; at best he
could stall it some days, under plea of pressure of work, since he had

just come back from his vacation. If he hadn't been away, he could have warned her two weeks ago, when the *requête* came in. "Well, give me as long as you can," she had said, and called Mathieu and Maître Cauchet.

She had known immediately what she had to do. But it was all a question of time. When they summoned her, which of course they would do, the new Family Council would have to be in existence already, as if it had no connection with anything Konrad had done. And that meant she had to work fast.

Her face darkened with anger as she remembered certain phrases in the document. Konrad had used the word "willful" three times. Willful disregard. Willful denial. Willful something else. He didn't know what willful was. He hadn't seen anything yet. She would make him sorry he had ever stuck his Jew nose into her door. She became furious every time she thought of the man, coming around with his big fisheyes years afterward, with his "How did you dare?" and "You didn't have the right." Where was he when she listened to her heart and took the boy in? Where were they all?

If it had been Pé. Or Léah. But not Michel, no, not while she had breath in her body.

The morning was fresh and bright. In a little while it would get hot, but the sun had not yet sucked up the chill of the September night. The streets were full of activity. A steady stream of bicycles flowed in both directions. On the sidewalks people walked with animation, popping in and out of the busy shops. Faces were gay, almost like before the war, when Touville was noted for its congenial atmosphere. The Vienna of France, tourists were told. Poor Jean! she thought with a dreadful pang. Her poor, poor boy! To die at twenty-one, when his life was just beginning, he who had always been so cheerful, so full of fun! Once he had walked like those she now saw in the streets, upright, smiling, his head full of projects and dreams. And now he lay in his grave, and everything was over for him.

The taxi entered the park before the *mairie* and wound through the shady curves under the tall, imposing trees. Even at this early hour the benches were full. Some read newspapers; a few, those who had brought little bags with them, had flocks of pigeons at their feet; the others stared idly about, following with their eyes those who crossed the green rectangle with a busy air.

As she paid the driver, he said with a little grin, "And the pigeons, mam'selle?"

She smiled at him. "No time today," she said pleasantly.

The gendarme on duty—Arthur, was it? the one with the frisky wife—saluted her as she entered. She heard the driver tell him, "She usually feeds the pigeons."

They knew her. Everybody knew her. Say "Mlle Rose" to almost anybody in Touville, and they would say, "Oh yes, the one at the Municipal Nursery"; or "The Orphan Lady"; or something of the sort. They knew her all right. And that was as it should be. It meant you belonged, that you had roots in your native soil. This was her city, her place in the world. She was French through and through. Even, she supposed, to her faults. People talked about those too. Frankly, she didn't much care.

In the cool inner courtyard she saw Maître Cauchet, chatting with two other men. They all carried briefcases.

"Good morning, Mademoiselle Rose," the lawyer greeted her, inclining his sleek, dark head. She nodded as she passed.

She felt their eyes on her as she went up the stairs. There had been a time when she had the finest legs in France. Or so her admirers would have her believe. The years, the years! Still, it was reassuring to a woman of forty-three when men stopped talking business to watch her go up a flight of stairs. She had filled out, but the shape was still there. And black had always become her.

On the second floor she entered a large paneled reception room tiled in black and white marble squares. Mlle Merlin was at her desk just inside the doorway; she looked up expectantly, then let her face go expressionless. They exchanged polite good mornings. Mlle Rose was instantly on her guard. There was something disquieting in the woman's eyes, a smirk, a look of triumph she could not quite hide. Mlle Merlin nodded to the guard seated before the mayor's door. Mlle Rose crossed the room, aware that the men waiting on benches against the wall were watching her with curiosity. The guard sprang to his feet and all but clicked his heels as he ushered her through the quilted door.

Mathieu was at his elegant glass-topped desk, his great grizzled head cocked sideways as he studied a sheet of paper that he held close to his face; with his other hand he scratched lazily beneath his alpaca jacket. "Ah, Mademoiselle Rose!" he said in bland joviality, letting the paper fall and swinging deliberately around to get up. "How nice to see you again! I trust our directress is well?"

"Quite well, Your Honor. And you?"

The guard shut the door discreetly. Mathieu grunted, and ambled up to her, taking her by the arm, his shrewd eyes peering at her face. "Well, Odette? How goes it?"

"Oh, Mathieu!" she began.

The *mairie* clock was striking ten as Mlle Rose stepped out into the sunshine of the street. As always, at the first chime the pigeons had come whirling out in startled flocks, and were now circling over the park.

She walked to the taxi station at the corner, entered the first vehicle, and told the driver to take her to the Temple.

Mlle Rose was thoughtful as she gazed out the window. The interview had not gone at all as planned. Hardly had she opened her mouth when Mathieu wagged his finger at her and said it was that priest, wasn't it? She ought to have known she couldn't get away with that sort of thing. At least, she might have told *him!*

She honestly had not known what he was talking about. Mathieu had seen that at once from her expression, and said, "Father Périer."

She repeated the name in bewilderment, staring at him. What on earth had Father Périer to do with Konrad and his *requête?*

"Well, well, well," Mathieu said softly. "Is it possible you haven't heard? Then prepare yourself, my dear. The sister has been talking. There are all sorts of ugly rumors going about. You told me he died at his sister's house. But she's been telling the neighbors that he was already dead when he was brought to her. And hinting at foul play into the bargain."

So that was what the Merlin woman was so happy about! It caught her so completely by surprise that she was speechless for a long moment before her indignation burst forth. "Oh!" she cried, "as if anybody—! Why, he died of a heart attack! Everybody knew he had a bad heart. He was sick for weeks before he died. It was the third attack. And that precious sister of his never once came to see him!"

"Then he *was* at the Nursery."

"But I told you that," she said reproachfully.

"You didn't tell me he died there."

Really, when Mathieu let himself be so obtuse she wanted to shake him. What difference did it make *where* the poor old man had died? "Well," she said, trying to keep her tone reasonable, "I couldn't put him out in the street, could I? Once he got sick he couldn't be moved. Anyway, I can just see that sister of his taking care of him! And then, once it happened, what was I to do? Put yourself in my position. I thought, Let's not have any scandal, there's been enough already. And so I sent Father Périer over there, with word to the sister to call a doctor, and tell him . . ."

Mathieu was regarding her with curiosity. "What a strange creature you are, Odette! Didn't you for an instant realize what an uproar there would be if you were caught carrying a corpse about in the streets? Suppose the neighbors saw him being taken into the house? And suppose the doctor refused to sign the death certificate? Do you know the trouble you'd be in?"

She resented that, especially from Mathieu. He of all people should have known she hadn't been thinking of herself. How easy it would have been simply to let things alone, call the doctor, let it be known that Father Périer had died in the Nursery, and give the gossipmongers a juicy bit to chew on! She could just hear them snickering, "And whose bed did he die in?" She didn't care what they said about her. But Henri? No, she had done the right thing. She had nursed him and fought to give him every minute of life his poor wasted body was capable of; and even after he had died, she had continued the fight, for his name, his reputation, so that he could rest in peace after his long remorse. The risk didn't count. There were certain things that were worth any risk. But Mathieu didn't want to see that. And so she answered simply, "Well, none of that happened."

Mathieu seemed to think that was funny. He began to laugh, taking off his glasses and squeezing the bridge of his nose with the tips of his fingers while she looked at him in perplexity. Then he wiped his glasses, put them on, and gave her a little lecture. She lived in her own little world, with her own set of values that had no relation whatsoever with the values of society. He had never known anybody with such a complete disregard for the law.

After that it wasn't any good, of course. Because there was only one way Mathieu could help her with Konrad, and he was already on his high horse about that. The procureur's summons? Mathieu might be the mayor, he might hold the city in the palm of his hand, but he couldn't interfere with the Parquet; nobody could. Changing the Family Council? That was a matter for her lawyer to handle, and Judge Cerval to decide. Why had she come to him then? Mathieu was no fool, he guessed at once, even before she finished her story, and she saw his face change. She knew that look—underneath his joviality he had his flinty side.

"See here, Odette," he said very seriously, "let's not have any of that. Konrad's a professional man, operating a perfectly legal business. A university graduate, a property owner, a taxpayer. He's within the law, he's tough and shrewd, and he won't be bullied. And as a Jew he's been persecuted enough already. I won't have it."

She protested that she hadn't asked for anything of the sort. But with a shady character like that, an agent for foreign powers, there was bound to be something in his past that could not stand questioning. Let the police look about. Perhaps that alone would be enough to make the man move on to other places. That was all she wanted. But if he didn't go, and the police *did* turn up something . . . But Mathieu had taken his position and wouldn't budge. She saw it was no use insisting. And so she changed the subject to him and his health, she scolded him with deliberate impertinence for not getting enough rest, until he was grinning at her; and then she left, calling back gaily through the open door, "Thank you, Your Honor," for the benefit of that cat Merlin, who no doubt was expecting a more chastened exit. And smiled sweetly at her going past her desk.

The smile was gone now, as she stared through the taxi window at the streets of Touville. Mathieu's homily was rankling within her. Disregard for the law, he had said. Which law? she might have answered. The law of the Third Republic, which had perished so miserably at a single vote at Bordeaux? Vichy law? Nazi law? The law of the Fourth Republic? Every day the laws and codes changed, every day new legislative acts poured over the land, and yet you were supposed to take it all seriously. A fine mess she'd have been in, and everybody else, if she had respected the idiotic promulgations of that senile old fool Pétain, urged on by his murderous Gestapo masters! Men, with their silly games! They said, The Law! and expected you to fall on your face in reverence. According to the law, she'd have turned away the Barshowanskis, and let them throw themselves in the river, as they had threatened to do if she, their last hope, failed. According to the law, she'd have given up Michel to the authorities to follow the fate of his parents, and have denounced Mme Quertsch and Mother Veronica. According to the law, her children would have starved and frozen during the terrible Occupation winters. In short, according to the law, they would all be dead now. She was not such a fool! The first law was to take care of yourself and yours, and it didn't matter what those too-smart government hairsplitters wrote down in their books. They would change it tomorrow. But there were things beyond their Codes, things no one could change. There was no law that could keep a belly from getting hungry, a heart from longing for love, a conscience from wanting to be right with God. Mathieu could prate all he wanted, there were things you did because you were a human being and not the sheep they had in mind when they wrote their laws.

Like with Henri. Mathieu had not wanted to understand. But Mathieu did not have etched into his brain, as she did, the portraits of the two priests, different yet the same, who had existed for her a quarter of a century apart. There was the Father Périer she had known when she was a fifteen-year-old girl on the threshold of womanhood, when she still wore her hair long and men had begun to look after her on the street. This one is standing in a pulpit, speaking with the voice of inspiration to a silent congregation. He is straight and slim, with a narrow, keen face, in the prime of maturity, with only a touch of gray about the temples. He has full, vigorous lips, an incisive yet delicate jaw, flashing eyes, the kindest yet saddest she had ever seen. This was the one portrait, separated from the other by heartbreak and disgrace, years of study and solitude and work, the thousands of petty daily acts that go toward raising children, making friends, surviving war and enemy occupation. And then, suddenly, the other portrait, against the background of an eventful winter day. Unexpectedly, without warning, Father Périer is standing in the doorway. Yes, this old man, with the hangdog lined face, the thin gray hair showing the waxen skull, the tired eyes and sunken chest, the collar yellow with age, the worn cassock—this old country priest, crushed by banishment, longing, and remorse—this ruin of a man is Father Périer. She had not seen him grow old. She knew nothing of him, had not heard from him since that day her father had run shouting through the streets to the bishop's rectory. He might have been dead. He was only an image deep in the past. Now this other image is there, like an accusation. She had done this to him. And yet he had come back. In spite of himself. In spite of

God. Humbly, at her mercy. Like a stab in the heart.

Mathieu had exploded when he heard about it, told her what people were saying, spoken mockingly of "that priest of yours." She hadn't cared. Henri had needed a home and she had given it to him. It didn't matter what any of them said. She was right with God, who knew what gratitude was.

How imposing the Temple was behind its fence of heavy iron spears and its garden of clipped shrubbery! The façade of white stone, the gleaming windows, the solid oak double door, the broad entrance steps of scrubbed marble, the neat walk of pale gray gravel, gave evidence of wealth, taste, and order. Mlle Rose had always considered the Temple, seated majestically in its green park fronting the boulevard, one of the most beautiful spots in Touville. It was always with pleasure that she entered the gate, leaving behind her the noisy street, with its cars and trolleys and vulgar motor scooters, the trivial cares and preoccupations of daily existence. It was like entering another world, where everything fell into a calm, intelligible pattern, the expression of a disciplined will from above. Will and organization—all the Temple convent schools were like that. Mlle Rose had not seen them all, of course—it was a vast order, with communities throughout the French-speaking world—but she had seen those of Lyons, Marseilles, and Biarritz, and while each was different, with its own architectural style and landscaping, they all revealed the same rich geometric nicety. Aristocrats, Mlle Rose reflected, going to the gatekeeper's wicket, where a nun's face, seamed and ancient under dazzling white, peered out at her mistrustfully.

She was in luck. Sister Louise, putting down the telephone, said that the mother superior was in and would see her. Mlle Rose walked up the gravel path to the door, which opened as she approached. Sister Blanche, her round face beaming, greeted her in the doorway.

From somewhere in the depths of the building came the sound of girls' voices singing a hymn. In the hallway, beneath the painting of the Saviour blessing a child, she paused to listen to it.

Sister Blanche said proudly, "Our converts."

"How beautifully they sing!" she said, genuinely moved.

Their voices were so young, so innocent! She too had been like that, she thought, walking at the nun's side. Life took the freshness out of everything. A mild regret flowed through her, for her forty-three years, for the struggles of the world outside, which coarsened and cheapened those engaged in them, for the fact that life was not the garden of the spirit that it appeared to be within the Temple precincts. She too had had her dream of purity. As a girl she had envisioned herself walking in some tranquil cloister, arrayed in spotless black and white, the bride of Christ, oblivious to the cries of the human jungle beyond the gate; and she had prayed to God for the vocation that would let her give herself to Him. But it was not for her, she was too much of the earth, with blood too proud and rebellious. Fortunately, she reflected, there were many ways to serve. Hers was not the least.

"And Michel?" Sister Blanche inquired.

"He is well, thank you, Sister."

"Such a dear child!" The nun crossed herself, and flashed a roguish sidelong glance at her. "Ah, that day, that day!"

Mlle Rose smiled, shaking her head. Yes, things had turned out well, in spite of everything. Who would have thought so in that black time?

In the waiting room, where Sister Blanche left her, she sat down in a polished mahogany chair and stared at the gold-framed portrait of Mother Miriam on the wall. The founder of the order. Could it be true that she was a Jewess, as they said? And they said that when she went to Rome she stammered so dreadfully that the Holy Father did not understand her at first. And now she was to be canonized.

Mother Veronica's erect, stately figure came noiselessly into the room. Mlle Rose stood up with a respect bordering on awe, overcome, as always, by the aura of the nun's presence. It was not the habit, nor yet her dignity as superior of the community. All her life Mlle Rose had had dealings with nuns, and found them in general to be simple-minded creatures, lost in their otherworldliness, and at the same time as petty as children. And she had learned long ago that the pomp of ecclesiastical rank, as in all other walks of life, covered those who were like all the rest, only vainer in their consciousness of power. Bishop Rebenty, for example, who, it was known, kept a tiny mirror fastened inside his mitred cap, and peered at it every chance he got. Mother Veronica was different from other nuns, different from anybody Mlle Rose had ever known. You could not imagine her as anything but what she was, so much was her flowing black costume part of her being, so pure her flesh, so candid her eyes, so alabaster-like her slender, tapering fingers, as if Nature had designed her above the accidents of substance. And yet she might have been anything she wanted, as those who knew her story remarked. With her breeding, her fortune, and her astonishing beauty, she could have had her pick of the rich and eligible males of Paris, where her mother, the dowager baroness, still maintained a fashionable salon. She might have been the mistress of a king, or made the fortune of a diplomat, a banker, a publisher, any of those who move in powerful inner circles, where a gifted, charming wife is an incalculable asset in the making of key decisions. Or she might have conquered in her own right, for she had brains as well as looks. Before her, Mlle Rose was disconcerted by her penetration, her calm, brooding intelligence, the multiplicity and power of her thought. But Mother Veronica had turned these bounties away from the world. From earliest childhood she had been sure of her vocation. She had entered the Temple at eighteen, it was said, and at twenty-eight had become the youngest superior in the near-century-old tradition of the order. Now forty, though ageless in appearance, it was probable that she would become mother general when next that post became vacant.

When Mlle Rose tried to put into words her opinion of Mother Veronica, the best phrase she could find was that the nun was "all of one piece." By this she meant that there was never any question, as with other people, about either her acts or her motives. Mother Veronica was transparent. She was deep but transparent. She said what she meant, gently, firmly, once. Her look went through you, and you inevitably made comparisons and were aware of your imperfections. It was nothing that Mother Veronica did or implied, it was what she *was* that made you feel that way.

"I am glad you have come," Mother Veronica said. "It was time we had a talk about Michel."

Mlle Rose replied that, indeed, that was why she had come. A certain situation had arisen in which the reverend mother's opinion would be invaluable. They sat down, and at the nun's invitation, Mlle Rose told her story. She did not mention Lespinasse by name, calling him only "a friend who works in the procureur's office." Nor did she say she had already appealed to the mayor. She dwelt only on the threat to Michel. Everything had been well, she lamented, until that Communist, that foreign profiteer, had showed up. The reverend mother knew that Michel had been ill, gravely ill, in the spring. It was Konrad who had done that, with his threatening appearance at the Nursery. Since then he had been making all kinds of inquiries, even going so far as to go to Sep and worming out of the unsuspecting Father Fonsac the information that Michel was attending St. Joseph's. And now the *requête*. Something had to be done to keep Konrad from getting the boy—even kidnaping was not ruled out—because she would not give him up.

Mother Veronica listened to her with grave, thoughtful eyes. When Mlle Rose had finished, she said, "There can be no question of that. You cannot give him up."

"I have no intention of doing so," Mlle Rose said, wondering at the nun's emphasis.

She explained her plan of changing the Family Council. She had already made an engagement for that afternoon with her lawyer, to take the necessary steps. It was not that that worried her, so much as the danger for Michel. She would never rest easy while he was at St. Joseph's.

She paused, hoping that Mother Veronica would make the obvious suggestion. She wanted it to come from her. Because it was Mother Veronica who had got Michel the scholarship to St. Joseph's. If Michel were to change schools now, with the re-entry to classes only weeks away, it would have to be she to find him another place.

Since the nun said nothing, Mlle Rose, sighing, ventured, "God knows, if I had the money!"

Still Mother Veronica was silent. Glancing sideways to see the effect of her words, Mlle Rose noticed a strange expression on her face. It was almost as though the mother superior were daydreaming. Her eyes, usually so penetrating, were fixed and vague; a tiny wistful smile hovered over her pale, perfect lips. Why, she's praying! Mlle Rose realized in astonishment. Had she even heard what she had said? Mlle Rose did not dare repeat it. She sat still, waiting.

"I have listened to you with great interest," Mother Veronica said at last, turning her head. "You are quite right, the man Konrad represents a great danger, perhaps greater than you suspect. It is not so much that he is a Communist. As a matter of fact, he is no longer, he has given up his party membership. He turned in his card in 1939, at the time of the Soviet-German nonaggression pact. But he has the Communist mentality, he is violently anti-clerical, which means that he is furious over the child's baptism. He will go far to try to nullify its effects. More important, he is a Zionist. You call him a 'profiteer.'

If he were that, he would present little difficulty. Profiteers can be bought. But M. Konrad is a man with an ideal, and it is this that makes him dangerous. It would be a mistake to underestimate him, or to antagonize him unnecessarily. It was not wise of you, for example, to have lost your temper, when he came to you at the Nursery. It would have been better to listen to him, promise to think about it, put him off. That would not have made him drop the matter, but it would have gained some time."

"You know him, then, Reverend Mother?" Mlle Rose asked, taken aback.

"I know *of* him," the nun returned quietly.

There was a pause, in which Mlle Rose wondered about the sources of the information she had just been given. She had never told Mother Veronica that she had lost her temper with Konrad. She had merely said that a M. Konrad had appeared at the Nursery on behalf of the aunt, and that by a slip of the tongue she had let him know the boy had been baptized. Who could have told her otherwise? And Konrad's turning in his Communist card. She hadn't known that herself, and yet Mathieu had the police records at his disposal, and had let her have a look at them. She did not doubt the fact, however; if Mother Veronica said it, it must be so.

"At the present moment," Mother Veronica went on, "I do not believe there is much likelihood that Monsieur Konrad will employ force to get Michel. It is not only the boy he wants. He wants vindication. This must come about through a recognition of his rights, that is, through justice. As a Jew he wants society to *give* him the boy. But if your plan of changing the Family Council works and the law will not help him, there is no telling what he may do. He is a man of resolution, and a Zionist. I agree with you that Michel must be kept out of his way."

She will help, then, Mlle Rose thought in relief. Why was she taking this roundabout way? What was on her mind?

"I must enjoin upon you," the nun said almost sternly, "to follow your lawyer's advice. How you manage the Family Council does not concern me. That is a civil matter. But it must remain within the law. There must be no claim that justice has been interfered with. In other words, there must be no scandal."

"But Reverend Mother," Mlle Rose began to protest. She was hurt. As if she were contemplating anything illegal! But Mother Veronica's eyes held something significant that made her fall silent. With slow emphasis the nun said, "Monsieur Lespinasse will not be able to help you here."

Now, how could she have found out about *that?* Mlle Rose wondered in amazement. There were only two people involved. Mathieu and Lespinasse. And herself, of course. There was no one else. Not even the secretary, who had merely recorded the receipt of the aunt's letters and sent them on for processing. It was inconceivable that Lespinasse could have talked; to have done so would have been to point the finger at himself. She had torn up the letters with her own hands, in the privacy of her room, and told no one but Mathieu. As tight-mouthed, cautious, and wily as he was, could *he* have—? No, it was impossible. Then how—? As her mind raced over these possibilities, another thought struck her with force: Mother Veronica had used Lespinasse's name. She was positive she had never mentioned the name herself. Mlle Rose did not know what to say. She wisely decided to say nothing.

Apparently Mother Veronica did not expect her to reply. She had risen and moved a little to one side, where she contemplated the portrait of Mother Miriam. After a moment Mlle Rose, uneasy at being seated, stood up.

"You know the purpose of our order," Mother Veronica murmured.

"Of course, Reverend Mother."

Mother Veronica turned with decision. "Mademoiselle Rose, I am about to make you an offer. You must think about it very seriously before you say either yes or no. But before you decide, I want you to know that I myself have given it a great deal of thought. I have made certain inquiries and certain preparations. As the child's guardian, however, you must give your consent. I would have spoken to you of this before now, except for the death of Jean. I did not want to intrude upon your grief. Now time is short. If you had not come here by tomorrow, I would have taken the initiative myself."

From beneath the folds of her habit the nun took out a photograph and held it out to her. Turning it to the light, Mlle Rose saw a charming outdoor scene. In the foreground was an uneven file of boys of varying ages, taking great strides, one behind the other, their bare heads thrown back and laughing. They wore simple gray uniforms with black ties. At their head marched a priest, looking back at them over his shoulder as if barking a command. Behind the boys was a gentle green slope leading up to a cluster of white buildings, out of which rose a slender spire. And beyond them, far away against the horizon, like a crown over the whole, was a shadowy tracing of snow-capped mountains.

Mother Veronica said, "That is St. Louis Gonzaga School and Seminary. It is at Cassarate in Switzerland, not far from the Italian border. Have you ever heard of it?"

Mlle Rose shook her head. Why was the superior showing her this? Surely she did not think that Michel—

"Outside of Rome itself," Mother Veronica said, "St. Louis Gonzaga is considered to be the finest, most intensive Jesuit school and seminary in Europe. It accepts only the most promising students from all over the world, those who have already exhibited a remarkable intelligence, and given evidence of a vocation for the priesthood. It accepts students of all ages, over the canonical age of seven. Instruction is in Italian. The life is monastic and severe, but not harsh. You can see for yourself that the boys are not unhappy. But the scholastic demands are extremely high and exacting. Only a few complete the training and are ordained. Those who fall by the wayside may go elsewhere and may eventually attain holy orders, of course, but it is not the same thing. For those who graduate from St. Louis Gonzaga have the world before them. You would be surprised, I think, to learn how many in the College of Cardinals are products of that seminary. Come," she added more softly, "let us sit down."

As they took their former places, Mother Veronica said, "You have already guessed why I am telling you this. It is up to you to decide and you must decide freely, without coercion. Michel is a remarkable child. I have observed him more closely than you might think. His teachers at St. Joseph's are unanimous in praising his abilities and his piety. I have the conviction that he will go far. No, that is not strong enough. I *know* he will go far."

As she uttered these words, a glow came into the nun's eyes, and a touch of color into her pale cheeks.

Impossible, Mlle Rose said to herself. She felt a keen sense of disappointment. The nun had completely mistaken her intention. It was only because a day school was too dangerous, involving as it did a daily exposure on the streets, that she had been reluctantly forced to settle for a boarding school. But it had to be in Touville, or nearby; Michel had to come home weekends and holidays, and be near enough for her to visit whenever she could get away for a couple of hours. What good was it to keep him from Konrad if it meant that she had lost him as well? Yet such was the nun's authority that Mlle Rose did not want to oppose her on personal grounds. She protested that Michel was only a child. How could he be sent out of the country, to find himself alone among a crowd of strange boys speaking another language? Michel didn't understand Italian. Besides, a seminary! She didn't want to force Michel to become a priest. If he wanted to, well and good, nobody would be happier than she—but suppose he wanted to be a doctor, like his father? And anyway, if St. Louis Gonzaga was so terribly exclusive, how could it be hoped that they would accept Michel? And on such short notice?

"They have already accepted him," Mother Veronica said calmly.

It was rare that the mother superior's face showed amusement. But Mlle Rose, glancing up sharply, her mouth open, saw something of the sort pass over those fine features. And then it was gone, and the nun said gravely, "I have taken that liberty. Not to present you with a *fait accompli,* but because there would have been no point in suggesting it if I did not know he would be accepted. But perhaps I was not clear. There are *two* institutions at Cassarate, on the same grounds, both called St. Louis Gonzaga. One is a school, the other a seminary. Michel will go to the school. Upon graduation, he will be eligible for the seminary, if he wishes. If he has a vocation. The Church forces no one to become a priest. If Michel has no vocation, he will realize it himself. In the meanwhile, he will be receiving the finest education in the world. But I have no intention of persuading you. You are free to choose. Say no, and some other boy will take Michel's place. There are hundreds waiting. Incidentally, it was not easy to win this opportunity for him. It will not be offered again."

As the nun spoke, Mlle Rose, recovering from her surprise, was considering a question that had been shaping itself in her mind ever since the beginning of the interview, and that now urged itself upon her with redoubled force. Mother Veronica had so much interest in Michel, then? Enough to have made her own secret inquiries about Konrad? To have had recourse to mysterious sources of information to find out things about her, Odette Rose? To have gone to a great deal of trouble, by her own admission, to get Michel into St. Louis Gonzaga? What a busy summer she must have had, and for Michel! True, the superior of the Touville Temple had always been kind about her boy; she had insisted that he be brought to her for visits, sent him gifts at Christmas and Easter, arranged for a scholarship to

St. Joseph's, bought him the communion suit, helped with cash at certain moments—but Mlle Rose had attributed it all to the natural desire of the nun to make a convert. Weren't the Temple Dames rich, and wasn't it their mission to bring the true faith to the Jews? Yes, but that was exactly it, they had made their convert! The boy was baptized, their purpose achieved. Why so much concern now? How much trouble the mother superior had gone to, and all without a word to her! Mlle Rose had the uncomfortable feeling that she had been an unsuspecting pawn in some deep game. She was filled with curiosity. Before she could stop herself, she had stammered out, "But *why*, Reverend Mother?"

Mother Veronica did not seem to think the question strange. "A moment ago I said to you, 'You cannot give the boy up.' You wondered why I said 'cannot' instead of 'must not.' I did not use the world lightly. You *cannot* give him up. Canon law forbids it. Michel is baptized. There can be no question of his not receiving a Christian upbringing."

Of course! Mlle Rose said to herself. There was the mystery explained. Canon law. Henri had mentioned it to her once, she should have remembered. The danger of apostasy, he had called it. Mother Veronica's thought had followed the same course as her own, but for a different reason. And, she admitted to herself, with far more foresight. From the very first it had been Mother Veronica who had urged her to have the boy baptized; she would take good care now to see that it was not spoiled by the family. Mlle Rose congratulated herself; she had got herself an ally, at the moment of need. But not Switzerland—that was out of the question.

She had scarcely begun to formulate her objection when Mother Veronica shook her head. Astonished, Mlle Rose insisted. She appreciated all that the reverend mother had done, more profoundly than she could say; but Michel was still a baby! She didn't rule out the possibility of Cassarate—but later, when Michel was a bit more grown up, and when the danger was more clearly defined. She wouldn't say anything about what such a separation would mean to *her,* although the reverend mother knew how she felt about the boy; but what about Michel himself? He needed her, he was insecure, he would be terribly homesick, and might even . . .

In reply Mother Veronica gently let her understand that it was Cassarate or nothing. If she had thought a nearer school would do, she would not have looked so far afield. Yes, she understood Mlle

Rose's anguish at the thought of separation. And Michel's as well. But there were three things to be said about this. Once Konrad got started, nowhere in France would be safe; Switzerland was the closest Michel could be and still be out of the country. Then, the parting was by no means final; at every long vacation—Christmas, Easter, the summer, even long weekends—Michel could come to the Mother House of the order in Paris, where Mlle Rose could meet him. Mother Veronica herself would take care of the travel costs. Finally, was this not a cause for which personal feelings ought to be sacrificed? Mlle Rose could find no better way of showing her devotion to Michel than by letting him go, for his own good.

Mlle Rose battled in vain against this reasoning. Mother Veronica was sympathetic but adamant. She would not insist, she said. Michel was well off at St. Joseph's, he could continue there. But she would not lift a finger to have him accepted anywhere else but St. Louis Gonzaga.

"But so far, Reverend Mother!" she implored.

"The choice is yours," the nun replied.

In the end, resentful and bewildered, she gave in. Mother Veronica's opinion that Michel would not be safe anywhere in France had frightened her. She herself thought the statement exaggerated; but she had never known the superior to be wrong about anything. For *his* sake, she thought. With tears starting to her eyes, she said, "So be it, I won't stand in his way."

"In God's name!" Mother Veronica exclaimed, with a gesture of satisfaction.

There were some details to be settled. In about two weeks—Mlle Rose would be notified later of the exact day and hour—Michel was to be brought to the Temple. From there two nuns would accompany him by train to Paris. An emissary from St. Louis Gonzaga would come for him and several other boys, for the trip to Cassarate. Mlle Rose was to prepare a valise with only what was necessary for the trip. The institution would provide for all his later needs. She was not to be concerned about the cost, the Temple would handle that part of it. As for St. Joseph's, there was no need to give them any more information than that Michel was being withdrawn for reasons of health. They did not have to know where he was.

"Let me impress this on you," Mother Veronica said. "You are to tell nobody. Nobody at all. Not Michel himself, we shall tell him at the right time. Only two persons in Touville will know where he is.

You and I. Nobody else. Michel is at a private boarding school. That is sufficient answer for any friend who is curious. It will be the truth, moveover."

Disconsolate, Mlle Rose promised.

The superior's face was expressionless at their leave-taking. Yet, escorted through the building by Sister Blanche, who had appeared at the right moment in response to some mysterious summons, Mlle Rose had the impression that she had left Mother Veronica in the grip of a radiant inner happiness. The more she thought about it, the surer she was that there was some strange emotional involvement there, that it meant a great deal more to the nun than one might have imagined. What could it be? It intrigued and baffled her. But one thing was certain, and that was that Mother Veronica was by no means as "transparent" as she had supposed.

Her appointment with Maître Cauchet was at three. Mlle Rose consulted her watch, and decided she had time enough to take the trolley. There was no need to be extravagant with taxis.

The trolley stop was opposite the Temple. She boarded one marked "University"; she would have to transfer at Place Chapelle.

Thinking over her conversation with the nun, and realizing with renewed force that she had actually agreed to send Michel away—in two weeks!—she almost broke into tears again. Nothing of the sort had been in her mind when she set out that morning to look for help. If only Mathieu had been willing to cooperate! she thought in anger. She was sure that a little spadework into that Konrad's past would send the fellow scurrying off. To think that a parasite like that could pry Michel loose from her when everything had been going so well! But not for long, she promised herself grimly. Oh no, she would take good care not to let that happen. She would finish that Konrad off in record time and bring Michel home again. Perhaps even at mid-term, she thought.

The trolley entered Place Chapelle. Mlle Rose stood up. As she did so, she saw through the window a tall ungainly figure striding among the noontime strollers on the sidewalk. They made way for him; several looked after him resentfully.

The devil's own, she thought with a little shock of recognition. A rush of anger blinded her. She hurried to the door and stepped into the street. If he should say one word to her! Just one word! But M. Konrad had already passed. Breathing hard, she followed him with her eyes. On his way to his lawyer, she supposed. Maître Paul. Mathieu thought the world of him, she knew. How did he dare take a case like this one? She watched Konrad until he had disappeared into one of the streets entering the square. What she could not understand was how the man had escaped being picked up during the Occupation. As noticeable as he was, with that skinny height of his, and that Jew face. They had missed him, and yet had got Michel's father. You could never tell how Providence would work out. Now *that* would have been a solution to all her problems. God knew she meant them no harm. But why did they make things so difficult for her?

Her trolley came along. She entered and sat down, fanning herself with her handbag. Troubles, she thought. She had her work cut out for her. Not only Michel. Renée. She would have to take some action there too. Because the girl had gone crazy, that was the only explanation. Moping in her room day after day, with that lovesick look in her eyes! What did the girl expect her to do, welcome the boy to her arms, give them a wedding, send them off on a honeymoon to Venice? And then what, if you please? What would they live on? Such romantic notions the girl had! At that age girls didn't know anything, love was what they saw in the movies and read about in those trashy magazines, moonlight and kisses and charming *tête-à-tête* that would last forever. And the boys with only one thing on their minds. Oh, he must have paraded himself in front of her, and rolled sheep's eyes, and made himself out to be a devil of an interesting fellow. Trust them to know instinctively how to get around a girl who had been sheltered all her life. You couldn't know until you had lived through it yourself. But you couldn't tell them, they didn't listen, girls were born these days thinking they knew everything. She could just see Renée living in a little garret in Paris, with that—that student! cooking, cleaning, washing diapers, haggling in the markets, without a penny to her name. Then she would learn what life was and would holler for her Maman Rose. And Renée thought she was being selfish about it! For not wanting her to ruin herself. Well, thank goodness it was only a few weeks longer, then that Mégret boy would be returning to Paris for the university year. And she would have time to talk to Renée, reason with her, take her in hand.

It wasn't as though she had forced the girl into anything. Renée had promised of her own volition. "Never!" she had cried. "I'll never leave you!" On the head of her dead brother. Even in the midst of her grief the words had sounded sweetly in her ears. And now, only a few months later . . .

Alighting at Place St. Lazare, she hurried past the church, crossing herself; she could not see it without thinking of Jean. As she approached the Nursery, she saw Michel sitting on the front steps. At least, she thought, he had given up that standing by the gate. How often, peeking out her office window, had she seen him there, gazing toward the square! It had broken her heart. She knew, of course, what he was waiting for; everybody knew, even the mothers, who couldn't help but notice him as they came and went. But what could you do? You couldn't tell him his father was dead, that would have been too cruel. Besides, strange things happened, sometimes they came back, after all hope had been given up. She had forbidden all at the Nursery to say anything about it to the boy, hoping that in time the realization would be borne in on him, gradually, so that the shock would be dispersed and absorbed. That Quertsch woman! What an idiotic thing she had done, to tell Michel that his father was at the Nursery! She had done it with the best of intentions, to keep him from crying and attracting attention on the way from the Temple, but she might have thought of something else. Because no sooner had they entered than he wriggled loose from her arms and ran about looking, his little face pinched and desperate, screaming "Vati!" And the only thing that would quiet him was to tell him that his Vati was coming. Tomorrow. And then the next day. And the next.

Michel stood up as she approached. She had never had to teach him that. He had natural good manners. Such a little man! Her heart smote her for what she was about to do to him. Overcome by emotion, she swept him into her arms, murmuring, "My boy, my little boy!" Then, sitting down with him on the steps, her arms about him, she told him the news. Strange, how his face lit up to hear he would not be returning to St. Joseph's!

"Where is it?" he asked.

"That's a secret. But it's a long way off. Imagine, you'll be making a trip on a train!"

"What kind of school is it?"

"A *good* school. Private, one of the best."

"But what *kind?*" he persisted, looking at her intently.

"Oh," she said, realizing what he meant. "Like St. Joseph's. Jesuits. But this is special, all the boys will be very intelligent. They want to be priests. Like you. It's a school and a seminary."

"Oh," Michel said. That was all. He gave her a brief sidelong glance and looked away. Seeing how sad and wistful his face had become, she was filled with remorse. What had she done? Not even the Nazis had been able to take him away from her, and now, for an imagined danger, in a France to which law and order had returned, she was sending him off herself. For the first time she felt a touch of resentment against Mother Veronica and her absolute ways. She had the impulse to march into the Nursery, to telephone the nun and tell her it was all off, and that Michel would return to St. Joseph's. But the image of Konrad came to her, sniffing about Sep like a bloodhound, lying in wait for a seven-year-old child and an idiotic servant woman on their way to school. She did not want to frighten him, but he *had* to know. She explained it to him gently, caressing his hair; it would not be for long, she said. She would fix that M. Konrad so that he would leave them in peace, and in the meantime Michel would be safe. Several times he seemed at the point of saying something; but though she encouraged him, asking him what was it, and to tell her what he was thinking, he did not open up but said in a small voice that if that was what she wanted he would go.

"Not what *I* want, Michel," she said. "I *had* to do it. You understand that, don't you?" When he didn't answer, she insisted, "You do, don't you?" and he nodded and said, "Yes, Maman Rose."

That Konrad! she thought grimly as she entered the hallway. What a mess he had made of things!

That night, at bedtime, Mlle Rose sat before her mirror, brushing her hair and mentally reviewing her day. She was tired, but with the sense of achievement that comes from purposeful activity. After her initial setback with Mathieu, and the persuasive *fait accompli* Mother Veronica had met her with, everything had gone as smoothly as she could have wished. Michel had his hideaway; that was the main thing, although the thought of his departure, still two weeks away, was already a thorn in her heart. And she had the answer to Konrad, which had shaped itself with astonishing ease. Maître Cauchet had readily fallen in with her scheme to change the Family Council. He had thought the grounds sufficient; in fact, had telephoned Judge Cerval and received the unofficial assurance that they would be so considered, if substantiated and presented in due form. She even had the members of the new Council; including herself, six of them, as the law required. Upon her return from the lawyer's office, she had spent the rest of the afternoon and evening telephoning, jotting down notes for her affidavit, conferring with Lespinasse, who had dropped in to see how the matter was going and had complimented her on the celerity of her action. She had also spent hours at what she herself, in mockery, called "daydreaming," by which she meant that process of undirected meditation that presented her with her best ideas. She simply let her mind wander. With unerring instinct, perhaps prompted by unconscious concern aroused by things too subtle or unsubstantial for thought—an intonation of voice, an expression, a gesture—her mind projected images of the possible, like a chess player mentally playing his opponent's game, in order to anticipate and thwart it. She might sit thus for a half-hour at a time, to all outward appearance merely looking out the window, searching for a phrase for a letter, brushing her hair; but she was plotting, weighing, selecting out of the contingencies of the future those sequences most likely to happen. Konrad's *requête,* for instance, had not surprised her; its possibility was contained in the word "justice" he had faced her with that Easter Sunday, and she had sensed the determination and drive that would make the man follow through. And so she was ready for it when it came, her course of action set in advance. If not for the death of Jean, she thought sadly, staring at her image in the mirror, she might even have prevented him altogether. But she had been prostrate for weeks, her timing had been bad, and Mathieu recalcitrant.

She was still disturbed about Renée. The girl was more upset than she had realized. She had not come down for dinner; and when, having thought the moment propitious to have it out, to speak sensibly and tenderly to her as a mother to her daughter, she went to Renée's room, the girl refused to confide in her. She was well, she had said. She had nothing to complain about, she just wasn't hungry. Yet there had been something in Renée's eyes, a hardness of decision, a sullenness, that called for decisions of her own. She might send Renée away for a few weeks, she reflected. Or descend like a storm on the boy's house, confront him and his parents, put the fear of God in them. Something had to be done to protect the girl against herself.

She sighed. It was late. Tomorrow would be time enough to find a solution. She would consult with Alain Béjart, whom she had to see anyway about the Council. Her image stared back at her in the mirror: the full, serious face, soft and unlined, except for the double vertical marks between the eyebrows, where life had bitten into her with its heartaches; the green eyes, still fine, still clear; the copper hair touched with a spidery tracing of gray. Odette Rose, she said to herself. God knew she had never wanted anything but what was hers by right. But how hard the world made you fight for what was yours! It was well, she thought, that she was a fighter. If not, she'd have gone under long ago.

Good night, she said to all her living and dead. Good night, Henri. Forgive me, I did the best I could. Good night, Jean, child of my youth. Renée, you bad, ungrateful girl, whom I still love. Pé. Léah. Manon, my little lieutenant. And Michel, child of my age, my last chance, my sweet, angelic boy, good night, good night.

What had awakened her? She had been sound asleep, when suddenly she found herself sitting up in bed, listening. She heard nothing, all was dark and still. Yet there was something. In some imperceptible way the peaceful rhythm of the night had been broken. She looked at her watch on the night table; it was four-thirty. She arose, put on a dressing gown, and went noiselessly into the corridor. Michel and Pé were asleep; through the half-open door she heard their breathing. She moved to the head of the stairs and peered down by the dim gleam of the night light, then continued down the hall, listening at each door.

In front of Renée's room she heard a faint noise, which she was at a loss to define. She put her ear to the panel. Had the girl turned over in bed? Or rather, wasn't the sound like the scrape of a shutter being closed? Suddenly, a monstrous suspicion struck her, and she darted to the window at the end of the corridor, which looked out into the playground. Pulling aside the curtain, she was just in time to see, against the darkness of the alley, something big and indefinable drop off the fence. At the same time she recognized the muffled slap of feet striking the pavement.

For a moment Mlle Rose stood staring out into the night. Then she swung around and faced Renée's door. Renée, the fairy child, standing in the corner of that room of death so many years ago, her doll's eyes shocked and bewildered at her first loss. Renée as she first said, "Maman Rose." Renée at school, in her white blouse and blue pinafore. Renée, grave and pale, at the first sign of womanhood. Renée the young lady, dreaming of the wide world. Renée, who took and took, and gave nothing in return.

Like another death. Henri. Jean. And now—

Oh, my little daughter, she groaned inwardly, as she advanced and rapped on Renée's door.

When Manon entered with the breakfast tray, Mlle Rose was sitting in the chair beside her bed. She had not slept since the scene with Renée; she felt that her face was drawn and haggard. Manon said something; she shook her head wearily, hardly listening. Suddenly she stiffened. "Door?" she demanded. "What door?"

Manon repeated patiently that Mlle Pasquier had found the front door unbolted this morning, and had accused her, Manon, of having forgotten to put the chain in place the night before. But that was not so, she went on, she had locked up as she did every night, she remembered distinctly having done so. Had Mlle Rose later opened the door for any reason?

Mlle Rose did not answer. She had seized her dressing gown and was hurrying into the hall, putting on the gown as she went. She flung open Renée's door and stepped inside. The room was empty, in the same state of disarray that she had seen a few hours before. No, not quite—the bed had been hastily made, and the photograph of herself that had stood on the top of the bureau lay on the floor, its glass panel shattered. And when she opened the closet door, she saw that Renée's suitcase and most of her clothing were missing.

Manon had followed her and now stood in the doorway, staring.

She had gone, then! After their quarrel Renée had packed her bag and crept down the stairs and out the front door into the night. Like a frightened animal. To get away from her hated mother, whose crime was that she wanted to save the girl from her own stupidity. What a hurry she must have been in! Yes, but not so much of a hurry but that she had taken the time for that last senseless bit of defiance, that hurling of the photograph to the floor.

Manon gasped and put her hand to her mouth. She had seen the photograph; she darted forward to pick it up.

Mlle Rose stopped her with a gesture. Gazing at her own likeness in its bent frame, she felt physically sick from the rage and shame that swelled in her heart. Eighteen years of her life lay on the floor. It was the sheer wantonness of the act, its unfeelingness, its gratuitous cruelty, that hurt the most. She could stand willfulness, impertinence, selfishness—but not ingratitude.

"Ah, no!" she cried out. She was not to be trampled on like this. Renée would come back—yes, and pay dearly before she was forgiven. She would go and get her herself, by force if necessary. She knew where the girl was. Pushing Manon through the door, she locked it behind her. It would stay locked until Renée came to open it. The photograph would remain on the floor until Renée picked it up. In her room she dressed quickly and went down the stairs and into the street, past two mothers who were entering with their children, and who stopped to gaze after her in surprise.

10

ᨀ

Louis!" Rina said. "Look at this!"

Konrad had just let himself into his home and was hanging his hat on the rack. He turned inquiringly to his wife, who came from the kitchen to meet him, with the newspaper in her hand. Judas was sitting in the middle of the living room, his face set in concentration as he added another piece of pasteboard to the card castle he was building. In the moment it took Rina to approach, he watched his son, admiring the steadiness of his hand.

"Where?" he said, giving her a kiss on the cheek.

The article she pointed to bore the caption ROMANCE IS NOT DEAD and the dateline "Touville, Sept. 5."

He sank into an armchair and, frowning, began to read.

> At an early hour this morning [the article said], the inhabitants of Rue Chauffours, a quiet residential street in the Pontchartrain section of our city, were treated to a painful spectacle: a woman of a certain age pounding on a locked door and crying out, "Give me back my daughter!"
>
> Before so unusual a scene a crowd quickly gathered, and there appeared a police agent, who, making his way to the now hysterical woman, invited her to calm herself and explain her strange behavior. After clutching his arm and screaming, "Arrest them! Break down the door!" the lady regained a certain measure of coherence, although still in an excited condition, and stated that she was Mlle Odette Rose, directress of a Crèche Municipale in Place St. Lazare, and that the young man, one Jules Mégret,

who lived at this address, No. 12, had first seduced and then kidnaped her daughter Renée, aided and abetted by the youth's parents. The crowd, which by now had grown quite large, sympathized with the distressed mother and urged the agent, Romain Ivert, to force an entry.

Agent Ivert rapped at the door and demanded that it be opened in the name of the law. At this the door was unlocked, and there appeared a man wearing a bathrobe, with the vestiges of lather on his face, who identified himself as Jules Mégret, Sr., the father of the young man in question, and stated that a few minutes ago he had forcibly ejected Mlle Rose from his house, out of a concern for the safety of his family, and that of Mlle Rose herself.

Questioned further, M. Mégret said that he had been shaving when he was startled by a loud rap at his door. He had hurried downstairs to open it, whereupon a woman unknown to him had burst in and in a loud voice had cried that she had come for her daughter, and would have them all arrested. He had assumed that the woman was Mlle Rose, foster mother of his son's fiancée, and had endeavored to calm her; but at that moment his son, attracted by the lady's cries, had appeared, and Mlle Rose had hurled herself upon him with evident intent to do him physical harm. Before so unreasoning an attitude he had had no recourse but to put the lady out, until she was in a condition to discuss their differences in a more civilized way.

At this juncture Mlle Rose, who had been restrained by those witnessing the scene, cried out "Kidnaper!" and had to be prevented from entering the house.

To Agent Ivert's demand whether Mlle Rose's daughter was in his home, M. Mégret admitted that she was, but added that she had come of her own accord. She had appeared in the dark hours of that same morning, carrying a suitcase, and in a pitiable state, asking for shelter. Her foster mother had struck her, she said, and threatened to have her shut up in a mental institution.

Agent Ivert now required that the young lady be brought forward, and pretty Mlle Renée Rose, her blond hair disheveled, her blue eyes brimming with tears, came to the door. She sobbed that Mlle Odette Rose was not her mother, but her foster mother, that she did not want to live with her any more, that she was twenty-one and free to do as she wished, and that of her own free will she had entered her fiancé's home for her protection.

Mlle Rose, beside herself with anger, cried out a name that modesty will not let us repeat, and stated that only last night this so-called protector had made his way to the girl's second-story room by means of a ladder, and had seduced her without a qualm. The daughter cried, "No, no," and the young Mégret now appeared at the door, exclaiming that he had not entered the room, but had only talked at the window. He had taken this drastic means of communication, he said, because Renée's foster mother had forbidden her to see him, and kept her shut up at home.

Before the distress of this remarkably handsome couple, and realizing that it was not a question of an abduction but of an *affaire de coeur,* the onlookers began to waver in their sympathy. An unidentified person called out, "Let them marry, and there's an end to it."

Agent Ivert then inquired whether the young Mlle Rose would go home with her mother, to which he received the firm reply, "Never!" Mlle Odette Rose, however, insisted, claiming that the girl had lied, that she was under age, and demanding that she be removed from the premises by force. This the police officer refused to do, saying that he had no warrant to enter the house, that so far as he could see no crime had been committed; and that while he could well understand her grief, he could not help her other than by advising her to swear out a complaint to the authorities.

The disappointed mother then withdrew, shouting that the girl was no longer her daughter, that she would disinherit her and let her go to the dogs where she belonged. The crowd, urged by Agent Ivert, dispersed, divided in its opinions; some supported the cause of the foster mother, who had been shamefully treated, they felt, by one who owed her all, and the others upheld the imperious claims of young love.

When peace had been restored, our reporter was able

to interview M. Jules Mégret, Sr., who expressed his regret for what had occurred. He had never met his son's fiancée before that morning, he said, but he of course could not turn her from his door when she appeared. He was convinced that Renée was a fine girl. Would the two marry? our reporter asked. The father replied that he supposed so, but that Renée could not marry without her foster mother's consent until December, when she would attain her twenty-first birthday. In the meanwhile she would stay with them, or with his sister in Paris, where young Mégret would soon return to pursue his studies at the university.

Our reporter begged M. Mégret to convey to the young couple his best wishes for their future happiness, and went about his business, musing upon the heroic measures young Mégret had taken to converse with his beloved. Shades of Abelard, Leander, Romeo! Romance, even in this prosaic age, is not dead!

Konrad put down the paper and reflected a moment. "When I went to the Nursery that time," he said, "there was a pretty girl at the table, with blond hair. She must be the one."

"Oh, the poor woman!" Rina said. "Imagine, so soon after the other one died, what was his name?"

"Jean," Konrad said. "But why do you call her a poor woman? She brings these things on herself. Oh," he went on, seeing Rina's expression, "I don't mean the death of the boy, although I've always thought there was something strange about that. But the girl that she kept locked up in her room. No wonder she ran away. And the other three brothers—there were five altogether—they've gone too. If she treated them the way she treated this one—"

"Well," Rina said indignantly, "if she was carrying on as Mlle Rose says. Coming like a thief in the night, with ladders!"

"Like mother, like daughter."

"Now Louis, that's not fair. How do *we* know—?"

"No," Konrad admitted, "it's not fair. The truth is, I don't like the woman, and the more I learn of her the less I like her. For instance, look how she carried on about the girl. The scandal, the shouting in the street, trying to hit the boy, and so on. It seems she can't control herself and goes berserk. Like with me. I wish you could have seen her then, you wouldn't feel so sorry for her now."

"What is it?" Rina asked, seeing the sudden frown that had come to her husband's face.

"Hm!" Konrad said ruefully, "she doesn't let go easily, does she?"

It was two minutes to ten. He was on time, the summons was for ten o'clock. Louis Konrad went up the worn stone steps, thinking of the countless human feet that had pressed them before him, to have scooped out those hollows in their surface. And how much human misery. For this building had once been the headquarters of the Vichy *milice,* through whose doors had passed so many unfortunates, never to return. Karl Benedek, for one. It must have been here, Place Chapelle was just around the corner. Since then the squat building in gray stone had been scraped and furbished and sandblasted from roof to sidewalk; a bronze plaque had been encrusted into the wall, bearing a bas-relief head of a young woman crowned with olive leaves and the legend "Liberté, Egalité, Fraternité"; and a sign had been put up over the door, reading "Commissariat de Police, 3e Arrondissement"; but there still clung to the premises an indefinable unpleasant air, an evil odor, as if part of the stone itself.

Five years ago his appearance here would have been the prelude to unimaginable horrors. Since then the world had changed. Freedom and justice had returned, and this very building was their symbol. Yet he felt a certain lack of ease. Unconsciously he squared his shoulders as he entered and addressed himself to the man in uniform at the desk beyond the railing. His name was Louis Konrad, he said; the commissioner was expecting him at ten o'clock.

The police officer spoke into the intercom in a bored tone. A metallic voice answered him, distorted beyond recognition. Konrad understood that he was to go in at once.

"Thank you," he said politely to the police officer, who had risen to point down the hallway, "I know where it is."

He walked toward the office, wondering with a vague disquietude what was coming now. It was his second visit. The first had been two weeks before, when in answer to a similar summons he had entered this same grim edifice, full of hope, already savoring the good news in his imagination, only to be left annoyed and baffled as to why they had called him at all. In the first place, in opening the door he had almost bumped into the Rose woman, who was coming out, and who shot him a vindictive look, tinged with smug satisfaction. And then the commissioner, a weather-beaten bulldog of a man with thick tufted eyebrows and the look of a retired top sergeant, had been unnecessarily dry, even curt, in his interrogation. He wanted to see the power of attorney, he said. Fortunately, Konrad had brought a copy with him, although he had included one in his *requête*. He remarked as much to the commissioner, who stared up at him as if to say, Who the devil asked *your* opinion? After that Konrad had confined himself to answering questions, in a tone as dry as that of his interrogator. He gave his name, address, profession, produced proof of identity. It was he who had drawn up the complaint to the Parquet in regard to the orphan Benedek boy? He was aware that the other side of the matter had to be heard as well? Very well, had he anything to add? Did he claim, for example, that the boy was being mistreated in his present domicile? To this he answered that he had no way of knowing, since he had not been allowed to see the boy; but that even if there was no mistreatment, the family— He had not been allowed to finish, the commissioner—by now Konrad had decided that he was an anti-Semite—pushed a sheet of paper toward him with one blunt, hairy finger, and pointed out where he was to sign. Konrad took his time about it, deliberately ignoring the pen the man held out to him, glancing over the paper as he slowly unscrewed the top of his own pen. It was merely a statement that he had appeared at the commissariat at the hour indicated, and been heard. He signed and pushed it back with one finger in the way it had been put before him. The commissioner's jaw had tightened with repressed fury, and Konrad was no less angry. An exchange of frosty good mornings had terminated the interview.

Now he had been summoned again. He did not know what to expect, nor did Maître Paul, whom he had telephoned upon receipt of the second summons. "It's too quick," the lawyer had said reflectively. "I suppose the only thing to do is to go there and find out. At least we're getting some action."

The door was ajar. Konrad rapped, and pushed it open. The commissioner was standing by his desk. Without preliminaries he said in a brisk but polite tone that he was authorized to read to him a communication from the Parquet. If monsieur would sit down? They both did so, and the commissioner, picking up a sheet of paper, began to read.

The message was brief, so brief that Konrad had hardly taken in its import before it was over. He sat still a moment, incredulous, his eye fixed on the patchwork of tiny red veins on the commissioner's right cheek. Then, scarcely realizing what he was doing, he reached forward and took the paper from the man's hand. He simply did not believe what he had just heard. But the words were there, just as they had reached his ears.

Concerning the *requête* of the Sieur Louis Konrad, engineer, domiciled at No. 137, Cours Berthet, Touville l'Abbaye, dated August 12, 1948, and asking change of guardianship of the orphan Michel Benedek, now residing at No. 8, Place St. Lazare, of this city, complainant is advised that no intervention in this matter can be contemplated by the undersigned, since for the tutelage of said minor there exists a Family Council, duly constituted in accordance with Article 142 of the Civil Code, which is alone empowered to make decisions of guardianship. Complainant is invited, if he so desires, to address himself to said Family Council, to facilitate which the accompanying dossier is to be made available to his inspection.

The document was signed in an illegible scrawl over the typewritten words "Procureur de la République."

The commissioner's mouth had tightened into an unpleasant grimace. He had been too abrupt, Konrad realized. But he was too taken aback to care. He asked what was the Family Council referred to. The commissioner muttered that it was clear enough. He began to read, ". . . there exists a Family Council, duly constituted in accordance with Article 142 of the—"

"I meant," Konrad interrupted, "very simply, what is a Family Council?"

He should have waited to ask Maître Paul. The commissioner allowed a look of outraged dignity to come to his face. He would have thought that every citizen had at least that much familiarity with the Codes, which were the glory of France. The Codes were Napoleon's great work, which still endured, long after his conquests had been forgotten. A Family Council was when a child had no parents, and the nearest of kin formed a group, a *Council* in other words, to select a guardian for him, and to advise the guardian about the care of the child. In the case of the Benedek boy, it would seem that there was such a Council, as the procureur said in his communication.

This Council had absolute authority over the choice of guardian for the boy. It had chosen Mlle Rose. If monsieur had any complaint to make about that choice, he could do as the procureur suggested: he could address himself to the Council. As for him, it was his duty only to make known the decision of the Parquet, and not to advise.

Konrad had not missed the slight emphasis on the word "citizen," nor the look of malevolent enjoyment in mentioning Mlle Rose. It was clear enough where the man's sympathies lay. Why? Was he a friend of the Rose woman? Had she convinced him, two weeks ago, with the same tissue of half-truths and display of wounded motherhood that had taken in Rabbi Notarius? Or was it simply the external aspects of the case, the outsider against the French woman, the Jew against the Catholic, his, Konrad's, unmistakable appearance, his accent? It made no difference, of course. The commissioner had nothing to do with his case; he made no decisions, he merely transmitted them. But staring at him, Konrad suddenly understood that what he had assumed was simple was much more complicated than he had imagined; and that in the procedural formalities that undoubtedly lay ahead of him, entrenched petty functionaries of this same stripe, too stupid, too impatient to understand the issues involved, would presume to judge, and to address him with this same insolence of official power.

He was full of questions. *What* next of kin, if the aunt was not a member? Where *was* this Family Council? When had it been constituted? By whose authority? He did not ask them; presumably the answers were in the dossier. At his request, the commissioner handed the folder over and busied himself with his papers while Konrad examined it.

There were three documents in the folder. The one on top bore this title: "Extract of the Minutes of the Recording Office of the Justice of the Peace, South Canton, Touville l'Abbaye, Judicial District of the Court of Appeals of that City, Côte-des-Alpes—Benedek Family Council." Konrad glanced through it rapidly. He learned that one Demoiselle Odette Rose, forty, spinster, etc., etc., having given shelter to an orphan child, one Michel Benedek, etc., and concerned for the well-being of said child, had appeared before Judge Jean-Jacques Cerval, etc., for the purpose of establishing a Family Council, in accordance with Article 142 of the Civil Code. There had also appeared the following persons: Maximilien Colbert, entrepreneur; Elémir Manfrédi, doctor of medicine; Wolfgang Manfrédi, doctor of law; Adolphus Instettin, baker; Jules Immermann, shopkeeper. After examining the credentials of said persons, etc., Judge Cerval had accepted them as members of the Family Council, which, upon due deliberation, had named the Demoiselle Rose as Provisional Guardian and the Sieur Wolfgang Manfrédi as Surrogate Provisional Guardian of the orphan Michel Benedek. Below the court seal was the date: November 12, 1945.

The second document bore exactly the same heading as the first, so that Konrad took it for a copy. But the spacing of the typescript was different, and so was the opening sentence. With growing astonishment Konrad read that the Demoiselle Odette Rose had appeared once more before Judge Cerval, this time to complain that the members of the Family Council created on November 12, 1945, had disappeared, been lost sight of, were nowhere to be found. She had need of advice in regard to the orphan entrusted to her care. She was therefore requesting the destitution of that Council, and the formation of a new one, with the following members: Alain Béjart, jeweler; Martin Mirebel, businessman; Mlle Camélia Deharme, nurse; Mlle Odette Rose, present Provisional Guardian; Mme Elsa Bordat, nurse; Antoine de Guèze, lawyer's clerk; all of whom were present and ready to offer their credentials. After some scathing comments on the lightness with which certain persons took their sacred duties, Judge Cerval had accepted those present as members of the new Family Council, which reconfirmed the Demoiselle Rose as Provisional Guardian, appointed the Sieur Alain Béjart as new Surrogate Provisional Guardian, and recommended that steps be taken to assure the French citizenship of the orphan in their care. The date beneath the seal was September 7, 1948.

Laying the two extracts side by side on his knees, Konrad studied them with more care. When he had finished he kept his head bowed for a long time. Then he looked at the last document. It bore the date September 14, 1948, and was a set of arguments addressed to the procureur by Mlle Rose, explaining why the orphan Michel Benedek should be left in her care.

Konrad's hand trembled slightly as he put the dossier on the desk. He wanted to borrow the dossier for a day or two, he said; it contained highly important information that he needed to discuss with his lawyer, since of course he intended to carry the matter further. He would return it intact. Frowning, the commissioner replied that it was impossible. These were official documents, part of the permanent record of the Parquet. Chaos would result if in every case . . . Konrad pointed out that the instructions of the procureur were that the dossier was to be made available to him. No, the commissioner said coldly, finding the passage and reading it aloud, the dossier was to be made available to his *inspection*. He had allowed monsieur to inspect them, and that was the limit of his authority. Now, if monsieur would sign here— Well, then, Konrad said, he requested permission to examine the documents again, and to take notes. The commissioner gave in with bad grace. It was very awkward, he said; he was extremely busy; but if monsieur would be quick about it . . . Konrad took up the dossier once more.

A half-hour later he was in the street again. He had intended, upon leaving the commissariat, to go directly to the shop. Instead, he went to Maître Paul's office, only to be informed by the secretary that the lawyer would not be in until two o'clock. He glanced at his watch. It was ten after eleven. It was just as well. He could use the intervening time to good purpose. He went home, explained briefly to Rina what had happened, and with an air of grim purpose picked up the telephone directory.

"In less than two hours," Konrad said, "and without leaving my house, I was able to establish the whereabouts of five of the six members of the first Family Council. Mademoiselle Rose could not have tried very hard. All she had to do was to lift the telephone. Two of them are still in Touville—Colbert and Instettin. Instettin has that little bakery shop across the street from the *lycée*. He doesn't have a telephone, but he's a member of a brotherhood or guild of bakers and pastry cooks, and they gave me his address and the telephone number of the café next door. When I called, Instettin couldn't come to the phone—he was at his ovens at a particularly crucial moment, it seems—but he was very much alive, the café owner assured me, and hasn't left the city in the past year, that he knows of. As for Colbert, I got through to him without any trouble. He's an importer. I knew him slightly before the war. He got very excited when he heard of the new Family Council, and said he was going to protest to the procureur. Mademoiselle Rose had certainly not tried to locate *him*, he said. In fact, he talked to her on the telephone only a couple of months ago, to ask how the boy was, since he hadn't heard anything about him since the Council met that one time in 1945; and she hadn't said anything about calling a meeting or making any changes."

They were in Konrad's home. Maître Paul had telephoned a little after two o'clock, and on learning what it was a question of, had offered to stop by. He had to be in that part of the city later on, he said; it would be convenient for both of them. He had been presented to Rina, whose hand he had kissed in polite gallantry, and had taken a chair in the living room, listening intently as Konrad, moving with nervous energy about the room, told his story.

"Colbert told me about the others," Konrad said. "Dr. Manfrédi —that's Elémir Manfrédi—is dead. His brother Wolfgang, the lawyer, is in Paris. Jules Immermann is in America. Colbert has been in touch with him, he gave me his address. He and his wife are staying with a brother of hers in a city called Cincinnati. Colbert couldn't give me Wolfgang Manfrédi's address in Paris, but suggested that I get in touch with his sister-in-law, the doctor's widow, who is still in Touville. I called her, and learned not only that she has the address, but that Mademoiselle Rose must have it too. Wolfgang Manfrédi sent the boy a gift from Paris last Christmas, she told me, and must have put the return address on the parcel.

"To sum up, then, of the six members of the Council, three, including the Rose woman, are here in the city. A fourth is in Paris, and could be summoned. A fifth could be consulted by letter. If Mademoiselle Rose did not take these steps, it was because she did not want to. Her claim that the members of the first Council have disappeared is a pure fraud, an excuse to constitute the second Council for her own purposes."

With a slight smile, Maître Paul said, "You sound like a lawyer."

Konrad spread his hands. "I'm only trying to be clear."

"You are being very clear. I'd like to know your conclusions. What are Mademoiselle Rose's purposes? Why did she need the second Council?"

Konrad studied the lawyer's long, lean, handsome head, the straight nose, the high, clear forehead, the hair with its appealing wave, boyish even though tinged with gray. A Gentile face. "I think you know," he said.

"I have my ideas. But I would like to hear yours."

Konrad shrugged. "Manfrédi, Instettin, Immermann. These names can't have escaped your attention. These men are Jews, all of them. Colbert as well. Five Jews, and Mademoiselle Rose, that was the first Council. She was being very careful, you see. The boy has no family in Touville. To show her good faith, she brings five Jews to Judge Cerval. These men will obviously act in the best interests of the child. Why not? One Jew is like another, these will be the child's 'family.' Only she summons them just the one time, to get herself named guardian, and she is clever enough to select men who do not know that the boy has an aunt who is claiming him. Except—" Konrad hesitated.

"Yes?" prompted the lawyer.

"Immermann," Konrad said with a frown. *"He* knew about the aunt. Madame Lindner wrote to his wife, and she answered her. Why didn't he bring *that* up at the Council meeting? It was called *after* their exchange of letters."

"Well," said Maître Paul, "let that go for the moment. What about the second Council?"

"I can't tell you much about that. I haven't had time. After I spoke to you, I looked them up in the directory. Two have telephones, Alain Béjart and Camélia Deharme. The Béjart number was busy. I called the other, and a voice answered, 'Charente Day Nursery.' I asked for Mademoiselle Deharme and gave my name. The woman went to call her to the phone. I waited for a few minutes, heard a click, and the phone went dead. Maybe we were cut off by accident, but I don't think so, I think she deliberately hung up on me. That's all I can tell you by way of fact. However, there's one point I'm virtually certain of without looking any further, and that is that there isn't a Jew in the lot."

Maître Paul said, "I think that's a fair conclusion. In fact, I *know* that three of them are practicing Catholics—Béjart, de Guèze and the Deharme woman. I know them. The Charente Day Nursery, Mademoiselle Deharme is the directress of that. She and Mademoiselle Rose got their diplomas in the same nursing school, in Marseilles, and are close friends. You can be pretty sure she hung up on you—she must know who you are—and you can be pretty sure that Mademoiselle Rose already knows of your call. As for Béjart, he has that elegant jewelry shop by the Palace Hotel; you might have noticed him through the window—a dapper, elderly gentleman with white hair, who affects English tailoring."

Konrad stopped walking and stared at the lawyer. "I might have known," he said at length. "There was a person of that description at the Easter party who quietly advised me to leave. And his name was in the registry book at Sep as the boy's godfather."

Maître Paul said, "It's just as well you didn't speak to him over the telephone, he'd have told you nothing. Béjart's known to be a bit of a crank, with his ideas. If he had his way he'd turn the clock back to the seventeenth century and Louis XIV, before all this nonsense of democracy and freedom of religion and thought. A believer in the sacred principle of authority from above. He used to write letters to Catholic newspapers to defend that old madman Maurras, and urging that France return to the Bourbon dynasty. And you could always find in them, I'm talking about the letters, a clear hint that the Jews are responsible for all our ills."

"An ideal godfather for a little Jewish boy," Konrad remarked dryly.

"I can also tell you about de Guèze, listed as 'lawyer's clerk.' The lawyer he works for happens to be Maître Cauchet, who's been doing Mademoiselle Rose's legal work for years. You can see what happened, of course. They need one more to fill out the six of the Council. They are in a hurry, yet they have to be careful to get people they can control. Cauchet's eye falls on his clerk. Why not old de Guèze? He's meek, obedient, a nonentity who depends on Cauchet for his bread and butter. *He*'ll do as he's told."

Konrad shrugged and consulted his notes. "That leaves Martin Mirebel, businessman, and Elsa Bordat, nurse. I take it you don't know them?"

"No, but I think the pattern is clear."

"Clear?" said Konrad. "It stinks to heaven."

Maître Paul drummed with his fingers on the arm of his chair. "Yes," he remarked, "I think you may say that. Here's how I see it. There exists a Family Council, of which the aunt knows nothing. The Council names Mademoiselle Rose as Provisional Guardian, and is never summoned again. Its work is done, Mademoiselle Rose has what she wants. For several years she has control of the boy, successfully resisting the aunt's attempts to take him from her. She is able to do so because no one is really following the matter up, not in person at any rate. Then a certain Monsieur Konrad enters the scene, and by appealing to the Parquet forces Mademoiselle Rose to reveal her status as guardian and the existence of a Family Council that gave her that status by due process of law. What will Monsieur Konrad do?"

"Do?" Konrad grunted. "He'll summon that Council, and set the facts before it, and demand—"

"Exactly," Maître Paul said. "And so Mademoiselle Rose has to replace that Council by one which will *not* take the side of the aunt and change the guardian. This she can do only if the first Council is incapacitated for one reason or another from—"

"Yes," Konrad said. "Yes, but how did she know?"

Maître Paul said carefully, "You are, I presume, talking about the date of the second Council? Because it's obvious—"

"It was the first thing that struck me, but apparently it didn't seem strange to the procureur, or to the commissioner either. *After* I hand in my *requête,* but *before* Mademoiselle Rose is summoned for a hearing—she must have been summoned around the tenth, to be heard on the fourteenth, as I was—she trumps up an excuse to replace the troublesome first Council by another one that will be more manageable, and that will confirm her as guardian. Why? How did she know her guardianship might be attacked? Or do you think it a coincidence that the second Council met on the seventh, only a week before the hearing?"

"Of course not," the lawyer said. "*Unless* the guardianship was going to be attacked, she didn't need a second Council. No, it's no coincidence. Someone warned her, that's clear. And she moved fast. I told you before. The lady is an old hand at the law and has friends everywhere."

"Damn her," Konrad said tersely. "And damn her friends."

"Amen," Maître Paul said with a little smile. "Now, what about that other document? Her arguments to the procureur?"

"The most shameless impertinence of all," Konrad retorted. "Full of lies, misrepresentations, twisted truths. Her bad faith shines through every word. If the procureur accepted them at face value, then I can't say much for either his intelligence or his good will."

"My friend," Maître Paul said gently, "let's not leap to conclusions. How do you know he accepted them?" As Konrad stared, the lawyer went on. "Don't forget, the procureur's hands were tied. So long as there is a Family Council, there's nothing the procureur can do. Mademoiselle Rose's arguments are no longer to the point. She didn't have to make them, in fact. And if they are as you say, then the procureur's action in making them available to you can be interpreted as a friendly interest on your behalf. Because just as Mademoiselle Rose didn't have to make them, he didn't have to let you see them. He is showing you Mademoiselle Rose's defense, the sort of thing she must have set forth before the second Council. He's saying to you, Monsieur Konrad, here is Mademoiselle Rose's self-justification. If you intend to approach the Council, you can have some answers ready. Now," the lawyer went on, studying Konrad's face, "weighing this, and knowing Procureur Hamard as I do, I think you can forget any idea you might have that it was he who gave the game away to Mademoiselle Rose. No, I know you didn't say so," for Konrad had started and turned a troubled glance on him, "but I suspect the idea crossed your mind. Hamard is a decent chap and takes his responsibilities quite seriously. So, incidentally, does Judge Cerval."

Konrad took a stand in the middle of the floor, his hands clasped behind him. "Now when," he demanded, "did I ever say the contrary?"

Leaning back in his chair, Maître Paul quoted at him, " 'One Jew is like another.' What makes you think that's what Cerval thought when the first Council was formed? As a matter of fact, nothing was more natural and to the child's interests than to have a Council made up of Jews. Perhaps Mademoiselle Rose was playing a deep game, but I see nothing in the proceedings to make me feel that Judge Cerval was, or that he has anti-Jewish feelings."

Konrad gave a short laugh. "I see," he said. "I am too sensitive, then."

"Understand me. I'm not criticizing you, I'm merely setting the record straight. If we proceed further in this matter, I have no doubt that we will run into more than a hint of prejudice and even hatred of your people. There is enough of that in France, God knows. But we must not find it where it does not exist. Can't you forget you're a Jew for a little while?"

"No," Konrad said instantly. "I can't. I don't want to. Can you forget you're a Catholic?"

"I imagine that's different," the lawyer remarked. "It's not constantly in the forefront of my mind. For instance, when you let me in a little while ago—I hope you'll pardon the personal allusion—can you deny that the thought that occurred to you was something like this: You are entering a Jewish home?"

Konrad said, "I won't deny that, if you'll be equally as sincere. Can *you* deny that what you were thinking was, I am entering a Jewish home?"

The two men stared at each other, and broke out laughing at the same time. Maître Paul said, "You have a point there. The chicken or the egg? Are you a Jew because I think you are, or do I think you are because you damn well are? Of course, in the case of the chicken at least, we have the Biblical argument. 'And God created great whales, and every living thing that moveth, and every winged fowl after his kind.' So I suppose the chicken came first."

"Well," Konrad said, taking up the other's bantering tone, "suppose I prove to you that Adam was a Jew?"

"Yes," the lawyer said. "We are all Jews. As a matter of fact, I might as well tell you that in my case that's literally true."

Konrad was sure he had not heard aright. The look he turned to Maître Paul was so perplexed that the latter could not prevent a smile. He said, "You spoke of Jewish names—Immermann, Manfrédi, and so forth. The name Paul, does that mean anything to you? There's one I'm sure you'll remember, the Jewish persecutor of the Christians until he became a Christian himself, and changed his name from Saul to Paul. I suspect that his example was in the mind of some ancestor of mine, some time during the sixteenth century. Our family came from Spain, at the end of the fifteenth century, at the time of the great expulsion of the Jews. But in France the family underwent conversion, not to Catholicism, but to Calvinism—the so-called Huguenots. The name had been Ibrahim; it was changed to Paul. The records show at least three of that surname killed during the St. Bartholomew Massacre of 1572. Since that time there has always been a Barthélemy in our family. I am the seventh of that name. However, the family religion changed again, some time in the 1680s, for what motives I can't say. I wouldn't be surprised if it were a simple case of bribery. The Church had set up what were known as 'conversion bureaus.' Any Huguenot who could show a certificate that he had been received into the Roman Church was handed the comfortable sum of twelve livres. Such are the historical accidents that govern our beliefs. My Jewish blood is considerably diluted, of course, but no doubt some remnant is left."

Konrad sank into a chair and stared at the lawyer, who met his look with calm amusement in his eyes. "Tell me," Konrad said at length, "as one Jew to another, how can any man in his right senses be a Catholic?"

"I'd be very glad to answer that question," Maître Paul said, "if I thought for one moment that you really wanted to know. Who can tell? I might even convince you that there is no other religion a man in his right senses, even a hardheaded Jew, could possibly adopt."

"Ah, spare me Pascal!" Konrad groaned. "Do you call *him* a man of sense, with his hair shirt and mortifications, and his reasons beyond the grasp of reason?"

Maître Paul said, laughing, "You *did* ask, you know."

"I did. But I didn't expect an answer. I asked for the same reason you brought up your family background. To clear the air. To understand each other. To let you know I appreciated the confidence. I imagine you did it just for that."

Maître Paul was suddenly serious. "As you say, to clear the air. So that you can say to me, bluntly, 'Why as a lawyer didn't it occur to you that there might be a Family Council?' And so that I can say to you, 'I understand your tender sensitivities as a member of a persecuted race, but let's not see bogeymen under the bed.' And to bring out into the open that lurking doubt in your mind, that perhaps it was I who gave the game away to the good Mademoiselle Rose."

The lawyer had not raised his voice, but something hard had crept into it with his last words.

Rina, entering at that moment with a tray, found the two men staring at each other in silence. She poured the coffee, glanced at her husband's face, murmured, "Excuse me," and left the room. Maître Paul, who had risen, sat down again.

Konrad said, "I won't deny that the thought crossed my mind. Perhaps it was unworthy of me. I didn't believe it, by the way. But the fact remains that *somebody* did. I didn't. You didn't. The procureur didn't. Then who did?"

"I intend to find out," Maître Paul said. "Because if, as I suspect, we are in for a long and troublesome procedure, we can't have that kind of leak."

Konrad gave him a queer look, rose to his feet and went to the window, where he remained looking out into the street. The conversation had taken an unexpected, personal turn. It would not have surprised him if, with the airing of his secret suspicion, the lawyer had offered to withdraw from the case. The man's last remark had set his mind at rest. Konrad liked the way he had faced up to the situation. He turned and said simply, "I'm glad I came to you."

"Now that that's settled," Maître Paul said with a faint smile, "do you think we could have some coffee? It smells good."

Some minutes later Maître Paul brought up the subject of Mlle Rose's deposition to the procureur. He wanted to know the arguments that had been brought forward.

"She put them under headings," Konrad said. "First comes the well-being of the boy. Here's what she has to say about that." He read from his notes: " 'The child was born in France. He is now seven, and has always lived in a French home, for he was separated from his parents when he was two. He speaks only French.' Of course," Konrad remarked dryly, looking up, "she is careful not to say that he was only three when the aunt first claimed him. But to go on. 'Can it possibly be to Michel's well-being to transport him to a far country whose climate might be harmful to him, to have him undertake a very long and fatiguing journey and then, suddenly, place him in surroundings totally different from those to which he has until now been accustomed, in the home of persons he does not know at all, whose customs and way of life are entirely different from ours?' She says more on the same subject, but the gist of it is contained in what I read. I didn't copy it all. Now comes the heading she calls 'National Arguments.' She says, 'Dr. and Madame Benedek, fleeing from the Nazis, found a land of refuge in France. They might have gone to England, to China, to Australia, like others of their family. They preferred France. Dr. Benedek felt the weight of gratitude toward the country that had welcomed him. It was his intention to repay her by seeking French citizenship. Since he is dead, it is for his son, born in France and under the protection of French authorities since birth, to repay that debt by becoming a French citizen.' "

"Go on," Maître Paul said, as Konrad paused.

"There are two more headings. What she calls 'Family Arguments' and 'Religious Arguments.' The only word I can find for them is that they are indecent. The family should not be given the child, she says, because it is dispersed. Oh, not in so many words, of course, but that's what it comes down to. The family has scattered over the globe. Therefore any claims in the name of family are invalid."

"Drivel," Maître Paul commented. "How could Cauchet have let her put that down?"

"Wait," Konrad said, his eyes smoldering. "Listen to this. I copied it exactly. I didn't want to lose a word. 'Religious Arguments: No arguments on this level have any force. The child's parents were Israelites, but that is no reason why the child must remain so. Religion is not like nationality. It must be freely consented to. When Michel has reached the age of reason, it will be for him alone to choose.' "

With a pained expression, Maître Paul said, "And this from the woman who had the boy baptized?"

Konrad spread his hands in an eloquent gesture. "There you have it," he said. "The arguments of Mademoiselle Rose. Such as they are. I could comment on them, but I won't. I think they speak for themselves."

"Her arguments don't matter much," Maître Paul said. "As I said before, they're the sort of thing she must have brought up before the second Council, which probably needed very little convincing in any case. On the other hand, arguments such as these, especially those related to family and religion, would only infuriate the members of the first Council. I think our course is clear. That is, if you wish to pursue the matter further."

The lawyer made his last statement so matter-of-factly that it was a moment before Konrad caught its import. "*If* I wish to pursue!" he said, startled.

"What I'm going to say to you may sound strange," Maître Paul said, "but I'm going to ask you to be patient and hear me out. A moment ago I remarked that I thought we were in for a long and troublesome procedure. The issue is more complicated than I had thought. I have no doubt that justice is on our side, and that eventually our rights would be acknowledged. But in the meantime what is going to happen to the boy? Please," he said quickly, as Konrad made a gesture as if to interrupt. He went on: "When you first came to me, I realized that the weak point in Madame Lindner's entire approach to the problem was that, for whatever reasons, she was trying to move other agencies to get the boy for her. Because Madame Lindner was not here to press her claim, Mademoiselle Rose was able to resist it successfully. And I believed that with you on the scene, that situation had changed; Mademoiselle Rose would be unable to stand up to a formal complaint following due process of law. It is true, I warned you against her, but I didn't really see where she could stop us. She has not stopped us, but she has delayed us. And it is that delay that worries me in regard to the boy, who may turn out to be the real victim of the coming struggle."

"If I may—" Konrad began.

Maître Paul said, "I'll have finished in a moment. From being a simple claim by the aunt that her brother's child be turned over to her as next of kin, this case has become, through the machinations of Mademoiselle Rose, a guardianship case like the one the Bible tells us was brought before King Solomon. Who is the real mother of the child? The one who has his blood in her veins, but who has done nothing for him? Or the other woman, who has no kinship with the child, but who took him in and acted like a mother to him? I say nothing about where true justice lies, only how the case must appear to a judge. I've seen guardianship cases; they are invariably painful, and seldom turn out as happily as the one that Solomon was called upon to decide. If only such cases were as simple as that! The guard raises the sword; the true mother says, No, no, *you* take him; and the truth is out. Do you know what happens in the majority of cases? The child is chopped in half, metaphorically speaking, of course. The child's loyalties are so divided that his personality is permanently harmed. Rightfully or wrongfully, Mademoiselle Rose has the boy. She has had him for more than four years. He has, in effect, grown up with her. Mademoiselle Rose has demonstrated that she is determined to resist to the end. The case may drag out another year or more. Are you prepared to face the consequences? I think you must weigh this before you make any other decisions."

"I suppose," Konrad said reflectively, after a long pause, "that you are only doing your duty in warning me. But you must realize that such a course is impossible for me. I mean that literally. Everything in me is revolted by what that woman has done to the boy and his family. And so the answer is no. I appreciate your motives. I won't do you the injustice of saying that it is easy for a Catholic to advise letting the status quo alone. But you must see that as a Jew it is impossible for *me* to let it alone. I can't and I won't. That boy will go to his aunt. And it's up to you to tell me what I must do to get him to her."

"As you say," Maître Paul returned, "I've done my duty. Now let me say that I agree with you. No, it's not a contradiction. It had to be you to make the decision. And so for a moment I took the part of the devil's advocate. Now I'll become yours again. What to do? Here's my advice. First, you obviously cannot present yourself to the second Council and ask it to award the boy to the aunt. They won't do it. They were chosen to meet such a demand. And so you must attack the legality of the second Council, and demand that the first be reinstated. On what grounds? On the basis of the fact that there were no grounds to destitute it in the first place. Its members have *not* disappeared; or let us say, rather, that only one of them has. The others are immediately available or can be reached. You must go to see the two who are still in Touville, and you must write to the other two. You must urge them to complain to the procureur that their rights have been improperly passed over, that Mademoiselle Rose made false representations to the judge in requesting a new Council. The procureur can order a rehearing before Judge Cerval, and Cerval will be obliged to reinstate the former members, since the disqualifying reason is obviously null and void."

"And Dr. Manfrédi?" Konrad asked.

"I was coming to that. He will of course have to be replaced. But by whom? In making this decision, we must take into consideration a change in circumstances of primordial importance. A Family Council, according to Article 142, is supposed to *be* just that: it must be composed of the nearest of kin, whenever possible. In this case there are three such persons—an aunt in Israel, an aunt in Vienna, an aunt somewhere in China. None of these has been represented in either of the Councils. Mademoiselle Rose could get away with that in 1945 by claiming that no relatives of the child were in existence; but now, three years later, she can no longer make that claim. The second Council is therefore invalid for another reason."

Konrad, who had been following the lawyer's rapid summation with attention, said, "Yes, but then the *first* Council is also invalid."

"Not at all," Maître Paul said, smiling. "It all comes down to a question of good faith. Mademoiselle Rose, without realizing it, created a Frankenstein's monster for herself in selecting the members of the first Council. She chose them in apparent good faith, which we shall be very careful not to assail. And this means that once the judge ruled upon them and accepted them, the choice must stand. She cannot rid herself of them. *You* will profit by her handiwork. There are three aunts to be represented? Very well, the members of the first Council will represent them. Let the aunt in Vienna delegate her authority to one of them, any one you recommend to her. Let the aunt in China do the same to another. As for the aunt in Israel, *you* are already her legal representative. The judge has no recourse but to name you to replace the member who is dead, Dr. Manfrédi. In this way, not only does the first Council regain its prerogatives, it is legally stronger than before, by fulfilling the spirit of the Code through whose provisions it takes its existence. And stronger in another sense —it has you as one of its members, to assure that *all* the facts are placed before it in its deliberations. And this time I think we can count on what it will do. After you have done the groundwork, the

Council will hand the guardianship over to Madame Lindner, and you, with your power of attorney, can simply go to the Nursery and demand the boy."

"One little detail," Konrad said. "Nobody seems to know the address of the aunt in China. But perhaps Madame Lindner can get it for me. In any case," he added gloomily, "I can see I have my work cut out for me. And quickly, too, since it has to be done before the first Council can be reinstated."

"Yes. There's work to be done. A great deal of work. But I haven't mentioned one other matter, another way we can attack the Councils, if all else fails. You'll notice I used the plural form. Because," the lawyer said, pursing his lips significantly, "Mademoiselle Rose slipped up in both cases in a trifling detail, a petty technicality, but one we can invoke if necessary, if it should become desirable to invalidate *both* Councils and summon a third. Judge Cerval has jurisdiction in the *south* canton of Touville. But Puy-le-Duc, where the boy was born, is in the *east* canton. The case should never have been brought before Cerval at all. We can attack the thing for the vice of form. It would be preferable, of course, not to do so, since we certainly don't want to impugn the first Council. And so, for the time being, we'll say nothing about it, but keep it as a final weapon in case of need."

Konrad took a deep breath. "Well," he said, "I suppose we'll win yet."

"Oh yes," Maître Paul assured him cheerfully. "It's just a matter of time."

11

❦

I N THE PLAYGROUND the children were at their games. Mlle Pasquier was with them, clapping her hands for attention.

"Sixteen, seventeen, eighteen," Pé chanted, as Léah, her braids flying, skipped and skipped. Michel, watching from the bench, saw him edge nearer, his eyes intent.

"Twenty-three, twenty-four, you're going to trip, you're going to trip."

"You'll hurt her," Michel said. Pé shot him a look of scorn.

"Pé!" Manon, sitting beside Michel, looked up from her knitting.

Léah got tangled up and fell to one knee, screaming, "You pulled the rope!"

"I did not!" Pé protested, aggrieved, glancing toward the bench.

"You did so!" Léah burst into tears.

Mlle Pasquier came up and seized Pé by the arm. He had been acting up all day. Why couldn't he behave himself, like Michel? If he didn't know how to play, he had better go inside.

"Inside," she repeated more loudly, as Pé stood his ground.

Muttering, Pé moved off. "Christ-killer!" he said under his breath as he passed Michel.

Astounded, Michel stared after him, then looked at Manon. She had heard, her face was flushed and angry. After a while Michel slid silently to the ground, crossed the playground, and went through the side passage to the front garden. He sat on the steps, then got up and wandered aimlessly among the shrubs. Some of the leaves had turned yellow and others red. Autumn is coming, he thought dully. And all the while his ears burned with that word. He had never dreamed a word could hurt so much. He felt betrayed and ashamed.

Maman Rose called him from the front entrance. Her voice was angry. When he entered the hall, he understood that her tone was not for him but for Pé, whom she held by the ear.

"Say it!" she commanded.

Pé whined. "I didn't mean it, Michel."

"Go to your room." Maman Rose released the ear, which was a fiery red, and smacked him with the back of her hand. Pé let out a howl and went scrambling up the stairs.

Michel turned away, with a sick feeling inside him.

"Forgive him, Michel. He's just a mean, nasty little boy." Maman Rose had put out her hand, beseechingly. There was an urgency in her face that showed she understood how he felt.

Yes, he said, he forgave him. He went out into the garden again and stood by the gate. Forgiving was easy. It wasn't that. It was the shadow that had somehow fallen over the world, which would never be the same again.

Looking down, he saw that grass had grown over the bare spot his feet had made on the earth by the fence.

PLM meant Paris–Lyons–Midi. It also meant Midi–Lyons–Paris. It depended which way you were going. The train started in Paris and went south, and then when it reached the sea it turned around and went back north again. It passed through Touville each time. Passengers got off, and others got on. Was this the train his father would have come on? He had never imagined it would be he, and not his father, to ride this train.

It was early morning, so early that the sun had not yet cleared the mountains to the east, but showed only its upper rim, like the top of a burning orange. Or like a crown, Michel thought, because of the rays that shot out and edged the clouds with pink. Yet the sky was light, and in the countryside the workday had already begun. The train moved with its persistent and monotonous clatter through a patchwork of farmlands, across whose many-colored surface crawled oxcarts and men in overalls and boots, made tiny by distance. Some of the farmers stopped their labors for a moment to watch the train go by. Could they see him? Michel wondered. To them he was only a face at the window. They did not know who he was or where he was going.

Michel Benedek, he thought, and turned his troubled gaze on the two nuns sitting on the opposite bench of the compartment. It seemed very strange to him that he could be the same boy, and yet have a different name. Last night, at the Nursery, he had studied himself in the mirror, and repeated several times, "Michel Rose." But the face that stared back at him was that of Michel Benedek. The face hadn't changed. Like calling an apple a pear. It was still an apple. Yet he would have to get used to it, because from now on he was Michel Rose. Maman Rose said so, and so did Mother Veronica. And he knew, because he had seen when Maman Rose gave it to the nun, that his new school identity card bore the new name, written clearly in black ink alongside his photograph. The card was in the little valise that now nestled at Mother Veronica's feet, and would accompany him wherever he was going.

Like him, Mother Veronica was looking out the window, but in the opposite direction, so that their lines of vision crossed. It meant that always he was aware, out of the corners of his eyes, of a half-oval of white and that pale, serious face that seemed unmoving in its contemplation of the landscape, yet must be aware of him as he was of her. Michel would have preferred to have the other one, Sister Marie Madeleine, sitting opposite him, for as soon as the first dim light came through the window she had crossed herself and buried her gaze in the little black breviary she was carrying in her hand. Mother Veronica made him nervous. She was so silent, so motionless, so lost in depths whose awful mysteries he could not even imagine; so—so *perfect,* as if the statue of the Virgin Mary had got off her pedestal and was accompanying him to Paris. And because he was sure, whenever her calm, impenetrable eyes rested on him, that she knew what he was thinking.

He was thinking of so many things—of Maman Rose, who loved him, and Renée, who loved her Jules, and Pé, who had changed, and Father Périer and Jean, who were dead, and M. Konrad, who hated him and wanted to make him a slave, and St. Joseph's that he was not going back to, and the new school, the seminary, that lay before him, and the Nursery, and his father. These things whirled in his head, in a strange kind of cadence that matched the rhythm of the wheels. The wheels went clickety-click, clack, clack, over and over as the train sped onward; and from his desolation sprang words that echoed so loudly in his brain that he wondered whether they were audible to Mother Veronica as well. The wheels said, Michel Benedek, Michel Rose, Michel Benedek, Michel Rose. And they said, Clickety-click, clack, clack, you are never coming back. And, North, south, west, east, I don't want to be a priest.

When you dream, things happen that sometimes make no sense.

You are talking to someone, and you look up and it is not that person, but someone else. Or everybody begins saying, It is time. You are filled with anxiety and go about asking what is going to happen, and they look at you with vague faces and don't answer. This morning everything seemed like that. Even the train itself, which was nothing like the pictures he had seen in books, but a huge, snorting monster, black and evil under the glaring lights and strong shadows of the station at that unreal, dark hour of the morning. Climbing the steps, he had bridled with fear at a sudden hiss that seemed to come from under his feet. And entering, he had found himself in a narrow, smelly corridor lit by a dim bulb, and passing glass-paneled doors through which he could see, by the bluish platform lights outside, compartments where people sprawled asleep in grotesque positions or met his gaze with unseeing eyes.

Like in a dream, he thought. Everything was like in a dream. Accompanied by the Virgin Mary, he was traveling on an unreal train to an unknown destination. But it was not he, it was a boy named Michel Rose who looked like him. And the wheels talked and chattered and clicked and sang strange songs that echoed in his brain.

Michel Benedek, Michel Rose. He had remained silent when they told him. It was one of those things that grownups do, that apparently can be done because grownups do them, and know better than little boys what is right. But he had not accepted it. It offended him. Was his name something separate from himself, like a wrapper, an identification tag, that could be changed when it got dirty? He *was* Michel Benedek. You couldn't choose to *be* someone else. Fortunately, he was still Michel; there had been no change there. Michel, he said to himself. And, as always, he heard inside him the broken voice repeating his name, the voice that had engraved itself in his memory in that dreadful moment of parting from his father. Only this time it was not alone. Maman Rose's voice was there too, saying, "Michel, Michel" in almost the same accents, as she had said it only a few minutes before, in the railway station. He must not disappoint her, she had said. He was the only one left now.

Maman Rose! He wanted to be with her, and not on this train at all. He didn't know why the wheels said he was never coming back. He would be back for Christmas vacation. And then during the summer. Yet the wheels kept up their monotonous cadence with that false, stupid rhyme, as if they knew better than he what was in his heart. As if they knew how much the Nursery had changed since

Father Périer and Jean had died, since Renée had run away, since Pé had called him that name. Of course he was coming back! Where else did he have to go?

North, west, south, east, I don't want to be a— No one had asked him. No one had ever asked him. It had always been taken for granted, and he had taken it for granted too. He had the vocation, they said. A vocation was when you wanted something very much, and were willing to devote your life to it. To serve, Father Périer had said. A priest was a servant, but a servant higher than the highest king. How fine that had sounded to Michel! Only a few months ago it would have seemed to him a splendid thing to go off thus into the unknown, secure in the radiant protection of God and His angels, to learn how he might serve. To prepare himself to stand before the congregation and lift the cup, and feel God flow down into his fingers. To turn and see his father looking at him with pride in his eyes.

It had all vanished, that world of illusion in which all was as it ought to be, in which all his loves went hand in hand, linked by the One Love that caressed him like an invisible hand from above—and his willingness had vanished with it. He had offered all he had for one little word. That word had not come. He would not ask again. He would go where they sent him, do what he was told—but he would maintain inviolate that little kingdom of conscience within him, that only his will could unlock. That part of him that was neither Benedek nor Rose, but Michel. No one could touch that. Michel, the wheels said. Michel, Michel, Michel.

Sister Marie Madeleine closed her breviary and lifted her rapt look out the window. "Oh," she said, with the pleasure of a child. "Lyons!"

Michel had not noticed that the train had left the flatland, and was now rounding a hilly curve. A fairy city had swum into view, fresh and lovely under the morning sun, which glinted on the waters of a broad river gliding under high stone arches. He gazed and gazed, filled with wonder, while the wheels sang, and Mother Veronica watched him with a gentle, melancholy smile.

Michel was asleep. He had resisted it for a long time, sitting upright in the uncomfortable angle that the wooden seat made with the wall. But little by little his small body had become slack, and he had slid down until he was lying curled on his side, his head on his coat that Sister Marie Madeleine had doubled under him. His feet touched the hip of the young woman who had got on at Lyons. Mother Veronica, silently observant, saw the woman's coarse face darken with annoyance as she glanced at him; then her expression softened and became protective, and she placed her hand at the seat edge as a safeguard.

He would go through life like that, Mother Veronica thought. It was the privilege of his beauty, his angelic radiance, that made people stay their eyes on his face, want to touch him, protect him. Could the Nazis have taken such a child and treated him like the others? Packed him in a sealed truck and carted him off to one of their infamous children's detention barracks? Shoved him into that frozen hell, to let him wither and rot like the rest? They would have done so, she supposed; she had no illusions about man's capacity for evil. How narrow an escape he had had! And yet, how safe he had been all the time!

Safe—as safe as the Christ child fleeing from Herod; as Moses cast adrift on the Nile; as St. Francis in the grave illness that turned his youthful mind to God; as Mother Miriam before the charging bull. In none of these cases had there been the slightest danger of the disaster that was so obvious to our incredibly shortsighted vision. What was Pharaoh's daughter doing at that precise spot of the riverbank? Had not God, in this infinitely intricate human chess game that is life, so fashioned the woman, so foreseen the conduct of her life—she had free will—that she would find herself at just the right place at exactly the moment when she could hear the child crying in his floating basket? More—before man was created, before the universe, before time itself, this woman was ineluctably willed, as implicit in Adam as Moses was. There was no need for the mind to reel at what would have happened if that daughter of kings had not been within sound of the cry—the continued enslavement of the Jews, the failure to reach the Holy Land, the failure to establish a nation awaiting a Saviour, the consequent not coming into being of Christianity, the complete alteration of history—all this was meaningless, for it was impossible for it not to happen. An accident! cried the worldly-wise. A miracle! said the narrowly pious. Neither one nor the other, a plan.

History was the working out in time of purposes contained within the eternal Godhead, purposes themselves independent of time, which was finite and created for the finite being that is man. Where those purposes tended was clearly established by Revelation, by the prophets, by the words of the Saviour Himself, the saints, the inspired teachers of the Church: that which had begun in heaven would end in heaven. Man, created in love, would—after being tried as to his worthiness of that love—return to his source. (In a sense, it was absurd to speak of beginning and ending, before and after, a journey and a return, since in God's mind all duration, all struggle, all tendencies and developments were ultimately merely a dimension —unknowable to us—of the foreseen and immutable. Yet it was impossible for man, shaped as he was, to think other than in terms of time.)

If the goal was clear, the wonderful edifice of event leading up to it was at best capable of only a backward interpretation. We knew where man was going, but we did not, could not know how he would get there. There was the Creation, the Fall, the Redemption—these we had witnessed and could understand. But the second coming of Christ, which had been promised us? It would come, of course; but no man could tell by what steps, by what pattern of happenings, by what interplay of lives, the consummation would be arrived at. Who could have foretold, when the youth Francis lay ill in Assisi, that out of that apparently fortuitous circumstance would spring the spiritual movement that would bring the Church and mankind closer to the purity of faith of the early Christian martyrs? It was when we saw the result that we could assess the instruments that had brought it about. And then we could see that what seemed fortuitous was nothing of the sort, that God had laid his hand upon that young man's heart, had wracked him with fever to set his soul afire, but that there had not been the slightest risk that he would die.

Not a single human being—the president in his palace, the Chinese coolie bending over his rice stalks, the American businessman in his Wall Street skyscraper, the nun in her chapel, the Indian with his blowgun in the heart of the Amazon—not an animal, a tree, a blade of grass, but what played a role in the tremendous pageant of God's reacceptance. We were all God's anointed. But only rarely could we glimpse what that role was, in those moments when human destiny took a lurch in a new direction, and there became apparent to our flesh-drugged eyes another tracing in the pattern, and the agency through which it came. For every saint who moved the earth there were countless millions who lived and died in obscurity, for the most part utterly blind to the fact that, acting in freedom of will—

God's gift to man—each contributed to a degree, however small, to the fulfillment of that which had been ordained for all time.

Sitting in the train that was taking her to Paris, watching the late afternoon shadows creeping over the land, Mother Veronica thought of the bull through which God had chosen to reveal one aspect of His plan. A bull, a cardinal, and a nun. It began, in human terms, with the nun, a plain, ungainly woman of Jewish parentage who, upon being converted and adopting the veil, had taken the name of Sister Miriam. One would have supposed in looking at her round, rather sheeplike face with its steel-rimmed glasses, and in hearing the stammer with which she spoke, that this was one of those obscure lives destined to spend themselves in muted orisons to God, who alone knew what purpose she fulfilled in His scheme of things. But there was a flame, a holy zeal, in this bride of Christ, which shone through the trappings of the flesh. In spite of her impeded tongue, her eloquence converted her entire family to the true faith, and found other hearers as well. Everywhere she went a ripple of conversions followed her. She became a mighty hunter for the Lord. Jews laughed at her approach, but they listened, and in the end kneeled down with her to pray. Some of her female converts she gathered about her as lay disciples, until she was, in effect, the mother superior of what was a religious sisterhood in all but the veil. Then the idea that had been slowly maturing in her all those years came to fruition. There were religious orders devoted to teaching, to silent devotions, to charitable good works, to nursing—but none whose primary purpose was to bring into the Christian fold the Jews who for more than eighteen centuries had systematically rejected the new covenant. Sister Miriam had already created the nucleus of such an order. She would go to Rome and convince the Holy Father to give it official sanction. She obtained leave from her superior and set forth on her mission.

She found Rome all but deserted, in panic at the news of Garibaldi's march on the Papal States. The Holy Father was no longer granting private audiences, she was told at the Secretariat. She produced a letter from her bishop. It had no effect. She returned day after day, to be given the same answer. Soon her permission would run out, and she would have to return without having been heard. One day she took a carriage to a little village a few miles from the city, where it was said there was a well with miraculous healing powers. As she walked along the unpaved single street in the huddle of earth-colored huts, she heard a shout and saw bearing down on her a bull that somehow had broken away from a neighboring field and was being pursued by a farmer who, his hat in one hand and a pitchfork in the other, was trying vainly to head it off. Sister Miriam stopped where she was and stared at the animal racing toward her. She did not move, although it was obvious that in that narrow space there was no room on either side of her for the bull to pass by. She was not frightened, she said later, only curious. And then the amazing thing happened. The bull stopped, grinding to a halt in a cloud of dust, its great shaggy horned head so close to her that flecks of foam from its nostrils spattered the hem of her robe. A moment later the animal, now meek, was led away, and the nun was surrounded by a shouting, jabbering crowd of women and children who cried, "Miracle! Miracle!"

Behind her a carriage had drawn up, and a hand was beckoning to her. Inside was a stout, extremely pale gentleman dressed in cardinal's robes, who questioned her. Who was she? What was she doing there? Why had she not run? As Sister Miriam stammered out her story, the cardinal, whose name she did not think to ask and never learned, gave her a queer look and told her to return to the Secretariat tomorrow.

The next day Sister Miriam was taken directly to the Papal presence. She talked for an hour. Never had she been more eloquent. That evening she was summoned again, before the Holy Father and three dark-robed prelates who took turns questioning her. Again the words flowed from her, broken, confused, but radiating a certainty that reduced her questioners to silence. She was told to go home and wait. Three months later she was granted permission to establish a sisterhood for the purpose of "making converts, primarily among the Jews, procuring a Christian education for young neophytes, and to that end conducting *pensionnats* and schools." Thus was the Temple born.

A bull, a cardinal, and a nun. Through them God had permitted the veil of His inscrutability to be lifted for a moment. That God had not let this humble creature of His be trampled to death; that her escape should have been the key to the Pope's private audience chamber; that from this incredible circumstance should have sprung the wide empire of Temples and their Dames—all this could mean only one thing: that somehow, through this new sisterhood, would come the divine force that would bend God's chosen but deluded people to His will. For this that unknown witness had been born, given a vocation and a cardinal's hat, and gone for an airing in the Roman countryside. For this that bull had been bred, and the bee that stung him. Sister Miriam, made the bearer of God's word, had played the exalted role in this juxtaposition of lives and events, and had died ecstatic with the knowledge of what she had accomplished. But the cardinal? Had he even suspected what his share of eternity was?

It was given to so few to know. Mother Veronica all her life had wondered what her part was to be. That it had to do with the conversion of the Jews she had no doubt. But, specifically, what? Was she to live and die in the seclusion of the cloister, just one more handmaiden of the Lord, lost in the anonymous mass of humanity, knowing she was being used—for all are used—but not glimpsing, even for one soul-shattering instant of happiness, the purpose of her being? If that were so, she accepted it in humility. It was enough for God to know. But constantly in her thoughts was the deathbed utterance of Mother Miriam, which she had thrilled to hear years ago as a schoolgirl, and about which all her secret hopes had centered ever since. "One will come!" that saintly woman, now aged and blind but still indomitable, had cried to the circle of sorrowing nuns around her. It was the last thing she said, and the only thing she had ever said without a stammer. "One will come!" A riddle to the world, but clear to the Dames who, like the founder, were waiting for the great conversion, "the" conversion for which God had ordained their order. These words, spoken while those weary unseeing eyes were opening to the glories of heaven, were a confirmation. Amid the souls yet to come to the world—in what time and place no one could tell, until the backward glance saw how all the pieces of the puzzle fell into place, until the signs were there to read—was the One who, allowed to be born to Jews, would through the Temple Dames embrace the true faith and bring his people with him.

Mother Veronica's secret hope was that of all her sisters in Christ: that it would be she to find the One.

She had not found him. He had found her.

Mother Veronica, sitting unmoving by the darkening window, let her eyes rest caressingly on Michel's face. The child's lips were softly parted, and she sensed rather than heard the breath that came and went. He slept in the hand of God. He had never been in any danger, no, not even when she had first seen him, sleeping thus, in Mme

Quertsch's arms, and the whole world was burning in a conflagration in which millions like him were perishing.

That was the setting for *her* miracle.

She had told no one. She never would. If it were her pride that had spoken, she would know how to chasten it. If it was God—He did not need her voice.

Dreaming in the twilight, Mother Veronica let her mind go back to February 1944. It was, she supposed, France's darkest hour. The occupying Germans, realizing that the war was lost, expecting from day to day the Allied invasion that in fact came with the warm weather, were feverishly ransacking the prostrate country. Their *rafles,* the dreaded manhunts of Jews and other undesirables, which hitherto had been sporadic, had become a daily occurrence, as if the doomed were determined to take with them into destruction as many of their enemies as possible.

For over two years now she had been working with the Resistance. Her task was to get Jewish children over the border into Switzerland. Gradually, a whole network of collaborators had been built up: the "recruiters," who hunted out those families and institutions to whom Jewish parents had entrusted their offspring for safekeeping, and who brought the children at appointed times to the pavilion in the Temple park; the "priests," who accompanied the children on their ride to the frontier in the bus; the innkeeper in the border village, who played host to their "picnic"; the Swiss agent, waiting at nightfall on the secret trail; the receivers, ready on the other side. The very daring of the method, its openness, insured its success. Periodically, the bus, full of children, went in broad daylight through the streets of Touville, and disappeared into the countryside. The following day it returned empty, by a different route; and one by one, the heroic Resistance volunteers, having exchanged their black cassocks for other garments, straggled back to the city by devious ways.

This might have been Michel's fate, Mother Veronica had often thought, except for the dreadful accident that occurred at this time. On a day toward the end of February, one of these Temple excursions—the last, as it proved—ran into a trap. It was never learned how it happened—possibly an informer had recognized one of the "priests" and had gone to the police—but when the men made their dash for the border at the usual twilight hour, they were gathered in by a net of armed SS guards waiting for them in the forest. The children, twenty-seven of them, were driven off in a covered truck, and disappeared from knowledge. The disguised Resistance agents were brutally tortured. It was not until the next day that the receiving agents in Switzerland were able to get word of the disaster to Touville.

How unfathomable are the ways of the Lord! And how easy it was to give way to human circumstance, to forget for moments that even evil serves! Her nuns, gentle, innocent creatures who had been participating in that risky game with fears they could not hide, were thrown into panic by this unexpected development. What would happen to them all? they cried. Among the captured agents was the mother superior's own "contact," the one through whom her orders were transmitted, and who knew her identity. Would he be able to resist the Nazi tortures? If not, they were all doomed. At any moment now might come the squeal of brakes in the boulevard, the irruption of hard-faced men in gray-green uniforms into their quiet precincts, with fearful indignities, pain, and death to follow. The nuns crowded about her, urging her to run, to go into hiding. She refused, saying, "God will give him the strength."

She said it to quiet them, and because it was inconceivable that she should avoid martyrdom at the expense of her duty; but she was under no illusions about either the efficacy of Nazi methods or her own individual value in the divine scheme. Everything depended, in a human sense, on the backbone of a man. If the agent resisted the torture and did not give her away, she and her nuns were safe for the time being, and reserved for other things. If not—well then, she had been wrong in her secret feeling about what those "other things" were to be, and she would go uncomplaining into God's presence, knowing nothing was truly lost.

Unknown to her, her destiny was already waiting at the gate. The founder's prophecy had begun to implement itself. Mother Veronica could not know, of course. The name Quertsch meant nothing to her. It was only natural, at that troubled moment when there was so much to be done, when the girls had to be sent home, when her nuns had to be schooled in their behavior under the coming duress, and word transmitted along the echelons of the underground, that she should have the gatekeeper tell the importunate woman that the mother superior could not see her now. Being destiny, the woman insisted; she held a child in her arms, bundled up against the cold; with the rage of the meek, she shoved the child under Sister Louise's nose and cried that it was a matter of life and death.

Unwitting mouthpiece of a higher purpose! Mme Quertsch too had been chosen; like Pharaoh's daughter, she had been at the right place at the right time, a human instrument by "chance" ready to hand. In her desperate phrase, she had spoken truly—but not as she thought. The life or death of Michel? That had already been decided, before the Word was flung into chaos. Mme Quertsch might have carried the boy to Nazi headquarters—she would have slipped on the way and broken her leg, and someone would have brought Michel to the Temple. She might have flung him off the bridge into the icy Char—an eagle would have brought him to the Temple. Michel was safe from all human powers; the issue was not his physical existence, but salvation or damnation, the eternal life or eternal death of his people.

Mother Veronica went to Mme Quertsch in the reception room. As she listened to the woman's tale, the chant of the nuns in the chapel came faintly to her ears; and at the same time her hearing was intent on the boulevard and the sound of traffic. Mme Quertsch did not notice her distraction; the poor creature, disheveled, her eyes asquint and staring with despair, was near hysteria as she spoke. The child's name was Michel Benedek. His parents, Jews, had been deported. Shortly before, however, the father, Dr. Benedek, had asked her, Mme Quertsch, to find a secure place for the boy. She had done so; at her instance, the nuns of St. Vincent de Paul's in Gade had taken him in. But when the Nazis got the parents, there was no one to pay the boy's keep, and in addition the nuns of St. Vincent's had lost their nerve. They sent for her to come and get the boy. This was the boy. For God's sake, what was she to do with him? Her neighbors had noticed; one of them was bound to talk. And then a friend had told her that the Dames of the Temple had certain contacts— She threw herself on the mother superior's mercy. A child's life was at stake.

How sharply Mother Veronica remembered her dismay, her incredulity at the irony of her situation! Of all the times the woman had picked! The boy had to be gotten out of there at once, and the less explained the better. She had never known the woman's name, but upon seeing her she recalled having come across her now and then, associated, in a humble capacity, with Catholic charity drives. It was not enough for confidences. She could not tell her that the Gestapo might be heading for the Temple at that very instant, that anywhere in Touville would be safer for a Jewish orphan than where he was. She pointed out instead, with calculated coldness, that the convent school was for girls only, and that the appearance of a male child—under school age at that—would arouse dangerous suspicions. She rose to her feet, terminating the interview. Speechless with the disappearance of her last desperate hope, Mme Quertsch gathered up the sleeping child, whom she had deposited on a chair. At the door Mother Veronica asked her if she was acquainted with Mlle Rose, at the Municipal Nursery. The woman was too lost in her fears to understand the significance of the question. She nodded dumbly and stood waiting. "Take the boy there," Mother Veronica said. "You may mention my name. Do you understand? Take the boy there. Hurry now."

What obscure curiosity or compassion impelled her at that moment to lift the end of the shawl Mme Quertsch had wrapped about the boy's head? She saw that gesture now, engraved in her memory as if it had been done with full awareness of its fateful consequence, as if she had known in advance that her whole life had been nothing more than a preparation for what was about to happen. Again, in her mind's eye, she saw the lovely face of a boy not yet three, fresh as a new leaf; the lips parted, as now; the eyelids, faintly veined in blue, quivering slightly as he slept. Something touched her heart; and a voice spoke, saying, "This is the One."

How long she stood, transfixed, she could not tell. She was holding her hands to her temples, staring at Mme Quertsch, who had recoiled from her and was edging toward the door as if to run. Had she cried out? If so, her ears, possessed as they were by the unbearable sweetness of that voice, retained no echo of her own. Certainly the woman had not heard the words that fulfilled the promise. Sister Blanche appeared at that moment, and Mother Veronica, with the last remnant of her self-possession, sent her for Sister Marie. She asked Mme Quertsch not to leave just yet, and sat down to gather her thoughts. When the two nuns came to her, eying her face in alarm, she sent them with a message to Mlle Rose. Then, telling Mme Quertsch to follow them and to allow them to arrive before her, she withdrew to her quarters and sank to her knees at the *prie-dieu*. "This is the One," she repeated over and over again. At last! She could have wept with joy. Her body still vibrated to that mighty sound, like a church bell struck by its brazen tongue.

Yet her part was not clear still. Why the voice? Why had she been told? She had already advised Mme Quertsch where to take the boy, and there was no safer refuge she could think of, even knowing its importance. Would the Nazis come for her? Then it was God's will that she should know what she had done, to make bearable the coming trial. If not, then that message was to prepare her to fulfill the further role for which she had been chosen.

Two days later she learned that the agent had died under torture, without giving her away. The prayer she said for the peace of his soul was also a prayer of thanks that God had found her worthy.

"Paris," said Sister Marie Madeleine, looking brightly at her superior. Mother Veronica did not hear her. Her eyes were fixed on Michel's face. Sister Marie Madeleine, seeing those unshed tears, sank back in her seat and crossed herself in wonder.

PART TWO

January 1949–January 1953

1

❧

Place Chapelle was almost deserted. The shopfront grilles, pulled down to the ground, presented their vacant, corrugated stare at the few passersby who hurried along, their heads bent against the edged wind that whipped over the surrounding rooftops and sent bits of debris and scraps of paper swirling in little eddies over the pavement. Standing on the traffic island in the square, Konrad waited until the streetcar he had just alighted from had gone on, then crossed over rutted crusts of gray ice to the sidewalk.

The clock in the church façade marked a little after nine; a bit early of a Sunday morning to be calling on people he hardly knew. The Immermanns would be tired after their long journey, were probably still asleep. But he was full of impatience. Colbert's telephone call had filled him with the need for action, now that the end was in sight and all that was lacking was the last link. He would listen at the Immermanns' door before knocking, he decided. He began to walk toward the Grand' Rue.

Colbert, he thought. Manfrédi through Lévy. Arnauld. Rose. Himself. That made five. Only Immermann was needed to make up the six, and now he had come, at last, just when Konrad was beginning to cast about in his mind for alternatives. He was glad he had not been forced into such a step. Immermann was important to him, for having been a member of the original Council. With Immermann he had a good team, one presenting a moral force and indignation that would crush the Rose woman's pretensions. Of course, he reflected cautiously, Immermann was somewhat of an unknown quantity; although the man had written to the procureur in protest, and demanded reinstatement in the Council, his reply to Konrad had had its note of reserve. He couldn't believe, Immermann had written, that Odette Rose would do such a thing, for the motives ascribed to her. Yes, but Immermann had been away and didn't know what had been going on; he would soon be convinced, as the others had been. All the others, that is, except that coward Instettin.

Striding along the sidewalk, his cheeks beginning to smart from the wind, Konrad made a grimace of distaste to think of Instettin, with his round, sly, floury face and his few wisps of hair plastered over his shiny skull. What kind of a Jew was this, who had learned so little from his own experience? "There will be trouble." And "I'm a baker, I bake bread, do you want me to lose my license?" A good tool for Mlle Rose, who had summoned him in the first place only because he had once supplied the Nursery with bread, and hoped to win her favor again. And because she needed a Jew, any Jew, to give color to her show of concern for the boy. Well, it was better this way, because, having got rid of that weakling, he had thought of the pharmacist Arnauld who, unlike Instettin, had known Dr. Benedek, and at this juncture carried additional weight for *not* being a Jew. Bake bread, Instettin! And if your right hand lose its cunning, for having forgotten Jerusalem?

There were Jews and Jews. Never in the history of his people had there been a time when circumstances pointed more ineluctably in a single direction than now; never had it been clearer that Jewry had to unite in a common aim, leaving petty differences for some future generation, which could apply to them the leisure and the peace that were being won now, in the jealously defended *kibbutzim* of the recovered homeland. Did an Instettin think, like the blackbird that challenged heaven on the first warm day of spring, that winter would never come again? He would go on shoveling lumps of dough into his ovens on his long paddles, until one day they would be wrenched from his hands by the robots of the new Hitler, whatever he might call himself. Surprise! Consternation! That this should be happening to an innocent man, who had always minded his own business! Or a Rabbi Notarius, who thought he was as French as the next man. But at least a Notarius worked for Zionism, he was blind only in one eye, he saw the way history was pointing, for the others, if not for himself.

On the other hand, there was Mme Manfrédi, the doctor's widow, who planned for herself and not for others. He had called on her because, when he telephoned her to ask for the address of the other Manfrédi in Paris, she had said she had to look for it and it would be best if he came by personally to pick it up. But he suspected, after he had been there a few minutes, that it was to have someone to talk to.

A tiny woman, lean and withered, with bright, indomitable eyes like openings in a parchment mask, her jeweled hand resting on a black-thorn stick. She was alone in the world, she said; and yet she had had three sons. She said it without self-pity, to explain why she was going to Israel. She wanted to die among her kind. She was studying Hebrew; she brought him her book, and haltingly read several sentences to him. The hope of Israel, she said, patting the book. A home and a language. Looking down at the woman, who stood hardly higher than his elbow, hearing the familiar words over which he had pored in his childhood, Konrad thought of his mother. What would she do in Israel, this frail old lady of seventy? Everybody served for something, she said, divining his thought. If all she did was to plant one orange tree . . . Very well, why not? Israel was for all, the land that would flow once again with milk and honey. But why did she deny that right to the Benedek boy? She knew why he wanted her brother-in-law's address; she gave it to him; but she balked at his purpose. Mlle Rose had earned the boy, she said; the twig was bent, let it grow. It was better for the boy to be a good French Catholic than a neurotic Israeli Jew. Wholeness was what counted. God would know how to sort out his own again when the time came.

He hadn't argued with her. Against such oracular platitudes there was no defense. But her words had rankled in him ever since, and in his own mind he had often answered them. Mlle Rose had earned the boy? And the Benedeks themselves? Driven from what they thought of as their homeland, murdered because they were Jews, hadn't they earned the right for their son to be a Jew and have a true homeland? Suppose, dear lady, that it had been one of your own sons? Would you have thrown him to the enemy so lightly? Bent twigs, wholeness, bosh! Who had bent the twig?

How blind they were, these people who couldn't see as far as to-morrow! Not even a Moses with his stone tablets fresh from God could make them all walk together to the Promised Land. There would always be some who longed for the fleshpots of Egypt, at the price of slavery and death. Now, come to think of it, there was a similar period for you. Yes, the times were much alike, then and now, times in which the fate of Jewry depended on the turning taken, and the answer staring them all in the face. Well, there were many who turned back, who perished in the desert; but the others, they were the ones worth fighting for.

Who did he think he was, Moses? Ha! He grinned mirthlessly at the notion, crossing the opening of Grand' Rue at the end of the square. A little way down the block a narrow street made a gap in the buildings. East end of Place Chapelle, Colbert had said. First street to the left, first door to the right. Top floor. Hardly a street, he thought. It looked more like an alley. He had passed it a hundred times and never known its name. There the Immermanns were, back from America, with no suspicion that their privacy was about to be invaded. What kind of Jews were they? Not like Instettin, surely, since they had protested; but would they be like Mme Manfrédi, say that the Rose woman had "earned" the boy, talk about leaving well enough alone? The remark in their letter about the Rose woman's motives worried him. And he remembered, too, that Hannah had written them a letter in the spring of 1945, before the Family Council was summoned, and in spite of that Immermann had voted along with the rest to make Mlle Rose the guardian. Well, he would soon see. Both Colbert and Dr. Lévy knew them, said they were fine people. Only he, Konrad, would be more reassured if they had ever showed up at any of the Zionist meetings.

He thought of the Immermanns as he remembered them in their shop, before the Vichy decrees had forced them out of business. They had stood behind the delicatessen counter, wearing aprons, big, fleshy, cheerful persons, both of them. She might have been anything, to look at her; a full, florid face with a humorous quirk to her lips, large, black eyes, a thatch of sandy hair. As for Immermann, his Jewishness was unmistakable, not only in his arched regal nose that reminded Konrad of the caricatures that appeared in German newspapers, but also in the sensitivity of the lip, the dark gentle air that accorded so strangely with the great, unwieldy stature of the man. They had a slight accent, he more than she, that indicated a German origin, like the name; they had waited on him with that glint of recognition that showed they guessed him to be of the secret brotherhood; and they made good sour pickles. This was the sum of his knowledge of them; almost nothing. How could he have told then that they would be so important to him now?

If his life had been different, he thought, he might have learned to be more outgoing, more amiable, more skilled in the human contacts that smoothed your way and let people accept you. If the Immermanns had remained strangers to him, it was his fault, not theirs. They had been friendly enough in the shop, would no doubt have responded to any overture of his. It had not occurred to him to make any such overture. He avoided people, had always avoided them, happiest when he was let alone. A hater, Rabbi Notarius said. A strange duck, in Dr.Lévy's term. Unsociable, cold, grim, even in his own view. Whose fault was it? Walking toward the alley, Konrad asked himself the question. Wasn't it this same twentieth-century world, which had molded him into what he was, with no concern for what he wanted to be? Plant a tree; then kick it, bend it, pour refuse on it, let pigs loose to root about it; and wonder why it does not grow straight and tall and give goodly fruit.

A Moses? Say rather a St. Paul, but in reverse. Saul of Tarsus, that visionary epileptic, had started out to save the Jews, and had ended by becoming the apostle of the Gentiles. Unable to rest until he had set the world on fire, he turned against his own kind and destroyed those he could not win over. A would-be messiah without a following, he made a god out of a poor, itinerant rabbi, who was as meek and lovable as he himself was not; and when the Jews wouldn't have this creature of his, concocted out of fragments of the myths of the Mediterranean basin, Paul softened the rigors of the Mosaic law to make it tolerable to those unfit to bear the yoke, foisted it upon the unsuspecting *goy,* and made the whole world Jew.

What a revenge! Konrad stopped for a moment to stare unseeingly before him. Nietzsche was right to call the man the greatest hater of them all; but Nietzsche, madman himself, thought Paul animated by hatred of the world, whereas it was his fellow Jews he was out to get. For, rejected by his brethren, he left them guilty of having turned up their noses at what their Roman conquerors themselves were soon to accept, and thus prepared the way for everything that happened to them since. Saul of Tarsus become Paul of Rome, progenitor of the ghetto and the pogrom—had he foreseen genocide, this latest spawn of his?

Continuing on his way, Konrad decided that he was no St. Paul either. There was no revenge in his mind, only the determination at whatever cost not to be trampled on any more, either in himself or in any of those the world had forced into a common cause.

He had come to the mouth of the alley. There was no sidewalk. Perhaps ten feet of rutted stone-block paving, covered with slicks and mounds of dirty ice, separated the building walls, which rose on both sides to uneven heights of three and four stories, their windows staring haphazardly at each other. An agile man, Konrad reflected, gazing up at the broken slice of sky between the jagged rooftops, could easily jump from one side to the other, far over the heads of those walking below. Perhaps more than one did, in those days when death stalked the land, and salvation sometimes lay in an emergency trap-door exit.

He walked down the alley, which curved off to the right a little way before him. Just beyond the curve, invisible from the corner, was the entrance he was looking for. You could come out and peer around at the street before deciding to risk it; or you could go the other way, down the alley, and lose yourself in the connecting maze. Konrad smiled wryly as he went up the stairs. The psychology of the field mouse, the rabbit, the mole—those creatures that burrow into the ground away from their enemies. Would he never lose that habit of mind?

He had arrived at the fourth-floor landing facing a closed door. From behind it came the sound of wrenched nails and the clatter of falling wood. They were at home then, and awake. He rang the bell.

"We just got in yesterday," Lise Immermann said. "I ran out to do some quick shopping for dinner, and bumped into Colbert. He was in a hurry too, and we could hardly exchange three words. But he told me the Council's going to meet soon, and that you wanted to see us. I'd have called you last night, but of course our phone's disconnected. So I'm glad you came, even though the house is a mess. But never mind that, we'll have a talk and get to the bottom of this. Jules! Put some wood on the fire, the man's frozen."

Immermann was already at the fireplace, poking up the smoldering log. So far he had not said a word. It had been his wife who had done all the talking. She had answered the bell, standing bulky in the doorway in a sweater and slacks, her face pink as with exercise, a claw hammer in her hand. In spite of the years, he would have recognized her anywhere; full-fleshed yet shapely, she had not changed. "You're Konrad," she had said, her shrewd, appraising eyes taking him in; and when he nodded, disconcerted by the bluntness of the greeting and wondering how she had put together the stranger who came to the shop so long ago and the signature of the letter he had written them, she had seized him by the elbow as if he might have escaped and had cried out, "Jules! Here's Konrad to talk to us about little Michel!" Over her shoulder he had seen a broad, low-ceilinged room whose furniture was covered with sheets; a large, half-open crate standing in the middle of the floor; and in the passageway at the rear, Immermann in a bathrobe with a barrel hugged to his chest, a look of mild curiosity on his dark, beaked, unshaven face. He had set the barrel down gently and come forward, beaming silent welcome, and then dedicated himself to clearing a space for Konrad on the sofa, removing boxes and wrapping paper, whisking off the dust cover, and gesturing for him to sit down. He was not a talker, Konrad decided, watching as the man broke slats of wood across his knee and placed them carefully on the log.

Lise Immermann had leaned across the top of the crate and was regarding Konrad with curiosity. "For heaven's sake," she said, "will you please tell us what this is all about? We've been wondering ever since we got your letter. How did you get into this anyway? Jules and I came to the conclusion that you must have known Karl after we went into hiding. Otherwise he'd have mentioned you to us. Of course, we knew you from the shop, although you were something of a mystery in those days."

"A mystery?" he said.

She laughed, showing splendid white teeth. "Nobody knew much about you. Or rather, they knew such contradictory things. The other customers, I mean. Someone said you were a scientist working with poison gas. Someone else said you made shoe polish. What else? Oh yes, you were a key man in the Communist party. Things like that. We couldn't place you, and then, of course, you had such a brooding look! Like Svengali, or something. You're from Silesia, aren't you? Someone told us your name was Konrad, and that he had seen you in a village somewhere in Silesia."

"That's strange," he commented dryly. "I've never been in Silesia. I'm from Austria originally."

"Ah!" she said. "Like Karl and Lili. But surely you didn't know them there?"

Immermann had sunk into a chair, after offering Konrad a cigar and at his refusal lighting it himself. Letting the smoke trickle from his mouth, he suggested, "Maybe you should give the man a chance, Lise."

Konrad surveyed them both in some perplexity. Why did the woman insist that he must have known the Benedeks? Was that the only reason she could conceive of that would make him take an interest in their child? But he had written them that he was acting for Hannah Lindner, who had given him her power of attorney. On the other hand, he had suddenly understood the cautious terms of Immermann's reply to his letter: they had associated his name with the stranger they had speculated about in former years, and about whom they had heard such contradictory things; they had no reason to have confidence in such a man. What a lot of idiotic rumors had passed about the Jewish community in those days! Like a bunch of hysterical women!

They were watching him expectantly; although their eyes were friendly, their attitude said clearly, Who are you?

"You know Dr. Lévy," he said. "Why don't you ask him about me?"

"Oh," she said blankly. "You know Lévy?"

"For a long time. So have you, I understand. He tells me he helped you escape in 1943. Ask him, I'm sure he'll give me a good name. In spite of my appearance." He could not help this last dig; the remark about poison gas had rankled.

"Oh," she said again. "I didn't mean—! They don't come any finer than Lévy. You know he was decorated?"

He nodded. "He's to be a member of the Council too, by the way. He'll represent Dr. Manfrédi, who would find it difficult to come from Paris for the meetings. And since Mitzi Benedek, Albert's widow, gave her power of attorney to Manfrédi, both aunts will have a voice in the Council. That should assure you that everything is open and aboveboard. No," he went on, seeing her gesture, "you were right to have your doubts. Why should you trust me, after all? Incidentally, since you attach so much importance to it, I did know Karl Benedek, though that's not the reason I became interested in his boy."

He told them about the visit the doctor had made to his home to tend to Judas. When he had finished, husband and wife looked at each other in wonder.

"You saw him only that one time?" she demanded. "And he said nothing to you about Michel?"

"Why should he?" he asked.

"But then, why are you after him? I mean, what reason would you have—?"

"Itzik and Hannah Lindner wrote to me. I knew Itzik as a boy, and when they found out I was living in Touville, they asked me to help. In the letter I wrote you—"

"They wrote to you *first*?" It was Immermann who spoke, leaning forward in his chair and removing his cigar from his mouth, while his wife came around the crate and stood before Konrad, her hands on her hips in the attitude of What next?

He stared from one to the other. He said slowly, "Yes, certainly. How else would I know? Or get involved in a family affair?"

"And so it was Hannah!" Lise Immermann's voice had an edge of bitterness to it. "And we thought it was your idea! That you had got after her to protest. We couldn't figure out why. It was Hannah after all. She can't make up her mind, it seems."

Where had he heard that before? It had a familiar ring. Rabbi Notarius' face came before him. It couldn't be, he thought. The woman wouldn't have dared! He was beginning to rise to his feet when Lise Immermann said, "First she tells Odette to keep the boy, and then she decides she wants him after all. No wonder Odette got mad."

Oh no! Konrad said wearily to himself, completing his movement and finding himself staring at Lise Immermann's angry face a few inches from his own. Are we going to have to go through this again? How many more, for God's sake? Let there be an end to it once and for all.

"Please sit down, Madame Immermann," he said grimly. "I have a long and somewhat complicated story to tell you."

"The poor woman!" Lise Immermann said.

Konrad gazed at her in some exasperation. He had expected annoyance, anger, recriminations—anything but pity. The Rose woman had deceived them shamelessly; he had laid the proof before them; and yet Lise Immermann's immediate reaction, like that of Rina, had been a surge of sentimental compassion for the deceiver. How much she must love the boy, to have gone to such lengths to keep him! The poor woman! And her husband said nothing, did nothing but chew reflectively at his stub of cigar.

He said coldly, "And Hannah?"

"Oh," she said, contrite, "I didn't mean— Of course, she must be desperate. All these years! We didn't know. We thought that if she could do a thing like that to her brother's child—well, we were pretty mad at her, Jules and I. We had wondered in the first place why she hadn't come for Michel, but there could have been a lot of reasons. After all, Australia! But then she does show up, at least that's what Odette told me, and refuses to take him. So this is Karl's sister, we said, the one he was always bragging about! His second mother, he used to say. She's quite a bit older than Karl, you know. And we were hurt, too. Maybe it was petty on our part, but to pop in and out like that, and not to come see her brother's closest friends! Or even let us know she was coming. We were pretty bitter about it."

Konrad said he could understand that, at that time. But why feel sorry for Mlle Rose now, after learning what she had done?

"My God, Konrad," she said, "what do you want? Didn't you ever tell a lie? She's human too. I'm sorry for both of them. You don't know Odette as I do. She's dedicated her life to her children. Michel isn't the only one. And now that the new Council is going to take him away from her—"

"Ah!" he said triumphantly, "you agree then?"

She looked at him in astonishment. "What else can it do? Family is family, after all. Jules?"

Immermann nodded, saying briefly, "Yes." And he added, shaking his head, "But I don't like it."

"Neither do I," she said, sighing. "But it can't be helped."

Konrad sank back in his seat. He had what he had come for. Immermann would serve, like it or not, on the new Council. His team was complete. Five against one. Or against two, if Judge Cerval persisted in voting as he had the first time. In any case, an overwhelming majority. And Lise Immermann might feel sorry for Odette Rose, but there was a kind of poetic justice in the woman's being trapped in the net of lies she had woven herself.

"Now," Lise Immermann said, "let's have some coffee."

They met the Benedeks in 1938, Lise Immermann said. They themselves had settled in France years before, first in Lyons, and then opening their delicatessen shop in Touville. It had been hard going in the beginning, but then things improved; and of course, when Hitler came to power in Germany, they congratulated themselves on having got out. After 1936 refugees began to trickle into Touville and found their way to the Immermanns' shop, to buy the kind of food they were used to at home, and to exchange impressions. Their place became a kind of clearinghouse for news and bartering. The Benedeks came after the Anschluss. One day Lili entered the shop, stayed to chat when she learned that they spoke German, asked if they knew anyone who wanted to buy a coat; she had a splendid wrap-around lined with mink, Karl's wedding present to her. It broke her heart to get rid of it, but of course they were in a bad way; they had been able to take out very little from Austria, and Karl's clandestine practice brought in next to nothing. The Immermanns found a customer for the coat, Karl came to thank them, and this was the beginning of their friendship.

The Immermanns helped the refugee doctor establish himself in Touville. They found him the room in Puy-le-Duc, introduced him about, recommended him to patients, coached him in French. Every day Karl came down from the hill across the river, and made his first stop at the Immermanns, to see what was doing. Sometimes he stopped in again on his way home. And every Sunday he and Lili came to the house, to this apartment, and spent the afternoon and evening, with dinner in between.

"And we talked," Lise Immermann said. "My God, how we talked! They trusted so few people, you see. When they came to us on a Sunday they had a whole week of bottled-up conversation to get through. We'd all be limp as rags when it was time for them to go. But next week here they'd be again, and we just as eager to see them."

Medicine was Karl's religion, she said. That was the one thing you couldn't joke about with him. He used to pace up and down here, in front of the sofa, explaining the great new things that were being done, that the war had interrupted. You'd think, to listen to him, that he was angry at the whole mess more for that than for anything else. What interested him above all was radiology; he felt that it was the coming science, and he was eager to get into research. But of course, with things the way they were . . . God? The soul? Heaven and hell? Don't bother him with that, he was a doctor.

And, incidentally, a good one, Lise Immermann said; and her husband nodded. In fact, more reliable as a medical man than as a human being. She had loved Karl like a brother, but that didn't blind her to his faults. The man was pigheaded, there was no other word for it. He'd swear that black was white, when the mood was on him, and shout you down when you tried to make him see reason. Why hadn't he gone to Australia when he could, for example? she demanded. His sister had begged him to come. But it had to be his way, or not at all. His brother Albert was like that, too, according to the stories Karl told about him. They sent the man to Dachau, gave him a taste of it. Then they released him and warned him to get out of the country. No, he said, it was *his* country. And now his ashes were in one of those urns they put them in to send to their widows. And imagine, Karl was proud of him for it.

He had his selfish streak too. In fact, that was the cause of their most violent quarrel. He came to them shortly before they went into hiding, all excited. For twenty thousand francs he could bribe someone and get a visa for somewhere in South America. It meant life for him and his family. He wanted the Immermanns to lend him the money, and promised to pay them back out of his first earnings.

"We refused," Lise Immermann said. "We had to refuse. It would have wiped us out. It wasn't a question of his paying us back. By the time he could do that it wouldn't matter if he did or not. We needed it to survive right then. It was all we had. In fact, we didn't have that much, although almost. Never mind, he said, give it to him, and he'd piece it out elsewhere. He just couldn't understand our attitude, and kept repeating it was his life. And Lili's and Michel's. Finally I had to tell him right out, in so many words, that it was his life and our death, and that it wasn't fair. He didn't have the right to ask us that. You'd have thought we were Gestapo, the way he looked at us. As though we'd stabbed him in the back. He went away furious, and we didn't see him for weeks. Jules couldn't stand it any longer and went over to Puy-le-Duc, and Karl threw him out. But Karl must have thought it over, because the next Sunday they came to visit us as if nothing had happened, and never mentioned it again."

Lili wasn't like that at all. She was a nice, sweet, gentle creature who looked at her husband when you asked her if she wanted the salt. A typical Austrian *Hausfrau,* Lise Immermann said, with a frankly self-conscious laugh at herself for being so different. Her solution for everything was to cry, as if that would change things for the better. But a good wife for Karl, who had a need to assert himself, someone to baby and dominate at the same time. But she had her moods too. There were times when despair got hold of her, and then there wasn't anything you could do with her, she saw everything black. Like when the baby was born. They put Michel in her arms, and even then he was a beautiful thing, and Lili began to cry and said, "He's too beautiful to live, he's going to croak." *Krepieren,* Lise Immermann said, in the German Lili had used, and Konrad winced at the harsh word.

She fell silent, her face suddenly sad. For the moment, lost in her reminiscences of her friends, she had put out of her mind what had happened to them. Her husband sighed, and lit a fresh cigar from the stump of the other. Konrad stared woodenly at the floor.

"He insisted on circumcising the boy, atheist and all. I think he just didn't dare not to. He was like the Catholic who does his Easter duty, and that's it for the year. So long as he goes that day he feels he still belongs, that there's some hope for him. There are Jews like that too. There's one," she said, pointing at her husband. "Dietary laws? Keeping a kosher house? Observing the Passover? That's all nonsense. But he fasts on Yom Kippur, and goes about the house wearing a skullcap and a long face. A Jew for a day."

Immermann observed mildly that an occasional fast was good for the system.

"Ha!" she said in scorn. "That's what Karl said too. He circumcised the boy for hygienic reasons. But he got mad when I asked him if he thought it was wise, at that moment. I mean, he got *too* mad, stomping up and down and hollering that he wasn't going to let those pigs stop him from doing what he thought he ought to do. So I thought, You and your hygienic reasons! Poor Karl!" she said, smiling, but with a sudden break in her voice. "He was really such a wonderful person. His moods and bad temper didn't mean a thing. It was just nerves. The responsibility. I used to catch him looking at Lili and the boy with a certain expression on his face, as if he were estimating his own strength. Once Lili came to me sobbing that Karl didn't love her any more, but that wasn't so. It was just that he took everything on himself, you see, because she was so—well, so helpless, and at times it got to be too much for him, and he flared up."

"Tell him about the boy," Immermann said.

"Now that," she said with sudden animation, "was really something! When it came to Michel, you never saw such a fussy old hen in your life. You'd have thought *he* was the mother, the way he held him, and fed him and took care of him. Nobody else could do a thing for him, not even Lili, not when Karl was around. They used to bring him here with them, and at the dinner table Karl would hold him on his lap and eat with one hand, one bite for himself and the other for Michel. When it was time for his nap, Karl put him on the couch in the other room, and every couple of minutes he'd go in there to look at him. He'd come out and say, He's asleep, or, He turned over. The whole world was at war, we didn't know whether we'd still be here tomorrow—but we always knew which side Michel was sleeping on. You know," she said to Konrad, "I went in there once after him, and he was sitting on the floor by the couch, holding

Michel's hand. The boy was asleep, he was maybe a year old at the time, and Karl had his hand in his, just looking at it. Like a fortune-teller or something. And his face was so sad that it made me want to cry. Later, when I heard what had happened to Karl, I remembered that expression, and that's how I remember him best today."

She looked at Konrad speculatively. "You know how they got him?"

Konrad nodded. He didn't want to hear that again.

By the spring of 1943 the Immermanns knew they had to get out. They had lost the shop, there was nothing to hold them in Touville. Besides, there were rumors that the Germans were going to take over the Free Zone from the Italians, who were too lenient. Dr. Lévy made the arrangements for them, placing them in a village in the Isère, where they worked in the fields by day, and by night shared an attic room in the village inn. Others had taken shelter in the area as well. Their identity was an open secret in the countryside, but nobody gave them away. On the contrary, the farmers and villagers, many of whom no doubt had grumbled against the Jews before the war, took a perverse pride in protecting them now. These were *their* Jews, let Vichy dare lay a hand on them! They posted lookouts, and if agents came snooping around, or if they heard a car approach— who had a car any more but the enemy?—a warning was sounded, and those who had reasons to do so took to the woods. It was not too bad a summer, especially since they were together.

After the harvest, however, there was little excuse for an able-bodied man to be hanging about the village; and that fall the Nazis *did* enter the Free Zone; and so, with his false papers, Jules took a job on the night shift of an electric plant several miles away. Lise stayed on at the inn, and to give color to her presence put on an apron and helped out in the kitchen. The joke of it was that the Germans quartered some officers at the inn, and Lise found herself in the position of cooking for them and even serving their table. To them she was French, of course, and couldn't understand what they were saying among themselves. It was all she could do to keep a straight face listening to their conversation, especially when one of them, a rather shy, middle-aged captain and not bad-looking either, got a crush on her, and the others kidded him about it in front of her. And poor Jules on his night shift, with his free hours during the day and not daring to show his nose at the inn, with those officers in and out at unpredictable times! He used to come afternoons and wait for her in the garden, and she'd run out to him when she got the chance. Standing in the snow, like a lovesick tomcat, with such a look on his face!

Immermann beamed fondly at her. "My feet freezing," he said, "and I should smile yet!"

It was not until their return to Touville after the Liberation that the Immermanns learned what had happened to Karl and Lili. It was a hard blow for them, and they reproached themselves bitterly for not having persuaded the Benedeks to go into hiding, as they themselves had done. Not that they hadn't tried, Lise assured Konrad; but there was no moving Karl, who got angry about it and said it was all very well for them, they had no children. Yet, perhaps, if they had tried a little harder . . . The ironic thing about it all was that Karl had managed to avoid being caught as long as he had, and then got picked up in that haphazard way only a few months before the Allied invasion. At least, they preferred to believe it was by chance; Konrad knew as well as they that there was many a man walking about Touville today who had sent Jews to their deaths with a word in the right quarter. And Karl must have aroused resentment among the other doctors for practicing on the sly as he did, to earn his crust of bread. It was best not to examine the ugly thing too closely. You found yourself wondering about other things. Whether the informer, if there was one, had also told them of the room in Puy-le-Duc. If so, why didn't they pick him up there? And if not, and the informer had simply pointed Karl out to them on the street, then what could one suppose but that it was Karl himself who—?

Lise's voice faltered and broke off. There were some things, Konrad thought, stealing a glance at her face, that ought not be put into words. He himself, in the many times he had brooded about it, imagining how the doctor walked off with a Vichy agent at each side, had deliberately not let himself dwell on what must have followed. Nobody had the right to judge Karl Benedek; nobody, not even his wife Lili, rocking in her chair with the capsule in her hand, waiting to see whether the police, having captured her husband, would now know where to find her.

She and Jules, Lise said after a long silence, had often wondered about Lili. You could never tell about people; who would have thought that she had the courage to do what she did? They would never know why she did it, that is, what went on in her mind. Maybe she simply gave up, lost her will to live, saw no way to survive without Karl to take care of her. That was the first thing that occurred to Lise when she heard the news, for as fond as she was of Lili, she had to admit that the girl lacked strength of character. But Jules, with the example of his mother before him, took another view. He had always felt that Lili had character enough, but had learned to subordinate herself to Karl, because his ego needed it and he took on so when he was crossed in anything. Spineless people didn't commit suicide; it wasn't that, but the child; she wasn't going to risk breaking down and telling them where he was.

Konrad had thought of that too. He looked down at his clasped hands, but not before he had noticed that Lise's face had suddenly become stricken, as if she had said more than she intended. Jules's mother? he wondered. Immermann's expression had not changed, yet there was a new tenseness in that big, ungainly body in the armchair. There was a story there, Konrad was sure; and he was just as sure that he would not ask about it.

Naturally, Lise said with a swift glance at her husband, they called at the Nursery to see Michel. In spite of their joy at finding him alive, it was an awkward moment, since the boy had no idea of what had happened to his parents and would have to be told something when he asked about them. Fortunately, he didn't ask, for the very good reason that he had forgotten the Immermanns in the year and a half they had been away; he was, after all, only two when they left. And so they hadn't had to give any explanations; they were his godparents, they said, and Michel accepted that without any fuss. He was well enough. A trifle thin, perhaps, but apparently in good health; quiet, well-behaved, remarkably handsome; and sad, as if he suspected the truth. And yet it would seem that he didn't, for during one of Lise's later visits he told her, with what seemed to be sincere conviction, that his father was coming for him.

"Well, now," she demanded, turning toward Konrad, "what were we to think of Odette Rose? I'll tell you what I thought, that she was an angel sent by God. I fell into her arms and blessed her and cried like a baby. And, if you want to know the truth, Jules cried too, even if he won't admit it. We were a bit hysterical, I think. If at that moment she had asked us to cut off our right arms, I believe we would have done it. You've proved that she lied to us about Hannah. All those letters and documents and appeals! The Red Cross, the

Foreign Ministry, the procureur and all the rest of it. All right, there's no arguing with facts. But if you think that lie can make me forget the Odette Rose who saved Michel, you're mistaken. I'll always be grateful to her for that."

"And so would I," Konrad said, "if only she hadn't kept him."

He ought to be going, Konrad reflected. It was getting late, and the Immermanns had their unpacking to do. But they showed no inclination to stop their flood of reminiscences; and as for him, he was eager to hear anything they could tell him to help fill up the background. There was one matter especially that still puzzled him: the Family Council. How could Immermann have voted for Mlle Rose, knowing what he knew? For all his wife's chattiness, she had not broached the subject; and Konrad had begun to feel that she was avoiding it deliberately. Were they ashamed? It *had* been a betrayal, in effect, if not in intention. And what could his intention possibly have been? Konrad did not want to ask. It was enough that the man was ready to rectify his mistake.

The question clarified itself unexpectedly. Lise Immermann, speculating about when Odette Rose had decided to keep Michel for herself, decided that it had to be some time during the year 1946. Konrad, who supposed that the woman had intended to keep the boy from the very first, asked what her reasoning was. The Council, she said. That was held in November 1945. And Odette told her that fib about Hannah in November a year later. The word "fib" jarred Konrad; but he let it pass by in his lack of comprehension of what she was getting at. What did the Council have to do with it? Didn't he see? she said. At that date Odette still planned to send Michel to Hannah. That was why she called the Council.

It was such a contradiction that he could only stare at her. Mlle Rose had called the Council to have herself elected guardian. To defy Hannah. How could Lise Immermann say—?

"Of course," she insisted, spreading her hands in an eloquent gesture. "Didn't you know that? Odette came to see us, in September, I think—"

"October," Immermann corrected softly.

"Was it October?" She frowned. "Well, in October, then. She said she had decided to set up a Council, because she had no official status in regard to Michel and couldn't get him his passport. To send him to Australia. Her lawyer had advised her that a Council could appoint her provisional guardian, and that would give her the authority she needed. It was just a temporary arrangement, to cut through the red tape and get Michel on his way. She asked Jules to be a member, and naturally—"

"Just a moment!" Konrad's voice was harsh. The woman's statement had caught him by surprise. Now he saw such a glaring flaw in it that he could not restrain his rude interruption. It was the aunt herself. Neither Colbert nor Manfrédi had known about her. Manfrédi, with whom he had exchanged several letters, had written from Paris with the testiness of the man of law who had been made a fool of that no one had told *him* of any relatives, and that if he had been fully informed, as he should have been, he certainly would not have allowed the meeting to proceed until the aunt was present, or at least represented, as the Civil Code provided. And Colbert had barked at him over the telephone, *"What* aunt?" and, at Konrad's insistence that Immermann knew of her, must have said something about her at the meeting, had rapped out an oath and replied angrily that he hadn't. In fact, Immermann hadn't opened his mouth during the entire two hours that the meeting lasted. That was inexplicable enough, Konrad had felt; but now it made less sense than before. What kind of a meeting was this, in which no mention was made of the aunt to whom the boy was supposed to be sent? What *had* they talked about, if not about Hannah? It was in this belligerent tone that Konrad put his questions, and Lise Immermann, who had been startled by his interruption, bridled and snapped, "Well, it did what it was supposed to do, which was to make Odette the guardian. Jules couldn't know then that she would change her mind and not send Michel after all. If he didn't say anything, it was because he didn't have the chance. But he wasn't the only one. No one said anything, except Odette."

"What?" he said. "For two hours?"

Immermann cleared his throat. It was a strange meeting, he said. If M. Konrad thought it important to know what happened, he— Yes, Konrad said. He was curious about what Mlle Rose could have told them in her two-hour lecture, without once touching on the purpose for which the meeting had supposedly been called.

Immermann's eyes twinkled under the sarcasm. Unruffled, he murmured, "As you say, a lecture. In fact," he said brightly, rubbing his unshaven chin with a rasping noise, "you might even call it mass hypnosis. I've often thought about it since. It's true we didn't say anything, but I wonder, given the circumstances, whether you wouldn't have done the same. I don't pretend to be anything but a grocer, but there were others there, you know. Good heads among them. Take Manfrédi, the younger one, the lawyer. He has quite a reputation at the Paris bar. His brother was a doctor, an educated man. Colbert—a sharp businessman, who knows his way around. Even Instettin. You call him a coward, but don't forget he's a coward who lived through the Occupation. We all did. I guess that constitutes a diploma of some kind. Forget me for the moment. But I think it would be pretty hard to put something over on the others. Smart Jews, all of them. But we kept quiet and listened, and when Odette finished talking, the judge called for a vote, and we all raised our hands and the meeting was over. We could have said a lot of things, but we didn't. We were ashamed."

"What?" Konrad said, wondering. He had listened with surprise and dawning respect. The man could talk, after all. Unlike his wife, who rattled on as though her tongue were hard put to keep up with her thoughts, Immermann spoke slowly, weighing and measuring each word. Words were precious, not to be wasted, were to be spoken with quiet relish, as if each had a flavor and an edge of its own. And he made sense. His beaming air of not-very-bright, sleepy good fellow was a pose. In that instant Konrad revised his estimate of this silent, mild-mannered giant.

Konrad had to remember just when it was that the Council meeting was held, Immermann began. It was in November 1945. A time that was like the awakening from a long nightmare. But the reality France had to face was scarcely less horrible. Reality was a barbaric name strange on French lips. Auschwitz. Or Belsen. Or Buchenwald. Reality was the faces of the prisoners returning from the east, or the emptiness left by those who didn't return. Reality was pillaged cities, farms without livestock, homes without a man, empty larders, fireless hearths. Rationing, and her camp follower, black marketeering. Brittle-boned children, with pipestem necks. The stark question in every newspaper: Can anyone furnish information as to the whereabouts of ———?

"We felt guilty," Immermann said, "and we couldn't bear it. We tried to justify ourselves, and we were hypocritical enough to blame Vichy for our own weakness. We could have stopped Hitler years before, at the time of the betrayal of Czechoslovakia, or even earlier, just by showing our fist. We didn't do it, out of cowardice. And so we had to bring Pétain, Laval, and the whole Vichy crew to trial, to find a scapegoat. Don't misunderstand me, they deserved to die. But for what they had done and not done, not to save the face of the rest. Pétain was tried, but it was France that was found guilty. It was a time of shame."

It was in this atmosphere, Immermann said, that the meeting of the Family Council was held. The same morbid introspection. The same sense of trial, the same shame. Five Jews met with Odette Rose to discuss the guardianship of a little boy, and found themselves being weighed in the balance.

Yet all Odette Rose did was to tell them of herself, and how she had survived the Occupation.

"The old story," Immermann said to Konrad. "Two strangers meet and tell each other how they survived the Occupation. Today we told you and you told us. Every Frenchman has told his tale to dozens. After a while the stories begin to sound alike. But I remember what Odette said, every word of it, and I imagine the others do too. And yet it couldn't have been more quietly told. It was as though she was talking to herself. As if we weren't there, and she was daydreaming aloud. And after a while you had the illusion she wasn't there either, and the voice you heard was inside you. Because we had all been through it ourselves. Everything she said—the hardships, the dangers, the fear of capture—struck memories in us that we'll carry about the rest of our lives. Why were we ashamed? Because Odette Rose isn't a Jew. She saved Jews without being one of us. It wasn't only Michel. There were others. That was in our minds the whole time she was talking. I was thinking it, and I could see it in the others' faces. She's not a Jew, I was thinking, but while we ran and hid and got false papers that let us pass for *goyim,* she stayed where she was and made herself a Jew. It amounted to that, because if she were caught, they'd have treated her like one. And we were thinking of those of us who hadn't been as lucky as we were. Of our families. Elémir Manfrédi lost his three sons, did you know? We had all lost someone—a brother, a child, parents. And I—I was thinking of my mother."

Immermann looked absently at his cigar, and put it in the ashtray at his side. "Lise mentioned her just now. In connection with Lili Benedek. You've probably guessed that they died pretty much the same way. Each for her son. Only with my mother it wasn't poison. She jumped out the window."

The quiet words hung in the air. Lise Immermann set down her coffee cup. The spoon rattled on the saucer. His mother, Konrad thought incredulously. He's talking about his mother. It happens every day: a shoelace breaks, a button comes off, a mother jumps out the window.

Immermann's voice went on, calm, unhurried, inflectionless, and terrible. "When Lise and I went into hiding, my mother refused to go with us. We were young, she said. It was safer for us to go, but it was safer for her to stay. She convinced us that she was right, and I still think so. But something went wrong, I don't know what. She was picked up somehow, and taken to the old warehouse by the river docks, that they used then as an interrogation center. You know those interrogations. When her turn came, she hurled herself at the window, and crashed through to the street. Three stories below. Cobblestones. She was badly hurt. The odd thing was that she didn't lose consciousness. There was a guard standing there by the entrance. She begged him to shoot her and put her out of her pain. He refused, and cursed her for blocking the traffic. If it had been a horse, or a dog . . . They pulled her aside to the gutter to let the trucks by. She died there, in the gutter. I don't know where she's buried. Or if she's buried. I wouldn't know this much if someone passing by hadn't recognized her lying there."

After a long silence, Immermann said gently, "You see, she knew the false name I was going under. And my address. I left them with her so that she could write to me. And she was afraid they would get that information out of her."

Konrad said nothing. There was nothing to say. What consolation would there be in saying, My mother too, a stone, more than thirty years ago . . . ? Perhaps he would tell him some day. Not now.

"To get back to the Council meeting," Immermann went on with no change in tone. "I sat there listening, and thinking that if I had known of Odette Rose and sent my mother to her, she would be alive now. Like Michel. And how different things would have been if there were more people in the world like her. And how different they would have been if *we* were more like her. We Jews. We were all thinking the same thing, and we were ashamed. It was illogical, I know, but no matter how hard I tried to justify myself, I couldn't drive the feeling away. Not if I wanted to be honest with myself. I told myself there was nothing I could have done. We were marked for slaughter, and each had to escape as best he could. There was no fighting it, except what we did. Any stand would have been suicide. The Benedeks stayed and died. So did my mother. The only way was to separate, scatter, and hope to live it through. I said all these things to myself, and then I looked at Odette Rose, and the shame was back, stronger than before. She had done what we didn't do. She risked her neck for my godson, and saved his life. She did, I didn't. I had saved my life, and not his. Sometimes you can be ashamed of just being alive."

Konrad stared into his cup. Immermann's story rankled within him. He had listened patiently to the end, curbing his rising anger as another piece of the puzzle fell into place and he realized with what contemptuous ease the Rose woman had got what she wanted. What she had always wanted, in spite of what the Immermanns might think. Yes, they had been ashamed, those five Jews who had managed to survive where so many among their families had not. He knew that shame, for years had felt it curling like a cancer in his own entrails; and he writhed inwardly to think how truly that taunting Jew-hater had judged them all, how skillfully she had measured and used their secret sorrows. You too, Immermann had said. You would have done the same thing we did. The thought was intolerable to him.

He knew now why Immermann had kept quiet, had not brought up the one piece of information that would have changed everything. Those five men who had been moved by that tragic tale that November day might admire the Rose woman's courage, might praise her, sympathize with her—but they were family men who would have recognized Hannah's claim without hesitation, if they had known about it. Mlle Rose took a big chance, and won. Because it was simply not true that she had called the Council as a means of sending the boy to Hannah. She had never intended to do so.

Did it matter? he asked himself. What difference did it make just when she had decided to keep the boy? The Immermanns had agreed that she had to be stopped; as reinstated Council member, Jules would vote against her now. Yes, but they were not angry enough. That lie, which had kept a child from his family, was a mere "fib," a peccadillo, and Odette Rose was still a saint. Let them know her for what she was, and thus be on guard in the future.

They were looking at him. He said to Immermann, "She deceived you twice. The lie about Hannah's coming to Touville was the second time. The first time was the Council itself. When she invited the other members, she said nothing about the aunt. And she counted on you not saying anything either. Her two-hour performance was directed primarily against you. To keep you quiet. Because she had no intention of sending Michel to Australia, then or any other time. Wait," he said, as Lise Immermann started to protest. "I have proofs. Take first the pretext for the Council. The passport. She said her lawyer had given her that advice. If so, he must be the same crooked lawyer who has helped her with her other shady deals. There was no need to summon a Council for that. I know something about passports. The boy didn't need one. The Red Cross would have taken him on the aunt's affidavit. Or, as an orphan, Mademoiselle Rose could have had him declared a ward of the state, and the government would have taken care of the necessary formalities for travel. But no, Mademoiselle Rose wanted the Council for her own purposes."

"But that doesn't mean—" Lise Immermann began.

"I know," he said. "It's a negative proof. But I have a positive one. The date of the Council—November 12, 1945. I thought of this before, but it seemed natural then, because the Council made her guardian. But now that I know what the purpose of the guardianship was supposed to be, what she told you it was, it sheds a different light on the lady. That's the date of the letter Mademoiselle Rose wrote to Hannah, the only letter she ever wrote to her, in answer to all her pleadings. The Council meeting was in the morning. That afternoon, or that night, Mademoiselle Rose sat down and wrote Hannah that she couldn't possibly send Michel now, he was too young. The very same day! How cynical and cold-blooded can you get? And no doubt full of triumph at her victory, and congratulating herself on how easily she had outmaneuvered five smart Jews. I think," he said meaningfully to Immermann, "that was your expression. And 'poor woman' was yours," he could not refrain from adding to the wife.

There was only one thing to do, Lise Immermann decided suddenly. She would go see Odette Rose and talk the whole thing out between them. Konrad replied dryly that he had tried that.

"Oh, not like you," she said. "Not as a stranger. And not as an emissary of the aunt either. As an old friend of hers who's known the boy since he was born. And his godmother."

Konrad shrugged. It could do no harm, he said; but he failed to see how it would do any good either.

"You men!" Lise Immermann's face had a look of amused pity. "Jules is like that too. Two and two are four. You can build bridges, but you're all like children when it comes to human relations."

"And according to you, how many are two and two?"

"Three," she said. "Three and a half. Five. Sometimes even four. It depends. That's what you call a lie, and you get all upset about it. To you Odette is a monster, because she doesn't play fair. As if life were a game! Who says you have to play fair, anyway? Men, with their codes and sense of honor! It's you who've ruined the world, if you want to know. Do you think I'm hurt because Odette lied to me? Not a bit. You could prove to me that she lied a hundred times instead of twice, and I'd still say 'poor woman.' Because that's what she is, a woman who's had to fight for everything she has. And to do some good in the world. If I were in her position, I'd lie too. Any woman would. In fact, I wouldn't be surprised if Hannah slipped a few things into her letters to you that aren't exactly so. Since she also wants Michel."

"Her story checks," Konrad said. "In every particular. But even if it didn't—"

"Exactly! She's his aunt, and ought to have him. They both want him, but Hannah has the better right. All right, I'll go to Odette and try to persuade her to give him up. No recriminations, no raking over the past, no threats. I won't say a word about what she told me. Just common sense. The good of Michel, family, his father's sister, that sort of thing. Odette must know what you're up to with the Family Council, and must realize that she can't hold out much longer. This is a good way for her to save face. She can tell people she wasn't forced to do it, she did it of her own accord. She's a heroine. Better that than come out of it with nothing but hard feelings. I know Odette, it might work."

Well, why not? Konrad thought. He saw little likelihood that such a move would succeed, but it was certainly worth a try. The worst that could happen was that the Rose woman would throw her out, as she had done to him. In that case he would be just where he was before, with no harm done. And it might have the salutary effect of teaching Lise Immermann a little basic arithmetic.

"When would you go?" he asked.

"Tomorrow," she said. "The sooner the better."

He was on the point of suggesting that she go today. Tomorrow morning he had an appointment with Judge Cerval to settle the agenda and date of the Council meeting. It would be good to know the result of the visit before then. But no, he decided, it made no difference. The Rose woman would not give in. And if she did, there was no guarantee of her sincerity, or that she would not change her mind again. No matter what promises she might make, she had to know that the Council was there, ready to take action.

"Please let me know how your visit goes," he said. "And incidentally, while you're there, you might try to find out from her where Michel is. He seems to have disappeared."

2

JUDGE CERVAL'S DESK was bare of everything except an inkwell, a blotter, a pen, half a dozen pencils, a ruler and a calendar. Not a single paper to mar its gleaming surface. An orderly mind, Konrad thought, noting how meticulously the pencils had been lined up side by side and with what care the ruler had been placed parallel to the inkwell. Too orderly. For it was clear, from the man's ramrod position in his chair, from the frown on his square-jawed, righteous face, that he was annoyed that the regularity of his proceedings had been called in question. It was not Konrad's first visit to the judge's chambers; it was, as a matter of fact, his third. And each time he had had to do battle against an attitude that boggled at details, that subjected every suggestion of his to a scrutiny that was overly meticulous. Konrad knew why, had been warned by Maître Paul to go easy and be patient. The procureur's order for a rehearing was, in effect, a reprimand to the judge who had presided over the second Council. Very well, Cerval seemed to be saying, it won't happen again. You complained? I'll show you what it's like to do it according to the book.

Thus, they had already spent a half-hour arguing over the agenda. The judge wanted to limit it to the question of the reintegration of Dr. Manfrédi as Surrogate Provisional Guardian, without prejudice to any other matters that might arise during the meeting. Konrad did not see why they should not call a spade a spade; the real purpose of the meeting was to destitute Mlle Rose as guardian and substitute Mme Lindner, and the agenda ought to say so. Cerval had thereupon entered into a maze of legal terminology that left Konrad bewildered; he gathered vaguely that there were certain forms to be observed, that it was not easy to destitute a guardianship once established, that to do so he would have to justify such a stated purpose in advance and officially cite Mlle Rose, etc. In the end they had agreed on a compromise. The meeting of the third Family Council was to "reconstitute the Family Council for the orphan Michel Benedek, and to reconsider the question of guardianship." After this Judge Cerval had consulted his calendar and set the date for the meeting: February 10, a month from today.

Konrad did not let his expression change, but inwardly he was seething. A whole month, when so much time had been lost already! How quickly Mlle Rose had prevailed upon this same judge to summon the fraudulent second Council! And how difficult everybody made things for him, when it was a matter of simple, obvious justice! It was as though he were the troublemaker, and not the Rose woman. No doubt the judge thought of him as that. Or perhaps, he thought, letting his eyes rest on the calendar, it was something else. That calendar had irritated him from the very first. It was one of those cheap inspirational printing jobs designed to appeal to the lowest intelligence: over the block of months was a picture, crudely colored in pink and gold, of a cowled woman blissfully gazing up to heaven, her clasped hands bearing a cross. Some saint or other, whom the truck driver—he could not have been an artist—had conceived of being made of sugar and cream, and not flesh and blood like everybody else. It was not Konrad's religious sense, but his esthetic one, that was outraged. How any man, Catholic or not, could bear to have that monstrosity staring at him day after day was beyond him. Konrad had often thought, if it were given to him to be an artist, what a pleasure it would be to paint the Madonna at the crucifixion as she probably was in reality. A fat, Jewish mother with sweaty straggling hair, her grubby face animal-like and wild-eyed with despair, squatting gracelessly to the ground to hold up her son's tortured head. She would wear an apron to which clung bits of chicken feathers, for she would have been preparing for the Passover Sabbath when they ran to tell her what was happening to her Joshua. And as for the Saviour himself, he would have a face like any of those you saw peering out at you in the photographs they took when they first opened up the concentration camps at the end of the war: narrow, cadaverous, blue-stubbled, ratlike, and shrewd. Only Konrad would add the earlocks of the Chassidim, to drive home his point, that this was a purely Jewish affair and as such completely alienated from the understanding of the Gentile onlooker.

These thoughts flashed across his mind again now, as he followed the judge's eyes to the calendar. He dismissed them, to wonder instead how far Cerval's position as a Catholic influenced his obvious reluctance to expedite matters on Konrad's behalf. Or was he being too sensitive, as Maître Paul had said? You could go as far in one direction as another. Well, there was no use making an issue of it. On the other hand, it wouldn't do to be too soft, to accept everything without a hint of protest. He said, "Isn't it possible earlier?"

"I'm afraid not," the judge said, making a notation on a sheet of paper, which he took out of a drawer and put back again. "Now," he said meaningfully, turning toward Konrad, "there is another matter which must be discussed, regarding the composition of the Council itself."

Konrad stared at him in surprise. The matter had been settled at their last meeting more than three weeks ago. Konrad had appeared with his list and all pertinent documents establishing the identity and qualifications of the proposed members. One by one Cerval had examined them, weighing and deliberating with irritating slowness, and had ended up by accepting all of them. Rose, Colbert, Immermann, Manfrédi represented by Lévy, as having belonged to the first Council and willing to serve again. Arnauld, upon his affidavit. Konrad, as bearer of Hannah's power of attorney. At that time the only flaw had been Immermann's absence, and the judge had agreed to wait for him. Now Immermann was here; Konrad had said so upon arrival at Cerval's chambers, and the judge had merely grunted. The Council was established. What problem of composition could there be?

"Monsieur Immermann," Judge Cerval said. "I'm afraid I am forced to reconsider his suitability for membership."

Konrad sat up so suddenly that his knee bumped against the desk. "What?" he said. "But Immermann is already a member. There's no reason to disqualify him."

"I should like to call to your attention that in matters of this sort it belongs to the presiding judge alone to pass upon the qualifications of proposed members. I have reasons to believe that Monsieur Immermann does not possess those qualifications."

"What reasons?" Konrad demanded incredulously.

"I have received an affidavit attacking Monsieur Immermann's fitness for the trust."

"Mademoiselle Rose!" Konrad said before he could stop himself. Judge Cerval glanced at him sharply, the corners of his mouth drawn down in disapproval. "Mademoiselle Rose has nothing to do with this. The affidavit is from a person who must be considered as the bearer of Dr. Benedek's last wishes in regard to his son. A Monsieur Pierre-Paul Houdy."

"Houdy?" Konrad echoed. "Do you mean the landlord? In Puy-le-Duc?"

"Do you know him?"

"I know a Houdy," Konrad said, bewildered. "The Benedeks rented a room from him across the river. If that's the one, I fail to see what he has to do with Jules Immermann. And he never said anything to me about Dr. Benedek's last wishes."

"You are at liberty to examine his affidavit, if you wish." Judge Cerval opened a drawer of his desk and handed Konrad a document stamped with a notarial seal. Taking it, Konrad glanced through the preliminary statement and began to read the text with attention. The undersigned had known Dr. and Mme Benedek for more than five years, and had every reason to believe himself to be in their confidence. He had given them shelter at the time of the persecutions of the Israelites, in full knowledge of the grave consequences to himself if he were caught. The Benedeks had been grateful to him, etc.

"In the course of a number of conversations," the document went on, "Dr. and Mme Benedek often told me that they wished to remain in France, and become naturalized citizens. One day, after having received a letter from relatives living in Australia asking them to join them there, they said to me that 'France was their adopted country, and that they preferred to die in France rather than go to a foreign country.'

"Both husband and wife frequently manifested to me their formal wish to install themselves in France and to raise their child as a Frenchman.

"When the Germans violated their treaty by taking over the Free Zone, Dr. and Mme Benedek entrusted to me all their family documents, as well as their family souvenirs, and told me, 'We entrust our son to you; if something happens to us, you will raise him or have him raised like your own child. Our formal desire is that he become a doctor, and, in remembrance of his father, that he establish himself in Puy-le-Duc, where everybody has been so kind to us.'

"Another time Dr. Benedek expressed himself to me as being extremely dissatisfied with the way he had been treated by his co-religionaries of Touville, saying that each was 'out for himself,' that they sneered at the country that had given him shelter, that they did not care who won the war so long as they were left in peace, and other things of this sort. At my surprise to hear him speak so bitterly, he declared that the last thing he wanted for his son was to be left to the mercies of such people, and that the worst of the lot were M. and Mme Jules Immermann, grocers who had become rich on the misfortunes of their fellow Jews. He repeated much the same thing on another occasion, saying emphatically, 'In no circumstances is my child to be entrusted to M. Immermann.'

"I believe that I am truly interpreting the last wishes of Dr. and Mme Benedek in saying that Mlle Rose should be allowed to maintain her guardianship of their son, and should be supported in her refusal to turn him over to strangers. Signed, Pierre-Paul Houdy."

"This man has been suborned!" Konrad cried angrily, tossing the affidavit on the desk. "It's a fabrication from start to finish!"

"Suborned?" Judge Cerval said. "By whom?"

"By the Rose woman, of course! The Benedeks couldn't have said the things attributed to them, because they didn't feel that way. Dr. Benedek didn't go to Australia because the medical association there wouldn't validate his diploma. And after that he stayed in France because he couldn't get out. As for the Immermanns, they were the Benedeks' closest friends. This is a plot, Your Honor. Look at the last paragraph. How does Houdy even know about Mademoiselle Rose? It's obvious that she went to him, and put him up to swearing to this pack of lies. She saw the chance to discredit one of the original members of the Council who had found out what she was up to and protested to the procureur. If she could find more Houdys, she'd do the same to the others as well."

Judge Cerval had listened attentively. "This is a very serious charge," he remarked. "Are you prepared to substantiate it?"

"Isn't it obvious?" Konrad retorted.

"I wonder if you realize what you are saying, Monsieur Konrad. It is just as well that you are making these accusations in a private conversation which will go no further, and not before witnesses. You are accusing two respected citizens of subornation and perjury, without a shred of proof to back up your charge. You say that Mademoiselle Rose urged Monsieur Houdy to make out this affidavit. There is nothing improper in that, so long as she did not prevail upon him to perjure himself. Can you prove, first, that he lied, and second, that the incentive to do so came from her? Do you deny that Monsieur Houdy must have been well acquainted with the Benedeks? That as their landlord he must have had conversations with them? If you admit this, how can you or anyone else prove that what Monsieur Houdy said passed between them did in fact not so occur?"

Completely taken aback, Konrad stared at the judge. He said, "If I understand you, Your Honor, you are prepared to accept this—this barefaced lie, unless I can *prove* that it is? That is, the burden of proof is on me, and not Houdy?"

"Houdy has made a sworn statement, under penalty of the law," Judge Cerval said. "Such a statement has juridical weight, unless attacked. You are free to attack it, of course. Prove to me that the affidavit is false, and I will accept Monsieur Immermann on the Council."

"Prove to me that it is true," Konrad said grimly, "and I will let Mademoiselle Rose adopt me too."

"You forget, Monsieur Konrad," Judge Cerval retorted with a faint smile, "that it is I who must be convinced." And he added with a certain enigmatic emphasis, "I have given this matter much thought."

Now, what did *that* mean? Was it an admission of doubt? Konrad said, "This is very awkward, Your Honor. We've already delayed the meeting too long waiting for Immermann. Now, if you insist on excluding him, I'll have to waste more time in finding someone to take his place."

Judge Cerval picked up the affidavit and put it away in the drawer. He seemed oddly embarrassed. "I thought you understood," he said. "If I accept Monsieur Houdy's affidavit, I must also take cognizance of the fact that he is the repository of the last wishes of the child's father. He will take Monsieur Immermann's place on the Council."

What a trap! Konrad thought. And to think that only yesterday he had spent hours winning the Immermanns to his side. "*If* you accept the affidavit," he said pointedly.

Judge Cerval met his eyes. Konrad believed he could see a certain sympathy in the other's face. "Monsieur Konrad, I have no alternative. As judge it is not my place to advise you on future contingencies of the law. I will suggest only that in the face of such a definitive statement as this, you run a greater risk in excluding Monsieur Houdy than in accepting him."

"I want to call my lawyer," Konrad said.

Five minutes later, in a public phone booth, he was answering Maître Paul's questions. Yes, the agenda was fixed. The date? February 10. The judge had not disqualified anyone else, only Immermann.

"Then don't argue with him," Maître Paul advised. "It's not worth it, and you won't get anywhere. Only Benedek himself could disprove Houdy's statement, and he's not coming back to do it. Instead, count your votes. You have yourself, Colbert, Lévy, Arnauld. That's four. Against, Mademoiselle Rose and, from all indications, this Houdy person. Four to two. Even if the judge himself votes with Mademoiselle Rose, which is not likely, you still win."

"Why do you say it's not likely? If he's willing to put out Immermann on a trumped-up story—"

"He *has* to accept the affidavit," the lawyer said patiently. "It's either that, or prove it's false, and he knows he can't, any more than you can. He may suspect it's a lie, but—"

"Suspect! After that story Rose told him about the first Council?"

"Well, don't make a fuss. If you attack the affidavit, you'll only delay the Council meeting. And if you jump on Cerval for accepting it, you'll only get him down on you for trying to teach him his business. Don't forget that he's going to preside over the meeting, and that he has a vote."

Konrad retorted that the judge seemed to be down on him already. As if he were the deceiver in the matter, and not the injured party! The lawyer said that it was, after all, the injured party that was calling attention to the judge's negligence in setting up the second Council. And the strange thing was that Judge Cerval was really a very capable and meticulous magistrate. The lady must have been very plausible with her story. Konrad said that nothing the lady did struck him as plausible, but then, *he* was immune to her charms. As for the judge, he was meticulous, but about the wrong things. By the way, what could the judge have meant by the risk of excluding Houdy? Of course, Maître Paul said. Did he want Houdy complaining to the procureur about being left out, as Immermann and the others had complained? Think of the strong moral position that would give Mlle Rose. The judge was right. It was better to allow Mlle Rose to win her small, meaningless victory over Immermann than to allow her to cry Unfair! after the decision. The repository of Benedek's last wishes! Konrad said bitterly. Where was the man more than three years ago, when the first Council was set up? But all right, he would take his lawyer's advice. Yet it was a nasty thing to do to Jules Immermann, who had a better right than any of them to be on the Council, and who was going to be hurt by Houdy's unjust accusation. What counted was the boy, Maître Paul rejoined. Get the boy, and all hurt feelings would be soothed quickly enough.

Konrad returned to Judge Cerval's chambers and told him that in the interest of quick action he would not protest the inclusion of M. Houdy in the Council. The judge said he appreciated M. Konrad's motives, and that he was being very wise. There was no obstacle to the meeting now, all the forms had been properly complied with. If M. Konrad wanted to prevent further delays, he suggested, it might be well for him to summon Mlle Rose and M. Houdy to the meeting officially, by court messenger. His tone was friendly, and Konrad, taking his leave, wondered whether he had not judged the man too harshly. Too fussy, certainly, and unpredictably weak or inflexible; but apparently he wanted to be fair.

In the other room Judas was practicing his scales. Konrad motioned to Rina to shut the door, and the thin, reedy sound of the violin was suddenly muted. "Yes?" he spoke into the telephone. "Madame Immermann? I was hoping you'd call."

"Well, I promised," she said. Her voice was tired and discouraged. They've quarreled, he thought. He felt let down, although he had not expected her to succeed. "I'm calling from the café. Jules is here too. I spent the whole afternoon talking with Odette, and since then I've discussed it with Jules. And we thought we'd better call you."

"She won't give him up?"

"Oh," she said. "I'm sick. I really do feel awfully about this. Five hours! I was with her for five hours, going over the same things a hundred times. No, she won't. She won't hear of it. And that's final. You can go ahead with the Council, if you want to, but— What?" This last was said away from the mouthpiece. Konrad waited, shaking his head at Rina, who made a gesture of resignation.

"Konrad?" Lise Immermann was back. "What did you say?"

"I'm still listening," he said.

"Jules wants me to wait. He says to think it over and talk to you later. But I wouldn't sleep tonight unless I told you this. I don't want it on my conscience. It's too late. Odette's had him too long. If you take Michel away from her, it will be like taking a child away from his real mother. It would destroy her. My God, Konrad, she cried until I felt like a louse. And I said to myself, What am I doing? Playing at God? You can't solve people's problems for them."

"I see," he said. "The twig is bent."

"I didn't say that," she said with a touch of anger. "Don't you think I see Hannah's point of view? I said I thought she ought to have him, and I still think so."

"Well, then?"

"Don't you understand? This is between Hannah and Odette. I can't have anything to do with it. It doesn't make any difference who's right. How do you expect me to live with myself if I take him away from one and give him to the other? I've been thinking about it all day. And so I said, Well, I'll call Konrad. Because if you have to make arrangements with Judge Cerval for the meeting, you have to know now."

"I see," he said again. "You mean that Jules——"

"We quarreled about it, if you want to know," she said defensively. "And finally he said that if I felt so strongly about it, he'd just back out. Only he asked me to wait a day or two until I calm down. But I'm not going to change my mind, and you've waited for us so long already, so it's only fair to you to let you begin looking for a replacement right away. Don't think we're doing this lightly. I know we gave you our word. But, my God, Konrad, I'm only flesh and blood."

And he was not?

It was truly ironical, he thought. Houdy's vicious slanders against the Immermanns had not been necessary, after all. The Rose woman had overplayed her hand, not knowing that Lise would be such an easy mark for a few tears.

"Konrad?"

He realized that he had been silent a long time. "Yes," he said. "I'm thinking." Was there any point to telling them now? In any case, Immermann was out of the Council, of his own volition. If he said nothing, they might never know about Houdy's affidavit. That lying paper would remain in Judge Cerval's files, and only he and the judge and Houdy— And Rose. There was also Rose. Lise Immermann would return to the Nursery to visit her dear Odette, who would look at her and think, These Jews! The more you insult them, the better they like it. He said, "Please let me speak to Jules."

"Yes," she said. "He wants to speak to you too."

Immermann's voice was low and hesitant. He was very sorry. He knew he had left Konrad out on a limb. But he had to have peace in his family.

Konrad said abruptly, "I went to see Judge Cerval this morning." He went on to Houdy's affidavit, quoting the passages that had to do with Immermann, which he had copied down from memory upon reaching home that morning.

"You know," Immermann said calmly, when he had finished, "Karl was quite capable of having said something of the sort to Houdy. About us, I mean. He was pretty mad at us there for a while. Lise told you about that. But he didn't mean it. He called me worse things than that to my face, and then he'd put his arm around my shoulder and laugh. Only I hate to have things like that put in writing and sworn to and put on record. Anyway," he added almost cheerfully, "this solves Lise's problem for her."

"Yes, it does," Konrad said.

"Except that it may make her change her mind again."

Konrad shrugged.

3

❧

Rain or snow, Mlle Rose thought, looking out the window at the rapidly darkening sky. The day had begun well enough, with fitful sunshine through a haze of scudding clouds, and unusually warm for that time of year, so that she had risked walking to the meeting. It was fortunate that she had set out early. The meeting was scheduled for eleven o'clock, still a half-hour off, and at any moment the skies would open up and cabs would be scarce as butterflies. She hoped it would be rain. She was tired of that everlasting snow, which was so white and beautiful as it fell, but which soon became a grimy mantle over the city, a trap for soot and mud. Touville was dismal enough in the wintertime without that, the Lord knew, with its gray stone buildings and shuttered windows. A warm rain, a downpour, to wash away the winter's hard usage, to sweep the rooftops and flood the streets, and leave them shining and clean again, the city that she knew and loved! If only, she thought wistfully, it could sweep the hearts of men, and leave them shining with charity!

But no, charity was too much to expect, she supposed. People went their way, each locked in his own little selfish world, without a thought for others. You could cut your heart out on a street corner, and they would shrink back in momentary horror; and then hurry home wondering what was for dinner. Bellies! she thought bitterly. Bellies and pockets. The rest was a romantic fairy tale to be fed to children.

It was monstrous that she was here at all. Dear God, what had she done? What crime had she committed, to be hounded like this? If there were not so much at stake, she would have stayed home, ignored them, let them have their meeting and come to any decision they liked. She had Michel, and all the arguing and debating in the world couldn't change that. This morning, upon awakening to the realization that this was the day she had watched approach for so long, she had been tempted to do just that, and not appear. But then her combative instinct had asserted itself, and her hunger for her far-off boy. She was sorry she had listened to Mother Veronica and sent him away. True, he was safe; but her days were empty, and he was growing up into a world of his own, away from her. Already, during Christmas vacation, she had noted changes in him, and the second parting, so soon, had been like a knife in her breast. It was then, looking ahead into a future of farewells, that she had decided that it couldn't go on, that it was not enough to be safe; he had to be with her. And to achieve this she had to win over the Council.

One vote! she had said to herself, sitting up in bed and listening to the familiar sounds of the Nursery coming to life below. One vote, she had said, as she set out for the cantonal court, envying those who thronged the streets about no greater business than a loaf of bread or a day's labor. She had three: herself, Houdy, Judge Cerval. One more, and all her heartaches would come to an end. Whose would it be? Konrad, that man without bowels, that obsessed scarecrow, was out of the question. It had to be Lévy, or Arnauld, or Colbert. Ever since this new Council had begun to take shape, she had been weighing them in her mind, seeking the chink in their armor that could be penetrated by a woman's despair. She had gone to see each of them to tell them her story, accepting in advance the humiliation of throwing herself on their mercy, not caring that her appeals would undoubtedly be reported to Konrad, who would gloat to know he had her on the run. She had not got anywhere, except perhaps with Colbert. Arnauld, on whom she had counted the most, for not being one of *them,* had bugged out his great, staring blue eyes, and sidled off to wait on customers, bellowing to his assistants, and returning to her to ask distractedly, "What were you saying?" Dr. Lévy had received her in his office with icy politeness, had listened in silence, and had terminated the interview by rising and saying simply, "I'm sorry." But the businessman Colbert, whose gruffness she suspected was a cover-up for a sensitivity he could ill afford, had argued with her, and thus given her the opportunity to meet his objections head on. She could not say that she had convinced him, but she had left him disturbed and shaking his head, unwilling to commit himself either way; and this was as much as she had dared to expect. You could never tell. It might be none, but if there were one, just one . . . She had done what she could, and now there remained only the final ordeal, the confrontation with them all, like a fox run to earth by a pack of hounds and facing them for his last stand.

A few drops of rain struck against the window with a spattering sound and left long streaks down the glass. Beyond those clouds, beyond the mountains and the border, high in his hilltop retreat overlooking the lake, Michel was in his history class now, unaware that the next hour would fix the course of his life. How quiet, pale, and withdrawn he had been upon his arrival, poor boy! It was the school, he said; it was terribly hard, with a discipline that made St. Joseph's seem like a kindergarten. Up at five-thirty, lights out at nine—and in between, study, class, and prayer with hardly a respite. The older boys were awakened at five, the seminarians at four. Demerits for everything, no excuses. But he was holding his own, and had already made astonishing strides in Italian. She had pumped him for hours, eager to picture every detail and circumstance of his life away from her, until, at his departure, she could follow him in her mind's eye to his journey's end; see the grassy fields of the school grounds on its wood-surrounded plateau, the Seminary on this side, the boys' school on that; trace his every step from dormitory in the morning to dormitory at night, through chapel, classroom, study hall, refectory, and playing field; and send him a good-night kiss as he kneeled beside his cot in the curtained cubicle. It would be Easter before she would see him again. Regardless of what happened today, he had to be allowed to finish his school year. But then, if all went well . . . She sighed, leaning her head against the cool glass, noticing at the same time that a car had pulled up across the street and that Dr. Lévy sat in the driver's seat. A moment later, Lévy, along with Konrad and Arnauld, were racing toward the door below, their heads bent against the rain, which suddenly came pelting down.

Behind her the door opened, and she turned to see Houdy enter and peer about him mistrustfully. It was quite dark in the long, narrow room, with its wainscoted walls and draped windows dim with water, and he did not recognize her until she had stepped forward. He had thought it was going to be in the court, he said, but the clerk had pointed out this door to him. She replied that this was the conference room, used for meetings of this sort.

"Where are you going to sit?" he asked, looking at the heavy rectangular table surrounded by chairs.

She had placed her purse and folder at the end of the table facing the judge's high-backed chair; now she sat down, and Houdy took the place to her right, shivering and saying gloomily, "It's damp in here."

Voices could be heard in the hall. Through the door, which Houdy had left half open behind him, Konrad stepped into the room, gazed coldly at the two of them, and went out again. To get his reinforcements, she thought contemptuously. Houdy hitched his chair closer to hers and said in a low voice, "He came to see me yesterday."

"Who?" she said. "Konrad?"

He nodded. "What is he, anyway? A lawyer?"

"A chemist," she said. "What did he want?"

"World full of crackpots," he said. "Want? To give me a lecture. To tell me about the aunt. I thought something was queer with him the first time, last summer, when he came to look at the room. He was so choked up then that he could hardly talk, just poked about and walked off and left me without a word. But yesterday! He brought a stack of papers this high, said that if I knew the facts I'd soon see the aunt had been wronged. And he began reading from his papers, and shoving them in my hands for me to see, and arguing himself dry in the mouth. Excuse me, I said to him, did you know Dr. Benedek? He hemmed and hawed and said he'd met him once. Well, that may be, I said, but he lived in my house for more than five years, and nobody knew him better than I did. I don't know what he may have told others about the boy going to his sister, but I know what he told me, and more than once. He wanted his boy to be French, I said, and nobody's going to talk me out of that. And he said, How can you call the aunt a stranger? His own aunt? Well, I said, where is she? And if you had ever heard the doctor talk about his people! I don't say the aunt, I said, but the Israelites of Touville. Jews, he said, we're not Israelites, we're Jews, there's nothing wrong with that word. And of course the doctor didn't want his son to go to a Jew, not during the Occupation, but after the war it was different, and surely I ought to see that. And then he began talking about you, and dropping hints right and left, until I had to tell him straight out, See here, the name at the bottom of my affidavit is Pierre-Paul Houdy and not Mademoiselle Rose. I signed it myself, I said, and I may not be a rich man but no one's going to get me into a pack of trouble over a paper with a notary's seal on it. I'm French, I said, and I have a respect for the law. And so he went away, and my wife came up to me and looked after him where he was walking down the Marché like a bean pole or something, and she said to me, Paul, what was that? And I said, Blessed if I know."

"Yes," Mlle Rose said angrily, "they don't mind making accusations, those people."

Houdy stared at her thoughtfully. He said, "What's eating them, anyway? The war's over. Why can't they be like everybody else? Let a person live in peace. They ought to be grateful you took the boy in."

"They don't know the meaning of the word," she said. "I swear I never had anything against them, but lately every one I meet! You try to treat them like anybody else, and they remind you of it themselves. You'd think they were proud of it. Polite and nasty at the same time."

"They don't let you be sorry for them," Houdy said.

There was a bustle at the door. M. Falère the recorder came in, saying over his shoulder, "Please take your places, gentlemen." Here they are, she thought. She opened her purse and busied herself looking for a pencil, wondering who would sit at her left. She heard whisperings and scraping of chairs. Arnauld's tousled head bobbed beside her; he sat down, glanced at her, and scowled at his fingernails. Beyond him was Dr. Lévy, and at the far corner of the table Konrad. Colbert had gone to the other side, had sat down in the recorder's place, caught M. Falère's eye, and shifted with bad grace to the seat next to Houdy. All wore their overcoats; Colbert in addition wore a woolen muffler about his neck; his poached-egg eyes were watery and he dabbed at his reddened nose with a handkerchief. They sat in strained silence as the recorder moved about the room. Setting his notebook on the table, he placed a battered floor lamp between his chair and the judge's and plugged it in, sending a pool of yellow light across the seamed tabletop and edging the profiles of the waiting faces. Then he went to a cupboard in the wall behind Mlle Rose and took out a small electric heater, which he set on the floor. After a moment a faint touch of warmth came to Mlle Rose's neck, and pink reflections tinged the ceiling and walls as the coil turned cherry red. M. Falère walked to the door, peered out, and rapped heavily. All stood up as Judge Cerval, wearing his robe, entered briskly and sat down, looking at his watch. "Eleven sharp," he said to M. Falère, who had followed him and taken his place, bending his gray head dutifully over his notebook. "Let us begin. At whose request has this Family Council been convoked?"

"Mine, Your Honor," Konrad said, beginning to get to his feet.

"If Your Honor please," she said, "I request permission to make a statement at this time."

His head bowed, his eyes fixed on the deep carving that edged the table, Konrad listened to Mlle Rose's voice. She was reading from her citation for services rendered the Resistance movement during the Occupation. After his first surge of impatience at the realization, he had settled back grimly, waiting for her to finish. He would then regain the floor and ask her point-blank why she had summoned the second Council, knowing that the first was available and willing to serve. After that the rout would be on.

Mlle Rose had dressed with care. She wore a black suit of soft woven wool, revealing a white blouse buttoned demurely to the throat. Her hair was thick and glossy and was swept back in coppery waves, accentuating the peak it formed in the middle of her forehead. She wore no make-up. Was she still in mourning? Her skin was very white, but puffy, and there were dark circles under her eyes. Severe. Maternal. Haggard. He had never seen her in repose, and from so close. Noting how large and expressive her green eyes were, he had to admit that she must once have been an attractive woman. A tomboy first; then a coltish, temperamental miss full of wild impulses; then the woman, temperament become passion, her coloring and complexion hinting at voluptuousness. Now he found her slightly grotesque, as if her air of tragedy queen had been borrowed for the occasion.

". . . This dauntless woman," Mlle Rose read, "with complete disregard for her own safety so conducted herself through the unprecedentedly difficult days of enemy occupation that she may well be held up as the model for all those who . . ." The words flowed on and on endlessly. Whoever had written it had not spared the adjectives. To Konrad it seemed slightly indecent, like a funeral oration. Between him and the woman he could see Dr. Lévy's cheek in profile, set in disapproval. Beyond him Arnauld was staring down at his hands lying loosely on the table; he breathed heavily, ill at ease. On the other hand, Houdy, his long, underslung jaw hanging loose, his eyes mournful as always, nodded in agreement, blinking, stealing swift glances at the others. You see? he seemed to be saying. As for

Colbert, he was decidedly under the weather, no doubt hoping that they would finish soon and let him go home; he listened patiently, with a sullen air.

In the middle of a phrase Mlle Rose suddenly stopped reading, and made a grimace. "No," she said, "it wasn't like that at all." She let the citation fall to the table, as all lifted their heads and stared at her. "This paper makes me out to be a heroine. That's not so. If you want to see some real Resistance heroes, you don't have to look further than this room. Dr. Lévy and Monsieur Arnauld. The chain they helped organize here in Touville saved hundreds and hundreds of lives. What I did can't compare with their work. I stayed home, that's all. Like millions of other Frenchmen, who suffered through it all and put their faith in God, and prayed and waited and resisted wherever they could. I deserve no credit for that. I came here today to tell you how it was, because I'm on trial here. Oh yes I am," she said to Judge Cerval, who had stirred and murmured, "Now, Mademoiselle Rose."

"Six judges," she said, looking at each in turn. "The agenda says we're here to reconsider the question of guardianship. That's a polite way of saying I'm to be thrown aside like an old shoe. Well, I thought, I'll defend myself, I'm not ready to be cast off yet, not while Michel needs me. I'll just go there and tell them how it was. They're gentlemen, they'll listen to me. Only the citation was a wrong move. I'm sorry I began to read it. We all know those citations. They read beautifully, but they leave you wondering where the truth is under the flowery language. We're here for the truth. And the best way is to speak from the heart."

"Your Honor!" Konrad said.

"If you please, Monsieur Konrad," Judge Cerval said frostily.

Mlle Rose took no heed of the interruption. "You have to know how it was," she said. "It all began with the Nursery. I wasn't just a private individual, I was a municipal employee, in charge of a Nursery run by public funds. People came to me. People in need, or in danger. I couldn't turn them away, I didn't have the right. Or the heart either. France wasn't France any more, it had been overrun by the Boche. Suddenly it was dog eat dog, everyone for himself, and the devil take the hindmost. Jews. Gypsies. Communists. Liberals. Intellectuals who couldn't silence their consciences. No, I thought, there's got to be a stand somewhere. The Nursery is still a piece of the old France. The new laws, they didn't apply to the Nursery. Occupation law—we all know what that is. I couldn't accept that. There comes a point where law doesn't mean anything, it's just legalized crime. And then you have to think for yourself, and pray that you're right."

At the judge's rebuke, Konrad had sunk back, furious, and stared at the windows drumming with rain. Now he found himself listening in spite of himself. The woman's voice was low, calm, reasonable. A bit monotonous, yet with its plaintive note. As though it were inside you, Immermann had said. Mass hypnosis, he had said. Was she going to try to do it again? Well, his turn would come; in the meanwhile it could do no harm to let her maunder on. Four to two, he thought, four to two. Five to two, if Cerval was a judge, and not a rubber stamp.

Mlle Rose had paused. It was really very simple, she said, when you looked at fundamentals. It was humanity against the barbarians. It was life against death.

Already at the start she had two youngsters in her care, the last of the five she had adopted before the war. And then the others began to come, directed to her by friends. People in trouble who needed a shelter, a moment's foothold before moving on. They stayed a week, a month, whatever was necessary to get their bearings. Later on, when the Resistance was organized, passing them on became less haphazard. But not all passed on. Some burrowed in and remained until the Liberation. Some were Jewish and some were not. With the non-Jews there was no danger: a homeless, deaf old woman, widow of a Polish musician who had left her without a penny; a teen-age girl sent to her by the Temple Dames, who earned her keep by helping with the children; later, an illegitimate boy abandoned by his mother. Trouble, yes, but no danger. Who cared about them? Human wreckage of the war, of a drowning society. But there were Jews who stayed too, and made of the Nursery a powder keg that could blow them all sky-high. The Barshowanskis, with whom she had only a casual acquaintance before they fell in on her one night, when the alternatives were the Nursery or the river; he was the Jew, she the Catholic wife who would not abandon him. A little girl named Léah, whom neighbors had found, gagged and half crazy with fear, in the closet of the room in which her parents had been arrested. And Michel . . .

Michel came at the lowest ebb of her fortunes. It was February 1944, the murderously bitter close of a winter that had seemed like a scourge of God. The shortages of food, fuel, clothing, medicine, soap, and all the rest were at their most critical point. No help anywhere—and there were already three persons in the Nursery who had no legal existence and were without ration cards. These gentlemen knew what that meant. Bad enough to spend half your day queued up before one shop or another, rain, shine, or snow. Bad enough to enter the shop, at long last, and get your few grams of bread, a handful of wilted turnips, or whatever it was the Germans allowed to get through to the people they had conquered. But when you hurried home with your prize, and thought of the faces that would be turned to you when you entered the door, and how many portions had to be made out of what was scarcely a single portion in itself, then your heart failed you and you wished you could just give it up. Just sit down and do nothing, and let what might happen. She didn't, of course. Another day, she said to herself. Another hour. Another minute. Somehow she kept going. She had friends, who helped her scavenge in strange places. A stroke of luck, a find in the black market, a bit of nourishment that came at the worst moment . . . She kept the key of their common store, and doled out share and share alike. Ration cards or not. They lived in a daze of near-starvation, and at night slept all together in the one room they could manage to heat. Her hands were almost useless to her, cracked and festering at the nails and joints from vitamin deficiency and the unrelenting zero weather. And here was another mouth to feed, another body to clothe and wash and bed, another person outside the law to hide. All this flashed through her mind in looking at the boy who had dropped from the blue with no warning, with no chance to refuse before she had him before her, with the knowledge that she might just as well cut his throat as put him out. And then she said to herself that if she were found out with one Jew or a hundred, her fate would be the same; that if she took in a hundred and turned away one, she would see that one's face forever after in her dreams. There was really no choice; she took him in.

Of course, Konrad said to himself. The same story she had told the first Council. It had worked once, why not again? And it was a new audience, all except Colbert and the judge. She had counted on that, and that these two would sit through it again. Sit through it? Colbert was spellbound, as he must have been before; he sat slouched in his chair, his handkerchief halfway to his nose, staring unseeingly over Konrad's head. Judge Cerval had withdrawn within himself, his eyes half closed. The others, too, were motionless and lost in thought.

Michel presented a special problem for her, Mlle Rose went on, in view of the periodic inspections by the Vichy police. So far as the others were concerned, she had already solved the problem: Maxim Barshowanski had carved out a niche in the cellar foundation, behind the coalbin panel, just large enough for him and his wife; and Léah simply mingled with the other children, left there by the working mothers. If they questioned the children, as they sometimes did, Léah could get by, she was French. But at that time Michel hardly spoke the language, and that with a pronounced accent; and was circumcised besides. Twice she was warned in advance of impending inspections; she placed Michel with a neighbor, a M. Lespinasse, for the day. But once they came by surprise, and gave them the worst hour of their lives. The Barshowanskis dived for the cellar, but Michel was trapped upstairs. She had time only to run up there and lock him in her room before the police were in the reception hall.

"As usual," she said, "I showed them around myself, room by room, pantry, closets, cellar, everything. They were very polite, but also very thorough, and my heart sank, because it was obvious that they were not going to pass over anything. They counted the children, wrote down their names, and asked them where their mothers worked. They even looked in the washtubs in the laundry shed, which we kept covered up when they were not in use. Well, it's all over, I said to myself, we're goners, all of us. All the time they were poking around downstairs I was racking my brain to think up some excuse for that boy's being in my room, but nothing came to me. When we went upstairs, I was praying for a miracle. I would open the door, and Michel wouldn't be there. God would make him invisible, or something. That's how far gone I was, and at the same time, strangely enough, I was beginning to get mad. It hits people different ways. Some get into a panic, or get hysterical, or just quit, like Michel's father. When I get into a jam, I get mad. Those who know me know that it's the way my nerves react, that it's just temperamental, and they don't hold it against me. But it's a fault, I suppose."

Konrad glanced up, saw how the woman's eyes had flicked over him, and thought in astonishment, Why, she's apologizing!

"Yet it was that fault that saved our lives in the end. Because when they came to my door and told me to open it, I balked. I just wasn't going to open it. It never occurred to me that I could get away with it. I think that all that was in my mind at first was this, that I wasn't going to make it easy for them. If they were going to get Michel, they would have to break the door down, and knock me down too. It would do no good, but that was the way it had to be. Naturally, I argued first, for the one chance in a million that I could convince them. I told them that they could enter everywhere else, that was municipal property, but this was private, this was *my* room. No, they said, they had to inspect everything. Look, I said, the city council furnishes me my quarters here, but suppose I just worked here and slept in a room across the street, would you have to inspect that? That would be different, they said, but their orders were to inspect the Nursery, and that meant the whole Nursery, so I would have to open the door. If not, they would break it down. And that's when I exploded. It wasn't only the inspection, but everything I had been through ever since the Occupation began. I must have been near the breaking point anyway, and now, with the feeling that all was lost no matter what I did, I let them have it. I put my hands on my hips and began to holler at them. The sergeant in charge had a flabby lower lip that hung a little crooked on one side, and all the time I was yelling I had the most awful temptation to claw at it and pull it loose for him, and when he blustered at me, that's just what I did. Or tried to do. I made a swipe at his face, and if he hadn't jumped back I'd have got him. In fact, they all jumped back and began to edge away from the madwoman. In that moment they weren't so far wrong. I had gone berserk. Completely wild. I went after them, and they backed down the stairs, looking up scared, and me on their heels with my hair flying, waving my arms and hollering and spitting in my rage. They went out the door, but I still wasn't going to let up. The nurses tried to restrain me, but I broke away and went after them into the street, screaming insults, and they slunk away and disappeared. Everybody in the block had stuck his head out the window and was enjoying the show. When I came to myself and realized that the miracle had happened after all, that we were safe, I sent Michel over to Monsieur Lespinasse just in case they came back, locked myself in my room and began to tremble. I couldn't control it, I trembled for over an hour until I feel asleep out of sheer exhaustion. But they didn't come back, then or ever. That was the end of the inspections. To this day I don't know why they let me get away with it."

The rain had subsided to steady drizzle, and the room had lightened perceptibly. A church bell tolled in the distance. Glancing at his watch, Konrad was surprised to realize that an hour had gone by. Perhaps, he thought grudgingly, Immermann had not been such a fool after all. He himself, in that time and place, with no knowledge of the existence of a family, or, like Immermann, in the belief that the woman's purpose was to send the boy to his aunt, would have been won over. And profoundly moved. As he was now, he realized with a start, in spite of what he knew.

Mlle Rose said, "Saving his life was only part of it. He had suffered a terrible shock. I had to give him a new life, a new identity, you might say. They tell you that children forget easily. That isn't so, they push their hurts deep down inside themselves and grow over them. You see them laughing and playing, and you think, Good! they've forgotten. And then they do something that shows you that whatever it was that hurt them is still there. Everything that makes a child suffer leaves a permanent scar. Even if they forget it consciously, it's working underneath, and comes out in odd ways. Little Léah, for example. She doesn't remember the closet, not with her mind; but her body remembers. I have to leave a light in her room all night. If she wakes up in the dark she gets hysterical. And if you embrace her too tightly, she goes rigid and panicky with fear. She doesn't know herself why she does it. Or the other boy, the one we call Pé, who's such a problem. He's illegitimate, an unwanted child, whose own mother treated him worse than a dog. I wish you could have seen the pitiful condition he was in when she brought him to me. He was half starved, wearing filthy rags, and was covered with scabs where the lice had bitten him and he had scratched himself. I don't believe he'd had a bath in months. She used to lock him in her room and go off to cafés with the American soldiers. And if she was having a good time and stayed away all day and all night, that was all right too. When she brought him to the Nursery, she didn't even kiss him good-bye, just told him to behave himself and went out the door, and he looking after her, not saying anything, but you could see it all in his eyes. A woman like that ought to be—well, that isn't the point. Imagine what that child's like inside. I've done my best for him, but she brought him to me too late. He breaks things, he's mean and callous and sneaky, he wets his bed, and he loves to make things suffer. We had a cat in the Nursery that used to hiss and run whenever she saw him. I wondered about it, until I caught him one day holding her upside down by the tail. And I can't get through to him.

He's obedient while you're watching him, but the minute he gets away, he's up to something else. Out of spite and resentment against the whole world.

"Michel's problem was different. Monsieur Houdy here can tell you how loving and protective his parents were. Overprotective, really, but you can understand that. An only child, and in mortal fear for his life. I don't mean that they spoiled him, not in the sense that people use the word. I mean, not pampered and selfish, or anything like that. He's the least selfish child I know. But it was as though—well, as though the umbilical cord had never been cut. He was two, going on three, and it was like being born at that age and not recognizing the world he found himself in. When they brought him to me he had been handed about from place to place, until it must have all seemed like a nightmare to him. He was absolutely lost. That's what I meant by a new identity. He had to find himself, start all over again, as though his previous life hadn't existed. Madame Bordat, that's our head nurse, used to say that if you took an angel and clipped his wings and put him on earth, he would look like Michel. It wasn't only that he was so beautiful, it was—I don't know how to say this—it was a different *kind* of beauty, as if he were made of different stuff from other children. It made your heart melt just to look at him. Everybody at the Nursery took to him right away. In no time at all he was everybody's favorite. Maxim, that's Maxim Barshowanski—he's dead now, he lived all through the Occupation, went back to Paris and died of a heart attack—used to call him 'the little prince.' And the boy so lost, so forlorn, so remote from it all! Grieving his heart out for his parents. Not that he knew what had happened to them. Suddenly they weren't there with him any more, and he was in a strange place, surrounded by people he didn't know, who spoke a language he didn't understand. When they brought him to the Nursery, they had told him that his father was there, so he would go quietly. Do you know, for weeks he used to go through the Nursery, looking for his father? It brought tears to my eyes to watch him, toddling from room to room, peeking in the doors. Well, I thought, poor little thing, I'll be your father and your mother."

Damn the woman! Konrad thought, looking about the table. Either she was a great actress, or she had forgotten they were there. As though she were dreaming aloud.

"His mother was dead. It wasn't likely his father would be coming back. It was a long time before I knew there was any family. And here was a child who needed love and attention *now*. Or the hurt he had already received would destroy him. It's easy to say now that I should have held back, that I should have tended to him without getting involved myself. It doesn't work that way. With a child it's everything, or nothing at all. I gave him the love he needed, I'd have been a monster if I hadn't. The night he came I sat up with him on my lap, rocking until he fell asleep. After that he wouldn't go to sleep unless I rocked him. For weeks and weeks, anyway, and when I gradually broke him of the rocking chair, I had to lie down on the bed at his side, or he wouldn't close his eyes. For days he hardly ate anything. I'd put the food before him, the little there was, and he'd look at it sort of helplessly. I fed him with a spoon, but even that wasn't what he wanted. One day he slipped out of his chair and came to sit on my lap. That's when he got his appetite back. One bite for me and one bite for him, that was the way it went. And no cheating! If I tried to give him two for my one, this little knowing smile would come to his face and he'd shake his head. And all day he'd follow me about. It didn't make any difference who I left him with, sooner or later I'd look up from what I was doing and find him there nearby, pretending to be occupied with something, but really in order to be near me.

"And all so grave and serious and grown-up in his ways! Like a little old man, moving quietly about, observing everything, listening to everything and not saying a word unless you spoke to him first. For one thing, he didn't know how to play. All the other children ran about, jumping and skipping, swinging on the swings, going down the sliding board, skipping rope, bouncing a ball, and so on. Michel wouldn't do any of that, not on his own initiative. Monsieur Houdy tells me now that his parents kept him very quiet in their room, for fear of disturbing the people beneath and calling attention to themselves. I didn't know that then, but I thought it wasn't healthy for a child not to play, and I took him out into the playground and taught him how. When I should have been doing my job I was out there with him, pushing him on the swing, or playing games, so that he'd learn and get enough confidence to continue on his own. For a long time he wouldn't stay there without me. The minute I'd stop, he'd stop too, and sit on the bench watching. And then he'd come into the Nursery to be near me. But one day I left him there with the other children, and he let me go. I watched him from the kitchen, and saw him playing with the others, and I can't tell you what it did to me to see him. I thought, Well, I've done it, I've given him a new life. He's accepted me and the Nursery, he's found himself. He had begun to grow around his hurt. I didn't deceive myself; I knew the hurt was still there, but I knew also that he would be able to live with it, and grow up to be a man."

Mlle Rose stopped and closed her eyes. No one spoke. After a while, she said heavily, "I came here to tell you how it was. But there are certain things that can't be put into words. Like the way he says, 'Maman Rose.' The way he puts his arms around my neck to whisper some little secret of his. The look in his eyes when you do something for him. Those of you who are fathers will know what I mean. Maybe there's someone here who has no children. I couldn't explain it to him no matter how hard I tried. What I have to say to you is this. I don't say that Michel is mine. My feelings don't count. He doesn't belong to me, I belong to him. What counts in all this is Michel. He's not an ordinary child, his attachments don't come easily, and when they do they're intense. I made myself his mother, not by saving his life, but by giving him my heart afterward. I made him over, not out of selfishness, but because it was the only way. He's French because I'm French. I gave him my country, my religion, my language, because that's what I had to give. Thanks to me he's a whole person again, with a place in the world, that same world that would have destroyed him. And I tell you this. You can take him away from me, but you can't take me away from him. If you try, you're going to break him into pieces again, and this time there'll be no putting him together. In a minute Monsieur Konrad is going to get up and tell you about the aunt in Palestine. He's going to tell you what a heartless person I am, to keep the boy from his father's sister. I want to ask, Where is the heart in this case? Where was the aunt when Michel needed her? Where is she now? Why isn't she here instead of Monsieur Konrad, who is nothing to the boy? Don't misunderstand me, I'm not criticizing her. But her feelings don't count, any more than mine do. It's Michel. They'll break his heart by tearing him away from his mother. Because that's what I am. They'll send him across the sea to Palestine. Another country, another set of strangers, another language, another religion. How many times can you make a person over? They'll put him on one of those Communist collective farms, a delicate city child like that! Bad enough to go from one mother to another. But to go to no mother at all! I've read about those farms. They separate the children from the others, like a chicken incubator. The children belong to the state, they say. Like in Russia. Which means that they belong to nobody. It would be the death of him. And in a country—"

Starting, Konrad said angrily, "Your Honor, I object. I request permission—"

"In a country at war!" Mlle Rose cried, shaking her finger at him. "If the Jews want to fight the millions and millions of Arabs that surround them on all sides, that's their business, and more power to them, I say. I hope they win. But is that any place for a seven-year-old child? Have you forgotten what war is like? He's been through one war already, isn't that enough? Oh!" she exclaimed brokenly, "why are you doing this? I wouldn't do this to your children." She looked searchingly at each of them in turn, and then said, "That's all I have to say."

He had made a mistake, Konrad decided bitterly. He should never have allowed her to have the first word, should have insisted on his right to speak, as the one who had summoned the Council. Even if he himself had not felt the power of her appeal, Colbert's face would have warned him. He did not dare look at the others. He rose slowly and opened the folder before him. He said simply, "Let's start at the beginning."

She was exhausted, as if some monstrous sea had washed over her and left her drained of her blood. She had been afraid that they would not listen to her, that the meeting would get out of her hands and put her on the defensive. That would have been fatal, she knew. Her only chance was to strike first, to make known to them, somehow, the injustice of what they were trying to do. Had she succeeded? She could not tell.

Konrad towered over the table. The lamplight gleamed on the edge of his gaunt jaw, and sent strong shadows over his fleshless cheeks. A grim face, taut and pitiless; the face of a fanatic. Could a man like that love? Have children? How harsh and inflectionless his voice was! And how thorough he had been! Like some devilish instrument of torture, his voice bored into her as he picked up paper after paper from the pile before him, read it, and made his commentary. Nothing had been left out, not even her motives for each act, which he analyzed as coldly as if she were a corpse he were dissecting in a laboratory. And he was all wrong! He spoke of Michel as if he were a gold trinket she had picked up on the street and refused to give up to its rightful owner. As if Michel had no feelings of his own! Where was the love in all this? The need he had of her? She wanted to cry out, to protest, to explain that these things had no importance; she had done them because she had to, not out of malice, but to protect the boy. But she restrained herself. To say anything would be to say too much, and she did not dare risk alienating these men. Konrad could not be silenced. If only he would be quick about it!

Finally Konrad closed his folder. Those were the facts, he said. Mlle Rose had systematically thwarted all attempts of Mme Lindner to unite her brother's son to her family; she had baptized the child against the known will of his parents, without consulting the Family Council she herself had summoned to advise her, and in contravention of the canon law of her own church; and she had fraudulently summoned a second Council, to prevent repudiation by the first. Mlle Rose had said nothing about all this in her statement, because there was nothing she could say. She had passed over this long record of deceit in silence, to dwell instead on what she had done for the boy, and her love for him. He, Konrad, had come to this meeting with the intention of asking Mlle Rose to justify, to explain, her strange behavior; but now that was no longer necessary. She had explained it by inference. For Mlle Rose the end justified the means. She had felt free to make a mockery of the truth, of the law, of religion, of the catastrophe that had befallen the Jewish people, of the sacred ties of blood and family, because she considered that the good of the boy required that he remain with her.

The good of the boy! he said in a voice suddenly harsh. Did Mlle Rose think that Mme Lindner was animated by any other concern than the good of the boy? This Family Council, was it not devoted to the good of the boy? Why were they doing this? Mlle Rose had asked. She would not do this to *their* children. No, and the Council would not do this to *her* children either. But Michel was not hers. The accidents of war and enemy occupation had cast the child up at her door—a trust, not a possession. The best thing that could be done for Michel was to return him to the bosom of his family, as his father had wished. It should have been done years ago, at Mme Lindner's first appeal, when the child was only three; there would have been little question then of the bond of affection that Mlle Rose insisted on so much. But it was still not too late. Michel was now seven, still a young child. He would take with him grateful memories of the woman who had saved his life and cared for him in his distress; but with the resilience of his age he would soon adapt to his new surroundings, and would grow up a whole person with his family in Israel.

Konrad paused, and then said with dry sarcasm, "Mademoiselle Rose is worried about the dangers Michel would be exposed to in his new home, which, incidentally, is called Israel, not Palestine. But she evidently knows little about the country. Russia does not govern Israel. Children are not raised in incubators. The *kibbutzim,* which she calls 'Communist collective farms,' are not concentration camps, as she seems to think, but experiments in communal living on a voluntary basis. No one lives in a *kibbutz* who doesn't want to. And children are not 'separated' from their parents. There is a type of *kibbutz* that provides special quarters for the children, to release the parents to do their jobs. Is this separation, or baby-sitting? Isn't that the function of Mademoiselle Rose's own Nursery? And there are other types of *kibbutzim,* where families live like families anywhere, except that their labors are directed toward the good of the community. All voluntary, I insist. But all of this has nothing to do with Michel. Dr. and Madame Lindner don't live in a *kibbutz,* but in a small town named Harad. Michel will not go to a *kibbutz,* unless he wants to, and with the consent of his aunt and uncle. And, for the benefit of Mademoiselle Rose, I'd like to point out that the war is over. The Arabs have been defeated. There is peace in Israel today. Where is the trauma in all this? Where is the danger? Michel will not be going among savages. The boy will be going to the country his father would probably have taken him to, if he had lived; Dr. Benedek was a Zionist. Michel will be joining his aunt and uncle and cousin, who are eager to take him in. He will grow up among thousands of children like himself, who have been uprooted by the terrible war we have been through, and who now have a country they can call their own. And I suggest that the quicker this is done, the better. Too much time has been lost already. I am sorry for Mademoiselle Rose, but she herself has said that her feelings don't count. I see no alternative but that this Council should do what it would have done in 1945, if he had had all the information before it, that is, send the boy to his aunt, where he belongs."

Konrad sat down. "Dr. Lévy?" Judge Cerval said.

"Whatever else this Council may decide," Dr. Lévy said quietly, "I feel that it should commend Mademoiselle Rose in the highest terms for having saved the Benedek child. We all know what courage and sacrifice were involved in such an action. Our society, however, is founded on the family as the indissoluble social unit. Children should be with their parents, or, failing that, their next of kin. Anything else is unthinkable, except in the rare case where the family is unable or unfit for the charge. This is not the circumstance here. I agree with Monsieur Konrad that the boy should go to his aunt."

Seeing that the judge's eyes had turned to him, Arnauld ducked his head and muttered, "The aunt, the aunt."

Houdy burst forth darkly, "May I speak, Your Honor?"

"In due course, Monsieur Houdy," Judge Cerval said. "Monsieur Colbert?"

Now, Mlle Rose thought. She felt stifled inside. Colbert's craggy face reflected indecision. Dabbing at his nose, he said hoarsely, "It should never have come to this."

Judge Cerval raised his eyebrows. "What do you mean, Monsieur Colbert?"

Colbert looked angrily about the table. "An impossible situation," he said in a loud voice. "It's either too slow or too fast. We met in 1945, and ever since then, nothing. And now, when we have a right to feel that it's all settled, they open it up again and want to rush things through. I don't want to blame anybody. If the aunt were still in Australia, I would say, Send the boy to her. But it's no use saying that there is peace in Israel. That's too simple. What they have there is an armistice. War could break out again at any moment. The Arabs are regrouping their forces. And I would want to think twice before sending the child there."

A flood of relief swept over Mlle Rose. She had a chance then! Glancing at Konrad, she saw his face tighten in a grimace of surprise and anger. He said harshly, "The war is over! If the Arabs haven't been able to crush Israel by now, they never will."

"I hope you're right," Colbert said. "But can you assure me they won't try again?"

"Of course they will!" she exclaimed, and Houdy nodded vigorously.

"Let them try!" Konrad said. He stood up and leaned forward on the table, addressing himself to Colbert. "If there is anything certain in the world today, it is that Israel will survive. We have passed the most dangerous stage. The British gave up their mandate and withdrew on May fifteenth of last year. Since that time the Arabs have hurled everything they had against the new nation, and have been driven back on all fronts. Technically you are right, this is an armistice. But in effect it is the end of hostilities. If there are border skirmishes, the Israelis will suppress them. Michel will be as safe there as anywhere. His parents came to France to escape from Hitler. Were they safe here?"

"We were betrayed!" Houdy said in sudden anger.

"By whom?" Konrad said insolently, his eyes beginning to smolder. "By ourselves?"

"Your Honor!" Houdy cried, struggling to his feet.

"There will be no such betrayal in Israel. It is the last chance of the Jews, and we know it. The Arabs are fighting for a piece of territory. The Jews are fighting for survival, for their lives, for their Promised Land." He shook his finger at Houdy as he cried, "Let me tell you this, sir! Hitler himself with all his might could not conquer Israel today!"

"Gentlemen," Judge Cerval said.

"Would you send your son to Israel?" Colbert asked.

"Now, that's enough," Judge Cerval said, rapping on the table. "Please sit down, Monsieur Konrad. And you too, Monsieur Houdy."

Konrad said, "I request permission to answer Monsieur Colbert."

"In just a moment." The judge turned to the recorder. "Do you have all that?" M. Falère held up one hand, while writing busily with the other. After a moment he nodded. "We will keep our tempers, please," the judge said, "and we will speak in turn. Monsieur Konrad, I consider your remark uncalled for. We are here to decide what disposition to make of the orphan boy Michel Benedek. No comparisons between France and Israel are necessary."

"Very well, Your Honor," Konrad said. "But it was not I who raised the issue of Michel's safety. If I have hurt anyone's feelings, I apologize. Now, with your permission—"

"Proceed," Judge Cerval said shortly.

"You ask an unfair question," Konrad said to Colbert, "but I'll answer it anyway. Why should I send my son to Israel? His father and mother are here, we are a united family. But let us suppose that my wife and I had died during the war, as the Benedeks did; and that my only blood relative were living in Israel. Would I want Judas sent to her? The answer, my friend, is yes. I would be proud to think—"

M. Falère held up a gray claw. "I beg your pardon. I didn't get that name."

"Judas," Konrad said. "My son."

"Judas!" Houdy said, his mouth open.

"Yes, Judas," Konrad said, turning toward him, his eyes narrowed. "Named after the most maligned man in history."

Houdy shrugged and looked at Mlle Rose; his expression said, What do you think of that? She suppressed a wild desire to laugh. It was so fitting, she thought. Konrad was still staring at Houdy. He continued, "I would be proud to think that my son was helping to build the new Jewish homeland. And everything I know about Dr. Benedek makes me feel that he would have felt the same way."

"Ah, no!" Houdy cried. "Let me tell you—"

"Order, please!" Judge Cerval said severely. "Your turn will come. Monsieur Colbert, do you have anything more to say?"

"Is this a vote?" Colbert asked, coughing and putting his handkerchief to his mouth.

"Not at all. You expressed some doubts, and Monsieur Konrad volunteered to answer them. Are you satisfied? If not, you are free to continue the discussion."

In the long pause that followed, during which Colbert stared unhappily at his handkerchief, Mlle Rose had the curious feeling that she was standing on a precipice, and that the slightest wind would topple her either way. "I just don't know, Your Honor," Colbert said at length. "This is a human life we are deciding. I've never been in a situation like this before. In 1945 there was no problem, everything was one way. Now I don't know. If we—" He hesitated.

"Yes?" Judge Cerval prompted.

"If we could question the boy?" Colbert said in an apologetic tone. "Maybe we could see—"

The thought had occurred to her during Christmas vacation, and she had dismissed it as too dangerous. If the vote went against her, what was to prevent Konrad from seizing Michel then and there? Anything was better than putting the child in their power. But now that Colbert was half convinced, Michel's presence might be just the thing to carry the day. And at the very least, it would give her that much more time to weigh alternatives. She said quietly, "Michel is a happy child. I am perfectly willing to let you learn that for yourselves. I agree to Monsieur Colbert's proposal."

"I object, Your Honor," Konrad said. "The test is unfair. Mademoiselle Rose has had possession of the boy for five years. Let Madame Lindner have him for five years now, and then ask him whom he chooses."

Judge Cerval reflected a moment, glancing around the table. "Very well," he said. "Let us put it to a vote. Mademoiselle Rose and Monsieur Colbert are in favor of questioning the child. Monsieur Konrad is against. Dr. Lévy?"

"No," Dr. Lévy said.

"Monsieur Arnauld?"

"No."

"Monsieur Houdy?"

"No!" Houdy said angrily.

Mlle Rose shot him a furious glance. What had got into the man? Didn't he realize that his negative vote, decisive as it was, played into their hands? Why was he betraying her like this? But Houdy would not let her catch his eye; he stared straight before him, breathing hard with repressed emotion.

The judge said, "I wish to go on record as being in favor of the proposal. However, the motion is defeated by a vote of four to three. Do you have any further comments, Monsieur Colbert?"

Colbert shook his head, and leaned back in his chair. Was he going to give up so easily? Or, on the contrary, had the Council's refusal to adopt his suggestion turned him against Konrad? If so, she had won! Please God! she thought, let it be so! What irony! Perhaps Houdy's unaccountable betrayal had actually helped her cause.

"Monsieur Houdy?"

Houdy shot to his feet and said in an aggrieved tone that he was profoundly shocked. For the last half-hour or so he had hardly been able to believe his ears. The arguments he had been listening to were really beside the point. A waste of time. Extraneous. It didn't matter whether the aunt had or had not done this or that. Or whether Israel was a safe place to send a child to. Or whether there were incubators there. Let them ask anyone who knew him, Pierre-Paul Houdy, if he was a fanatic or a religious bigot; they would soon learn that he was not. But a thing either was so or it wasn't. M. Konrad had said that Mlle Rose's feelings didn't count.

"No, sir," Konrad interrupted. "It was Mademoiselle Rose herself who said it. I merely agreed with her."

Well, it didn't matter, Houdy said. He wanted to say that the aunt's feelings didn't count either. Or the boy's. Right was right and wrong was wrong.

"Please come to the point, Monsieur Houdy," Judge Cerval said, looking at his watch.

Houdy said hotly, "I voted against bringing the boy here because it is unnecessary. It wouldn't do any good. Even if he said he wanted to go to Palestine with his aunt, I wouldn't pay any attention to it. What does a child know? They could tell him anything and he would believe it. The boy is what he *is*. He's French, he was born here."

The fool! Mlle Rose thought, noting with dismay how all had stiffened and turned wondering faces toward him. She waited for the objection, which came, not from Konrad but from Lévy, who said, "Just what are you insinuating, sir?"

"Just a moment!" Judge Cerval's voice was sharp. "Your remarks are out of order, Monsieur Houdy. That question has already been decided. The Council has voted not to bring the Benedek child here for questioning. But I wish to point out to you, further, that your attitude pays little honor to the members of this Council, and to the court itself. If the decision had gone the other way, this court would have established conditions for the child's appearance that would have precluded any undue influence. You wrong these gentlemen by your suggestion. If you care to offer an opinion on the disposition of the Benedek child, please go ahead. But I must ask you to avoid inflammatory remarks."

If only Houdy would look at her, to read the warning in her eyes! But he would not. Thrusting out his jaw belligerently, he said, "Maybe I was out of order, Your Honor, but I was coming to something that ought to be said. We've been talking about everything but this. Dr. Benedek wanted his son to be French. He told me so himself. The boy was born and raised here. The doctor wouldn't have wanted him sent to a lot of strangers on the other side of the world."

"Your Honor!" Konrad cried, rummaging among his papers, "I have here a letter—"

"I know that letter!" Houdy retorted, with a wave of his hand. "You showed it to me yesterday. I don't care what it says. I know what the doctor told me. When he had to get out of Austria, he didn't go to Australia or to Palestine, he came to France. France became his country. The last thing he wanted for his boy was to fall into the hands of strangers. None of you knew Dr. Benedek. How can you tell what he wanted?"

For the past few minutes Arnauld to her left had been shaking his head and muttering under his breath. Now there was a bellow at her side, and the pink-faced pharmacist was on his feet. *He* had known Dr. Benedek and the boy too, and by Christ! he had never heard the doctor so much as mention the name Houdy! His jowls quivering, his head lowered like a bull, he demanded that his statement be put in the record. While the judge rapped on the table with the butt of a pencil, Dr. Lévy said in acid tones that a person as misinformed as M. Houdy would do well to listen rather than to speak; Konrad and Colbert both said something Mlle Rose did not catch; and M. Falère threw up his hands and looked about him in distress.

"For God's sake, Houdy!" she exclaimed, aghast. He looked at her then, and she shook her head, saying in a low, urgent voice, "Please don't say any more!" For a moment he wondered at her; then, with a gesture that included all at the table, he said, "If you were French, you'd know what to do." And sat down.

The stunned silence that fell was so sudden that Judge Cerval struck the table twice more before he could stop himself; then, letting his pencil fall, he whipped off his glasses with a startled air. But it was Colbert who spoke. Slewing around in his chair, he said, "What do you mean, sir? I am as French as you."

Dear God, she thought dully. And I brought him here myself.

4

THERE WAS a little girl sitting on a bench in the front garden; she looked up as the gate creaked, and then, with a flirt of her pigtails, she had slid off and disappeared into the shrubbery beside the building. Moving up the walk with Jules and the bailiff, Konrad saw that she was no longer in the garden. She must have headed toward the back through the narrow space between the Nursery and the wall. Was this the same child he remembered seeing at the table that Easter Sunday, wearing a ribbon in her hair? What was her name? The girl who had been locked in the closet. Léah. Perhaps she still remembered him, and had run away from fear. Konrad the ogre, the child snatcher. Poor thing! And if she had a family somewhere, like Michel?

They had reached the steps. The others let him go first, and mounted after him as he raised the knocker and let it fall. Almost a year ago, he reflected, he had stood before this same door, listening to the sounds of festivity within, phrasing his greeting in his mind. An innocent, with no idea of the complex chain of human events that would spring from that simple act of letting the knocker fall. Well, he was a year wiser now. What a wide circle he had had to go, to be able to return today, no longer a supplicant, but with the power of the law behind him! How much trouble the woman had caused him!

The door was opened by a girl wearing a nurse's cap, who fixed her eyes, startled, on Konrad's face. "Good morning, Manon," Jules said over Konrad's shoulder. The girl gave no sign that she had heard. "Would you be kind enough to tell—" Konrad began. But she was no longer there; at his first word a strange grimace had crossed that sallow, broad-cheeked face, and with a little curtsy she had disappeared, leaving the door ajar. Was it fright he had seen in her eyes? he wondered, beginning to become angry. From within came the sound of children's voices and the clatter of dishes. A woman's voice, not Mlle Rose's, authoritative, scolding.

"They're in the dining hall," Jules said softly behind him. "Ten o'clock recess." Konrad nodded, glancing at his watch. His mouth was suddenly dry. There'll be a scene, he thought, remembering Mlle Rose's face as he had last seen it, the lips trembling. To be saying something, he asked about the girl who had opened the door. Surely she was not a nurse? She couldn't be over eighteen.

"Who, Manon? No, she's one of Odette's orphans. A sort of general helper in the Nursery."

Behind them the bailiff muttered something.

"What?" Konrad asked.

"Wholesale," the bailiff repeated. "She takes them in wholesale."

"Yes?" a voice said in the doorway.

Konrad turned and found himself staring at Mlle Rose. He removed his hat and said politely, "Good morning."

"Yes?" she said again. "What is it?"

At least she's calm, he thought in relief. Was he mistaken, or did she too seem surprised, like Manon? He presented his companions, who had also bared their heads. She knew M. Immermann, of course, he said. M. Immermann had been kind enough to accompany him, to ease matters for Michel. The other gentleman was M. Moyroud, an official of the court, who had come to witness their transaction.

The bailiff, a hangdog little man with a tight-lipped, bony face, said cautiously, "Delighted."

"Michel?" she said in an odd tone. "But I— What's today?" she interrupted herself, her eyes widening.

Could she have forgotten? No, no, it was impossible. The Council *procès-verbal* was explicit. She had received her copy. And, following Cerval's advice, he had sent her official notification that he would come for the boy during the morning of the first day after her month of grace. March 10. Today.

"March tenth," he said, staring.

"We've brought the papers," the bailiff said.

"And so you've come after all!" she exclaimed.

"Mademoiselle," he began, and stopped. "After all?" he said, frowning. "What do you mean? You were notified."

He had come expecting an emotional outburst—cries, insults, hysterics, anything. But he was quite unprepared for the glint of amusement that came suddenly to her eyes, and the dryness with which she said, "I see. It's you who haven't been notified, apparently. I've appealed the Council decision to the Tribunal. Of course I did!" she snapped, at his involuntary gesture of surprise. "I couldn't accept a decision like that. And so you've made your trip for nothing. I'm coming," she added in another tone to a woman in uniform who had appeared behind her.

For a moment he could not speak. "Odette," Jules's voice said.

"If you'll excuse me," she said. "I'm very busy." She turned as if to enter.

"Look here!" Konrad said harshly, recovering himself and taking a step forward. "What does the Tribunal have to do with this? The decision of the Council—"

"Ask your lawyer," she said, and shut the door.

"My father's coming," Judas said.

The stout man in the doorway was fumbling in his worn leather portfolio; he glanced up and nodded.

"Are you a policeman?" Judas asked, looking at the uniform.

"Lord no, sonny," the man said, a smile creasing his heavy face. "I'm a court usher. Do you know what that is?"

Konrad, crossing the living room to the hall, heard the question, and Judas answer, "Yes, sir. Something like a notary." He stopped to listen.

"Oh, nothing so grand," the man said. "But you're not so far wrong at that. You're a bright boy. What's your name?"

"Judas."

"Really?" the man asked, surprised.

"Yes, sir. Judas Konrad."

"Well, well," the man said softly. Konrad stepped into the hall, frowning. The man turned toward him, still wearing his grin.

"Yes?" Konrad said curtly.

The man straightened up and said in a businesslike tone, "Monsieur Louis Konrad? Chemical engineer? Rue Berthet, 137?"

"That's right."

"Court usher Régnier. A writ from the Tribunal. Sign here, please."

Konrad signed the acknowledgment that was held out to him. "This writ is dated February twenty-second," he said, after breaking the seal and glancing at the first page.

"So it is," the usher said.

"Three weeks," Konrad said. "Three weeks to cross town."

"I don't send them," the usher said. "I just deliver them." He turned to Judas with a wink. "Most people wish they didn't come at all, eh sonny?"

"His name is Judas," Konrad said.

The usher's smile faded. He looked at Judas and back to Konrad. "Well, good-bye," he said stiffly, and marched down the steps, shaking his head.

Rina came from the kitchen. "What is it, Louis?"

"A court usher," Judas said proudly.

"Oh?" Rina came forward, wiping her hands on her apron. "Is it from her?"

Konrad had flipped the first page over and was rapidly scanning the second. "Listen to this!" he said. Pointing, he read, " 'It is obviously not to the interest of the minor Benedek to entrust him to an unknown person, who will take him to a destination equally unknown, but rather to leave him to his guardian, whose background and way of life are readily accessible to inquiry, and who is and will remain under the permanent control of French law.' Unknown!" he said angrily. "She means me, of course, Louis Konrad, who crawled out from under a rock! A gnome, a troll! French law, indeed!"

"July!" Konrad said. "No one's laid eyes on him for over a year! Vanished from the face of the earth! And all she'll say is that he's all right."

"She's changed," Lise said. "She's become bitter and suspicious of everyone. We used to have good long talks, in the old days, I mean, before all this happened. Now she just sits there and waits for the visit to be over. Look here, Odette, I told her, put yourself in Hannah's place. How you settle this in the courts doesn't concern me. But at least let me see him. I'll write to Hannah, and her worries will be over. What have you got to lose? And all she'd say was, Look around, if you want. He's not here. And, What is she worried about? I tell you he's all right."

Rina said, "What would it hurt to let you see him? Or at least a photograph?"

"Well, I tried," Lise said, pushing away her plate. "You can't reason with her now. I suppose she's afraid I'll grab him and run. What I don't understand is, if he's not at the Nursery, where is he? School's over, if that's where he's been."

"That's what I said to Louis," Rina said indignantly. "What kind of a mother is she? Well, she claims to be his mother," she said to Konrad, who had grunted. "It's vacation time. Where's Judas? Right here with us, that's where."

"And stuffing himself, too," Jules said.

"You should talk!" Lise said.

"Hannah won't come right out and say it," Konrad said, "but she's afraid he's dead. She keeps hinting at it in her letters. Oh, I know it doesn't make sense, but it's natural at that. She's seen all the others go, one after the other. It colors all her thinking. She can't forget it."

Rina rose from the table. "No, no," she said to Lise, who had also pushed back her chair. "Please, don't bother."

"It's all so delicious," Lise said, sighing and leaning back. To Konrad she said, "No, and I can't either. Sometimes it just doesn't seem to be true. I mean, that we can walk about, go anywhere we want, visit a friend, and all without fear. Sometimes I'm afraid I'll wake up and find that things are what they were. Like a nightmare, in reverse."

"Some nightmare!" Jules said. "With your German captain."

"Did you know a German captain, Aunt Lise?" Judas asked.

"Yes I did. And he had nice straight legs, too. Not like your Uncle Jules."

"A fine court system!" Konrad said angrily. "She appeals in February, and they set the trial for June of the following year. Almost a year and a half! And in the meantime she's got him, and nothing we can do about it. Where is he, in God's name?"

Jules said, "Why don't you hire a detective?"

Rina entered from the kitchen, bearing a tray. Jules leaned forward as she placed it on the table. "Hear, O Israel," he said appreciatively. "A real Viennese strudel!"

Confidential Inquiries, Inc.
Rue Maçon, 112
Touville l'Abbaye, C. d. A.

TO: M. Louis Konrad

IN RE: Whereabouts of minor Michel Benedek—Third Report, October 2, 1949.

DEAR SIR:

We hasten to place at your disposal the following summary of our investigation to date.

Domicile of Subject: Findings, negative. No child answering description of subject has been seen at or near premises. Observation from rented room opposite Nursery has revealed no suspicious or unusual activity. Surveillance of playground from alley shows routine operation only. Discreet inquiries in neighborhood have led to no result.

Investigation at Sep: Domicile to which we were referred in Sep is inhabited only by caretaker, known as Mme Thérèse. An attempt to enter into conversation with her under a pretext led to no result, in view of the person's suspicious nature. Our operative was threatened with a pitchfork. Results from questioning villagers, negative. Parish priest, one Father Fonsaq, knows child, but has not seen him for past two years.

Investigation of Schools: To date our organization has made inquiries in 63 schools, lay and religious, within a 50-kilometer radius of Touville. Results, negative.

Kindly let us know if you wish to continue the investigation.

In the meantime, we beg to remain, etc., etc.

DECEMBER 31, 1949

DEAR HANNAH AND ITZIK,

On this New Year's Eve I find myself thinking of you and yours, and my heart aches to think how cruelly your dearest hopes for this past year have been deceived. Some ten months have gone by since that day in March when I set out for the Nursery in the expectation of embracing your nephew and taking him to my home; and still there is a half-year to wait. We are helpless, our hands are tied by the malice of a woman and the tortuous delays of the law. I cannot tell you how slowly the time has passed for me. Each day brings us closer to that day in June when the Tribunal will at last chastise the pretensions of Mlle Rose and quash her claim forever; but each day also is another bit of Michel's life that is under her control. With her disregard for the truth, there is no telling to what extent she may be poisoning his young mind against you, against me, and his future home in Israel. With her narrow Catholic piety—she is known, for example, to have relationships among the more bigoted element of Action Française, and to be useful to the Franciscan priesthood for her participation in their parochial camps for children—she is sure to turn him against the religion of his fathers. And who knows what unedifying spectacles the child has been and will continue to be exposed to at the Nursery itself?

In this last connection a certain notoriety has been given here in Touville to the strange death of Mlle Rose's brother. The man, whose name was Joseph, was shot to death by his partner in the café which they owned and operated together, in mysterious circumstances not yet fully explained. It seems to have been a dispute over money. The newspaper reports and rumors this has occasioned have brought to light some astonishing things about Joseph Rose and his police record. A onetime wastrel, petty smuggler, and brothel keeper, he nonetheless earned a citation for exemplary courage in battle against the German invasion. During the Vichy régime, however, he was convicted of black marketeering, and would have been harshly dealt with except for Mlle Rose's influence. He got off with a year in prison. At one time he lived at the Nursery, and Dr. Lévy, who has a long memory in such matters, assures me that his scandalous behavior was such that on one occasion Mlle Rose herself had him arrested. It seems that in a drunken stupor he urinated down the stairs on the children below, who were making too much noise. To such company your brother's son has been exposed. Yes, and to the company of the renegade priest who died in Mlle Rose's bed, and whose body was carted off in an attempt to hush it up. And this is the woman who dares to set herself up as the only suitable "mother" for Michel, and to question your right and fitness to care for him! But there is nothing we can do about it. The law must take its course, it does not see what everybody knows, it is concerned only with the provisions of the Civil Code and with maintaining its outworn and burdensome procedures, which strangle justice. What does the Tribunal care for the tender soul of an innocent child? Its docket is full. We must wait a year and a half, as if Michel were a stone, and not a growing boy who needs love and care.

And while we wait, where is he? Nobody knows. Or rather, everybody knows, for Michel has been seen by a number of people. Manfrédi, driving by the Tuileries gardens in Paris, saw him walking with a woman wearing a fur coat. (But Manfrédi has not seen Michel since the boy was four, and caught only a glimpse now.) Jules Immermann is positive he saw Michel in a taxi, here in Touville, and says that the boy saw him and seemed to recognize him. (But it was night, and Jules should wear glasses but doesn't.) Arnauld saw him in the railway station, going through the gate to the Paris train accompanied by two nuns. (But he saw only the back of the boy's head amid a crowd.) Even Rina, who has never met Michel, saw him in a movie theater. In short, we all have Michel on the brain, and see him in our dreams. We are as ignorant of his whereabouts as ever. By now I am convinced that Mlle Rose has put him as a boarder in some school at a considerable distance from Touville. Short of combing every school in France I see little likelihood of locating him. The police will not help us, since, until the Tribunal has pronounced, Mlle Rose remains his guardian and we have no rights. As if the rights of blood and family required express approval by the law!

Each day I ask myself how I might have handled matters so as to avoid this intolerable delay. I look back over the year that is now coming to an end, and wonder whether I should have always followed my lawyers' advice. For example, Mlle Rose's refusal to obey the Council decision laid her open to a complaint of non-presentation, which is a delict and would have brought her up before the Correctional Tribunal. My lawyers persuaded me not to make the complaint, on the grounds that there would then have been *two* cases pending, one civil and the other correctional, and the conflict of jurisdiction would have produced a drawn-out debate over priority, itself a matter to be decided by the courts. More red tape, more delay, etc. They were convinced that this was precisely what Mlle Rose and her lawyers wanted, and that the courts would in any case give priority to her claim of annulment against the Council, which would automatically wipe out our complaint against her. I gave in, because they are lawyers and I am not; but now I am filled with doubts, if only because of the nuisance value of such a complaint to Mlle Rose, who has had matters entirely too easy in her plots. However, it is too late now for such an action, and at this stage there is nothing we can do but wait.

You ask why we must have two lawyers. I have no choice in the matter, it is a requirement of French law. As an *avoué,* Maître Paul concerns himself with procedure, with seeing our action through the courts, with the preparation of documents and conclusions; but he cannot plead before the judges. For that an *avocat* is required. Now that our claim has passed on to the courts, we need both. But you need not worry about the expense. Perhaps I was not explicit enough about it in past letters. The Jewish War Orphans Relief Society, which approached Maître Lanson at Dr. Manfrédi's request, will foot the bill for his services. As for Maître Paul, I believe I told you that he will charge no fee. As for myself, I have yielded to your insistence, and am keeping a record of the small sums which I am out of pocket in this matter. Really, I am ashamed to jot down such trifles, but I understand and appreciate the delicacy which prompts you to insist, and must admit that in your place I would do the same. You will pay me the total when Michel is in your hands, and at your convenience. You must believe me when I say that these expenses represent no hardship whatsoever to me.

In fact, to set your mind at ease, I may tell you that, in a small way of course, and quite to my own astonishment, I seem to be on my way to becoming what our French bourgeois calls *commode,* that is, well-to-do, if not rich. It is amusing that this should be happening to me, and in the way it has. For in self-defense against society I have become a petty capitalist, and am living off the fruits of others' labor. I had the misfortune of beginning my professional life, upon graduation from the university, in a world stagnating in economic depression. For every post requiring a chemical engineer there were hundreds of applicants, and I the least considered of them all, for my accent, my race, my appearance, my lack of connections. The world had no need of me, it seemed, yet I had a need to live and to support my wife, whom I had just married, on the strength of my diploma. In desperation I set up a miniature laboratory in my cellar and began some washtub experiments with lanolin, which has since become a household word. I found I could make some acceptable hair oils, shoe polish, and so forth, and set an old derelict vaudeville actor to hawking my products from door to door, on commission. Within a year or two I was able to set up a production line in an old stable and go into business, I, Louis Konrad, who believed that the capitalistic system was responsible for the ills I had been suffering! The war and its aftermath closed me down, of course; but I had taken the precaution of patenting certain of my processes, and with the German defeat I was able to start up again. Now I have a small but modern factory, a staff of trained employees, a trusted foreman, a delivery truck—in short, I have become the picture of the man I used to hate with the virulence of the young, who believe the world can be cleansed by shouting slogans in meeting halls. I suppose it is not too late for me to become an engineer again, that is, to practice the profession for which I was trained, but now the prospect has little attraction for me, in spite of the opportunities that the new economic upsurge has made available. I have been an outsider too long, I am set in my ways, and—I am told to my face—I am impossible to get along with. So be it! It is we impossible Jews who will make a homeland for all of us; those who, like you, give yourselves to the new nation, and those who, like me, give of their surplus. There is even a delicious irony in the thought that the world of barbarians, which permitted one-third of our people to be wiped out before allowing us to build a haven for the rest, is helping to underwrite Israel. For in the ultimate analysis, the money for Israeli guns, agricultural machinery, irrigation projects and foreign bank credits comes from the *goyim* at large.

Forgive me this digression.

Let me point out that, for all my despair over the impasse in which we now find ourselves, there is one cheerful note. Our cause is slowly but surely attracting a certain amount of attention, and winning friends and adherents. Scarcely a week goes by but I receive an inquiry about it, sometimes from complete strangers. For example, about two months ago, I received a letter from l'Argentière in the Hautes-Alpes, from a man who signed himself simply "Bira." He asked for information about "the Benedek affair," which he had heard about in the editorial offices of *Homeland,* the Zionist weekly. I made inquiries, and learned that "Bira" is the pen name of a retired Jewish lawyer of the Paris bar, who has settled in a mountain retreat to devote himself to journalism and literature. I set down a brief account of our case and sent it to him. A few days later I received a similar request from the Jewish Consistory in Paris, and shortly afterward another from the Jewish Children's Welfare Society here in Touville, the organization that furnished an interpreter to Mitzi during her visit to Touville. I had my account mimeographed, and sent them each a copy. The replies were interesting. Bira sent a highly indignant letter, saying that your difficulties in obtaining your nephew formed part of a nationwide pattern which he had been observing for some time now, and which left no doubt in his mind that it was a deliberate plot on the part of the Catholic Church to win proselytes by any means. There were hundreds of such cases, he told me, whose circumstances were suspiciously alike. In each case the Catholic authorities smothered the issues, discouraged publicity, and dragged the matter out, hoping to win through human weakness and inertia. "Cry scandal!" he urged me. "That is the only language Rome will listen to." In contrast, the acknowledgment of the Consistory expressed sympathy for the "bereaved family," and advised moderation, calling Mlle Rose's action that of a "misguided individual," which could be "quietly settled through friendly, dignified negotiation." The Welfare Society made no official reply, but I received a telephone call from Mme Bianchini, president of the chapter. She took no sides, was sorry for all concerned, praised you for your "pioneering" in the "Holy Land," praised Mlle Rose for her "charity," and added a detail that I have been puzzling over ever since. It seems that the Society, upon learning several years ago that Mlle Rose had taken in a Jewish orphan, sent a social worker to the Nursery and offered to pay a monthly stipend for Michel's care. Mlle Rose refused. Why? An honest pride in not accepting handouts? Or did she already anticipate trouble with the Jews, and want to owe us nothing? I don't know. Nothing that woman does is clear to me.

But to return to Bira and the Consistory, what do you think of such divergent views? Don't they represent the two extremes of Jewish opinion today, that of the mouse and that of the lion? As it is, I am not in a position to follow either counsel. Cry scandal against what? Bira exaggerates. Where is the plot here? The character of Mlle Rose explains everything. Yes, she found a senile country priest who was narrow-minded and complacent enough to baptize Michel; but I have not forgotten, nor have most Jews who lived through the Occupation, the courageous stand taken at Avignon by the Catholic

Primate of France, Cardinal Loriol, who openly denounced the Nazis and Vichy for their persecution of our people; Father Tellier, the priest of Lyons who organized the chain to get Jewish children into Switzerland, of which Dr. Lévy and Arnauld formed a part; the Temple Dame who risked her life to warn Lili; and a host of others. I despise the Christian church, which is a corruption of our own (everything in it that is *not* borrowed from Judaism is worse than corrupt, it is idiotic); but let us not see bogeymen under the bed. As for the Consistory's "dignified negotiation," it is Mlle Rose herself who has closed the door to that approach. There is nothing to attack, and no defense possible other than that of the law. I wrote again to Bira, thanking him for his interest and saying that, in the early stage of our quest, a public outcry might have intimidated Mlle Rose into obeying the Council, but now that the Tribunal has taken it up, our lawyers and I felt it best to minimize the Jewish-Catholic issue.

Incidentally, Rabbi Notarius of our city, with whom I have maintained an armed truce ever since our quarrel, has taken it on himself to approach Bishop Rebenty of the Touville diocese on the issue of Michel's baptism. You will remember that I dissuaded Maître Paul from doing so, for reasons I explained in a letter. Apparently the unhappiness of a family moves Notarius little, but he *is* preoccupied by the theological implications. He reported to me that Bishop Rebenty knew nothing of Michel, had not authorized Fonsac to baptize him, and promised to have the old priest up for questioning and disciplinary action. So much for that. It is Mlle Rose alone who is responsible for our problem.

But I have let my pen get the better of my intentions, which were merely to greet you at the passing of the old year, and to assure you that even though we have not yet produced your boy for you, our interest continues as keen as ever. It is strange how this matter, to which, after all, I am really an outsider, has taken hold of me and my friends. It is as though—but there! The bells are ringing, it is midnight, the new year has come, and Judas, who has insisted on staying up to welcome it in, is calling me to wish me happiness in 1950. It is just as well, I have said all that I have to say, except to pronounce the old Jewish cry, wrung from the heart by centuries of oppression, which for you will have a double significance—"Next year in Jerusalem!" Amen! my friends, with all my heart and soul!

Louis Konrad

Judge Minotard read rapidly. His face stern, his great silver-streaked head bent closely over the document in his hand, he read in so reedy and monotonous a tone that Konrad, seated in the first row of the courtroom, could catch only a phrase or two. At his side Jules muttered, "I can't hear him." Konrad leaned forward, aware, out of the corner of his eye, that Mlle Rose across the aisle had done the same. A sigh ran through the room and the judge looked up. He cleared his throat and continued more loudly.

"Whereas, at the time of the disappearance of the Benedek couple, which has given rise to the issue of guardianship, they were domiciled at Puy-le-Duc, and the domicile of their child, the minor Michel, was Puy-le-Duc, a commune dependent upon the east canton of Touville;

"Whereas, the Council decision which is here impugned was reached under the presidency of the justice of the peace of the south canton, who was radically incompetent in this matter *ratione loci;*

"Therefore, the Tribunal pronounces, for vice of form, the annulment of the decisions taken by the Benedek Family Council, which took place on February tenth, 1949, under the presidency of the justice of the peace of the south canton of Touville, and finds the defendants liable to all the costs."

For a long moment Konrad remained in his tense position. It was only when Jules touched his arm that he realized that a bell had rung and that all had risen to their feet. Then he rose and walked up the aisle, through the door that the usher had opened wide and into the hall, where Jules joined him, looking at his face in alarm.

"I'm all right," he said. "Let me alone."

There had been few spectators in the courtroom. They came straggling out, talking softly. Colbert came out, looked at Konrad, hesitated, and came over, saying, "Tough luck, old man." Konrad nodded. Through the open door he could see Mlle Rose, her face flushed in triumph, coming up the aisle with Maître Cauchet. He swung on his heel and walked away. Jules, with an apologetic smile at Colbert, hurried after him.

It was hot in the street. The sun, glaring down on the pavement, sent little shimmers of heat into the sultry, motionless air. Konrad, stepping into the shop, found the relative darkness a relief to his eyes. A large ceiling fan, rotating lazily overhead, moved a breath of air against his cheek. Jules was behind the meat counter, whose glass front was misted over; he was in his shirt sleeves, his face perspired, his armpits stained and damp.

"Well, hello," Jules said, beaming. "Lise! Come see who's here."

Lise came through the curtained opening to the rear room, thrusting back a straggling lock of hair with her hand. She stopped at the sight of him and stared at his face.

"Well, you look all right," she said harshly.

"Why shouldn't I?"

"Jules told me yesterday you were at the point of—"

"That was yesterday," he said.

She shrugged and came forward. Her face was red and angry. "What sort of fool lawyers do you have, anyway? I never heard of anything so silly in my life! They should have known Cerval was incompetent. Did you have to lose all that time for the Tribunal to tell you?"

"Of course they knew," he said, wondering at the rage in her voice. "That was our reserve weapon. Only since Mademoiselle Rose used Cerval for her two Councils—"

"Yes," she said. "You thought she didn't know. That you could get away with it. Take a short cut. A smart old fox like her! And so she turned the tables on you. Some reserve weapon!"

"She's not smart," he said. "She's stupid. Only—"

"Ha!" she said sarcastically. "Even better! How does it feel to be outmaneuvered by a stupid woman? Jules!"

A woman had entered the shop, carrying a market basket over her arm. Jules, with a wink at Konrad, went to attend to her. Konrad waited, perplexed; why was Lise being so disagreeable?

Jules asked the woman if that was all. Lise stared out the window, tapping with her foot. The cash register rang.

"We're closing tomorrow," Jules said.

"I know," the woman said vaguely. "I saw the sign."

"We're going to the mountains," Lise said in a loud voice. "The whole month of August. I'm sick of this place."

"That's nice," the woman said. She went out, glancing at Konrad. Konrad looked questioningly at Jules.

"She's mad," Jules said fondly. "She quarreled with Odette this morning."

Lise turned angrily. "Lawyers! Chemists! All so damned smart! Yes, and you too," she said to Jules. "Pussyfooting around with that look on your face!"

"You went to the Nursery?" Konrad asked. "Why?"

"Why not?" she said.

Konrad shrugged and turned to Jules. "I have to talk to you a minute."

"Go ahead," Lise said. "Only get him out of here, or I'll— Go away, both of you. Big secrets," she said, as Jules took his apron off and came around the counter. "Had a meeting with your lawyers, no doubt. Haven't had enough yet, I suppose."

"No," Konrad said shortly. "Come on, Jules."

Lise bit her lip. "What are you going to do, take it to Appeals Court?"

Konrad shook his head. "We're going to summon another Family Council. Only this time— It's a bit complicated. If you want—"

"No. Tell it to Jules." She stared at him, her eyes narrowed. "Another Council! And you want Jules?"

"Yes. Instead of Houdy."

"Well, take him! Only get that boy, do you hear?"

"Bye, dear," Jules said.

In the street Konrad said, "Let's go down by the river." What had they quarreled about? he wondered as they walked. Whatever it was, Lise had changed her mind. He had expected an argument, and instead of that Lise had said, Take him. And suspiciously bright about the eyes as she turned away.

"What happened at the Nursery?"

"She just got back about a half-hour ago," Jules said. "Just finished telling me about it when you came in. Odette all but threw her out. I say, Louis, do you have to walk so fast?"

"Sorry." He slackened his pace.

"She figured it was the psychological moment. You know, after Odette won her case. If Michel was there, she'd let her see him. And the funny thing is that right away Lise got the impression that he was there. From the way were acting. Lise says that Manon had a funny look about her, and as soon as Lise entered Manon went upstairs and stayed there. Odette was jumpy too. Jumpy and belligerent. Well, she says to Lise, what do you think of your friend now? I didn't come to talk about that, Lise told her, I came to see Michel. Odette said he wasn't there, but just the way she said it made Lise surer than ever. She insisted, and that's when it started, with Odette saying that Lise had called her a liar, and Lise arguing that she was Michel's godmother and was entitled to see him, and what could

Odette lose since she had won the case? Before it ended, Odette practically accused her of being two-faced, trying to be friends with both sides and bearing tales from one to the other. Lise exploded, and said what about the way Odette got me off the Council? If that wasn't two-faced, what was? Because you know," Jules said, shading his eyes with his hand and squinting sideways at Konrad, "that's been rankling in her ever since. When it reached that point it wasn't any good, of course, and Lise said that if that was the way Odette felt about her, she was going and wasn't coming back. Odette said that was fine with her, she could do just that. And Lise marched out, and Odette called after her, Tell Judas' father he can take it to Appeals, I'll be waiting for him."

"She said that?" Konrad seized Jules by the arm. At Jules' nod, he released him and stood staring. "Come on," he said shortly, and strode off. Jules followed after, wiping his face on his sleeve. "Here," he protested, "are you a man or what? In this heat?"

On arriving at the river Konrad turned to the right and walked along the cobbled embankment until he could see the bridge and the hill beyond. There, in the shade that reached them from a roof cornice across the way, he hoisted himself to the rough stone parapet and sat gazing at Puy-le-Duc. After a while he stirred and said bitterly, "Judas' father!"

"I shouldn't have told you that, I suppose," Jules said. "But she did say it. And of course, it does strike people as strange. Naming your son Judas, I mean. What on earth possessed you, anyway? Damn!" he muttered, patting his shirt pocket, "I've come away without a cigar. Now what am I going to do?"

Konrad turned to him angrily. "We're all Judases. Ask them! That's the way they think of us. We betrayed their Messiah. Only Judas happened to believe, and I agree with him, that that particular son of David betrayed him, and all of us. But I didn't come to talk to you about that," he said, turning away.

"What?" Jules said. "Is it a paradox, or what? Jesus betrayed—?"

"She *wants* me to take it to Appeals. She's having the time of her life. She's enjoying it. Talk about paradox!" Konrad said. "Do you know, I felt sorry for her. At the Council meeting. That pathetic story she tells! And afterward, when even the judge voted against her, she was so crushed she didn't have the strength to get up from her chair. She was still sitting there when we walked out. We all felt like brutes. Now she's eager for more."

"No, no," Jules said. "That isn't what I meant. You said—"

Konrad shrugged. "It's just a theory of mine."

"Out with it, man."

"It's all there," Konrad said. "Matthew, Mark, Luke, and John. All you have to do is read them. Judas was an idealist, a patriot, or else he wouldn't have followed Jesus in the first place. He was one of the twelve apostles, remember. One of those who dropped what they were doing and devoted their lives to become fishers of men. Do you think a man like that would betray the great leader for thirty pieces of silver? The apostle John tells us that when Judas repented and gave back the money to the Sanhedrin, they bought a potter's field with it as a burial place for strangers. Judas sold his leader for only enough money to buy a potter's field. I don't believe it. A man like that would have to have another reason, and a good one. It's a pity he didn't write a fifth gospel, and tell his side of the story. But the reason is clear enough without that. It was because Jesus wasn't the messiah he started out to be."

"I never thought of that," Jules said. "I mean, about the money. It was damned little, wasn't it?"

"The most surprising thing about the New Testament," Konrad said, "is that none of them offer any explanation as to why Judas did it. You'd think they'd all be eager to explain it away, to show how wrong he was. They pass over it in silence. Except John, who suggests feebly that Judas was a thief. A fine thief, whom they had selected to hold the purse, and who gave back the bribe money! If they don't explain, it's because they didn't want to, or didn't dare. History has a way of corrupting itself. By the time the Gospels were written, decades after Jesus died, the argument was whether Jesus was or was not the Son of God, and a great new religious movement had been born. But in its origins the movement was political, and only incidentally religious. Palestine was an occupied country. You know what that means, think back a few years. The Roman rule must have been just as harsh as Hitler's in France. What kind of messiah were you looking for six or seven years ago? Somebody who would get you into heaven after you had starved to death in a concentration camp, or one who would drive the Germans out?"

"Well," Jules said, grinning, "I know what I wanted *first*."

"So did the apostles," Konrad said. "And they thought they had found it with Joshua, the carpenter's son. He was a Jew of Jews, who had spent his boyhood listening to the graybeards disputing in the synagogue. And argued with them himself, we're told. He went into the desert, and came out with a great new weapon, a Jewish weapon, the only one that might possibly work against an empire as strong as Rome: passive resistance. Others have used it since. Gandhi in India, for example. But Jesus invented it. Turn the other cheek, he told his people. Be meek and humble. Let them kill you, trample you down with their horses and chariots, only follow our law, not theirs. When they see they can't do anything with us, they'll go away. And a handful of men followed him, including Judas. Why not? What other hope did they have?"

Jules's great dark face was intent, his beaked profile turned slightly away. "I see," he said, as Konrad paused. "They can't kill us all." He added brightly, "No gas chambers then."

"But the others wouldn't go along. The idea was too new for them. It must have seemed silly. What, turn the other cheek? To the Romans? Far from letting us alone, they'll . . . And they heckled him with questions, like the one about the coin and the tribute. Or what was worse, they were indifferent. That's when Joshua ben Joseph began to change. He got moody and petulant. The Gospels are full of little hints of it. He loses his temper and threatens to use the sword. He curses a fig tree, like a spoiled child. He breaks the Sabbath, he who had said that the earth would fade away before one jot of the Law was changed. He scolds the Jews, and says that if they won't listen to him, others will, he who had told the Samaritan woman that his message was not for the likes of her. And he begins to drop obscure hints that maybe he's not just an ordinary mortal like other men. The apostles are disturbed and demand signs. They don't believe it, which is the best proof that it was not for that that they had followed him. And Judas begins to see his hopes of freeing his country go down the drain. His leader has gone mad, the poet with the strange, compelling dream has delusions of grandeur, the great hypnotist with his faith cures to spellbind the yokels has begun to believe his own propaganda. Now Palestine can go to hell, *his* kingdom is in the other world. Judas, the treasurer of the cause, sees a whole bottle of costly ointment poured on Joshua's head, and the man browbeating those who murmur—he who had told his apostles to sell all they had and give it to the poor. Already Judas must have spoken out, complained, made his attitude known. Jesus was aware of it. At the last Seder—"

"Seder!" Jules said.

"It was the Passover," Konrad said simply.

Jules snapped his fingers. "Of course! Why, they must have gone through the whole ritual. Who asked the Four Questions, I wonder?"

"John," Konrad said. "The youngest. The favorite. He was sitting at Jesus' right hand. Which explains why it was to him that Jesus said that one of them would betray him. It must have been on Judas' face. It was a bitter feast for him, no doubt. All that talk of heaven, when it was right there on earth that the problem was! And the last straw was that bit of mummery at the table. The bread was his body—"

"Bread!" Jules said. "You mean matzoh."

"Yes. The matzoh was his body, and the wine was his blood. Already the man had apotheosized himself. Judas couldn't take any more, and he did what Jesus had said he was going to do, he went to the Sanhedrin and offered to lead them to the rebel leader's hiding place."

"Jesus the Maquisard," Jules said.

"As a matter of fact," Konrad said, nodding, "the comparison is not inexact. What was the Sanhedrin afraid of? Jesus the blasphemer? The one who said he could tear down the Temple and build it up again in three days? The one who claimed to be God? They could have taken care of that themselves. Why drag the Roman authority into it? Why was it expedient for one man to die for the people? A strange argument any way you look at it. Why for the people? Wasn't it because Jesus was the leader of a resistance group that could get them all into trouble with Pilate, the Otto Abetz of Jerusalem? You'll notice what sign Pilate put over Jesus' head on the cross. Not Jesus the blasphemer. Jesus, King of the Jews. The man who set himself up against the power of Rome. That was the only kind of king they were worried about. The rest was just Jewish nonsense."

Weary of the topic, Konrad made a gesture and turned to stare at the river. The water flowed sluggishly, filmed over with dust. It was the drought, he thought. The hills from which it sprang were parched and dry. Like the hills of Galilee. And if he had been Judas? What would he have done?

"It's an interesting theory," Jules said. "But now, just to round it out, why did Judas repent?"

"Because he was a human being," Konrad said, "and because the matter went further than he expected. I imagine he thought Jesus would be imprisoned, disgraced, exiled. Not crucified. Crucifixion was a Roman game. He didn't go to the Romans, he went to the Sanhedrin. Who knows what they promised him, those collaborationists? Bring us to your leader, and we'll have him up for questioning. We'll put a scare into him, make him recant. We won't hurt him. Judas was a Jew and thought as one. It was a purely internal affair, a matter of discipline, to make Jesus come to his senses. But Jesus didn't recant, and the Sanhedrin turned him over to Pilate with the complaint that he was stirring up the people. Which he was, of course. Judas hadn't bargained for that. Matthew tells us that Judas, seeing that Jesus was condemned, repented. A giveaway, that phrase: 'seeing that he was condemned!' And the final blow must have been the strange words the leader said on the cross. Eli, Eli, why have you abandoned me? It must have broken Judas' heart. Yes, his leader had come to his senses, but too late. Maybe, if he hadn't betrayed him—? But now there was no hope, and he went and hanged himself. An idealist who was betrayed. A man who set his life at stake for his idea, that of freeing his country from the hated Gentile occupier. The most hated man in history, and the one who has been least understood."

Jules was regarding him with warm, friendly eyes. Konrad passed his hand over his forehead, pressing his fingers deep into the brow. Had Jules understood? If not, who would? What had happened, really, at Jerusalem that Passover? Fantastic, that because of that he was sitting here overlooking the river Char, casting about for ways and means to unite a family!

"Well," Jules said, beaming, "so you have an idea about Judas. Maybe everybody's wrong. Good. But, you fanatic, why saddle your son with it?"

"He was born in 1938," Konrad said wearily. "The Jews in Germany were wearing the yellow star, and were called Isaac, no matter what their names were. Isaac or Sarah. And I thought, Not Isaac. Not that sacrificial lamb. Not that plaything for a whimsical God. Better Judas, after a man who devoted his life to looking for a king to defy Rome, and wouldn't accept a false one. They call us Judas anyway. Let's *be* Judases, and maybe the world will begin to understand what we Jews are after."

"Poor kid!" Jules said.

"I've explained it to him," Konrad said. "He knows what he has to live with. And he's accepted it. Proudly. You don't have to be sorry for him."

After a while Jules sighed. "We have no children, Lise and I. I used to be glad, in those days, but now—now I don't know. I wouldn't have named mine Judas, though," he added, laughing. "I'd have named him Solomon. That's the difference between us."

"Yes," Konrad said dryly, "the one who died full of years and wisdom, among his concubines."

Jules shrugged, still laughing. "Why butt your head against the wall?"

Both looked up at Puy-le-Duc. "See there," Jules said, pointing. "That's Karl's window. Do you see that square roof? Just below it, with the white curtain."

Konrad said, "I've wondered which it was."

They were silent a long time. At length Konrad said, "Last night, when you called, I was at Maître Lanson's office."

"Rina told me."

"Maître Paul was there too. He feels pretty bad about yesterday's decision. He spotted long ago that Cerval was incompetent, but held back on it to use against the second Council, if necessary. And now they've used it us. We could appeal, but we're not going to. There's a better way. We're going to call another Family Council, but with a new idea. Until now the three Councils have been concerned with naming a provisional guardian. Now we're going to name a definitive guardian. Hannah, of course. Our position is that so long as there was the possibility that the father was coming back, Mademoiselle Rose had the boy in temporary trust. But now there's no reason for her to continue, not with an aunt who wants him. It comes under a different heading of the Civil Code. There can't be any legal objection. If the third Council is invalid because of jurisdiction, they all are. It's just as though no Council had even been called. We start from the beginning. A new reason, a new judge, a new guardian."

"But the old members," Jules said.

"Yes. All except Houdy. We've had enough of that crank. I imagine Mademoiselle Rose has too. If she had any chance of winning us over, he lost it for her with his stupid chauvinism. I want you to take his place."

"How are you going to get rid of him?"

"Easy. We don't invite him, that's all. The Rose woman didn't summon him for the first two Councils, why should we?"

"Hm," Jules said. "If you could only get rid of Odette in the same way!"

"We could, you know. We don't have to invite her at all. But both Paul and Lanson feel it would be better to let her sit in on it. To placate her, they say. As if we haven't placated her enough as it is! But all right, her one vote won't mean anything. There's only one complication about calling the new Council. Before we can appoint a definitive guardian, we have to prove that the parents are dead. That's why it's definitive, as a permanent replacement for the parents."

"How are you going to do that?" Jules demanded. "Lili, yes, people saw—what happened to her. But Karl just disappeared."

"Just a lot of red tape, that's all," Konrad said gloomily. "More time lost, but it can't be helped. First we have to get an affidavit from the Ministry of Veterans and War Casualties to the effect that Karl was arrested and deported. We turn this in to the Tribunal, with our plea. There have been any number of precedents, on the presumption that a deportee who hasn't appeared in all these years may be presumed dead. Once the Tribunal has pronounced—and of course they take ages—the judgment is turned over to the procureur. If no evidence to the contrary is turned in to him in the following month, Karl is declared legally dead, and we can go ahead with the Council. A matter of another year, perhaps more. But there's no other way."

"All of that!" Jules exclaimed in awe. "To prove what everybody knows!"

"I didn't make the law," Konrad said.

"Why don't you just grab him?" Jules suggested. "Kidnap him. And let Odette go to law to get him back." His tone was joking, but Konrad turned on him angrily. "And where is he, may I ask? Besides, suppose I did, what would that prove?"

Jules regarded him strangely. "Just what is it that you *want* to prove? Oh!" he said, clutching his brow, "Oh, for a cigar!"

Konrad said, "You haven't answered me. Whether you'll serve on the new Council."

"What else?" Jules said reproachfully.

"Benedek?" the clerk said. "That sounds familiar."

"Very likely," Konrad said. "There was a Tribunal hearing last summer over the guardianship of the son. But this has to do with the parents. A certificate of decease. I have this affidavit—"

"But that's what I mean," the clerk said. "I seem to remember . . . It was only a short while ago. Just a moment while I look it up."

"I don't think so," Konrad said patiently after the man, who had already got up from his desk and was moving toward his filing cabinets. The clerk paid no attention; he pulled open a drawer and ruffled through the papers in it. Konrad waited. The man had made a mistake, of course.

"Yes," the clerk said, returning. He had a document in his hand. "Just as I thought. A declarative judgment was handed down two months ago. In August. See? Dr. Karl Benedek. Wife, Lili Weiss Benedek. That's it, isn't it?"

Konrad looked at the document in stupefaction. There could be no doubt. On August 14, 1950, the Civil Tribunal of Touville had ruled, on the basis of an affidavit furnished by the Ministry of Veterans and War Casualties, that Dr. and Mme Benedek were dead. He could only stammer, "But—but when—?"

The clerk pointed. "January eleventh, 1950. By petition of a Mademoiselle Odette Rose. Do you know her?"

"Excuse me," Konrad said, and hurried out the door.

"She did the job complete," Konrad said over the phone. "Once she got the declarative judgment, she took it to the procureur, and waited out the month. There was no appeal, and the procureur allowed the certificate to become valid. Now it's recorded in the Puy-le-Duc civil registry. I went up there myself to check it. The Benedeks are legally dead. She did exactly what we planned to do ourselves, except that she started almost a year ago and followed it through. Only I don't know why, because—"

Maître Lanson's slow, measured tones said, "It's obvious, I believe. She intends to call a new Council herself."

"That's what I thought," Konrad said. "But there's only one place she could call it, and that's before the justice of the peace of the east canton of Touville. The Tribunal settled that once and for all. And she hasn't, or at least, not yet. I've just come from there. Judge Bourget tells me he has no such case pending. He's familiar with the matter, or heard about it at any rate, and would know. Maybe she thought of doing it and changed her mind. Or maybe she hasn't got around to it yet."

There was a long pause. At length Maître Lanson said, "We must get ahead of her. You must make formal application for the new Council at once."

"That," Konrad said, "is just what I have done."

What a break! he thought, hanging up the phone. Mlle Rose had done his task for him, shortening his labors by as much as a year. It was October now. By next month, or December at the latest, the fourth Family Council could meet. The fourth and the last. Because this time, he thought grimly, there would be no month of grace; this time he would get a court order to implement the decision of the Council, demanding delivery of the boy within twenty-four hours, and he would appear at the Nursery with a police escort, ready to break down every door, if necessary, to find him. And suppose she were to take it to the Tribunal, as she had the last Council decision? Ha! On what grounds? This time the Council would be foolproof. There wasn't a court in the land that would annul it.

"Annulled!" Konrad said.

He was sitting up in bed, propped against pillows; for the past three days the fever and aches of the grippe had raged through his body, leaving him weak and cotton-limbed. It had been out of the question to attend the Tribunal hearing. Early this morning, to test his strength, he had got out of bed, and had saved himself from collapsing only by grabbing the back of a chair. Dr. Lévy had had to go in his stead, and had promised to come report to him on how the trial had gone. Now the ringing of the doorbell had announced, not Lévy, but his lawyers, bringing with them the raw damp of a rainy November afternoon and bearing on their faces the haggard expression of defeat. "Annulled!" Maître Lanson had cried, lifting his arms and letting them fall in a gesture that sent a spray of droplets to the floor. And Konrad, shocked, incredulous, could only repeat the word, his voice, muffled and hoarse, sounding strange in his own ears.

"Louis!" Rina said in alarm. "Where are you going? Get back in bed."

Without realizing it, he had pulled the cover aside and was groping with his feet for his slippers. Rina knelt beside the bed and tugged at his feet. He sank back against the pillows, breathing hard, suffering her to shove his feet under the blanket. A dull rage began to rise up in him, as he fixed his eyes on Maître Lanson's bloodless, lined face.

"But why?" he cried.

"Easy now," Maître Paul said. "It's a long story. It won't do any good to get excited. Allow me," he said to the older man, who muttered, "Yes, yes, I'm chilled through." He helped Maître Lanson remove his coat, which glistened with moisture, and then slipped out of his own. "Thank you," he said to Rina, who had stood up, panting, and came to take their coats. "Let me get you a towel," Rina said to Maître Paul, who replied quickly, "No, no," and took out his handkerchief. Mopping his face, he said, "A real downpour."

Maître Lanson had moved to the fireplace and run his fingers over his drooping, silky, yellowish-white mustache, then rubbed his hands together and held them out to the glowing coals. Over his shoulder he said in slow anger, "Boy scouts! It's time to retire, I think. What is left of the Republic, when there is no more justice?" His spare figure turned. "A French court! And I have lived to see it!"

"He's catching cold," Maître Paul said in a low voice to Rina. "If you had a drop of brandy, perhaps?" Rina nodded and hurried out. To Konrad he said somberly, "We didn't have a chance. They were waiting for us. It was all cooked up beforehand, regardless of the evidence."

"Evidence!" Maître Lanson cried in scorn. "What is evidence to a Minotard? What are facts? With their rag of a newsletter and their Catholic picnics! A word down the line, and they dance like monkeys on a string!"

"But," Konrad got out, bewildered, "she had no grounds."

"Do you want to know the grounds?" Maître Paul said. "Baptism, that was the grounds."

"What?" Was it a joke? At a time like this, when every breath sent pain through his chest? But Maître Paul was serious; his eyes gleamed strangely in his pale face. Konrad looked from him to the other, who nodded, coughing and waving his hand. "He dared," he said. "He took Paul aside and as much as told him so. He knew better than to say it to me. Do you know what I'd told him? Do you?"

"But who?" Konrad demanded. "I don't have the slightest—"

"Minotard," Maître Lanson said. "That hiker! Are you a judge? I'd have asked him. Which law are you sworn to uphold, civil or canon? That's what I'd have said. Madame," he said, turning to Rina, who entered at that moment, "I am a Catholic. Today, I assure you, I make the statement without pride."

Rina, offering him the tray, looked questioningly at Konrad, who said with difficulty, "Please!"

"Yes, yes," Maître Lanson said, tossing off his brandy with a little birdlike movement of his head. "Come, Paul, let us tell this man the worst. Sick as he is. Let us sit down."

They drew up chairs at the bedside. Rina offered a glass of brandy to Maître Paul, who first demurred and then said suddenly, "Yes, by God, I believe I will," after which Rina retired unobtrusively to the far corner of the bedroom, where she sat down and listened.

"First of all," Maître Lanson said, laying his thin hand on the cover over Konrad's knee, "it would have made no difference if you had been there. There is nothing to reproach yourself with. Lévy made a perfectly splendid civil party. Calm. Dignified. Articulate. But it didn't make any difference what he said, or anybody else for that matter. It was a foregone conclusion, as Paul told you. It was all set in advance. I've been in the law too long not to know the signs. The hearing was a farce. They didn't even bother to hold off the verdict to another date, as they usually do. They were too eager to put the Council in the wrong. They had the opinion already written. Boy scouts, with their road maps!"

"What do you mean, already written?" Konrad said. "How could—"

"When the judges came out," Maître Paul said, "the same thought occurred to me. They were in chambers eighteen minutes. They couldn't have weighed the evidence in that time, let alone write the verdict. Yet the verdict had four points to it, each fully developed. And the paper it was written on creased twice across. It must have been under Minotard's robe the whole time."

"But what points could they make?" Konrad cried. "There was nothing wrong with that Council!"

"Not a valid argument in the lot," Maître Lanson said. "The first was the aunt. Eva Weiss, the one who went to China. They said—"

"But first tell him what Mademoiselle Rose said," Maître Paul interrupted.

"Eh? Yes, yes, of course. Minotard asked her why she claimed that the Council decision did not truly represent the wishes of the family, and she said that no attempt had been made to learn the wishes of the boy's aunt, his mother's sister. Aunt Weiss, the only representative of the maternal line."

"But no one knows where she is!" Konrad said. "She's disappeared."

"Which is what I informed the Tribunal," Maître Lanson said. "And Paul here produced Hannah's and Mitzi's joint affidavit, which states the same thing. Minotard asked to see the affidavit, and he and the other two judges bent their heads over it, and mumbled a bit among themselves, and the hearing continued. We thought that was the end of it. And yet the first point of the verdict was that. Against all logic, against all common sense. And against the explicit instructions of Article 409 of the Code. Aunt Weiss was not present or represented at the Council, therefore the Council was invalid."

"But in the name of God!" Konrad cried angrily, "the woman may be dead! It's years since anyone has heard from her. How can—?"

"We said that too," Maître Paul said. "It didn't make any difference."

"Second point," Maître Lanson went on. "The Council was invalid because no member of the Office of Wards of the Nation took part in its deliberations, as required by the law of April twentieth, 1945. Oh yes," he nodded solemnly, as Konrad stared at him wide-eyed, "there is such a law. Where these learned gentlemen are off in their reasoning is that it has nothing to do with our case. That law, which is only a few years old, concerns provisional guardianships only, not definitive ones, like ours."

"Then how does it apply?" Konrad demanded.

"It doesn't apply. But they invoked it anyway."

"I see," Konrad said, his voice thick and uncertain. "Out-and-out robbery, then."

Rina said from her corner, "Please, Louis, you shouldn't—"

"Go on," he said. "What was the third point?"

"Strangers," Maître Paul said, with a mirthless smile. "Arnauld and Lévy. Mademoiselle Rose claimed they had no right to participate in a Family Council, as not being family and not having been close enough to the parents to sit in as friends. Lanson here jumped up and went after Minotard about Lévy's representing one of the

·278·

aunts by power of attorney, and had to be called to order. Then Lévy demanded to be heard, and told the whole history of his and Arnauld's relationship with Dr. Benedek as far back as 1939. Minotard ragged him, but Lévy held his own, and even had the spectators murmuring in sympathy. Useless. It did no good. The Tribunal ruled both of them out. And the fourth point was Houdy. The repository of Dr. Benedek's last wishes. Minotard pretended to be scandalized. 'What, sir,' he said, 'you were allowed to participate in the third Council, and passed over for the fourth?' And Houdy answered, 'Yes, Your Honor, in favor of a stranger.' "

"Yes," Konrad said. "In favor of the boy's godfather." He drew a deep breath, wincing as the pain struck at his chest. He felt oppressed and sick at heart. His fever had certainly gone up, he thought. He should have gone to the trial. Even if he had had to be carried in on a stretcher. To see with his own eyes and hear with his own ears the incredible things he had just been informed of. And so the judges had reached their conclusions before the trial, and had written out the verdict in advance! All of Mlle Rose's illogical arguments swallowed entire and copied out point by point, in a barefaced denial of the facts. Like a Nazi court. Like Vichy. There is still justice in France, he had said to Mlle Rose that day, so many disillusionments ago. How she must be gloating now, telling her friends how she had taught those Jews a lesson!

He leaned back and closed his eyes, feeling bitterness flow over him. Was there any use in fighting any more?

Maître Paul began to speak. Never in his life had he seen such a blatant subversion of the law, he said. Until now, in all their brushes with Mlle Rose and all their defeats, there had been some pretense of adherence to the forms, however unfair the decisions were. It had been possible for a man to find excuses for them. But now no excuse was possible. The judges had determined to come out into the open. The boy was not going to be given to his family, regardless of the law. A baptized child was not going to be turned over to Jews. They *wanted* the family to know that. That was the meaning of the fantastically prejudiced hearing today. They had deliberately let their bias be seen.

"And just in case we didn't get the point," Maître Paul said, "just in case we had the ridiculous pretension of carrying the matter further, Minotard waited for me in the corridor. And asked me point-blank if I didn't know the boy was baptized."

"I think," Konrad said suddenly, opening his eyes, "I'd have knocked him down."

"I said to him, 'Of course I know. The child was given an invalid baptism by a fanatic, against canon law. And only the moderation and decency of my client has prevented me from taking the matter to higher authority, to Rome if necessary.' Minotard flew into a towering rage. 'Now I see,' he said, 'the stories they tell about you are true.' And went off stamping his feet and waving his arms."

"Stories?" Maître Lanson said.

"I come from a family of converts," Maître Paul said simply.

"By Jove!" the older man said, blowing out his mustache, "I never knew that. And he had the nerve—!"

"Tell him about the bishop," Konrad said.

Maître Paul regarded him thoughtfully. "Yes," he said, "it does fit in, doesn't it?" He turned to the other lawyer. "There's a pattern being formed here. Tell me what you think of it. About a year ago Konrad wrote to the aunt in Israel, and mentioned that the local rabbi here, Rabbi Notarius, went to the bishop to complain about the boy's baptism. Rebenty said he didn't know anything about it, and promised to take disciplinary action against the priest who did it. Notarius was convinced that the bishop was sincere about it. Quite concerned, in fact. Admitted that it was against canon law. Well, several weeks later Konrad received a letter from the aunt, with several enclosed documents. She was furious. The bishop was a liar, she said. He knew about the case as far back as the spring of 1948. Right after they baptized him."

"Or before," Konrad snapped.

"Possibly," Maître Paul said. "I'm not trying to whitewash him. But it could well have been after. It seems that in the winter of 1947, when the aunt and her family were still living in Australia, the aunt went to the archbishop in Sydney and told him her story. She hoped that Mademoiselle Rose, being a Catholic, would listen to persuasion by the Church to give up the boy. The archbishop of Sydney wrote to the archbishop of Westminster in England, asking him to see what he could do. And, in his turn, the archbishop of Westminster wrote to Bishop Rebenty."

"Wheels within wheels," Maître Lanson commented.

"And wheels that turn slowly," Maître Paul said. "By now months had gone by. The boy had already been baptized. With or without the bishop's knowledge. Rebenty called Mademoiselle Rose in, in accordance with the archbishop's instructions, and that's what she told him, in addition to her own highly colored version of the facts. Rebenty thought it over for some time, and then wrote to Westminster, saying that Mademoiselle Rose said she had saved the boy's life after the family had abandoned him, and that she refused to give him up. It seemed to him, he said, a matter for the civil authorities to decide. A very cautious letter. He said nothing about the baptism."

"Then how do you know that's what Mademoiselle Rose told him?" Maître Lanson said.

"From the bishop himself," Maître Paul said. "The aunt in Israel sent Konrad the chain of letters. They had finally caught up with her in Harad. Konrad and I discussed the matter, and agreed that I ought to talk to Rebenty. To get a ruling on the validity of the baptism. And to suggest that this priest in Sep be given a little instruction in canon law. But I wasn't going to be put off as Notarius was. I took along the bishop's own letter to Westminster, and assumed from the start that he was familiar with the matter. He didn't like it at all. He hemmed and hawed—"

Maître Lanson said dryly, "I can just see him."

"And finally he admitted that Mademoiselle Rose had told him about the baptism. His hands were tied, he said. Once the boy was baptized there was nothing he could do about it. It was 'over his head,' he said."

A frown creased Maître Lanson's forehead. "Over his head? What does *that* mean?"

Konrad said harshly, "This diocese is under the jurisdiction of the archbishopric of Avignon. Cardinal Loriol, archbishop of Avignon, Primate of France. Bishop Rebenty's immediate superior, and the highest church authority in France."

"By Jove!" Maître Lanson said. "And does he have a finger in this pie?"

"We don't know," Maître Paul said. "We're only interpreting Rebenty's phrase. Of course, it could mean simply that the canon law involved would have to be analyzed by someone higher up, perhaps the cardinal, perhaps Rome. You could take it either way. But after what we saw today . . ."

After a long silence, Maître Lanson said thoughtfully, "a half-century. Give or take a few years. That's the time I've spent at law.

I'm seventy-four, and still able to hold my own, thank God. I was already a law student at the time of the Dreyfus trial, the second one, in 1899. I sat in on that trial, one day, at any rate. And this case reminds me of that one. It has the same stink of interests higher than the law. Pressures behind the scenes. The same feeling that what is going on in the courtroom is only a puppet show for the real drama taking place in hidden quarters. Do you suppose Minotard's instructions came from the cardinal himself?"

"Instructions?" Konrad said, staring.

"I'll wager," Maître Lanson said, "you never heard the term 'boy-scout magistracy.' No? I thought not. Perhaps only one in a hundred Frenchmen has. And that one probably a lawyer or a judge himself. Strange expression, is it not? And meaningless, you think. It is not meaningless, my friend, it is a fact. And what you've told me about the bishop simply confirms it still more."

"But what does it mean?" Konrad asked, puzzled.

"The Church in France is desperate," Maître Lanson went on, without heeding the interruption. "It is fighting a rear-guard action. I believe that is the correct military term. It has never gotten over 1789. Every year fewer men enter the priesthood. There are hundreds of churches in remote country districts that have no priests. The movement to win over the working classes has failed. More than one priest, taking part in the plan to approach the laborer on his own level, by wearing the same clothes and doing the same work at his side, has ended up by abandoning not only his soutane, but holy orders as well. True, the Church won a great victory two months ago in the Barangé law giving government subsidies to religious schools; but at the cost of alienating its liberal affiliations. And in its struggle for existence, to maintain itself, the Church has penetrated into strange places. Yes, into the magistracy itself."

Shaking his finger, he said indignantly, "Until now France had every right to be proud of its judiciary. No country in the world could point to a finer body of men of the highest professional competence and integrity. Catholics for the most part, and devout ones too, they administered the law regardless of creed. They were aristocrats, many by birth, all by nature. They would have repudiated with the utmost scorn any attempt upon their independence. It would have been unthinkable for them to take orders from anyone, or to submit to the influence of any group, religious or otherwise. I say 'would have.' Because we who have been associated with the law have seen a change taking place. You ask me, what does this strange combination of words mean. Boy-scout magistracy! That is the title given a secret freemasonry of magistrates, judges and procureurs within our court system, those who as boys and adolescents belonged to Catholic youth organizations, scouts or hikers or whatever you want to call them. In every courthouse there is a nucleus of them, or at least a correspondent. And they receive bulletins and circulars purporting to bear news and information, under cover of which they receive their instructions as to the attitude they are to take in certain matters. I have no doubt," he finished quietly, "that Minotard is one of them, perhaps the other two judges as well."

Konrad's head ached. So this was the meaning behind the old man's odd epithets! He found himself thinking of the letter he had received from the man who called himself Bira, almost two years ago, with his claims of a Catholic conspiracy, claims which he had dismissed as exaggerated. Bira too was a lawyer, he remembered; perhaps he too had noted, in the tribunals of Paris, the same web that Lanson was talking about now. Of course, Bira was a Jew, and would have been kept in the dark as far as possible; but Lanson was a Catholic. And so was Paul, in spite of his ancestry. Perhaps they had even been sounded out for membership in the clan. They ought to know. And here Lanson was making an indignant accusation against his own church. And Paul, he who had repeatedly urged him not to be hypersensitive, not to see slights and prejudice where there were merely misunderstandings and bad breaks—Paul said nothing now, but regarded him steadily, without expression, as if unwilling to affirm but unable to deny. What if it were so, then? Would it not explain those astonishing miscarriages of justice, those monstrous defeats coming upon the heels of petty victories, rendering them meaningless? Would it not explain how easily, how smoothly, the Rose woman wound her way through the juridical maze that for him, with the finest legal advice of Touville, had proved to be beset with so many difficulties and unforeseen obstacles?

A Catholic conspiracy in the court system! How tempting it was to accept the explanation on the face of it! Too tempting, in fact. Like the Communist conspiracy, which existed, as he knew from his own youthful errors, but which was blamed for a good many things that would have surprised Stalin himself to hear of. Or like the Elders of Zion, that myth perpetuated by the Nazi cynics to explain the so-called Jewish stranglehold on the world.

But if it were not so, then how could he understand the fantastically prejudiced hearing his lawyers had just come from, in which all
logic and justice had been openly flouted by three judges sworn to
uphold the law? Which law? Lanson had said. Which law is supreme
in France, civil or canon?

Perplexed, troubled, feeling his breath wheezing in his chest, he
rubbed his eyebrows with papery fingers, staring down at his blanketed knees. At last he looked up and said, "What is to be done?"

"Appeal," Maître Lanson said.

"Oh, yes!" Rina said, and fell silent in confusion, as all looked at
her.

"Ah?" Konrad said, with a crooked smile. "And go through it all
over again?"

With an intensity that made his voice quaver, Maître Lanson
said, "Fortunately, in our tribunals, and certainly in the higher
courts—Appeals and Cassation—the majority of our judges have
remained immune to the influence of Catholic ideology upon their
verdicts. The boy-scout magistracy is relatively new, you will find it
primarily among the younger set, that is, among the judges of the
courts of first instance. It is there that you have lost both your cases.
But I will stake my life on the supposition that the Touville Court of
Appeals will resist any pressures that may be put upon them. Four
points, and not one of them valid! You will see what Appeals does to
them!"

Konrad looked at Maître Paul.

Maître Lanson said, "If not, I will retire from the law. I think," he
added reflectively, "it's about time anyway."

"I have two lawyers," Konrad said.

"Appeal!" Maître Paul said with unexpected harshness. "And if
you lose, I won't leave the law, I'll take the matter to Rome."

Peering over the top of his round, steel-rimmed glasses, his great
grizzled head bent over his desk, Mayor Crisenoy studied the papers
that the woman laid before him one by one. Konrad, standing just
inside the quilted door, waited in silence, gazing out the window into
the heavy foliage of the trees in the square. The mayor seized a pen
and rapidly signed the papers, pushing each impatiently aside with
the back of his hand. The woman murmured something. "No," the
mayor said, putting his palms on the desk and pushing himself to his

feet. The woman gathered up the papers and came toward Konrad. "Please be brief," she said in a low voice as she went out the door. He started and looked after her angrily.

"Don't pay any attention to Mademoiselle Merlin, Monsieur Konrad," the mayor said, putting out his hand and smiling. "She guards me like a watchdog. At times too well, I'm afraid. You may have as much time as you need. However, you come at an unfortunate moment. I have been away, and upon my return—" He nodded ruefully toward his desk.

"I am aware of that, Your Honor," Konrad said, shaking hands and, at the mayor's gesture, sitting down on the chair beside the desk. "Mademoiselle Merlin told me so more than two weeks ago, on August thirty-first, to be exact, when I came to see you on a matter of the utmost urgency. Since then I have come back several times. Only today was it possible for me to see you. It concerns a municipal employee, Mademoiselle Rose, directress of the Nursery at St. Lazare."

"Ah," the mayor said noncommittally.

He knows all about it, Konrad thought. He said, "Your Honor is no doubt aware that for several years now I have been engaged in litigation with Mademoiselle Rose over an orphan child in her care, whom I am trying to have returned to his family."

"All Touville knows it," the mayor said, as the telephone rang. "Yes?" he said, picking it up and listening with a frown. "Well, find him and have him at the meeting at three."

"I assure you," Konrad said, as Crisenoy's portly bulk swung toward him again, "that it is not my wish that it come to this. However, I will be brief. The courts have recognized the justice of my claim. On July thirty-first the Appeals Court passed judgment, ordering Mademoiselle Rose to turn the boy over to me, as representative of the family, on or after August thirty-first, upon my first appearance. On that date, accompanied by a police officer of the arrondissement, by a bailiff of the court bearing the court order, and a friend, I presented myself at the Nursery. I was met by a Mademoiselle Deharme, who informed me that she was temporarily in charge of the Nursery and that Mademoiselle Rose was away on sick leave. I told her that I had no need to see Mademoiselle Rose, that I had come for the child, Michel Benedek; and I showed her the court order. 'I know the child,' she told me, 'but he is not here.' And that was all we could get out of her. She didn't know where the boy was, nor where Mademoiselle Rose had gone to recover from her illness. If we—"

A buzzer sounded on the mayor's desk. Konrad checked himself, and listened to Mlle Merlin's voice announce that M. Fontaine had to catch a train. In irritation the mayor said that M. Fontaine could wait five minutes more, M. Konrad had already waited two weeks.

"If we wanted to know where Mademoiselle Rose was," Konrad resumed, "we would have to go to the mayor, her direct superior."

There it is, he thought, remembering the bailiff's malicious expression of two weeks before, when, leaving the Nursery, Konrad had insisted that they appear in a body at the *mairie*. "It's no use," the man had said, "he won't tell you anything." And the police officer looking at him pityingly sideways: "Haven't you heard what all Touville knows?"

"But my dear fellow," Crisenoy said in mild astonishment, "I don't have the slightest idea where Mademoiselle Rose might be. I was away myself at the time. I didn't even know that Mademoiselle Rose had been sick. Upon my return I found a brief report from her to that effect, but as far as I remember—wait a minute. Mademoiselle Merlin," he said into the intercom, "would you please find Mademoiselle Rose's last report, the one concerning her sick leave? And bring it in here."

A moment later Mlle Merlin entered the office and laid a sheet of paper before her superior. The mayor glanced at it and handed it to Konrad, saying, "There, you see?"

The letter stated briefly that the undersigned, finding herself temporarily unable to fulfill her duties at the Municipal Nursery because of poor health, and upon the advice of her physician, had decided to use her accumulated sick leave time of thirty-three days to improve her physical condition. There would be no interruption to the Nursery services to the community, since Mlle Camélia Deharme, R.N., would assume the direction of the Nursery during the incumbent's absence. It was signed Odette Rose, R.N., Directress.

Konrad laid the paper down on the desk. Mlle Merlin picked it up, and, at a glance from Crisenoy, left the office.

Konrad said, "Is it not usual, Your Honor, that when a municipal employee, and especially a department head, goes on sick leave, he inform his superiors where he may be reached?"

"Yes," the mayor admitted cheerfully. "It is usual. But it is not a hard-and-fast rule. We leave a great deal of latitude to our personnel. A great deal. The essential thing is that community service not be interrupted."

Latitude to defy the law. To kidnap. "I find it strange," Konrad said dryly, "that Mademoiselle Rose's illness coincided so exactly with the date on which she was to turn over the child. In any case, she left me no alternative. I have been forced—"

The telephone rang. With a patient grimace, the mayor answered it. Konrad sank back into his seat, nursing his hands. These repeated interruptions were annoying. Were they doing it on purpose? Well, it didn't matter. It was quite clear that the mayor had no intention of helping him. He would make his offer and go.

"You were saying?" Crisenoy said, hanging up the receiver.

"On August thirty-first," Konrad said deliberately, "unable to find Mademoiselle Rose or learn of her whereabouts, and convinced that her disappearance had no other object than to defy the judgment of the Court of Appeals, I entered a charge of kidnaping against her before the Procureur of the Republic. The case has already been put before an examining magistrate, and I have already testified. When Mademoiselle Rose returns to Touville, and I suppose that sooner or later she will have to return, she will be summoned in her turn. Unless she either gives up the child in accordance with the court judgment, or finds some argument stronger than the pronouncement of the highest court of the land, she will be remanded to the Correctional Tribunal on a criminal charge. She will inevitably be found guilty, for the Appeals Court judgment is executory."

"You would go that far then?" Crisenoy said, peering at him curiously.

Konrad spread his hands. "What can I do?" he demanded. "I have no wish to send her to jail. What good would that do me? I want the boy, nothing more. As I told the examining magistrate, the moment she gives him up I will drop the kidnaping charge."

The mayor drummed on the desk with his fingers, and sighed. "I admire your persistence, Monsieur Konrad," he said. "But I have already said that I don't know where Mademoiselle Rose is to be found. When she returns, she will have to extricate herself from your charge as best she can. Mademoiselle Rose is a city employee, but she is also a woman. Her problem with the law has nothing to do with her functions as head of the Nursery. It is part of her private life. I can have nothing to do with it, even if I knew where she is.

Once the *mairie* begins to interfere with the private lives of its employees—"

The buzzer rang, and Mlle Merlin announced fretfully that M. Fontaine was leaving. "No," Crisenoy said. "Send him in."

Konrad rose to his feet. "I'm sorry," he said. "I had hoped—"

"It was a pleasure to meet you, Monsieur Konrad," the mayor said, heaving himself up and thrusting out his hand. "I do hope that this unfortunate affair can be settled to the satisfaction of all."

Releasing the hand, Konrad bowed slightly and strode to the door. It would be a long time, he thought grimly, before anyone would unseat Crisenoy at the mayor's desk.

5

THE DRIVER had stopped at the edge of the road, by a hedge, over which Mlle Rose could see a wide expanse of treetops. The hedge gate was open; a narrow dirt road led from it into the park, curving into the trees and disappearing from sight. This was the entrance, he told her. The monastery was about fifty yards in. Did she want him to drive her to the door? He would do so if she wished, but at the other end it was a bit difficult to turn around. No, she said, she preferred to walk.

She got out and paid the driver, turning to face the park as the taxi drove off. How lovely it was! The leaves had begun to turn. They rustled gently in the breeze, yellow and bronze and red amid the green. The trees were like stately sentinels, with their thick girths and lofty branches. They must be hundreds of years old. Like the monastery itself, whose photograph you saw reproduced on picture postcards, one of the prides of Strasbourg. She had bought one in the railway station last night, admiring the ancient, weather-beaten walls, the thick, X-shaped beams showing black against the white, the crooked red tiles of the low-slung roof. Fifteenth century, the legend said.

She began to walk down the dirt road. Ahead, through the foliage, she could just make out the building. She was grateful for the solitude that closed about her as she moved away from the highway. Like in a cathedral, she thought, looking up at the leafy arches towering overhead. All was hushed, as if time had stood still. How wonderful it would be if it were so! Back in Touville that bloodhound Konrad and his police would be frozen in their tracks, helpless to move a foot. And here, in this wooded sanctuary, over which so many centuries had rolled, and left untouched, she could dwell, free from preoccupation and care. With Michel, of course; forever young, unchanging, hers. What to others might seem like death would be life to her.

Daydreams, she told herself, sighing and shaking her head. Time would not stand still, it moved on with terrible speed, and every minute brought her closer to the dreaded day when she would have to go back and face the consequences of her defiance of the law. Already her month of leave was half over, and only now had she got the news she had been waiting for, and that gave her a new hope. Her last hope. If this failed, there was nothing more she could do.

Nothing, she told herself. She had tried everything, grasping at every straw, fighting for time. Did that Konrad never get tired? Had he nothing else to do but to persecute her? What was Michel to him, that he should dedicate his life to destroying him? Twice the Tribunal had saved her and forced her enemies to regroup their forces and start again. But then her luck had run out; the Appeals Court had brushed aside her arguments; Michel was to go to his aunt. That was final. And now she was outside the law, with nothing but her wits to help her.

She walked slowly, burdened by thought, yet savoring the calm freshness of the grove. Her mind was full of Michel. She had spent the last two weeks with him, at the Mother House in Paris. A wonderful time, in spite of the worry that lay like a stone on her heart. How pleasant it was to awake in the morning, and look ahead to a whole day with her boy! To come down the stairs to the nuns' refectory, and find him waiting for her at the breakfast table. To plan their day together over her coffee cup, knowing that this much at least was hers, that whatever might lie in the future, these precious hours were certain. Yes, she planned in days and hours now, she who, only a few short years ago, had put away Michel's satin armband in camphor against the day that it would serve for Michel's first-born. She had until the thirtieth of September, when Michel would board the train for Cassarate and the new school year, and she would return to the Nursery and—what? She did not know, she refused to think about it; and, after the first day of her stay in Paris, when she had talked to Michel about their case and given him his instructions, by tacit mutual consent they had avoided the subject. This was their time together; each day, each hour, was a self-contained eternity, to be made the most of. Perhaps, she realized now, there had been a touch of hysteria in their togetherness these past two weeks, as if their very exclusion of time from their reckonings had made their nerves pay the penalty in a greater awareness. Certainly, there were times when Michel's eyes gave away his despair. So serious, so grown up, so unsmilingly attentive, her little darling! There were moments, indeed, when she could forget he was a boy of eleven, and she talked to him openly, unreflectingly, without any of the safeguards that adults reserve in their conversations with children. He had to know the world that wanted to swallow him, and there was so little time!

"Can't we run away?" he had blurted out once; and she, noting how pale he had become, and how fixed and staring his eyes were, understood that he had been thinking about it for some time, and had spoken now because he couldn't hold back any longer. "Where?" she had asked. "Anywhere!" he had said fiercely. "Just you and I. Away from all of them. Where they can't find us." She had had to resume her tone of grownup then, and point out that it wasn't so easy to disappear just like that. Besides, he had the safest of all hiding places right now. "But what about you?" he had interrupted her. She had laughed then, to cover up the tug of gratitude in her heart, and told him he was not to worry about her, she still had a trick or two up her sleeve, and they were after him, not her; nothing was lost so long as he was out of Konrad's clutches.

That night, however, her assurance had deserted her, and she had sat in her room staring at the calendar, counting the days left to them. "September fourteenth," she repeated to herself several times. Half her time was gone. The other half would go even more quickly, like the last grains in an hourglass. It was then that Mother Veronica had telephoned from Touville and given her new hope.

She had stopped by a clump of bushes, beneath which clusters of tiny blue flowers winked up at her. What were they? she wondered, admiring the delicacy of their thin, crisp petals. How did they survive the chill of the changing season's nights? She herself, lying on her cot last night in a cell of the Strasbourg Temple, to which she had gone from the station, had awakened shivering, and had had to hunt for another blanket. Moved by an impulse, she bent over and touched a flower with her finger. Like touching God, she thought, going on her way again, cheered. It was a good sign to have found flowers in her path.

The road opened up into a small clearing of hard-packed claylike earth, beyond which she could see the monastery unobstructed. It was even lovelier than the photograph, which had not captured all the mellowness time had given it. There was moss at the joinings of the roof tiles, and swallows' nests in the greenish copper eaves. A flagstone path led between dwarf hedges to a heavy, bolt-studded door, beside which dangled a knotted rope.

Her heels sounded hollow on the flat stones. How many women have crossed this threshold? she wondered, as she tugged at the rope and listened to the brazen clang within. How still everything was! And if there were no one here? Perhaps they were out in the fields, gathering in their harvest. Hard-working, humble monks, dedicated to poverty, chastity, obedience. The Cornelians minded their own business; not like some, the Dominicans or Jesuits, say, whom one saw everywhere, mixing in the world and its affairs. Yet strangely enough, it was one of these unworldly Cornelians who had found the woman, when even the family didn't know where she was. A sound interrupted her musings; behind the patch of crossed bars on the door a panel had opened and a face could be seen. The next moment the door had opened, and a young monk stood before her.

Why, he's only a boy! she thought in astonishment, noting the curious look he gave her, and his timid, almost awkward air.

"I'm Mademoiselle Rose," she said. "Father Bosch is expecting me."

He let her in without replying, stepping around her to shut the door. With a slight bow, and blushing, he led the way down the dark hall, his long reddish-brown robe whispering softly over the uneven, polished tiles. The blush amused her. Fixing her eyes on the shaved spot amid his hair, she followed him gravely until he stopped by a closed double door and rapped gently.

"Mademoiselle Rose, Father," he announced in a low voice, having opened the door a few inches.

"Show her in," a voice said at once.

Mlle Rose found herself in a narrow, high-ceilinged room furnished in startling simplicity. The pitted white walls, except for a single crucifix, were bare. A rough wooden bench, three or four chairs of rustic design, an oak table as desk, a window seat on which lay a number of books—that was all. She might have stepped into the fifteenth century, she reflected, as she advanced toward the monk who rose from behind the table to greet her. He was of middle height and lean, with a narrow, hard-muscled face on which the cheekbones stood out prominently, and with tiny, whipcord lines about the mouth. His eyes, set close together, were of an intense blue, and had something fixed and penetrating about them, at once dreamy and alert. An extraordinarily handsome man, she realized, and one whose decisive movements and cut of jaw suggested power. Like an admiral on his bridge. Or rather, a horseman, used to dominating his mount. Obedience? she could not help wondering, as she sat down in the chair to which he motioned.

"I have received your telegram," he said, without preliminaries. "What is it exactly that you wish me to do?"

"You have located her, Reverend Father?"

"Yes. It was not difficult. Naturally, I said nothing of her whereabouts in wiring Mother Veronica. I note, however," he said, regarding her with curiosity, "that your telegram came from Paris."

"Oh," she said bitterly, "I have had to leave Touville. Like an outlaw. A bandit. And all because I would not give up my son to . . ."

He listened calmly as she explained; he too had sat down, his hands quiescent on his lap, his eyes intent on her face. "I see," he said, when she had brought her account to a close. "The Appeals Court decision is executory, then?"

"Yes, Reverend Father. I have appealed to the Court of Cassation, but I am required to give Michel up pending their decision. You can see that this is impossible. Suppose I win? I'd have to go whistling to Palestine to get him back. Do you think *they* will obey a reversal, once they have their hands on him? Oh, they had it all thought out," she went on. "They even asked to have me put under arrest, as a guarantee that I would comply with the decision and hand Michel over. But the court wouldn't go that far. They gave me a month, until August thirty-first. That was the day they were to come for him. And so I left on the thirtieth, the day before."

"And the boy?" he asked.

"He is safe. He is not in Touville."

"Thank you," he said. "I did not know the details. Mother Veronica wrote only that you had lost a case in law. And that the boy is baptized. It was enough, of course."

"You had to know," she replied. "It was only fair. I couldn't ask you to go into this blindly, without knowing the risk you were running."

He smiled then, unexpectedly. "These ancient walls have withstood greater risks, mademoiselle," he murmured. "They will not crumble yet a while. And as for blindness, we shall see who it is that is blind. There is more at stake here than they realize, with their lay bodies and their pitiful human justice. The issue is not who has the boy, although that is the most important to you, of course. In a wider sense the issue is more than the child's salvation, although that is its immediate cause. But there is the question of the Church itself. There is an irreducible conflict here, mademoiselle. Your case is a signpost of the times. Much will depend on its outcome."

She was not sure she understood him. Conflict, yes, but what did he mean by the rest? He did not choose to explain, but said abruptly, "The woman I was asked to locate is in Lautern, a small town in Austria, a few miles southeast of Vienna."

"Austria!" she said. "Surely she could not have been there all these years. She went to China. When did she come back?"

"Hong Kong," he corrected her. "If it had been the mainland, it would not have been so bad. But Hong Kong is under British rule."

She looked at him in bewilderment.

"I see," he said. "You know nothing of her, then?"

"Very little, Reverend Father. I only know that she went to China and disappeared. Or rather, Hong Kong. The family admitted in court that they had lost track of her. Why is Hong Kong worse than China?"

"Did you know she was a nurse? No? She worked in the American hospital in Hong Kong. She was there when the Japanese entered."

"Oh!" she said blankly.

"It's not a pretty story," he said, getting up and going to the window. "At best it's not clear what happened. Apparently the Japanese treated the American staff with little ceremony. Some of the nurses were molested. Eva Weiss of course had an Austrian passport, but in all probability it was stamped with the J. Eventually she was released, and returned to her job. Shortly after, however, she had a breakdown of some sort and was hospitalized. She seems to have passed from one institution or rest home to another. She was at Kowloon, on the mainland, for a while, perhaps elsewhere as well. Her last stay was at Macao, under the care of a Portuguese doctor. Then, about a year ago, she returned to Austria and settled in Lautern."

Mlle Rose had followed this narrative with growing horror. "Breakdown!" she said. "Do you mean she's crazy? Out of her mind?"

Father Bosch smiled thinly. "It's a matter of definition, I suppose," he said. "You understand that I have not seen her myself. I can only go by the reports furnished me. It seems, though, that she is not out of contact with reality. It's more a question of nerves. At times she becomes highly excitable and says some strange things. Most of the time, however, she is quite calm. Quiet, bitter, and disagreeable. 'Lost' was the word my informant used. As though she were living in some private inner purgatory of her own. She took up nursing again in Lautern, but had to leave it. Now she does sewing, and earns only enough to keep herself alive. She lives alone, goes nowhere, receives no visits, except those of her clients, receives no mail, does not read the newspapers—in short, seems to have withdrawn within herself. Except for a walk in the evening, she never leaves her house."

"Oh, dear God!" she said involuntarily. She had not foreseen this complication. On the one hand, the woman's mysterious disappearance was explained. She had gone to pieces, poor thing, and had retired to a quiet corner of her native land to live out her days in peace and be let alone. What had the Japs done to her, to bring about a change like that? But while her mind dwelt in pity on that shattered life, she had her own dilemma to consider too. Was it really true that the family did not know where she was, as had been said at the last Tribunal hearing, and as the Appeals Court had believed? Or, in view of her condition, had the family decided to leave her out, as being not quite there, difficult to manage? Would not she, Mlle Rose, be playing into Konrad's hands by contacting the woman? And even if Konrad's lawyer had told the truth, how much validity would the courts give to a statement by Eva Weiss, with her medical history? It didn't make any difference, she decided. She had to take the chance. She had no other choice.

Father Bosch was regarding her expectantly. She produced the letter from her purse. She wanted this delivered to Eva Weiss, she said. She could not send it through the mails, because accompanying her letter was a document that she wanted the woman to sign. And, human nature being what it was, she would not sign it unless someone were at her side to urge her to do so. Someone who spoke German, and could answer the questions that were bound to be asked. The letter, which she had had translated into German, explained everything. If the Reverend Father could read German—?

Gravely he took the letter from her hand. He glanced through it and returned it to her, saying thoughtfully, "Yes, I see where you are going. I must confess I had no idea before. By the way, her signature should be notarized. But that can be arranged. I will send one of our friars, Brother Anselm. He is most discreet, is an Alsatian who speaks French and German with equal fluency, and was a lawyer before entering our order. Will that do?"

"Oh!" she cried, filled with gratitude. He cut her short. "I suggest also that I send a letter along with yours. The woman does not know you. She may be readier to listen if you are vouched for."

She could only nod, her eyes suddenly smarting with tears.

Brother Anselm, when he appeared, startled her with his resemblance to Father Périer. But the monk, though bowed, was cheerful and robust, with a tanned, leathery face. While Father Bosch dictated to him in German, Mlle Rose sat in the window seat and looked out into the tiny garden below. What could Mother Veronica have written, for this abrupt, domineering man to be so willing to help her? What connections the Temple Dame had! Two of a kind, she thought, noting the superior's thin decisive lips with those odd lines about the corners, the calm intensity of his gaze, the strong, tapering, aristocratic fingers. Mother Veronica had every confidence in him. "If anyone can find her, he can," she had said, and she had been right.

Father Bosch had finished, and was reading through the letter that the monk had handed him. Obligingly he translated it for her, and she nodded in approval. Then, at the superior's invitation, she gave Brother Anselm his instructions. He must not be put off, she told him. Eva Weiss was to sign the document, preferably before a notary, but without that formality, if necessary. Mlle Weiss would undoubtedly ask questions about her, Mlle Rose, and how her nephew happened to be with her. It was all in her letter; it would be well for Brother Anselm to read it and familiarize himself with the details.

"One more matter," Father Bosch said as the monk was about to leave. "The lady is nervous, and given to irritability. And she is not a Catholic. She must be led gently."

When Brother Anselm had gone, Father Bosch asked after Mother Veronica. It was years since he had seen her, he said; a most remarkably intelligent person, and with a depth and intensity of devotion such as one found in the saints. He was pleased to be able to be of service to her in this matter. "She takes an extraordinary interest in your child," he said thoughtfully, fixing Mlle Rose with his gaze.

Yes, that was true, Mlle Rose admitted. The reverend father

might judge from that what an unusual boy Michel was. She described Michel to him, and, emboldened by his interest, related the story of how he had come to her. He was more thoughtful than ever when she had finished. "Some are born with a destiny prepared for them," he said. "Michel may be one of those. And though God loves all the souls that come from His hands, He loves some more than others. This is a mystery we cannot penetrate. We cannot measure infinities. We must consider all souls to be of equal value, a value so immense that the meanest human creature on earth is worth more than all the stars. And that is why Mother Church is jealous of all her children. We cannot afford to let one escape us. We must fight for the soul of your boy as though it were that of all humanity, as though it were a question of the salvation or damnation of all mankind, as though God's immortal work in the creation of Adam and his offspring were to stand or fall by this alone. That is the motivation behind Mother Veronica's interest, mademoiselle, and mine as well. Of course we will help you! If you could not count on our help in such a cause, it were better the Church had not been founded at all. I tell you this: If there were no other way to save the faith of your boy, I would crawl on my hands and knees to Lautern for that woman's signature. And the monk who would not do this is not fit to bear the cloth."

Father Bosch's voice had taken on such intensity, and his eyes such a gleam, that Mlle Rose was disconcerted. "What did you mean by conflict?" she dared to ask. "A moment ago you said—"

"The lay spirit," he caught her up. "It lies over the world like a fog. It is the greatest enemy of our age. Every day our sky becomes darker, and the light of Mother Church is seen more dimly."

Yet once, he went on, it was not so. There was a time when Mother Church dominated the known world to the point where one might almost have thought that the millennium was at hand. It was in the time that has since become known as the "Middle" Ages, a name set down in books with a touch of condescension, as though it were merely the uncivilized transition to something better. But it might well have become the final age, the time of the second coming of Christ, the fulfillment of the Apocalypse, except for man's cursed propensity to play with the devil.

"It has become the fashion today," Father Bosch said, "on the part of the so-called liberal thinkers, to sneer at the devil and rationalize him away. According to them, the devil does not exist, hell is a myth, damnation is a state of the mind. Nothing could be farther from the truth. It is the devil himself who has turned our heads with this pretty logic. Reason, God's greatest gift to man, had been turned by Satan to his own uses. For reason is pride, and pride is Satan's home. The devil is real, mademoiselle. This is the lesson that the world has forgotten, and this is our downfall."

The Church was locked in a battle to the death with the lay spirit. For the Church, repository of God's truth, no longer held the power over men's minds it once had. Power was now in the hands of civil governments, civil law, uniformed police, the general at the head of his army, the dictator, the soulless earthbound philosophy committed to the fulfillment of material wants, the wealthy entrepreneur, the scientist, all of those who, puffed with pride, never for a moment questioned their right and ability to rule, judge, and decide the fate of men. History spoke with enthusiasm of the Renaissance, the Age of Enlightenment, as though they were triumphs over the power of darkness; whereas, the truth was that these themselves came from the Prince of Darkness, and there never was a more enlightened age than that of the Middle Ages, when men knew what they had to know and left the rest alone. What other desire was more God-given than the eagerness to return to the heaven whence one had come? What other knowledge was more important than the way of life that would achieve that blessed end? The earth might have become one universal theocracy, with priest and ruler merged into the single person of the Holy Father; it had almost done so; but it was the lay spirit, the misuse of reason, that had conquered. Today there was only a small patch of land by the Tiber River where His Holiness could command; throughout the rest of the world he could only recommend. And this was the result: Mlle Rose, in difficulties with the law, to which heartless abstraction the soul did not exist and only bodies counted, was not to be allowed to continue the instruction that would save her child's soul, and had to resort to subterfuges to carry out God's will.

"There is only one hope for the world," Father Bosch said. "The ascendancy of the Church. The lay spirit must be destroyed. It will not happen in our time. But it will happen. Otherwise God's word is made a mockery, and if there is anything that history has taught us, it is that God will not be mocked. For us there remains only to do His will, and to wait."

Mlle Rose had followed this ringing tirade with bewilderment. She felt out of her depth. All this over Michel! But he's only a boy, she thought, with a touch of resentment. She supposed it was natural for Father Bosch to feel the way he did; he was a monk. Her wants were much more simple. She wanted Michel, that was all. She smiled uncertainly, and said, "Thank you, Father, for explaining it to me."

"What will you do now?" he asked, in an abrupt change of tone. "It is a long way to Lautern. Brother Anselm will not return for two or three days."

"I am staying at the Temple here," she said. "I will go there and wait."

He promised to notify her immediately upon the monk's return. At her departure she tried to thank him. He turned away from her with a gesture, leaving her to the young monk, who escorted her to the door and blushed once more at her good-bye.

"Bring her the boy?" Mlle Rose's voice echoed her dismay. "But what for?"

"She wants to see him," Father Bosch said. "He is her sister's son. She had all but forgotten his existence. What was her expression, Brother Anselm? A treasure found?"

"Yes, Reverend Father," the monk said.

"But I don't understand," Mlle Rose said, bewildered. "What does she want to do with him? Is that her condition, or what? If I bring her the boy, she'll sign the release?"

Father Bosch looked at the monk, who said gently, "There was no promise, Mademoiselle Rose. You must understand," he went on at her gesture of impatience, "that I was dealing with a person who is not completely normal. I don't quite know how to describe it. It is as though her spirit had died, and only the body is alive. She is completely remote from this world. Remote, and filled with a sadness that is quite pitiful. At my explanation she showed no emotion at all, simply listened and asked me to leave your letter with her. She showed no interest in the paper to be signed, said she needed time to think, told me to return in two days. I thought it best to comply, and not to insist as yet. When I returned two days later, she showed me a letter her sister had written to her when the boy was born, in 1941. She had hunted it up among the things she had brought with her from Hong Kong. 'They are all dead,' she said. I assured her that Michel was very much alive, thanks to Mademoiselle Rose. That was when she used that expression, 'a treasure found.' But I had the impression she didn't quite believe me, for several times during the course of the conversation she repeated that they were all dead. Once she even said 'we.' 'We' are all dead."

"Good heavens!" she said. "Then she *is* mad."

"I suppose so," the monk rejoined. "And yet, if not for her apathy, one would not know it. She is not stupid, by any means. It's obvious that she had suffered a great deal. If you want my opinion—"

"Oh, please!" she said.

"I think," the monk said slowly, "that if she were to see the boy, she would sign the paper. She cannot quite accept the fact that he is alive. It goes against her obsession, you see."

"But suppose it's a trap!" Mlle Rose exclaimed.

Father Bosch and the monk exchanged glances. "That has already occurred to us," Father Bosch said with a smile. "Brother Anselm agrees that it would be a mistake for you to take the boy to Lautern and under the jurisdiction of Austrian law. And so he has made a suggestion to me, which I present for your consideration. Why not offer to bring her here to meet her nephew?"

"Here?" she said. "At the monastery?"

"Why not? Brother Anselm will return to Lautern with your offer, which will include her traveling expenses. She can spend the night here and return home the next day. It will cost her nothing. But our condition is that she sign the paper first. Brother Anselm will buy her ticket for her and travel with her. Here," Father Bosch said meaningfully, as Mlle Rose hesitated, looking from one to the other, "we are in control."

"Let me think," she said. It could be done, she realized. Today was the twenty-first. Michel was in Paris. She had nine days in which to handle it, nine days before Michel had to be on the train for Cassarate, for the beginning of the new school year. She could bring the two together for a few hours, to satisfy that mad aunt of his and fulfill her part of the bargain, and get Michel back to Paris on time. And by the first, when her own leave of absence ran out, she would be back in Touville, with that precious document in her pocket. She did not like the idea, but it could be done. Which meant that it *had* to be done, since there was nothing else she could do.

"Thank you," she said. "I accept your proposal."

6

❦

J ULES?" Konrad said into the telephone. "Can you come over
here? Something important has come up."

"Now?" Jules's voice was incredulous. "At this hour? And in this
rain? Are you out of your mind? I'm in my pajamas."

"I tell you it's important."

"Come over and get me in your car."

"I can't. I have a guest here."

"Who?"

"Eva Weiss," he said, and hung up.

One minute to get out of his pajamas, he reflected, entering the
living room. Another minute to be out in Place Chapelle, racing for
the cab station. Ten minutes to arrive at Cours Berthet. In twelve
minutes Jules would be bursting through the door, to see the mysterious aunt who had turned up, after so many years, out of nowhere.

He himself had not yet got over the shock. He had been reading
the newspaper, yawning, too lazy to go to bed, when the doorbell
rang. He had hurried to the door to prevent a second ring, which
might wake Judas up, wondering who would come calling at eleven
o'clock on a rainy Sunday night. The woman who stood on the dripping doorstep had come without an umbrella; her coat was sodden
with rain, as was the dark beret she wore over her mannish gray hair.
He had gaped at her harsh, lined face, which was streaked with
water and as expressionless as a mask, and could only nod at her
question, "Herr Konrad?" At the same time he had noticed the small
valise at her feet.

"I was told to come to you," she had said in German. "I am Eva
Weiss. Lili's sister." And she had added, with no change in tone, "I
am wet."

In the next few minutes, before Rina led the drenched visitor to the bedroom for a change of clothing, he had learned only that Eva Weiss had come from Austria, having received a cablegram from Hannah, and that she had walked from the station. Now he stood staring at the damp patches in the carpet, wondering what the woman was telling Rina in the bedroom. Could she really have walked from the station, carrying that bag? He had seen no sign of a taxi in the street. Why hadn't she telephoned him? He would have gone to pick her up.

Rina came out, her eyes wide with excitement. "She's drying herself," she said. "I gave her my bathrobe, she was soaked through and through. She'll stay here with us tonight." She came closer and said in a whisper, "Louis, I don't think she's—well, *normal*. Did you see her eyes? I thought maybe she walked because she had no money, but when I asked her about it she said it hadn't occurred to her. To take a taxi, I mean. And when she opened her purse, I saw some bills in it. She said a monk gave it to her."

"A monk!" he said, staring.

"And she said that Mitzi gave her some more."

"Mitzi? She saw Mitzi in Vienna?"

"That's all I could get out of her. She talks so strangely. It will be a wonder if she doesn't catch pneumonia. I'm going to give her some brandy."

Left alone again, Konrad went to the window and stared out, puzzling over this strange creature who had fallen in on them in that unexpected way. Where could she have been all these years? She had said that Hannah had sent her a cablegram, yet in her letters Hannah had written that she did not know where she was. Not that it mattered now, he thought grimly. But a year ago, or a little less, he would have given much to have been able to produce her at the trial. What could have brought her to him now, without so much as a note announcing her arrival?

A taxi had pulled up before the house. Konrad went to the door, glancing at his watch. Fourteen minutes had gone by since his phone call. He had not been so far wrong. He opened the door, and Jules backed in, shaking his umbrella outside.

"A fine thing to do to a man," he said reproachfully.

"Lise didn't come with you?"

"She's in bed, with grease all over her face. Or whatever it is women put on at night to charm their husbands. Anyway, she's coming down with a cold. She wouldn't stir out tonight for anything.

Give me a handkerchief, will you? Forgot mine. By the way," he added, mopping his face, "this isn't a joke, is it? She's really here?" Seeing Konrad's face, he shrugged. "All right, but why?"

"That," Konrad said, "is what we're going to find out."

Eva Weiss sat on the sofa. She wore Rina's flannel robe and fur-lined slippers. She had toweled her hair and combed it straight back. Her face, which wore no make-up, was seamed and lined like carved wood. She had been ill, she said abruptly. She had had no idea that anyone had been concerned about her, or worried over her disappearance, until she had talked to Mitzi. But that was part of her illness. She had been in Hong Kong when the Japanese entered. It was like the end of the world. She had had the delusion that she had died. She knew now that it was a delusion; the doctors had explained it to her; it was a defense mechanism. Something frightful had happened to her. She had been forced to watch certain things in a torchlit room, in which laughter and screams had been mingled together, until it was her turn. She had tried to tell them she was not an American, but that didn't make any difference. Then the pain began, and that was all she remembered until much, much later, when the doctors convinced her that she didn't have to play dead any more. She took up her existence again, but her past was wiped out. She had put it all out of her mind. There was no one left but her. That was why, when she returned to Austria, she had settled down quietly in an out-of-the-way little village and not tried to look anybody up. What was the use? She bothered no one, and no one bothered her. Until one day last week a monk came to see her.

"I thought he was begging," she said. "I told him I had no money. No, no, he said, he had a letter for me, from Strasbourg."

Konrad had been listening in growing horror and compassion, aware of Rina's stricken face and Jules's narrowed eyes. Another victim, he told himself savagely. They had thought that she was one of the few who had escaped. Did you see her eyes? Rina had said.

Then he stiffened and stared at her incredulously. For in the same inflectionless voice she had added, "From Mademoiselle Rose."

"What?" he said stupidly. "Mademoiselle Rose? In Strasbourg? She wrote you a letter from Strasbourg?"

The next moments were full of confusion. All spoke at once, while Eva Weiss looked from one to the other. It was Konrad who recovered himself first. He had risen to his feet. Now, with a great effort, he sat down again and said, "Please, Fräulein Weiss, tell us about this letter. Begin at the beginning and tell us everything. We will try to be patient."

"I don't understand what is going on," she said. "But I will tell my story, and you will tell me what is behind it all. At first I thought it was a mistake, the letter was not for me. I do not know a Mademoiselle Rose in Strasbourg, I told the monk. He insisted that the letter was for me, that it explained itself. And so I read it while he waited. It was not a mistake. The letter said that Lili's boy, Michel, was alive. Mademoiselle Rose had saved him from the Nazis and cared for him all these years. But now she wanted to send him to a state school, and in order to do so she needed an official declaration from me. She was sending the declaration for me to sign. At first I couldn't believe it. I had forgotten Michel's existence. Even if I had remembered him, I'd have thought he was dead, like the rest. But the monk assured me it was true, and while he was speaking, I remembered a letter I had received from Lili at Hong Kong, telling me she had had a little boy. Was it possible that he had survived? I couldn't take it in. The monk put the declaration in my hand, and I looked at it, but I was so confused that it didn't mean anything. I kept telling myself, Lili's boy is alive. The monk took the paper from my hand and read it to me and explained it; he wanted me to sign it at once. Finally I told him that I had to think it over, to come back in two days. He was very disappointed; it was important for Michel's career, he said, but very well, he could give me two days."

She stopped, and pressed her fingers to her temples. Konrad watched her grimly. What trick was this? What was this "official" declaration the monk had brought for her signature? A woman who, by her own confession, was or had been mentally ill. He waited, hiding his impatience.

"That night," Eva Weiss said, dropping her hands, "I went down to the cellar where I kept the box I had brought with me from the East. I found Lili's letter. It was dated May 1941. I can't tell you what it did to me to read it again, after so many years and so much unhappiness. It was like a blow. For the first time I realized what had happened to me. It was as though I had truly died during that time, and my world had died with me. I sat on the floor and cried. I don't know how long I stayed there. The light bulb burned out, and I stayed there in the dark, remembering things. It was like giving them existence again. Lili, my baby sister, I said to myself. The last time I saw her was in 1938. Fourteen years ago. She wouldn't recognize me now, I thought. I am an old woman now. But of course, she couldn't see me now, she was dead. And then I began to wonder whether it was really so. I had taken it for granted, but how did I know it was true? And then I remembered that Mademoiselle Rose's letter said that she had saved Michel after the death of his parents. And so Lili *was* dead, and her Karl was too. It was a terrible moment for me. Lili had come alive for me for an instant, and I had lost her again. I cried some more, and then began to wonder about the others. Maybe some had escaped, like Michel. And all the time I was thinking, underneath my sadness, that I was well again, at last. Because I couldn't realize how sick I had been until I was well enough to realize it. It was the strangest feeling in the world. I'm well again, I told myself over and over. And suddenly a great curiosity came over me, a hunger to know everything about those years I had lost, to see Michel and any others of the family that might have survived. I fell asleep there in the cellar, on the floor, thinking that now things would be different, that I could begin to live again.

"The next day I reread Mademoiselle Rose's letter, and studied the declaration she wanted me to sign. It was very puzzling. It was really two separate statements on the same sheet of paper. The first had a place for me to sign, identifying myself as Michel's aunt on the maternal side, and authorizing him to study medicine at a state school."

"Medicine!" Konrad cried out. "But the boy's only eleven!"

"Wait," she said. "The second said that I entrusted the education of my nephew to Mademoiselle Rose and that I officially appointed her his guardian."

"For heaven's sake!" Konrad cried angrily, jumping up. "I hope you didn't sign it!"

She replied with dignity, "I have been sick, but I am not a fool."

Konrad turned to Jules. "Do you see what she's after? She's defied the Appeals Court. She knows she can't get away with it, and that I'll be waiting for her when she comes back. Somehow she managed to locate Fräulein Weiss, how I don't know. Just imagine what she could do with a signed statement like that! It would open up the whole case again, or at least throw a wrench in the machinery. And she has the nerve to go to her with a proposal like that, knowing that this aunt has been out of touch with the case and might be induced to sign. And to use a monk for her messenger boy!"

"Clever," Jules said briefly.

"But Louis," Rina said. "Can she get away with such a thing? Even after the Appeals Court—"

"Who knows what she can get away with?" he caught her up. "These courts will listen to anything she has to say, even the most obvious lies and nonsense." He turned to his visitor, insisting, "But you didn't sign?"

"No," she said. "I wasn't going to sign anything without seeing the boy. I told the monk that when he returned. But it wasn't only that. There was a little detail that bothered me. You mentioned it just now. I couldn't believe that in France medical studies start at the age of eleven. It made the whole thing suspicious. I didn't say that to the monk. I simply said I wanted to see Michel; then I would consider what to do. He had to be content with that. He went away, saying that I would soon hear from him again.

"A few days later he was back. He had an offer to make to me, he said, on behalf of Mademoiselle Rose. She was perfectly willing for me to meet Michel, but he was just getting over the measles and was not to fit to travel. Why didn't I come to him? Mademoiselle Rose would pay my expenses to Strasbourg and back. I could spend the afternoon—"

"Just a moment," Konrad said unsteadily. "Let me get this straight. The monk told you that Michel was in Strasbourg, with Mademoiselle Rose? Are you sure of that?"

"Why, yes," she said. "Or else why should I go there?"

"Strasbourg!" Jules said. "So that's where he's been!"

Rina said ruefully, "Louis, you never thought to look there?"

"Why should I?" he demanded. "But please go on, Fräulein Weiss. Did you go to Strasbourg?"

"No," she said. "I came here instead. The appointment was for today. Sunday the twenty-eighth."

"But how—?" he began in bewilderment.

"But let me tell you. The monk was all for my leaving then and there. This was on Thursday. No, I said, I have to get ready first. I'll come on Sunday. I wasn't satisfied, you see. I thought, I'll go to Vienna, to the old Benedek house in the Leopoldstadt. Maybe someone there will be able to tell me if any of the family are left. And that's what I did, the next day. I went to the door and rang the bell, and Mitzi answered it. Albert's widow. You can imagine how we both felt, staring at each other. Each of us thought the other was dead. After the first excitement was over, I brought up the question of Michel. She was astonished. She thought that Michel was with Hannah by now. There had been a lawsuit between Hannah and this Mademoiselle Rose, and Hannah had won. We didn't know what to do. Finally we decided to send a cablegram to Hannah, asking about Michel. That same night we received the answer. It said that Michel had disappeared with Mademoiselle Rose, and for us not to do anything without first contacting Monsieur Konrad in Touville. And that's what we decided to do. On Saturday—yesterday—I sent a telegram to Mademoiselle Rose in Strasbourg, telling her I couldn't come until the thirtieth. I asked her to confirm by wire that she would be there with Michel at that time. As return address I gave the name of a hotel in Vienna. Late that afternoon the answer came. Mademoiselle Rose said she and Michel would be at the Cornelian monastery in Strasbourg at noon on the thirtieth, waiting for me. And I have come here instead. Now, Herr Konrad, perhaps you can tell me what is going on here."

Staring at Eva Weiss's harsh, ravaged face, Konrad felt a surge of gratitude. How well the poor woman had managed everything! For once the Rose woman had outsmarted herself. Setting a trap for the boy's aunt, she had fallen into one herself. For the first time since Michel was spirited away from the Nursery four years ago, Konrad knew where he was. And it was Mademoiselle Rose herself who had given his whereabouts away! Eva Weiss's rendezvous was for Tuesday, two days from now. Just time enough to make all the arrangements, talk to his lawyers, lay his hands on the Appeals Court judgment in Maître Paul's office, contact the police in Strasbourg, and make the trip. Because he was going with Eva Weiss to Strasbourg. He would have to work out the details, but the basic fact was simple. The courts had awarded the boy to him, for delivery to his aunt in Israel, and he was going to take him. Right out of the walls of the Cornelian monastery, whose monks had lent themselves to the shameful game of trying to split a family and defy the law!

Jules was regarding him gravely. "You'll come?" Konrad asked.

"Of course," Jules said.

Konrad looked at his watch. It was after midnight. Maître Paul was probably asleep. Well, it couldn't be helped. "Fräulein Weiss," he said. "I'm going to call my lawyer now. After that I'll be glad to answer your question. But I suggest that we get to sleep as soon as we can. We have a long couple of days before us."

The taxi in front of him was slowing down. Konrad eased down on the brake, watching as the driver's arm thrust out and pointed across the highway to where the row of hedge was broken by a gate. As he passed in front of the gate, Konrad saw a dirt road curving into the tall trees of the park. "That's it," he said. At his right Eva Weiss peered over his shoulder at the park as they went by. From the back seat Jules grunted, "I don't see it."

"Aren't we going in?" the bailiff asked.

"Not yet," Konrad said. Ahead of him the taxi edged to the right and halted on the gravel shoulder beside the ditch. Konrad pulled up behind him. The driver got out and came up to him. Konrad opened the window.

"That's the entrance," the driver said. "The monastery is behind those trees, like I told you."

Konrad let his glance move along the veil of foliage across the road. "It's a big place," he remarked.

"Used to be bigger," the driver said. "This whole area was theirs. Goes back to the fifteenth century. It was nothing but wilderness then, they tell me. They've been selling pieces of it ever since."

"How far in is the building?"

"Not far," the driver said. "I could throw a stone that far, when I was younger."

Konrad turned and spoke softly to Jules. "We can't risk going in. But if we stay out here, we won't be able to see her signal. She would have to come down to the highway, and they might get suspicious."

"We could hide among the trees," Jules suggested. "Cowboys and Indians."

Konrad grinned mirthlessly. "No," he said. "No tricks. They're the ones who have to hide, not us." He considered rapidly. A little way ahead an earth embankment crossed the ditch to a field fringed with shrubs. From there the entrance to the monastery would still be in sight. But the taxi driver would have to help. "Jules," he said, "put the bag of toys in the taxi, will you?" To the driver he said, "You'll drive the lady to the monastery and park as close to the door as you can. She will enter without taking the toys with her. You stay there and wait. Leave your meter running. She should be out again in a few minutes to get the toys. When she does that, you leave and come here, and I'll pay you. I'll be parked off the road, over there, behind those bushes." He pointed to the spot. The driver followed his finger; he seemed puzzled.

"You're not going in?"

"No," Konrad said. "Just the lady."

The driver considered that for a while, looking from one to the other. "I don't get it," he said. His face, which was round and pleasant, had become watchful. "Are you detectives, or what? I don't want to get mixed up in anything. You hired me to show you where the Cornelian monastery was. You told me to point it out to you and drive past. I did that. But the rest—"

"Look," Konrad said. "What are you worried about? This lady is coming to see her nephew, who's visiting the monastery. She brought him some toys. You picked her up at the station and brought her here. You're a taxi driver, you're doing your job, that's all. You don't know anything about us."

"Why can't you pay me now?" the driver said. "I'll drop her at the door and go on my way."

Konrad said patiently, "The toys. If she comes out and takes the toys, it means that the child is there. You come and tell me that, and I'll pay you off."

The driver whistled under his breath and pushed back his cap. He looked frankly worried. "How do I know you're not kidnapers?"

The bailiff leaned forward in the back seat. "I'm an agent of the court," he said. "We're executing a court judgment, that's all. There's no question of kidnaping."

"We're losing time," Konrad said. "Here, look at this." From the seat beside him he picked up the thick folder he had gotten from Maître Paul and removed a document. "Here's the judgment," he said. "Here, you see? Appeals Court, city of Touville. July thirty-first, 1952. I'm from Touville. This gentleman is an usher of the Strasbourg Tribunal. He's going to serve the paper for us. It's all quite legal."

"Well," the driver said, taking a deep breath. "I guess it's all right. You had me worried there for a minute. Hiding in the bushes. What was I to think? If I understand you, you want me to wait by the door until the lady comes to get the toys. And then come and tell you."

"That's right. It will probably be only a minute or two. But it may be that the boy hasn't arrived yet. Then you'll have to wait longer. Maybe an hour, maybe more."

"It's your money," the driver said.

Konrad spoke rapidly in German to Eva Weiss. She nodded, her face expressionless. "Poor boy," she said. "I will frighten him. This face of mine." She got out of the car and entered the cab. The driver made a U turn, moved down the road, and, swinging wide, disappeared through the gate.

Better get off the road. If the Rose woman were to arrive now and catch a glimpse of him . . . He started the motor and crossed the embankment, making a circle and stopping just short of the shrubs lining the ditch. Through the branches he could just make out the monastery entrance. Glancing at his watch, he saw that it was twelve-thirty. At noon, the telegram had said. He had deliberately arrived a little late. Whatever else the Rose woman was, she was punctual. She would be waiting inside, looking impatiently at her watch, as he was doing now. There! In the distance he heard a car door slam. Eva Weiss had gotten out of the cab. Another few minutes, and their hunt was over.

He could hardly believe it. Four years! he said to himself, incredulously. More. Four and a half. April 1948. September 1952. For all that time Odette Rose had led him a dance through more legal labyrinths and byroads than he imagined existed. Four Family Councils! They had made legal history, Maître Paul had assured him. Their case would be studied by law students throughout France. Professors from their podiums would analyze all the details, pointing out in their pompous way just where the mistakes had been made. "If at this point the representative of the family had taken the precaution to . . ." Yes, it would be easy for them, after the fact, to construct a theory of action that would have avoided all the pitfalls he had stepped into. They weren't dealing with Mlle Rose. Who could have foretold this little stunt of hers, for example? Even the Appeals Court decision hadn't stopped her. How could he have supposed that she would be able to locate Eva Weiss, when her own family didn't know whether she was dead or alive? And the Cornelians—where in the lawbooks did it say that monks would help a woman defy the courts?

By now Eva Weiss was face to face with Odette Rose. And the boy—what would the Rose woman have told him about his aunt? About all of them, for that matter? Did he even know of the efforts the family was making to bring him to them? Did he know he was a Jew? Mlle Rose had had him baptized. No doubt she had taken good care to make a good Catholic of him; that is, to fill his head with ridiculous mummery and hocus-pocus. The Virgin birth. The Resurrection. The Father, the Son, the Holy Etcetera. Everything by threes, the magic number. Ritual to replace the unseen God, whom the Gentiles couldn't believe in otherwise. Had the boy swallowed all that? With what eyes was he looking now at his aunt? More than eight years the Rose woman had had him. It was the aunt who was the stranger, the person to be regarded with suspicion, whose face and hands and flesh were alien. No doubt he had come up to her, at his foster mother's urging, and reluctantly given her his hand; even more reluctantly suffered the embrace the woman would give him; and then retired to the familiar safety of the other woman's side. The foreigner, the stranger, the alien Jew—his own mother's sister! He felt sorry for the boy. It would take a long time before he could accept Hannah and the others as his family. It would probably be years before he realized what the Rose woman had done to him.

Five minutes had gone by.

If only Eva Weiss played her cards right! He had warned her of the woman's foxlike cunning. On Sunday night, after talking to Maître Paul on the telephone, he had given her a brief outline of the principal stages of his quest. And during the long, uneventful drive from Touville, he and Jules had filled in the details. Eva Weiss knew the person she was dealing with. The Rose woman was desperate, but that would not make her forget caution. She had chosen the Cornelian monastery for her rendezvous, for example, and not, say, a hotel room. There would be a back door, no doubt; perhaps even a monk posted at the entrance to give the alarm in case of need. Konrad would not even put it past her to show up without the boy, except for one thing: Eva Weiss had made it clear that she would not sign the paper without seeing her nephew, and Mlle Rose needed that document too badly to run the risk. No, no, the boy would be there. The important thing was for Mlle Rose to be convinced that the long-lost aunt had come in good faith, to embrace her sister's son, and nothing more. Mlle Rose too would know whom she was dealing with; since she had located Eva Weiss, more than likely she knew her background; and the monk would have reported Eva Weiss's condition. That ravaged look. Those deep-sunk eyes, empty of all but a terrible sadness that struck to the heart. The woman who for so many years had thought she was dead. Ready-made for the Rose woman's plots. Yet she would be cautious. Konrad would never again make the mistake of underestimating her.

Jules had been conversing softly in the back seat with the bailiff. Now he leaned forward and said, "It's taking her a long time."

"Nine minutes," Konrad said. His eyes narrowed, he studied the hedge gate through the thin screen of leaves before his windshield. No one had come in or out since they had taken up their vigil. All seemed still and peaceful, except for the cars that sped by on the highway. A quiet country scene. What was going on in that invisible building beyond the tall trees? He had told Eva Weiss not to delay, to come out for the toys as soon as possible. The natural thing to do. Had she come up against something unexpected? Something to make her postpone the signal? Did the Rose woman suspect the trap? He stifled the sudden irrational urge to start his motor, barge up the dirt road and burst into the monastery. For better or for worse, they had made their plan and would stick to it. Only it was unbearable to sit there idle by the side of the road, helpless to do anything but wait.

Far away a car door slammed. Jules had moved to the front seat beside Konrad. He gave a sudden movement and tossed the butt of his cigar out the window. "Did you hear that?"

Konrad nodded, looking at his watch. Fifty-two minutes. What in God's name could have happened? Well, he would soon find out. He turned the key in the switch and started the motor. A moment later the taxi nosed out of the hedge gate, paused, and swung left and came toward them.

Jules's hamlike paw tightened on Konrad's arm. His jaw had gone slack with disbelief. "She's there!" he said.

As the taxi crossed the embankment, Konrad saw Eva Weiss sitting in the rear, her head flung back against the seat; her mouth was open, and her face was furrowed with tears. Abruptly he turned the ignition key and got out.

Eva Weiss did not look at him as he strode to the side of the taxi. She looked unseeingly before her. "Well?" Konrad demanded.

"She came out like that," the driver said apologetically. "She got into the cab and just sat there. I didn't know what to do. So I came here."

Konrad opened the back door. "Fräulein Weiss," he said. "What happened?" She looked at him uncomprehendingly. "Give me a hand," he said to Jules, who had come up beside him and was staring, a look of pity on his dark, beaked face. Between them they half lifted her out by the elbows. No sooner was she on her feet than she pulled away from them and screamed, "He's dead! Lili's boy is dead!"

"This is highly irregular," the notary grumbled.

Konrad said patiently, "You will not be responsible for the validity of the affidavit. I merely want a record of what happened today, in case it should be needed in the future. The deponent is a citizen of Austria. It will not be easy to summon her to testify if the occasion arises. There is the factor of time. We must leave Strasbourg today. And there is the lady's condition. She has suffered a severe emotional shock. What we need is your seal and signature to the effect that this lady is the person she says she is, and that under my questioning she made the statements attributed to her. You are free to qualify her declaration in any words you want on the document itself."

What was it, he wondered, that made all French officialdom find objectionable irregularities in all his proceedings? A notary was a man who, among other things, was empowered to receive and certify affidavits. He, Konrad, wanted an affidavit; what was simpler than that? Yet Notary Emile Forst, whose name Konrad had picked out at random in the telephone directory, had shaken his bald head and pursed his lips disagreeably under his toothbrush mustache. He was not qualified to receive a statement of the kind Konrad wanted; Konrad had to present himself to the Tribunal with a *requête* for an audition. Besides, an affidavit on the basis of questioning by a third party—! However, at Konrad's last words, Notary Forst unexpectedly gave in. He would draw up the affidavit, he said, on the condition that he himself make an affidavit describing the circumstances.

"Very well," Konrad agreed at once.

While the notary was dictating to his secretary, Konrad turned his attention to Eva Weiss, who was sitting quietly in an armchair by the window. Jules was at her side, speaking to her in a low voice. She had gotten over her hysteria, thanks to the tact and gentleness of this ungainly giant, who had never stopped talking to her in that monotonous, hypnotic tone all the way to the city. But what a time they had had with her until they could get her into the car! Michel was dead! And it was their fault! She should have gone to him on Sunday, as she had originally agreed; it was the delay that was responsible for everything!

By the time they got back to the hotel, Eva Weiss had gone to the other extreme. She was quiet and docile, she did what she was told like an obedient child; but her vacant eyes showed that she was far away. Yet she could answer their questions. Only then did they learn what had happened at the monastery. Mlle Rose had been there, but not Michel. Insisting now, and taking turns interrogating her, they realized simultaneously that there was no reason to suppose that anything had happened to the boy. Mlle Rose had simply come without him; another of her tricks, for which she had another of her lame excuses; it was Eva Weiss's mania that had done the rest.

Jules, visibly shaken, had muttered, "Thank God!" and turned away to clear his throat.

Konrad, relieved, had continued his questioning. When it was through, his face was dark. "That bitch!" he had said thickly.

Now he said to Eva Weiss, "This gentleman will hear your deposition. I want you to repeat what you told us in the hotel. I will ask you questions. Do you understand?"

"Yes," she said.

The notary asked for the deponent's passport and identity card, glanced through them, studied the photographs, and dictated rapidly to his secretary. "Now," he said significantly to Konrad, "please hear this." To his secretary he said, "The deponent, who dictated in my presence the declarations contained in the document signed by her and annexed to this *procès-verbal,* appeared, accompanied by two gentlemen who identified themselves as Monsieur Louis Konrad and Monsieur Jules Immermann, both of Touville i'Abbaye, who insisted that Fräulein Weiss's deposition be in the form of question and answer, conducted by Monsieur Konrad, for the reason that the lady was in a state of emotional disturbance and unable to depose otherwise."

"Very well," Konrad said, "but after the words 'emotional disturbance' add 'as a result of her encounter with Mademoiselle Rose.'"

The notary hesitated and said, "'As a result, in Monsieur Konrad's opinion, of her encounter with Mademoiselle Rose.'"

Konrad shrugged. Word splitters. "Now can we get on with it? Thank you. Incidentally, I will conduct the questioning in German. I imagine that your secretary—"

"We are in Alsace," the notary said with a faint smile.

"Fräulein Weiss," Konrad said without preliminary. "Why are you in Strasbourg today?"

She did not look at him. In a voice without inflection she said, "To see my nephew."

"Who is your nephew?"

"Michel. Michel Benedek. The son of my sister Lili."

"Why did you believe that your nephew would be in Strasbourg today?"

"I received a letter."

Rapidly Konrad led her through an account of the monk's visit, the letter Mlle Rose had sent her, along with the letter of the Reverend Father Wilhelm Bosch, and the exchange of telegrams. Eva Weiss answered briefly and directly, without hesitation; but in so mechanical a voice and so frozen an attitude that she might have been a great gray doll wound up with a key. The notary was watching her face in a kind of fascination; and once the secretary, an angular, spinsterish woman of indeterminate age, looked sideways in curiosity, and bent over her pad again with a tiny shudder.

Yes, Eva Weiss said under questioning, she had had every reason to suppose that her nephew was to be found at noon today at the Cornelian monastery here in Strasbourg. But upon arrival at the designated place, she had been ushered into a large room in which there were two monks and a woman. There were no children in sight. Who were the monks? One was Father Bosch, who had written her the letter. The other was the monk who had come to see her three times in Lautern and who had paid her traveling expenses to and from Strasbourg. She did not remember his name. The woman identified herself as Mlle Odette Rose, guardian of her nephew. Had she used the word "guardian"? Yes, she had. The monk did; he acted as interpreter between them.

"Did you inquire after your nephew?"

"Yes."

"What did Mademoiselle Rose say?"

"Many things. Lies."

"What was the first answer?"

"She said that Michel was in Touville. He was still sick with the measles. It would be harmful to him to travel. I said, 'You promised. I did not make this long trip to see you.' She said, 'Come with me to Touville. You will see him then. You will see what a fine boy he is, and you will sign this paper for him to study medicine.' 'I sign nothing until I see him,' I said. And she said, 'Come to Touville.' 'Is he in Touville?' 'Yes,' 'No,' I said, 'he is not in Touville.' 'Yes, he is.'

'Very well,' I said, 'I will go to Touville with you.' 'No,' she said, 'he is not in Touville.' "

"What did you say then?" Konrad asked, at her pause.

"She spoke in French to the monks. It was very rapid. I said, 'I do not understand French.' The other monk said to me that Mademoiselle Rose had paid me a compliment. She had said that now she saw that I was truly Michel's aunt; that I would do anything for him. I said, 'Please do not speak to me as if I were a child. I have come to see my nephew. I do not like these tricks. He is here, he is there. Where is he?' 'I will tell you the truth,' she said. 'If you had come Sunday I would have brought him. He is a schoolboy. Classes begin tomorrow. School regulations in France are very strict. He was here, but I had to put him on the train. Why did you postpone our meeting?' I said, 'What school?' 'Chambéry,' she said. 'He is at a pension school at Chambéry.' 'Very well,' I said, 'let us go to Chambéry.' 'It is not permitted. Once classes have begun no one is allowed to visit the children.' 'No,' I said, 'that is not the reason. You are deceiving me. He is dead. That is why I cannot see him.' "

For the first time a trace of emotion appeared in Eva Weiss's voice. The notary exchanged a glance with the secretary, who had looked up. Without prompting the woman went on, "She said to me, 'No, he is not dead. Why do you say such a thing? He will come home at Christmas! You can come visit us and see him then.' I was angry. 'Christmas!' I said. 'That is a long way off. I am here now, after a long trip.' 'You postponed the meeting,' she said. 'And you,' I answered, 'sent me a telegram saying Michel would be here with you.' "

She was speaking rapidly now, her head high. Konrad, who had been standing, sat down unobtrusively off to a side, nodding at Jules. He would not be needed any more. Eva Weiss said bitterly, "I was very disappointed. I thought, I have nothing to do here, in a monastery, talking to two monks and this lying woman. I wanted to leave. I did not believe anything she said. I looked at the robes the monks wore, and felt ashamed for them. Mademoiselle Rose did not want me to leave. She began to speak; a long tale, about how she had saved Michel, and while the monk translated she stared me in the face. She has big green eyes, like a cat. She studied me and studied me, and all the while her fingers were twisting and turning something in her fingers. A piece of paper, I thought. Finally I got up to go. She came to me then and put something in my hand. It felt like a cigar.

'What is this?' I said. It was money. French thousand-franc notes, rolled up. I did not understand. I said, 'But he gave me the money already for the trip.' I meant the monk. 'No, no,' she said, 'this is for you. For your trouble.' 'What is it that you want?' 'Nothing,' she said. 'Nothing for myself. I am thinking of Michel. He wants to be a doctor, like his poor father. A signature, that's all. His future depends on it. Ask Father Bosch, he will tell you. I will make a doctor of him, he will be famous. This document—' I let the money fall to the floor. I felt dirty, as if I had picked up a worm. 'You are mistaken,' I said. She said, no, no, I did not understand. It was for Michel. 'You are the one who does not understand,' I said. I was trembling with anger. 'You are trying to buy me. You think a Jew will do anything for money.' 'I am not rich,' she said. 'It is all I have. But wait! Dr. Benedek had a bank account in Switzerland. I found the papers among the effects he left. It is for Michel. But if you will sign, I will give you the papers, and you can dispose of the bank account until Michel is of age. You must do this, you must! For Michel!' She took me by the arm. She seemed desperate, about to lose control. I felt nothing but disgust. She hadn't even heard what I had said. She thought I refused the money because it wasn't enough. I didn't answer her. There was nothing I could say. I turned around and walked out. When I entered the taxi I found my face was wet. I didn't know how long I had been crying."

Eva Weiss's voice trailed off. Konrad got up. "Fräulein Weiss, did Mademoiselle Rose at any time during your interview say that Michel was dead?"

After a long pause she shook her head. "Please answer aloud," Konrad insisted gently.

"What do you want?" she burst forth. "I don't know. Maybe she didn't say it. But I am afraid! She is desperate, she will do anything. If he is alive, he is in danger."

"If he is alive," Konrad caught her up, "what do you think should be done with him? You are his aunt, his mother's sister. What do you think is best for Michel?"

"He should be taken away from that woman," she said. "He should be given to you, to be turned over to Hannah in Israel."

"That's all," Konrad said shortly.

Late that afternoon Konrad drove out of Strasbourg and headed southwest. Jules Immermann sat beside him. Eva Weiss sat huddled in a corner of the back seat. After a short while she fell asleep. Konrad drove in silence, his mind going over the past two days. At long intervals Jules made a remark, which Konrad answered briefly. Traffic was heavy; it was ten o'clock before they arrived at Besançon. After a dispirited dinner at a hotel dining room, during which they nodded in exhaustion, they retired to the rooms they had booked and went to bed. The next morning, refreshed, they set out at an early hour. Konrad drove grimly; it was a fool's errand he was on, and he knew it, but, as Jules said, one of these days Odette Rose would slip up and tell the truth and he couldn't afford to let a single lead pass by.

They arrived at Chambéry at one o'clock in the afternoon, having decided not to waste time on lunch. After several inquiries, they located the police station they were looking for. For once Konrad found easy sailing; the commissioner, shown the Appeals Court judgment and the Strasbourg affidavit, flipped open the telephone directory, jotted down six numbers, and reached for the telephone. In each case the results were the same. In none of the schools of Chambéry was there enrolled, whether as boarder or day student, a child named Michel Benedek. For the moment they had come to the end of the trail. Konrad thanked the commissioner and left.

"Now what do we do?" Jules said, as they stood beside the parked car.

"What is there to do?" Konrad replied. "We will go home."

What a fiasco! he thought, as he drove off. Another disappointment to add to the long list of heartbreaking defeats the Rose woman had handed him. But at least there was no victory for her this time. She hadn't got the signature she so desperately needed. Things remained as they were, except for the cruel wrench to their emotions. But even here Odette Rose hadn't got off scot free; she had failed in her last gamble, and would be feeling damned miserable, knowing what was waiting for her when she returned from her sick leave. Only one question remained. Where was the boy? Where was the boy he had been hunting for more than four years, and never laid eyes upon?

7

❧

Behind him, to his right, a voice hallooed through the wood. It hung amid the scrub oak and scented pine, drowning out their whisper. Standing by the fence, Michel lifted his head. Signor Maas's voice. There it came again, floating in the thin October air. "Martyrs!" it called. "Saturninus!" A scattered chorus of joyous shouts answered him. A crow, perched on the fence a little way ahead, startled Michel with a flutter of black wings as it flew off, made a swoop and came to ground, where it strutted in the leaves.

That was two. St. Stephen and St. Saturninus. Stephen was the easy one, of course. It had been found right away, under a pile of stones. Where had they found the saint of Toulouse? Michel had been puzzled about that one. Saturninus was a bishop. There was the city itself. The statue of Jupiter. And the bull. But as clues they didn't lead anywhere. Well, but that was two. He listened intently, wondering how the other teams were making out. Between Stephen and Saturninus he had heard a faint, far-off cry that was not Signor Maas, but because of the distance he could not distinguish the name. Women Saints or Poets? In any case, it was only one, unless he had missed hearing others. The Poets were pretty far away, at the northern end of the strip. Then Martyrs were ahead, and would likely win. Not that it mattered, though; it was only a game, a way to get through a Sunday without thinking too much.

The crow hopped closer, flirting its tail and making a scrabbling sound amid the leaves. Bold as brass. As if it owned the whole world, and Michel were an intruder. How black it was! In spite of himself, Michel thought of the seminarists and suffered a guilty pang. He stamped his foot on the ground, not letting himself wince as the pain shot up his leg. Again, harder this time. The crow flew off with an outraged chatter. Michel followed it with his eyes. The mind was the hardest part. You could control what you did; that was easy. But you could sin through thought, and there was no guard against that, because you couldn't know the thought was coming until it was there. He had wanted to confess it the first time. He had been standing at the dormitory window with Kevin, looking out over the roof of administration, to the part of the Seminary field visible beyond the treetops. The seminarists were there, strolling about the cinder path that circled the field. They walked by twos, talking with flapping movements of their wide-sleeved arms; some had their hands clasped behind their backs, and walked slightly bent over. They look like crows, he thought. He told Kevin, and asked his advice. Kevin said no; what counted was the intention. He hadn't thought it in deliberate malice, had he? Well, then. Why did he have to out-Pope the Pope? And so he hadn't confessed it; but that night, after lights-out, he got out of bed and stood on one foot with his arms outstretched at shoulder level, in the attitude of the crucifixion. He stood until the burning in his shoulders and leg became intolerable, and the sweat poured down his face, before he forgave himself.

Through the wire mesh of the fence and the trees that thinned out ahead, Michel could see the white stucco of the Seminary buildings. He gazed at them with respect. So close, and yet so far off! He still had four years to go. What a long time that was! Still, the time passed. While you were living it, time moved terribly slowly, so that the future seemed never to get any closer. But when you looked backwards, you could see how really quickly it had gone by. It seemed like yesterday that he had gotten off the train at Cassarate, a new boy, already homesick and apprehensive at what lay before him, and followed with his eyes the priest's pointing finger to the very top of that steep wooded hill. Yet now he was an intermediate, halfway through. There would come the moment—still distant, but it would come—when he would look back and reckon not four but eight years behind him; and, diploma in hand, he would go through the gate into that new, mysterious world, the Seminary. The boys' school led to the Seminary. For the chosen few, those who had been found—

Heavy-hearted, Michel stared through the trees, recalling the monsignor who had come from Rome to interview him. Was it two years ago, or three? No, two; he remembered that when they summoned him to the rector's office he was afraid that it had to do with the decision of the fourth Family Council, and that they had come to get him; and that was in December 1950. He had told the monsignor that he was studying hard so that they would accept him at the Seminary. Yes, Father, to be a priest. If God found him worthy. He had said it with conviction; at the moment, under the penetrating yet kindly gaze of the distinguished visitor, it had seemed so simple. It was only when the door closed behind him that fear came, and he said to himself, fiercely, that he would have to be found worthy. He would *have* to!

He tried to picture himself at fifteen. He would be tall, with his hair cropped close, and his face would have the same keen brooding look that all the seminarists had. The solitary confinement of the Novitiate would be nothing to him. His austerities would astound the masters. There! he would tell his cringing coward flesh. This is for my father! And Father Périer! And Jean! And fainting in an ecstasy of pain, he falls to the icy floor, while angel faces, invisible to his mortal eyes, lean down to pity the Son of Man.

He straightened up in disgust, his eyes fixed on the white buildings. He, the Son of Man! A fantasy, nothing more! How could he atone for the sins of others, when he could not atone for his own? Murderer! he said to himself, pressing down on his foot. How they must all despise him!

A whacking sound and boys' voices behind him made him turn around. It was Angelilli and Horst; they had branches in their hands and were poking in the bushes. Horst had torn the leg of his uniform; a strip of muddy gray hung down. His eyes were wide with excitement.

"There's Rose. Find anything?"

Michel shook his head and limped up to them. Horst indicated the other with his thumb and said, laughing, "Angelilli found Saturninus. Did you hear us hollering back there? Signor Maas had t-tied it to—" He shrieked with laughter, choking and prancing in his eagerness to get it out.

"What?" Michel said.

Horst's baby skin had turned pink. "To a—a rabbit's tail," he gasped, putting his hand on Michel's arm. "And we ran all through the forest trying to catch it, until it ran under Angelilli's feet and he fell on it."

For-r-resta, he said. Deep in the throat. Bavaria, he said he came from. A German. His father could have been a Nazi. Michel supposed that they had children, and loved them, like other people. He had often looked at Horst and wondered. Blond, pink, blue-eyed, soft. An Aryan. If he only knew what he was touching. Michel gently disengaged his arm. St. Louis Gonzaga boys did not touch each other. Horst had been had up twice for that already.

There was a grin on Angelilli's dark ferret face. He hadn't even known it was a rabbit, he said. Nobody knew. Signor Maas had sneaked down to the hutch first thing in the morning and turned it loose in the wood before anyone was about. And so he had been caught completely by surprise. He had seen something red in the underbrush, and reached in for it. It was the banner, all right, but as he put his hand forward it sprang away from him. He let out a yell, and Giorgetti and Horst came running. They helped him corner it. And Signor Maas watching and slapping his leg at the fun. What an idea of his, to tie the banner to a rabbit! Did Rose get it? Did he? The bull was the clue; they had tied St. Saturninus to the tail of a bull.

"Look here!" Angelilli said proudly, showing his wrist. It was furrowed by a thin red line. "Those things can kick, did you know? He did that when he got away from me. I got the banner off him, but he fetched me a kick with his hind legs and got away."

"Anyway, we're ahead," Horst said. "Three more to go. What are you looking for?"

"St. Tarsicius," Michel said.

"So are we," the two said together.

"In the bushes?"

"That's what you know," Angelilli said, his grin growing wider. "A master hid him there once, six years ago. A fellow out of senior final told me. And when they said it wasn't fair, he said, Sticks."

"Come on," Horst urged. The two moved off.

Kevin's red head appeared in the clearing. He waved and went on. Michel considered briefly. It was true that they had beaten St. Tarsicius with sticks. But he had set out from the Catacombs, and that was where they buried him. That was much more likely. Michel had a hunch about the outcropping of stone at the deep corner, where the fence turned off. He had been on his way there when he stopped to look at the Seminary. He turned to the left, imagining that he was Tarsicius, and that this was a Roman street. The scene he had read about in the *Book of Days* came to life in his mind.

"Upon completion of the ceremony, Sixtus recalls to the faithful their imprisoned brothers. It is necessary to take the mysteries to them, to sustain them in the hardships of the prison, and a generous soul must be found to offer himself to confront the danger. A hundred imploring glances turn toward him. Old men, women, maidens veiled in white, all want to take the bread of life to the martyrs. Before the priest is a boy who, without daring to utter a single word, extends his hands in supplicating gesture. There is so much innocence, so much ardor, such vehement desire in that face, that Sixtus can do no less than exclaim, 'You also, my son?' 'And why not, Father?' the boy responds. 'No one will suspect my tender years.' Moved by that faith, the old man takes the divine food from the table, and places it in the hands of the little one. The child's name was Tarsicius. He was eleven years old."

Eleven years old. Like him. Michel squared his shoulders and marched through the wood. That clump of bushes is a group of boys playing a game. They turn toward him inquiringly. Where are you bound, Tarsicius? Head high, his hand pressed against his chest, Michel does not answer. Let's see, Tarsicius. Michel hurries on. What's he holding there? Where's he going? He's up to something. Hold on there! What have you got under your shirt? If you don't show us, we'll . . . They rain blows on him. No! he cries, sinking to the ground. Though you may kill me, I will never . . . Unsullied, pure in heart, his eyes fixed on heaven, Michel clutches the Most Holy Host to his bosom, a living ciborium, while around him echo screams of rage. A Christian! He's taking a magic charm to the prisoners! Kill the Christian! Now and in the hour of our death, amen.

Michel stopped, his unseeing eyes staring straight ahead. Did Tarsicius have a father? The story said nothing about him. But no doubt a Christian. Right there at the mass, proudly urging his son on. And the future Pope himself handing you the Host for safekeeping. What an opportunity! And what about St. Saturninus, pushed by the enraged crowd before the statue of Jupiter and ordered to bow down and make sacrifice? Things were different today, a boy didn't have any chance at all. Christ had conquered the world, and the opportunities just weren't there any more. Nowadays they hid little banners in the wood, red for martyrs, white for women saints, gold for poets, and the team that found its five before the others got inspirational books as awards. Nowadays everything was according to rule, from the moment Father Scala snapped on the lights in the still-dark dormitory, calling out, *"Laudetur Jesus Christus!"* to the time he turned them off again at night to the cry of *"Deo gratias."* And from dormitory to chapel to refectory to class you marched silently in file, your head bent down, not free for an instant in this tamed world to find the way to let God and yourself forget the taint you bore like a cancer within you. You could study hard and win prizes at the end of the term; you could refuse the meat that your belly hungered for; pray more than anybody else; put stones in your shoes until the skin broke and festered. And then what? The masters praised you, Maman Rose was happy, Mother Veronica nodded reserved approval—but your own heart knew how little it all meant.

"The banner!" he said aloud. He had promised himself to make today an outing. No thoughts. An afternoon in the wood, in the fresh air. He walked on. He came to the swampy area, where bushes grew thick and rank, and made his way around it. Beyond, the ground sloped upwards, and became firm underfoot. A little way more, and he came within sight of the stone outcropping he was looking for, just within the corner of the fence. By now Michel was breathing hard, and his foot was throbbing painfully. Have you heard about Rose? His foot got infected, gangrene set in, and now they're going to have to amputate up to here. Yes, pebbles in his shoe, to mortify the flesh. Nobody knew how far gone he was, except Kevin Rory.

What had Kevin meant? "It's all very well, Rose," he had said, "but you do it for the wrong reasons." He had protested, but Kevin hadn't wanted to discuss it. He knew what he knew, that's all.

Behind him a shout arose. He could not make out the words. He was in the furthermost corner of the school's broad acres, the southwest corner of the fence, past which the hill plunged abruptly down through thick forest to the town on its lake. Had they found another banner? He hoped it was not Tarsicius; he had set his heart on that himself. He had better start looking. But he felt a curious disinclination to move. This little pocket of the wood had a quiet, detached air about it, as if no one knew it was there. The afternoon sun, penetrating through the delicate tracery of the tall evergreens, lay peacefully on the seamed granite that jutted through its blanket of earth. How wonderful it would be to stretch out on that mossy bank, and dream in this tranquil solitude!

Michel has disappeared. He has built a tiny hut in this secluded spot and been lost to sight on earth, in heaven and hell. Here he remains while the decades pass, his food and drink what the forest and cloud yield; bronzed by the summer sun, nipped to the bone by the winter snows; until, purified, wise, and holy, the white-bearded hermit with the eyes of flame is glimpsed at last by God, who tenderly stretches forth His hand, and . . .

As if to remind him of his duty, a silvery chime penetrated the deep wood. Three o'clock by the chapel bell. Four was the deadline, so as to be on time for Benediction. Had an hour gone by already? Would it never end? On, carcass! Get on!

St. Michel, the one-legged hermit, clambered up the few yards of slope to where a little pouch in the stone filled with pine needles afforded a natural seat. And suppose it were really so, about the gangrene? Oh, that would be a fine thing! That would bring back the dead, wouldn't it? Sinking into the spongy depression, Michel stared at his shoe. It was no good. It just wasn't any good. In sudden resolution he bent over and pulled the shoe off. He had not put in the pebble this morning because it was Sunday. The sole of his thick woolen sock was sticky. He took that off too, and examined the wound. It was red and angry, with yellowish crusted edges, and it hurt abominably. He wrapped his handkerchief around it, put the rolled-up sock in the inner pocket of his jacket where the bulge wouldn't show, and, tugging gingerly, put on his shoe again. Perhaps he had better report to the infirmary in the morning.

Getting up, he began to explore among the crevices of the rock. On the other side, at the bottom, there was a wide crack that Signor Maas might well have thought of as a niche in a catacomb. He put his hand into the dark opening, and fell back uttering a cry. His hand had touched something warm and furry, which squealed and moved under his groping fingers. A rabbit darted out, gave a clumsy hop, and floundered down the slope to the fence, where it made indecisive dashes to one side and then the other, and even leaped once futilely against the wire mesh. Michel let his breath out. What a scare, and it was only a rabbit! Why did it not run? Michel approached warily, his fingers still feeling the softness of the fur he had so unexpectedly touched. Still the rabbit did not run. It cowered to the ground, its round flanks quivering. Kneeling, Michel stroked the long, soft, brown ears lined with white that lay flattened against the skull. The rabbit whimpered, and then Michel saw the paw. It was the left forepaw, and it had been crushed to a pulp. Tiny raw splinters of bone showed through the red-blotched fur. It looked as though someone had taken a stone, and simply . . .

The flood of compassion that swept over him was so keen that for a moment he felt sick. Mechanically he continued stroking the rabbit's ears, waiting for the revulsion of his stomach to subside. Then he took his hand away, and sank down to the ground. The rabbit did not move. Only the rapid pulsing of its soft, pouchy sides showed it was alive. Its eyes, glistening dark oval buttons, were half closed. Was it fear? Pain? What could be done with such a bloody mess of a paw? Vilella, the boy from Argentina, had broken his arm in the gym, and they put a cast on it and after some months it was good as ever. Could you do that to a rabbit? Even as he wondered, he knew the answer. This was the Saturninus rabbit that Signor Maas had taken from the hutch behind the school kitchen. It had the same brown fur, touched with white under the neck and on the belly. They would laugh at him in the infirmary. Rabbits were for eating. If he took it back, it would be slaughtered for Tuesday night's dinner.

The rabbit stirred. It licked its paw and whimpered. Michel winced and looked away. Kevin's jaunty figure stepped from behind the rock; he approached, a look of curiosity on his pale, freckled face.

"What is it?"

"Look!" Michel said, pointing.

Kevin whistled and kneeled down beside him. "Now that," he said critically, "is a really fine job of smashing. That was done by an expert. Angelilli, I suppose? He's a clumsy oaf. I've always said so. Well, old man," he said, addressing the rabbit, "there's no help for it, it's the stew pot for you. Forgive my bluntness. Rory is frank. Straightforward. He's very fond of rabbit stew. It's the only decent meal they serve in this vinegar college. I'll have this piece, I believe. Yummy!" He poked the rabbit's hindquarters with his forefinger.

"Don't!" Michel protested.

"Why not?" Kevin demanded in mock surprise. "Are you a materialist, or what? Do you believe in pain? Do you know what pain is, my boy? A curling of the nerve ends, nothing more. A purely private affair of no importance. It has no existence outside your skin. Do the stars care? No. And then you die, and it's just as though you never felt a thing. Wiped out. Retroactive. Never was. Incidentally, how's your foot? Do you limp on purpose, or can't you help yourself?"

Kevin was in one of his moods. Michel did not answer.

"Tender-hearted Rose!" Kevin said. "He goes soft over a hurt rabbit, and bears his own pain like a hero. A saint, that's what he is. St. Jerome and the lion. St. Michel and the rabbit. But that's not why Rory likes you. Blunt, straightforward Rory regards that with suspicion. But he likes you anyway. Do you know why I like you, Rose? Because you're the only person in this highly overrated abode of learning who understands even a scintilla of what I say. Scintilla! Isn't that a lovely word? Should be stincilla, of course. Example of metathesis. I'm in love with words. Rory, the boy genius with the rapier-like wit. Tell me, Brother Rabbit," he said sternly, looking down, "do you see any significance in putting the mind of a genius in a head covered with red hair? No? I thought not. And then they speak of Providence!" He shook his head sadly, and turned his mocking, colorless eyes on Michel. "I need you as an audience. And then even you fail me. Vinegar college! You let it pass right by. Isn't that a gem? That's Erasmus talking about the school he went to in Paris. I mentioned Erasmus to Signor Maas, and do you know what he said to me? That the old gentleman was of doubtful orthodoxy. And he a Dutchman too! I think I'll join the Dominicans. What are you going to do with the rabbit?"

"I don't know," Michel said. "In a little while the paw's going to get infected. I was thinking—"

"Speak up, my boy," Kevin said, as Michel hesitated.

"Well, couldn't it be amputated, or something? They did that to a dog once in Sep. It got its leg caught in a tractor, and they called a vet and he had to cut it off to get the dog out. But the dog lived. It gets around on three legs and is all right."

"Splendid!" Kevin agreed. "Who's going to cut it off?"

Michel looked at the rabbit and said nothing.

"Go ahead," Kevin urged. "You may be a great surgeon some day. You've got to begin somewhere. But tell me, Doctor, after the operation, what then?"

After a while Kevin sighed. "I see I have to play the part of Socrates, and drag it out of you. Plato, sit up straight! We have here one three-legged rabbit. The problem before us is as follows, ergo, to wit: How can such a creature continue to exist in a hostile world? Answer, please. No? You are silent? Let me help you, although I know nothing. Enlighten me with your wisdom. Would you take it to the school and keep it as a pet? Pets are not allowed at St. Louis

Gonzaga? Ah! Then we must examine this more closely. Is it not true that a thing must be either here or there? Certainly. Then if it cannot be there it must be here? That is correct. Then why not leave it here?"

"But it can't run," Michel protested.

"It speaks!" Kevin crowed. "A talking Rose! Enlighten me still further, oracle. Why must a rabbit run?"

"It's all right for you to make a joke out of it," Michel said, nettled. "But if I leave it here, it's going to die. The foxes will get it. Or if not the foxes, the hawks will. Look!" He pointed up to the sky, where tiny black specks wheeled lazily against cottony shreds of clouds.

"Oh!" Kevin cried indignantly. "If the great god Pan could hear you! Are you going to upset the balance of nature now? Hawks too must live. Hawks and foxes and seminary crows. And you, a mere mortal, are taking sides. Favoritism, by Jove that thunders! Rose is anti-hawk! Rose sides with the rabbits! Now, in the name of all that's holy," he snarled in a sudden change of tone, thrusting his face close to Michel's, "why are you carrying on like a blathering crybaby over this animal?"

"But it's hurt," Michel said, shrinking back. "Don't you see it's hurt?"

"Never mind what I see. I see more than I say. It's what you see. Or rather, what you don't see. You don't see it, do you?"

"What?" Michel said, bewildered.

"Never mind. On second thoughts, forget it." He stood up, stretching his rawboned frame and smoothing down his lapels. He smiled coldly down at Michel. "It's only a rabbit, Rose. Just a rabbit. It was bred for the table. This Tuesday, or the next, or the next. What's the difference? If Signor Maas hadn't got hold of it for this silly game, you'd eat it one of these Tuesdays and smack your lips over it. You can't save it. Take it back, it's eaten. Leave it here, it's eaten. So let it go about its business, and come help me find St. Tarsicius." His good humor suddenly restored, Kevin said gaily, "Apparently you had the same idea I did, you clever chap! I may make something of you yet. Up, disciple, up! When I'm Pope I'll make you Primate of France. Or send you out to the pygmies in Africa for target practice. One of the two, I haven't decided which."

Michel rose slowly to his feet. What was Kevin getting at? What did he see that was such a mystery? With Kevin you could never tell.

Still, he was right, of course. Why get so upset over a rabbit? Yet it seemed cruelly unfair, because of the paw. Bad enough that the little creature's only defense against the teeth and claws that lay in wait for it was to run; but now even that possibility had been taken away from it. Very well, life *was* unfair. Who ever said it was not? It was only a rabbit. Let it get along the best it could. He hadn't made the world.

"A riddle!" Kevin exclaimed. He had turned and was facing the rock. "A psychological riddle, the best kind. If I were a Dutch Jesuit with a grim sense of humor and an aversion to Erasmus, where would I hide the banner of St. Tarsicius? Answer, the Catacombs. End of riddle. But *which* catacomb? Beginning of extrasensory perception. Did you know I have extrasensory perception?" he inquired of Michel. "I do. It's one of my many amazing attributes. Last summer I baffled three psychologists in New York. They took turns holding decks of cards to the back of my neck while I was blindfolded. They found I could distinguish the reds from the blacks every time. Extrasensory perception. Don't you love the sound of it? Say it aloud. Roll it on your tongue. What learned ignorance! I will now give you a demonstration. Because the banner is definitely there. Oh yes, it's there. I sense it through my extrasensory perception. There is an aura of red floating about that rock."

"I looked," Michel said.

"Oh you of little faith!" Kevin said with a reproachful glance. "Follow me, sir. Don't interfere with the wave lengths." He approached the rock, his face intent. Michel took a few steps behind him and looked back. The rabbit had not moved from its place. As soon as they had left, one of the hawks would come. It would peel off like a dive bomber and shoot downwards with incredible speed, its great steely talons ready to strike. Michel shuddered and turned away. Kevin was standing facing the rock. His eyes were closed dreamily and his chin was thrust out. Watching him, Michel felt a thrill of admiration. There was no explaining Kevin. He was a genius, certainly; but that was not all, that didn't explain the other things. His ability to glance at a mathematical problem and come up with the answer, whereas everybody else, including the math master, had to work it out on paper. His trick of "photographing" a page with his eye, and reading it back to you out of memory. The time he was booting a ball about the playing field, and the spring squall struck unexpectedly; Kevin stopped, with much the same dreamy expression that he now had on his face, and pointed to the gymnasium chimney. And then lightning shot down and smashed it with a terrific splintering noise that sent bricks and slates flying and left a smoking hole in the roof. And his visions, in which he saw God and the angels, all the hierarchy of heaven. Nobody could explain those. "Touched by the finger of God," Father Latouche said.

Could he really sense a color without seeing it? Michel watched, entranced. Kevin moved off to one side and bent closer to the rock. His eyes were still closed. "It's here," he muttered. "I know it's here." Suddenly he straightened up and pointed before him. "Look there," he said. Michel moved up beside him. Kevin's finger indicated the crevice where the rabbit had taken refuge. Kevin opened his eyes. "Go on," he urged. "It's in there, I tell you. Put your hand in and fish it out."

"You do it," Michel said.

"Disobedient brat! Very well, the pygmies for you, I promise you." Kevin stooped over and thrust his hand into the opening. When he stood up he had the banner in his hand. "Tarsicius!" he exclaimed in triumph, waving the bit of red cloth. "Extrasensory etcetera never fails." Then he examined his fingers, and a puzzled expression came to his face. "What's this?" he said. "Blood? Is Tarsicius bleeding, or what?"

"The rabbit was in there," Michel said.

Kevin gave an exclamation of disgust and wiped his fingers on the ground.

Michel looked at the rabbit. It had sat up on its hindquarters; the forepaw dangled in the air, limp and useless. "Rory," Michel said in a choked voice. It was no use. He walked quickly toward the fence, feeling Kevin's eyes on his back. The rabbit shrank at his approach. "I won't let them eat you," Michel said. Sitting on the ground, he took off his shoe and removed the handkerchief he had wrapped about his foot. Then, as gently as he could, he bound it loosely about the paw and lifted the rabbit to his lap, stroking it and making soft murmuring sounds.

"Very pretty," Kevin commented. He was leaning against the rock, and his lips were tightly compressed in an angry grimace. "A charming *pietà*. That foot of yours makes me want to vomit." He stared for a moment and then said shortly, "Good-bye." He walked away without looking back.

A *pietà* was the Madonna holding the crucified Jesus in her lap.

That was like Kevin. Why did he have to make a remark like that? He didn't feel like any Madonna. It just wasn't fair, that was all. It was Signor Maas's fault, and Angelilli's, and somehow his own too for being part of it. How would Kevin feel if he were in the rabbit's place, waiting for the claws to sink into his soft flesh? Well, this was one rabbit no one would eat, not even in a stew. No one. It was important. He didn't know why, but it was important.

Kevin was back. He walked down the slope, kicking the stones out of his path, and stood tall over Michel. "Are you trying to destroy yourself? Is that it? What do you want to prove, anyway?"

"What?" Michel stammered, staring up at him. Kevin was really angry. "I'm not—"

"Listen to me and stop pretending to be dumber than you are. You've had this coming to you for a long time. I've been watching you. Do you think you can fool me? Shall I confess this? Shall I confess that? Little sanctimonious Rose! Michel the curly-headed rosebud, like a painted angel. The class model! But it eats at your inside, doesn't it? And so you have to be holier than anybody else."

The attack was so sudden that Michel could only gape in wonder. And then the import of the words sank in; something cold tightened in his stomach. "What?" he said again, stupidly, dreading what was coming, asking himself, How? How does he know? And astonished that Kevin, bantering, sarcastic, superior Kevin was so venomously angry.

As though from a great distance he heard that pitiless voice say, "That trick of yours, keeping your underpants on when you put on your pajamas! Don't you think the whole school knows you're circumcised?"

The rabbit gave a convulsive start under Michel's hand. He kept his eyes fixed on the long, twitching ears, hearing the shameful word echoing in his head. What an ugly sound it had! And what an ugly meaning! Branded. Branded for life, indelibly. All his little devices had been in vain, then. His way of standing in the shower stall, his back to the opening. His way of putting on his pajamas. His dressing for gym in the angle of his locker door. The whole school knew. How they must have snickered at him behind his back! He remembered suddenly the sharp, inquiring glance the doctor had turned on him, the time there was the typhus scare and all the boys were examined; and the kindly voice of the man saying, "You can put your clothes on, son." Had the doctor guessed what he was thinking? But the whole school knew. That's what Kevin had said. How was it that he himself had noticed nothing? Nothing? The color rose to his cheeks as he remembered little incidents he had dismissed from his mind. Giraud asking him with that smirk which was more important, the Old or the New Testament? Giorgetti's glancing at him as he protested to someone that Mussolini was not a Jew-hater but had been forced into it by Hitler. Inexplicable silences as he approached groups. Coolnesses he had thought were caused by envy. He had not let himself see these things for what they were.

And Kevin! How long had he known? There had been no change in him, Michel was sure of that. Kevin had never avoided him, been suddenly different in any way. He had always been the protective upperclassman who had taken a lower-form boy under his wing. Supercilious, condescending—but that was his right, the prerogative of his amazing brilliance and the four-year difference in their ages. Michel well knew the honor bestowed upon him by their friendship. Yes, but then why turn on him now? He had done nothing, was what he had always been. He said this to himself; but he knew that it was his foot, and that Kevin had understood.

Kevin had squatted down and was studying his face under pale, reddish lashes. "What are you ashamed of, you little fool?" he exclaimed roughly. "Don't you know that Our Saviour was circumcised too?"

Michel protested. He was *not* ashamed. He was not the only one to put stones in his shoe. Other boys did it too. The masters knew, and didn't say anything. They said the flesh had to be chastened. Only with him it had gotten infected, that was all. It could have happened to anyone. It didn't mean anything. "You don't understand," he said lamely.

He saw that Kevin was not really listening to him. That raw, freckled face, which had always seemed to Michel to need a final patting into shape, a smoothing down, before it was finished, had that queer, inward look that came over it sometimes when Kevin was brooding. "You know," Kevin said at last, "I've often wondered why Christ was born to the Jews. I mean, why did He *have* to be a Jew? Do you know why it was? It was because at that time the Jews were the only ones to have an idea of the true God. And so they got mad at the Saviour, because to them what He said was blasphemy. You know, that about the divine taking human shape. They were a holy people, and they thought he was mocking their God. And so they crucified

Him. Yes, but then came the resurrection, and that proved He was right. He rose from the dead, and then His disciples could really and truly believe He was the Son of God, and because they were Jews too and had been brought up to know the true God they suffered martyrdom to found His church. Now that's interesting," Kevin said with sudden gaiety. "A lovely paradox! He had to be a Jew because only the Jews were capable of understanding Him. But once they understood Him, only the Jews were capable of not believing Him. A marvelous, holy, contradictory people! God knew what He was doing when He picked on them in the first place. He looked about the earth until He found the simplest, toughest, stubbornest, hardbittenest desert rat of them all, and He said, 'Abraham! Get ready!' Because that was the stuff He needed to make martyrs of, so the rest would understand. The first Christian martyrs were Jews, you know. Like their father Abraham. 'Cut my head off,' they said, 'but we won't give in! Damned if we do!' And the rest are just as stubborn, but in the wrong direction. Why don't they let themselves be baptized and get it over with? You have that same stubborn streak in you, you know," he said, turning to Michel. "Oh yes, you do. Look at that foot! But at least you're baptized. Of course you are, or you wouldn't be here."

"Oh, yes," Michel said. "I'm baptized."

He had not meant his tone to be so bitter. But he did not like being lumped together in the other's mind with "the Jews," as if he were indistinguishable from the rest. Could Kevin really not see he was different? Kevin looked at him questioningly.

"Hm!" he said. "Yes. I remember something. Rory's steel-trap mind. I wondered at the time, because it didn't make sense. It still doesn't. Do you remember when Giorgetti asked Father Latouche about the Chinese? And Father Latouche said that no one ever got into heaven except through baptism? I thought you were going to faint. I never saw a sicker face in my life. Why? If you're baptized?"

And so Kevin had seen him after all! He remembered the moment very well; he would never forget it. Father Latouche's absolute statement, said in the tone that admits no exceptions, had been the blow that destroyed any last, lingering hope he might have had. It had hit him hard, and he had felt the blood drain from his face. And in that instant of dizziness, he had looked up in time to see Kevin's eyes turn away to fix themselves inscrutably on the priest. A touch of panic welled up in him, as if the other's curiosity were a probe moving dangerously near his inner pain. Why was Kevin prying like this? What was it to him? He turned away, muttering that he didn't remember that.

Kevin shrugged. "Just as you wish, Rose. I'm just trying to help. I'm worried about you. That's why I lashed out at you a while ago. It makes me mad to see what you're doing."

"Oh," Michel said. "You don't have to worry. The foot will be all right. I'll go to the infirmary, and they'll—"

"Try to understand, will you? It's not the foot. It's *why* you do it. What's driving you? If I were a Jew, I wouldn't—"

Michel started angrily. "That's got nothing to do with it. You're mixing everything up. Why don't you leave me alone?" He struggled to get up, putting his bare foot to the ground in his haste and wincing at the pain. Kevin put his hand to his shoulder and pushed him back. The rabbit, dislodged from Michel's lap by the movement, squealed and hopped to the fence, where it crouched, its sides heaving.

"Steady, youngster," Kevin said. He had gotten very pale, so that the freckles stood out in great dark blotches. "I'm not through yet. I have to do this. Because you're sick, Rose. You're sicker than you think."

"Let go! Let go, or I'll hit you!" He clawed at the hand on his shoulder and wrenched himself free.

"Bite, scratch, what do I care? But you're going to listen. It's not your foot, it's your head. Don't you know that you walk in your sleep? Stop squirming and listen. I said, you're a sleepwalker. I've watched you myself. You get out of bed and walk about the dormitory in your bare feet in the dark. Oh yes, you do," Kevin insisted, as Michel stiffened and turned to him, his eyes wide with disbelief. "You always do the same thing. You go to the door and try to open it. And when you can't, because it's locked, you go up to the door of the prefect's room and look at the crucifix. You just look and look. And then you go back to bed."

"It's a lie!" Michel burst forth. "What's the *matter* with you?"

"I knew you would say that," Kevin said. "I didn't believe it myself. I thought you were awake, because you had your eyes open. And so the first time you did it, I asked you next morning if you had felt sick during the night, and you said no, why? Because I heard you getting up to go to the bathroom, I said. And you said no, you hadn't gotten up."

Michel remembered that conversation. He was too stupefied to speak.

"You walked again last night. Barefoot. On that sore. Now tell me again you're all right."

Lady Macbeth, who had helped her husband murder the king while he slept in their castle. Nobody knew, until she began to walk about the castle at night in her sleep, rubbing her hands to get the blood off them. Her own conscience gave her away. Well, why not? There was blood on his hands too. He had let his father die for him. He had killed Father Périer. If not for him, Jean would still be alive. What a horror! Michel Rose, offspring of a corrupt line of infidels, whose father was in hell, walks the night to escape from himself. What if the dormitory door were not locked? Where would he go? He began to sweat. He said wildly, "I murdered my father!"

Kevin gaped at him. Then Michel saw those pale eyes take on a cruel slant as the other scrambled to his feet and seized him by the hair. "Don't you ever say that again! Don't you ever think it! You know damned well your father died in a concentration camp!" Kevin's shove toppled Michel over backwards, his feet in the air, involuntary tears starting to his eyes from the outrage to his scalp. He lay still for a moment, blinking, hearing those incredible words repeat themselves in his ear. Kevin could not have said them. He couldn't know. Nobody at the school knew. He was dreaming. Yet the ground was hard beneath his back, his head hurt; and here was Kevin's face bending over him, pale and stern, the lips moving, uttering words he did not listen to. He said, "What?" sitting up. "What did you say? You said something . . ." He got up, taking the other by the arm. "Rory? What did you say?"

"I said I was sorry, I shouldn't have done that. And you'd be right to report me."

"No, no, before that."

"Here, don't stand on that bare foot like that." He pushed Michel gently down, and, taking out his handkerchief, dabbed at the wound. "It's bleeding," he grunted.

"Rory," Michel said quietly, staring at the whorl of red hair only a few inches from his eyes, "Rory, *how did you know?*"

"Oh, damn!" Kevin said. He tied the handkerchief around the foot and plumped himself on the ground. "Be a good kid and forget I said it, will you? It never happened."

"But you said—" Michel began, bewildered.

Kevin butted himself on the forehead with the palm of his hand. "Rory, the great amateur psychologist! The boy who broke the I.Q. barrier!" He grinned shamefacedly sideways at Michel. "I snooped, that's all. I read your newspaper clipping. About the trial."

After a long time Michel said, "Oh!" in a small voice.

"If it's such a secret, you really shouldn't carry it about with you like that, you know. Not with busybodies like Rory around. But you can rest easy. I haven't told anybody, and I won't. I wasn't going to say anything to you about it either, only it slipped out when you said that about your father. Why did you want to say a thing like that for? You don't mean it, Rose. You can't mean it. You're not crazy, only hurt inside. And that makes you think these unhealthy thoughts. You know that, don't you?"

Kevin had read the clipping. He knew everything then. It was all there: his name, his story, his shameful past; Maman Rose; M. Konrad; the courts; everything. What a fool he had been to bring it with him! Dear God, if anybody else had read it too! He would tear it up as soon as he got back. And in the meantime he would make Kevin swear the solemnest oath there was that he wouldn't . . . But he had promised already. Kevin was a decent fellow, he wouldn't go back on it, he had done it only because he was worried about him. Because things were not right with him. Because Kevin was really a friend. What was that last part? Thing like that for? And not meaning it.

"Oh," he said, "I didn't mean with a knife or anything like that. But lots of them ran and hid and got away. And my father—"

"Them?" Kevin asked.

"Jews," Michel said. "They hid out from the Nazis and the militia. But my father couldn't because of me. He was afraid for me because I was so little. So he took a chance and stayed where he was. It says so in the clipping. He—" His throat tightening, horrified at what was forcing itself through his shattered reserve, unable to keep his voice from breaking, he blurted, "He must have hated me!"

It was out now, that thought that had been festering within him all summer, ever since the Appeals Court trial, when the newspapers had got hold of it and played it up into a local scandal. He had saved one of the articles, because it had photographs of his father and mother. And there, in the middle, at the spot he skipped over in his rereadings, was that bald, terrible statement that stuck in his heart like a claw. "Because of the child, Dr. and Mme Benedek . . ." Even now he could not bring himself to complete the sentence in his mind. But the poison was there, working at him. At first in Sep, and then, when that got too dangerous, the rest of the summer at the Mother House in Paris, he had thought and thought about it, until he could not bear to look at the photographs any more because of the accusation he saw in their eyes.

"Hated you?" Kevin said, staring. "When they wouldn't run because of you? They must have loved you very much. You're getting it all mixed up."

"Oh," Michel said. "I know. My father cried when he— I meant there at the end. They found a safe place for me. For me, but not for them. Don't you see? They took care of me, and they got caught instead. In my place. Isn't that f-funny?" he said hysterically. "My mother killed herself. You didn't know that, did you? She took poison and died in the street. They just stood around and watched her die. And she was thinking—"

"Stop it, Rose! That's enough now!"

But he couldn't stop, not now. "And then they took my father to—" His face screwed up and tears burst from his eyes as he shouted, "—to Drancy, and he was thinking about me too, how they saved me but not themselves. And he hated me!"

"For God's sake, Rose!" Kevin shook him until his teeth chattered, but he twisted himself away and screamed in Kevin's face.

"They're in hell! You said it yourself! They're burning in hell because they're Jews!"

Kevin's breath came with a sudden hiss; he stumbled backwards and fell to his knees. Michel crumpled to the ground, burying his face in his hands, sobbing, wishing he were dead, and knowing, miserably, that there was no way, no way at all, that he could atone for them, or for himself.

Through his sobs he heard Kevin's voice whispering. When at last he could bring himself to lift his head, he saw that his friend was praying; his eyes were closed, and his cheeks were wet.

"It's no use," Michel said dully. "Praying can't help them."

Kevin crossed himself and stood up. "I was praying for you," he said. He remained for a moment looking down at Michel. "Forgive me," he said. He walked away shaking his head.

The three-quarters bell rang out in the distance.

His face was dirty, and crumbs of earth had stuck to the back of his head. He fished for his handkerchief, but it was not in his pocket. He wiped his face on his sleeve, and passed his hand over his hair, feeling his fingers tremble. Curly-headed rosebud. His uniform was a mess; he would surely get a demerit for that. He felt too wretched to care. Empty. Sour. Like when you're sick to your stomach, and you heave everything up and you sink back, panting, with the poison out of you but your insides still retching upwards and that taste in your mouth. Aside from that sick feeling, he was aware of a vast astonishment. One minute he had been stroking the rabbit, feeling sorry for it, wondering how he could save it; and then, with no warning, Kevin had turned on him, with one relentless surprise after another, until he wanted to scream. He *had* screamed, and rolled on the ground like a child in a tantrum. His face burned as he thought of it. Jew. Baptism. Sleepwalker. His father, who was in— No, Kevin hadn't said that. It was he, Michel, who had said it. It had been torn out of him, he didn't know how. Kevin probing, digging, questioning without mercy, one thing leading to another, until in his agony he had said what he had not even let himself think all this time. He had said— Cover it, bury it, pile other thoughts over it. Quick—think of something else. The handkerchief. The rabbit had that. See? All you had to do was . . .

There it was by the fence, almost within reach. Here, rabbit. Here, bunny, bunny, bunny. You soft thing. You hurt thing. I ate your father, but I won't eat you. Nobody's going to eat you. Hawks, and foxes, and seminary crows. That was Kevin, teasing him, while he was still in that joking mood. Crows didn't eat rabbits, did they? Well, but they were scavengers, weren't they? If they found a dead animal, like a cat in a gutter . . . Why did he think about a cat? This was a rabbit. Here, bunny.

Doubling his good leg, Michel dug his heel into the soft earth and pushed himself up to the fence. He leaned against it and took the rabbit onto his lap. The handkerchief fell off. Well, that didn't matter. And if he got blood over his uniform, that didn't matter either. Funny, the face Kevin made when he got blood on his hands. After what he said about pain. It was easy to say that, about somebody else's pain. But when the blood got on your hands—he wouldn't think about that either.

A snatch of a song curled in his mind. Father Brighi had chanted it for them in the Latin class, softly so as not to be heard in the hall, his hand marking time in wide sweeps: *Gaudeamus igitur, juvenes dum sumus.*

Juvenes. That was youth. Like himself. Like the rabbit. There really wasn't any way out for the rabbit. He had to decide quickly, because if the bell he had heard a little while ago meant quarter to four, the game would end in a few minutes, finished or not. But there was nothing to decide. Yes, but he couldn't go off just like that and leave it. Yes, but if he took it with him, that would be just as bad. What was that shouting? That must be Kevin, showing up with the banner. What had taken him so long? But perhaps it hadn't really been long at all, only he felt that way because his thoughts were coming so fast. As if everything in the world but himself had gone into slow motion.

What long ears you have, little bunny! Bunny Benedek. Bunny Rose. The better to hear my enemies with. Could you hear a hawk? Maybe their wings made a whistling sound. Michel pushed his fingers through the fur the wrong way, admiring the softness of the inner hairs. Da, da-*da,* da, da-da-da . . . The song went on in his brain. How did the rest of the words go? *Post jucundam.* Something. It was the eating that bothered him. It was being brought into the world just for that purpose, to be eaten. They were born inside a fence, and when they were taken out it was into the kitchen, to have their throats cut, and be skinned, and be hung up on hooks, like ripped-open babies. And if one got out, there were other teeth waiting for it. Teeth, and beaks and claws. To let just one escape, was that so much to ask?

What was he to do? What on earth was he to do? The foot was nothing, at the infirmary they would paint it with something and put a bandage on it, and maybe give him a crutch to walk with. Holier than anybody else. Ha! That was nothing. But the other thing that Kevin had said, that about—about— Did he really do that? It made him shiver to think of himself walking in the night with his eyes open and not seeing anything. Or even knowing he was doing it. And if he took a notion to open the window and . . . Or get hold of the prefect's key, unlock the door and come out to the woods. Walking.

Like a ghost, like a damned spirit, like the lady who . . .

He rocked back and forth, cradling the rabbit in his arms, crooning the first line of the song over and over, part of his mind searching for the other words while he contemplated himself walking in the night. Why did he try to open the door? Where was it he wanted to go? Home? Maman Rose would send him back again, if M. Konrad didn't get him. He was safe here. This was the only place in the world where he was safe. Except if Kevin—but he wouldn't do that. No, no, he wouldn't do that. No one knew, only Maman Rose, and Mother Veronica, and now Kevin. And the rabbit. He giggled, blowing gently into one of those long ears and watching it twitch. The rabbit had heard everything. Oh, but there were others. How could he have forgotten the others? There was God, who allowed soft, furry things to come into the world to be eaten, without a chance to fight back. There were the spirits of the dead, torches that once were human, who screamed and called his name. There was himself, who got out of bed and walked and didn't know it. He could get rid of the clipping. But if the prefect found him and asked him where he thought he was going, he might answer, "I murdered my father"; or "Don't you hear the screaming?"; or, "Why do you call me Rose? My name is—"

But why did he think of that now? There was time for that. There were four more years to go at the boys' school; then six at the Seminary. Six years as a crow. The rabbit was now. Why couldn't he think of the rabbit? He kept sliding from one thing to another, and in the meantime the precious minutes were passing. He was caught. This was as far as he could go, with his back jammed up against the fence, his useless paw stretched out before him. The world lay wide open to his eyes, and the sky overhead, but there was no place he could go. If they didn't catch him, his thoughts would. God would see to that. God, who had murdered His own Son. What a joke! He would have to ask Father Latouche about that. Which was worse, to murder your father or your son? Had his own father thought about that? Now, that would have been a way out. They could have gotten away then, free of the hated burden. He would have forgiven him for that. Because he was slowly being destroyed anyway.

Gaudeamus igitur, juvenes dum sumus
Post jucundam juventutem,

Post molestam senectutem,
Nos habebit humus.

The words had come to him. He sang the song aloud, waving his arm like Father Brighi. *Humus* meant earth. How beautiful the earth was! And the pale blue sky bending over it all, blandly warm with the sun. Like a golden liquid. God had given man such a beautiful place to live in! Then why didn't He let man live?

They were calling him. His name was in the air. Why was he dreaming like this? He had to go back. The game was over, and they were calling him. They would come for him, and find him by the fence. There was always a fence.

"Rose! Where are you?" The boys' voices. And then Signor Maas, a deeper tone. "Benediction, Rose! Come in!"

Benediction. Didn't they know he had been to hell and back?

"Poor bunny!" he whispered. He held it up to his face, feeling the fur tickle his nose, wondering why the fur was wet. They couldn't forget him, then. Wherever he went, there would be those voices. Of love or of hate, it didn't matter, since they both strangled. Be my son. No, be a slave. Be a Jew. No, be a Catholic. Be a priest. Be a Jesuit. Be Rose. Be dead.

"Rose!"

Michel started, his hair on end, anguish in his throat. Michel! he thought. There was only Michel. His hands tightened. A drop of sweat rolled down his clammy cheek. He felt its wet splash on the back of the hand that squeezed and squeezed. The rabbit's hind legs drummed in a brief spasm against his knee until he heard the muted crunch and something gave.

He did not look at the rabbit. Hastily he slid forward and put on his shoe, pulling it roughly over Kevin's handkerchief. Then, picking up the limp, furry flesh and his own handkerchief, he hobbled to the rock and shoved them into the crack. Tarsicius' catacomb. *Juvenes dum sumus.* The boulder he selected a little way below was almost beyond his strength, but it had to be big. He heaved and shoved, scrabbling behind him with his feet, feeling the hot blood spread in his shoe and not caring, until with a last wrench that left him dizzy he got it into place. It fit well enough. No fox was going to get in.

He had hardly headed down the slope toward the marsh when Kevin came to meet him. Kevin had been running; he panted as he spoke. "Come on! Signor Maas is fit to be tied. He says—" He stopped, staring at Michel's face and then his uniform. "My God!" he said. "What have you been doing? Did you cut yourself or what?" Then his eyes widened. He looked over Michel's head up the slope, and down again. Michel met his eyes. It was Kevin who turned away. "All right, youngster," he said. "You can't walk like that. Here, let me help you." Supported by Kevin's shoulder, limping, but strangely at peace, Michel went through the wood.

8

❧

M Y DEAR BIRA,

Almost three years ago you and I exchanged letters in regard to the efforts of the Benedek family to obtain possession of their orphaned nephew Michel. At that time you gave me some advice which I did not consider expedient to follow. To be frank, I believed then that your opinion concerning the role of the Catholic Church in this affair was exaggerated. Now I am not so sure. The further this matter has gone, the more I have become aware of a hidden hand behind Mlle Rose's machinations, and the sickening smell of incense.

If I may try your patience once more, allow me to sum up our activities of these three years and to state our present situation; you may be sure that any advice you care to give will fall upon more receptive ears this time. At the end of 1949, when you wrote to me . . .

This, then, was the state of affairs until this past summer. Four Family Councils, two trials in courts of first instance, and one, definitive, in the Touville Court of Appeals. Victories interspersed with heartbreaking defeats, until we won the big battle, and Michel was declared legally ours. But this, incredible as it may seem, has not proved to be the last stage of our struggle. Upon my presenting myself at the Municipal Nursery to receive the boy, on the day appointed by Appeals, I learned that Mlle Rose had left town on "sick leave," destination unknown. She stayed away more than a month, and no efforts on my part succeeded in discovering her whereabouts. Yet by an odd combination of circumstances, Mlle Rose's own activities revealed her. It seems that she had managed to locate Fräulein Eva Weiss, another aunt of the Benedek child, who had disappeared from the knowledge of the family some years ago . . .

As you can see, the attempt was abortive, and we were back

where we were before, except for a tragic aftermath. As a result of her encounter with Mlle Rose, Fräulein Weiss has had a relapse. During our return from Strasbourg I noted that she was in a strange, dazed condition. Once home she retired to our guest room, and we supposed that she had gone to bed. The next morning, however, we found her sitting in a chair staring out the window; it would appear that she had spent the night in that fashion, for she had not undressed. She was like stone, unhearing and unseeing, and nothing that we could do elicited the faintest reaction on her part. Naturally, we called a doctor, who in turn summoned a psychiatrist. The upshot is that the poor woman has reverted to her former condition, in which she simulated death in order to avoid an awareness that her oversensitive mind refused to accept. At least, this is how I understand the diagnosis, which was couched in rather more technical terms. She could not stay with us, of course. After several days of negotiation, a place was finally found for her in a nursing home in the vicinity of Voiron. The specialist says quite frankly that her illness may be incurable at this stage; or at best may yield incomplete results after long treatment. She was taken away a week ago, and I am still haunted by the memory of her deathlike face as she was carried to the car waiting for her.

In the midst of the excitement and worry occasioned by the presence of the sick woman in our home, I learned that Mlle Rose had returned to Touville. I telephoned the examining magistrate into whose charge my complaint of kidnaping had been referred, and the woman was summoned for a hearing. Her deposition makes strange reading, being full of outbursts of temper and disobliging remarks about her opponents, whom she calls "opportunist Frenchmen of new vintage"; and shows, moreover, no attempt on the part of the magistrate to call her to order. But let that pass. The magistrate, whatever his feelings in the matter, could not do other than remand her for trial before the Correctional Tribunal, altering the charge, however, from kidnaping to that of non-presentation of children; a lesser charge, unfortunately, but in his opinion more relevant, since he finds Mlle Rose's action more clearly defined under Article 357 of the Penal Code than under Article 354, as we alleged. The date of the trial has been set for November 18.

It would seem, therefore, that justice is about to be done, and that I have no need to have recourse to you or anyone else. Mlle Rose will be tried, and she will be found guilty. It cannot be otherwise, since the only issue before the Tribunal will be whether she did or did not comply with the executory verdict of the Appeals Court. She will be given the alternatives of producing the child or going to jail. Yet, since I believe I know the lady now, I cannot convince myself that this will be the end of it. She is an *exaltée*, incredibly stubborn, and has come to look upon herself as a martyr to motherhood. She will go to jail, and we will be no further than before, since all our efforts since 1948 to discover the boy's hiding place have been unavailing.

This is why I am writing to you. The equivocal attitude, not to say downright dishonesty, of the bishop of Touville; the brazen distortion of justice at the hands of Judge Minotard in the name of his religion; and now the meddling of the Cornelians to help Mlle Rose make a mockery of the law—all this, in addition to the otherwise unaccountable delays, obstacles, reluctance on the part of officialdom to perform their duty, etc., point to the conclusion that Mlle Rose is not alone in her fight. She will not yield; and if, as I suspect, the Church is behind her, the consequences are incalculable. Cry scandal, you advised me. Very well, but how? I have a few ideas on the subject, but they seem pitifully inadequate. I am most anxious to hear yours . . .

Louis Konrad

October 16, 1952

My dear Konrad,

Your letter has reached a man who had all but withdrawn from the "business" of a world rushing to destruction. Yes, I am convinced that the world has gone mad. When the American bomb fell on Hiroshima, I awoke as from a long sleep and said to myself, "I am sixty, alone among men, with a small income sufficient for my modest needs. I do not belong where I am. I will go away and do only what I want to do." I came away to my mountaintop here at l'Argentière, where I live like a hermit, with my sunsets and my beloved books. My company is the few sane men who have left their thoughts and their dreams behind them throughout the ages. With them I commune during the slow, peaceful days and nights, and now and then I set my ideas about them down in writing. I have nothing more to do with the market place and forums of the world.

Yet I have been a fighter. And in reading your long letter, I felt the oldtime anger curling inside me, as Voltaire did upon learning of the injustice done to Calas. Like him I am impelled to cry, *"Écrasez l'infâme!"* There is one more fight left in me after all. Yes, I will help you, in the measure of my powers. I cannot and will not bustle about; but my pen is still able. This tiny instrument, in spite of the horrible engines of destruction invented by man, is still the most powerful weapon in the world. When the time comes that it is not, then indeed there will be no hope for man.

You say, "Now I am not so sure." I do not know you personally, and so cannot tell whether you are given to understatement, or really still have doubts. If it is the latter, then I must ask what it takes to convince you. If I had not left my habit of sarcasm in the folds of my lawyer's garb (now only a dusty, wrinkled reminder buried in the closet), I would say, Are you waiting for the Pope himself to tell you? Good Lord, man, what more do you want? If you were not convinced by my first letter, you should at least have made inquiries, sounded out Church authorities, asked other opinions. No, you have waited until it is all but too late; until they have perhaps irreparably molded the boy's religious convictions; until he has been fully exposed to the systematic teaching of hatred the Christian Church has always directed toward our people; until the voice of public opinion, which is slow to awaken, can hardly reach the necessary pitch before they will have whisked the boy away forever from your grasp.

But it is not my intention to scold you; but rather, to convince you, and then offer suggestions as to remedies.

Let me put it bluntly. *Unless you take energetic action immediately, you will never get that boy.* Perhaps the early steps of Mlle Rose's resistance to the claims of the family were hers alone. But once the baptism was performed, the full weight and power of Catholicism, with its hierarchy of thousands and its half a billion faithful, became her ally and your implacable enemy. This is not conjecture on my part. For proof you need only go to the one source of information that cannot be impugned or doubted, the Church itself, with its canon law and exegesis and body of precedent.

As I write this I have before me a book entitled *Jews and Christians,* published shortly before the war. Its author is the Jesuit priest Bonsirven, it boasts the imprimatur, thus representing the official view of the Church, and it is designed to serve as a manual for those dedicated to the conversion of Jews to Catholicism. You should read this book, if you have not already; it will teach you how much you and I and the rest of our people are in the thoughts of these zealous missionaries; by what ruses, hypocrisies, and opportunist charities they hope to penetrate our doors and persuade us of their message. Beware of the Catholic visiting nurse, social worker, teacher! Such visits are, in Bonsirven's own words, "pretexts to cover another purpose," they are the "bait" to catch the unwary. All means serve, in the Jesuit view, to attain the desired and holy goal; even means unholy in themselves.

Bonsirven's book would be merely amusing were it not based on a Catholic creed stated in canon law (Can. 1350.1), according to which one learns that the Church considers the whole world to be its parish. Yes, I am the parishioner of the good priest of the church of l'Argentière; you, and along with you all the Jews, Protestants, atheists, heretics, Moslems and what have you in the area of Touville in which you reside, are the parishioners of your local priest, whom you may not even know by sight. This may mean nothing to you, who do not recognize his authority. But, in the eyes of the Church, *the authority is there!* It is a right the Church has allocated to itself, and nothing can shake it from its position.

What does it matter? you will say. The right the Church may claim is a purely spiritual one; I will get into heaven none the less readily for following the practices of my own religion; in the meanwhile, so long as this so-called right does not encroach upon my civil liberties, I will ignore their claims.

History gives the lie to such an attitude. What happened to the civil liberties of the countless thousands of Jews (Moors, heretics, agnostics, etc., etc.) who were put in ages past to the cruel alternative of conversion or death? The Reverend Father Bonsirven mentions these violent methods himself, in order to point out that *tempora mutantur, et nos mutamur in illis;* the Church, geared to eternity, knows how to adapt itself and wait. The political emancipation of the Jews since the time of the Crusades "has obliged the Church to follow other paths." Note that the emancipation that the Jesuit talks about has taken nothing away from the "rights" of the Church; it has merely forced it to change its methods. The Church has never abandoned its hope and ambition to "save" Israel. It considers this mission divinely decreed. "A Christian," cries Bonsirven, "cannot desist from leading Israel back to Christ, however he may annoy Jews as a whole by so doing: relations between Christians and Jews will therefore always be affected by this inevitable principle of friction."

Not "should not"; "ought not"; but *"cannot"* desist. And this by canon law.

Do not be deceived by those Catholics who may agree with you that the baptism of the Benedek boy was ill-advised, or improper, or "that it should not have been done." They may be sincere, but they are speaking for themselves, and not for the Church. Even if those who have the authority to speak—for example, your bishop of Touville, who did not hesitate to lie in the name of a higher truth—express their concern over the manner of the act, do not be deceived. In reality they are rejoicing. Another soul that was lost has been admitted to the great brotherhood of the saved. It does not matter how this was accomplished. What matter a few human tears, so long as God be satisfied? They are the only ones who know what satisfies God. Do they not have their rights?

Let us examine a bit this matter of the baptism. Your Maître Paul expostulated with his bishop, who admitted that according to canon law the boy was not eligible for the sacrament. This is true. Canon 751, no doubt as a result of the changing times, imposes self-limitations upon the Church. No one is to be baptized by force. In the case of children, baptism is not to be conferred without the consent of the parents. (Paragraph 1 of the canon provides an exception to this rule: "One may licitly baptize the children of infidels, even against the will of their parents when, by reason of the state of health in which these children find themselves, one envisages with all prudence that they will die before having attained the use of reason." We shall see some interesting results of this exception.)

Why this softening of its "rights" on the part of the Church? *The Dictionary of Canon Law* gives the answer: ". . . because of civil legislation which is often hostile to it, also because of popular prejudices, the Church cannot exercise all its rights." And goes on to explain that, except in the case of imminent death, the baptism of infidel children will lead to apostasy, for the parents, upheld by "civil legislation" and "popular prejudice" (!), will not allow these children a Christian upbringing. Such baptisms are therefore rendered "illicit."

Illicit. An interesting word. Does it mean null and void? Wiped out, as if it never happened? Not at all, and here is where your difficulty is. . . .

In practice the Church maintains the strange doctrine *that all baptisms are valid*. It does not matter by whom performed, or in what circumstances. Let the village idiot sprinkle me with water while I am asleep or unconscious, or otherwise unable to stop him, mutter the magic words, and presto! I am baptized and belong to Mother Church. It is true that he would be reprimanded severely by the priest, and told it "should not have been done," it is "against canon law," etc., etc.; but I am baptized nevertheless. For baptism is a sacrament, it leaves an indelible mark upon the soul; and the human instrument, however erring and misguided, does not matter. In the ultimate analysis, it is the Holy Ghost who baptizes, and there is no way for humans to undo the spook's work. And note for what reason the baptizer would be scolded: not because of his attempt against my individual liberty; not because I, as a free being, may not *want* to belong to Mother Church; but because, not having my consent, the baptizer has made a bad Christian, an "apostate."

I exaggerate, you say? On the contrary, I have not stated the worst of it. For what is meant by "belonging to Mother Church"? It means just what it says, being a possession of the Church, body and soul. And for proof I cite you the Mortara case. In 1858, in the city of Bologna, a Jewish child, Edgar Mortara, fell gravely ill. His age was between six and seven. The servant woman, a fervent Catholic named Anna Morisi, was certain that the child was going to die, and that his death would mean eternal damnation. She secretly baptized him. But the child recovered, and Anna Morisi, disturbed by the spectacle of this new Christian following the religious practices of his Jewish family, went to her priest. The matter was placed before the Inquisition of Bologna, and eventually reached the Pope himself, Pius IX. It was decided that the baptism was valid. The solution was simple. Was the boy not in the Papal State, where the pontiff was temporal as well as spiritual ruler? The order was given to remove the boy from his family, and was carried out by the archbishop of Bologna. The protests of the family were disregarded. The boy was taken away by force and placed in the college of San Pietro in Vincoli in Rome. The story became public, and there was an immediate, indignant reaction by the press in almost every country in Europe. This was not the Middle Ages! How could such a monstrous thing occur in our enlightened nineteenth century? The English and French governments made representations to the Vatican, and old Moses Montefiore himself went to Rome to see the Pope. Useless. Pius IX maintained, in an attitude that can only be qualified as cynical hypocrisy, that the question at issue was a spiritual one, outside his temporal jurisdiction; and declined to take any action. In the meanwhile, of course, while the battle raged, Edgar Mortara was being stuffed with Catholic dogma, and the Pope, pleased with his progress, made him his ward. Several years later the Mortara family, attempting to keep the case alive, persuaded the Italian government to demand the prosecution of Anna Morisi. Useless. She had become a nun. Prussia threatened to intervene, and the Vatican, by what inducement I do not know, got the Mortara family to withdraw its complaint against her. Edgar Mortara was never returned to his family. In 1870 Italian troops captured Rome, and the young man, now eighteen or nineteen, was given the opportunity to revert to Judaism. But they had had him too long, and he refused. He became an Augustinian monk, and died, if I am not mistaken, in 1940, at the advanced age of eighty-nine, still faithful to the Church that had kidnaped him and broken his parents' hearts.

By what authority did Pius IX do this? He was simply following Church precedent, as laid down by Benedict XIV a century before, whose papal bull *Postremo mense* had dealt with a similar case (see *Dictionary of Canon Law,* II, col. 141). Benedict had also ordered a newly baptized child removed from his non-Catholic family, and his rule was approved by the Sacred Congregation in 1777. These are the comments of the *Dictionary:* "It is the necessity of assuring a Christian education for the baptized that renders separation from the parents indispensable. The Church is a mother too: she has the right and the duty to safeguard the religious formation of her children and to avert the obstacles that might oppose it; she cannot permit the baptized to be exposed to the imminent danger of apostasy."

May the God of Israel shield us from such mothers!

I quote from the book by Franz Leenhard, professor at the University of Geneva, entitled *The Church and the Realm of God.* Considering the Mortara case, Professor Leenhard (a Protestant) says in biting sarcasm: "The archbishop was right to remove the child from his parents, after the servant had rightly baptized him against their will and unknown to them. Those who refused to return him to his parents were right. Pope Pius IX, who had approved all this and who had participated in the drama, was right. All were right, they say, because they had done nothing more than conform to the principles established by Benedict XIV. The explanation is not even an excuse."

An isolated case, you say? But before this there was the Montel affair, and before the Montel affair who knows how many similar cases buried in the Vatican archives, which created their little local stir and were forgotten. The Montel case goes back to 1840, and involves the French Jew of Nîmes, Daniel Montel, who with his pregnant wife set out on a trip to Rome. At Ostia, however, the wife gave birth to a daughter. When Mme Montel had recovered her strength and was in condition to travel, the trip was resumed. No sooner had the young couple and their infant arrived at Rome than they were placed under guard until their case had been decided by the Holy Office. The astonished parents learned that at the inn at Ostia, where the child was born, a servant woman who had assisted at the delivery had secretly baptized their daughter at the moment of birth, in the fear that she would not live. This was the beginning of a long and dogged debate between Rayneval, our *chargé d'affaires* at Rome, and Cardinal Lambruschini, Secretary of State to Pope Gregory XVI, reported fully by Rayneval to Thiers, President of the Council and Minister of Foreign Affairs. In Lambruschini's arguments the position of the Church emerges clearly. This was for His Holiness "a matter of conscience, covered by canon law and established by various precedents," the cardinal stated. Rayneval argued in vain. At his insistence, the cardinal replied, "You may threaten us with all the guns at your disposition, you may invade our shores with all your fleets, but on this matter (the removal of the child from her parents and her education at Rome under the surveillance of the Holy See) we remain unshakable." The outcome of the matter? The child was returned to France, but only after a solemn promise had been exacted from the French government that it would make itself responsible before God to raise her in the Catholic religion.

This same Cardinal Lambruschini was responsible for an even harsher application of this pernicious canon law in Genoa, whose archbishop he was before going on to Rome. There an oil merchant baptized a Jewish boy of twelve or thirteen, claiming that the boy had given his previous consent. The Holy Office declared the baptism valid (of course!), and ordered the child removed from his family, in spite of the intervention of the King of Sardinia, who happened to be at Genoa at the time. It was small consolation to the parents, who never saw their son again, that the merchant was imprisoned for having administered an improper baptism. Improper, yes—but valid.

Do you still say I exaggerate?

The same thing is happening to your Michel Benedek! The only difference is that the Church has cleverly kept out of sight, preferring not to render open battle. France is not Italy, nor much less the Papal State, and this is the twentieth century. Ask yourself these questions. Does not Mlle Rose's incredible obstinacy argue a support in which she has every right to have confidence? More, is that support not rather a threat? Does she *dare* give in, with a pistol at her back? How has she managed to hide the boy so successfully for so many years that no one has caught a glimpse of him? The boy must go to school—what does he do during Christmas? Easter? The long summer vacation? Does he come home? Or does he move from one hiding place to another? If so, does not this argue some collusion with some institution or other? A pension, a convent, a summer camp such as the Franciscans operate for children? Mlle Rose, a municipal employee, cannot be rich. Who pays her lawyers? Her court costs? Her travels?

I am afraid there is only one answer. The Church is engaged in this to the hilt, ready to do anything rather than turn a baptized child over to Jews. The examining magistrate who changed your charge of kidnaping for that of non-presentation of children knew what he was doing. The first is a crime; the second is only a delict, punishable at most by one year in prison. Mlle Rose must be found guilty, yes; but she may be given a suspended sentence, or less than the limit. But even if it is the limit, she will go to jail laughing at you. And the Church will take over and continue to hide the boy.

What is there to do? Cry scandal, I repeat. In matters of this kind, secrecy is the Church's best friend. The issue is this: civil law vs. canon law—which is supreme in France? Ever since the Revolution Frenchmen have become accustomed to believe that civil law governs all. *The Church has not accepted this!* Only by necessity has it pretended to yield and put a good face on matters; it has, in other words, gone underground. If you succeed in bringing this to the attention of the public, there is a chance that of two evils the Church will choose the lesser, give up the boy rather than expose its pious fraud. You must, to put it simply, force the public to reassess the place of the Church in France today. And this the Church will not tolerate.

You ask me for my ideas. In one word, publicity! Now! Don't wait until Mlle Rose is brought to trial. The whole world must wonder, Where is Michel Benedek? Every boy of eleven who moves in the public domain—on buses, trains, airplanes, in automobiles—must be an object of suspicion. Perhaps then the Church will think twice before exposing itself. Summon your Family Council, present the problem to them, have each member call a gathering of friends to tell the story. Bombard the newspapers with letters for publication. Summon a press conference, compare your case with the Dreyfus Affair, give them a photograph of the boy for circulation. Write down an account of the family's struggle from the very beginning, have it printed or mimeographed, and send copies to the Jewish Consistory in Paris, to the Jewish Children's Welfare Society, to the Jewish-Christian Alliance, to the Federation of Israelite Organizations of France, to the Jewish War Orphans Relief Society, to the mayor and every member of the city council of Touville, to the prefect of the Côte-des-Alpes, to the members of the Chambre des Députés, etc., etc. Form a Committee for the Defense of the Benedek Child, with a headquarters and a secretary. On October 27 the Conference of Jewish Organizations will begin a week-long symposium in Paris, sponsored by the French Section of World Jewry. The corresponding secretary, Maître André David, is a friend of mine from my years at the bar. Upon finishing this letter I shall write him a brief account of your case and ask that you be put on the agenda to address the Conference. Tomorrow I shall compose a letter of introduction to him on your behalf and send it to you. It will then be up to you to write him, or telegraph him, or call him on the telephone to complete the arrangements. If you can get World Jewry interested in your case, you will have come a long step forward.

For my part, I will begin a series of articles on the Benedek Affair and fire them off to various periodicals with which I am now collaborating. (Please send me, in this connection, a copy of your mimeographed account. From time to time I may also write you asking for clarification or additional information.)

Gird yourself, my friend. Your battle has only just begun.

BIRA

9

❧

D EAR HANNAH AND ITZIK,

What a trial! A scene from a grade-B movie on the melodramatic side! A farce! A wrestling match! To think that I, Louis Konrad, could have been capable of— But no, this is not the way to tell you, I must put myself into some calm and recount the whole incredible event from the beginning. Forgive my penmanship. My hand is still trembling.

Very well. The trial was today. It lasted four hours. The decision will be announced in two weeks, on December 2. What that decision will be is anybody's guess. Now let me begin the tale, which is called "The Baiting of the Bull," or "Whom the Gods Destroy . . ."

The controversy grows. This morning there were knots of men and women on the steps of the courthouse, arguing heatedly. I was recognized as I approached, heads turned toward me, reporters came running. One, a man named Pletzel, was from the *Touville Gazette;* I knew him from the first press conference, when he showed himself sympathetic to our cause. He told me that the phones have been ringing day and night at the editorial room, asking information about the boy. There were reporters from Paris, he said. Two of them, already inside. I thanked him for his articles. Photographers took my picture as I answered questions. Where was the boy? they wanted to know. "Ask Mlle Rose," I replied. "If I knew, I would not be here today." The crowd around us thickened. Someone called out, "Communist!" and there was a brief scuffle. On the other hand, as I pushed my way into the building, several people I did not know wrung my hand. Everyone is furious, on one side or the other. A good omen, I thought. Anything rather than that indifference against which I have been battering my head like on a stone wall for almost five years! Our campaign is succeeding beyond expectation.

People were milling about the corridors, unable to find place in the courtroom, which was filled to overflowing. I had to force my way in, followed by the reporters, who have a privileged bench. They sat jammed shoulder to shoulder. And the audience, what a cross section of opinion! Our attacks had brought out the clergy: one whole row was filled with Roman collars, with a scattering of others among the laity. One was the adjutant of Bishop Rebenty, I learned later. There were even two nuns, Temple Dames, sitting discreetly in the back row. And in the loges, surrounded by a coterie of yes-men, none other than M. Forgues, deputy from Grenoble of the MRP, the rightist Catholic party, sporting his Legion of Honor ribbon. Yes, but across from him, locking glances like a swordsman, Georges Reschling, Communist party-boss of Lyons, who accompanied Thorez to Russia two years ago on the occasion of the surgery that failed. And in between, shades of all banners, right, left, center, center-right, center-left: Lévy and Colbert, of our Council; Jules, at my side; the jeweler Béjart, monarchist reactionary, who sponsored Michel at the baptism; Zionists from our local chapter; Mlle Merlin, the mayor's secretary (he wouldn't come himself, of course); Socialist rank and file; a Gaullist or two; a professor from our university law school; and many, many others I did not recognize, predominantly ladies, moved no doubt by the motherhood issue. There was a murmur as I entered. I could not tell whether it was hostile or not. I was the last participant to arrive. Mlle Rose was on the defendant's bench, the lawyers in their robes at their bar.

One thing was sure, I thought as I sat down. Whatever direction this trial took, whatever bias might be revealed during the hearing, it would not pass unnoticed, like last year's, under Judge Minotard. I remembered what I had been told about Judge Pochet, president of the Correctional Tribunal: a Catholic, yes, but a man of principle, noted for his fair decisions. And I prepared myself for any eventuality.

Except the one that happened.

Hardly had the usher announced the entry of the judges and they had seated themselves at their desks on the dais, than Pochet revealed himself in his true colors, by questioning my capacity to serve as civil party against Mlle Rose.

"In France, nobody pleads by proxy," he stated categorically.

It was a bombshell. Those in the audience were bolt upright. Was the case going to be thrown out before it had started? Someone clapped his hands; another said angrily, "Shame!" Whispering broke out, which Pochet stopped with a glare. As for me, I was thunderstruck, and the optimism with which I had entered disappeared at once. But I must be brief, I do not have the patience to recount for you all the legal wrangling of a four-hour trial. My lawyers countered this move by changing the civil party to you, making your domicile Maître Paul's law office. Pochet then struck his second blow: M. Konrad had no right to represent the civil party, since his power of attorney was outdated, going back to 1948! Very well, we found another power we had had prepared for the Fourth Family Council, of 1950. Pochet professed himself satisfied, and the trial was allowed to continue.

Another surprise! Their Honors demanded to know in what circumstances I became interested in the Benedek child, and I had to rehearse the whole weary business over again, before three judges who watched me with bleak eyes and interrupted repeatedly to verify trivial details.

Do you understand the significance of this procedure? They were trying the case all over again! A court of first instance, and in the criminal jurisdiction, reviewing a decision handed down by a higher, civil court! It is unheard of. My lawyers were aghast, but were squelched when they tried to raise an objection. The massacre went on. Everything I said was taken as though I were a hostile witness; they pounced on every detail that could possibly be given a dubious interpretation. For instance, my admission that it was I who first suggested that you provide me with a power of attorney, and not you to me. As if it makes any difference! Your consent was involved in any case. But no—Pochet all but cried Aha! and repeated it for the sake of the recording clerk. And smirks on the faces of the priests— they now knew the secret key to the whole affair! The reporters scribbled furiously, the room filled with electricity, and all the while I asked myself incredulously, "Who's on trial here?"

Patience! I counseled myself. I must not let them get me angry. But a person can take only so much. No sooner had I been put through the wringer, than the president invited the defendant to tell her side of the story. *Her* side, in the name of—! But the purpose of the trial was to determine whether Mlle Rose had obeyed the order of the Appeals Court to deliver the boy to the family, *and nothing else!* No matter, Their Honors, in their wisdom, had decided on a retrial, as a rebuke to the higher court, no doubt, for having overlooked canon law in their decision. And so there I was, already smoldering dangerously, forced to listen to that woman, in her weepy, self-pitying voice full of false sentiment, parade the same pathetically transparent set of lies that I have disproved so many times that they have become like the Hydra-headed monster to me, cropping up afresh every time they are destroyed.

She took Michel in, at a time when, etc., etc. She already had six Jewish children in her care. (The last time she told it there were only two; they grow like rabbits, those children; but wait, there are more astonishing fables to come.) She spoke of M. Houdy, and Karl's "last wishes"; the boy called her "Mother"; no one ever offered to help pay her expenses in caring for him. And so on and so on, the same old tune, her claims growing more extravagant as she proceeded, unchecked by the judges, who drank it all in and asked for no corroboration and doubted no word. There were sneers in the audience; Lévy was clutching his head; beside me Jules growled. Yet there were those whose faces showed tender belief. On she went: none of the Benedek or Lindner family had claimed the boy after the Liberation. If they had, she would have given him up without any fuss, since she was not yet emotionally attached to him. It was not until after the baptism that they showed any interest at all. As a matter of fact, Mme Lindner had come to see her in 1946, and told her to keep Michel, since she was unable to take care of him.

Hitler's technique: the bigger the lie, the more it will be believed. There are still some people in Touville today who are convinced that you came to the Nursery and "gave Michel away to Mlle Rose." And now she dared to try it again! But this was a court of law. I looked indignantly at Lanson, and started to rise. He shook his head, and spoke up himself. Mme Lindner, he stated, had never set foot in France. Mlle Rose insisted; so did he; she added an embellishing detail that tripped her up: Mme Lindner had come accompanied by an interpreter of the Jewish Welfare Society.

"But that aunt was Mme Mitzi Benedek, widow of Dr. Benedek's brother," Maître Lanson exclaimed.

It was the Rose woman's own lawyer who made her back down. He had evidently begun to worry at his client's excesses. Better not go too far! He suggested that the defendant had perhaps confused the two aunts; a natural error, since she had never seen either before. Mlle Rose wavered, caught the savage look Cauchet flung her, and accepted the possibility.

The representative of the Ministry of Justice, M. Passy, substitute of the procureur, also gave Mlle Rose a look; but it was one of curiosity. Could it be that he did not share the attitude of the judges? He had listened to me, I remembered, with close attention. This, at least, was encouraging.

A moment later Lanson interrupted again. Mlle Rose had said that it was not until M. Konrad had appeared in the case that she had heard from Mme Lindner. Before that there had been nothing: no communication of any kind, no hint of any wish on your part to take Michel, no letter, no package, no gift for him. "The liar!" Jules muttered; the judges frowned in our direction, not certain who had said it. Lanson was more polite. "There are letters in existence to prove the contrary."

"Produce them," the president said.

Of course Lanson did not have them with him! Why should he? The Appeals Court had seen them all, ruled on them, disposed of them forever, one would have thought. Lanson conferred with Maître Paul, and announced that the documentary evidence to prove his contention existed, and would be turned in to Their Honors before decision was rendered. He had not anticipated this line of argument by the defendant, believing it extraneous to the issue as described in Article 357 of the Penal Code.

As you can see, he restated his previous objection, this time indirectly. The judges ignored it.

Having got away with her whopper, at least for the moment, Mlle Rose triumphantly continued her story. Astonishing creature—accused of a lie, of which proof was forthcoming, she went on to others, of stupefying audacity. I am convinced she is insane. It was all a cabal, she said. The Communists, the Zionists, the Freemasons! (Why not the Mafia? the Black Hand?) But the boy had *asked* to be baptized! Could she refuse him the Kingdom of Heaven, when it was his own wish? The last Family Council—this was part of the plot too, having been packed by members who did not represent the true wishes of the family, which had been deceived by their agent, M. Konrad. She knew this to be so, because only last month, in October, she had met the third aunt of the boy, Mlle Eva Weiss, in Strasbourg, and Mlle Weiss had thanked her for having taken care of her nephew, and asked her to continue to provide for him.

Until this point I had been able to restrain myself, with difficulty, it is true. But at that monstrous lie my self-control snapped. Could decency be more outrageously flouted than this? And with our grief so fresh over the tragedy of that poor woman! I frankly do not remember what I shouted as I leaped up. Jules told me afterwards that I bellowed like a bull and that everyone started, caught by surprise, since they had been looking at Mlle Rose. Jules too uttered an exclamation, but it was lost in the uproar. The president pounded his bell, someone pulled me by the sleeve; and Maître Lanson was on his feet, waving a paper and crying out, "May it please the court!"

Jules whispered, "For God's sake, sit down and let him read the affidavit!" I came to my senses and sat down, and Pochet tore into me. Such outbursts would not be tolerated! This was a court of law! Etc., etc. Jules tells me that I muttered "Old fool!" I don't remember that; saying it, I mean.

Lanson's reading of Eva Weiss' affidavit was a *coup de théâtre*. The words fell into the hushed court like hammer strokes. No one drew a breath. The deputy Forgues was leaning forward, his eyes glittering. In all his years at the bar, Lanson assured me afterwards, he had never had a moment like that one. It all came out: Rose's letter to Eva Weiss at Lautern, their exchange of telegrams, the conversation in the monastery, the part played by the monks, the attempted bribe; everything Eva Weiss had sworn to under my questioning before the notary. As Lanson read, Mlle Rose slid lower and lower on her bench, like a punctured balloon, and her two lawyers stared at her and at each other in consternation. Was it possible? Could that incredible woman have kept her Strasbourg attempt a secret from her own lawyers? I am convinced of it. And the judges! Their faces were something to see as Lanson, punctuating his words with an accusing finger pointed at the Rose woman, read the closing, damning statements of Eva Weiss's deposition: "I am afraid! She is desperate, she will do anything. If he is alive, he is in danger. . . . He should be taken away from that woman. He should be given to you, to be turned over to Hannah in Israel."

I quote this from memory, but I am sure the words are exact. I still hear them in my ears, not as read in court—I was too busy watching the expressions chase themselves over the faces of the spectators—but as spoken in Strasbourg by that victim of the Rose woman's mania.

In the stunned silence that followed there was a minor diversion. One of Rose's lawyers, Cauchet, collapsed. Perhaps it was a true fainting fit—his client had given him enough cause. Or perhaps he wanted to distract the attention of the audience and the court from Mlle Rose, whose blanched cheeks proclaimed her guilt. If the latter, it succeeded all too well. The release of tension was carried off with a burst of laughter, as people half rose and craned their necks to see Cauchet on the floor. Again the president's bell, and the threat to clear the courtroom. Cauchet came to in a few minutes, and sat out the rest of the trial with a sick face.

I refuse to take the blame for what came after. Mlle Rose had committed a brazen perjury before the court. There was no possibility of an honest confusion, as the court had chosen to believe over the identity of the aunt who visited Touville. She had lied under oath and had been caught out. Would the Tribunal allow itself to be openly deceived and ridiculed to their faces? Would they not order her arrested on the spot?

They did nothing of the kind. The president asked for the affidavit, studied it interminably, consulted with the assistant judges at each side, ignoring the murmur of the spectators who had begun to argue among themselves; and finally pointed out that in the body of the text itself was the deposition of the notary, Emile Forst, to the effect that the deponent was suffering from some kind of nervous disorder at the moment of testifying; was, in fact, not of sound mind. Therefore, the gravest doubt . . .

You will remember in what circumstances Eva Weiss dictated her affidavit. It was the cruelest mockery to rule that her emotional state —produced by Mlle Rose herself!—invalidated her report.

It was enough to restore Mlle Rose's confidence. She is nothing if not resilient. She snorted and straightened up, nodding her head as if to say, See how they have maligned me, these scheming Jews!

Maître Lanson tried to argue, but Pochet cut him short. "This is not the best evidence. Let the lady be brought. Let her testify in person."

And I was on my feet again, this time beyond control. "What do you want?" I ranted, waving my arms. "What is evidence in a French court? Who's on trial here, Eva Weiss or that perjurer on the bench there, with her lies and her bag of tricks? Why don't you ask her where is the boy she kidnaped? You want to know where Eva Weiss is? Ask *her!* Ask her how she destroyed Eva Weiss with her lies and her bribes, until she lost her mind and took her own life! Eva Weiss is dead! And her murderer is sitting before you, hungry for more blood! And she'll kill the boy too, if you don't stop her. The affidavit is not enough for you? You want to corroborate it? Do you want me to dig her up? This trial is a farce, an inquisition . . . !"

This is more or less what I said, but with such violence that I could feel the veins start out on my neck and foam fleck my mouth. My throat is still hoarse from it. And in the midst of my tirade, Mlle Rose's hateful face danced before me, and I lunged across the floor toward her, to do what I don't know. Fortunately, the usher grabbed me, several pairs of arms came to his assistance, and I was hustled down the aisle, struggling and yelling, to the corridor outside, where they walked me up and down like a nervous race horse until my bile had subsided somewhat.

I still don't know why I was not locked up for contempt of court. Perhaps it was the very violence of my reaction that saved me. Or perhaps the startling nature of my announcement, and the accusation I had shot at Mlle Rose. The judges were so taken aback that they sat frozen long enough for me to spew it all out. By the time Pochet came to and shouted for order, I was outside, and there was nothing to do but to declare a recess and pick up the shattered remnants of the court's dignity. The judges withdrew, weighed all the pros and cons, and decided, I suppose, not to make a martyr out of me.

Not one of the audience budged from his seat during the recess, which lasted perhaps fifteen minutes. There was, however, a fist fight, which the ushers broke up, throwing both men out of doors.

At the reopening of the hearing Pochet ripped into me for contempt, and everyone was sure I would be sentenced, or at least fined. But at the end he announced that the court would be satisfied, this one time only, with an apology.

I got up and said, "I apologize," and sat down.

The trial continued, but now it was all anticlimax. The lawyers presented their conclusions. (Not Cauchet. He left it all to his colleague, one Maître Tercy, who outdid himself in rehashing all of Mlle Rose's stale arguments, and even went her one better by combining two of the supposed conspirators in the phrase "Jewish Freemasonry.") As for Lanson, he brought the trial back to sanity by presenting a good, solid case against the woman for non-presentation. As I had guessed, the substitute, on behalf of the Ministry of Justice, associated himself with the civil party, and demanded the application of Article 357 of the Penal Code, since the Appeals Court decision was not suspensive, but executory. To be truthful, I hardly listened. I felt sick from the violence of my outburst, and had begun to tremble uncontrollably.

It was almost amusing to see how a path cleared before me when the trial was over and I walked out.

Lévy, who came to my home in the evening, reported that the discussions continued in the corridors and the street a long time after the session closed, amid insults and brandished fists.

Other friends came too, including Maître Paul, and we spent the evening weighing the fantastic event. There is of course no telling what the judges will do; but we are agreed that matters look bad. We may present all the documents we want to the judges (French law permits the introduction of new evidence between trial and verdict), in order to corroborate our contention that the family's attempt to get the boy goes back to 1945; they can always find a way to dismiss the charge. From the direction of the hearing itself, I have no doubt that that is what they will do. Paul thinks the same. I have never seen him so furious. He cries, "The law will not be mocked!" We must appeal, he says. I suppose that is what we will come to— but I am too exhausted now to decide anything. I am convinced only that, no matter how the decision goes, our chief hope is the publicity we have given and will continue to give the affair. It must eventually rise up to become a tidal wave, to swallow up those who urge an interest higher than that of humanity. If this does not happen, then there is no hope for the world. . . .

LOUIS KONRAD

10

❦

THAT MORNING it was not Father Scala's boomed *"Laudetur
Jesus Christus"* that awoke him, but a confused hubbub that
penetrated his drugged senses gradually until he realized that something was wrong and sat up abruptly in bed. The overhead light was
on, but the darkness of the window had no hint of morning about it,
and his body was limp and aching as though he had not had his sleep
out. Surely it was too early. But the prefect's voice sounded angrily
in the corridor, "Out! Everybody out! You, Angelilli!" What could
have happened? Michel slipped out of bed and thrust his head
through the curtain. In the harsh glare of the naked light bulb he saw
that some of the boys were already standing in their pajamas before
their cubicles. Others, like himself, were peering fearfully out. Father
Scala, his massive jaw blue with stubble, his unruly hair uncombed,
was darting into the cubicles of the dilatory ones, clapping his hands
and crying, "Look lively, now!" He seemed dreadfully angry, and
Michel hastily stepped out.

"What is it? What's happened?" The boys whispered nervously
among themselves, dazed at the harsh awakening, and shivering with
the cold.

Father Scala had taken up a position in the middle of the double
row of boys, who stared at him with misgiving. His eyes were wide
and shocked as he looked at each of them in turn. His shout was so
sudden that it made them jump. "Who did it? I want the one who did
it to step out this instant and confess! If I lose my patience!"

Michel was mystified, and so were the others, who looked about
them in bewilderment.

"Was it you, Magruder? You are amused, you smile?"

Magruder, a wiry, dark Irish boy, had made a nervous grimace;
now he shrank back. "I haven't done anything, Father."

Father Scala took a deep breath. "Look!" he said, pointing.

A chorus of gasps went up as the boys followed his finger. The crucifix that had been fastened to the door of the prefect's room was missing. Where it had hung the door was discolored in the outline of a cross, with two tiny dark holes top and bottom where the screws had bitten into the wood. Michel gasped too as the enormity of it sank in. Someone had removed the crucifix during the night, for a prank. Someone had dared to lay his hands on that holy object, and of course the prefect had noticed it the moment he stepped out of his door; and now he was going to find out who had done it, and the boy, whoever it was, would be severely punished. Awe struck him to think that any of them could have been capable of such a thing. The boys had surged forward to see better, and Father Scala ordered them roughly back into line. He strode up and down before them, waving his arms, and shouting that the culprit had better confess now, the longer he waited the worse it would be for him, and for all of them. They would all stay where they were until the crucifix was found and the guilty one discovered.

"In your pajamas!" he cried. "All of you! Without breakfast!"

Who could have dared? Michel asked himself in fear. A crucifix! Was it possible that among them, boys selected for their intelligence and piety, was one who had no fear of the wrath of God? The others seemed overcome by the same doubt. All looked at each other, wondering. Only Kevin seemed composed. He stood, his raw, pale face set in a dreamy expression, looking down at the floor. As Michel stared at him, he lifted his head and gazed back. There was something in his eyes. . . . And suddenly, as though he were back in the woods again, sitting on the ground and looking up at his friend, Kevin's voice came back to him. "You walk about the dormitory in your bare feet in the dark. You go to the door and try to open it. And then you go up to the door of the prefect's room and look at the crucifix. You look and look. And then you go back to bed."

No! he almost cried aloud as the thought came to him. Had he walked again last night? No, no, he hadn't! He couldn't have! And even if he had, he wouldn't have touched the crucifix! Why should he? You look and look, Kevin had said. Very well, he looked, there was no harm in that. That was very different from laying violent hands on the cross, with its tiny figuration of the Son of God. It sent a surge of nausea to his stomach just to think of it. He tried to see himself doing it: standing before it in the dark; staring at those tortured eyes a few inches from his own; deliberately, driven by some crazy impulse, reaching upward with desecrating fingers . . . He could not, it was impossible, it was not he, he was not mad!

Michel's heart jumped. Father Scala had stepped close and cried, "Was it you?" But it was not to him that the words were addressed; the prefect was pointing to the boy to his right, Nigri, who twitched violently and cried, "Oh no, Father!" with lips that trembled. Fear shot through Michel as the prefect turned away, glancing at him. What would he answer? A desperate denial gathered in him, ready to burst forth; yet his own dreadful suspicion had robbed him of strength, and beyond the priest he was aware of Kevin's eyes burning into him. It was only a moment, but it seemed an age that the priest's glance held him suspended.

"Very well, then," Father Scala snapped. He strode away, crying, "Let no one move!" He unlocked the door and shouted down the stairs, "You, down there! Yes, you! Tell Father Pace I must see him at once. At once, do you hear? Now," he said grimly, turning back, "we shall see! All morning! A week if necessary! The crucifix is here, and will be found, make no mistake. One of these beds will be empty tonight."

They were in the common room, where they had been conducted after refectory and made to sit at attention under the impassive eyes of Father Pace, the prefect of discipline. But Father Pace had been called away, and left Signor Maas in his place. Then Signor Maas had left them too, unaccountably, and after a bit of timorous whispering among themselves the boys had crowded to the window, from which the entrance to administration could be seen. They were all angry and weak and full of gloom as they gazed out and conversed among themselves. Michel had remained seated; but feeling himself too conspicuous, he had risen and joined the others. All talked at once, watching administration, waiting for Horst to come out.

What a weary and miserable morning they had spent, still in their pajamas, faint with hunger, in agony because of their unemptied bladders, while the rector himself, pale and angry, had walked up and down the line to examine their faces, and the prefect and other priests had ransacked each cubicle to find the holy object! They had turned everything inside out, ripping the beds apart and heaving the mattresses over on the floor, rummaging through every article of clothing, shaking the curtains, even crawling about on their hands and knees. Michel had watched them progress toward his cubicle with a fear so palpable that he could taste it in his throat, all the while praying that the crucifix would be found before they got to him, and cursing himself for the cowardly wish. Besides, it was useless. Angelilli? Horst? Chamfort? Longhi? Nigri? None of them could have done it. And that left him, the sleepwalker, the one who was all twisted inside and full of hatreds he himself couldn't understand. He had gotten up again during the night, as Kevin had seen him do before, he had gone to stare at the crucifix; and this time he had done more than stare, he had— And the screws? How had he removed them? With his bare hands? No matter, he had done it somehow, and if so, then the crucifix had to be in his cubicle somewhere, and in a moment they would find it and let out a shout and come out and fix him with a terrible look and he would wish he were dead and out of it all.

The rector had come and stood before him, regarding him with sorrowful gaze, and he had waited for the accusation to come. He had lifted his eyes, and the world had been blotted out by that stern but kind face he had never seen so close before, the face of a demigod so holy and removed and above them all that the boys instinctively lowered their voices to speak of him. In that instant, in which he took in the aged but firm-fleshed countenance, with its crown of short-cropped, stiff white hair, the still youthful eyes with their clear, uncompromising gaze, that august figure suddenly became for him merely a man suffering for the unruliness of his children; and he was aware of a surge of pity within himself for the problem now facing him. But Michel had had no time to think of that. The rector had moved on, and the others had come and pushed aside his curtain and entered his cubicle. Then his agony had begun in earnest. He had braced himself, feeling the blood withdrawing from his face, listening to the obscure noises coming from behind the curtain, wanting to scream that it was not he, but that other Michel, the one he had no control over, who had done it while the real Michel was asleep. Kevin would back him up, tell what he knew; they couldn't blame him for what he couldn't help. Yet even if they didn't expel him, it wasn't any good. They would question him mercilessly. *Why* did he walk in his sleep? What was tormenting him? Why? Why? What the consequences might be he didn't dare imagine. When, after what seemed to be a much longer time than they had spent in other cubicles, they emerged empty-handed from behind the yellow curtain, it had taken the last remnant of his self-possession not to show the relief that flooded over him, and he realized how close he had been to fainting.

Horst! They had all turned in astonishment as the outcry came from the German boy's cubicle, and had seen Father Scala seize his arm, and the rector hurrying to them, and the knot of black-clothed men forming around the hapless baby face that had gone white with panic. Michel had had a moment of shocked disbelief, followed by a pang of shameful joy. He had watched Horst being propelled toward the door, his ear gripped in the prefect's hairy fingers, a spreading wet stain at the front of his pajamas; and he had thought, Then I didn't do it!

But the search had continued. It was not the crucifix they had found, but a forbidden knife.

It had not been until noon that the hunt was called off, and it was acknowledged that the crucifix was not in the dormitory. The boys had been allowed to get dressed and had been led to refectory by a grim, still unshaven Father Scala, and then confined to the common room. All but Horst, who had been taken to administration and had not come out.

The boys argued among themselves. It was the screws, Giraud said. Just having the jackknife in his possession would have been good for a whipping and a week's loss of privileges. But they supposed he must have done it because the knife had a screwdriver in it. No, Chamfort said, it was because it was a wooden crucifix, and it hadn't been found, and with the knife . . . The others looked at him, not understanding.

"He cut it up," Chamfort said. "And flushed it down the toilet."

They were silent, contemplating with awe this additional sacrilege. Michel thought of the row of white, smelly receptacles in the lavatory, and felt sick. How short-lived his relief had been! Now he was back where he had been before, in the same incertitude and fear, except that now there was a new mystery as well. If his hands had done the terrible deed, what had he done with the crucifix? Could he have done what Chamfort had said? But he had no knife.

"No, that's not it," Angelilli said decisively. "Horst's a fool. I told him to get rid of that knife. But he didn't take the crucifix."

"Then where is it?" someone asked.

Angelilli jerked his thumb. "Out the window."

They turned on him in protest. Hadn't he seen them searching?

They had routed out all the boys on the first floor of dorm, and they had scoured the terrain on all sides of the building.

Kevin spoke; Kevin, who had remained off to one side, listening without comment; and there was a sudden, respectful hush.

"It's on the roof," he said. "They looked down, but not up. The fellow leaned out and threw it up and over. What do you think, Rose?"

It was the first time Kevin had addressed him today. Michel wondered at him. Was it a trick? "No," he said, his throat dry. "The eave sticks out. You couldn't lean out far enough to throw it over."

He had the impression that Kevin expected him to continue. Those elfin, colorless eyes were fixed on his; then Kevin shrugged and turned away. Michel looked after him resentfully. What did Kevin want of him? That he give himself up?

"Why doesn't he come out?" Nigri complained. "They'll make him say he did it, even if he didn't."

"Yes, and we'll all be punished whether they find it or not," Chamfort said gloomily.

Giraud groaned. He wanted no more mornings like the one they had just had, he said.

There was a bustle at the window. "Here he comes!" Angelilli cried. Horst had appeared at the door of administration. Someone had brought him his coat, and he had put it on over his pajamas. He walked unsteadily toward the dormitory. "He's confessed," Chamfort said. "Look at his face."

"No, he hasn't, you'd look like that too if—"

"We'd better take our places."

"Look, the rector is coming out."

"Sit down, everybody, he's coming here."

"No he's not, he's heading toward chapel."

Signor Maas appeared in the doorway. They turned toward him, clamoring at once.

"Did he confess?"

"What are they going to do to him?"

"Can we go now?"

"To chapel, everyone," Signor Maas said severely. "Come now, line up."

"Come on, Signor, tell us!"

"Be a good sport!"

They fell into line, protesting. Chapel at this hour! What was up? "You find out," Signor Maas said. "You'll catch it now."

The rector was praying. Hushed in their seats, the boys fixed their eyes on the back of his head and waited. Slowly the great snowy crown bent forward as, still kneeling, the rector raised his arms sideways. He stayed in that position a long time, then painfully rose to his feet and came toward them. His face was bloodless and haggard, and his voice seemed oppressed by a great sadness as he spoke.

"I have prayed God for illumination and forgiveness," he said. "I have been guilty of a great lack of charity. And now I will ask you for your forgiveness as well."

He searched them with his eyes. Michel held his breath. What did he mean?

"When I summoned you here," the rector began again, "it was in the spirit of anger and vengeance. Anger, because of the desecration done to the sacred image of Our Lord's Passion, a passion which he suffered for us, that we might redeem ourselves from sin. Vengeance, yes—that is not too strong a word for what I contemplated. For I reasoned thus. The boy who took the crucifix from Father Scala's door could not have done so inadvertently, since he had to remove the screws with which it was fastened. It had to be one of you, since the outer door was locked, and the crucifix was in its place when Father Scala retired. Could it have been a prank? I wondered. And my answer was no, for while you are playful, being boys and high-spirited, you come from Christian, God-fearing homes and have been taught to treat as holy that which is holy, to regard with reverence what partakes of the divine. I said to myself, This act was not a childish prank, it was a deliberate and calculated act of protest against the God who created him and against His Son, His Church, our school and its holy purpose. The boy who did this sacrilegious thing has put himself beyond the pale, has called down God's curse on himself, and must be rooted out at once before he can contaminate the rest of you. This is how I spoke to myself in righteous but shortsighted anger, and my purpose in calling you before me was to scold you, threaten you, bully you with menaces until the guilty one had been discovered and had restored the crucifix. Then he was to be summarily expelled, as one casts out devils for the health of the soul."

The rector stopped. The boys sat in silence, waiting. "And then I entered this holy place, in which my soul has never failed to find truth and peace, and I looked upon the face of Our Redeemer, whose effigy, fixed to the cross as He was in life, is looking down upon us all, and I seemed to hear the words 'Vengeance is mine!' And I was ashamed, for I understood that in my indignation I had allocated to myself that which is the Lord's.

"It is not in anger that I speak to you now. I look upon you, and I wonder, not which one of you is guilty of the deed, but why he did it. Everything lies in the motive. You will remember that the Pharisees complained of our Saviour because He healed the sick on the Sabbath. And His answer was that the Sabbath was made for man, and not man for the Sabbath. I myself would break down the door of this chapel if it were necessary to do so in order to reach the side of a dying person in need of the last sacraments. For just as the Sabbath was made for man, the Church was made for man, and not man for the Church. One of you took the crucifix. Why? It is too easy to reply that it was a prank. We must still ask ourselves why that spirit of playfulness should have directed itself toward a holy object. It is too easy to say that it was an act of protest against God. We must still ask ourselves why one of you, whoever it was, should be imbued with rebellion against One he should love with all his heart and soul. Can there be one among you whom our teaching, instead of enlightening and setting on the path to God, has, through the perversity of Satan, corrupted and twisted and soured? If this is so, then we must inquire whether it is not our fault; whether we as teachers have not failed in our duty; whether we have not become complacent and dull of soul, so that Satan could find a chink in our Christian armor to do his evil work.

"But this is not all," the rector went on. "Could there not be some other motive, one which, even though ill-advised, might justify such a deed in a pure mind in need of guidance? Let us suppose that one of you has a mother who is sick. Let us suppose that this poor woman has a particular cult and reverence for Christ Jesus. Let us suppose that this boy, knowing of her illness, addresses a prayer each night to the crucifix which is most in evidence before him, the one on the prefect's door; until, his imagination inflamed by the knowledge that nothing is impossible to the Son of God, that He can save her if He will, he removes the crucifix in order to send it to her, hoping that contact with the holy effigy will effect one of those miraculous cures of which our scripture is witness. Can we say that such a boy had evil in his heart? No, that boy is not evil. What he has done is a foolish thing, for it is not in man to force God to work a miracle, to urge Him to bend His inscrutable will. He has used an unworthy means for a higher purpose. He has taken God's law into his own hands, when faith would have been enough. For it is written that faith, even though it be no greater than a mustard seed, is enough to move mountains."

The rector clasped his hands behind his back and stood brooding before them. "This example I have given you," he said, "is of course only a hypothesis. But it is enough to show that we must not leap to conclusions. It is possible that the theft of the crucifix was the result of an evil intention. But it is also possible that it was not. St. Joan of Arc was chided by her inquisitors for having left off her maidenly garments and assumed the clothing of a man. It was immodest, they said, and a proof that the voices she heard were prompted by the devil. Her reply was that God had chosen her to be a soldier among men; and that, being the only woman amid a host of rough-tongued, brutal soldiers, she had put on trousers so as not to flaunt her womanhood before them. It was more modest, she said. And so you see, dear children, we must not judge by appearances. Reality may be the very opposite of what it appears to be. After the last judgment, Our Saviour has told us, the first will be the last and the last the first. Appearances are not enough. We must look deeper than the outward semblance. And for this we must be moved and guided by charity. It was for this that I prayed, for while we are all in need of charity, there is one amongst us here who is in special need, and we must find him out so as to offer it to him."

Charity. How sweetly the word echoed in Michel's ear! Charity meant loving forgiveness for anything a person might have done. How good it would be to open up one's heart, to pour forth everything that lay choked up within! A great longing welled up in him to confess, not only his probable theft, but every sullied thought he had ever had, and come forth a new person, pure and ready for a new life. The voice of the rector, soft and sad, seemed to be speaking within him. The other boys, too, were entranced; they sat motionless, their lips parted, their eyes fixed unwaveringly on the one who spoke to them in that kindly fashion. If he were sure he had done it; if, searching his sleeping memory, he could bring out of its hidden depths one corroborating image of himself in the act, Michel would have risen then and there and fallen to the rector's feet in self-accusation. But he could not. He sat, troubled, and waited.

"But charity must not be misplaced," the rector said. "There is forgiveness for all those who turn to God, aware that they have done wrong. But there can be no forgiveness for him who, having sinned, compounds that sin by rejoicing in it. How else can we name that attitude which, once evil has been committed, locks itself up within the evildoer's breast, and refuses the mercy of God which is accessible to a single word? A man has done horrible crimes all his life without repentance. In the hour of his death his soul is moved to cry out, O my God, I am heartily sorry I have offended Thee. That man is saved. So little is enough. Even less. Let him cry, God! Or Jesus! Or Mary! That man is saved. But as it is said that a horse may be brought to water, but cannot be made to drink, so it is that salvation is offered to a man for a single word, yet he cannot be made to pronounce that word. Charity is not for these. Such a man is cast into the outer darkness, out of God's kingdom, for he has refused to drink of the living water which would have saved him; that living water which may be refused a thousand times, but not the last."

The rector's voice had grown stronger and more resonant. Now, raising his arms, he cried out, "This is my great fear! That the boy who has done this thing, for whatever motive, good or bad, may in his dread of reprisals so harden his heart that he cannot bring himself to confess it. What would have been easy at first becomes more difficult as time goes on, for each denial is an additional impediment in the way of confession. And the fault is mine, for in the first shock of realization I permitted myself to give way to anger, I bullied you, I made you suffer acute discomfort, until the guilty boy must have been overcome by fright to think what would happen to him if he were found out. I have been as guilty as he. No, dear children, I have been more guilty, for he is a boy whose understanding is not yet completely formed, but I have reached my maturity and have failed in charity, the virtue without which I am nothing but a tinkling cymbal. And for this I ask your forgiveness."

"No, no," several of the boys cried out together. They leaned forward, eager to deny, shaking their heads and holding out their hands. Michel was as moved as the rest. He felt ashamed. If only he could lift the weight of guilt from that noble, haggard head!

"Thank you," the rector said gravely. "And now let me tell you how I, and my colleagues in Christ, hope to overcome our blunder.

We shall make it easy for the boy to admit his deed. We shall not ask him to do so here and now, before his companions. Instead, beginning now, you will come to my office one at a time, in alphabetical order, for questioning. While awaiting your turn, you will stay here to examine your conscience, and you will return here when you are through. Afternoon classes are suspended. At five o'clock, having passed the previous time in meditation, you will go to confession, in preparation for tomorrow morning's mass. If the guilty one first admits his act to me in secular fashion, before he does so to God through his confessor in the secrecy of the confessional, so much the better; but admit it he shall and must, for his own deliverance.

"You are asking yourselves," the rector went on, looking at them keenly, "what will happen to the boy who admits the deed. I shall tell you. He will be placed in retirement for meditation. He will be reasoned with, so that he may understand the nature of what he has done. He will be asked to search his soul and explain why he did it. We are ready, no, we are eager, to plumb the deepest recesses of his soul and to appreciate his motive, for, I repeat, we cannot believe that, however mistaken he may have been in his means, his motive could have been evil. This will be taken account of in our ruling in this matter. If his purpose was to mock God, to strike a blow on behalf of Satan, then we shall make every effort to bring about a true repentance, we shall pray for him and with him, and after due penance we shall send him home. With heavy hearts, I assure you, but there can be no alternative, for while such a person may be fit for some great office in life, he cannot be a soldier of God. But no, it cannot be, I cannot, will not believe it. There *must* be some other motive. And if there is, we shall find it, we shall understand it, and we shall be charitable. That is all I can tell you, dear children, for I cannot bind myself in advance to a decision which must reflect the will of my colleagues in Christ in assembly.

"Let us suppose that the boy still does not admit his deed. Then I shall ask you to do it for him. There is a schoolboy code of honor which belongs to your age and is not without value in forming your characters. That is the code that says that you must not inform against any of your companions who may be guilty of some minor infraction of the rules. I have no doubt but that some of you must have known of the pocketknife in the possession of your companion Horst. It would have been commendable to bring this to the attention of your superiors, yet I cannot blame you for not having done so. But surely you must see that this code does not apply in the matter of the stolen crucifix. For in the latter case someone has committed the sin of sacrilege, and for his own salvation must be brought to account. To reason otherwise is to say that any of the eleven innocent apostles who knew of Judas' plan of betrayal should not have informed the Master of them, supposing that He did not know it already. Could such an apostle dare to take on himself the awful responsibility for what followed that betrayal? Can any of you know the identity of this misguided boy in your midst, and be silent? Would you not be haunted the rest of your life by the knowledge that through your weakness you contributed to a friend's delinquency and endangered his salvation? It is your duty to God, to your school, to yourself, and to your friend to speak up. He who knows and is silent is, in the eyes of God, as guilty as the one whose hands perpetrated this deed. But again, I do not ask you to do so here. When you are being questioned in my office, that is the time. You need not have certainty in the matter. Perhaps you overheard a chance remark, or noticed an undue interest in this particular crucifix, or know of some secret problem one of you has; tell us your suspicion, and we will do the rest. Your identity will be kept secret."

All were silent. Michel felt his breath coming and going quickly. He did not dare look at Kevin, who was sitting nearby, to his right. He felt overwhelmed by the rush of events. He needed time to think, to convince himself he had not done it, to find a way out. He was sure that Kevin thought him guilty. How else could he interpret Kevin's watchful silence, his enigmatic air? Would he be moved by the rector's appeal? Could he resist the forthcoming inquisition in the rector's office?

"And now," the rector said quietly, folding his hands before him, "I wish to speak to the boy himself. One of you knows to whom my words are addressed. What I have to say is this. You have done a dreadful thing. Yet you are our brother in Christ, and we love you as ourselves. Even now the angels in heaven are looking down upon you with sorrow and pity in their hearts. Even now the Mother of God is bending her hands in supplication toward the Lord to ask forgiveness for you, just as your earthly mother would do to know of your deed. And God, who loves you as He loves all of us and all mankind, His children, is waiting for that first slight motion of your heart that is the beginning of repentance and remorse. Forgiveness is ready for the word. Speak this word, my child, remove this horrible burden from your conscience, give yourself up to the infinite mercy of God. Your failure to do so is worse than the original deed, which may have its explanation. But there can be no explanation for your refusal of God's mercy, for your refusal to accept the intercession of the Blessed Virgin, for your disappointment of the hierarchy of heaven, which is hanging on your lips. Do not harden your heart, beloved child. There is mercy for you. But you must ask for it. To those that ask, all shall be given. This is the Lord's promise, and has never been refused."

The rector sank to his knees. "Dear God," he cried, closing his eyes and lifting his arms above his head, "pour your grace upon this erring heart, that it may understand the error of its ways and seek forgiveness through *contritio cordis, confessio oris, satisfactio operis*. Let not this sheep be lost through failure to understand Your infinite mercy, through pride or shame. I beg this of You, I in whose charge this tender soul has been placed, and who have failed in my duty. And if it be not so, if it be not Your will that Your grace should sustain this child in his hour of need, let his sin fall upon my head, for the shepherd is responsible for the strayed sheep. And in my affliction I will bless Your name, now and forevermore. Amen."

Michel's heart turned over, and he felt a sharp pang at his eyes as if tears were ready to burst forth. In dull misery he waited. The rector rose to his feet. In a low voice he said that the prefect of discipline had something to say to them. Then he walked slowly to the door and stood looking out.

Father Pace came from the rear of the chapel and stood before them. He placed on the bridge of his nose the heavy horn glasses he wore on a chain around his neck, and opened the Bible he held in his hand. He said, "I shall read to you from St. Paul, First Corinthians, Chapter 11, 23–29: 'The Lord Jesus, the same night in which he was betrayed, took bread, and giving thanks, broke, and said: Take ye, and eat: this is my body, which shall be delivered for you: this do for the commemoration of me. In like manner also the chalice, after he had supped, saying: This chalice is the new testament in my blood: this do ye, as oft as ye shall drink, for the commemoration of me. For as often as ye shall eat this bread, and drink the chalice, ye shall show the death of the Lord, until he come. Therefore whosoever shall eat this bread, or drink the chalice of the Lord unworthily, shall be guilty of the body and blood of the Lord. But let a man prove himself: and so let him eat of that bread, and drink of the chalice. For he that eateth and drinketh unworthily, eateth and drinketh judgment to himself, not discerning the body of the Lord.' "

Father Pace closed the book. "I give you these verses to meditate upon," he said. "They must be uppermost in your mind all this day, and especially at five o'clock, when you enter the confessional to unburden yourselves of your sins. I hardly think I need stress their meaning. The boy who laid his impious hands upon the crucifix must confess it, or he will not be able to take holy communion. To do so would be the gravest of mortal sins. To do so would be to eat judgment and damnation to himself. It is not I who tell you this, but God Himself, speaking through the mouth of His inspired prophet and saint, St. Paul. Lay these words to your soul. You have all afternoon to do so. And now we will begin our interviews. Who is the first boy?"

Angelilli, visibly shaken, stood up.

From the doorway the rector said gently, "Follow me, my child."

He was in the chapel again, having returned after his interrogation in the rector's office. The questioning was behind him. It had not been the inquisition he had feared. During the long period of waiting, as boy after boy arose and walked out and his own turn approached, Michel had decided that, whatever happened later, he would say nothing under the immediate ordeal. At confession, if at all, he had told himself. He was not sure he had done it; he did not remember it; why should he accept the blame for something so dreadful when it was only a doubt in his mind? Confession was a different matter. There the doubt was enough, for the suspicion that one had committed a sin had to be brought out into the open, be left for the confessor to decide. In the meanwhile, the rector's interrogation might produce a surprise. Perhaps there was another boy among them who was as sick as he. What did he know about them, after all? The outward piety, the innocent face, these were not enough. No doubt the others judged him as he judged them. Was he not the curly-headed Rose, the boy saint, the class model? Yet he knew himself to be full of uncleanliness and festering resentments, which drove him from his bed at night to wander in the darkness like a damned ghost. One of the others might have done it, in spite of appearances. It was a slender hope; but he had clung to it with the desperation of one who has no other. It was enough to take him through the grilling, which, though thorough, was not ungentle. It reminded him, in fact, of that other questioning he had undergone two years ago in this very room, by the monsignor from Rome. Why was he at St. Louis Gonzaga? Did he feel he had a vocation? Did he realize the sacrifices involved in the religious life? It was only after a long series of questions like these, which he allowed himself to answer with gradually increasing enthusiasm, as though he had forgotten the true purpose of the inquiry, that they asked him outright if he had taken the crucifix. He replied with a ringing, "No, Father!" and further denied with emphasis having awakened last night, or gotten up for any purpose, or knowing the whereabouts of the holy object, or having any knowledge or suspicion of anyone else. Perhaps they too remembered the interest of the monsignor, for the rector bent forward and spoke in low tones to the other priests, who nodded and glanced at him sideways with a calculating, solemn air. Then they had let him go.

In truth, his worst moment had not been the interrogation itself, but the moment preceding it, when Kevin came out of the rector's office after his questioning, and crossed the tiny anteroom toward him. But Kevin had deliberately not looked at him before going out the door, and Michel, gazing fearfully at his face in spite of himself, could not tell whether his friend had betrayed him or not. Then the dark-robed figure of Father Scala had appeared in the rector's doorway and beckoned to him; he had entered and, seating himself in the solitary chair before the semicircle of inquisitors, had sensed no condemnation in their waiting attitude; and had known that for the time being, at least, he was spared.

But now, seated at the back of the chapel, he felt the trap closing about him. He had got by these men of God, but he could not get by God Himself. No one had admitted to the crime. He reached this conclusion, for all were there, even Horst, who had appeared, grinning shamefacedly, and taken a seat; and he noted the gloomy look on the face of the rector, who had come in, conferred with Father Latouche, and disappeared into the sacristy. In a few minutes they would be summoned to the confessional. The human hunt was over, and now God would have His turn. Michel's resistance was gone; the long day, with its emotional upsets and nervous strain, had left him limp; it was not in him to make a false confession. This was not like the other times, the scores of times in the past, when he had kept his doubts to himself, and confessed by the book. This time a sinful crime had been committed, and he had reason to suppose that it was he who had done it. He had to speak up. The consequences didn't matter: the gasp on the other side of the lattice; the first condemning words of the priest, under which his soul would writhe and crumple with shame; the penance, which would certainly include returning the crucifix—how could he, when he didn't know where it was?—and leaving the school, whether or not he had to report himself to the rector; the disillusionment of Mother Veronica; the agony of having to face Maman Rose, already at her wits' end to keep him from M. Konrad's clutches, and who would be forced to find him another refuge, or even to give him up to the slavers of Israel—all of this didn't matter, compared to the alternative, which was damnation.

And so his mind was made up when Father Latouche called them forward for prayers. The other boys, moving down the aisle, were cheerful, after their long inactivity. "Move lively, Rose," Chamfort whispered to him, in imitation of Father Scala; and Michel forced himself to grin back, feeling his lips stiff and ghastly under the grimace. He envied them as they took their places. They would confess their peccadilloes, and be liberated to rush back to the snug, friendly dormitory and then to the evening meal; he was a condemned man going to his execution. Tonight they would gather and wonder at his absence; they would guess at the truth, and chatter and gossip about it; then they would say their prayers, sink into their beds, and be instantly asleep. And he? He didn't know where he would be. In the retirement the rector had spoken of, with priests grimly wrestling with Satan over his soul? On the train going back to Touville? Very likely. He had no sick mother to plead, no excuse, no reason at all. Charity was not for such as he. Whatever they did, he knew that he would be covered with confusion and shame, and beginning a new life in which happiness was not to be imagined.

Was the hell of the other world much worse than this?

How quickly the prayer was over! And once the confessions began, how quickly the others went, confessed, and left! To Michel's troubled senses they seemed to pop in and out behind the velvet curtains like puppets on a string. Only one confessional was in use. Two boys went in, one at each side; and then, as one came out, another took his place. Father Latouche, sitting with them, told them off, pointed to the next in turn. Now! It was his turn. With knees that seemed unhinged, Michel approached the box, feeling Kevin's eyes on the back of his neck, trying to phrase the words that would destroy him, the irreparable words that would be the signal to the disaster to follow. He opened the curtain, and sank to his knees on the padded bench; the musty smell of thousands of dead sins swallowed him up. The lattice was closed. Michel waited, noting dully in the glimmer of light that penetrated a crack in the curtain that a tiny spider moved along a single dusty strand of web overhead. He envied the spider. The lattice panel slid back, and he heard the quiet breath and a dull rustle as the priest turned toward him. Who was it? Did it matter? He had to speak. He had to! He swallowed hard, and said, "I—I have sinned, Father."

The *Confiteor* fell from his lips, mechanically, while a part of his benumbed mind wondered at the sweat that poured down his neck to his back. Yet his hands were very cold. He kept them crossed tightly before him, pressed against his chest. A soft, sad voice spoke to him behind the lattice, and for an instant Michel stopped breathing, while his scalp crawled and his hair seemed to come alive with movement. It was the same voice that had spoken to him earlier of charity; the voice that had asked him if he had taken the crucifix, and to which he had replied emphatically, "No, Father!" In the sudden, abject fear that came over him he did not understand the words. The rector repeated them: What did he have to confess?

What dreadful plot was this? In his four years at St. Louis, Michel had never known the rector to hear confessions himself. No wonder the boys preceding him had come out of the confessional with startled expressions. What did it mean? Michel's mind raced with this new problem, while his lips stammered out a confused tale of an evening prayer he had not said before retiring. Was this a way to get around the secrecy of the confessional? No priest could reveal what was said to him under that seal; no priest could report to the rector that he had found the boy who had stolen the crucifix. Yet no boy could be expelled without the order of the rector himself. Was it this that had prompted the rector's move? For if the rector knew it of his own knowledge, he could order the expulsion without any explanations. Was that it? Michel didn't know. He knew that the knowledge gained in confession was sacred. But how far could a priest act on that knowledge?

His penance for the missed prayer was to say double prayers at bedtime for a week. And then the rector said, "Is there anything else, my child?"

Charity! Michel thought. Had it all been an act, then, to persuade the boy to admit his crime? To soften him up, to suggest possible motives, to hint that they would be kind, only to fling him out without mercy when they knew who it was? No, he answered himself. The rector would not do a thing like that. Again in his own mind's eye he saw the noble, suffering priest kneeling before them all and before God, raising his arms in supplication that the sin of the boy fall on his own head. No priest could have done such a thing just to impress them. No, no, it was impossible. It was only because the rector was so profoundly disturbed about the sacrilege that he had wanted to hear confessions himself. Besides, what did it matter? Michel had already accepted expulsion as the cost of winning God's grace again. He would have to speak up. It didn't matter whose human ear heard him.

The rector insisted gently, "Is there anything else?"

The soft urgency of the voice stung him to speech. I think I stole the crucifix, he opened his mouth to say. But, to his own astonishment, the words that came out were "No, Father."

What had he said? But that wasn't it at all! Quickly, there was still time to retract them. He could say, "I beg your pardon, Father, I spoke without thinking, what I meant was . . ." Yet at that moment something closed like a tiny door within him, his throat locked stubbornly, and with clenched teeth he listened to the rector's benediction and request that Michel pray for him. Then, his scalp prickling, the chill of damnation already striking at his entrails, yet powerless to stop himself, he stumbled out of the confessional and walked blindly out of the chapel.

Michel knelt at the altar rail. His gaze was fixed before him, on the life-size crucifix whose outstretched arms seemed to envelop the chapel in a protective gesture; yet out of the corner of his eye he could see Father Latouche's characteristic movement of the sleeves in shaking the wafer before he administered it to the first boy. There were six before him. Christ had had his fourteen stations on his way to the crucifixion; for Michel there were only six steps to damnation. He knew it; his mind was perfectly clear. Through the long, agonized night, during which he had lain like an inanimate thing while his mind had butted against the impenetrable walls of his dilemma, he had foreseen this Calvary of his in precise detail. He had seen himself facing the image of the Christ while his lips ate of His Body. He had known that every fiber in him would shrink from the terrible sacrilege, but that he would stay rooted to the spot and unprotestingly open his mouth. He had guessed that the rector would be there, watching in grim foreboding, for no one could have confessed. He had heard the phrase from St. Paul about eating and drinking damnation echoing in his ear, and had closed his heart to it. He had gone too far. There was no backing out now.

What he had not foreseen was the sudden, unexpected memory that came to him of his first communion, so long ago, when he had knelt in the chapel at St. Joseph's and expected the Kingdom of Heaven to open up to that great outpouring of love within his soul. All his "family" had been there: Maman Rose, Renée, Jean, Pé, Léah, M. Béjart, even Annette and Félicité. The chapel had been filled with lilies, he remembered, and his heart had swelled to the beauty of the organ and choir. He had put all that out of his mind, to concentrate instead on the act of will that would bring his father down to him from heaven, that father in whom he had seen the Father of the world; for in his innocence he could not imagine that the man whose memory he adored could be in hell. All that was gone now, and in its place he felt an unbearable sense of loss. How had it happened? He had wanted nothing more in life than to share his love, to offer himself up to God the Father; yet here he was, at yet another communion, kneeling in abject misery, self-condemned to hell, like his father, yet unable to prevent himself from taking the last irreparable step. Why was he doing this? He did not know. He had tried his best, but things had happened to him, acts springing from some obscure depths within him and mastering his will. Why did he think of the rabbit? The rabbit was now no more than a heap of moldering bones within its catacomb, dead and out of its misery. Its brief agony was over, for there was no question of heaven or hell for such a creature. For Michel there was no such escape. The soul was immortal, and its sufferings lasted forever.

Father Latouche was before him, waiting, his hand lifted. I am coming, Vati, he cried to himself hysterically. He opened his mouth, felt the paper-thin wafer on his tongue, and swallowed. Then, as if he were still alive, he went back to his seat and sat down.

When mass was over, the rector spoke to them briefly. The sorrowful, gentle priest of yesterday was gone. In his place was a terrible menacing figure who said that God would find him out. He and his colleagues in Christ had done everything they could to soften his heart. But he could not escape from God.

They filed out of the chapel in silence. In the quadrangle there was confusion. The priests had gathered in the doorway, their heads bent together, their faces drawn and somber, while the boys milled about in little groups. Kevin approached him and said, "Michel." It was the first time his friend had addressed him by his Christian name. A sudden anger took hold of Michel. "I know what you're thinking," he flared. "But I didn't do it. Do you think I would take communion?"

"Sh!" Kevin said warningly, laying his hand on Michel's sleeve. Michel looked down at it, and a lump came to his throat. But he stared back at Kevin's questioning look and said, "I was awake all that night. So I couldn't have done it."

Kevin's brow suddenly cleared, and his eyes showed unmistakable relief. He patted Michel roughly on the shoulder and said, "All right, youngster. I should have known." He turned away.

Michel followed him with his eyes. His mouth felt dry and bitter. What did a lie matter, to one who was already damned?

11

THREE DAYS before Christmas vacation was to begin, Michel received a letter from Maman Rose. Good news! she wrote. That dreadful trial, in which she was accused of kidnaping—she had won! She had been much more afraid of the verdict than she had let him know in her previous letters; but the judges had proved unexpectedly human, had seen her side of the matter, and had thrown the case out of court.

There were complications, however. Konrad had immediately appealed, and the Appeals Court, moving with astonishing rapidity, had set the date of the hearing for January 8, only a few weeks away. And so they would have to go all through it again, with one great difference: Konrad had demanded the presence of Michel at the trial, and the court had accepted his demand. Michel would have to appear before the judges for questioning, or Maman Rose would be charged with contempt of court.

"I have accepted the condition," Maman Rose wrote, "not because of the contempt charge, which is meaningless, but because this is the moment I have been waiting for. They think they are making things difficult for me, they are crowding me, forcing me to knuckle under; they plan to worm all kinds of horrible admissions out of you —they don't realize they are letting me play my trump card, which is *you*. It's too complicated to explain in writing. I'll tell you all about it when you come home. Yes, my darling boy, you are coming home at last, after such a long time! You will be perfectly safe, because I made such a fuss in my reply to the court that they have agreed to let you appear under safe conduct, which means that no one can lay a hand on you during the trial. We are all dying to see you again, we have missed you dreadfully. Let us hope that this is the last of these trials, and that after we have won it—we must win, we *will* win—we will be united again forever."

Michel was to go from Cassarate to Paris, where he would stay at the Mother House of the Temple until it was time for him to be brought to Touville. The letter ended with a million hugs and kisses from "the one who loved him best in the world."

Michel read this letter with mixed feelings. Maman Rose's opening announcement sent a thrill of joy through him. She had won the case, then! Didn't that mean that the nightmare of the trials was over, that he was free at last to live like other boys, that he could stay with his Maman Rose? No, M. Konrad had appealed. That meant, unaccountably, that the case was going on. Michel couldn't understand it. Why did it take so long? Why did they have to go from court to court, persecuting his poor Maman Rose over and over again? Michel had only the vaguest idea of the legal processes involved. He envisaged the Law as some kind of shadowy, intangible monster hovering over the land, set into motion by evil men to help them fulfill their evil purposes. The Law had been after him for years, urged on by M. Konrad. It was Maman Rose who had fought back, who had managed to keep him out of their clutches. But now he was going to testify, he would have to appear in court and be asked questions. The thought sent a surge of fear through him; yet Maman Rose seemed to make light of it—she had been waiting for this moment, he was her trump card.

Well, but that was almost a month away; and in the meantime, he was going home! For the first time in two years he was going to his Maman Rose at the Nursery, and sink into its warm, loving, familiar atmosphere, where no one would be spying on him, where for a little while, at least, he could go to bed nights without dread. Three days! he said to himself with a little shiver. He had three more days to wait before vacation began. Could he hold out that long? He didn't know. He knew only that a dreadful change had come over his life, that death had entered his soul, that he was in greater danger of being caught than ever before.

Ever since his sinful communion he had thought of nothing else but how to undo the harm he had done. Many times, alone in his cubicle at night, he had forced himself to kneel in an effort to pray, only to feel his own self-condemnation hanging over him like an incubus, sucking his brain dry and leaving him in despair. It was as though a roof of iron had closed over his head, beyond which his repentance could not reach. How could he repent, he asked himself, if he had not cleansed his soul as God had prescribed? True repentance meant the undoing of what you had done, or equal atonement for it if it could not be remedied. He had done neither. He had lied to the rector, he had made a false confession, he had eaten damnation unto himself by unworthily receiving the body of the Lord. And as if this were not enough, he had gone through all the forms of worship established at St. Louis, in the full knowledge that he was compounding his sin still more by his hypocrisy. He had not truly prayed since that fateful November day; he had kneeled with the others without actually saying the words. He could not. Yet he had to go through with the pretense, all the while his heart felt choked up inside.

If only he could return the crucifix! But he did not know where it was. It had disappeared as though some spirit had snatched it up. Once, indeed, about a week after that day, he had had a dream in which he had been filled with an intense premonition that the crucifix was within his grasp. He saw himself standing in a dark cave in which a single beam of light shone down from a crack overhead. The light fell on a small wooden box lying on the ground. The crucifix is there, he told himself. He kneeled down, full of growing excitement, and tried to lift the lid. But it was nailed down tight and did not budge. Suddenly as he wrestled with it, it worked loose and fell with a great clatter to the stone floor. Inside was a doll dressed in black, lying face upward in the attitude of the dead. Yet as he stared at it, struck numb by the familiarity of the tiny features, the doll turned its head and looked at him, and he realized that the face was his own. He fell backwards, a cry choked in his throat, and he awoke. He lay awake a long time in the silent dormitory, trying to understand the meaning of his dream, but could come to no conclusion.

What was he to do? He had managed to escape detection, but things were worse than ever. How long could he keep up the masquerade before he broke down and gave himself away? Tormented in conscience, scarcely eating, tossing restlessly a good part of the nights, he had seen the physical change in himself: the pallor, the hollowness in his cheeks, the blue bruises under his eyes. Yet he did not feel weak; on the contrary, he was sustained by a nervous energy whose source was a mystery to him, and that at times made him feel lightheaded. He seemed to float effortlessly through everything. He even managed to be gay, knowing it was the surest way to divert suspicion from himself, although more than once his laughter seemed shrill and false in his own ears. Whited sepulcher! he groaned within himself. Yet he had to go on. The alternative was to confess it all, and he knew he could not face it; less now than ever. The rector was right. Delay had made it even more difficult than before. No, he had to go on, and hope for the best.

But even this was becoming more difficult. The atmosphere at St. Louis had changed. The mystery of the crucifix had not been allowed to die. The priests were grim and uncommunicative; they did not refer to the crime again, but their eyes were suspicious, and when they addressed a boy, there was an unspoken question in their tone: Are you the guilty one? The boys themselves, on the other hand, talked of nothing else. Their imaginations had been stirred by the uncanny nature of the disappearance, and in their few free moments they gathered together to air their theories. It was God Himself who had removed the crucifix, as a test. When He was satisfied, the crucifix would take its place again, as a miracle. No, others said, it was not God, but Satan. The rector had said so. Satan had entered the soul of one of them, and caused him to perform the sacrilege. He was still there, because he had not been driven out by confession and penance. But the devil could not long be hidden; his presence marked the flesh with unmistakable signs, especially in the eyes, the nails, the shape of the ears. It was Magruder who insisted on this. He had seen cases of demonic possession, he affirmed roundly, in his native Ireland. Angelilli, on the other hand, could not believe that any one of them could have done it. If it was Satan, then the old fellow had done it himself, directly, without intermediary. The others scoffed at him. What! Satan touch a crucifix? He would tuck his tail between his legs and run at the mere sight of one! Well, Angelilli conceded, but something funny was going on; he had heard strange movements in the dormitory at night; if not Satan, then it was a ghost. At this some of the other boys chimed in. They too had heard noises, and some had seen the curtains of the cubicles move, although the windows were shut and there was no wind.

The crucifix on the prefect's door had been replaced; and this was the occasion of another rumor. This crucifix, the boys said, was wired to an alarm. Just let some unlucky individual touch it, even by accident. The prefect would pounce on him in a second, and much good it would do the fellow to protest that he had nothing to do with the other matter! It would be all up with him. The rector's patience was exhausted. He had given the boy every opportunity to set things right, and the boy had refused. Now he would send him packing, no matter what story he might tell. And at this stage he didn't much care whether he got the right one or not. Any scapegoat would do, to clear up the thing once and for all.

And so Michel's escape, bought at the cost of his salvation, was only temporary. Sooner or later he would be caught. The ghost that the boys talked about—was it not himself, still walking in his sleep, the demon within him still thirsting for more unholiness, more sacrilege? Now that everyone was suspicious of everyone else, it needed no more than a glimpse of him for his secret to be out. It was unbearable to go to bed at night and wonder whether this night would be one of *those,* to struggle against sleep, to sink into exhaustion, feeling himself slide into darkness and know he could resist no more. But waking was even worse. What horrible revelation would be waiting for him? And if there was none, there was still the day to be got through, with its classes, its prayers, its study and meditations, during which he must be perpetually on his guard not to give himself away, not to let his agony peep through for a single careless moment. More than once he found himself half wishing that they would catch him at it, and get the cruel suspense over with. And then he dismissed the thought with horror; he could not permit *that,* whatever happened.

Maman Rose's letter gave him new hope. Here, at least, was something to cling to, an oasis promised in the near future where he could take shelter from himself. Perhaps, once he was away from St. Louis, he could clear his thoughts and find a way out. Perhaps, he reasoned with himself, he might even confess what he had done, to some priest in Touville; the penance would be hard, no doubt, but so long as it did not require him to reveal himself to the school authorities he could endure it. It was only necessary at this moment to hold out a bit more. Three days! And nights. Somewhere he would have to find the strength to keep himself under control.

I'm going home! he said to himself over and over during that time. He said it each morning when, groggy from his few hours of tortured sleep, he crossed the dark quadrangle on his way to mass in the chapel; at the grace before meals, when he bowed his head like the others, and stared down at his folded, impious hands; at each moment that his guilty thoughts overcame him and he started in the realization that he had allowed his preoccupation to show in his face; and at night, when the curtain of his cubicle closed behind him and he stared dully at his cot and knew that he had got through the day but that new dangers lay before him.

It was not until he stood on the platform of the railway station, with his suitcase at his feet, and gazed up the snowbound, wooded slope to where the school lay invisible on its plateau, that the full realization came to him that he had endured and that he was free.

That was the moment Kevin chose to speak to him.

Michel had not deceived Kevin for long, and he knew it. He had told Kevin the first lie that came to his head, when his friend approached him after chapel that day; and he had seen the relief in Kevin's face. But the next day Kevin was impassive again, and in the weeks that followed he did not speak to Michel but kept to himself, wrapped in moody silence. Michel made no further attempt to convince him. What was the use?

Michel did not see Kevin come to him. He was standing somewhat apart from the others, looking up the hill, when Kevin's voice said behind him, "Don't come back." Michel jumped and turned around. Kevin's face was pale and deadly serious. "What?" Michel stammered.

"Don't come back," Kevin repeated. "You don't belong here, Rose. No, don't say anything, just listen to me for a moment. I've been watching you. You're heading straight for a nervous breakdown. You know why as well as I do. Go home and stay there. If you come back—"

"What?" Michel said. "You'll tell on me?"

"No," Kevin said quietly. "You'll tell on yourself." He walked away. Michel followed him with his eyes, much disturbed.

What did Kevin mean? All the way to Paris Michel brooded on it. Tell on himself? Not for anything in the world! What? Reveal his guilty secret *now,* when he had bought the right to keep it with his own salvation? At the very beginning of the affair, when the rector was disposed to be lenient—that was the time for such a step, if at all. And for Kevin's advice, he could not help but feel with a certain bitterness. But perhaps Kevin did not mean it in quite that way. He had said something about a nervous breakdown. Michel knew what that was; he had not forgotten the strange illness he had undergone when M. Konrad first came to the Nursery that Easter Sunday. Perhaps Kevin meant that he would get sick, and that the sickness itself would give him away. Or that he would be caught sleepwalking.

Yes, Michel thought; but it was easy for Kevin to tell him not to come back. Kevin didn't have to hide, he had no Konrad after him to sell him into slavery. And Kevin was almost a man, he was fifteen, and about to enter the Seminary. He could speak lightly about making such momentous decisions. But Michel was only a boy; his decisions were made for him by his Maman Rose, who had his good at heart and knew far better than he what was best for him.

Kevin was going to Paris too, where he was to be met by an uncle who would take him to London. Fortunately, he sat with two older boys in another compartment of the train, and Michel did not have to face him during the long ride. It was night when the train arrived. For a moment Michel stood next to Kevin as their little group, led by the priest, alighted on the platform; then they filed into the great bustling terminal, where Michel spied the two Temple Dames waiting for him by the information counter. When, a minute later, walking with them toward the taxi stand, he paused in the doorway and looked back, he saw Kevin standing beside a stout gentleman with a reddish beard; his friend was staring after him with an expression of sadness on his face.

He was a prisoner. He had supposed, from Maman Rose's letter, that he would stay at the Mother House a day or two and then go on to Touville. But the days passed, and still he stayed on. Each morning he awoke to the sound of the bell that resounded through the ancient high-ceilinged halls of the great house, and gazed resentfully at the antiseptic white walls of his tiny cell on the third floor, still shrouded in the darkness before dawn. Perhaps it would be today, he said to himself each morning. His vacation at home, on which he had counted so much, was slipping away from him, and still he did not move. There were reasons, he knew. After the first week he had received another letter from Maman Rose, lamenting that he could not come to her just yet; Touville was buzzing with the forthcoming trial, and it was not wise for him to arrive too much ahead of time. And Mother Raïssa, head of the Paris community, had to wait for a moment in which it was convenient to send someone to accompany him on the train. Nonetheless, each morning, Michel arose with a sense of anticipation and hurried downstairs to the convent chapel for mass, hoping that after the ceremony, when Mother Raïssa made a point of greeting him, she would tell him the news he had been so eagerly awaiting. Then, hiding his disappointment as best he could, he returned to his cell for his hat and coat, so as to cross the cloister, go through the gate at the other end, skirt the park that lay behind the residence of the mother general of the order, and through another gate that led to the quarters of the order's lay sisters, where he had his meals.

Three times a day he made this trip within walls; these, along with a daily walk in the cloister, were his only outings. The rest of the time—the long, long hours of the day, marked by the mournful bell, the slow fading of daylight yielding to the early wintry dusk, the first nostalgic hours of the night after the evening meal—he was the prey of Sister Marie des Anges, who had been assigned to him as his tutor. The stout, bright-eyed nun, who was the convent librarian and had free time on her hands now that classes were suspended for Christmas vacation, seemed far more anxious to keep him busy than to teach him anything. She piled the assignments on, and demanded an accounting of his every hour. How much time had he devoted to his reading? How long had it taken him to write the essay? How had he spent the afternoon? In the beginning Michel answered truthfully, with the result that the nun doubled her requirements; whereupon, for his own protection, he added an hour to every task, until his tormentor professed herself satisfied. Inwardly Michel raged; it was hard to sit chained to his desk with his thoughts dwelling in longing on home, while everyone else was on vacation. But there was no escape; little boys, Sister Marie des Anges told him every day, must not be idle. In this boredom and annoyance, Michel began to slip little remarks into his essays to see their effect on the nun. In one paper, devoted to the topic "Man the Homemaker," which Michel suspected was taken from the curriculum of the girls' school with the word "man" substituted for the word "woman," after a number of earnest platitudes, he wrote that just as the wife owes obedience to the husband, the husband has the right to enforce that obedience, even to the point of using his superior physical force. Sister Marie des Anges returned the paper to him with the vague remark that it was not bad, but that he must strive for greater clarity. Had she read it? he wondered. After that he let himself go further, deliberately writing in the most pious strain but always including some outrageous parenthesis toward the end. Honesty was the best policy, he explained for three pages, but on the fourth he wrote that a man could steal if he were hungry. He praised St. Alexis, who lived unrecognized in the guise of a beggar in his parents' house for seventeen years, watching their hopes and fortune wither as they looked for him, but added that even for sanctity he thought the price too high to pay. On another occasion he wrote an entire page in Italian. Sister Marie des Anges noticed nothing. Michel derived a great deal of pleasure out of this perversity, and actually began to look forward to his daily essay, which at least took his mind off his own problems.

His previous visits to the Mother House had not been so restricted. Then Mother Raïssa had made it a point to let him get out into the city whenever he could be accompanied, saying that boys must play. But now things were different, it seemed. There was danger, even here. His case had been made into a national scandal, Mother Raïssa told him; all through France people were talking about him, and wondering where he was hidden. She had called him to her office shortly before Christmas day, to ask him to help with decorating the common room and the chapel for the celebration; but after he had agreed, willingly, she kept him there, chatting. Occasionally her eyes rested meaningfully on a magazine lying on her desk, bearing the title *Homeland* in blue lettering on a white background. Michel was filled with curiosity, but the nun made no move to show it to him, and he did not dare ask any questions. Later he saw what seemed to be the same magazine in the hands of the nun called Sister Petra; she stood with two or three other Temple Dames, their heads bent together over the periodical, talking softly and earnestly among themselves. It seemed to Michel that they regarded him with peculiar interest as he passed.

The next morning, instead of returning to the Temple immediately after his breakfast with the lay sisters, Michel waited outside the refectory door until the hall was clear, then walked boldly through the lobby toward the *conciergerie,* and out the front door. No one stopped him. Once outside, he hurried to the corner two blocks away, where he remembered having seen a kiosk during his last visit. An old man sat in the tiny space, his face half covered by a greasy shawl. Behind him, among a festoon of periodicals clipped to a line of wire, Michel saw the familiar blue and white cover. He pointed to it silently.

"Jew paper," the old man grunted through his scarf as he tossed it on the counter.

Five minutes later Michel slipped unobtrusively into the doorway, passed unseen before the *conciergerie,* and made his way back to the Temple. The magazine nestled under his coat, held in place by his arm. He had also bought *Le Figaro,* and yesterday's *France-Soir.*

Once in his room he sank down on his bed and unbuttoned his overcoat. He had not looked at *Homeland* as he bought it. Now he was startled as the magazine fell to his knees, and his name looked up at him. There it was, in the same blue letters as the rest, toward the bottom of the cover, amidst a list of contents. Michel read, "BIRA: THE BENEDEK AFFAIR IMPERILS THE HONOR OF THE CHURCH, p. 7."

For a long time Michel stared at these strange words, too unnerved to turn the page. What did they mean? The Benedek affair! Could that be about him? There was a dreadful mistake somewhere. What did he have to do with the honor of the Church? After a while he opened the magazine to page 7 and began to read.

"On November 18," the article began, "the Correctional Tribunal of Touville was the scene of the pleadings in 'a delicate guardianship case,' to use the euphemism employed by certain newspapers whose eagerness to avoid commitment does strange things to their expressed desire to keep the public informed.

"A certain Mlle Rose, directress of the Municipal Nursery of that city, was being tried for non-presentation of a minor, as the result of her refusal to obey the executory order of the Touville Court of Appeals. To anyone with the slightest acquaintance with the law, the issue could not be in doubt. Yet the hearing was conducted in an atmosphere that reminded the onlookers of nothing so much as a kind of court procedure familiar to all Frenchmen who lived through the recent Occupation, in which the tendentious philosophy of an alien and monstrous political creed took precedence over our admirable body of native law. Throughout the four-hour procedure were heard strange slogans and malicious insinuations, of which the phrase 'Jewish Freemasonry' will give the flavor.

"The verdict was to be rendered on December 2. It was actually given four days earlier, on November 28, almost clandestinely and in haste, thus obviating the necessity of taking into consideration corroborating evidence submitted by the plaintiff. To those who assisted at the hearing, and noted the evidence of tension and bias, it came as no surprise to learn that Mlle Rose was exonerated of the charge against her. Of course, there will be an appeal. The case will be heard again, it is to be hoped with an entirely different result. But regardless of the outcome, it is time that the attention of France be drawn to the real significance of this human drama, which in one form or other has been fought out for almost eight years, and which in reality lies outside the realm of the judiciary. For we are in the presence here of a scandal. The word is not too strong. Here are the facts."

At this point the author plunged into a long recital of dates and details, which Michel skimmed over quickly. Most of them were familiar to him, having appeared in the Touville papers at the time of the Appeals trial last summer. He would read them again at more leisure; for now his eye leaped ahead to where he saw the word "conscience" in an italicized sentence.

"It is no longer a question of law or of justice. It is a question of the Church. A certain ecclesiastical doctrine, domineering and totalitarian, has unmistakably become apparent. I say it without hesitation: *The Catholic conscience is on trial here.* The long legal battle we have just outlined is only the rear-guard action to cover the true purpose behind the Benedek affair. The Benedek child is now eleven years old. He is being kept in hiding in the care of priests, in some monastery of France, Spain, Switzerland, or Belgium. Let the court battle last a little while longer, and the verdict will not matter, it will be too late, definitely too late. The child will take holy orders, in accordance with Mlle Rose's vow. What is to stop her in her designs? Jewish Freemasonry? Would to God that the Jewish solidarity implied in that phrase really existed, it might take action to prevent this monstrous violation of a child's conscience. But as matters stand, the fight against the secret power of the Church has been conducted by one man, so far in vain. What is to stop her then? The law? But not even this awful power, which we suppose to be supreme in France, can have any effect upon the child's singular guardian. The maximum penalty that can be visited upon her is a year's imprisonment. She would welcome such a verdict with the enthusiasm of the martyr to a cause. And the Benedek boy will remain in hiding, daily subjected to the systematic indoctrination that turns him more and more irrevocably from the faith of his fathers, his inalienable right.

"No, only the Church itself can have any influence over the child's fanatic keeper, for it is inconceivable that Mlle Rose could so long have stood up to an entire family without the resources of the Church to advise, to relieve, and support her.

"The accusation must be made. It is not I who make it. It is the

Benedek child himself whose voice rises from his secret lair to cry out:

" 'I accuse the Church of an abuse of its power.

" 'I accuse the Church of violation of conscience.

" 'I accuse the Church of having failed to respect human integrity, the rights of a natural family, and the innocence of a child.'

"These would be the words of the victim of this plot, if he could be made to understand what has been done to him.

"Are there no authorities to whom appeal can be made? Yes, there are. The first of these is the true Christian himself, he who will not let Church expediency take precedence over that saying of his Master on which his faith is based: Love thy neighbor as thyself.

"I appeal to true Christians, who cannot accept that profit be taken from the exceptional circumstances of the last war and the deportation and death of the parents, by a woman who secretly converted a child whose parents made him a Jew by circumcision and whose family has never ceased to claim him. In the final analysis, it is simply Christian honor that is involved.

"I appeal to the directors of Universal Jewry, to the directors of the Jewish Consistory, and to all the Jewish organizations of France, to face their responsibilities and bring aid to a man who has exhausted himself in a single-handed fight against an all-powerful and malicious adversary.

"I appeal to the organizations of deported persons to undertake the defense of a child whose parents knew the agony of a concentration camp.

"I appeal to the Municipal Council of Touville, for it is from that council that the directress of the Municipal Nursery takes her authority, and it was in her quality of city employee that the child was entrusted to her in 1944, when he was not yet three years old.

"I appeal to the Jewish-Christian Alliance, made up of reflective men dedicated to a mutual comprehension, to reveal by its action that it has a reason for existing.

"I appeal finally to all free men, whether Jews, Catholics, Protestants, or agnostics, to all those who still believe in the dignity of the human being, to intervene and put an end to the scandal created by these kidnapers of children."

Michel put down the magazine and drew a deep breath. He was aware of a vast astonishment. Why, the man had everything all wrong! How cleverly he had distorted the truth of things into the exact opposite! Now it would appear that it was Maman Rose who was the kidnaper, and not that M. Konrad who for years had been trying by all means to get his hands on him, Michel, so as to sell him into slavery. And Bira himself! What did Bira have to do with him? And that bit about the honor of the Church! How did that enter into it? If not for the Temple Dames and the Jesuits of Cassarate, that evil man would have tracked him down long ago! To think that a magazine would publish a mass of lies like this!

Michel heard a familiar step in the hall and hastily shoved the periodicals under his bed. It was Sister Marie des Anges, come for her daily session. Michel was troubled during the entire hour. The nun, finding him distracted, lost her patience and scolded him. Michel made no reply. When the class was over and the nun had gone, he kneeled down beside the bed and fished out the papers.

He read the article again and again, becoming angrier all the while. Certain things in it were true, and this made it all the more abominable. The man, whoever he was, had juggled his facts well, so as to give an air of plausibility to his point of view. But how did he dare speak in Michel's name? If Michel accused anybody, it was M. Konrad, who had forced him to hide and live like a criminal under an assumed name. Had the judges read the article? Did they believe it? For the first time Michel understood the monumental struggle his Maman Rose had been engaged in during all these years. And now he was going to take part himself! It made him weak to think of it.

That Sunday in October Kevin had said to him, "Don't you think the whole school knows you're circumcised?" Now, Michel reflected dully, his face red with shame, all France knew. For the man had dared even that, had not hesitated to put down on paper for all the world to read the most secret, the most shameful fact of all, which Michel himself did not permit his thoughts to dwell on.

"Don't come back," Kevin had said. But no, at the school he was Michel Rose. No one would associate him with the boy Bira was talking about.

He had forgotten the newspapers. Now he found himself looking at a portrait of a man on the front page of *France-Soir*. Suddenly Michel stiffened and stared in utter disbelief at the caption over the picture. Had the whole world gone mad? There was his name again! "Famed Academician to Plead for Benedek Family at Touville," the caption said. At the bottom of the photograph Michel read, "Maître

Hector Gens, who has the distinction of being the only lawyer in the Académie Française, when queried as to what he hopes to achieve at the Touville Court of Appeals on January 8, answered succinctly one word: 'JUSTICE!' " That was all; there was no article, only the picture with its captions. Michel studied the face, which was that of an old man, long and narrow, with large, fine eyes that stared directly forward with hypnotic intensity. His hair was white, brushed straight back and lying flat and silky against the skull; yet the eyebrows were black, and arched high over the eye sockets, standing out incongruously against the whiteness of the skin.

The Benedek family, the caption said. Then this lawyer was on Konrad's side, and was his enemy. Michel felt overawed. An academician, no less! One of the forty immortals. Michel had studied about the Académie Française in history class. It had been founded by Cardinal Richelieu in the seventeenth century, and since then the best brains of France had belonged to it. Great men like Voltaire, Boileau, La Fontaine, Montesquieu, Victor Hugo, Alfred de Musset, François Mauriac constituted its membership. Names that were the honor roll of the glory of France. And this man was one of them; this Maître Hector Gens with the lean, intelligent, dangerous face was going to Touville, to ask Michel questions in front of the court! Michel felt his world crumbling around him. How could such a man have lent himself to play Konrad's game? What values were safe when one of the great of France—for there was no disputing Maître Gens's greatness, it was part of his definition as academician—could condemn Michel unseen and unheard, and call it justice?

It was a long time before Michel could bring himself to look at *Le Figaro*. He was relieved to find no mention of himself.

That afternoon he was summoned to help with the Christmas decorations. He plunged into the work eagerly, overcharged with energy from his enforced idleness and glad to be doing something, anything, to take his mind off the articles he had read. He scampered recklessly up the ladder to reach the chandelier and cornices that the nuns found difficult of access, while they exclaimed in fear at his audacity. When the work was done, they praised him to Mother Raïssa, who patted him on the head and told him that he would be the guest of honor at the "little festivity" they would have on Christmas Day, three days from now.

Michel's enthusiasm vanished at once. He would be here at Christmas, then, and not at the Nursery.

In the days that followed, Michel slipped out each morning to the kiosk and bought the daily papers. Every day something appeared: an article, a photograph, a letter to the editor. His astonishment grew. Why were these strangers so concerned about him? And where did they get their information, which, though it had to do with him, often aroused so little response in his memory that he wondered whether they had not confused him with some other boy in similar circumstances? His pile of periodicals, added to daily, soon became difficult to hide. He clipped the articles that referred to him or the case, and hid them in his valise; what was left of the papers he disposed of on his way to breakfast, in the waste bin behind the mother general's residence; and he pored over his collection of clippings until he could have recited them by heart.

He soon learned to distinguish among the periodicals and their points of view. *Le Figaro* and *La Croix* took Maman Rose's side, whereas the others, notably *France-Soir* and *Le Monde,* while reporting the facts without comment, generally managed to avoid mention of Maman Rose altogether, and played up the activities of M. Konrad and his lawyers. It was in *La Croix,* for instance, that Michel found an explanation for M. Konrad's indefatigable pursuit. Michel had an uncle who had never acknowledged him, it seemed, a rich banker named Jerome Benedek, who had been established in Paris until the war but had emigrated to America. But Jerome Benedek, in a deathbed change of conscience, had left a huge fortune to his orphaned nephew, on condition that he be removed from Mlle Rose's care and entrusted to his family. M. Konrad was to receive 20 per cent of the fortune, or some eighty million francs, upon succeeding in his mission. This, the author of the article concluded, was the sordid motivation behind the so-called Benedek affair; M. Konrad's pretended concern for the child's relatives was nothing but the veneer over his real desire, which was for the banker's hard cash.

It did not occur to Michel to doubt this story, since it answered a question that had always puzzled him: Why was M. Konrad, a total stranger, going to such enormous trouble to persecute him? Yet at the same time he did not quite believe in this belated phantom of a millionaire uncle. He had an aunt in Palestine, who had visited him once when he was a child, given him some toys, and told Maman Rose to keep him; but no one had ever mentioned an uncle. No doubt some such millionaire existed, because there it was in black and white for everyone to read; but he was some other boy's uncle.

Michel felt cheered by this article. When the judges read *that*, it would make up for the vicious conclusions of that M. Bira.

In *Le Figaro* Michel found a long feature dedicated to Maman Rose, printed with a large photograph of her seated in her office and looking up with a challenging air. He studied the photograph longingly. The camera had "seen" her, he reflected, much more recently than he had. The last time he had been with her was in September. There she was, with her soft, kind features, her high forehead now showing a few lines, the little peak of hair dipping down in the center to form a perfect Cupid's bow. Moved by a sudden impulse, he lifted the paper and kissed the photograph. Then he read the article. It dwelt on Maman Rose's long history of private charities, and the fact that she had saved the lives of eleven Jewish orphans during the war and the Occupation. This was the woman who was being pursued through all the tortuous byways of the law as a monstrous criminal. Yes! she *was* a monster, in the original, etymological sense of the word, that of "divine warning"; she was a monster of charity, a portent to show the rest of mankind, lost in selfishness, what the human heart was capable of. But this meant less than nothing to M. Konrad, to the family lawyers, or the atheist press. "In all the long and troublesome proceedings in the Benedek affair, which has gone from one Family Council to another, from court to court, the one element which none of the persecutors of this noble woman has ever taken the slightest account of is the passion that broods in the maternal heart of the sorrowful Mlle Rose."

Reading this, Michel's heart swelled with pride. He was a bit puzzled, however, about the eleven Jewish children mentioned in the article. There was himself, and Léah. The others—Manon, Pé, Reneé and her brothers—were not Jewish. Perhaps, he concluded, there had been others before him that he had known nothing about.

In the same paper he found a letter to the editor in answer to Bira's article. It was couched in fury. "The honor of the Church! Has the critical M. Bira, safe in his hermitage in the Alps, ever considered the role of the Church and its servants in sheltering the Israelites when they were the object of the Nazi manhunts? Does he know how many priests and nuns, yes, and the higher prelates of the Church as well, not to mention the countless thousands of lay Catholics, risked their lives for those who refused to accept the dispensation that gives life eternal? Let us not speak of honor, but rather of gratitude! When the balance is cast in the eternal reckoning, it is not the Church that will be found wanting!"

In *Le Monde* Michel read that the first president of the Touville Court of Appeals, M. Bouhours, concerned over the great demand for seats at the Benedek-Rose hearing on January 8, and fearing that the hall usually reserved for such civil proceedings was too small to accommodate it, had announced that the much larger Assizes court-room would be used. Even this court would be insufficient, however (the reporter went on), for the news that Maître Gens would present himself at the Touville bar on behalf of the plaintiff had caused a stampede for places on the part of those who wanted to see the great lawyer in action. M. Konrad, interviewed as to his opinion of this sign of public interest in the case, interpreted it as a reawakening of the French conscience, now beginning to reassert its innate sense of justice, which had gone into hibernation during the war and its aftermath.

Michel read these reports, and brooded over them, and with growing apprehension watched the days go by that were taking him closer to the trial. His attitude had changed. More than anything he wanted to go home; but now that longing was mixed with fear. Rereading Maman Rose's letter, and noting the tone of optimism in it, he wondered how she could hope to triumph over a Maître Gens. And then, regardless of the outcome, there was the ordeal itself. Michel could form no mental picture of a courtroom and its proceedings— but he knew that there would be judges wearing black robes and strange red-banded caps, and lawyers who argued, and spectators listening to every word; and that before this multitude, already curious about him because of the outcry in the newspapers, he would have to appear and support the questioning of all those eyes. . . . His heart sank in dread to think of it.

Christmas Day came, and with it the "little festivity" promised by Mother Raïssa. He dined that day in the Temple refectory and not with the lay sisters. There were gifts by his plate—a book, a carved ivory rosary, a holy medal; he was singled out to read a chapter from the life of the Blessed Mother Miriam, founder of the order; he was urged to propose a toast, which was greeted by applause and smiling faces. He was made much of, and grew confused. They are kind, he thought. If they only knew!

By New Year's Day Michel had accepted that his vacation was

irretrievably spoiled. At most he would have a couple of days before the trial, and a week after it. Classes at St. Louis Gonzaga began again on the sixteenth.

It was not until the evening of the sixth, when Michel had begun to wonder whether there had been a change of plan and that perhaps he would not be called upon to attend the trial at all, that Mother Raïssa took him aside and announced that he would be leaving early the next morning. She had received a telegram from Touville. He would be accompanied on the Paris–Lyons–Midi train by two nuns, who were on their way to Tunis via Marseilles, and who would turn him over to Mother Veronica at Touville. Michel took the news calmly. Whatever was going to happen was going to happen. At least, he thought with a touch of bitter amusement, he would be rid of Sister Marie des Anges and her daily inquisition.

As the car turned into the dark alley, M. Béjart switched the lights to dim, but not before Michel had seen a figure in a nurse's cape standing just inside the fence. Was it Maman Rose? he wondered. The car stopped beside the gate, which swung open, and Michel saw that it was Manon. "Hurry!" she urged in a whisper. But M. Béjart had already opened the door and was stiffly clambering out, hampered by his thick overcoat. Michel slid out after him. Manon embraced him briefly, and with her arm in his walked quickly with him across the dark playground, whose surface was mottled with slicks of ice.

A faint gleam of light shone from the back door. Maman Rose, a shawl over her shoulders, was peering out. "Thank God!" she exclaimed fervently. She took Michel into her arms, pressing him to her and rocking back and forth, making little crooning sounds. "My boy, my boy," she said tearfully. Michel's throat contracted. He was home again. "Oh, Maman Rose!" he stammered, burrowing his face into her softness and holding her tightly. All the despair and longing that had been pent up in him during the past weeks went into the strength of his embrace. She murmured soothingly in his ear. If only he could stay where he was forever and ever, and never have to lift his head and face the world and himself again! But, after a long while, Maman Rose gently loosened his grip and held him at arm's length, studying him hungrily.

"You're taller," she said, "but so dreadfully thin! But I can't see you properly in this light."

Behind them M. Béjart coughed discreetly, and asked if everything was all right. For his part, he was sure they hadn't been seen. "Oh, Alain," she said with emotion, taking his hand, "how can I ever thank you! If it weren't for you and a few other friends, I don't know what I'd do. If I have the strength to go on, it's because . . ." She gave his hand a little shake.

M. Béjart's fine white mustache quivered. "My dear lady!" he murmured. "We'll beat that rabble yet."

"We will!" Maman Rose said. "We have to!"

"Hello, Michel," Léah said shyly. She was standing in the kitchen doorway. Beside her stood Pé, grinning at him. They had both grown; Pé stood half a head taller than Michel. Two years! Michel thought, approaching them. It had been two years since he had seen them. It had not been safe for him to come to the Nursery, Maman Rose had said. And so Maman Rose had come to him in Paris, as often as she could. He had thought often of Pé and Léah, as his brother and sister; but he had remembered them as they were then. He embraced them awkwardly, suddenly timid, as though they were strange children he had just been introduced to. They stood grinning at each other, not knowing what to say.

Behind him M. Béjart said he would just run along, his part was over for the day. Until tomorrow, then. Oh, by the way, they hadn't come back, had they? Maman Rose replied grimly that they hadn't and if they knew what was good for them, they wouldn't. M. Béjart laughed, and called out, "Happy homecoming, old man." Michel started to say, "Thank you, sir," but not trusting his voice, cleared his throat and nodded. M. Béjart tipped his hat to Maman Rose and went out the door.

Maman Rose cried, "Remember, one o'clock sharp tomorrow."

"Count on me," he called back gallantly, going down the steps. Through the open door Michel watched the dapper figure fade into the darkness of the playground, making his way carefully, his stick probing before him. Manon followed him. Then the car door closed quietly, and the motor coughed and started.

Someone stood lean and tall in the dim corridor, staring at him. Michel saw the fringe of iron-gray hair and the long, leathery face, and recognized Félicité. "Why, it's Michel!" she said with a foolish grin of welcome. "Where have you been, Michel?"

"He's been away," Maman Rose said. "But now he's come home for a visit. Come, Michel, you must be frozen. There's a heater in your room. We'll go upstairs." She turned to Pé and Léah. "Michel and I are going to have a little talk. Help Manon in the kitchen, and when we're through, we'll have our party."

As they went up the stairway, Michel heard the old servant's cracked voice exclaiming to Manon, who had entered and bolted the door behind her, "It's Michel, Manon. Did you see him?"

"Poor creature!" Maman Rose said. "She keeps asking about you."

Divine warning. Monster. What was the story behind Félicité? Michel wondered. He had always taken her for granted. Now it occurred to him that the simple-minded servant woman must have been another of Maman Rose's charities, long ago, before he came to the Nursery. For him she had always been there. She had taken him to St. Joseph's mornings, when he was a little boy with a new schoolbag, and the world was a garden in which wonderful miracles happened. He had put his hand in hers and trotted along happily at her side. How far away those days seemed now! Yet Félicité had not changed; it was he who had changed, he who had grown older and corrupt and learned to live with sin in his soul. In that instant he was aware of a queer doubling of perspective, as if the boy he had been then had come up to stand at his side. He was filled with shame. But he would not let himself be sad, not now. It was good to come home, and find everything as he had left it, and be at peace for a little while.

Entering his room with Maman Rose, he was overcome with emotion. A faint light from the street lamp outside, filtering around the drawn shade of the window, showed him his bed by the window, his desk and chair side by side with Pé's, the bureau he had shared with Pé, and the other bed by the wall. The room and its furnishings were just as he had pictured them in his memory, yet all different somehow, smaller and touched with strangeness. He had been away too long. But he would settle in again; one night's sleep in his own bed, and he would awaken in the morning to find that everything had become familiar to him once more.

His hand groped for the light switch. "Wait!" Maman Rose said. She crossed the room swiftly, and peered out from behind the shade. Then she beckoned to him, and he knelt down on the bed beside her and looked out into the street laced with harsh light and dark shadows from the arc lamp overhead. Two men in overcoats stood in the doorway opposite; he could see the pale blur of their faces, and the glow of a cigarette. "Photographers," Maman Rose said. "They're dying to get a picture of you. They take turns. For a week now there's always been someone." As they watched, the cigarette flew into the street, and went out in a tiny shower of sparks; and one of the men thumped himself with embracing movements of his arms, stamping his feet. "It's cold out there, poor chaps. Last night I sent them out some coffee with Manon. She told them there was no use waiting about, you weren't here. But they said they had their jobs to do." She shrugged and drew the curtain over the shade.

Michel said nothing. Driving through Touville a little while ago with M. Béjart, on his way to the Nursery from the Temple, he had been surprised when the old gentleman had said they would enter through the alley. He had asked why, and M. Béjart had snorted and said, "The Fourth Estate. Photographers." But in circling Place St. Lazare, he had stared down his street and seen nobody, and wondered at the precaution. Now fear struck at him, chilling his joy at being home. He was the hunted, even here.

Maman Rose uttered an exclamation of dismay. She had snapped on the light, and turned to him. "My poor baby! What have they been doing to you?"

He muttered that it was nothing, he felt a bit tired, that was all. No, she exclaimed, it was more than that. He was thin and pale, and had great dark circles under his eyes. She was sorry she had ever let him out of her sight, she said. Fortunately, the end of their troubles was in view. She sat down beside him and pulled him to her shoulder, stroking his hair. He closed his eyes, remembering those nightmarish last days of his at St. Louis; he felt the sudden urge to cry, thinking how she would look at him if she knew. She was all he had in the world.

Manon came into the room and approached with a worried smile. "How you've grown!" she said. Manon had changed; her face had lost its roundness, and the sallow skin was tight against the bones. A thin vertical line had rooted itself between her eyes.

"Look at him!" Maman Rose said tragically. "They'll say I starve him, or keep him chained up in a closet, or something. How was your trip, Michel? Did anyone notice you?"

"All right," he said hesitantly. "I don't know. There was one man."

He told her briefly about the man who had boarded the train at Mâcon and settled in their compartment. He had brought a newspaper with him, and after reading it he had entered into a conversation with the two nuns, saying that his niece was a novice with the Benedictines. He had asked them what they thought of the Benedek case. *Le Monde* was full of it, he said, and showed them an article on the front page. Michel could read the caption, which read, "The Benedek Affair: A Bank Account in Switzerland?" Then the man noticed Michel, called him a fine lad, and asked him his name. Michel answered "Jean Dupont," as he had been told to do, and the man screwed up his face in doubt and said, "It's not Benedek, is it?" "No, sir," Michel said, and the man laughed and looked around at the nuns, who had frozen on their seats, and said it was only a joke. But when they reached Touville, and the nuns helped him with his bag and accompanied him to the platform where Mother Veronica and Sister Blanche were waiting, the man got up and stared at them from the train window. The two nuns who had brought him had to board the train again, because they were going on, but they were nervous and said they would change their compartment.

Michel did not mention something else the man had said. Talking to the nuns, he had shaken his head with a cynical grin and said it was all nonsense. Did they know what was back of it all? Money, he said. The boy's father was a doctor, and had made a pile during the war. He had put it in a bank in Switzerland. Now that the parents had been declared legally dead, the money would go to the boy. Just like the Jews, he said; trust them to have it and keep it. That was the secret behind it all. If it had been a poor boy, no one would have made any fuss about him at all; the family would have been glad to fob him off on Mlle Rose. And as for Mlle Rose herself, she was no fool either, she knew "where the honey was." Michel, staring at the man's sly, hateful countenance, had wanted to cry out that it was not so, but knew that he would only be giving himself away. He had resolved not to say anything about it to Maman Rose; it would only make her angry.

Maman Rose praised him for his presence of mind in having answered the man as he had. They had made a circus out of it, she commented bitterly. Every day now there was something in the papers. It was all that Konrad's doing. He was deliberately seeking publicity, so as to rally to his side all the scum of France. But Michel was not to worry. She had allies too. Konrad would learn a lesson he would not soon forget, in spite of his Paris lawyers. Did Michel know who was her greatest ally? *He* was.

"Me?" Michel said.

"You're a big boy now," she said, nodding. "You'll soon be twelve, Michel, and now you have to play a man's part. I've been waiting for this day, delaying and fighting for time, and praying that you'd be ready for them when the time came. Now it's come, and I know I can rely on you. That's why I sent for you. And the beauty is that they've asked for it themselves, thinking they were trapping me and that I wouldn't give in. But with the safe conduct there's nothing to worry about. They won't dare touch you. At the proper time you'll appear in the courtroom, testify, and then leave. That big fish of a Konrad won't be able to do a thing about it. You'll walk out right under his nose, and he'll never lay eyes on you again."

"But Maman Rose," he said, thinking in fear of what lay before him tomorrow, "what will they ask me? Why do I have to be there?"

"That's where you have to be smart," she said. "I can't tell you the exact questions. You can be sure they'll beat about the bush and do their best to trip you up. But no matter what they say or how they say it, there are certain things you have to be firm about and not let yourself be shaken. Sooner or later the court is going to get around to them, and that's where you take your stand. There must be no doubt how you feel. Three things," she said, holding up three fingers to catch his eye. "Three basic things, and the rest doesn't matter. First, do you want to live in France or Palestine?"

Could there be any doubt? he wondered, looking at her. Then he saw that she expected him to answer, and he said, "France."

"Two," she said. "Do you want to stay with me or go with your aunt?"

"With you," he said instantly.

"Three. Do you want to be a Catholic, or a Jew?"

It was not doubt that made him hesitate, but a pang of guilt that shot through him. "A Catholic," he said meekly, recovering himself.

"You see?" she said. "That's your bedrock. That's the position you can't be shaken from. But you mustn't answer like a namby-pamby, you have to hold your head high and speak with conviction. With fire. You have to make them feel that they'll be shattering your life if they try to force you to be what you're not. And it's the truth too, but you must make them feel it inside as you do. Above all, don't be intimidated. They'll try and twist your words and make you say that black is white. Don't try to argue with them. You can't do it. You only know three things. You want to stay with me in France and be a Catholic. It's as simple as that. Tell them just as you told me.

There's a lot more to the law than paragraphs in the Code. The judges are human too. Underneath their robes they're only men. And when you and I stand up to them together, they'll think twice before breaking your heart by sending you to an aunt you've never seen."

These were the basic things Michel had to insist on, Maman Rose went on. As far as the details were concerned, Maître Cauchet would brief him on those. Maître Cauchet would come to the Nursery tomorrow morning at nine o'clock, to go over it with him. The trial was not until one-thirty. But there was one thing she wanted to tell him now. A warning.

"This is important, Michel," she said. "Don't mention the name of your school, or say anything about the Temple Dames. You see why, don't you? You've got to understand what's involved. Because once you're before the court, you're on your own, and there's no turning to me for answers. You can never tell what a court's going to do. I expected to win at the other Appeals Court hearing, and I lost. But the last trial at the Correctional Tribunal, I thought I didn't have a ghost of a chance, and I won. You've got to look ahead. We *might* lose tomorrow, and then where would you go? If you tell them about St. Louis, you can't go back there any more. They'd have a swarm of police waiting for you."

Michel glanced swiftly at Manon, who smiled and nodded. "Oh, Manon," Maman Rose said. "I told her ages ago. I trust her as I do myself. If I didn't have her to talk to, I think sometimes I'd lose my mind. But nobody else knows, so be careful what you say. Not a word to Pé or Léah. And at the court, you have to weigh each word ten times before you speak. Not only about the school, but the nuns too, because—"

"I know," he said. "I won't be able to travel with them any more."

"That's it," Maman Rose said in satisfaction. "I knew you'd understand. And now, the children have waited long enough. Is everything ready, Manon?"

"Yes, Mademoiselle Rose."

"Then come on."

Mystified, Michel rose and followed the two women out of his room. Maman Rose rapped lightly at the door to her own sitting room, and then opened it. In the middle of the room Michel saw a small square table covered with a cloth, and a cake with candles in the center of it. Pé and Léah were seated, wearing gay paper hats. They had turned expectantly toward the door. "Happy New Year, Michel!" they cried.

"Tomorrow is another day," Maman Rose said. "Today we celebrate. Happy New Year, Michel!" She kissed him, and so did Manon.

Michel burst into tears.

It was as though a huge tight knot had loosened inside him, and left him ravenously hungry for food and drink, for laughter, for companionship. How terribly lonely he had been, he realized with emotion, seated at the table and looking at the faces about him! Léah's face, pert and pretty, with its fresh baby skin and dark, tender eyes. Pé, with his snub nose and freckles, choking with laughter as he stuffed cake in his mouth. Manon, watchful, smiling. And Maman Rose, his Maman Rose, who loved him more than anything else in the world. Michel felt cradled in a sea of tenderness such as he had not known since he had left the Nursery that fateful day four years ago. There had been no such tenderness at St. Louis Gonzaga. Such emotions were not for the little soldiers of God they already were; already they had left that behind them, in preparation for the hard lifelong test that lay ahead, in which they would be set aside from the rest of men, sneered at by the impious, made the target of temptations they had to be strong enough to resist; in which they had to be tempered like steel to dedicate themselves to God to the exclusion of all else, including human love. And at the Mother House in Paris, where he had just spent the loneliest three weeks of his life, there had been nothing the nuns could offer him but food and shelter, prayer, study, and impersonal kindliness. His heart was hungry for affection, love for the boy that was Michel, for himself alone because he was theirs and not an object of training. Even his meetings with Maman Rose in Paris had not been like this. There they could never forget that they were in an alien atmosphere; Maman Rose could never stay more than a few days at a time; and Manon, Pé, and Léah were not there. His family! How he loved them at that moment, drinking in their features with shining eyes! A whole week he would be with them! Or even eight days. True, there was the trial tomorrow, but that would be soon over and he would be home again, like in the good days before the troubles started, to meditate in peace on his problems, solve them, and heal himself again.

"The little minx!" Maman Rose cried, laughing and shaking her head. Léah, who was a boarder at the Temple, was imitating Sister Blanche. She had got up from the table and was waddling across the room, sighing heavily as with asthma and making solemn blessings with her hands. Michel began to laugh; it was Sister Blanche who had turned him over to M. Béjart, only an hour ago. Léah had caught her gestures exactly.

"And here's Mother Veronica," Léah shouted over their laughter. "Pé, help me!"

It was obvious they had played this little skit before. Léah drew herself up until her back was straight and stiff as a poker, bowed her head, pouting so that her cheeks were drawn, and half closed her eyes as though she were reading a breviary in her hand. Manon giggled and said in awe, "Goodness me!" Pé struck the table and shouted, "Boom!" Then in a falsetto voice, "Mother Veronica, the furnace has blown up!" Léah slowly raised her head, her face impassive, stared briefly at Pé, and bowed her head again, saying softly, "I have ordered a new one."

"But Mother Veronica," Pé cried again, "the school is on fire!"

Léah lifted one arm with a gentle sweep to allow for a wide sleeve, delicately turned an imaginary page, read intently for a moment, and without looking up said, "I have already summoned the fire department."

Pé screamed, "But we shall all be burned to death!"

The breviary snapped shut, Léah's head shot up and she stared in mild reproach at Pé. "God's will be done," she said.

Léah exploded in a screech of laughter and pranced around the table, pulling Michel's hair as she passed.

"That's nothing," Pé said in excitement. "You ought to see my math teacher! Look, he walks like this." Pé got up in his turn and walked about, his hands behind his back and his belly thrust out. Michel and Léah clapped, but Maman Rose said that Léah's performance was better, that Léah had the stuff to be a great actress.

"She's very intelligent," Maman Rose said. "Did you know, Michel? Léah is the first in her class. All my children are smart," she went on, with a glance at Pé. "Only one of them has a little difficulty with discipline."

"That's me," Pé said unabashed.

Michel listened to them with delight. He felt lightheaded with happiness. How good it was to laugh again! His old-man's gravity, so carefully cultivated at St. Louis, so expected of him at the Mother House, fell from him, and he was a boy again, free to make impulsive movements and say the first thing that came into his head. Léah began to sing, "Sur le Pont d'Avignon," and Michel joined in with her, waving his arms. In doing so he upset his glass of wine-and-water. It didn't matter, it didn't matter at all. You could spill things in your own home, and it was all right. Manon mopped it up with a cloth, while Léah screamed in mock fear, "We'll be drowned!" and Pé shouted, "God's will be done!" and Maman Rose rocked with laughter.

"Here," Maman Rose said, getting up and seizing the wine bottle. "We'll have a toast." She poured water into Michel's glass and added a dollop of wine. Pé and Léah held out their glasses, and Maman Rose added some wine to them. "Who'll make the toast?"

"Michel!" the children said at once.

Urged by them, Michel stood up. With a toast you were supposed to say something clever. But he didn't feel clever, just warm and secure and full of love. Tomorrow was very far away. He raised his glass, having no idea of what he would say. He would open his mouth and try to keep his voice steady as he made it clear that he was very happy and wanted to be with them always.

Through the expectant silence came the sound of the doorbell.

"What on earth . . ." Maman Rose began. She stared at Manon, who had suddenly paled. "Do you suppose . . . ?" Manon said. "Oh, no!" Maman Rose said, putting down her glass.

"I'll look out the window." Manon hurried through the passageway into Maman Rose's bedroom.

"Félicité!" Maman Rose muttered under her breath, and rushed out to the landing. A moment later Michel heard her whisper fiercely down the stairs. "Félicité! Go to your room! Never mind the door. I'll answer it myself. Go to your room!"

Michel looked at Pé and Léah, who had become very grave. What was happening?

"You know who it is?" Pé said solemnly. "It's that Monsieur Konrad, that's who. He came here three times today already."

Michel couldn't take it in. His danger had been so far from his mind at that moment that he could only stare stupidly from Pé to Léah and back again. Incredibly, Léah nodded.

Manon entered from the bedroom just as Maman Rose stepped in. "It's their car," Manon said. "It's parked right in front. And the photographers are in the garden, watching the door."

Maman Rose's face went red and then white. Michel recognized the signs of one of her monumental fits of anger. "All right," Maman Rose said in a low voice. "They're asking for it. They want to make a big show for the newspapers, do they? I'll give them a show! I warned them. Manon, take the children into Michel's room. Then you know what to do. But then you come back and lock the door from the inside. No matter what happens, stay there with Michel until I rap at the door and tell you to open it."

"Yes, Mademoiselle Rose," Manon said. "And the photographers, suppose they—"

"Why not?" Maman Rose said. "The more the merrier. I'll stay here."

"Come, children." In bewilderment Michel rose and followed Manon out the door, across the corridor, and into his own room.

"Who is it, Manon?" he asked.

The bell rang again. "Ring, ring!" Manon said. "There's no hurry. Who? It's Monsieur Konrad."

"You see?" Pé said.

"Konrad and your aunt," Manon said. "They want to talk to Mademoiselle Rose and to see you."

"My what?" he said. "My aunt? My aunt from—from *Palestine?*"

"Big as life. I almost fell over when I opened the door and saw them, the first time. This morning. I recognized her, from her picture in the paper. I opened my mouth and looked at them and couldn't say a word. I ran and told Mademoiselle Rose, but she wouldn't let them in."

"My aunt!" Michel repeated. It was a severe jolt. In his mind the words "aunt" and "Palestine" had always gone together. The two had fused into a dreadful menace hanging over him, but that menace was personified in M. Konrad. His aunt had remained in the background, anonymous, remote, fixed in the faraway country she wanted to drag him to. Now, incredibly, she was here; she was a living woman, not just a name, and she was standing at the entrance door below, ringing the bell to be let in.

The bell rang again. Manon put her finger to her lips. "Don't make any noise," she whispered, and went out the door. There came the sound of a key turning in the lock.

"I saw her," Léah said. "Your aunt. She has gray hair. But Monsieur Konrad doesn't have any hair at all."

"Yes, he does," Pé affirmed. "He has some around the ears."

Léah sniffed scornfully. Pé had run and hid, she said. He was afraid M. Konrad would think he was Michel. And so Pé had never laid eyes on him.

"I saw him from the window," Pé said hotly. "I'm not afraid of him."

"But what do they want?" Michel said fearfully. He felt trapped. Surely they would not try to force their way in and seize him, with the trial tomorrow! Was that their purpose in insisting that he appear to testify? To lure him out of his hiding place and grab him the night before, when they knew where he would be? But Maman Rose would not let them!

As if in answer to the doubt, he heard the jangling of the bolt as the door was opened below, and a murmur of voices. Manon had let them in! Why? "You know what to do, Manon," Maman Rose had said. Then it was Maman Rose who had told her to open the door. And she had said angrily, "I'll give them a show!" Was she going to scold them and send them about their business? At any rate, he reasoned with himself, they would be unable to get past his locked door. He was safe. But he could not put down the feeling of uneasiness within him to know that they were in the same house with him.

Michel jumped. He had heard a furtive fumbling at his door. The lock clicked, and Manon entered, her eyes wide and solemn. She locked the door behind her, and turned to him, whispering, "They're here. I put them in the reception room. Has Mademoiselle Rose come out?"

He shook his head and whispered reproachfully, "But *why,* Manon?"

"You'll see," she said mysteriously. "But don't worry, they can't get in here. Anyway, they're sitting as quiet as can be in their chairs, waiting for Mademoiselle Rose to come down to talk to them. They'll wait a long time. That Konrad. And your aunt, Madame Lindner, her name is. And Monsieur Immermann. And a woman I've never seen before." She giggled suddenly. "Maybe she's Konrad's wife. There's nobody so ugly but what some woman will marry him. And the photographers came in too. One of them asked me for coffee. Imagine! Said his ears were frozen. I didn't even answer him. I can just see myself making coffee for that lot."

Léah clapped her hands, and then put her hand to her mouth in contrition for the noise she had made. "You brought your scrapbook!" she said. "Let's see it, Manon!"

"Come on, Manon!" Pé urged.

"Speak softly," Manon said. She had a large black notebook in her hand. "Look," she said to Michel, holding it up with pride. "I began it last summer, when they printed your parents' pictures in the paper. And since then lots of things have come out, and I've got most of them. The nurses help me, they're awfully excited about it all, and when they find something, they cut it out and bring it to me. Michel," she said, sitting on his bed, "do you realize you're the most famous boy in France? Well, you are. Everybody's talking about you, and wondering what you look like, and where you are. The mystery boy, they call you. It's all so—well, it's thrilling!"

"Thrilling!" he said, starting. "Here they want to—" He choked. "And you—you call—"

"Oh, don't be a goose, I didn't mean that. Of course it's terrible what they're trying to do to you. But we're going to win, and in the meanwhile millions of people read about us in the newspapers every day. Millions! The whole country! Here we were, just like everybody else, and now suddenly all France wants to know about us, and our names come out on the front page, as though we were—well, truly important, like General de Gaulle or somebody like that. My name too," she added with awe in her voice. "Manon Colin, just like that, and how Mademoiselle Rose took me in from the Temple Dames. I felt so funny when I read it, and I thought, This is me, and everybody in France is reading my name this minute, and now they know about me, whereas they didn't before. It was terribly exciting, and somehow sad too at the same time. Did you ever feel like that, Michel? I mean, sort of—why, what's the matter?"

He had turned a piteous look on her and shaken his head. "I don't want people talking about me," he said miserably. "I just want to be let alone."

"They'll let you alone, Michel," Léah said reassuringly. "You'll see. After the trial."

"Sure," Pé said. "You've got nothing to worry about."

Manon still had the notebook in her hand. She looked at Michel uncertainly, then opened it and asked him if he wanted to see. This picture was of his aunt.

Michel found himself staring at two figures standing in an open space, and behind them, in the distance, the nose and part of the wing of an airplane with the words "El Al" written on it. The photograph had been taken close up, and only the head and shoulders of the two could be seen. The one on the right was that of a man wearing a hat and overcoat, with a scarf wrapped around his neck. Could this be M. Konrad? Yes, because the caption said: "The Benedek Affair: M. Louis Konrad Greets Mme Hannah Lindner, Aunt of the Benedek Orphan, at Orly Airport." But how different he looked from the man Michel remembered! Only the heavy-lidded eyes seemed vaguely familiar. The other figure, that of a woman, was looking straight into the camera. She too was wearing a hat, and a coat with a fur collar. The hat sat back on her head and revealed a lock of gray hair in front. The face told Michel nothing; it was that of a middle-aged woman, with full lips set somewhat unevenly and heavy lines curving up from the corners of the mouth to the nose. Otherwise, the features were indistinct. This is my aunt, Michel told himself. His father's sister. The woman who had been battling Maman Rose all these years to take him away from her. In the instant of letting his eyes rest on her face, he had supposed that he would recognize her somehow. Yet it was anybody's face.

"Let me see, Michel," Pé said.

"Wait!" Manon admonished him.

Michel glanced through the article that accompanied the photograph. Yes, his aunt had told the reporters who questioned her, she had come to France to attend the trial of Mlle Rose, and to embrace her nephew, whose guardian she was. The courts had awarded her custody of her brother's child, and she had come for him. He would accompany her back to Israel, she said, where he would have been years ago, if not for the fanaticism of Mlle Odette Rose. The article concluded with the statement that Mme Lindner would spend the night in Paris, and the next morning would take the Paris–Lyons–Midi for Touville, where she would be the guest of M. and Mme Konrad, her representatives in her nephew's case. In cutting out the article, Manon had included the dateline, which was January 6, 1953.

January sixth. Yesterday. Then it was this morning that M. Konrad and his aunt had boarded the train for Touville in Paris. The same train that Michel had taken. All during those long hours in which he had sat opposite the two nuns, staring out the window or listening to the conversation of the man with the newspaper, those two had been on the train with him, maybe even in the next compartment! They might even have passed each other in the corridor, or alighted in Touville one behind the other, or gone out the gate together. And suppose—Michel's blood ran cold at the thought— suppose they had happened to be in the same compartment with him? Would he not have recognized M. Konrad, seen from so close, and in his fright have given himself away? And if they had a description of him . . . He did not finish the thought, but turned haunted eyes upon Manon. But she was not looking at him. She had lifted her head and seemed to be listening to something far away, her face keen with secret amusement. Michel listened, but heard nothing. "What is it?" he asked. She shook her head vaguely.

Pé and Léah had got hold of the notebook, which they spread out on their laps and were studying together. "Look at this, Michel," they cried, turning the pages. But most of the clippings were already familiar to him. "Later," he said. How much longer would the visitors remain in the reception room, he wondered, before they began to get restless? M. Immermann, Manon had said. Michel remembered him—a big man who smoked cigars. His Jewish godfather. Maman Rose was angry with him, he knew, because he told lies about her, and had gone over to their side. Why had he come here now? And who was the other woman, whom even Manon didn't know? It was fantastic that they should be in the same house with him, and only the thin locked door separating them. And still Maman Rose had made no move.

Suddenly Manon stiffened and turned toward the window. At the same time there came a screech of brakes in the street, a sharp voice calling commands, and the commotion of boots striking the pavement. Manon lifted the shade, and her jaw fell. "My God!" she breathed. "It's a whole truckload of them! And here they come, running up the walk!"

"What?" Michel stammered.

"Police, silly!" Manon cried, clapping her hands. "What did you think? Mademoiselle Rose told them she had nothing to say to them. And they kept coming back! Now they're for it!"

The bell rang and did not stop, and at the same time there came a heavy pounding at the entrance door below. As they stared at each other, they heard the sound of the bolt being flung back with a great clatter, the tread of men entering, and the indistinct murmur of voices. Léah uttered a little scream, and covered her ears with her hands. She had become deathly pale, so that Manon seized her in her arms and whispered urgently to her, "But Léah, it's nothing. It's only the police. They're on our side. Léah baby, don't cry!"

Pé was looking pale himself, but he muttered in disgust, "Girls!"

The voices grew louder and louder, until a great cry penetrated to them, and Michel realized that Maman Rose was shouting. A man's angry voice answered in the same tone. What were they saying? The floor quivered, as if heavy weights were being thrown about below and shaking the building. Then there was a loud thud that made the window rattle. "They've opened the door!" Manon cried. "They're on the steps!" Now they could hear what the voices were saying. A man was sputtering, "What? What? The woman's mad, I tell you!" Another male voice thundered, "Move along there!" Maman Rose, her voice easily distinguishable from the rest, cried, "Violation of domicile! Arrest them all!" "Come *on!*" someone urged. Then there was a roar in which Michel could make out only the words, "No, you don't!" And all during this heated exchange strange blooms of light flared along the edges of the window shade.

"Oh dear!" Manon cried. "Léah, be a good girl and stop carrying on. No one's going to lock you up. I want to see this. Michel, put out the light!"

Michel did as he was told, and Manon, forcing Léah into a sitting position on the bed, kneeled at the window, tugged at the shade until it rose a few inches, then slid the window up. A current of icy air swept into the room and set the curtain billowing. With the room dark behind them, Manon, Michel, and Pé kneeled and looked out.

A cluster of men moved down the walk toward the street, arguing and waving their arms. In the darkness of the garden Michel could not distinguish their movements clearly, but it seemed to him, from the scuffing and heavy breathing, that someone was being shoved along and was resisting. Then they reached the gate, which opened with a shove, and milled about the car parked in front. In the center of the knot of bodies Michel could see two men wearing civilian hats; one of them was waving his fists over his head and shouting, "But they opened the door themselves! They let me in, I tell you!" This was M. Konrad; he seemed beside himself with anger, and was glaring at a man in uniform, who seemed to be the one in authority. Around them were perhaps a dozen more policemen, shifting their feet and watching. The raw light from the street lamp picked out the metal of their insignia and glimmered palely on their leather harness. As Michel watched, someone climbed onto the running board of an open trucklike vehicle stationed in the middle of the street with its headlights on, and held up a dark object; then there came a blinding glare that threw the group into mountainous relief. It was followed by another flash from the fence, where the other photographer had perched himself. Maman Rose was nowhere to be seen; but then, from the doorway below him, Michel heard her cry, "Breaking and entering! Arrest them all!" Where was his aunt? After a while Michel made out the figures of two women huddled by the gate alongside the knot of policemen, their coated backs to him. They stood silently watching M. Konrad.

The man in uniform laid his hand on M. Konrad's arm and said something that Michel could not hear.

M. Konrad let out an anguished roar. "It's a lie! What door, in the name of sanity? All you have to do is look at it!"

"You broke your way in here!" Maman Rose shouted across the garden. "Arrest him, officer!"

In fury M. Konrad pushed his way to the gate, where several of the men in uniform grabbed him. "Yes, arrest me," he shouted back. "Arrest me, and we'll have you tell your lying story under oath! We'll see who goes to jail!"

"Breaking and entering!"

"Arrest me! I want to be arrested!"

By now lights had gone on in the houses across the street, and a number of people had thrust their heads out. Others had gathered on the sidewalk opposite to watch. In the midst of the general clamor, Michel saw the officer in charge remove his cap and pass his hand wearily over his forehead.

Another voice arose, stilling the rest abruptly. The other man with a civilian hat had pushed his way forward, and called out, "Odette! Give us the boy, and we'll drop the charges against you. It's not too late. That's what we came to tell you."

"That's Monsieur Immermann," Manon whispered. But Michel had already recognized the dark face with the great beaked nose.

"Never!" came Maman Rose's answer.

"Be reasonable, Odette," M. Immermann called back. "For your own sake. If it gets to court, you'll go to prison. We don't want to do that. This is your last chance!"

All those in the street had turned to face the doorway of the Nursery. They stood still, waiting for the reply. Michel felt his chest tighten; he could hardly breathe. They were talking about him.

When Maman Rose spoke, it was no longer in a shout, but in a tone of quiet resolution.

"Then I'll go to prison," she said. "I'll rot in prison the rest of my life, but I won't give him up."

The door slammed, and the bolt slid into place.

A man standing in the middle of the street, with the glare of the police car lights on him, shouted, "Bravo!" Several of the police turned menacingly toward the sound, and the man faded into the shadows beyond.

M. Immermann straightened up slowly, and spread his hands in a gesture of resignation. M. Konrad turned again to the police officer, and the circle of uniforms closed in again as the two argued. They had lowered their voices, and Michel could no longer hear what was said. After what seemed to be a long time, M. Konrad shoved his hat back on his head, and said, "All right, then. If she does, I'll sue her for false arrest. But I insist that you examine that door."

The police officer spoke, gesticulating earnestly. M. Konrad shrugged and opened his car door. The two women came forward, along with M. Immermann. A moment later the motor started, the car lights came on, and the car moved down the street, disappearing in the distance. The police made shooing motions toward the onlookers, who sidled away reluctantly, looking over their shoulders. Then the officer uttered a command, and the police boarded their vehicle, which headed toward the square; those standing in the rear continued waving their arms in dismissal to the men in the street.

Pé was asleep. He lay in his bed, the covers pulled up to his neck, one arm flung back over his head. Lying on his side in his own bed, Michel watched the blanket rise and fall gently with his friend's breathing, and remembered Pé's hopeless longing for his mother in America. His mother had abandoned him shamelessly, and run off with an American soldier. Since then nothing had been heard of her, and Pé had stayed on at the Nursery. There was no one to claim him. How lucky he was!

Michel was heartbroken. How brief had been his few moments of happiness! A piece of cake, a bit of laughter, the beginning of a toast—and then had come the frightening interruption, which had ruined the party. But that was not the worst blow. That had come after the police had sent M. Konrad about his business, and Maman

Rose, flushed with her victory, had returned to him again. It was then that she had let slip the remark that had left him stunned. As soon as Michel had testified, she had said, he would go in M. Béjart's car to the Temple, and would leave that same night for Paris. He had stared at her, unable to remonstrate; and she, interpreting his look correctly, had swept him into her arms and murmured that she knew how hard it was for him, but it was all for the best. Touville was simply not safe for him, not until the court had given its verdict, which wouldn't be for several weeks, in all likelihood. He did understand, didn't he?

There had been nothing to say but that he understood; but inside himself he repeated over and over, One day! He had come home for one day! This was his Christmas vacation, in which he had promised himself to think through his dreadful problem, perhaps even make a new confession and do penance for his sin. This was his homecoming, his dream of love and affection in the midst of his "family"!

Tomorrow night he would be on his way to Paris. Then would begin again those lonely days at the Mother House, until it was time to return to Cassarate. He would arrive there as he had left, tormented in conscience, unrested from his ordeal, to begin the torture all over again. There would be no respite until Easter, months away. But he would be expelled long before then.

For a moment he had the wild impulse to rush into Maman Rose's room, throw himself at her feet and beg her to— But it was no use. Maman Rose would not listen to him. Only a few months ago he had pleaded with her to run away with him where no one could find them, and she had dismissed the idea with so many adult reasons and pointed out so many insuperable difficulties that it was impossible to insist. She would do the same now. And there would be no change in the plan: He would have to testify tomorrow, he would be taken to the Temple Dames, then to the train, which would take him to Paris. Whether or not his soul rebelled at the thought of it, he would stay at the Mother House until it was time to move on. Whether or not it meant detection, disgrace, and expulsion, he would find himself returning to St. Louis Gonzaga and the old agony. There was nothing he could do. He was only a boy, caught up in something too big for him.

He lay back in his bed, thinking of Kevin and the sad look on his face as they parted.

Mlle Rose could not sleep. In spite of herself, she was worried about the coming trial. Always in the past, in her dealings with that Konrad and the labyrinth of the law, she had been able to see one more step left to take, if her present action should fail. But this was the end. Tomorrow she either won or lost. It was for this reason that she had played her trump card, had allowed herself to be "forced" to bring Michel to court. It had got her in wrong with Mother Veronica, who was against the idea at all costs. Never before had she gone against the reverend mother, who had insisted that while the court might hold her in contempt for failing to produce Michel as ordered, this would not affect the course of the hearing, which would be conducted on the merits of the issue. She could win just as well without Michel as with him. And if she lost, she would not have exposed Michel to their view, where photographers could take pictures of him, and thus make hiding him in the future immeasurably more difficult. She could not expect Michel to hold his own, the nun had said, against the kind of questioning he would be subjected to in that court. But for once Mlle Rose had not yielded; her boy would not only hold his own, she had replied, he would confound them all by his testimony. She was not afraid of the contempt charge. That wasn't it. She needed Michel to win, and with him she *would* win. As for the photographers, they were not allowed in court; and she would make sure that Michel made his entrance into the courthouse through a side door, unnoticed. The decision had led to a coolness between the two women, but that couldn't be helped. It was Mlle Rose's decision to make, and she had made it.

Now, suddenly, she was not so sure. How pale and run-down Michel had looked on his arrival at the Nursery! He was a bundle of nerves. Could he resist a Maître Gens? Had she done the right thing to bring him to Touville? Was it too late to follow Mother Veronica's advice, and send him away? She lay in bed, propped up by pillows at her back, frowning and staring vacantly before her. By now the actors in tomorrow's drama were asleep, each secure in his own plans for the coming battle. Only she was awake, tormented by her doubt, wondering whether she had not made a colossal mistake, which might ruin everything. She tried to picture Michel standing before the court, a small, pale figure, towered over by relentless men in their black gowns and with wily, experienced faces. Could he do what she had dreamed he would, raise his boyish voice and defy them with the certainty of his desire to stay with her, to be what she had made him? Had she put too much on his shoulders?

Perhaps it would be better, she thought, to have Michel questioned privately, in the judges' chambers. Just Michel, the judges, and the lawyers. That would make Michel less nervous, and do away with the goldfish-bowl atmosphere that came from being in the center of hundreds of faces ringing him around. It meant, of course, that she would not be present; but once the interrogation started, she could not help her boy anyway, and in the judges' chambers Maître Cauchet would be there to see he got fair play. The more she thought of it, the better she liked the idea. She would sleep on it, she decided, and speak to Cauchet in the morning. There was still time for the request for a private hearing to be made.

Somewhat cheered by the thought, Mlle Rose got out of bed. She went to her dressing table, opened a drawer, and took out an envelope. The letter had arrived over a month ago, and since then she had read it a hundred times. She studied the return address on the flap, which was that of a street in Paris. There, in a narrow, slanting hand, was the name of her disinherited daughter: Renée Mégret.

The letter was brief. It addressed her as "Dearest Mother," it announced that her husband Jules had graduated engineering school with honors, and was now working with a large company that offered every prospect of advancement. They had had a difficult time at first, but things were well with them now. And—this was the big news!—she had had a baby daughter, who was now three weeks old, and the cutest darling in the world! She had named her Odette. She hoped her mother would write to her as proof of her forgiveness, and that all would be well between them as before.

For a long time Mlle Rose stood reading and rereading the letter. When she finally put it back in the envelope, her eyes were wet.

She was still weeping silently as she opened her door, crossed the hall, and entered Michel's room. He was asleep. She stood beside him, studying his face in the pale light that filtered through the window. How innocent and young he looked! Pale and somewhat drawn, yes, but with a breath-catching purity that shone through the flesh. Little David, she thought, about to face Goliath. Well, it was in his hands now, his and God's. She had done everything she could. Now it was up to him.

As she turned to go out, she noticed something thin and white at the foot of the bed. It was a piece of heavy string, tied to the rung of the footboard and disappearing under the blanket. She gave a slight tug at it. It tightened but did not come out. Michel stirred and moaned softly. Now what on earth was *that* for? she wondered.

12

❧

I T WAS a quarter to one.

There were perhaps twenty people across the street from the Nursery. A few sat on the steps of the houses, while the others stood about in small groups, talking. Michel could see the frosty vapor of their breath. All wore heavy coats and were muffled up against the cold, standing hunched with their backs to the wind. Some had cameras slung over their shoulders. There were two or three women among them. Those passing by looked at them and turned to stare at the Nursery.

Michel let his hand drop from the window shade and sat down on the edge of his bed. He felt trapped. At intervals throughout the morning he had peeked out and seen how the number of reporters and photographers had gradually increased, until they took up all the sidewalk area across the street and scarcely left room for others to go past. Some had even had the nerve to ring the bell of the Nursery and ask for an interview with Mlle Rose or with him. They had been sent about their business, and now they were congregated in front, waiting for him to come out to go to the courthouse.

In a few minutes he would be leaving. His suitcase, which he had never really unpacked—he had merely opened it last night to remove his pajamas and toothbrush—was already downstairs. He was fully dressed. His coat, with the muffler and mittens in the pockets, was lying across his chair. They would come for him at one o'clock, and all he had to do was to pick up his coat and walk out. He sat quietly, looking about the room, and thinking over the events of the morning.

From the dark before dawn, when the creaking of the gate announcing the arrival of the mothers with their children had awakened him, he had scarcely had a moment of privacy. Pé, aroused at the same time, had begun an animated conversation about his school, and was full of questions about the school that Michel went to. "You can tell *me*, Michel," he urged. "I wouldn't tell anybody." He had been hurt when Michel refused, but got over it when Léah and Manon entered, full of excitement, with the morning paper. They had all huddled over it together, marveling at the photograph spread over half the front page. It had been taken from the street and showed the scene Michel had looked at the night before, but in reverse. There, in front of the gate, was the knot of policemen surrounding M. Konrad and M. Immermann, the two women standing forlornly off to one side, the other photographer perched on the fence, his camera poised before his face; in the background, on the steps, an indistinct figure that had to be Maman Rose; and up above, in Michel's window, three heads side by side, hardly rising above the level of the sill. A tiny white arrow pointed to the figure in the center of the group in the street, that of a man with his arms flung over his head and his face distorted with anger, with the legend, "M. Louis Konrad." Another arrow pointed out Maman Rose. And still another, placed against the front of the Nursery over the second-story window, asked the question: "Is One of These the Mystery Boy?"

Fortunately, Michel realized upon studying the picture, it was impossible to distinguish the features of any of the three. The heads were merely three dark blobs against the lighter color of the shade. Nonetheless, their indiscretion led to a lecture from Maman Rose, who came in shortly afterwards. She had not realized the extent to which they had exposed themselves. Michel had to be very, very careful, she said, not to let his picture be taken by anybody. With the kind of publicity Konrad had been giving their case, Michel's portrait would be flashed across the front pages of newspapers throughout France, and there would be no hiding him after that. Maman Rose seemed disgruntled this morning, and from the remarks she let drop, Michel understood that her annoyance was caused by the article accompanying the photograph. It was openly hostile to her, quoting M. Konrad to the effect that Mlle Rose had summoned the police on false pretenses as one of her self-dramatizing stunts, but had not dared press charges on her claim of "violation of domicile," knowing she could not substantiate it. And the reporter had gone so far as to refer to her as "the fantastic Mlle Rose."

At nine o'clock Maître Cauchet appeared and grilled Michel for an hour. He was not content to repeat the warnings Maman Rose had expressed the night before, but had Michel run through what he called "a little rehearsal." He had Michel stand with his legs apart and his hands behind his back, his head held high, and fired questions at him. Michel apparently passed this test well, for the lawyer patted him on the shoulder and called him a bright boy.

After that people came and went with scarcely a halt. The Nursery staff, who had already left for the day when Michel arrived last night, now clamored to see him. The first was Annette, who entered with a broad smile, but became emotional after her greeting and clutched him fiercely to her, stammering endearments. Michel, almost smothered in the cook's grasp, was also overcome and found his cheeks wet when she had gone, yielding her place to the head nurse, Mme Bordat. Then came Mlle Pasquier, whose hair was now, astonishingly, bright yellow and peeped out in curls underneath her white cap. Marie, the washerwoman, her mottled red arms bare to the shoulder. One of the sewing ladies, the other having fallen ill with a "weakness of the chest" and retired to live on her pension. A new nurse whom Michel had never seen before, who said she was dying to meet him, that he was every bit as handsome as people had said, and that her friends wouldn't believe her when she told them. Dr. Peyrefitte, whose beard was now more white than gray but whose breath was as disagreeable as ever. Félicité, who entered three or four times and stood looking silently at him. And of course, Manon, and Pé and Léah, who dashed in and out in great excitement.

For the last half-hour, however, he had been alone. Maman Rose had had some lunch sent up to him, with strict orders that he was to be left in peace, to take his nourishment and rest a bit before the trial. Michel had spent this time in forcing down a few mouthfuls of food, in peeking out at the photographers massed before the Nursery, and in taking leave of his room. He had the premonition he would never see it again. He let his eyes wander over every detail to impress it into his memory, telling himself at the same time that he was being silly. It was inconceivable that they should lose the trial; and even if they did, it was clear that Maman Rose had no intention of giving him up. He would be safe at Cassarate, and sooner or later he would be able to come home for a visit. Yet his heart was heavy, and he found his eyes dwelling on his room with peculiar insistence.

The trial, which last night had seemed so far away in his joy at coming home, now loomed over him as a menace that turned his blood cold. France. Maman Rose. Catholic. Those were the three magic words he must never let out of his mind for a moment. M. Konrad would be there. And his aunt. And the great Maître Gens, who would shake his finger at him as Maître Cauchet had done, but this time it would be the real thing, and shout, "Now, do you mean to tell me . . . ?" But he would have to resist, to defy him, to stick to his guns no matter what. France. Maman Rose. Catholic. If only— But he must not think of that. There was no way out. It had all been arranged. He would testify at the trial, he would go in M. Béjart's car to the Temple, he would take the train to Paris, and then, when the time came . . . Don't come back, Kevin had said. But what else could he do?

Manon, wearing Maman Rose's blue nurse's cape draped around her shoulders, appeared at his door. "It's time," she said.

How quickly the last quarter-hour had gone! He was full of things he had to think over. But it was time. He slipped on his coat and followed Manon down the hall. At the foot of the stairs he saw a strange man standing just inside the entrance door. The man was bulky in a thick coat; his hat, which he held in his hand, had left a red welt across his forehead. Was he guarding the door? The man stared at Michel in open curiosity, then closed one eye in a wink. Michel turned away self-consciously.

The children were in the dining hall. Michel heard their voices and the rattle of dishes. As he passed the doorway, the nurses saw him and came hurrying out. Pé and Léah came out of the kitchen, then all the others came crowding around. By the time he got to the back door, he was surrounded by the entire household. "Are you going already, Michel?" "Good luck, Michel." Léah kissed him, and turned away blushing. Pé shook his hand. "Good-bye, Michel."

Maman Rose came out of her office, pulling on her gloves. She looked down the hall at them and called softly, "Michel!"

He came to her, and she put her gloved hands to the sides of his head and looked at him earnestly. "We'll say good-bye here, Michel," she said. "You're going with M. Béjart. You know what you have to do. There's only one more thing. After you've testified, they'll let you go and you'll walk out with M. Béjart. But before you leave, I want you to come to me where I'm sitting in the court and give me a kiss. You must do this in front of everybody. It's important, so don't forget it. You know why, don't you?"

"Yes," he said.

"Be brave, Michel," she said, embracing him. "This is the last time. Now go quickly."

She released him and walked toward the front door, which the strange man opened for her. She went out and the man followed her, slamming the door loudly behind them. "Now!" Manon said. Michel went toward the back door through the crowd that put out their hands to touch him as he went by. Manon had opened the door, and stood waiting for him. Michel crossed the deserted playground with Manon beside him. There was an automobile in the alley, its motor running; M. Béjart sat at the wheel. Manon unlocked the back gate, and Michel sprang into the seat beside the old gentleman. He had barely time to wave at Manon before the car started. M. Béjart did not speak; his eyes were fixed ahead, on the figure of a man who stood at the end of the alley in a curious attitude. He had his back to them and was bent slightly forward staring down Place St. Lazare, at the same time holding his hand up with the palm facing them. Then the hand signaled to come on, the man stepped aside; as the car reached him, he opened the back door and sprang in.

"Slide down in your seat," M. Béjart said, as the car moved into Place St. Lazare. Michel did so, and the car picked up speed. In a moment they had crossed the square and turned left. Behind them Michel could hear a confused shout in which he could distinguish a note of anger. M. Béjart chuckled softly and looked at Michel. "All right, lad. You can sit up now. We got away from them."

The man in back grunted. He must be a policeman, Michel thought. And the other one too. It was all arranged. How easily Maman Rose had fooled that crowd! M. Béjart gave a brief peep on his horn. The woman sitting on the rear seat of the car in front of them turned around and looked back. It was Maman Rose. She smiled and faced front again.

M. Béjart was fuming. He brandished his walking stick as he cried, "The scoundrels! Oh, the scoundrels!" His hat was askew and his overcoat had come unbuttoned; through the opening Michel could see his fat gold watch dangling loose on its chain.

"Are you hurt?" the man in the black braided uniform said.

M. Béjart uttered a contemptuous snort. "Hurt?" he said, bristling. "Ask *them* who's hurt! I almost did for one of them. I hit something, anyway. Riffraff! Did you see that? Almost jostled me off my feet."

The man in the black uniform said no, he had opened the door when the police guard rapped, and had only seen people running.

"Well, I did," M. Béjart said, breathing hard.

"Calm yourself, sir," the man said.

"Alongside the courthouse, and under the eyes of the police! There were three or four of them, with their cameras. Did they take your picture?" he asked, turning to Michel.

"I don't know," Michel answered. "I—I don't think so."

It had all happened so fast that he was not sure of anything. From the first moment of approach to the courthouse, he had been filled with amazement, as if the tumultuous scene he was witnessing were something out of a movie, and not happening to *him*. Maman Rose's car swinging into the small plaza before the building with the tall, round columns, and the faces in the crowd turning toward her. Then the open mouths and the fingers pointing, and the cry of voices merging into a dull threatening roar as a wave of humanity surged toward the car, which had stopped before the steps. Flashbulbs were going off around Maman Rose's car as M. Béjart drove past the edge of the crowd facing the other way and pulled up at a side door, where a police officer was standing. M. Béjart said something he did not catch, and he was running toward the door, now open, seeing with a quick turn of his head that there were several men pointing cameras at him on the broad sidewalk that had seemed deserted at the moment of opening the car door, that the man who had been on the back seat had thrust out an arm and with the other was striking at something with his hat, and just catching out of the corner of his eye the glitter of M. Béjart's cane as it swung in an arc and hearing the sharp *thwack* as of wood on metal. He had plunged into a dark hall, where the man in the black uniform had seized him by the shoulders and bundled him into the room where they now were.

He had never seen M. Béjart like this. "Ha!" the old gentleman cried, stamping his foot. "I let him have it, by God! Rushing up like that! Where did they come from, I'd like to know?"

"Calm yourself, sir," the man in the black uniform said again.

"Thirty years I've had this cane," M. Béjart cried in satisfaction, "and I've never appreciated it until now. A good piece of wood, that. See here." He pointed to the dent.

"I must beg of you," the man in uniform said.

"Yes, yes," M. Béjart said. "Of course. Court of law. I understand."

"Your watch, sir," Michel said.

"Eh?" M. Béjart looked down at the watch dangling free, seized it and put it to his ear. A slow smile spread over his fine features. "Well, we gave them what for, eh Michel? A blow for freedom, what? I wouldn't have missed it for the world. But a bit too stimulating for the system." He looked about the room, taking in the dark, paneled walls and the ancient chairs lined stiffly against them. "Where are we, sir?"

"Assizes, first chamber," the man said. "Across the hall, that is. Do you hear that?"

Michel now noticed a door in the opposite wall. Through it came an indistinct sound of voices and scraping feet. "Trying to get in," the man said. "Court was jammed hours ago. They even brought their lunches, some of them. The others will wish they had. Is this the boy?" He turned friendly, curious eyes on Michel, who looked down, confused.

The door opened, and another man in braided uniform thrust his head and shoulders through. "Everything in order," the first man said.

"They'll be coming in now," the man in the door said. He cocked his head, listening to the noise in the hall behind him. "Madhouse," he said with a grimace, and slipped out, shutting the door behind him.

Michel had been waiting for two hours, and was bored, restless, and cold. At first M. Béjart, still animated from his encounter with the photographers, had chatted with the court attendant, and Michel had listened, admiring the old gentleman's distinguished manner and the precision of his language. But after a while the attendant had yawned and gone to the opposite door, where he stood listening to the murmur outside and gazing vacantly at the floor. M. Béjart seemed offended. He addressed a few questions to Michel, who answered, "Yes, sir," or "No, sir," and then lapsed into silence, occasionally looking at his watch. What were they waiting for? He asked M. Béjart, and was told that the trial was going on. The attendant looked up at this. "They'll call you, never fear, sonny," he said. Michel sat still, looking around the gloomy room, feeling the damp chill slowly penetrate his body. His fingers were cold, and he put his mittens on. His hands trembled as he did so.

The door opened suddenly, and the other man in uniform thrust in his head and said briefly, "All right."

"Come along, little one," the first attendant said, straightening up quickly.

Michel got to his feet, and so did M. Béjart, who said, "Now remember, look for me when you're through. I'll be standing just inside the door."

In that instant Michel was filled with panic. It was not what M. Béjart had said, but the realization that the moment he had been dreading ever since he had received Maman Rose's letter in Cassarate was *now;* that he would have to go out into that hall full of strange, shuffling noises, and then into a courtroom filled with people who would stare at him greedily and say to themselves, So *that's* the mystery boy! And the judges would question him, and he would say stupid things because his mind was as stiff and cold as his fingers, and he had forgotten everything that Maman Rose had told him. He felt a wild impulse to run. But M. Béjart had already taken him by the arm, and the attendant had already opened the door and was looking at him impatiently, snapping his fingers.

Michel drew a deep, shuddering breath and walked through the doorway. The attendant took him by the hand and almost pulled him into the midst of a tightly packed cluster of men and women who stood facing a huge double door chased in gold. "The court, if you please!" the attendant cried, shouldering his way among them. They turned protesting faces toward him, faces which gaped with astonishment upon seeing Michel. "Here he is!" someone cried. By the time Michel had penetrated among them there was a hubbub of voices behind him, and a score of hands had reached out to touch him. In the press of bodies around him Michel stumbled and then recovered himself. He stifled a bleat of fear as their momentum shoved him through the door that the attendant, with the help of the other uniformed man who had reached it before them, managed to open at the right moment.

Michel took a step forward and stopped. He was in an enormous bowl of a room that to his first startled glance seemed filled halfway to the ceiling with human beings, who had turned their heads toward him and were craning, moving, shifting to see him better, in a silence that was more ominous than the noise outside. The room seemed to flow toward him, as if he were at the bottom of the bowl and those fixed, intent eyes had the weight of gravity behind them. Then he saw that a dais ran around three sides of the room and that those who had been seated on it had risen to look over the heads of those filling the floor seats in the center. As he took another step forward, urged by the attendant, the insistent ringing of a bell came from the far end of the room before him, where a row of men wearing black robes sat high behind desks on a raised platform. The judges, he thought. Behind them, against the back wall, stood men looking over the others' heads at him. Above them were two crossed flags against a dark, figured tapestry. He lowered his head in confusion and moved down the narrow aisle toward them, horribly oppressed by the weight of humanity on both sides. The attendant kept his hand on Michel's shoulder, waving the other before him and whispering harshly, "Be seated, gentlemen! Be seated, if you please!" A chorus of murmurs rose behind him, and a woman's voice said clearly, "Oh, the darling!"

Suddenly there was a sharp cry, and all heads skewed around front, where a woman had stood up and stretched forth her arms toward Michel, her face working and her mouth open. "Karl! Karl!" she cried. Michel stopped in his tracks, and shrank back as though she had touched him, although she was a good distance away. She was a middle-aged woman with marcelled gray hair under a black toque hat, and deep-sunk eyes full of tears. Was it his aunt? he wondered in astonishment. Why did she call him Karl? Karl was his father's name. A bell rang out, and the woman collapsed with a moan out of Michel's sight. Voices rose all about him. "What is it?" "What happened?" "Who is she?" The bell sounded again, and the judge in the center of the row of desks said angrily, "Another outburst like that, and I shall order the court cleared."

"No, no," several people muttered. Those who had risen sat down and all were still.

"Madame," the judge said, turning toward the woman who had cried out, "the court understands your emotion, but you must control yourself."

Incredibly, from beside the woman, a tall, bony figure uncoiled itself, and M. Konrad's voice said, "We beg the court's pardon. It will not happen again." Michel stared in fascination at that bald head, with the ladder of wrinkles continuing from the forehead high up the skull. He had seen M. Konrad last night, but in the dark and at a distance. He looked harmless enough now, amid the crowd. Then the woman *was* his aunt, if M. Konrad was speaking for her.

Michel had stopped in the aisle at the outcry. Now the attendant's lunge caught him off balance and almost spun him from his feet. The man had brushed Michel's shoulder in thrusting himself into a row of seats and seizing the coat lapels of a stout, swarthy man with glistening black hair, who struck at his hands and muttered viciously, "What are you doing? I beg of you! I've done nothing!"

"Your Honor!" the attendant cried, without relinquishing his grip, "this man has a camera! He was taking a picture!"

Now several things happened at once. A policeman came hurrying down the aisle toward them, as the swarthy man stumbled into the aisle and the attendant triumphantly held high a small, shiny object hardly larger than a cigarette lighter, while the judge pounded the bell and cried out, "Eject him! And confiscate his camera!" At the same time Michel, who had been staring in astonishment at this scene, was aware of a whisper at his side, which came from a man seated on the aisle only an arm's length away. Michel had noticed him before, for his strange, shriveled face and the terrible intensity of his eyes, which were like black coals amid a scattering of ashes. Now the man had leaned toward him and opened a toothless mouth to whisper, "Marc!"

He said Marc! Michel said to himself. The man had called him Marc! He stood rooted to the spot, unable to move as a clawlike hand reached out and took him by the wrist. This can't be happening, he thought, dazed. He was dreaming it. The commotion around him receded into some dim background of heavy breathing, pounding steps, and a voice in the distance shouting, "Take the film but give me back my camera!" That dreadful mouth with the pale gums had thrust itself forward and was slobbering, "Marc. My son. I'm your daddy." He felt his coat sleeve being pushed up and scraping fingers on his wrist. Why did nobody help him? He was surrounded by a sea of faces, and yet nobody saw that this monstrous creature with the prunelike head had slid off his seat and was kneeling before him, pushing, pushing, pushing at his sleeve, with those mad eyes only inches from his own. The image of death flashed across his mind. And then, like awakening from a nightmare, Maman Rose's voice cried out, "Who is that man? What's he doing there?"

Michel reeled back as the man's grip was suddenly loosed, everything swam into focus again, the bell rang, voices cried, "Outside!" the toothless man was being shoved violently up the aisle by the attendant; and looking up in a flood of relief, he saw to his left, in the front row of benches, Maman Rose standing, her green eyes ablaze, pointing her finger at him.

There was no transition. He was standing in the open space before the judges' desks, looking up at the five severe faces gazing down at him, outlined against the crossed flags. The judge in the center, the one with the great leonine head and the tiny white pointed beard, was saying, "By request of the defendant, this child will be questioned in judges' chambers. The court is recessed." Behind Michel was a loud murmur of disappointment. The judges stood up, and to Michel's right four black-robed figures also rose from a double tier of benches behind a polished counter, descended a step and walked toward him. One was Maître Cauchet, his face sternly impassive. Guided by a hand on his shoulder, Michel walked forward, up two steps to the dais, through a curtained door and into a dark, silent hall. A moment later he had entered a quiet, chair-filled room with a fireplace where a glowing bed of ashes gave out a grateful warmth. The hand pushed him into a chair by the fire, where he sat shivering, not daring to look around. He was thoroughly frightened.

A voice said, "Mr. President," and another answered, "Just a moment, sir, if you please."

Voices murmured, chairs scraped, there was a rustle of paper. "Thank God!" a deep voice said. Someone rubbed his hands together with a dry sound.

Louis Konrad looked at his watch. The judges would be out at least half an hour, he reasoned. He leaned back and said to Jules, "I'm going out for a minute. Look after Hannah and Rina, will you?" Jules nodded. Konrad stood up and stepped out into the aisle. As he moved toward the door, those seated in the audience followed him with their eyes and leaned toward each other to whisper. To the usher who stood with his back against the door he said, "Where did they take that man? The one who was molesting the boy?"

The usher shrugged. The policeman had taken him in charge. With that mob in the hall he hadn't dared leave the door for a moment.

Konrad stepped out as the usher opened the door for him. The crowd in the hall surged toward him. "There's Monsieur Konrad," someone said. "What's happening?" another voice asked. Konrad answered that the court had recessed, and pushed his way through. He asked his question of a man at the edge of the crowd, and the man pointed down the hall to his right and asked eagerly, "What did he do?" Konrad answered that the man had created a disturbance, and walked down the hall.

In the great columned lobby he found a knot of men and women milling about a bench under one of the columns; in the center of the group was the tall figure of a policeman who seemed to be engaged in a heated discussion with someone. Coming closer, Konrad could see that he was talking to a young woman, and that the man with the strange, wrinkled face who had seized Michel by the wrist was sitting on the bench a few feet away, staring woodenly at the floor and now and then running the tip of his tongue over his lips. Konrad pushed his way into the midst of the crowd; he was curious about the person who had done such a mad thing in court. Whatever his motive, the man had seemed to know Michel, and might furnish some information about him.

The policeman recognized him, and touched his cap. "There's the man, Monsieur Konrad," he said, nodding toward the bench. "This lady's his daughter. She wants to take him home. Says he's harmless. But I don't know, after attacking the boy the way he did."

The young woman had turned to Konrad at the policeman's salute. She was dark, almost dusky in complexion, like a gypsy, with full sensuous lips and a straight, flared nose. In her mid-twenties, he guessed, although the lines about her eyes made her seem older. In spite of the icy wind that moved through the lobby, her face was moist with perspiration, and her hair, black and coarse, straggled down over her ears. As the policeman spoke, she pushed at her hair with a distracted gesture and cried out, "Please, sir, tell him to let us go." There was despair in her voice, and her eyes had the dumb appeal of a tortured animal. Pity stirred in him.

"There was no real harm done," he said to the policeman. "He only touched the boy's wrist. But I'm curious to know why."

"He didn't hurt him," the woman cried. "He wouldn't hurt a child for anything in the world. Let me take him home. We don't let him out. Only today he got away from us, because of the trial. He's been reading about it in the papers, and he got the idea—"

"Yes?" Konrad said, as she stopped.

She made a vague gesture. "That it was Marc. His son. My brother."

"Marc?" said the man on the bench, stirring and looking about him eagerly.

Behind Konrad someone muttered, "He's crazy. Look at him."

The woman started and said fiercely, "He's *not* crazy. How would you be if you lost a son?"

"Here!" said the policeman. "Let's have no remarks."

"You're Monsieur Konrad?" the woman said to him. "The one who's looking for that boy?" At Konrad's nod, she said, "Then maybe you'll understand. You're a Jew, like us. Maybe the same thing happened to him as to Marc. No, no, Daddy," she cried to the man on the bench, who had moaned and tried to get up. "It isn't Marc, it's a different boy. We'll be going home soon." She produced a handkerchief from her pocket and dabbed at the sweat about her nose. "He's been like this ever since the war ended. Before that he was like everybody else. We're from Algiers. He had a business there. We're two sisters, and the boy. I won't say his name because he gets excited. My mother died when the boy was born. She was too old for it. I'm the younger of the girls, and I was already thirteen. It hit my father hard, but he got over it because he had the boy. My father adored him. You know, a son to carry on the name. It meant everything to him. Well, when the boy was old enough we took a trip to France, all of us, and the war broke out and trapped us in Marseilles. We couldn't get back home. We managed to get along and stay together until the Germans moved into Free France, and then we had to go into hiding. My father was wild with worry about M— I mean, about the boy. He finally put him in with a family he knew, Catholics they were, and we thought he was safe. But when the war was ending and the Germans left, he went back and found that the family had disappeared. All we ever learned was that they had moved north. But they didn't take the boy. A neighbor told my father a priest had come and got him."

The spectators had become quiet and were listening intently. Another one, Konrad thought. The same old story.

"We looked everywhere," the woman said. "We went to every church in Marseilles. Nobody knew anything. He was still all right then," pointing to her father. "There was still hope. His boy was alive. It was just a question of finding him. Finally someone told us that in Nice there was a kind of summer camp where there were forty or fifty orphan children that priests were taking care of. Some of the children were Jewish, they said. They hadn't been called for after the war. I went there with my father. It was on a hill that's called Piol. A house and a garden with a wall around it. We could look through the gate, and it was true, there was a group of children playing and doing exercises, and there was a priest directing them and blowing a whistle. We called to him, and he came over. We told him what we wanted, that our boy had got separated from us during the war and that we had been told that there were Jewish children among this group. And we asked permission to enter and see if we could identify him among the others. The priest said he couldn't take that responsibility himself, and that he would go ask his superior. He entered the house, and we waited about ten minutes. I wanted to call my brother's name through the fence. If he was there he would come and we would recognize him. But Father said no, we would make the priest angry. I shouldn't have listened to him. The priest came back. He was very polite, but he couldn't let us in. His superior was not in, but would be there on Sunday morning. If we would come back on Sunday, we could talk to him and would probably be allowed in. This was a Thursday. On Sunday we returned. This time my sister came with us. We found the house closed, boarded in. There was no sign of the children or of the priests. There was another house nearby. We went there and rapped on the door. The woman who answered told us that on Thursday night two buses had come and had taken the children away."

A murmur arose from the crowd. The woman glanced at them defiantly and said, with a gesture toward the man on the bench, "He's been like that ever since. He went berserk, and we had to struggle with him to get him home. Now he slips out every chance he gets and looks for his boy. He looks at their wrists because my brother had a birthmark there. On the left wrist. A small mark shaped like a pear. But he's harmless, don't you see? He wouldn't hurt his boy."

"My God!" the policeman said. Several voices spoke up. "Let them go." "The poor old man." "No wonder."

Konrad felt sick inside. "Here," he said, producing a scrap of paper and a pencil. "Write down your name and address. If I come across anything . . ."

The woman shrugged and made a grimace. "Forty million Frenchmen," she said. "But all right." She placed the paper against the column and wrote. "Here," she said. Konrad glanced at what she had written and put the paper in his pocket. "Just you and your sister," he said. "How do you live?"

"How do you think?" she replied, with a touch of defiance. "We get along. You don't have to worry about us. Come on, Daddy," she said. "We're going home."

The policeman made no move to stop them. Konrad pushed his way through the crowd and returned to the courtroom.

An electric stir ran through the audience. Three-quarters of an hour had gone by since the court recessed. During that time hardly anyone had left his place; they had all settled back and talked quietly among themselves. Now the curtained door through which the judges had disappeared opened partway and stopped; for a couple of minutes it stayed in that position, moving slightly as though someone had his hand on the knob on the other side. The spectators craned their heads and watched. After a long while the door opened and an usher appeared, followed by Michel. A murmur arose, and the boy, looking up startled as though he had forgotten the existence of those waiting in the courtroom, shrank back momentarily.

Konrad drank in his features. How ironical it was! he thought. To have labored all these years, to have forced the resourceful Mlle Rose to produce the boy in court, and to be obliged to sit helpless while the boy walked out under his very nose! And with a court order in his pocket authorizing him to take the child into his custody at any time and wherever found! But it would only be for a little while, he thought grimly. And now at least he knew what Michel looked like. White skin, almost girlish in its purity; light brown hair, rebelliously curled, with golden reflections at the tips; wide-set gray eyes. These he had expected from the descriptions given him by the Immermanns and others. But he had never imagined the sheer beauty of the boy, the brilliance of those eyes now filled with panic, the transparency of the flesh. The image of Karl Benedek as a child, Hannah had told him at the boy's first appearance, when she had been shocked out of her calm and risen to her feet crying out her brother's name.

After the first excited whisper an absolute silence had fallen over the audience. All watched as the boy crossed the judges' dais toward them, the usher at his side. A man hurried down the aisle; an elegant old gentleman with a pale, fine face, blue eyes, a bristly white mustache—M. Béjart. The liaison man, no doubt. Rage filled Konrad as he watched the old crank approach the boy. They would walk up the aisle, disappear through the door, and his heartbreaking task would begin all over again, no matter what the verdict was. It was all Konrad could do to keep his face composed, with the Rose woman only a few feet away across the aisle and no doubt looking at him mockingly.

But no, he was mistaken; she was not looking at him at all. Her eyes were fixed on the boy as he passed by, and with what seemed to be very much like surprise in her face. As Michel passed between Konrad and Mlle Rose, Konrad saw him glance quickly at her and look away again; and she, half rising, opened her mouth as if to speak and remained in that attitude as the boy went up the aisle with Béjart and out the door.

Jules had seen it too. "What's eating her?" he said to Konrad, leaning forward.

The lawyers were coming out. There was a polite hesitation at the door, then Maître Gens's tall figure appeared, followed by Cauchet, Lanson, and Tercy. Maître Gens went immediately to his bench and whispered to Maître Paul, who had remained behind and had spent the time of recess busily writing among his papers. Konrad saw Paul's head jerk up and the look of incredulity that crossed his face. What did it mean? Konrad wondered. But Jules said urgently, "Look at Cauchet!" And Konrad, turning his head, saw that Mlle Rose's lawyer, his face pale and stern, was bent over speaking softly in her ear; and that her face had blanched and her lips begun to tremble.

What could have happened? Konrad was about to rise and approach the lawyers' bench when the usher cried, "The court!" the judges filed in, all stood up and sank down again as the judges took their places and President Bouhours said, "The court is in session." He would have to wait, Konrad decided. Cauchet hurried past. The Rose woman had sunk into her seat, her chin lowered on her chest, staring straight ahead. Was he mistaken, or were there tears in her eyes?

"May the court please." Maître Gens had risen.

"Maître Gens," President Bouhours said.

A sigh ran around the courtroom. The great lawyer from Paris was about to begin his argument. This was the moment all had been waiting for.

"Gentlemen," Maître Gens said to the judges, "the case that concerns us today is indeed a strange one. I have become familiar with it only recently. My colleagues Lanson and Paul, seated beside me, have followed its astonishing ramifications from the beginning. They have asked me to join them today, hoping by our united efforts to put an end to an affair which has become a public scandal.

"That this matter goes far beyond the simple guardianship of a child is amply attested to by the repercussions it has aroused in your fair city. No crime has been committed. The defendant, Mademoiselle Odette Rose, is accused of a delict, the non-presentation of a child under the provisions of Article 357 of the Penal Code. She is not a Bluebeard, a Landru. Why then do the newspapers of Touville, and indeed all of France, follow the course of this case on their front pages? Why this extraordinary interest on the part of the public, which has filled our audience chamber to overflowing and left hundreds in the street, exchanging rumors and awaiting the court's decision? Is it not because we all know what has never been openly said? Is it not because the dispute between two women over the guardianship of a child, which is surely a private matter, touches upon something else, which is the domain of all of us? It is time that the true motivations of the defendant be examined. It is time that her actions be seen in their true light. It is time that what has been the subject of gossip, rumor, and innuendo emerge before you, backed by incontestable evidence, so that you may give it its due weight in the decision that is yours to make.

"Gentlemen, you have heard the testimony of Madame Hannah Lindner, civil party in this painful affair, who has come from Israel to give her statement. Mademoiselle Rose has recounted for you her part and justifications. Most important, for the first time in the years that this matter has been the subject of legal procedures, the boy himself has been brought forward, and in the private hearing just concluded has made surprising revelations, which substantiate the argument I am going to put before you.

"The facts are these. In 1938 Dr. and Madame Karl Benedek, fleeing Nazi persecution in their native Austria, found asylum in France, settling in Puy-le-Duc, suburb of Touville. They were Jews. They were attached to their religion and practiced it. A child, Michel, was born to them in April 1941, and true to their beliefs they had their son circumcised. Such an action cannot be construed other than as a clear indication of their wish to see their child grow up in the cult of his parents. In 1941, in countries to which the Nazi racial philosophy had penetrated, to circumcise children was to mark them with an indelible sign exposing them to the persecutions to which, at that time, the Semitic race was subject.

"On February fourteenth, 1944, Dr. Benedek was arrested by the Gestapo, imprisoned in Touville, transferred to Drancy, and deported to Germany, to one of those slaughter camps from which hundreds of thousands of unfortunates have never returned. Madame Benedek's fate would have been the same, were it not that at the moment of arrest, and for motives all too clear for those who lived through those years, she took her own life.

"Dr. and Madame Benedek left a family, which had been dispersed by misfortune. Can we reproach the Jews, forced to flee, for having gone to the ends of the earth? What region of Western Europe has provided them a safe home in the last thirty years? So many of them died through having remained faithful to the land where they were born that it is the height of cruelty or bad faith to blame the others for their flight. Dr. Benedek had a sister. You see her here before you, Madame Hannah Lindner, née Benedek. She and her husband, the veterinary doctor Isaac Lindner, escaped to Australia, and thence to Israel. They were accompanied by their two sons. One of them died en route, of a disease brought on by the unsanitary conditions of their forced escape. The other son contracted the same illness, but survived in a steadily weakening condition until two months ago, when he too succumbed, at the age of twenty. Dr. Benedek's only brother was murdered by the Nazis. His widow escaped to England, and is now living once more in Vienna. Madame Benedek's only sister, Mademoiselle Eva Weiss, found refuge in China, returning to Austria after the war. She too is dead now, like her sister by her own hand, as the result of the indelible mental scars left by her barbarous treatment at the hands of the Japanese. Of the older generation, the parents of Dr. Benedek and those of his wife, two died natural deaths. The fate of the other two is shrouded in mystery, but there is every reason to believe that the irruption of the German Nazis into Austria was the reason for their disappearance. Gentlemen, these two families, united by a marriage, were all but destroyed. Of the Weiss branch, to which Madame Benedek belonged, there are none left, it has disappeared completely. Of the Benedek branch, there are only two—a bereaved mother who has lost her two sons, and the orphan who is the subject of our procedure here, Michel Benedek, the only bearer of the Benedek name who can transmit it after him. Is it any wonder that these few survivors, when the end of the war made such a quest possible, should have set about the heartrending attempt to discover what had happened to the others, and to reunite the family? Is it any wonder that their hopes should have centered about the young son of Dr. Benedek?

"A short time before the arrest of the parents, this child, Michel, had been entrusted to a nursery of St. Vincent de Paul. For lack of resources—the Benedeks had left practically nothing of value—Michel could not be kept there. A family friend, Madame Quertsch, tried to place him with the Dames of the Temple. That institution does not accept male children. Madame Quertsch thereupon entrusted Michel to Mademoiselle Odette Rose, directress of the Municipal Nursery. This was, I repeat, in February 1944. Michel then had not yet attained his third birthday.

"Who is this Mademoiselle Odette Rose, who thus entered upon possession of the Benedek child? She is a strange person. Some consider her to be a saint. Others see her as a visionary, not to say fanatic, somewhat irresponsible. We must be on our guard against appreciations that go to such extremes and are so lacking in subtlety. Certainly she has the reputation of being a worthy woman, and a devout one. In accepting the care of the orphan child she acted well; more, she gave proof of her great courage and humanity. No one has ever denied this, and on more than one occasion the family and its representatives have made full acknowledgment of this virtue on the part of the defendant. Because of her fine qualities, she has established extended connections in all circles. Everyone in Touville knows the charitable directress of the Municipal Nursery. She is greatly appreciated among Catholics; she is protected by the mayor and city council; she has friends in the magistracy. Yet this is not the whole story. The many splendid aspects of her character have their reverse side. Her many connections have led her to intrigues, not always scrupulous, to gain her ends. She is of an imperious nature, and conducts the Nursery with an authority above the rendering of accounts. Although generous, and with a fund of maternal affection that has led her to adopt and raise children, she is unable to tolerate any check to her sovereignty, and sometimes quarrels with these children when they are of an age to make decisions for themselves. This is the cause of the scandal she created when one of the protégées wanted to marry.

"This violence of character, which will bow to nothing; this intolerance, which does not permit her to respect the convictions of others; are they not two of the principal causes of the case now being tried before you?

"If there are those who regard her as a saint, I must decline to place myself in that category, for I cannot imagine a saint capable of lying.

"Lying, gentlemen. That was the word I used. For among the many myths that have arisen in this case, and that have found too ready acceptance in the public ear, is one that was deliberately, and with malicious intention, propagated by Mademoiselle Rose, in denial of facts in her possession. Mademoiselle Rose has affirmed, not only to all who would listen, but under oath in courts of law, that the family made no move to recover the orphan child for a number of years after the Liberation. She has made that same statement before you today. She has told other courts, and she has told you as well, that the only contact she had with the family was the visit of an aunt of the child, who begged her to continue in her care and education of the child because the family did not want him. She has said that only in 1948, when Michel had reached the age of seven and had undergone baptism, did the family manifest itself, implying thereby that it was anger at the baptism and not interest in the boy that was its motivation.

"All this is a pure lie. The documents I have in my hands, certified copies of which you have on your desks before you, prove exactly the contrary.

"I will not take the time of this court to read these documents. I will limit myself to pointing out certain salient features of some of them."

A good beginning, Konrad thought in satisfaction. A hint of secret motivations. A statement of family losses, all the more impressive for its lack of sentimentality. Praise of Mlle Rose, balanced immediately by the bald announcement that she was a liar. Here are the facts. The tone was exactly right. That quiet yet impressive voice filled the courtroom without effort. Glancing about him, Konrad saw that all were listening intently. Even Hannah, who did not understand French and had had to testify through an interpreter, had her eyes fixed unwaveringly on that tall spare figure in the flowing black robe. If only, he thought wistfully, he had had Maître Gens with him at the beginning! But of course, at that time it would not have interested him. It had taken the long, slow years of muted struggle to make clear what kind of case it was. Only after he had exhausted the recourses of the law, and by so doing proved that Mlle Rose had hidden powers behind her, had he persuaded Bira to take a hand. And it was Bira, the former Paris lawyer, working through Maître André David, corresponding secretary of the Conference of Jewish Organizations, who had got Maître Gens for him.

Maître Gens had begun his exposition of the documents before him. The familiar names and dates and places flowed before Konrad, reminding him by their very clarity and sharpness of detail how painfully he had amassed them, assimilated them, made them part of his case against the Rose woman. And how easily the great lawyer wound his way among them and fitted them unerringly into the damning pattern! What a mind the man had! Thinking back to the night before, when he had gone to the railway station to meet Maître Gens, after that fiasco at the Nursery, he remembered how dismayed he had been to learn that the lawyer had made his first detailed study of the case on the train to Touville. But early this morning, when he and Maître Lanson had called on the visitor at his hotel, his dismay had changed to amazement at the man's easy familiarity with all the ramifications of the case. And now, listening to him addressing the court, Konrad's admiration grew at every word. He himself, who had lived with the matter all those years, knew no more about it; nor could speak with anything like the tone of absolute assurance and conviction that Maître Gens displayed.

"Gentlemen," the lawyer was saying, "the conclusion is inescapable. As soon as the enemy wall was breached and a letter inquiring as to the fate of a Jewish refugee could reach its destination, Madame Lindner wrote inquiring about her brother. As soon as the war was over and civilian mobility restored, Madame Lindner took official steps to bring her nephew to her, in compliance with her brother's wish and her own. Does this not destroy the myth that Mademoiselle Rose, for her own purposes, has so artfully disseminated?

"If these facts do not destroy it, if there is the slightest doubt in your minds, Mademoiselle Rose herself will dispose of it. I will pass over without comment the various documents of the next six months —the letters, the appeals addressed to Mademoiselle Rose, to friends, to officials—not because they are unimportant but because they merely confirm what I have already established, and will call your attention to a letter written by Mademoiselle Rose on November twelfth, 1945. To whom did Mademoiselle Rose write this letter? To Madame Hannah Lindner, to the aunt whose existence she denies knowing of until a year later; the aunt who is supposed to have said, a year later, that she did not want the child. This letter is worth reading in its entirety, for it has never been given consideration in a court of law during the progress of this affair. You will note that I do not say it was never presented to a court of law. It was so presented at the trial held before the Correctional Tribunal on November eighteenth, 1952, of which this hearing is the appeal. But by a strange set of circumstances, which I shall discuss later, it was never given consideration. The authenticity of the letter is beyond dispute; it is in Mademoiselle Rose's hand, and signed by her. It begins as follows: 'Dear Madame, I know that a number of persons have taken it on themselves to give you news of your little nephew.' You will see that Mademoiselle Rose's very first words condemn her. 'I know,' she says. 'I know that you are alive, I know who you are, I know that the boy I have in my care is your nephew, and that you have expressed concern for him. I know your address.' Is there need to read more? Yes, because in the course of this interesting letter a number of things will emerge worthy of comment. It continues as follows: 'They have even told you that his parents are dead, although there are still a number of deportees and prisoners who have not yet returned, kept in captivity by the Russians.

" 'You should know that your nephew had been placed in a paying day nursery by his parents. Fearing to be molested by the Germans, Dr. and Madame Benedek turned over all their possessions—jewels, money, clothing—to friends and neighbors, in the hope that in the event of their disappearance all these valuables might go to their child or their family. These so-called friends took good care to safeguard the valuables, but took no interest whatsoever in the child. When the parents were arrested by the Gestapo two years ago, the day nursery did not want to keep the boy, because there was no one to pay his board and besides it was forbidden to shelter Jewish children, under penalty of severe reprisals by the Germans.

" 'I am a city employee, unmarried, and fourteen years ago I adopted five orphan brothers and sisters. Since then I took in a little Jewish girl who is now three and a little boy who is going to be five. Madame Quertsch of Touville knew this, and came to see me to ask me to take the little Benedek boy because she could not keep him herself, and she told me that there were people who had the parents' money, but that none of them wanted to take the boy or give up the money. Because I have a conscience, and am Catholic, I took your nephew under my care and faced all the risks involved at that time in sheltering Jewish children. I took care of him as though he was my own child. He was sick when I got him, but he grew strong and healthy. I hoped to be able to return him to the arms of his parents, and if not, to keep him and raise him until grown up.

" 'This a little later bothers the so-called friends, who all have more or less things belonging to the child. They can hardly wait for him to leave for far away so they can appropriate what does not belong to them.

" 'I must tell you that you owe nothing whatsoever to any of those who write to you asking for packages or other things. No one ever gave your nephew anything since he has been with me. Before, he had his father and mother and had no need of outside help.

" 'Your nephew is too young to travel by himself. For his sake, you must wait until travel is easier, so that a member of the family can come to take him, and to recuperate all that belongs to him. This would certainly pay the costs of the voyage. On the other hand, the boy would grow stronger, and who knows if at least one of the two parents might not return.

" 'I tell you this without any personal interest, since I have raised your nephew completely at my own expense, never having received any help from any agency, Jewish or otherwise. Useless to tell you that the only sentiment that motivates me is the affection I have for him. I took him in sick, wretched, abandoned by all, when there was no other alternative but to turn him in to the Gestapo, as was then required.

" 'No one then had the courage to take him. I took him in, not knowing him, not knowing his parents, his family. I took him in with nothing, or practically nothing. This is a bond of affection that no one has the right to break just like that. His money I sneer at. He has become my own little boy, and I am heartbroken to see that people, the so-called friends of the family, want to take him away from me in order to divide up his valuables.

" 'I am French and Catholic, and besides this boy have adopted or taken in seven other children whom I raise the best I can, without asking help from anyone, with the fruit of my labor and my own money. The affection of my children is my recompense, I ask for no other.

" 'Your nephew is a Jew, that is, he has remained in his religion.

" 'This letter stating things as they are, and having no more to add, I beg you to believe, etc.' Signed: 'Odette Rose.' "

Maître Gens paused. Raising his eyes, he gazed at Mlle Rose. Along with the others in the courtroom, Konrad too looked at her. She gave no sign of having listened to the reading of her letter. She was in the same attitude as before, sunk low in her chair, staring straight ahead of her.

"This letter," Maître Gens resumed, "reveals its author by more than the signature. There are expressions in it that show the courage, the nobility of a woman who risked her life to save that of a child. The sentiment that motivated her was the affection she had for him. She sneers at his money. She asks only love as recompense. This is noble. It would be nobler if Michel Benedek had any money. Where is this money to which we find so much reference throughout what I have read to you, and in certain recent newspaper accounts that are mere exercises in fantasy? The Benedeks left nothing, not to Mademoiselle Rose, not in a bank account in Switzerland, not anywhere. There is no millionaire uncle in America. I will hazard no guess as to the origin of this fairy tale, other than to say that it was not the civil party which I represent. Michel Benedek was left nothing, because there was nothing to leave. If there ever was anything, it went long before February 1944, to keep these unfortunates alive at a time when they had no legal existence and could not obtain ration cards without fraud and extreme danger. Why then speak so much of what does not exist? Because Mademoiselle Rose already at that time had no intention of returning the child to his family. The letter is an eloquent appeal to be allowed to keep the child a little longer. Perhaps the parents will return. Wait until the boy is older, stronger, until travel is easier. But in the meantime you must realize that I, Mademoiselle Rose, am the only one you can trust—all the others are after money. Does this not reveal the woman of intrigues that is Odette Rose? Already she envisaged the family and the friends of the family as her enemies. Why else should she attempt to sow the seed of discord among them? Why else should she ascribe greed where there could be none?

"I should also like to call the attention of the court to the brief, curious statement at the end of the letter, referring to the religion of the boy. Your nephew, she says, has remained in his religion, he is a Jew. At the time this was written, it was the truth, a simple statement of fact. Whatever instruction in religion Mademoiselle Rose may have given the child, she had not yet had him baptized. It is not the fact that is in question here, but the implication. All through this letter we find the repeated assurances to the worried aunt that the child has fallen into good hands: Mademoiselle Rose is a municipal employee, that is, a responsible person; she is a Catholic, that is, a person of moral principles; she loves the child and is concerned with his welfare, etc. Does not the remark that the child has remained in his religion convey an unspoken promise that he will continue to do so? It is as though Mademoiselle Rose had written in so many words: 'In case you are concerned lest little Michel, the son of Jewish parents, may be led from the faith of his fathers through his residence in a Catholic home, you may put your mind at rest; I have not caused him to change his religion, I shall not do so in the future.' And yet, so artfully is it said, Mademoiselle Rose could proceed some time later to have Michel baptized and maintain that she had broken no promise. Does not the very manner in which the statement is worded suggest that even so early in the negotiations Mademoiselle Rose was already planning the religious conversion she here denies?

"If you feel that this conclusion is one that falls within the realm of conjecture, let me call your attention to a strange omission in this letter, one which destroys utterly the good intentions it professes. This letter was written in the afternoon or the evening of November twelfth, 1945. It was not written during the morning, because that morning Mademoiselle Rose was occupied with something else; she attended the meeting of the Family Council she herself had summoned for the purpose of providing for the child Michel Benedek, a meeting held before the justice of the peace of the south canton of Touville.

"What a strange meeting that must have been! Mademoiselle Rose represented the boy as an orphan. She said nothing about an existing family. She summoned none but strangers. These men, knowing nothing of the claims of the family, impressed by the courage and enterprise of Mademoiselle Rose, agreed to name her provisional guardian of the boy. And a few hours later, having through deceit received legal sanction for her possession of the child, Mademoiselle Rose wrote a letter to Madame Lindner, the letter I have just read to you, in which nothing is said of the Family Council nor her appointment as guardian; a letter, in short, whose only purpose was to mislead, to create dissension between the family and its friends, to gain time.

"Gentlemen, this letter is sufficient in itself to nullify any defense that Mademoiselle Rose and her able counselors may put up to justify her actions in this matter. It shows that Mademoiselle Rose lied to you when she claimed that she did not know of the existence of the family, and that the family did not want the boy. It shows further that from the very beginning of the negotiations she had already determined to do everything she could to resist their just desire. Nothing in this document can be taken at face value, not even the implicit promise about the child's religion."

Maître Gens let the letter in his hand drop to the counter before him, and picked up another sheet of paper. His indictment of Mlle Rose did not rest on her letter alone, he said. There was more, much more. There was, for example, the part played by Mlle Rose in the investigation of the case by certain ministries of the government. For perhaps a quarter of an hour the lawyer dwelt on the correspondence Hannah had had with the Ministry of Foreign Affairs, the letters that had crossed between that Ministry and Mlle Rose, and Konrad's attempt to find some ray of reason for the bureaucratic indifference that had at a certain point settled over the affair. Only one conclusion could be reached: It was Mlle Rose who had sidetracked the governmental inquiry, through her misinformation and lack of cooperation. There was the intervention of the International Red Cross, rendered fruitless by Mlle Rose's refusal to give the boy up. There was the visit of Mitzi to Touville, of which Mlle Rose had made shameless use, converting one aunt into another and maintaining that it was Mme Lindner who had come to her and refused to accept the nephew who was offered to her. Could anyone believe any more in the good faith of Mlle Rose? Maître Gens asked reasonably. To do so was to fly in the face of all evidence, even that of Mlle Rose herself.

But this was only the beginning, the lawyer went on. After two more years of vain appeals, Mme Lindner decided that a more personal intervention was necessary. Unable to come to France herself because of her sick son, who needed her constant care, she entered into correspondence with M. Louis Konrad, engineer, a friend of the family since childhood, who was now residing in Touville. Out of loyalty to his friends, and moved by his sense of justice, M. Konrad devoted himself to the task of restoring the Benedek child to his family. The appearance of this new threat became known to Mlle

Rose shortly after she had had little Michel baptized, and was less willing than ever to give him up. She resolved, by a bold stroke, to consolidate her position.

"We enter here," Maître Gens said, picking up a separate folder and removing a sheaf of papers from it, "into a long and complicated phase of this affair that may well go down in the legal annals of France as 'The Battle of the Family Councils.' I have no desire to be the historian of this battle; it is enough for our purpose to trace its major developments briefly. I recommend its study, however, to all those who wish to learn how far a disrespect for the law can use the resources of the law to defeat the law."

Ignoring the snicker that arose at this sally, Maître Gens plunged into an analysis of the struggle that Konrad knew only too well. Step by step he traced the formation, the decisions, the frustrations of the various Councils. The hearings before tribunals. The Appeals Court trial. The definitive decision, and the refusal of the astonishing Mlle Rose to bow to it. The Strasbourg episode, designed as a last-ditch desperate measure to set the family at odds within itself. The trial before the Correctional Tribunal on the grounds of non-presentation.

"This trial," Maître Gens said, "has a direct interest for this court, since our hearing is a review of the procedure and verdict of that tribunal. The chief argument of the defendant was her claim of disinterest on the part of the family, a claim which was totally unexpected by counsel for the civil party, and with reason, for it had been disproved many times before in other legal hearings. The Tribunal had announced that it would render its verdict on December second. Profiting by the disposition of law permitting the introduction of evidence at any time before the verdict, Monsieur Konrad and his legal representatives devoted the days following the hearing to the gathering of documents that would prove what one would imagine was no longer necessary to prove, that is, that the family had made every effort since 1945 to obtain possession of the child. A most impressive sheaf of testimony was gotten together, consisting of some eighty-three pieces, each one of which was a damning indictment of Mademoiselle Rose's fable and her veracity. You have that dossier before you. I have read some of the items to you, and taken excerpts from others. Never has a more convincing body of proof been submitted in support of a contention needing none. This dossier was turned in to the Tribunal on November twenty-eighth, that is, four days before the date announced for the verdict, and with previous notice in due form."

Speaking with slow emphasis, Maître Gens said, "Gentlemen, the Tribunal did not even consider this evidence. Two hours after it had been submitted—time enough for a gathering of heads and a hasty glance through a few pages—the Tribunal rendered its decision, upon the pretext that one of the magistrates was about to be called away on unavoidable business. Its only reference to the new documents was this: '. . . that various items of corroboration were delivered on November twenty-eighth, less than two hours before the delivery of the verdict and ten days after the closing of the hearing, so that they could not be the subject of analysis and debate.'

"After such a sleight-of-hand with the purposes of the law, it was to be expected that the decision would be in favor of Mademoiselle Rose, and it was.

"Even more remarkable than this weird verdict were the terms of the judgment. Not only did the Tribunal question the validity of Monsieur Konrad's power of attorney on behalf of Madame Lindner, it criticized the Court of Appeals for not having done so during its hearing. A rare audacity! Since when, in France, does a Correctional Tribunal pass judgment on an Appeals Court? The Tribunal observed that the power of attorney was dated 1948, and expressed its astonishment that it should be used to give effect to a court decision dated 1952; as if it were the fault of Monsieur Konrad that he had been unable to obtain justice during those four years! Following the unbased insinuations of Mademoiselle Rose, the Tribunal further expressed doubts as to the legitimacy of Monsieur Konrad's claim— that is, whether he truly represented Madame Lindner as he pretended. Let me state here before going on that it is not for the judges, when they are in the presence of a duly authenticated power of attorney, to verify the relations between principal and agent. It belongs by unquestioned right to the principal to choose his agent. Yet the Tribunal, so jealous in its concern for verification in regard to Monsieur Konrad, accepted without demur the allegations of Mademoiselle Rose that the family had shown no interest in the child until 1948.

"It is obvious, gentlemen, that the Tribunal had decided, at all costs and whatever the evidence, to acquit the all-powerful Mademoiselle Rose. What remained was merely to find a pretext for so doing. It found that pretext in a sophomoric quibble over a word, the

word 'guardianship,' which had not been expressly stated in any judicial decision to date. The Appeals Court decision of July 1952 had
named Madame Lindner guardian without stating explicitly that the
guardianship of the child was to be conferred upon her. Such a contention on the part of the Tribunal defeats itself, yet since the Tribunal actually used it as the basis for its decision, I must place a formal
refutation in the records of this appeal hearing. It is elementary law
that the function is inherent in the duty, that one cannot be designated guardian without the power of guardianship. It was sufficient
for Madame Lindner to be appointed guardian by court order for her
to have the authority that goes with it. If any legal precedent is necessary to validate this argument, you may find it in Cassation, April
fifteenth, 1904—D. 1906.1.323, and Cassation, October nineteenth,
1935—D. 1937.1.12."

Maître Gens put aside the documents piled before him on the bar,
and deliberately removed the glasses he had put on to read them. His
long fine face took on a reflective cast. A sigh ran through the audience. It was evident that the documentary stage of the discourse was
over. Now would come the analysis and conclusion. It would be dramatic, they sensed. Konrad glanced at Hannah, to whom Rina was
whispering in German. He caught her eye, and nodded reassuringly.
He felt jubilant. What a lawyer! What presence! What weight he
gave every word! Konrad remembered a remark that Hannah had
made shortly after her arrival in Paris, while they were still at the
airport. "Sometimes these smart-alecky lawyers are too smart for
their own good." He had been shocked to realize that she was referring to Maître Gens, of whose acceptance of the case he had informed her in a hurried and optimistic note. But he's a member of
the Academy! he had wanted to protest. But glancing at her, he had
held his tongue; he had sized her up; and indeed, their long correspondence had already given him the measure of the woman. She
was one of those women called "practical" or "down-to-earth,"
whose function in life is to be a wife and mother; to whom bread is
bread, and roses foolishness; and all hairsplitting smart-alecky. A
Jewish mother, he had thought. And if from his long experience with
the type—Rina was, after all, one of these, and so was Lise Immermann—he had learned to recognize their limitations, he was also
aware that in those very limitations, the narrowness of view, the
mistrust of all abstractions, the clinging to the material and familiar,
the centering of the family within herself, lay that adhesive force

which, as much as the Torah, had kept Jewry alive. What do you say now? he wanted to cry.

"When the Benedek dossier was brought to me, only a few days ago," Maître Gens began, "I was deceived in my first reading of the material into believing that this was just another guardianship case, marked only by the extraordinary ingenuity of the defendant in avoiding the just claim of the family. Led astray by long experience, I imagined a situation that was heartrending, as they all are, but not new. I envisaged Mademoiselle Rose as a spinster endowed with a great maternal affection that had no outlet with children of her own, and who had attached herself to this child with the same desperate bond of love that unites any mother to her offspring. I believed that she had identified his flesh with her own, and that to take the child away from her would be doubly cruel in that it would bring home to her the reality of her sterility. It is always saddening to see persons confronted by alternatives of this nature, and I have never been able to harden myself to look upon them with equanimity.

"Upon studying the matter with more care, however, I was struck by a number of details that suggested a different interpretation. This child, whom Mademoiselle Rose professes to love with such jealous devotion, does not live with his foster mother. It is years since he has done so. No doubt she is responsible for his care, but this is not the same thing as having him constantly at her side. I noted also the various facets of Mademoiselle Rose's character, upon which I have already touched; her violence of disposition, her insistence on making her whim her law, her reluctance to surrender any degree of her control over the lives of others. And I wondered whether Mademoiselle Rose were not more concerned with keeping others from getting the child than with keeping him herself; whether her ingenuity and astounding generalship in the labyrinth of the law were not the result of a love of litigation for its own sake. From the pages of the dossier, moreover, rose a definite aura of anti-Semitism, revealed not only by disobliging remarks about the race and religion of the family, but also through such claims, which I have shown to be false, that the interest of the family in the child began only when it was learned that he had been baptized. I asked myself whether this case would be the same if the Benedeks had not been Jews, but, for example, Catholics who had become refugees for political reasons. And I was led to wonder whether this case were not the result of religious fanaticism rather than one of mother love.

"I confess that upon arriving at this court this afternoon I did not know which of these interpretations was the right one. That the cause of the family was just I had no doubt; otherwise I would not have accepted to appear here before you on its behalf. The Benedek child must go to his family. That is beyond question, or our law is meaningless. Yet we are men of responsibility, aware of the gravity of the duty society has laid upon us. It may matter little to the family why Mademoiselle Rose acted as she did, whether by affection or religious conviction. But it matters to this court. We are dealing here in human lives. A child is not a piece of property, to be bandied about with the same cold and unfeeling justice as would be applied, let us say, to a house, a diamond, an automobile whose title is contested. A child, the product of love, must live in love; a child, who satisfies the needs of parenthood which are part of our nature, has needs for affection and care on the part of his parents, or those who take the parents' place. And so I came here today sorely puzzled, convinced from my study of the case that the civil party is in the right, but wondering what would be the effect of such a decision upon Mademoiselle Rose. And this in turn depended on her true motivation in this matter.

"Gentlemen, I have listened to Mademoiselle Rose's testimony and observed her with care as she explained her part in this affair. If there is anything of which my long years at the law have convinced me, it is that the accents of true passion cannot be simulated. I have no doubt whatsoever that Mademoiselle Rose loves this child, with the same love as any mother for the child that grew within her and whom she has brought forth into the world. All the evidence to the contrary can be explained away. If little Michel does not live with his foster mother, it is because, first, he must go to school, and second, that school must not be in Touville. I ask you to put yourselves in Mademoiselle Rose's position for a moment. For years she has fought a running battle to keep the child that chance has brought to her; she is willing to risk everything to keep him: her health, her fortune, defiance of the law, lies, deceits, intrigues. But since she is capable of such extremes, she believes that her enemies, those who want to take the child from her, will go to the same extremes to get him. Tired of the delay, or the law failing, they may take him by violence. And so Mademoiselle Rose is forced into a difficult compromise, which has its irony. To keep Michel, she must lose him; to have him, she must send him away; to prevent her enemies from getting him, she must not have him herself. At most she can see him for brief intervals far apart, during his vacations. But, as a municipal employee, she too is chained to her duties, and can go to him seldom."

Where was he going? Konrad wondered. No doubt the great lawyer knew what he was doing, but this dwelling on the affection of the Rose woman seemed to him a bit excessive. Several people near him were nodding, as if in agreement; and even the Rose woman herself, still sunk in her strange apathy, had looked up once and regarded the speaker oddly.

"But human motivation is never simple," Maître Gens said. "Just as I am convinced that Mademoiselle Rose is motivated by a true love for the child, I am also convinced that she betrayed that love through her religious fanaticism. The question is not, as I originally supposed, affection or religion; it is both. If an impartial examination of the circumstances of this unusual case reveals that the defendant's affection for the child is genuine, it reveals as well that against all law, civil as well as canon, Mademoiselle Rose forced that child's conscience in a way that cannot be defended. Using her own egotism as her guide, she reasoned that since she regarded herself as his mother, he was hers to do with what she wished. Since she was Catholic, he would be Catholic too. Perhaps she felt that this community of religion would bind him to her still more; perhaps she reasoned that the family would lose interest in a child whose faith was no longer theirs; perhaps she reasoned that the act of baptism would make the Catholic Church her ally in defending herself against the claims of the family. It may be that it was all of these. The one thing she did not take into consideration—and this is unforgivable, this is what proves her love to be of the kind that smothers and destroys— was what such a conversion might do to the boy himself."

It was all right, Konrad thought, settling back in his chair. Maître Gens had set up a straw man in order to knock it down. The love that destroys. A new argument, a good one. In all their court actions to date, he and his lawyers had set about proving that the Rose woman had had only a temporary trust, which she had extended illegally by deceit; her feelings didn't matter. Maître Gens's argument was that they did matter, but in the wrong way. What next?

"Let us examine for a bit this element of religion, which has made itself a part of what would otherwise be a relatively uncomplicated guardianship case, like so many others. Mademoiselle Rose, for the reasons I have alleged, or for others beyond my grasp, had Michel Benedek baptized. Can anyone seriously maintain that she was within her rights in doing so? It has already been clearly established before this court that her guardianship was only a provisional one, and that fraudulently obtained through a contraband Family Council presided over by an incompetent magistrate. Certainly this provisional guardianship did not authorize her to govern the conscience of a child placed in her care only by the accidents of war and enemy occupation. Even a guardian properly designated with a permanent status does not have the authority to change the religion to which a child belongs by birth and family. More than one notable precedent can be found in our legal annals. I mention specifically that of the Court of Colmar, November nineteenth, 1857—D. 1859.2.36. I read you an excerpt from that decision. 'The selection of the religion in which a child is to be raised may not be considered purely as an educational matter. Just as jurisprudence denies to the guardian the power to make exclusive decisions in regard to the education of his ward, in the same way, and with even more reason, it should refuse to the guardian the right to select his religion. In accordance with the ideas on the subject that are generally accepted but nowhere expressly formulated, the adoption of a religion is very similar to the adoption of a nationality. This is a matter decided by birth; and only the child himself, when he has reached a maturity permitting self-determination, can abandon the faith into which he was born. It is nevertheless understandable that the privileged bond pertaining to parenthood might admit an exception to this general rule; for example, if the father, in changing from one cult to another, were to raise his children in the new religion he had embraced. But such a concession, made in the interest of that harmony which is the foundation of domestic life, may not be pretended to for any reason by either the guardian or the Family Council.' "

Looking up, Maître Gens said, "This is civil law. Is there any conflict between this law, which is the law of France, and canon law, the law of the Church? No, gentlemen, the Church itself condemns Mademoiselle Rose. Canon 750 states clearly that except in danger of death no one has the right to baptize an infidel child; and for those who are in good health, baptism may not be administered without the consent of their parents.

"The religious conversion of the minor Michel Benedek, certainly not in accord with the will of his parents, evokes an old controversy, which one might have hoped was extinguished long ago. In this matter the Church has always showed itself to be prudent, and has always opposed the frenetic intolerance of Catholics who refused to understand that the only legitimate method of conversion is that of persuasion. But not even persuasion is permissible in the case of those who do not have the full use of reason, such as children.

"Early in the history of the Church there were those who, carried away by the fervor of their faith, attempted to force Jews to accept baptism. This was forbidden by the Council of Toledo in 633, by the decretals of Pope Innocent III and Pope Innocent IV, and by a decision of Pope Gregory X.

"The Church has always opposed the violation of conscience. Those who set themselves up against this rule did so in defiance of ecclesiastical authority. In 1764, at Cavaillon, a Catholic baptized the son of Rabbi Crémieux. Four Jewish communities addressed a protest to Rome. The Holy Office expressed its solemn disapproval of this proceeding, and forbade the baptism of Jewish children without the consent of their parents, under penalty of prison for men and whipping for women.

"And here we find a Mademoiselle Rose, who, violating natural law, seeking to undo the ties of blood, not only took it on herself to change her ward's religion against the rules of the very religion she professes, but also dared to hide him in contravention of the decisions of justice so that he could not be returned to the religion of his fathers.

"I say that such an action is dishonest and monstrous.

"Does she allege that she was merely obeying what she believed to be her conscientious duty? The fact that she may have been animated by a sincere faith does not give her the right, in the name of that faith, to violate the moral law. Christianity has never taught children scorn of family, disdain of parents, desertion of the ties of kinship. No one has the right to do evil, even in the conviction that good will come of it.

"Such, gentlemen, is the religious issue which complicates this case. It is the history of an error committed by Mademoiselle Rose and concurred in by a priest who should have known better. It is an error which has aroused secret animosities on the part of certain of Mademoiselle Rose's Catholic defenders who, no doubt out of a sincere religious fervor praiseworthy in itself, have been so carried away as to set the requirements of the faith above those of simple civil justice. It is this compounding of the original error that has made this case what it is today. I am absolutely convinced that without the religious issue, this case would never have reached the courts at all, or aroused the slightest public interest. Without the religious issue we would not find in it any of those singular indulgences toward obvious untruth or those strange apathies in the application of justice that have plagued this affair from the very beginning. Catholic versus Jew; there you have the essence of the matter—the coming into conflict, in the person of an innocent and unwitting orphan child, of two sets of beliefs, each of which precludes the other. Because this child was baptized, there was set in motion a wave of resistance in Catholic circles to the claims of the family. The capacity of persons of strong convictions to believe whatever flatters those convictions is unlimited. How else can we explain the pattern I have already hinted at? The persistence of the myth propagated by Mademoiselle Rose? The eagerness to accept her every statement, against all evidence? The delays, the tortuous proceedings, the halting judgments, the unwillingness to move against an outrage crying for remedy? The collaboration of certain Cornelian monks in an enterprise of bribery and subornation, which the most elementary morality should have made repugnant to them? The fantastic verdicts, which have no relation to the testimony?

"It is too simple to say that Mademoiselle Rose was animated only by maternal passion. I do not deny that this passion exists; but it exists along with a religious fanaticism which is inseparable from it and which has done strange things to it. Mademoiselle Rose took in a Jewish child, she had him baptized, she believed that by so doing she had opened to him the path of salvation, and she has pushed her religious intolerance to the point where she dares to flout all law, human and divine. And she has been aided and abetted, tacitly no doubt, since few men will admit a shameful motivation to themselves, by those who believe as she does; by those who think, These are only Jews; by those who feel, as if their feelings and not the most rudimentary justice were what counts in the lives of others, that the boy is better off with a Catholic foster mother than with a Jewish aunt.

"These are truths that have never officially entered the pleadings of the civil party in any court. The civil party, however much it may have resented the highhanded actions of Mademoiselle Rose and her intolerant accomplices, has felt it best to ignore them, in the certainty that its claim for justice was so well founded, that its case was so clear, that a French court could not but recognize it, regardless of its own religious convictions. If I bring the matter up here, it is because that hope has been deceived. There has been a miscarriage of justice, and all evidence points to the religious issue as its cause. Very well, then, I say to this court, let us bring these secret things out into the open, let us examine them, let us give them their due weight in the decision that is yours to make. This is the reason why I have dwelt on matters which belong more properly to the field of moral theology than to civil law.

"But, gentlemen," Maître Gens went on with a peculiar intonation in his voice, "once this subject is opened, we must follow it to its end. It is not enough to analyze the motivations of Mademoiselle Rose, or to express before this court the profound resentment of a family whose integrity and religious scruples have been so summarily violated. In this clash between wills, in this stubborn, long-drawn-out struggle between two women over what each conceives to be her rights, are we not forgetting something which in the ultimate analysis is more important than either? Are we not forgetting the object of this struggle? This object, over which such a storm of controversy has arisen, which has been made the prize in a war of so-called higher truths, which has unleashed a chain of morbid emotions more suitable to a barbaric age than our own—this object is not merely a receptacle of hopes or a symbol, it is a child, a human being who has rights and feelings of his own. And now, for the first time in the years that this case has been in litigation, the testimony of that child is available to us, and we may see what are the results of Mademoiselle Rose's care of him."

At last! Konrad thought, aware of the stir that passed through the courtroom. This was what all had been waiting for. An unbearable tension rose within him as he leaned forward in his seat. At the same time he noticed with astonishment, glancing at the windows, that it was quite dark outside and that all the lamps were lit in the courtroom. At what point had they been put on? He did not know. By his watch he saw that it was a quarter after six. Maître Gens had been speaking for two hours. But now the important part was to come.

"Until now," Maître Gens said, "the child in question has remained hidden from the public eye, from the civil party and from the courts that have passed upon his fate. He has been surrounded by mystery, not only as to his whereabouts, but also as to his own opinions about that fate. He has never been consulted by anyone, not even Mademoiselle Rose, about the disposition to be made of him. But this court, to its credit be it said, in its determination not to be made game of any longer by a woman who has shown nothing but scorn for the law, ordered that the boy be produced as a condition of the hearing, under pain of imprisonment for contempt. Great as is the daring of Mademoiselle Rose, she did not dare disobey such an uncompromising mandate. She brought the boy from his hiding place, under safe-conduct it is true, but she brought him. And at long last the court has heard what he had to say.

"Gentlemen, you have heard the testimony of Michel Benedek. You will remember the very first question put to him: 'What is your name, my child?' It was a mere formality, for the sake of the record. No one expected the answer that was given. I will ask you what each of you felt in your heart when the boy, unthinkingly, following the practice imposed upon him by the woman who now sits before you as defendant, replied, 'Michel Rose.' Did you not feel surprise, a sense of outrage, a stab of shame? Did you not ask yourselves how the child's parents deserved this? Was it not enough that the Benedek family should have been all but wiped out by the barbarity of man, and the remaining members scattered throughout the world, without the theft of its name? Mademoiselle Rose had no right to attach her name to the Benedek boy; she never adopted him. What was her motive in doing so? Was it the blind egotism of the spinster determined to perpetuate herself, even if by so doing another name was to be erased from history? Was it for the purpose of enabling her better to defy the law? I cannot tell. I am baffled by the monstrosity of such an act."

The lawyer's voice had become hoarse. The calm, reflective tone had disappeared; in its place was the urgency of the man who is shocked and angry. Looking at him, Konrad saw that his face had become flushed, and that the veins stood out on his neck. Konrad's own cheeks began to burn. Michel Rose. She had dared even that. He did not trust himself to look at Mademoiselle Rose.

"Mother love!" Maître Gens cried. "Is this not the kind of love that crushes its victim, that swallows its own offspring? Is this the result of that tender care about which Mademoiselle Rose has boasted so much? The Nazis, in doing their fiendish work, could not quite wipe out the Benedeks, they left one alive. It remained for Mademoiselle Rose to complete their task and steal the only inheritance of his fathers. But let us hear the rest of the boy's testimony. Questioned further, Michel Benedek said that for the past four and one-half years he has been a boarder in a school. You asked him what was the school he was attending, the school so hidden that for all that time no one had caught a glimpse of him, the school so closed to the outside world that no one there suspected that Michel Rose was Michel Benedek, the most discussed boy in France. And the boy answered that the school was St. Louis Gonzaga, a Jesuit school and seminary in Italian-speaking Switzerland. And when, scarcely able to credit your ears, you asked whether he was studying to be a priest, this offspring of parents murdered because they were Jews answered yes."

The words rang through the courtroom, leaving a stunned silence behind. Then an inarticulate sound arose from the audience. At the back of the courtroom three or four men hurried out the door. Heads were turned toward Mademoiselle Rose, who had suddenly struggled to her feet, shouting, "You don't understand! I had to do it! It was only . . . !" So choked was her voice that Konrad could not make out the rest of it. "Switzerland!" Jules breathed behind him. The ushers converged on Mlle Rose, who flung up her arms and sat down abruptly. The president's bell, which had been ringing ever since the first signs of the commotion, finally imposed itself. The ushers, after a glance at Judge Bouhours' angry face, withdrew to one side.

"Mademoiselle Rose!" the president said harshly. But then he muttered under his breath and motioned to Maître Gens, saying, "If you please!"

"We have felt sorry for Mademoiselle Rose," the lawyer said. "We have heard her speak, and we have admired her courage, and we have admitted to ourselves that without her this child would in all likelihood have suffered the fate of so many of his race, victims of a holocaust that staggers the imagination. And we have admitted that she loves the child to whom she has given a second life. Love, yes; but what kind of love? I refuse to qualify it as she does. I refuse to couple it with the word 'mother.' A mother is one who gives life, not destruction. And again the child himself is the best witness. He had said that he was studying for the priesthood; but he said it with such diffidence, such lack of conviction, that the same question occurred to all of us; and you asked him whether he *wanted* to be a priest. None of you will forget the look of inner torment that crossed that child's face as he struggled for an answer, the despair that sprang to his eyes. His inability to speak. The tears that burst forth as he hung his head and muttered, 'I don't know.' "

"Oh my God!" It was Mademoiselle Rose who uttered it, in a whisper that carried throughout the courtroom. But Maître Gens, after his last words, had turned to face the audience; and the judges, frowning at the defendant's bench, let their eyes come back to him.

For a long moment Maître Gens mused on the faces uplifted toward him. Then he said gravely, "I have lived a long time. Along with many of those who hear my voice I have suffered through the national shame and fear of two enemy invasions. There is scarcely one among us here today who does not have written in his soul the bitterness of the more recent of them. You have not forgotten that time, you will never forget it. You will remember, as I do, how we were obliged to bear, hidden and choked up within us, the love of country, the patriotism, the sense of national identity that was endangered by a barbaric people. Some took comfort from the consolations of religion, and the beatitude 'Blessed are the meek' took on a new meaning. But all, I think, repeated to ourselves, like a talisman, the phrase 'I am a Frenchman.' This was our rock, the fixed point of sanity in a mad world. For France is more than a word. It is a way of life; it is the sum of our history, our culture, our relationship to God and man.

"But never, I assure you, has the awareness that I am a Frenchman, part and product of a nation that is a light to the world, been more present to me in spirit than now. I stand before you to defend an outraged family which is not of our country, and I think, We are French. We are a just and generous people, we are intellectually honest. Let the Spaniard vaunt his courage, the Italian his arts, the Englishman his orderliness. We are the men of reason, of clarity, of logic, of justice. I have presented my argument to this court. I have said all that is in my knowledge and power to say. There remains only one more word, and this word I address not only to the learned judges, but to all those present, and to all France. It is this. Has our beloved country been so debased by her misfortunes, by the reverses of war, by her economic and spiritual straitjacketing by a vicious enemy, that we are no longer capable of justice? Of a logical process of thought unimpeded by extraneous considerations? Of kindness and generosity? Great as was our need at the time, the Benedeks came to us in a need far greater than ours, convinced that France would take them in and return love for love. We did not fail them.

We opened our doors to them in accordance with the sacred laws of hospitality, and shared our crust of bread with them. But we too were overrun by the enemy, as Austria was, and as a result the Benedek parents were destroyed. We could not save them. The evil power rampant in the world had made our sovereignty a myth, and we were forced to watch in utter helplessness as so many of our guests, along with our own, were dragged off to destruction.

"But if we could not help it then, we can help it now. France is once more free. Our only duress today is the urging of our own consciences. In a juridical sense, the question before this court is, What shall we do with this boy? But in a larger sense, the question before the entire country is whether, having unwillingly betrayed the trust of the stricken parents, we shall willingly betray the trust of their child. What has happened to the conscience of France?

"Mademoiselle Rose has answered these questions in her own way. Her answer was to take the child and mold him according to herself. The child was a Benedek, but she robbed him of his name. The child was a Jew, but she made him a Catholic. Whatever ambition or talent may form within him, whatever dreams of his future life as a man and citizen of whatever country, she has determined that he shall be a priest, whether he so wishes or no. Is this hospitality or imprisonment? Is this mother love, or betrayal of the fundamental right of any child, to become what he has the potentiality to be? I cannot feel that Mademoiselle Rose speaks for France. I cannot believe that the ancient virtues that have made our country great can have been so utterly lost. I cannot believe that this is the image that France has of herself. If this were so, then it were time indeed that the barbarians overrun our land and put an end to our nationality, for the France of our hearts is no more.

"The Benedeks were born in Austria, took shelter in France, and died, one here and one in Germany. They learned, at the expense of their lives, that there was no place for them among the most civilized countries of the world. But today there is a place for them, and if they had lived they would have found it. They were Zionists, they dreamed of the rebirth of the spiritual and geographical home promised them in our Scripture. That home is now called Israel, and but for a historical accident the Benedeks would today be living useful and happy lives as pioneers in this newest and yet oldest of nations. And Michel Benedek, that challenge to our consciences, would have been born there into the inheritance that is his by inalienable right.

"Men and women of France! We are speaking here of love, of need, of the most fundamental requirements of the soul. Where is the greater need? Is it with France or with Israel? Let us not be blinded by self-pity. Poor as we are, crippled by the dreadful wounds of the recent conflict, weakened by the loss of the flower of our manhood, we are immeasurably richer than that tiny desert land whose only wealth is its history, its men and their determination. Has France so great a hunger that it must look abroad for its citizens? Must we steal children of other peoples to populate our cities?

"Where is the greater need? Is it with Catholicism or Judaism? We Catholics are a mighty host numbering half a billion, while the Jews, who a scarce two decades ago comprised eighteen millions throughout the world, now have been reduced by one-third, destroyed by a supposedly Christian people. Shall we rejoice because ours is the only true religion? Or shall we say that the God of Abraham, of Jacob, and of Isaac, who is also our God, cannot have failed of His promise to His chosen people, and that there is hope and salvation for them as well? Chateaubriand said, 'If you wish to create mockers and hypocrites, show yourselves to be intolerant and fanatic.' Nothing will create more enemies of the Catholic faith than to have it believed that it is intolerant enough to force consciences and to persecute those who do not share the same beliefs.

"Two women stand before you, neither one the natural mother of the child in the sense that she gave the child birth; but each of them having claims to foster motherhood; and this court and you who have heard the evidence must decide between them. Where is the greater need and the greater right? Is it Mademoiselle Rose? She who has done her best to destroy this child? The one who by her own admission has many other children in her care, so that the loss of one will make little difference to her? One whom she has already grown accustomed to be without? Or is it the foster mother, Madame Hannah Lindner, who has no other child around whom to build the remaining years of her life? You have pitied Odette Rose, because she is one of you and you understand her. Is there no pity and understanding for anyone else? This woman here before you speaks another language and professes another faith. But is she not a woman with the same heart, the same needs as any other? Since fate has made us judges between them, and we are forced to measure the hungers of human souls, put yourselves in the place of Hannah Benedek Lindner. You are the sister of this child's father, you have the same blood in your veins as he. He is dear to you not only for his own sake, but also because his father wished him to go to you in case of disaster. He is dear to you because he is a relic of your beloved brother, to whom you were a second mother in his childhood. He is dear to you because, being both Benedek and Weiss, he is the last of both lines and the only hope of their continuance. He is dear to you because you have seen your own sons die one by one, and you have no one else on whom to expend that fund of maternal affection that was called into existence and then cruelly denied. He is dear to you because he represents the hope of the country you have made your own. He is dear to you, in short, because he is yours, and only the selfishness of a single woman has prevented you from gathering him to your arms.

"Gentlemen of the court, men and women of France!" Maître Gens cried, raising his arms. "The law has already decided that Michel Benedek must go to his family. The question before us is whether we shall confirm that decision. I ask you to keep before you the realization that by this choice France will judge herself, will decide whether we are what we were; whether all persons are equal before the law, whether of alien blood or our own, whether Catholic or Jew, protected by powerful friends or poor and alone; whether we act in justice or intolerance. I ask you to weigh your decision with great care. I ask you to allow me, along with every other fellow countryman of mine, to keep my head high in the days to come, to say to myself, 'I am a Frenchman!' "

Amid a total silence Maître Gens lowered his arms and sat down.

13

❦

W HY DID he do it?
The question had leaped to her lips in that shattering moment in which Maître Cauchet came to her from the judges' chambers; but the lawyer had merely shaken his head, and indeed there was no time to go into it, for the session had resumed immediately. Why? Why? she had asked herself as the Paris lawyer talked on and on, the words going over her head like so many meaningless sounds. She had slumped listlessly in her seat, so utterly stunned and crushed that it was as though there was no longer any relationship between her body and her thoughts, which raced in frustrated circles around the incredible fact: Michel had given himself and her away! She could not understand it. The possibility had never even entered her mind. She had had doubts, yes; but they had concerned Michel's timidity, his power of self-assertion. Why, only last night she had explained it to him, and he had understood. Don't mention St. Louis Gonzaga or the Temple Dames, she had said. And just as though the scene were recurring before her now, she saw in her memory how Michel had glanced at Manon, worried that his Maman Rose had made a slip and given away their precious secret. No, no, he had understood, there was no question of that. And yet, incredibly, he had blurted out everything before the judges and the lawyers, like a ninny! Her Michel could not be such a fool! But the alternative was that he had done it on purpose. If so, why? Why had he betrayed her?

The rest of the trial was a meaningless jumble to her. Only once did her will assert itself over her numbed senses, and that was when that pitiless voice recounted what they had wormed out of Michel, and put the worst possible interpretation on it. In the realization that all was lost, that her sacrifices over the years were now turned against her as if they were crimes, she struggled to her feet to answer her tormentor. None of them had understood! She, a religious fanatic? But it was Michel who wanted to be baptized! It was Michel who had wanted to become a priest! And since she had had to hide him, what better place——?

But it was no use. She had sat down again, and the trial had gone on and on. After Maître Gens it was the turn of her lawyers. She did not listen to what they said. What did it matter? Shrewd little black-frocked monkeys disputing over a straw! Michel had betrayed her. Why?

When it was over, she did not have strength enough to rise. Maître Cauchet had to help her to her feet. "Here!" he said in alarm. "You'd better let me take you home." She walked slowly up the aisle, leaning on his arm. In the corridor Maître Gens stood talking to a group of men who crowded around him; some had notebooks in their hands. Konrad stood at the edge of the group. He glanced at her expressionlessly and turned away.

In the car the lawyer tried to cheer her up. It was bad about Michel, he said. The boy seemed to have lost his nerve. But they had not lost yet, not by any manner of means. Gens was devilishly able, you couldn't deny it; but now that the oratory was over, the judges had to consider the guardianship issue, which Gens had dismissed a little too summarily. The guardianship was *not* automatically transferred with the naming of a new tutor; a specific decision of the court was required, and this had never been handed down. Anyway, there was doubt whether the case properly came under Article 357. That argument had made them sit up and take notice! Had Mlle Rose seen the public prosecutor's face?

She did not answer, but instead asked if Michel had said anything about the nuns.

"What nuns?" Cauchet asked in surprise.

Her mind felt drugged. How heavy her thoughts were! But she had to think! Something had to be done about Michel. He could not go back to Cassarate, that was clear. Not after having told their secret to the whole world. Some other place would have to be found. She couldn't decide that now, not in her present state. Mother Veronica would have to help her. Michel was at the Temple, where Alain had taken him in accordance with instructions. That lawyer of theirs had brought up the issue of the name, and made a big fuss about the school; but he hadn't said anything about the Temple Dames, and

Cauchet apparently didn't know about them either. And so Michel hadn't said anything about them. Which meant, she reasoned sluggishly, that for the moment at least he was safe. She ached to confront him. Why? she would ask him. Why did you do this to me? It *had* to be fear, confusion, emotional upset! Because if it were not, if he had done it deliberately—her mind refused to follow this train of thought. Yet why had he walked out of the courtroom without coming to kiss her as they had planned? By then, if not before, he certainly understood what he had done. He was ashamed, she thought, drawing what little comfort she could from the realization; he was ashamed, and would not give her the Judas kiss.

At the Nursery she got out of the car without a word. Cauchet hurried ahead of her to open the gate; she ignored him, brushed past Manon, who greeted her expectantly at the door, and went to her room, where she stood with her hands to her head, trying to clear her thoughts. She had to see Michel. It was too dangerous to have him brought to the Nursery. She would have to go to the Temple. But first she would telephone Mother Veronica. Oh God! she thought. She had remembered the nun's warning. Don't expose him to it, she had said. He's no match for those lawyers. The risk is too great. How right she had been! Yet who could have foretold that Michel, her darling, clever boy—! Mother Veronica would be furious at her. Well, that was the least of it. She was reaching for the telephone when it rang. She sank down on the edge of her bed and picked up the receiver. Mother Veronica's voice said, "Mademoiselle Rose?"

"Michel," she croaked. "I must see him. Have you talked to him? Did he—?"

The nun interrupted her. Her voice was cold. "There's no use going into that. What's done is done. And there isn't time. I want you to listen to me carefully. I am calling you from the railway station. Michel is already on board the train. It leaves in two minutes. In a moment I will join him. I am taking him away."

Mlle Rose opened her mouth but could not speak.

"Michel must go to school," the nun continued. "He cannot go back to Cassarate, and he cannot stay in Touville. The only solution is to find another place for him, at least temporarily. The court will give its verdict on the twenty-ninth. If it is favorable, which I doubt, we can consider the advisability of his returning to St. Louis—"

"But—but—" Mlle Rose stammered.

"If not," the nun went on inexorably, "other plans must be followed. As yet I cannot tell what these will be. I shall notify you at the proper time. And now I must leave."

With a tremendous effort Mlle Rose gathered all her forces and cried, "But where are you taking him?"

There was a long silence at the other end, broken by the soft click of the receiver being placed carefully into its cradle.

Early the next morning Mlle Rose received a telephone call from Camélia Deharme. Had she seen the papers yet? Michel's picture had appeared! In the *Eveilleur des Alpes*. All the other papers were full of the case, but the *Eveilleur* was the only one that had Michel's picture. It was spread over half the front page.

Mlle Rose did not receive this daily, which had a Communist tinge. Disturbed, she sent Félicité out to buy it. In the meanwhile she examined the other newspapers, which Manon brought to her room. All of them had front-page stories of the trial, along with photographs of Maître Gens—the great lawyer entering the court, leaving the court, shaking hands with Mme Lindner, who was weepy with gratitude, waving from Konrad's car. Damn him! she thought. The things he had said! When Félicité appeared, breathless, she snatched the paper from her hand, looked at it and groaned. It was Michel, clearly and unmistakably Michel. He was wearing his coat and mittens, and was sprinting across a sidewalk toward a door that a policeman was in the act of opening. At the left appeared a man's arm brandishing a cane, and in the background a man with a camera in his hand, his mouth open in protest and alarm, pedaling backward from some invisible menace. The courthouse! she thought. They had caught him entering the courthouse. And the worst of it was that Michel's face, turned toward the camera in three-quarters profile, was perfectly recognizable. And so was the distinctive carriage of his head, along with his light curly hair. It was unforgivably stupid of her. Why hadn't she made him wear a hat?

In spite of herself, Mlle Rose had to acknowledge again that events had proved Mother Veronica right. How quickly the nun had acted! She must have arrived at her destination, whatever it was, before anyone could have seen Michel's photograph in the paper.

That afternoon Mlle Rose telephoned the Temple, only to be told that the reverend mother had not returned. No, it was not known where she had gone. Yes, the reverend mother would be requested to call Mlle Rose immediately upon her arrival. She was given the same answer the next day, and the next. But the days passed, and still no word came. She must be back, Mlle Rose decided in despair. Why didn't she call? Did she think Michel was hers, to dispose of him so high handedly, without so much as an explanation to her? Well, if she would not come to the telephone, she would certainly have to receive her in person! And so one morning about a week after the trial Mlle Rose took a taxi to the Temple and asked humbly at the gate to see the mother superior. Even as she did so, her heart sank; for Sister Louise, who had always welcomed her at the gatehouse with a smile and reached for the telephone, made no move but regarded her in reproach. "The reverend mother will notify you at the proper time."

"Sister," Mlle Rose beseeched, putting out her hand.

"Those are my instructions," the ancient nun said coldly, turning away.

There was nothing to do but wait. She returned to the Nursery and went to her room. There she stayed in the days that followed, consumed by anger and worry, letting the Nursery run itself as best it could. She lived like a caged animal, talking to no one. Manon brought her her meals, her face sad and drawn, and hung about uneasily, waiting to be spoken to, until she was dismissed. Where was Michel? Mlle Rose asked herself a thousand times a day. Where had Mother Veronica hidden him? Why didn't she call and tell her? Did she think she wasn't to be trusted? She wasn't Konrad, she was the child's mother! Very well, they had had a difference of opinion, and the nun had proved to be right. Was this a reason to lock herself up out of reach, as if she were punishing a naughty child? Not a word! Not even that a place, wherever it might be, had been found for Michel, and that he was well. That he was sorry for what he had done. That he missed her. Anything to relieve her of her anxiety about her boy!

During these weeks a controversy raged in the newspapers. So-called experts solemnly guessed which way the court would decide. Each day there were a number of letters to the editor, on one side or the other. For the most part Mlle Rose glanced at them distractedly and tossed them aside. How weary she was of it all! It was as though something had snapped within her, leaving her broken and useless.

The night before the announcement of the verdict Maître Cauchet telephoned her. By then she had made up her mind not to attend the court session. The bad news would come to her soon enough, without her going to meet it. He could telephone her when it was over. The lawyer tried to reassure her; she listened to him in silence and hung up.

After this conversation she studied herself in the mirror. The face that peered back at her was haggard and sick. She was old, she realized dully. How yellow her skin had become! There was no life in it. And her eyes looked like those of a lost soul, sunk as they were in darkness.

It was not Maître Cauchet who called her the next day, but Lespinasse. He lived only a few houses away, and she had seen him often since he had helped her more than four years ago in the matter of the Family Council. Occasionally he had dropped in at the Nursery to inquire how matters were going in regard to the boy. He had come to the trial, and had smiled at her encouragingly when she caught his eye.

He was telephoning her from the courthouse, he said. The verdict had just been announced.

"Is it bad?" she asked, at his hesitant tone.

"Well," he said, clearing his throat, "yes and no. It's a bit complicated. The court has declared itself incompetent. Cauchet will explain it to you. He's going to the Nursery to talk to you in person. But I thought I'd better—"

"Incompetent!" she repeated, not understanding.

Lespinasse launched into an explanation. The court hadn't been able to get around Article 357 of the Penal Code, which required a specific judgment on the question of the guardianship; but at the same time recognized that the boy's aunt had been legally given the right of guardianship by a proper Family Council, according to Article 450 of the Civil Code. It was a legal dilemma, he said; he confessed that he didn't understand it too well without doing a bit of research.

"But what does it mean?" she said, puzzled but yet suddenly filled with the unexpected hope that it was not over after all, that she still had a fighting chance.

"Well," he said, "the incompetence comes about because the court ruled that your refusal to turn over the boy doesn't come under Article 357 at all, but under Article 354. And that's not a delict. It's more serious. They said that fraud was involved, which qualifies it as a crime. That takes it out of the civil jurisdiction, and puts it under the jurisdiction of the Court of Assizes. So you'll have to be tried again."

"But that's wonderful!" she cried. "It means I still have a chance!"

"Odette," he said in an odd tone, and stopped. "It's not so simple," he said after a pause. "The public prosecutor was furious. The court handed the case back to him with instructions to prepare a better brief, and he didn't like it at all. I hate to be the one to tell you this, but I thought you ought to know as soon as possible. The prosecutor demanded that you be imprisoned, to prevent you from continuing to hide the boy. He said that you've gotten away with it for eight years, and it was time you were stopped. And," he continued apologetically, "I'm afraid the court agreed with him."

"You mean," she said, as these words sank in, "that I'm to be arrested?"

"I'm afraid so," he said.

"When?"

"Today, I guess," he said. "Look," he went on quickly, "don't take it too much to heart. Cauchet can get provisional liberty for you in a couple of days. They won't keep you there long, there'll be such a public outcry that they'll have to let you go. You have a lot of friends, Odette. More than you think. The public isn't going to like this one bit. You'll see."

"Yes," she said brokenly. "Friends. All I wanted—"

"I know. You don't have to tell *me*."

"A home," she said. "I just wanted to give a child a home. And for this I'm to be . . . . All right. If that's the way it has to be."

It was seven o'clock when they came for her, and quite dark outside. They had waited until the mothers had gone, they told Manon, to be as discreet as possible. They hoped that Mlle Rose would appreciate their consideration and go quietly. Oh yes, Manon told them brokenly. Mlle Rose was upstairs, waiting for them. She started up the stairs slowly, but was running by the time she got to the top, and the tears had started to her eyes. When she had rapped and entered, and sobbed out her message, Mlle Rose told her roughly not to be a little fool. Crying for what? Because she was going to prison? She was glad to go! Anything was better than staying night after night in this great empty building. It didn't make any difference what they did to her. She was an old shoe that had been cast aside. An old, broken woman fit for nothing any more.

But as Manon stood helplessly before her, her sobs caught in her throat, Mlle Rose wilted suddenly and cried out, "He needs me, Manon! God in heaven, what am I going to do?" And darted out the door. Holy Virgin! Manon thought, terrified, and ran after her, down the dark hall. She caught up with her by the window overlooking the playground, where Mlle Rose had stopped and stood wringing her hands. "Don't you understand?" Mlle Rose said in a piteous voice. "If I go with them, I can't find Michel. And I've got to find him! Nobody can take care of him the way I can."

In her fear Manon began to reason with her. The men were downstairs, waiting for her. She *had* to go with them. She couldn't get away. And where would she go? She didn't know where Michel was. Please, please, Mlle Rose!

"I'd find him," Mlle Rose said. And then she began to laugh, with a hysterical note that made Manon shudder. "For my sins!" she cried. She let herself be led down the hall, weeping softly. As they passed the head of the stairs, Manon saw that one of the men had climbed halfway up and was staring up at them with a strange expression. "Oh please!" she cried. The man muttered and turned away.

"This is the end, Manon," Mlle Rose said, weeping. "There's nothing left of me."

"I'll get your bag," Manon said. "It won't take but a moment. You wait here." She was startled as Mlle Rose clutched her by the shoulders and cried, "What did I do wrong? I don't understand. I've lost him, and I don't know how."

Manon stamped her foot. "Jesus, Mary, and Joseph! Do you think I *want* to do this?"

Leaving Mlle Rose staring at her, and surprised at her own daring, Manon darted into the bedroom and seized the bag she had helped Mlle Rose pack that afternoon. Please God, she thought, racing out, let her go quietly, if she must. Mlle Rose was standing where she had left her, but now her head was lifted in a listening attitude. "Listen!" she said.

Manon stopped short, the bag bumping against her knee. She heard nothing. "Oh, Maman Rose!" she said reproachfully. I've called her Maman Rose, she thought. I'll always call her that now.

"Empty!" Mlle Rose said. "It's empty again. I filled it with people, and now they're all gone. Why? Why, Manon?"

Manon shook her head. Downstairs, by the entrance, a man cleared his throat loudly and shifted his feet. Leaning on the railing, Mlle Rose walked slowly down the stairs.

PART THREE

January–May 1953

1

WHEN THE TRAIN, hissing gently, drew to a stop, Mlle Isolde Vincent slid her bag out of the overhead rack, buttoned her coat, and stepped into the corridor, where the other passengers were hurrying toward the door. She had dozed a little after Avignon, but she was wide awake now, and aware of an inner excitement that reminded her of her Resistance days. It was ridiculous, she knew; there had been good reason then for that tenseness in the pit of her stomach, that heightening of the senses, for one instant of carelessness made the difference between life and death. But now? France was at peace. The Germans had gone. Vichy was a thing of the past. On the train no one had spoken to her except the conductor who had demanded her ticket, and he could not have cared less who she was or where she was going. She had passed no check point, there had been no search, no irruption of men in uniform, no look of suspicion in anybody's eyes. And from the hills north of Marseilles, as the train rounded the last curve and began to descend, the lights of the city had blinked up at her reassuringly, as if the great seaport had never been stilled and darkened under a curfew, and prostrate under the heel of an invader.

On the platform she put her bag down, ostensibly to button her gloves, but in reality to make a quick survey of the terminal. The area where she stood was in semidarkness, ill lit by widely spaced lamps that cast a harsh bluish glare over the passengers moving toward the exits. An electric baggage truck, operated by a robot-like figure in padded overalls, slid forward in its own shadow like a monstrous beetle. By the wheels of the locomotive, bathed in steam, a crouching man held a lantern over his head and with the other hand made sharp motions that sent the clang of metal echoing from the high-raftered ceiling. A railway station on a winter night in peace-time. Everything quite normal.

Mlle Vincent sighed and, picking up her bag, walked toward the gate. As she did so, she was aware of a man and a boy standing just beyond the grille, staring at her. She recognized them with a touch of annoyance. Why couldn't that fool of a priest follow directions? He had been told to wait by the *contrôle*. Not that it made any differ-ence, in the circumstances; but there was a right way and a wrong way to do things. In the old days, she thought with contempt, he wouldn't have lasted a week. She glanced at them expressionlessly as she passed. Cancialotti's swarthy face was sullen; his short, squat figure was enveloped in a black overcoat with the collar turned up, and he wore his dark, broad-brimmed hat pulled down low. In spite of herself, she was amused. The picture of a conspirator! At least the boy had done what he had been told. He was wearing his glasses, and had pulled the soft knitted cap she had bought him over his ears, covering his hair completely. How pale and sad and wistful he looked through the grille! For all the world like a prisoner looking out! Poor Luc, she thought, surrendering her ticket at the gate. How much did he understand of what was happening to him?

The priest was muttering under his breath as she approached. "Two weeks!" he said, his eyes glittering in fury. "She said it was only for a few days, and it's been two weeks. I'm not running a hotel. I'm sorry I got mixed up in it. You people—"

"Good evening, Father," she said calmly. "Hello, Luc."

The boy gave her a startled look, and responded in a low tone.

Cancialotti drew his breath with a sharp hiss. "Lies! Nothing but lies! She said the case was pending, and there wasn't anything illegal about it. I should have known she wouldn't have been so upset about a photograph if that was all. She was pretty careful not to say any-thing about the warrant."

"Warrant?" said Mlle Vincent. "What warrant?"

"You people think I'm a fool," he said hoarsely. "She wouldn't even come to the phone the second time I called. I wrote a letter and I sent a telegram. Nothing! Like hollering in an empty room! Do you think I can't read? It's in all the papers. My housekeeper smelled something fishy the first day. She's got the biggest mouth in Mar-seilles. There's a warrant out for him. The court awarded him to the aunt."

"Oh, that." Mlle Vincent sniffed in scorn. "That was last summer. The case was being tried again. The verdict was given today. That's why we couldn't take him off your hands before. No one lied to you. It's *still* not settled. The court declared itself incompetent, and it'll have to be tried again. You were in no danger. That's right, Luc," she said to the boy, who was staring at her. "It's not over yet. But we'll make sure you're safe until it is." She had better not tell him about his mother, she decided. Not yet, anyway. He looked miserable enough without that. It could not have been very pleasant for him, considering the priest's mood.

Cancialotti pushed up the brim of his hat. His face was drawn and blue with stubble. "I haven't slept in three nights," he complained. "The whole parish knows about it. They keep dropping hints. One of them had the nerve to tell me, It's a fine thing you're doing, Father. I don't know what you're talking about, I told him. It's been like that the whole time. All this week I've been expecting the police to come rapping at the presbytery door, that would be a fine thing too, wouldn't it? I'm sick of it, I tell you. If you hadn't been on that train, I'd have turned him in. What do you think of that, eh? Moving children in on people, like nothing at all. Like here, hold my hat for me a minute. Phone calls. Telegrams. Grocery bills. Do you think I'm rich? She promised—"

Mlle Vincent was aware of a stirring of disgust. "Here," she said, taking the envelope from her pocket. "She's not one to forget her promises. You'll find she's been more than generous."

"Keep your money!" he said violently. "Do you think I would take it now? I want nothing more to do with it. Take him, and welcome."

She shrugged and put the envelope back in her pocket. "All right. I'm a little short of cash anyway. And I have to buy two tickets to Belfort. Do you know when the next train leaves for the north?"

He pointed his finger at her, backing away. "I warn you! I have no intention of lying. I didn't ask where you were going. I don't want to know. If the police come—"

"Oh, for heaven's sake!" she snapped, suddenly angry. "What are you worried about? You're in the clear. You took in a child, out of charity. You didn't know who he was. The child was called for. As for the rest, you don't know anything about it. Is that so hard to do?"

For a moment they glared at each other. Then the priest turned on his heel and walked away.

A fine specimen, she thought, watching him cross the waiting room and go out the revolving door. But Mother Veronica had sized up her man well enough. He would grumble, she had said, but he wouldn't dare go back on his word. And she had known he would refuse the money.

"You have your school card?" she asked, turning to the boy.

"Yes, Mademoiselle Vincent," he said. He looked worried.

"What's the matter?"

He hesitated, then blurted out, "He'll tell. Where we're going, I mean."

"Of course he will," she agreed, grinning. "That's why I told him."

"Oh," he said blankly. A tiny smile came to his lips and disappeared. Like an old man, she thought.

"Come along, youngster. Let's get our tickets."

In the waiting room Mlle Vincent deposited the boy on a bench, put their bags at his feet, and strolled over to the ticket window. Although it was after midnight, there were a half-dozen people before her, and she stood so that she could keep the boy in sight. Not that it was likely that anyone would pay any attention to him. Just another child making a trip with his mother; slumped forlornly and sleepily on the bench, occasionally reaching up a mittened hand to push his glasses higher on his nose. Those who hurried by were preoccupied with their own plans. The policeman who stood by one of the exits was staring out into the street, his hands clasped behind his back.

When she returned, the boy opened his eyes and sat up straight. "Take a nap, if you want," she said to him. "We have almost an hour to wait."

He shook his head and asked her what it meant when a court declared itself incompetent. She explained it to him, adding that the case would probably not be heard for several months, and in the meanwhile another school had been found for him where he would not be known. "And don't forget," she said. "You're Luc Casella now. That's what's on your school card, and that's your name. You've got to stop looking surprised when people address you as Luc, or you'll give yourself away." He had listened intently, his eyes fixed on her; and something stirred within her to contemplate the intelligence that gleamed within them. A prize worth fighting for, she said to herself, just as she had when she first saw him ten days ago. Strange, that he didn't ask about his mother. He must surely miss her. This was one of the silent ones, she decided.

The policeman had left the door and was moving aimlessly in their direction, stifling a yawn. He was a burly man, with a pock-marked good-natured face. Mlle Vincent talked softly to the boy, keeping the man in the periphery of her vision. He glanced at them, passed by, stared after a young couple walking toward the gate, said something to a porter, who scratched his head and laughed, yawned again, and strolled back. He was passing the bench on the other side when he stopped, studied them for a moment and said, "That's a fine-looking boy you've got there, madame."

"Mademoiselle," she corrected him, looking up. "I'm his aunt, his mother's sister."

"Oh," the policeman said.

"It's a natural mistake." She smiled up at him with timid eager-ness. "I mean, seeing us here like this. Yes, he's a good-looking boy, although he's vain enough without being told. Like his father. Now, there was a handsome man for you! Italian, God forgive him! He was a prisoner in Africa, and never came back. I warned Marie—that's my sister—when he asked her to marry him. As well marry Rudolph Valentino, I said, and it wasn't so farfetched at that, be-cause Giorgio—that was his name—looked enough like him to make you catch your breath. Women used to follow him in the street."

"Is that so?" the policeman said politely.

Mlle Vincent clutched her purse and edged nearer on the bench. "She almost lost her mind when he didn't come back. Marie, I mean. She used to look at the boy and cry. He's just like him, she used to say. It got too much for her. She just lost her interest in life. Fortu-nately, mother was with us then. It was she who raised the boy. You wouldn't believe this, but he loves his grandmother more than his own mother. When he found out today that she was sick, he insisted on going to her. She's in Montpellier, that's where we come from, only when Marie married . . . Nothing would do but he had to see his Nonnina—that's what he calls her—and if I hadn't promised to take him, I believe he'd have gone on his own. Hitchhiked, or walked even."

"That's too bad," the policeman said, glancing up at the clock.

Mlle Vincent edged still nearer, patting her hair with a gloved hand and smiling coquettishly. "Influenza," she said. "I declare, there seems to be another epidemic starting, like after the First World War. Marie's been flat on her back for a week now. Everywhere you go, it's influenza, or the grippe, or the virus, it's all the same thing. And then we got the telegram about mother. It's no joke, she's seventy-six, and even though she's as spry as can be it doesn't take much—"

"Excuse me," the policeman muttered. "I have to—"

"Never been sick a day in her life before. Except for her false teeth, you'd never know—"

But the man in uniform had fled, after a furtive salute, and now stood in his former position by the exit, scowling through the plateglass at the night.

Mlle Vincent turned to the boy, who was staring at her openmouthed, and closed one eye in a great wink.

Some minutes later a metallic voice echoed through the station announcing the imminent departure of the Montpellier–Toulouse–Pau–Garonde–Biarritz train, and the heavy figure by the door turned and looked at them. "Come on, my boy," Mlle Vincent said with satisfaction, seizing her bag. "Let's go see your poor sick grandmother."

Michel Benedek. Michel Rose. Jean Dupont. Luc Casella.
He sat huddled in the corner that the wooden seat made with the carriage wall, staring out into the dark countryside that rolled past him like a wheel, fast at trainside, slower the further away he fixed his gaze. He had been cold on entering the train, but once it had started a grateful warmth filled the car and he had unbuttoned his coat. He felt worn and drained of energy, but he could not sleep. He was thinking of his names. One Austrian, two French, one Italian. A little bit of everything. A little United Nations. The image of a ladder came to his mind. Each name was like a step taking him further away from—from what? From himself. The first change had been bad enough, but at least he had still been Michel. Now he was not even that, he was Luc, a short, ugly monosyllable that jarred him with its harshness. Like an exclamation, not a name. But he would have to get used to it. Benedek, Rose—both were impossible now, with the whole country alerted and curious about him. And Jean Dupont, even though he had used the name only a few weeks, was known as well, now that the photograph had appeared and forced

them to remove him from his new school. It was Mlle Vincent who had invented the latest one. She had called for him at the presbytery that Monday afternoon, sent by Mother Veronica, and they had gone for a walk in the Vieux-Port. There, gazing at the three English destroyers anchored at the Quai des Belges, they had discussed his new identity. He had best be of Italian descent, she had said, since he spoke the language; from Savoy, originally, being so fair of complexion. Casella would do as well as another. Mathieu, Marc, Luc, and Jean. Let it be Luc, she had decided with a laugh. Luc Casella. How did that strike him? But it would be Luca, he had protested. She had disagreed. Best not to flaunt it too much. Luc let it be, his mother was French. And she had created a genealogy for him with the same ease as the tale she had routed the policeman with a little while ago. After that had come the barbershop, where he had been shorn of his curls; the glasses she had produced from her handbag; the itinerant photographer with his tripod set up on the cobblestone quay, calling to the sailors on leave; the tobacco shop, where they had bought the blank school identity card; and finally to Notre-Dame for the director's signature. And lo and behold! he was Luc Casella, born July 1, 1941, at St. Dié, Vosges, of Domenico and Anne (née Brizard) Casella, certified as a student at Notre-Dame-de-Lis, Marseilles. As easy as that.

Michel sighed and glanced at Mlle Vincent. They were alone in the compartment, and she had stretched herself out on the hard seat, tucked her coat under her knees, and dropped off to sleep in an instant. The compartment light had been turned off, but from the corridor came a dim glow that lay softly on her strangely pursed lips—like a Pekinese, he had thought, the first time he saw her—her plump, faded cheeks, the lank gray hair that stuck out like a fringe under her black beret. How calm she was about it all! It was her Resistance training, he supposed. That day on the docks she had told him stories that had left him wide-eyed with amazement. Smuggling children over the Alps to Switzerland. Accompanying the British aviator with the broken jaw on the train to the Spanish border, embroidering her story at every inspection, and turning him over to the Basque smugglers at the other end. The sabotaged troop transport, when the Boche were retreating from the American landing at St. Tropez. Like a flower, she had said merrily; a screaming flower; the truck had split apart and spilled men in uniform like petals from a daisy. She had even killed a man once with her own hands, one of *them;* but here she had refused to elaborate.

It was not the adventures themselves that had so impressed him. He knew, like all French children, that such things had happened during the Occupation. It was the thought that it was this mild lady, this small, somewhat round-shouldered middle-aged lady who walked smilingly with his hand in hers, who had done them. Could speak of them so lightly, and with such pleasure. She's enjoying this, he had thought suddenly, as she joked with the street photographer, and had been confirmed in his opinion by the glee with which she had accepted the policeman's idle challenge in the station.

The thought brought a certain resentment with it. But that was unfair, he decided. She had no share in him; she was a stranger who had volunteered to help him escape, at some risk to herself. It didn't matter if she made a game of it. Mother Veronica had chosen her ally well.

Not as she had with Father Cancialotti. It was incredible to think that such a mean man could be a priest. Why did he say two weeks? It was eleven days. It was a Monday morning that Mother Veronica had taken him to the presbytery. Monday, January nineteenth. That afternoon Mlle Vincent had appeared, and they had gone for their walk. After that he had been kept indoors, out of sight upstairs. And hardly had three days passed but he was in mortal fear that he would be turned in. Even the housekeeper had hinted at it, talking on the telephone to one of her friends. Trembling in his boots, she had said contemptuously of the priest. Each night Father Cancialotti returned from his parish duties in a more vicious state of mind, until Michel shrank to hear his steps in the vestibule and to catch sight of that dark, sullen face. Meals were a torture, what with the angry silence at the table and the sickening smell of rancid oil from the kitchen. And at night, when he was locked into the icy cubbyhole on the third floor, forbidden a light that could be seen outside, he had sat for hours at the window, a blanket around his shoulders, staring down into the dark street, while morbid thoughts chased themselves through his mind. Maman Rose would lose the case, and the police of all France would be after him. That tall, shadowy figure striding along the sidewalk was M. Konrad, looking for the presbytery. On every newsstand in the country his photograph stared out at the passersby, who bought the magazine, studied his features and looked curiously at every boy they met. At Notre-Dame-de-Lis the boys in his class whispered to each other, Have you heard? The new boy,

Jean Dupont, is Michel Benedek, his picture is in *Paris-Dimanche*. Why was this happening to him? he asked himself fiercely. And he answered, Jew! Accursed of God! Hypocrite! Damned for sacrilege and false communion! He groaned to think that he had brought it on himself. Was this better than St. Louis Gonzaga? Was he doomed to spend the rest of his life locked in the attics of priests like Father Cancialotti, who couldn't stand the sight of him, who begrudged him every mouthful, who never spoke to him directly but said to the housekeeper in his presence, as though he were an object, Let him go to bed, or, If he gets sick now, that's all we need?

No, he thought now, listening to the song of the wheels that were taking him away from that evil place, Mother Veronica had been misled about her man. But it was also true that she had not had much choice in the matter. He had had to be removed from Notre-Dame that same Sunday night, before the day students returned to class Monday morning. And the next morning, once Mother Veronica had arrived from Avignon, she and Mother Celeste of the Marseilles Temple had made a half-dozen telephone calls before one Father Cancialotti had grudgingly consented to keep him "for a few days," until a more suitable place could be found.

Michel started and turned his head in fright. Someone had rapped sharply and slid the door back. A stern voice said, "Tickets, please!" It was the conductor. Michel let his breath out and looked at Mlle Vincent, who in one motion sat up and reached for her bag. "When do we arrive?" she asked, blinking as the conductor's flashlight shone over the tickets she had handed him.

"Garonde?" he grunted. "One fifty-six, afternoon."

"Slow train," she commented.

"If you were in a hurry you should have taken the express." The flashlight swung up briefly and dazzled Michel's eyes. The darkness enveloped him again. The conductor turned away. "Pretty thing. How old is she?"

"Thirteen," Mlle Vincent said, yawning. "And imagine, yesterday I caught her putting on lipstick!"

The conductor muttered something about a spanking, and stepped out into the corridor. Michel gazed after him resentfully. In the semidarkness he saw that Mlle Vincent was grinning at him. "It's the cap over your hair," she said. "And those prissy glasses. I'll have to get you a better pair. Were you asleep?"

"No," he said. The question that had been in his mind ever since

Mlle Vincent appeared trembled on his lips. How is Maman Rose? But he did not ask it. She must be very angry and disappointed in him. He felt too weak and broken up to hear Mlle Vincent say so. Tomorrow, he said to himself. If she hadn't brought it up herself by then, he would ask her.

Even as he thought this, he knew that he would not.

Mlle Vincent fumbled in her bag. "Here," she said, handing him something. It was chocolate. Michel took it gratefully; he had not realized how hungry he was. "Eat up," she said, reclining again. "And then you'd best go to sleep. You'll need all your wits about you tomorrow."

"I will," he promised. As he bit into the sweet-smelling chocolate, he was suddenly flooded with a feeling of relief. Marseilles, with all its discomforts and terrors, was behind him; so was Cassarate. Nothing could be worse than those. Before him lay Garonde, a new school, a new life. M. Konrad would never find him there. Mlle Vincent, Mother Veronica, Maman Rose were too clever for him. In time the world would forget about him, he would grow, become a man, make his peace with God—and some day he would look back at this time as Mlle Vincent looked back at her Resistance activities: something he had lived through and could talk about in that same offhand, joking tone. He imagined himself saying to Maman Rose—by then he would have explained to her why he had given away their secret at the trial, and she would have understood and forgiven him—He thought I was a girl, because of the cap and those glasses, you see, and he said to her, How old is she? And she, quick as a wink, answered . . . He had finished the chocolate. He leaned back, shaping the story in his mind, and fell asleep.

They were sitting in the hotel terrace room, a glassed-in balcony that overlooked the plaza they had crossed walking from the station. Mlle Vincent wanted to see the trees, she had said, and had argued with the waiter until he reluctantly consented to serve them there instead of the coffeeshop to which it was appended, where the other customers were. The weak winter sunlight that penetrated the glass panes had no warmth to it, and Michel shivered a little, waiting for their tea to come. But Mlle Vincent rubbed her hands in satisfaction and stared greedily at the bare trees in the plaza and spoke of the "view." Garonde had many memories for her, she said. Many a time she had crossed the square that lay before them, on her way to a little leather and harness shop at the foot of the hill beyond the station, close by the river. That was her "contact" in Garonde, the place where she met Philippe—although his name was no more Philippe, she said laughing, than hers was Cleopatra, but one of those outlandish Basque names that only a native could say. It was Philippe who was the northern end of the smuggling ring to which she had entrusted the British aviator. The Basques were all smugglers, every mother's son of them. They had got the Britisher over the mountains into Spain and safety. If she had time this afternoon, she added, she would take a stroll down by the river and see if Philippe was still around. Little had she thought in those days, when the average life expectancy of Resistance agents was a few months, that she would be sitting here on this balcony in the year 1953, having a cup of tea!

In spite of his chill, and the stiffness of body that was the result of his long trip, Michel felt a pleasant sense of expectancy, as though he were living an adventure. He had been charmed with his first view of Garonde, with its quaint village air, its curving, hilly streets barely wide enough to let an automobile through, the twin spires of its cathedral towering over all, the men wearing blue berets walking purposefully in the streets, the thick-walled, green-shuttered houses with broad, round arches through which he could glimpse interior patios that in the summer, no doubt, would be full of flowers. He was very far away from the cities where danger was, where he was being hunted. At this distance he could almost feel, with Mlle Vincent, that he was living a game. And so he had not been truly alarmed when they entered the hotel where Mlle Vincent's brother was to meet them and the bell captain winked at him slyly and said, "Playing hooky, eh?" He had half turned toward Mlle Vincent in readiness for one of her inventions, which would send the fellow about his business. But she had merely said, "Doctor's orders," had left their bags with him, and gone to do battle with the waiter.

He hoped that he could stay in Garonde. St. Ignatius was the name of the school, Mlle Vincent had said. Jesuits, of course, with that name. And her brother, Father Vincent, was one of the teaching staff, and would look out for him.

The waiter brought their tea, with great snowy buns and pats of butter, and Michel sipped the hot, steaming fluid and felt his discomfort disappear. When they had finished, they sat quietly waiting, looking up every time there was a movement near the entrance, which they could see through the glass doors.

St. Ignatius of Loyola was a Basque, Michel suddenly remembered. The founder of the Jesuit order had been born near Azpeitia, in Spain. He remarked on this to Mlle Vincent, who nodded and said that Loyola's companion, St. Francis Xavier, was also a Basque. She supposed, she added with a laugh, that there were a *few* exceptions. And when she had called them smugglers, it had been with genuine respect. They were a remarkable people, she said. No one knew where they had come from—she had read somewhere the theory that they were the remnants of the lost Atlantis, which had sunk beneath the sea—and their language was like nothing else on earth. Jammed in between France and Spain on the west coast, living in parts of both countries with the Pyrenees in the middle, they refused to acknowledge the existence of a border; and so their smuggling, aside from being profitable, amounted to an assertion of their national integrity, it was patriotism and business at the same time. They were all noble, she said; at least, that was their claim, and they certainly carried themselves as though they were.

Michel had studied about the Basques in school, but that was different from being among them in person, and listening to someone who knew them through experience, and he listened with interest and respect.

In the midst of a sentence Mlle Vincent said, "Here he is," and half rose from her seat, waving her napkin. In the coffeeshop a tall, black-cassocked figure looked about him hesitantly, caught sight of them and came through the door.

"My dear, my dear," Mlle Vincent murmured with emotion, seizing the priest's hands and holding her face up to be kissed. "And this," she said, releasing him and turning toward Michel, "is Luc, the boy I told you about."

Father Vincent shook hands gravely with Michel and said, "Hello, son," and Michel replied, "How do you do, Father."

He was late, Father Vincent said to his sister, taking a seat. It was a bad hour. He couldn't get away until now, because of classes. Otherwise he'd have met her at the train. In order to come at all he had had to find someone to take his two-o'clock class for him, but he had to be back by three. After six he was free, and could spend the evening with her. He had the same warmth of voice as his sister, although in appearance he was quite different. His face was lean and ascetic-looking, and his hair had something electric about it, curling stiffly up and out, like a mushroomed cork. As if it would crackle at the touch of a comb, Michel thought. He liked Father Vincent at once.

"Then we'd best be going," Mlle Vincent said. "It should be settled this afternoon. The canon is expecting us?"

The priest looked at her guiltily and hitched his chair closer. "Now, don't fly off the handle, Soldie. He isn't, and I'll tell you why."

Mlle Vincent was aghast. She said with a little wail, "Oh, Tristan! How *could* you? After what you—"

"Now, now, let me explain. You don't know the canon. I thought it over after I got your call, and the more I thought about it the more I realized that you're up to something. I know you, and I know him. I can just see myself in the middle of it. He'd start asking questions. Where's he from? Why does he want to transfer? Why didn't he get here at the beginning of the trimester? Your sister, you say? What is she to him? And I'd be groping in the dark. You know I'm no good at that sort of thing. He's as fussy as an old hen. Oh, dear!" Father Vincent glanced at Michel, and a shamefaced boyish grin came to his face. "You didn't hear that, did you, son?"

"No, Father," Michel said.

"What I'm getting at is this. If he smelled any sort of irregularity about it, he'd come out with a flat no, and there'd be no moving him after. But if we simply pop into his office and say, Here we are, I mean, present him with a *fait accompli,* what is he going to do? Tell you to get right back on that train again? He won't do it, he's too— And you can always blame me. You arranged it all with me, and I simply forgot to tell him about it. He'll grumble a bit, and be sarcastic—with me, not with you—and then he'll throw up his hands and say, Oh, very well."

Mlle Vincent thought that over, while Michel regarded the priest in secret astonishment. Was he really planning to—to—*deceive* his superior? Was it possible? He had given no thought as to how he was to enter St. Ignatius; he had assumed that it was all arranged. They're like everybody else, he thought; and suddenly felt very grown up and worldly wise, and a little sad.

"Perhaps you're right," Mlle Vincent said finally. "You know your man and I don't. And at this stage there's no alternative. Well then, let's get moving. I'll call the waiter."

"Just a minute, my dear." There was a new tone in Father Vincent's voice, and Michel looked at him curiously. "Come on, give."

"What?" Mlle Vincent's face was all innocence.

"I know the signs. You're too happy about this. You didn't cross half of France just to get a stray boy to school. You're up to something. What is it?"

"Tonight," she said, smiling. "We'll have more time then. I wouldn't hide anything from you."

"Now!"

She shrugged, still smiling. "If you promise to let me do the talking. Or better yet, just introduce us and get out."

"I have a class, remember?"

"All right." She leaned forward and said significantly, "Does the name Benedek mean anything to you?"

Father Vincent remained staring at her as if hypnotized. Then slowly his head swung around and he studied Michel's face. "Oh my God!" he said in a voice suddenly hoarse. "Sister, what have you got yourself mixed up in? Do you realize—?"

"Of course!" she said gaily. "What do you know about the case? You're a priest, aren't you? The boy is baptized."

"A heathen like you! Since when—"

"Oh, it's not me. I'm just helping a friend."

He groaned, clutching his head. "Soldie. Dear Sister Soldie, bane of my life! Why didn't you tell me?"

"Over the telephone?"

"You could have written. It's been more than a week since you— You could have told me the whole story and given me the chance to think it over before I got myself involved." He shook a finger at her. "No, that wasn't it, you wanted—"

Grinning, she said, "All right. Tell us to get right back on that train."

"To me?" he said reproachfully. "To your own brother?"

"I *had* to, sugar-pie. If I had told you the truth right off, you'd have hit the ceiling. Like your canon. And even if you had agreed, you couldn't have been casual enough about it in putting it up to him."

"But he'll be recognized!" he cried.

"No he won't. *You* didn't recognize him, and you already suspected I was up to something. It's too far away. Nobody's *expecting* to see him here. Nobody here knows him, he's only a name in the newspapers. Why, Hitler himself could walk down the street—"

"I won't do it!" he said in sudden determination. "You have no right to put me in a spot like this, Soldie. This thing is dynamite."

"Now, listen," she said persuasively, lowering her voice and moving her chair closer. Michel looked from one to the other. They were arguing in low tones, and he could not hear what was being said. Was he to be turned away now, after congratulating himself on his escape? A feeling of anxiety took hold of him. Where could they go, if not here?

At length the priest gestured wearily. "Trapped!" he said. "By my own flesh and blood! All right, against my better judgment. We'll probably both be sorry later on. But I can't send you away again now, and you know it." He brooded a bit, then turned to Michel. "The Lord protect you, son. I'll do what I can. What's your name, by the way? Benedek what?"

Michel had let his breath out in relief. "Luc, Father. Luc Casella."

"Good boy!" Mlle Vincent said with emphasis. "Remember that. And you too, Tan-Tan. And now let's be going. Remember your three o'clock. And it's quarter to now."

They rose, and Father Vincent hoisted up his cassock to fish in his pocket. His sister told him never to mind, she knew he didn't have a penny to his name, and tossed a bill on the table. Seeing how pale the priest had become, Michel felt sorry for him, and grateful at the same time. What a great deal of bother he had become to people! But the image of M. Konrad came to him, standing up in the courtroom, and he shuddered; not that, anything but that! As they walked out, Father Vincent muttered that the school was only five minutes away. So far as time was concerned, it would just work out. He would take them to Canon Sombre's office, introduce them, bow his head under the scolding, and hurry off to class. And Soldie would be on her own. And by God! Her story had better be a good one!

"It will be," Mlle Vincent said grimly.

Michel, trotting along beside them, was sure it would.

At four o'clock Michel, his bag and overcoat stored away in his dormitory cubicle, fell into the line of boys that was forming for the march to the chapel for Benediction. Curious faces turned toward him as he took the place the priest pointed out to him. Behind him a chunky boy with a red-cheeked impish face nudged him and whispered, "What's your name?"

"Luc Casella," he whispered back, wondering whether talking in line was permitted at St. Ignatius. It would have earned him a demerit at Cassarate. And at Notre-Dame too.

"What are you, Spanish or something?"

The priest was staring at them. Michel held his tongue. He did not want to get in bad the first day. But the priest walked to the head of the line, and the boy insisted, nudging him again.

"No, Italian. But I'm really French. I was born here."

"Where?"

"St. Dié. That's in the Vosges."

"Oh. Wasn't that the place that was wiped out during the war? Every building? A hole in the ground?"

Michel turned his head slightly and nodded.

The line started to move. A priest walked at the head of it, and another at the end. But there was a momentary confusion at the door to the chapel, and the boy whispered, "What about your family?"

"Gone," Michel said simply. The boy's face seemed stricken, and he pressed Michel's arm. They entered the chapel together.

Bless Mlle Vincent! He was safe.

2

FATHER VINCENT stood at his window, staring up at the leaden sky. He had put on his overcoat and picked up his hat before he noticed that it had begun to snow. At the moment it was only a sparse scattering of tiny granular bits of white that pinged softly against the windowpane; but from the looks of the overcast it could turn into a real storm, and the walk that he had been looking forward to was no longer so tempting. But the prospect of remaining in quarters, prey to his gloomy thoughts, had even less appeal. It was Sunday morning; mass and breakfast were over. The boys with passes for the day were making a great to-do in the nearby dormitory, whooping and calling to each other as they dressed for their outing. In a few minutes a deadly hush would fall over St. Ignatius, and while ordinarily Father Vincent found the quiet soothing and conducive to the reading he saved for weekends, he was filled today with the need for physical activity. He would go out, he decided, snow or no snow.

As he stepped into the hall, boys ran out of the dormitory and past him, their faces merry and excited. "Good-bye, Father!" "Until tonight!" The Benedek boy, or rather, the Casella boy—he mustn't make that mistake again—was not among them, of course; he had no one in the neighborhood to go to. Every child who boarded in the school had to have a correspondent, someone who could be notified in case of illness or problems, and who would receive his visits. Soldie had run over to Biarritz after talking to the canon, and had arranged for the Temple Dames there to accept the obligation, but the boy certainly couldn't go there on his own. In fact, he thought, going down the stairs, the less he stirred out the better. It meant lonely Sundays for him, but that couldn't be helped. Perhaps later, when he had returned from his walk, he would stop by and see how the youngster was doing. He seemed to be a quiet, intelligent boy, although rather withdrawn. He would be grateful for a little attention. None of this was his fault.

Problems! Problems! he said to himself. How peaceful his life had been before it was so radically altered on Friday! The day before yesterday! It seemed that he had been living on a powder keg for ages. At the very first step he had put his foot in it. What had possessed him, at the moment of introducing Soldie to the rector, to add that she was from Touville? Who had asked him that? What a look she had shot him! It was all very well for her to play her little games, but he was not used to that sort of thing, and he foresaw in that instant how many pitfalls and deceits he had laid himself open to. Fortunately, the name of the city had meant nothing to the rector, and he himself had escaped before he could do more harm.

The boys were milling by the great barred portal, urging Brother André to open up. From the doorway of the glass-paneled lodge the old gatekeeper scolded them surlily, his nose red with the cold, a coarse gray woolen shawl over his shoulders. Jangling his keys, he hobbled among them, grumbling, "Shove, shove! You'll not get out any the faster for it." In the lodge a round-bellied stove crackled and smoked, sending a villainous, acrid smell into the hall.

The boys piled out, and Father Vincent followed them. The snow was dry and powdery and lay on the icy sidewalk without melting. He stood still a moment to choose his direction, and had taken two steps when the outer wicket shot open and Brother André's anxious face peered out. "Ah, there you are, Father!" he cried in his cracked voice. "You're wanted in the rector's office. At once, the canon said. God be praised! And I thought I had just missed you!"

The wicket slammed shut. Father Vincent gaped up at it before he recovered himself. Nonsense! he thought angrily. Was he to start every time someone looked at him? Yet a premonition of disaster chilled him as he hurried through the door that was opened for him, and made his way to the rear, cutting through the cloister to save time. The enormity of what he had done was like a stone in his chest.

At the door to the rector's office he paused to brush away the snow that clung to his coat, and to compose himself. Then he knocked and entered.

The rector was sitting at his desk. His face, usually pink and bland, had a purplish tinge, and his hair was ruffled. There was something ominous in his voice as he said without preliminary, "Come closer, Father. I want you to look at something." But he had already recognized the newspaper that the canon's hand was lying on. It was Friday's *France-Soir,* which he and his sister had pored over at the hotel, after the boy had been accepted at the school. "This is the crucial moment," Soldie had said. "If he doesn't connect this up with Luc the instant he sees it, he never will." Even from the doorway Father Vincent could read the headline, "ODETTE ROSE GOES TO JAIL!" and remembered the subheading, "Whereabouts of Benedek Boy Still Unknown." And the two photographs, the one of Mlle Rose entering the gate of the prison in Touville, and the other, damning one, of the boy himself running in the street.

"Closer," the rector said.

He stepped forward, and then he saw what the rector had in his other hand. How had he ever imagined, he asked himself incredulously, that they could have gotten away with it? He could not take his eyes from the card that the rector, with great deliberation, laid down on the newspaper, alongside the boy's picture. From the upper left-hand corner of the card Luc Casella's face stared up at him, young and solemn with its glasses. The resemblance between the two was obvious.

"Well?" the rector said.

He did not reply.

Leaping up, the rector struck the desk a terrible blow with his clenched fist. "Good heavens, man!" he shouted. "Are you mad, or what?"

Fifteen minutes later Father Vincent walked out of the rector's office. His face was pale, and he repeated to himself, "My God! My God!" At the portal he did not wait for Brother André, but opened the door himself. The gatekeeper called after him, "It's coming down now, Father." He did not look back. He had gone half a block before he was aware that it was snowing heavily, and that he still had his hat in his hand. He clapped it on and continued walking. After a while he felt the melted snow from his hair trickle down under the hat and mingle with the perspiration on his cheeks.

At the hotel he placed his call with the operator and sat down to wait. His shoes were wet. He stared at them, thinking he should have put on his rubbers. In a few minutes he rose and approached the operator. "It takes time," she said. "I'll call you." Nonetheless, he came back again and again, patiently, humbly, until the woman, ready to snap at him, studied his face in alarm, and asked if he were unwell. Oh no, he assured her, it was just that— He left the sentence unfinished and sat down again. When at last she called out, "Touville! Booth three!" and he passed her, muttering, "Thank you," she eyed him with concern, shaking her head.

"Hello!" he cried into the mouthpiece, his voice loud and unnatural in his own ears.

His sister's voice said, "Hello? Hello? Tristan?"

"Oh Soldie," he said with a groan. "Thank God! I've just come from the rector. The boy—"

"What is it?" she asked sharply, as he paused and swallowed. "Pull yourself together. And no names!"

Names! he said bitterly. As if that made any difference now! It was all up with them. The rector knew, and was going to the police. There was no doing anything with him. He had tried to argue, and been screamed at for his pains. The man was close to hysteria. It was, How did you dare? And, She lied to me! And, You, a priest! He hadn't been able to get a word in edgewise. Baptism, he tried to say, but the rector brushed that aside with, This is the *law!* There was nothing more he could say. He was in a terrible jam.

"All right," she said. "All *right*. We're all in a jam. Did you admit anything? I mean, about the party who sent me? No names!"

He did not answer. He had suddenly realized that he had come away without money. He winced, thinking of facing the operator again, and the long-distance charges.

"Tan-Tan?"

"What?" he said. "Admit? No, of course not. I tell you, I didn't have a chance to say anything. All I could do—"

"How did he find out?"

"Crossword puzzles!" he cried. "He does crossword puzzles. He had Friday afternoon's paper, and he opened his drawer to get a pencil, and the boy's card was there with his picture and so he saw the two pictures together. I knew we couldn't get away with it. If it wasn't that, it would be something else. I'm sorry I ever—"

"Now listen!" she interrupted him. "There's only one chance. How long ago was this? Have the police come?"

"The police?" he said. "No, not yet. Not when I left. I tell you, I've just—"

"And the boy?"

"At the school."

"Tan-Tan," she said after a long pause. "I hate to do this to you, but there's no help for it. There isn't time for anything else. If I were there—but I'm not, and you are. Get him out of there. It doesn't matter where, the hotel, the railroad station, anywhere he can stay for an hour or two. Then—"

"No!" he cried.

"Then scout around and find a family that's willing to put him up until we can send someone to—"

"No, no! I won't!"

"It's his salvation, Tan-Tan," she reminded him quietly. "You must know some good Catholic family in town that would be willing. Since you're in trouble about this already, you might just as well—"

"That's enough!" he shouted. "I won't do it, and that's final! I didn't ask for this. You—"

She hissed at him. "Listen to me, and stop interrupting! If you don't do this, you'll be the sorriest person who ever lived. Do you think we're doing this on our own authority? Use your head, man! If nothing else can make you see reason, let me tell you that we've seen a certain party in Avignon. Do you understand now? Do you?"

"Avignon?" he said. "Do you mean the arch—?"

"Oh!" she cried in disgust.

For a moment he was thunderstruck, then choked in a blinding rage. Another of her stories! "I won't hear any more," he said hoarsely. "You got him into this, not me. Now you find a way to get him out of it. But I'm through!" He slammed the receiver down and sat there breathing hard.

Emile Fontanel, Procureur of the Republic at Garonde, sat at his desk staring down at the newspaper and the school card. His head was splitting, and there was a sick, acid taste in his mouth. He had spent most of the previous night in the company of a few fellows from the Jockey Club, splendid men with a dash of sporting blood, who had taken him under their wing and promised him a pleasant evening. He was new in Garonde, having been transferred from Pau only four months ago; and a bachelor; and had accepted their invitation gladly. They had had dinner at the count's château up in the hills, accompanied by four vintage wines. Then came a few rounds of cards, with cognac, and he had won a pile, which he lost at the casino they drove to afterwards. By the time they arrived at the brothel his head was reeling, but he kept drinking champagne after the others had stopped. He did not remember how he had got home. He had been explaining to one of the girls why the government had closed down establishments like this one, and then the telephone was ringing, and it was ten-thirty in the morning and he was in his own bed with a wretched hangover, and a man's voice was saying Benedek, Benedek to him until the message got through to his befogged brain.

Now, an hour later, his eyes bloodshot and his stomach threatening to wrench itself loose, he supported his unshaven chin on his hand, studying the boy's photographs and listening to the two priests who sat before him. He wished them and the boy at the devil. If the boy was going to be found, why did it have to be on a Sunday? The Parquet had been locked and empty, and nothing would do but he must drive in himself to attend to them. How the key had scrabbled at the lock before he got the door open! And the priests behind him, waiting, pretending not to notice.

The one from the school—what was his name? Sombre—was doing most of the talking. Fontanel listened wearily, looking from one picture to the other. They did not seem to him to be much alike. Yet Sombre said that the priest who was sponsoring him, one of his teachers, had admitted it, or not denied it, at any rate. He scratched his head, trying to remember where he had seen a larger picture of the Benedek boy, on the cover of some magazine or other. Yes, he recalled, his secretary had showed it to him and had got quite sentimental over the "poor motherless child." "Yes, yes," he said, holding up his hand, and got to his feet. He groaned to himself as he bent over the shelves behind the secretary's desk, and rummaged among the untidy papers on them. There it was. *Paris-Dimanche*. He had not been mistaken. It was the same pose as the one in *France-Soir,* but head and shoulders only, and blown up to a large size. Now the resemblance was clearer. He put the magazine down on the desk, and the priests bent over it and nodded. They hadn't seen that one, they said; but it was the same, no doubt about it.

Canon Sombre was indignant. They had taken him in completely, he said. What a fantastic tale that woman had told him! "Lies!" he said, his florid cheeks quivering. "From beginning to end! She said the boy was in St. Dié when it was bombed. Smashed flat, like an ant's nest someone had stepped on, she said, and the child pinned in the rubble for two nights and a day, between the dead bodies of his

father and mother. When the rescue team got to him he was screaming with terror, and half crazy. And the boy sitting there, listening to
it all with a sad expression on his face. And there I was, in a mortal
fear he was going to break down, and blaming the woman for her
indiscretion in reminding him of it all again. I accepted him out of
pity. She must have counted on that. I never even got around to
asking why he was being transferred from his other school. It was
only later that I thought of it, after she was gone. Oh, she's an artful
one, all right! But how was I to know? Father Vincent's sister! I had
him up on the carpet as soon as I put two and two together, and let
him know in no uncertain terms. And I'd have had an interesting
conversation with that sister of his too, only she's left town. I called
up the Grand Hotel, where she was staying, and was told she had
checked out. The same night. Oh, by the way, I brought you this."
He laid an envelope on the desk. "Thirteen thousand francs," he said
with a significant air. "She paid that for the trimester. I don't want
any part of it. I'd like you to take charge of it, please."

Fontanel hesitated, then swept the envelope into a drawer. "I'll
have my secretary send you a receipt for it," he said. What was he to
do now? he thought. If only he could lie down for a while, long
enough to shake this thing off and get some solid food into himself!
He had to pull himself together. But the priests were looking at him
expectantly.

With an effort he said, "We ought to question the boy."

"But I did," Canon Sombre said. "I told you over the phone."

"Oh," he said. "What did he say?"

"He had been well coached, never fear. That's the damnable thing
about it all. Once one opens the door to falsehood! They've made a
liar out of him, like themselves. I had him summoned and I asked
him, What's your name? Luc Casella, he says. All right, I say, that's
enough of that. What's your *real* name? He never even blinked. Luc
Casella, Father, he says. No, I say to him. Don't lie to me, your name
is Benedek. Oh, he says to me, the little hypocrite! You mean that
boy who's missing? No, Father, maybe I look like him, but I'm Luc
Casella. Look at my school card, my name's there. I'm from the
Vosges—and he starts in on the same story the woman told me,
looking me in the eye the whole time."

Fontanel's stomach gurgled loudly, and he winced and coughed.
"And so he wouldn't admit it?" he asked, looking down at the magazine.

Canon Sombre's pink face expressed triumph. "Oh, he came around. He didn't have to say a word. I flipped the newspaper open in front of him. You should have seen his face! His eyes bugged out and he got as pale as death. Jail, he says in a whisper. *Jail!* And then he began to cry and wouldn't answer any more questions. But that was enough. I sent him to the dormitory and called you on the telephone."

It seemed conclusive enough, Fontanel decided. Still, neither that Vincent fellow nor the boy had actually admitted it in so many words. Should he interrogate the boy himself? Tomorrow, he thought.

"This is a very serious matter, monsieur," the other priest said. There was a look of distress on his pale, scholarly face. This was Canon Blevitz, the bishop's adjutant, a small, deprecatory man who wore glasses. Fontanel had never met him before, but in the course of his duties he had once had occasion to telephone the bishop's rectory and had spoken to Blevitz, and found him cooperative and willing to help. Both of them, he thought. They were taking it in the proper spirit. They had come to him immediately, as they should have. There had been quite a stink in the papers, he recalled, about the Church keeping the boy from his aunt. Gossip, he decided. The best proof was the presence of the priests before him, concern written all over them.

"Very serious," he agreed. It occurred to him now that with the discovery of the boy the attention of all France was going to be directed to Garonde and its procureur's office, and that his name was going to get into the newspapers. And in the Ministry of Justice in Paris one higher-up would say to another, Fontanel, eh? Seems to run a tight department down there. Best keep an eye on the fellow. The thought made him almost cheerful. "The bishop sent you, I suppose?"

Canon Blevitz said no, the bishop was out of town for the day. It was quite by accident that he had heard of this unfortunate business. Canon Sombre had bumped into him on the street on his way to the Parquet and had told him the story. He had decided to come along as moral support. Besides, the bishop would want a report on the matter. Might he ask what the procureur had in mind?

"Well," Fontanel said, "it's not really our baby, you know. It's in Touville that he's wanted. I'd best notify them up there, and ask for instructions."

"If I may make a suggestion?" Canon Blevitz said courteously. "I've already mentioned this to Canon Sombre and he is in agreement with me. It was very natural for the canon to speak to the boy to verify his suspicion, but as a result the boy knows he has been found out. For safety's sake—"

"Good heavens!" Fontanel exclaimed, blinking. He hadn't thought of that. If he should get away now! "Where is he at this moment?"

"Quite safe," Canon Sombre assured him. "You need have no fear on that score. There's only the one exit, and that's kept locked. Before I left I spoke to Brother André, the gatekeeper, and told him in no circumstances is the Casella boy to be allowed out. But what Canon Blevitz had in mind—"

"The responsibility," the other priest said. "Canon Sombre is naturally quite upset about this, and would like to be relieved of the care of the child as soon as possible. It's not really a question of his running off. Where would he go? But the canon wishes it to be a matter of public record that he turned the boy over to the authorities as soon as he discovered the truth. The same day. And so we thought of bringing him to you."

"To me?" Fontanel said, astonished. "And what would I do with him?"

"Surely there are facilities . . ." Canon Sombre said tentatively.

He could, he supposed, put the kid in the orphanage for a day or so until the matter was settled; but the thought of the red tape involved made him wince. And even if they accepted him, he had no one to delegate the matter to, he would have to do it himself. The orphanage was out in the country. He would have to wait about until the boy was brought, then drive out in this snowstorm—no, that wouldn't do at all. The only other alternative that occurred to him was to take the boy home with him. He shuddered and said, "I have a better idea, gentlemen. He's well enough off where he is. You tell me yourselves he can't get out. I'll send the telegram, and within a few hours we'll have our instructions. By tomorrow they'll have come for him, and it's off our shoulders. Here, I'll write it off now." He seized a pencil and blocked out letters on a pad. When he had finished, he consulted the directory, silently cursing the tiny letters that seemed to squirm and blur under his forefinger. When this was over, he thought longingly, he was going to make a beeline for home, he was going to get down a good, stiff brandy to settle his stomach, disconnect the telephone, and fall into bed until tomorrow. Ah, there it was! Jeanpré. Gustave Jeanpré.

"How's this, gentlemen? 'Procureur General Jeanpré, Palais Justice, Touville l'Abbaye, Côte-des-Alpes. Superior reports Benedek boy probably boarding pupil St. Ignatius Garonde Stop Awaiting instructions Fontanel Procureur Republic Garonde.' "

"Why 'probably'?" Canon Sombre asked.

"Well, I don't want to stick my neck out on this. So far nobody's actually admitted anything definite." He stood up, and to his relief so did the priests. "Canon," he said to the rector, "I'm leaving the child in your care. That's best all around, and for him as well. He's your responsibility. He's not to be allowed out or receive visitors. Will you accept this responsibility?"

The canon was reluctant. He had hoped— However, if the procureur insisted. He did? Well, then, yes, he would accept it, and he could assure the procureur that when they came for the boy, they would find—

"I'm sure of that," Fontanel said. "I'll drop this off at the telegraph office on my way home." It ought to be in code, he thought, then shrugged. To hell with it. Oh, his head! his head! "Thank you, gentlemen. This way out, please."

Procureur General Gustave Jeanpré, wearing his overcoat, sat at his desk, holding a square of paper in his gloved hand; his long, saturnine face was composed, but Konrad noted a tiny smile under the neat gray mustache and sensed an air of satisfaction about him.

"I'm sorry to have made a mystery of it," Jeanpré said, "but in the circumstances I had no choice. You'll see why in a moment. A little after three o'clock today I received this telegram from Garonde down by the Spanish border, from the Procureur of the Republic there, a Monsieur Fontanel. The nature of the telegram was such as to require you to be notified at once, and at the same time it was not something that could be explained over the telephone. And so I asked you to come here to discuss it with me."

At seven o'clock? Konrad wondered. If the telegram had arrived at three, or a little after, why had the procureur set the time of their meeting so late? Maître Paul was thinking the same thing, he was sure; out of the corner of his eye he caught the slight movement of the lawyer's head that he read as an indication of surprise. Paul was sitting to Konrad's right, in front of the procureur's desk; to Konrad's left was Hannah, and beyond her Jules, who had leaned over and was whispering to her in German. Hannah nodded. Her face was very pale, and she had fixed her eyes on Jeanpré's face. There was no heat in the office, nor in the rest of the Parquet, which was dark and deserted, and they had not removed their coats upon entering. Hannah also wore a heavy scarf and Rina's fur-lined mittens, yet still shivered. The flanges of her nose were red and her eyes gleamed feverishly; she was coming down with what promised to be a wretched cold or worse, and yet she had insisted on coming along with them to the procureur's office. Poor woman! Konrad thought. How she had jumped that afternoon when the telephone call came! "They've found him!" she had cried. "They've found Michel!" And then her shoulders had sagged, and she said in a miserable voice, "That was a stupid thing to say. I don't know why I said that." It was because the same incredible idea had occurred to him that he had replied impatiently, "It's probably not that at all. Let's not get our hopes up without reason." And turned away so as not to see the tears starting in her eyes.

Jeanpré waved the telegram. "I'm going to read it to you. It's addressed to me, and says the following: 'Superior reports Benedek boy probably boarding pupil St. Ignatius Garonde Stop Awaiting instructions Fontanel Procureur Republic Garonde.'"

"Oh!" Hannah cried faintly. The name, Konrad thought. She had caught the name. She had been right. He himself was conscious of no surprise, only a dull feeling of satisfaction. The words "At last!" shaped themselves in his mind. He did not look at Hannah, who was whispering excitedly to Jules. Jeanpré leaned forward and handed the telegram to Maître Paul, who glanced at it and said, "Probably? What does he mean by 'probably'?"

Konrad had been about to say the same thing.

"I know no more than you," Jeanpré said gravely. "Of course, that was the first thing that struck me. Probably! I said to myself. What does the fellow mean by it? It's either the Benedek boy or it isn't. You can guess what happened. They've got some boy at St. Ignatius whose identity is suspect. They think it may be the one we're looking for. The obvious thing to do would be to verify before sending out an alarm like this. It would be easy enough, it seems to me. But no, the man rushes to the telegraph office and sends off the wire and says, 'Awaiting instructions.' What am I supposed to tell him? Dear Colleague, if it's *probably* the Benedek boy, you can *probably* take him in charge? This Fontanel must be some kind of prize idiot. Aside from not making the most elementary check of his facts, he sends the telegram in clear, not in code, for all the world to read. Heaven knows how many hands it's passed through! Right now telephone lines must be buzzing throughout Touville and Garonde, and by tomorrow you'll see it in the newspapers. The damnable thing about it all is that it's Sunday. Ordinarily the telegram wouldn't have taken more than an hour to get to me, and I'd have got through to him at once on the telephone and got him to explain himself. But today it took more than three hours—he handed it in at noon—and when I put in a call to his office, there was no answer, of course. Or at his home either. The phone there seems to be out of order. And so I sent identical telegrams to both places, telling him I would telephone him at his office at seven tonight, and to be there to take the call."

The mystery was explained. The procureur had done the only thing he could do. There was certainly no point in rushing off to Garonde unless they were sure. Konrad was suddenly assailed by doubt.

"I think it only fair to tell you," he said, "that this may be part of an elaborate hoax. Yesterday I received two phone calls, and this morning another, about the boy. They were from friends of mine who had gotten wind of his whereabouts. One of them, Arnauld the pharmacist, had heard that the boy was in a religious institution in Alsace. He was all excited about it, insisted that it was true, because he had heard it from a scrubwoman who works at the nursery on Rue Charente, which is run by a friend of Mademoiselle Rose. She said it was common knowledge at the nursery, and everybody was talking about it. But Dr. Lévy, the chest specialist, got a tip that the boy is hidden in a Dominican monastery in Voreppe. And someone else called to say that he was seen in Marseilles, taking a train for Belfort, where a private family was ready to take him in. And when I pinned them down, it turned out that the source was also from the circle of the Rose woman's friends or employees. I think they're doing it deliberately, to send us off on wild-goose chases. Not my friends, they were perfectly sincere and trying to help. No doubt the Rose woman engineered it before she was locked up. Even in jail the woman's a menace."

Jeanpré weighed the point, his eyes narrowed. "Fontanel's telegram seems to be quite a different thing," he remarked. "Although that 'probably' does stick in my craw. However, if it turns out to be a false lead, I'll have the others investigated. One of them may just be true. We'll know soon."

Konrad looked at his watch. "It's seven-ten now."

"The call is going through," Jeanpré said. "It's already been placed with the operator. We must be patient."

Konrad made no reply. How easy it was to counsel patience when one stood on the outside of events! For years now he had learned that virtue out of necessity, and had learned as well to bear with those who urged it on him. But in the last three weeks, ever since the trial, he had been aware of an increasing sense of irritation with those who used the word so glibly. The Appeals Court decision of last summer still stood, was still executory, pending the verdict of Assizes; the boy had been flushed from his hiding place in Switzerland, and was on the run; the Rose woman was in jail—all these counted as victories in the agonizingly long struggle, and yet their quarry still eluded them, little Michel was still not in their hands, had put in his tantalizing appearance at the court and been swallowed up once more. It was only a matter of time, all assured him, and in the meanwhile he must be patient. But time now brought a double suffering. Hannah was with them now, and it was intolerable to see how the woman was wasting away, mooned about the house with only one thought on her mind, and jumped at every ring of the telephone or doorbell. And he had been patient enough, he supposed, with all the well-wishers, curiosity-seekers, busybodies and reporters who had thronged his home recently, with whom he had gone over the facts as he had a thousand times in the past, unwilling to let pass a single opportunity to scotch the lies the Rose woman had spread about through the years. Oh yes, he could be patient! But it was one thing to possess one's soul in waiting, and another to allow oneself to be made a fool of, to be given the runaround. And that was why he had refused to accede to Mlle Rose's demand for provisional liberty. And, to stimulate the hunt, sworn out a complaint against the woman for kidnaping and murder.

Hannah plucked at his sleeve. He turned to her, forcing a cheerful smile to his lips. It had to be true! she insisted. A procureur of the Republic! An official! He would not send such a telegram without being sure. She held a handkerchief in her mittened hands, and was twisting it into knots. Very likely, he said, and Jules nodded, patting her shoulder. A little while longer, Jules assured her, and she would have her boy.

It was seven-fifteen.

Jeanpré and Paul were discussing the request for provisional liberty. No, the lawyer said, they would not agree to it. In fact, they had filed their answer with the court this morning, within the twenty-four-hour deadline. Mlle Rose claimed to be sick, to be suffering from uremia, but her appeal had no medical opinion attached to it. She claimed to have eight adopted children at the Nursery who needed her care, but when you counted those she named there were only three, two of whom were away at school, and the other was a young woman of twenty. She claimed that the Nursery could not operate properly without her, but who had taken care of the Nursery during the month of her so-called sick leave and the many other trips she had made to see Michel?

"We have no desire to be vindictive," Maître Paul said. "If she's really sick, they'll put her in the prison infirmary, and she'll be well taken care of. We simply can't have her on the outside and pulling strings to flout the law. Why," he said, "where would she be now, if she were at liberty? With her network of spies here in town, don't you think she'd have heard about the telegram within a matter of minutes? At this moment she'd be on the train for Garonde, racing to get the boy out of that school before we come to claim him."

"Unless," Konrad said, "it was she who had the telegram sent."

"Oh, come now!" Jeanpré said.

Konrad shrugged. "Anyone can send a telegram. You don't have to prove identity."

The telephone rang. Jeanpré swung around in his chair and stared at it for a moment before picking it up. "Hello," he said. "Hello? What? Jeanpré here. I can't hear you. What? Speak louder. I'm shouting too. Fontanel? Is that you? You got my telegram? Good. Yes, of course I got yours, otherwise— Now listen, I have to be sure about this. You wrote that it was probably the boy we're looking for. What do you mean by 'probably'? Didn't you verify? What? How?"

For perhaps thirty seconds the procureur listened in silence, frowning, his eyes intent. Konrad's throat was suddenly dry. What was Fontanel saying? This much was sure—he had sent the telegram and it was not a hoax. But was it really Michel? It seemed an age to Konrad before Jeanpré's mouth twitched and relaxed, and he nodded significantly at them. An inarticulate sound came from Hannah. Konrad let his breath out and exchanged glances with Maître Paul.

"All right," Jeanpré cried. "What have you done with him? Where is he?" Again he listened, and this time his eyes opened in incredulous shock. "You did *what?*" he all but shouted. "You *left* him there! But why didn't you—? What? I didn't get that name. Canon what? Sombre? Yes, but— Yes, I know that, but— Don't you read the papers? Do you realize what the issues are? I tell you, you don't know these people, they're capable of anything. I advise you most strongly to take him out of the school at once, and make yourself personally responsible for him. You should have done that immediately. What? Now look here, Fontanel, it's *your* responsibility. You can delegate it if you want to, but if there's any slip-up you'll catch it, not him. I won't argue with you. I've given you my opinion. Now, here's what we're going to do. Monsieur Louis Konrad, legal representative of the guardian, is catching the next train to Garonde." Jeanpré's raised eyebrows interrogated him, and Konrad nodded. "He'll identify himself to you, and bring the court order with him. You're to turn the boy over to him, and no one else. I'll forward precise instructions in the meanwhile. And until Monsieur Konrad gets there, the boy is to be kept *incommunicado*. Impress that on the headmaster. And one more thing. In the future, if any further communication is necessary, put it in code. All right. Good-bye."

Jeanpré turned to them, his face flushed. "It's the boy all right," he announced. "Extraordinary type, that Fontanel. Did I say probably? he said to me. No, no, it's the Benedek boy, the rector questioned him and he admitted it. If he had said so in the first place, you'd be on your way by now. He's left the boy at the school. I know," he said, as Konrad made a gesture. "You heard what I told him. And he answered that it was the headmaster himself who came to tell him about the boy, and that the man will certainly take good care not to let him get away. We're in Basque country, he said. A Basque priest doesn't break his word."

Jules grunted.

"I beg your pardon?" Jeanpré said.

"He said, Jesuits!" Konrad said. "St. Ignatius. It must be a Jesuit school. Like the one in Switzerland. Basques or Swiss, they're Jesuits. But all right, we've no choice in the matter. I'd better see about trains."

Please, Hannah said. She wanted to go to Garonde with him. Konrad shook his head. It was her right, she insisted. She was his aunt and guardian. Konrad took in her worn face and watery eyes, and refused. It was a long and tiring journey. Bad enough, for her sake, if her condition worsened, became flu or pneumonia; but then he would have to take care of her, and be hindered in getting Michel. She had better stay with Rina. He would bring Michel to her there, and she would have him the rest of her life. This was not his real reason, as he well knew; he had remembered his ill-fated trip to Strasbourg with the boy's other aunt, and its tragic aftermath. No more of that!

Hannah turned away, dabbing at her eyes.

"I'll go with you," Jules said.

Konrad asked permission to use the telephone to call the railroad station. He was in luck. An express train left at eight-thirty. There were many changes and long stopovers on the way, but even then it was the fastest on the timetable. It arrived at Garonde at two-fifteen the following afternoon.

They made their plans hurriedly, for it was already twenty to eight. Konrad telephoned Rina, broke the good news to her in a half-dozen words, and interrupted her rejoicing to tell her to pack him a light bag. Then Jules called Lise. They thanked Procureur Jeanpré and hurried out of the office and down the stairs of the courthouse. Konrad was to drive Hannah home, pick up his bag, and go to Maître Paul's office. For his part, Maître Paul was to drive his own car to his office, dropping Jules at his home on the way, and dig the court order from his files. He would be waiting in the street with it, and Konrad would pick it up without loss of time and head for the station. Jules would meet him there, arriving by taxi. They had just time to make it.

A nun was walking across the concourse toward the gate where Jules was waiting. He recognized the costume. A Temple Dame. No doubt from that snooty school on the Lyons highway, half hidden behind its immaculate shrubbery. They were dedicated to converting Jews to the one true religion, he had heard. Christers, Lise called them. The things she came out with! This one was a looker. She certainly was! And the way she walked! She didn't walk, she floated. Like a queen or something. Such a waste, he thought philosophically. The vows they took. He turned aside so as not to seem to be staring, but as she passed him he stole another glance at her and their eyes met. A little shock went through him like an electric current, although the nun's face was completely expressionless. In grudging admiration he watched her go through the gate and board the train. Then he sighed and looked at the clock suspended from the ceiling.

Eight twenty-five, and no sign of Konrad.

Inexorably, the great minute hand made its little jerking movements with a slight click. At eight twenty-nine the ticket taker blew his whistle and asked if he were taking the train or not. He replied that he was waiting for a friend. "Suit yourself," the man said. A few moments later he slammed the gate, a light flashed by the locomotive, and the train departed. Jules looked after it regretfully, and put the tickets in his pocket. When he turned around, Konrad was running toward him, his bag tucked under his arm, his coattails flapping. Jules smiled at him. "We missed it," he said. "What took you so long?"

"Damn!" Konrad muttered, staring tight-lipped through the grille. Then he put down his bag and took off his hat, running his hand over his forehead. It was the court order, he said shortly. It was not in Paul's files as they had thought, but in Lanson's. They had had to wait until the old lawyer got to his office, and quick as he was about it, it was still a fraction too long. But there was no use going without the court order. Fontanel would be within his rights to refuse to deliver the boy.

"Oh well," Jules said. "Don't take it to heart. There's another train at eleven fifty-six. Of course, it's not an express. It takes a few hours longer. But we'll get there. And in the meanwhile we can get something to eat. I'm starved."

"Damn that Fontanel," Konrad said, "and his 'probably.' "

3

A SINGLE CHIME rang out from the clock tower as the taxi arrived at the entrance to the Temple in Biarritz. Alighting, Mother Veronica looked up at the graceful cupola dark against the leaden winter sky. It was two-thirty. She approached the gate lodge and demanded to be shown immediately into the presence of the mother superior. The nun on duty, astonished at being addressed by her name, and flustered under the unswerving gaze of the visitor, whose silver crucifix proclaimed her rank, broke the rule of the order by leaving the gate unattended and ushering her in person to the superior's office.

Three nuns gaped at her as she swept into the room. They were standing by a small round table on which lay a newspaper, which they had evidently been discussing when the gatekeeper rapped at the door. Their faces were worried.

"Mother Marie-Candelaria," she said to one of them. "I must speak to you in private. Return to your duties," she added to the gatekeeper, who started and beat a hasty retreat, crossing herself. A moment later, two nuns passed her, bowing, and went out the door.

"Do you know me, Mother?" the other nun said uncertainly, taking a step forward.

"I am Mother Veronica, of the Touville community," she replied.

"Oh, thank God!" Mother Marie-Candelaria cried, clasping her hands.

Approaching, Mother Veronica looked down at the newspaper. The headline was, "BENEDEK BOY FOUND IN GARONDE!" Under it, in smaller capitals, were the words: "HELD UNDER SURVEILLANCE PENDING ARRIVAL OF M. KONRAD." The paper was the *Sud-Ouest,* and was dated Monday, February 2, 1953. An afternoon publication, she thought; in the morning papers, which she had picked up during the stopover in Toulouse, there had been no mention of the new turn of events. Although the "Benedek affair" still held the front pages, the only new facts she had learned were that Mlle Rose had been removed to the prison infirmary, and that her lawyers were drawing up an appeal to the Court of Cassation. Was it possible, she had wondered as the train sped through the snowy countryside fresh and radiant under the morning sun, that the rector of St. Ignatius had changed his mind and had not gone to the police after all? True, the grocer Immermann had been waiting by the gate in the Touville station when she boarded the train last night; but it was just barely possible that it was a mere coincidence. And he had not taken the train. He was still standing by the gate when it left.

Now she saw that her momentary optimism had been unwarranted. The worst had happened, because of a Jesuit headmaster who did not know canon law, and that weakling brother of Mlle Vincent, who had been unable to stand up to his superior in a moment of crisis. And these, she thought in a rare surge of bitterness, were the Lord's anointed. Had she come too late? Was the boy out of her reach? Sinking down into a chair, she picked up the newspaper and read the article with care, ignoring Mother Marie-Candelaria, who started to speak to her, then interrupted herself and sat down, watching her anxiously.

When she had finished, her hope had renewed itself. The boy was not yet in the hands of the police, if the article could be believed; he had been left at the school until Konrad should arrive to take him. And Konrad at this moment was speeding on his way to Garonde, the reporter stated; he had taken the eleven fifty-six train from Touville and would arrive at ten-fifteen on Monday night. She had not been mistaken, she realized. Immermann had been waiting for Konrad, who had not arrived on time, and they had missed the train. She looked at her watch. It was two-forty. God's will, she thought. She had eight hours.

She turned calmly to the other nun. "Thank you for being so patient," she said. "I understand how you feel. You received the note I sent with Mademoiselle Vincent, and agreed to act as correspondent for a child whose name was Luc Casella. And now you discover in the newspaper that you have been deceived as to the boy's identity, and have unwittingly become involved in a scandalous affair. I ask your forgiveness for this. You can readily understand that I could not commit such a secret to writing. I intended to pay you a visit in the near future and give you a full explanation. Unfortunately, the boy's identity has become known through an unforeseen coincidence, and he is in great danger of being lost to us. And so I have come to talk to you, and to ask your further cooperation. Listen!"

First, Mother Veronica decided, the newspapers—all of them—to see if any had gleaned any scrap of information she did not yet possess. Mother Marie-Candelaria, who had been immediately won over and expressed her eagerness to help, sent out for them, and Mother Veronica spread them out on the superior's desk, which the other had ceded to her as her right. They added nothing to what she already knew, except that it was Canon Sombre himself who had given out the secret to the press. This appeared in the *Dauphiné Libéré*, whose reporter stated that he had been summoned by the headmaster of St. Ignatius late Sunday night, in order to be sure, the priest said, that "the facts were not distorted and his innocence in the matter clearly understood." With a man like that, Mother Veronica decided instantly, there was nothing to be done.

She would have to use Father Vincent.

But was the boy really at the school? Or had there been a change of plan? She had to find out. Mother Marie-Candelaria brought her Gervaise, a plump, brassy, loud-voiced country woman who worked in the convent kitchen, and who could be relied upon for a mission of this sort. The woman entered, wiping her hands on her apron, her face guarded as though expecting some reprimand. Mother Veronica spoke to her briefly. She was to go to Garonde at once; her only purpose was to learn whether the boy was still at St. Ignatius. Nothing else. She was not to try to see him or speak to him, or arouse suspicion in any way. Could she do this? Gervaise, glancing at Mother Marie-Candelaria, bobbed in an awkward curtsy, and swore that the reverend mother could rely on her.

When the woman, delighted with the assignment, had gone on her way, Mother Veronica placed a telephone call to Mlle Vincent in Touville. Were there any new developments there? Yes, Mlle Vincent said. The boy's aunt, having filed a charge of kidnaping and murder—what a ridiculous business! Murder!—against Odette Rose, had now amended her complaint, in view of the discovery of the boy's whereabouts, to kidnaping alone. And Odette was quite sick, had suffered some sort of breakdown. Nerves, apparently. Yet she had been refused provisional liberty.

"Very well," Mother Veronica said. "Please inform the community that I have arrived safely at my destination, and have every hope of completing the task I have come for. Tell Sister Blanche, and no one else, that I shall almost certainly be arrested within a day or two, and—please don't interrupt," she said coldly, as Mlle Vincent's voice squawked in her ear. "Tell her that the police will come to the Temple to question them about the boy. They know nothing about the matter, and are to place the entire responsibility on me. Do you understand? Very well. And now I need a legal opinion. Mademoiselle Rose has appealed the recent decision to the Court of Cassation. I must know whether the original Appeals Court decision of last summer is still executory, in view of the new appeal. There will have to be a *règlement de juges*. Does this affect the first judgment?"

"Maître Cauchet," Mlle Vincent began cautiously.

"No. There must be no doubt about this. Go to the Procureur General himself. You are a member of the city council. There has been some talk of suspending Mademoiselle Rose from her job—you can say that one of Konrad's Communist friends is behind it, without mentioning any names—and a vote of no-confidence will be brought up for the council's consideration. Your conscience is troubling you, you do not know how to vote if that eventuality occurs. If the decree is still executory, Mademoiselle Rose continues to be in opposition to the law, and that will affect your vote. That is your cover. Jeanpré will accept it, and will talk. He will be in a good mood today, you can be sure. Do this at once, and call me back without delay." She paused a moment, then added, "Incidentally, you will be arrested as well."

A smile formed on her pale lips as she hung up and turned to Mother Marie-Candelaria, who was watching her in awe. "Do you know Father Vincent at St. Ignatius?" she asked. The nun shook her head. "No matter," Mother Veronica said. "He will know of course who you are. Telephone the school and ask to speak to him. They must allow you to do so, for you are the child's correspondent, and you are calling to inquire about his welfare. Insist if you must: Father Vincent, and no one else. Tell him that he must come to Biarritz at once, on a matter of the greatest urgency. If he is recalcitrant, and he will be, tell him briefly that it concerns his sister."

While Mother Marie-Candelaria placed her call, Mother Veronica consulted the railway timetable she had asked to have brought to her.

Garonde–Biarritz–Bordeaux–Orléans–Paris, there it was. A train left that night at ten twenty-three. Eight minutes after Konrad's arrival in Garonde. If God willed, she would be on that train, her mission accomplished. She would be in Paris before the news was out. Time enough to report to the mother general. But no doubt the police would be waiting for her at Touville, on her return. By then it would not matter.

"I can't tell you over the phone," Mother Marie-Candelaria was saying. She was speaking to the priest. From the way the nun glanced sideways at her, her eyebrows raised in dismay, Mother Veronica gathered that Vincent was proving difficult. "It's terribly important, Father, I wouldn't call you if it weren't. It's—it's about your sister. I can't tell you any more." Even from where she sat, Mother Veronica heard the man's voice raised in expostulation. The nun covered the mouthpiece with her hand and whispered, "A little after six?" Mother Veronica nodded, and Mother Marie-Candelaria said, "Very well, Father, if you can't come earlier. No, it must be in person. Good-bye."

"Now," Mother Veronica said, as the other hung up, "I must ask you to go to Garonde yourself. I would not ask you to do this if anyone else would do. It is imperative that I speak to the bishop. You must arrange it for me, either directly with His Excellency himself, or with his adjutant Canon Blevitz. Tell them only as much as is necessary for the appointment to be granted. You may have difficulty with the canon, since he has already taken a stand by going with the rector to the police. If he is unwilling, call me from his office, and I will speak to him. But I do not think that will be necessary. By now certain doubts will have occurred to him." She made a rapid calculation. A half-hour with Vincent. Fifteen minutes to the station. A half-hour to Garonde. "Make the appointment for seven-thirty. Later if necessary, but not earlier. And wait for me at the rectory. I want you to be present as well."

No sooner had Mother Marie-Candelaria gone than the telephone rang. It was Gervaise, calling from the station at Garonde. Yes, she said breathlessly, the boy was still there. She had had no trouble at all in finding that out. She had brought along a bag of cookies, and told the gatekeeper she had read about the poor orphan child in the newspapers, and her heart had had the urge to bring him a present. The gatekeeper, who was not a priest but a brother and a scowly fellow, had told her to be off, that no one was permitted to see the boy;

but the prefect of discipline had happened to be entering at the moment, had listened to her story, and taken the cookies to give to the boy, saying he was in the dormitory.

"Thank you," Mother Veronica said. "You have done well."

"My Christian duty, Mother," the woman said.

It was four twenty-five. Two of her precious hours had gone by.

At quarter to five Mlle Vincent called from Touville. She had been to see Jeanpré, who had received her readily enough and merely nodded at her problem of conscience. The question was an academic one, he said. In a matter of hours, he said, the boy would be with his aunt, and all charges against Mlle Rose would be dropped. The arrest had been preventive rather than punitive. Once the boy was found, there was no reason for the woman to be held any longer, and no doubt the vote of no-confidence would be forgotten. But, for her information, the Appeals Court decision was still executory; the appeal to Cassation made no difference, being concerned only with the question of jurisdiction, that is, whether the case, if continued—and there was no reason to do so—would be a civil or criminal one.

"Mother," Mlle Vincent said, when she had completed her report, "what am I to say when I'm arrested? I mean, about—"

"The truth," she replied. "As little of it as possible. And only what you know of your own knowledge, that is, what you did yourself. For the rest, refer them to me."

"Oh, Mother!" The woman's voice came in a little wail. "I don't mind for myself. But to think that *you*—"

Abruptly Mother Veronica hung up. The decree was still executory then. Not that it mattered to her. But Bishop Reynaud—would he be willing to defy the law? Was he a Canon Sombre? Or a Father Bosch? Well, she had an ultimate weapon in case of need.

It was not until almost six o'clock that Mother Marie-Candelaria called from Garonde. She must have been speaking from the rectory, for her voice was guarded as she announced that Monseigneur would see her, not at the hour she had requested, but at eight-thirty. Canon Blevitz was listening, Mother Veronica decided, and had needed persuasion. "Very well," she said gravely. "I shall be there."

And now Vincent, she thought. All the pieces of her puzzle had fallen into place. She sat in the dark, waiting. She had not slept since Saturday night, and then only four hours; but she was not tired. On the contrary, her spirit was lifted up in a song of praise to the All-

Powerful, who had given her these hours in which to do her part. Her mind, fresh and confident, went over her plan. It would work, she had no doubt. God could not have let her move so far toward the dream He Himself had instilled in her soul, only to fail her now. Michel was hers! And through her, the instrument created before time was, he would be the world's. In a few moments, when the power of persuasion was needed to spur her human helpers to do what she could not do herself, the words would be there, as they had been for Blessed Mother Miriam. She was absolutely certain of this, and as she sat in the dark room, waiting, she rejoiced to feel that He to whom she had given herself as a bride should allow her, in the measure of her powers, to become one with His ineffable will.

At six-twenty she heard a motorcycle roaring up the incline of the road before the Temple. A few minutes later, one of the nuns rapped at the door and announced timidly that a Father Vincent had asked to speak to the mother superior.

Mother Veronica crossed herself. "Let him come in," she said.

Father Vincent arrived at the Temple half frozen. Prey to all sorts of morbid fancies after the nun's telephone message, he had asked Father Morsan, almoner at St. Ignatius, to take him to Biarritz on his motorcycle. But he had not counted on the force of the wind they created by their passage. Mounted behind the other priest, who had a leather windbreaker and goggles to protect himself, Father Vincent had found that his overcoat was no protection at all. No matter how he crouched and buried his head between his shoulders, the icy air knifed its way with demonic power through every opening, from below, up his sleeves, down his neck, ballooning his coat behind him and wrapping his chilled flesh in an ironlike mantle of cold. When he dismounted before the Temple, he staggered from the stiffness of his limbs, his face was raw and red, and his eyes smarted. The hem of his cassock was crusted with mud. He was furious at Soldie for having brought her peck of trouble into his peaceful world, and at himself for having run like an ingenuous boy to the rendezvous. What could the nuns of Biarritz tell him about his sister? It was another of Soldie's tricks. And yet underneath his anger was the nagging doubt.

Ushered into the mother superior's dark office, he took a step forward and stopped. Then a lamp went on, and he saw a nun standing before him. She stood motionless, her hands at her sides. Her face was like marble, smooth and white, her lips a thin, pale line. Was it the reflection of the light, or were her eyes really flashing? The aura of force that emanated from her was so strong that he felt his resentment vanish. He knew at once that this was not the nun who had spoken to him on the telephone. This was Mother Veronica, as Soldie had described her.

"You are Father Vincent, brother of Isolde Vincent of Touville," she said. It was not a question, but a statement, and her voice was cold and harsh. Father Vincent nodded wordlessly, his eyes fixed on her face.

She took a step forward. "A soul was entrusted to you. You accepted that responsibility and promised to guard him. Yet you have not done so."

He could only stammer, "My superior—"

She cut him off, her voice hardly raised yet lashing in its intensity. "You are a priest. You wear the Jesuit habit. A soldier of God. You have studied canon law. Yet you let that child be taken from you without a struggle because a misguided man, frightened for his own skin, gave you a scolding. You should have resisted. You should have gone to the bishop. All else failing, you should have removed the boy from the school, as your sister begged you to do. You did nothing. You are a disgrace to the cloth you bear."

His body aching, his eyes bleary and unfocused, Father Vincent heard these words more in astonishment than anger. Never had a nun spoken to him in that tone. And yet, such was the authority of her bearing, it did not occur to him to protest. She was quite near to him now, although he had not seen her move. It was not the light. Her eyes were full of fire. It was unbearable to look at them. He repressed the urge to cross himself, aware that his hands had begun to tremble. It was the cold, he told himself fiercely.

"That boy belongs to God," the nun said. "He is baptized. It is not for you or anyone else to let him fall into infidel hands. It is years now that we have labored to keep him within the Church. You in a moment of weakness have imperiled his salvation. But it is not too late. There is one chance to save him. We must take that chance."

What did she mean? Canon Sombre had already gone to the Parquet, the story had come out in the newspapers, the whole world knew the boy had been found. But his thoughts were so disorganized that he could only mutter, "The law."

She repeated the word with such scorn that he took a step backwards. "There is only one law! God's! The law you are sworn with your whole being to maintain. At the cost of martyrdom, if need be."

He turned from her, staring at the floor. He well knew what a miserable figure he must cut in her eyes, with his disreputable muddy cassock, his grimy, windburned face, his uncombed hair. Like a penitent boy, cowardly and ashamed. But he could not help himself, he stood rooted to the spot as she continued to speak, her terrible words burning into him. He hardly knew what she said, only that in measure as she spoke he saw himself with his shell of human vanity stripped away, in all his ugly nakedness. He had taken the easy way out. He had accepted the boy, not from conviction, not to rejoice heaven with the lamb that might have strayed, but because Soldie had outtalked him. He had let Canon Sombre bully him, dismissing for the sake of expediency the moral scruples that nagged at him. He had handed the whole package back to Soldie with a telephone call, washing his hands of the matter like another Pilate. He, the man of God, the weakest of all His children! This fantastic nun, raging at him with whispered words that struck like blows, was right. He had failed the boy, himself, and God.

And yet . . . Smarting under his own self-condemnation, he suddenly became angry. He had not asked for this, had not volunteered in the game they were playing. They had come to him, had caught him by surprise without adequate preparation, and expected him to perform miracles. They had not let him into their councils; they had handed him the boy, saying in effect, Here, he's yours, protect him. How, in heaven's name? He was a priest, a teacher, a man of meditation and prayer, not one of their Resistance heroes. He should have done this, he should have done that. It was unthinkable that he should defy his superior. And anyway, regardless of what he should have done, the police knew now and the fat was in the fire. There was nothing he could do about it now. Why hadn't they kept the boy to themselves, if it was so important? By what authority did she speak to him like this?

With the violence of the timid man who is pushed too far, he wheeled on her. Before he could speak she held out her hand. There was an envelope in it, unsealed. He took it wonderingly, and at her gesture opened it and took out the single folded sheet of paper it contained. What was this? His eyes took in the engraved letterhead, in fine, spidery letters; the salutation to "Our Beloved Sister in Christ, Reverend Mother Veronica"; the apostolic benediction; the brief message; the signature, ending in a wavy scrawl; the Secretarial seal, which he recognized. The letter was an unequivocal command to the addressee and to all religious and lay Catholics of whatever degree to do all in their power to prevent the minor Michel Benedek of Touville, Côte-des-Alpes, France, from being forced into apostasy by falling into the hands of those who would interrupt his Christian education.

"Rome!" he muttered. He felt the blood drain from his face, and was close to fainting. God, God, what had he done? The nun took the letter from his nerveless fingers. "Your sister tried to tell you. You would not listen. Yet you can redeem yourself."

He had to sit down. He let himself collapse in a chair. After a while he leaned forward and buried his face in his hands. He remained in that attitude while Mother Veronica told him what he must do. Everything rested on him. It had to be someone *inside* the school. The boy had to be gotten out. Immediately, before he was turned over to the police. The emissary of the family was arriving late tonight, which meant that the transfer of the boy would probably take place the first thing in the morning. He had until daybreak. She didn't care how he did it, that was up to him. No doubt some of his colleagues at the school would help him. He must know someone in the city who could be relied upon to keep the boy under cover—a parish priest, say, who would understand the importance of the matter, and who could be told, in strictest confidence, of the letter she had just showed him.

He listened, breathing hard. What she proposed was so foreign to his nature that he could not envisage himself doing it. Yet the Holy See had spoken. It *had* to be done, and he was the only one who could. Canon Sombre's face came to him, apoplectic in its wrath, and he shuddered. If he had the bishop behind him! Rome was far away. He stammered as much to the nun, who said, "Make your plans. I will speak to the bishop. He will get word to you."

After a while she said, "Go now." Her voice was kindly at last, and he felt an irrational surge of gratitude as he rose to his feet. At the door he looked back. The nun was standing in the same attitude, except that she had lifted her face, as if in prayer. He had the impression that only a tremendous effort of will kept her from sinking to the floor.

Only after he had left did he realize that he had forgotten to ask about his sister.

Bishop Reynaud sat in a high-backed chair covered in black leather. The lamplight glinted warmly on its rich surface and sent strong shadows over the features bent over the letter. His mouth was set in a tiny, rueful smile. A Renaissance head, Mother Veronica thought. The long, narrow cast, the smooth hair touched with silver above the ears, the predatory nose with its thin-ridged arch, the eyes keen and tolerant at the same time. This one would make his own decisions, she had concluded on first meeting him. And once he had decided, he would carry out the plan with strength and discretion. She need not have been concerned, this was no Canon Sombre. She herself had to fade out of the picture; but her replacement was at hand.

Canon Blevitz, standing uneasily at the edge of the circle of light, stepped forward at the bishop's motion and took the letter. His pale face tightened as he read, and a sigh escaped him. Wordlessly he handed it back and returned to his former position, his head bowed.

Bishop Reynaud said, "We shall obey, of course. There can be no question about that. The injunction is categorical. I am only sorry matters got as far as they did before I was informed."

With distress in his voice Canon Blevitz said, "I have already explained to Your Excellency—"

"Yes, after the event," the bishop said. "I know I was away. But it was a hasty move. Sombre is a hysterical old woman. You know my opinion of him. That's neither here nor there, however. The good sisters are right. The boy must be removed at once. But I am concerned with the legal aspects of the matter. The Procureur General of Touville states that the decree is executory. But there are some unusual circumstances connected with this case. If the decree is carried out, the boy will be taken away to a foreign country, out of French legal jurisdiction. Yet the final decision is still pending. Cassation will pronounce, the case will be heard again. And if the foster mother, this Mademoiselle Rose, wins, what then? Will they return him? There is a manifest injustice here."

Mother Veronica offered up a silent prayer of gratitude. He was all she had hoped he would be. "I have always thought so," she said.

The bishop mused, tapping the letter on his knee. "A most delicate situation," he said. "There will be a great public outcry. We must be prepared for slanderous attacks in the newspapers. They will call it a kidnaping, I'm afraid. And yet we are only protecting our own. Could the Procureur General possibly be mistaken?"

"If I may suggest, Your Excellency," she said.

"Please."

"I believe we should ask for a higher opinion. That of the Minister of Justice. If he should support our view, the public clamor will be stilled, and Michel will be safe from the law for the time being. It is unlikely, I admit. But even the request will have its uses. We shall all be questioned, we must remember."

She saw from his face that he had understood. He nodded and said, "The suggestion is a good one. And it so happens that we may be in a position to implement it. His Excellency Monsieur Fouquet-Quarles is now in Garonde. He is leaving for Paris tonight, having been selected by Premier René Mayer to form part of his new cabinet. If he will, he can reach the ear of the Minister of Justice with our request for an opinion. Canon Blevitz, I'll ask you to reach him by telephone. From your office. When you are connected, pass the call to me here."

Mother Veronica watched the priest's slight figure hurry to the door.

"This letter," the bishop said, holding it up.

"It should remain with you, Your Excellency. You may have further need of it. As for me, my part is done with my visit here. I must not have the letter with me when I am taken into custody."

"You have taken it all on yourself, Reverend Mother," he said. "It will go hard with you."

"The child is my responsibility. He has always been, from the beginning. In any case, my part cannot be hidden. And the law will need a scapegoat."

"Nonetheless, it remains that you have chosen the harder part, that of self-sacrifice."

She permitted herself a smile. "It was not I who chose."

He spread his hands, and she knew he had expected that answer.

They sat in silence, waiting. At length a buzzer sounded. Bishop Reynaud rose and picked up the telephone. For perhaps ten minutes he spoke softly into it, then hung up and returned to his chair. A moment later Canon Blevitz entered the room.

Bishop Reynaud said, "Dear Sisters, you have done well to come to me. If Canon Sombre had done the same before taking his ill-advised action, we would not be in the predicament in which we now find ourselves. But it is still not too late. Tomorrow the Minister of Justice will be asked for an opinion. In the meanwhile I shall take steps to assure that the boy is not lost to us pending that opinion. What these are need not concern you. It is better that you do not know. The police will learn of this meeting, and will inquire as to its purpose. We shall of course speak the truth. And the truth is this: You heard that the boy who was in your care was about to be turned over to his family. You could not believe that this was in accordance with the true spirit of the law, in view of the new appeal to the Court of Cassation. You were naturally disturbed. You came to consult your superior in Christ. In your presence he in turn consulted by telephone with His Excellency Monsieur Fouquet-Quarles. Then he spoke to you in these words: Mother Veronica, Mother Marie-Candelaria, return to your duties. You have done what you believed to be right, but there is nothing more you can do. Let the law take its course. If an injustice has been done, the Minister of Justice will take the necessary measures. If not, we must bow our heads to the inevitable. Do you understand?"

Mother Veronica stood up, and her companion, staring at the bishop, caught her movement and also rose.

The bishop said gravely, "Leave all the rest to me."

Downstairs, the telephone was ringing. It had to be the private phone in the rector's office, which by a peculiarity of construction of the school building could be heard on the second floor. The canon was out; he had left in a great hurry a half-hour earlier, rousing Brother André and telling him he could be reached at the bishop's residence if necessary, and that no one not a member of the staff—did he understand, *no one*—was to be permitted past the door.

There were three priests with Father Vincent in his tiny quarters. "You had better answer it," one of them said to him.

He nodded and hurried out the door. By the time he got downstairs the telephone had stopped ringing. But Brother André was hobbling toward him in the dark corridor. "It's for you, Father," he said, panting. "Telephone. In the rector's office."

"Who is it?" he asked.

Brother André shrugged and spread his hands. So much the better, Father Vincent thought. He walked quickly ahead. The rector's door was open, and his desk lamp was lit. The hands of the little clock beside it pointed to ten. He picked up the receiver and said breathlessly, "Yes?"

A voice in his ear said, "Who is speaking?"

"Father Vincent."

"This is Canon Blevitz," the voice said. "Monseigneur is now in conference with Canon Sombre, who has made a full report to him concerning the child Luc Casella. Monseigneur has instructed me to inform you that you are to consider yourself severely reprimanded for your part in this affair. There will, however, be no further disciplinary action. Do you understand?"

"Yes, Canon," he said, bewildered. "But—"

The voice went on, marking each word with peculiar emphasis. "Monseigneur has also requested me to tell you that he has full confidence in the religious who spoke to you in Biarritz this afternoon. I am referring, in case it has slipped your mind, to the person who requested you to visit her to give you greetings from your sister."

Father Vincent remained glued to the telephone, his eyes staring ahead of him in despair. He had a vile headache, and they were proposing conundrums for him to solve. The nun had said that the bishop would communicate with him. Well, now he had, and . . . Full confidence. That could only mean that he was to go through with it. But he wanted to hear it in so many words. He blurted out, "If I understand you, I'm to—"

"Monseigneur," the voice cut in sharply, "has no further interest in your movements in this matter. More, *he does not wish to know*. Is that clear?"

The sound that came from him had its hysterical note. "Clear? Oh, it's clear enough. The letter—"

"There was no letter," the voice said. The receiver clicked in his ear. For a moment Father Vincent stood motionless. Then he put the receiver gently on the hook. He walked softly out of the office, closing the door with care behind him, and went upstairs. The others were waiting for him. They turned their heads as he entered. He had no speech left. He nodded.

"Here," one of the priests said. "I've drawn a map of the school." He kneeled on the floor, where a sheet of paper covered with black lines was laid out. He put his finger on it. "At seven-twenty tomorrow morning, when the line forms for study hall . . ."

Mother Veronica, sitting by the window of her third-class compartment, heard the announcement bellowed raucously over the loudspeaker system, and felt the trembling of the track beneath. A train was arriving. At the same time a group of people came into view on the platform beneath her window. They were well dressed, even elegant. The men wore expensively tailored overcoats that allowed a glimpse of starched white collars and silk cravats at the neck. There were two or three women among them, wearing fur coats. One of them carried a nosegay of flowers, which she smilingly presented to the man around whom they were clustered. He took off his hat and bowed gallantly. Mother Veronica recognized him; his photograph had been in all the papers at the recent announcement of his appointment to the cabinet. He was on his way then. Tomorrow the Minister of Justice would have an unexpected visit. There would be a polite exchange of formalities, a promise would be made to look into the matter, and that would be the end of it. The Procureur General of Touville knew his business. But Bishop Reynaud would be in the clear. Had not his adjutant accompanied Canon Sombre to the police? Had he not advised them to let the law take its course? He could not be held accountable if a hotheaded priest refused to obey orders and snatched the boy away. As for Vincent—she shrugged. Weaklings deserved no pity.

In the next track the train pulled in. Even before it had come to a complete stop, compartment doors opened and passengers jumped out, swinging their luggage awkwardly in their haste, and racing toward the train in which she sat. She waited, her eyes moving back and forth until she spotted them. The grocer got off first, then put up his hand for Konrad. In the glaring light from overhead their faces seemed worn and bloodless, and they moved with weariness. Konrad put his bag down on the platform, settled his hat on his head and looked about him. For a moment his face was turned in her direction. She did not move. There was no need; if he distinguished her at all among so many faces, he saw only a nun, like so many engaged in the Lord's business. And if, tomorrow when the news broke, he remembered having seen her and realized how narrowly they had crossed in their missions, let him; she owed herself that small personal triumph. It would be the last for a long time.

Immermann made a gesture, Konrad took up his bag, and they

walked off in the stream of the other passengers moving toward the gate.

The party beneath her window had disappeared amid cries of farewell. Now compartment doors slammed throughout the train, and in the corridors the new arrivals, having made the connection with the Paris train, passed by, peering through the glass-paneled door.

Mother Veronica sank back in her seat. She had done what it was in her power to do. It was up to a higher power now. She held a rosary in her hand. Kissing it, she closed her eyes and began to pray.

4

KONRAD AWOKE with a shudder and looked in alarm about the dark, unfamiliar room. In that moment of returning consciousness he did not know where he was, and he sat up sharply in bed. Then it came back to him. He was at Garonde, in the hotel, after that dreadful train ride of almost twenty-four hours. Jules lay in the other bed, his hands under his face, snoring gently. It was still night. Why had he awakened with such a start? Then it came again, that muffled rapping at the door. Konrad swung out of bed, groped with his feet for his slippers, realized that he had not put them out, and trod gingerly over the icy tiles in his bare feet to the door. Opening it a crack, he saw a man in uniform standing in the dim light of the hallway.

"What?" he croaked, not hiding his annoyance.

"Monsieur Konrad?" the policeman said. "Monsieur Louis Konrad?"

"Yes. What is it?"

"Identification, please."

Had they awakened him in the middle of the night for such a silly routine formality? Muttering angrily, he went to his valise and took out his passport. The policeman studied it briefly, his eyes going from the photograph to Konrad's face, then handed it back and saluted. "A message from the Parquet, sir," he said. "Procureur Fontanel is expecting you in his office at eight o'clock. To get the boy."

Konrad's anger vanished. "Thank you," he said.

The policeman saluted again and turned away.

"What is it?" Jules was sitting up in bed.

"Fontanel," Konrad said, sliding under the still-warm covers of his bed. "We're to be at his office at eight o'clock."

Jules grunted incredulously, snapped on the light and looked at his watch. "Five-thirty," he said. "Now that's what I call efficiency. How well run things are here!"

"And so thoughtful!" Konrad said, yawning.

"Well," Jules said reasonably, "it might have been at four. Or three."

"Or he might have had someone meet us at the train. It was in all the papers."

"Mystery," Jules said. "Cloak and dagger. Don't do the obvious." He turned over, the bed protesting under his weight. "How do you feel?"

"Rotten," Konrad said. "I ache all over."

"Me too. What do you say we sleep another hour or so?"

Konrad reached up and put out the light. Burrowing under the bedclothes, he lay staring at the ceiling, listening to Jules sighing as he shifted on his pillow. He knew he would not be able to sleep more now. The message had been like a shot of adrenalin to his nervous system. It came to him now with extraordinary intensity that his quest was all but over. In a couple of hours he would present himself at the Parquet, identify himself, hand over the court decree, and walk out with Michel. As easy as that. Who could have foretold, that Easter Sunday so far behind him now, that it would be at the other end of France, in this remote border town, that he would finally catch up with the boy? It was incredible, he told himself. So many wasted years, so much heartbreak, so many frustrated hopes, so much expense! And all because of a stubborn woman who had got that quirk in her head. Well, she had got what she deserved. Compared to Eva Weiss, she had got off lightly.

Wasted years? No, they had not been wasted. His health had suffered, the profits of his factory had slipped badly, he was all but a stranger to his own son—but had he not established a great principle, that all are equal under the law? He had not changed society, nothing but time and the slow labors of millions of obscure people struggling toward the light could do that. Anti-Semitism still existed, none knew better than he. But was it not a triumph that he had forced the very *goyim* to recognize the sanctity of families other than their own, that he had returned one soul to Israel, that he had challenged the Goliath that was the Church and won? His labors had served to give notice to the world that another Dreyfus case was no longer possible in France, and that the Jew was no longer docile prey, he would fight back. Judas, he thought; and if it had been his own son Judas? Who would be the Konrad who would fight for him? Probably none. Well, but it hadn't happened. They had survived. Judas was fifteen now, straight and tall, already a young man. Incidentally, he reflected, he had better see a bit more of his son, now that the Benedek affair was all but over. Judas had been somewhat sullen and standoffish with him lately. They all deserved a holiday after this. Perhaps they could take a trip together somewhere during Easter, and get acquainted again. How good it would be to return to a normal life, one in which his only purpose in picking up a newspaper would be to read the news about other people!

He looked at his watch. It was a quarter to six, and still dark. But he had begun to fidget, and knew that it was no use, he would have to get up. He slid out of bed quietly, so as not to disturb Jules; but he heard the other bed creak, and Jules said, "Oh hell, let's go camp on his doorstep."

"Eight o'clock is time enough," he said. "I'm going for a walk, and see if I can get some breakfast."

"Me too. Who'll shave first?"

Twenty minutes later they walked downstairs to the lobby and peered through the glass doors into the coffeeshop, which was dark and deserted. A waiter coming on duty told them that they could be served in half an hour. They went out into the plaza, where the street lamps were still lit, crossed it aimlessly, wandered into the maze of streets beyond, past silent, shuttered houses until the ground sloped noticeably and they emerged into a narrow esplanade overlooking a stream whose borders were rimmed with ice. Jules looked at it in disgust.

"This is a river?" he asked. "The Char is a river. But this?"

They stood watching the water, shivering a little in the gusts of wind that whipped over its black surface. It was still dark, but to their left a pale sheen of light began to appear in the sky.

"Say, Louis, how do you feel?"

He gave a short, nervous laugh. "I don't know," he said. "I don't seem to feel anything. I can't believe it, I guess."

"I feel like yelling," Jules said. "I feel like waking up the whole damn town and lining them all up to watch us pick up the boy."

"No, you don't."

"Yes, I do. And if I were a Catholic, do you know what I'd do? I'd buy a million candles and light them all, and sit in the church crossing myself."

"All right."

"All right then."

It gradually grew lighter, and they could see in the distance a looming mass of black that had to be mountains. The Pyrenees, Konrad said. Jules couldn't believe it. Those, the famous Pyrenees? Why, they were only hills! The Alps, those were mountains. Then he grinned shamefacedly and asked if he was fooling anybody.

"Come on then," Konrad said.

Jules clapped him on the shoulder. "You old—*Konrad,* you!" he said affectionately. "You're as nervous as I am."

They turned and began to retrace their steps.

A hand shook him gently by the shoulder, and a voice whispered, "Are you awake, son? Listen, and don't make any noise. You have to leave the school." He struggled to sit up, but the hand pressed downward. "Don't move, just listen. Do you understand?" He nodded, and Father Vincent whispered, "Good boy! Now pay attention. We're getting you out of here. You must do exactly as I say, or the police will get you. You don't want that, do you? They've found you out, and Monsieur Konrad is coming for you." For perhaps five minutes the priest, kneeling beside his cot, spoke in that scarcely audible voice, and Michel nodded, memorizing the details. But he too had something to say, and when the other had finished and silently blessed him, he beckoned and whispered in his turn, "If I let them take me, will they let Maman Rose out of jail?" Father Vincent shook his head, put his finger to his lips warningly, and answered, "Be ready."

Was it a dream? he wondered as he awoke to the sound of the bell, and this conversation flooded into his memory. No, it was not, it had really happened. And he was surer than ever when, marching to chapel, he caught a glimpse of Father Vincent hurrying toward the sacristy, and was shocked at the man's ravaged appearance. He wished he could talk to him; there was so much he had to know. Why had they sent Maman Rose to prison? How had the rector found out who he was? Did Mother Veronica know that M. Konrad was coming for him? Where were they sending him? What would become of him now? And why hadn't Father Vincent answered his question? A shake of the head wasn't an answer.

During mass he answered the question himself. That night before the trial, Maman Rose had told M. Immermann that she would rot in prison the rest of her life, but she wouldn't give him up. She had let herself be arrested so as to give him his chance to get away. It was what she had wanted for him, and he couldn't spoil it now. Noble Michel! he sneered at himself in Kevin's tone, noting the relief with which his coward soul accepted the excuse. But he couldn't help himself. Fear lay on his stomach like a palpable thing. The very thought of finding himself in that evil man's clutches was intolerable to him. He would do what Father Vincent had said. He was only a boy. He couldn't foresee what would happen. They might not let Maman Rose go even if . . . Maman Rose and Mother Veronica and Mlle Vincent and the priest knew better than he.

And so, returning to the dormitory after mass to get his books for study hall, he was quite prepared. At the bell, he allowed the others to fall out before him; then, when the line was already formed, he slipped through the curtains of his cubicle and went unobtrusively to its end. The prefect of studies clapped his hands, and the line moved out of the dormitory into the hall. Several of the boys turned their heads, wondering why he was not in his accustomed place, but Father Echegoretta, walking beside Michel, said sharply, "Eyes front!" and the boys faced forward again.

At the head of the stairs Father Uscátegui, smiling, fell into pace beside the prefect, gesticulating, his head bent forward to ask a question. The line slowed, then picked up again. It reached the head of the stairs and began to pass it. Father Echegoretta took Michel by the arm, squeezed hard, seized Michel's books, and stepped a pace forward. His pulses hammering, Michel went down the stairs hugging the railing. The entrance door was open, and several day boys were entering, subduing their giggles, their faces shiny with the cold. Brother André was not in sight. Feeling horribly conspicuous, expecting a shout behind him at any moment, Michel loitered in the hall, glanced through the window of the gate lodge, saw Father Vincent talking earnestly to Brother André; then, seizing his opportunity, he darted out the door, leaving it open behind him. Once in the street, he turned left, fighting down his impulse to run, and walked toward the far corner. In his school uniform without a coat, he felt that the very houses were staring at him. Overhead towered the twin spires of the cathedral. A laborer's cart, drawn by a pair of horses steaming under their blankets, plodded by. The driver turned his head to look at him, frowning. Michel's breath came quickly, forming frosty clouds before him. But he was not cold. Would the driver call out? The distance widened between them, and still there was no sound but that of the horse's hooves and the strident grinding of the iron-rimmed wheels. Michel did not dare look back. He had come to the end of the school wall and reached the row of shops where the street began to curve. He darted into the first open doorway he saw. It was a bookstore. Good. The driver would think he had been sent on an errand. He stared at the display of books with their meaningless titles until the noise of the cart had died away.

Footsteps and voices sounded in the quiet street. They came nearer and nearer. Michel shrank forward against the cold glass and fixed his eyes on the books. The voices were those of men. There were two of them. They appeared at the edge of Michel's vision, walking slowly, their shoulders hunched, their faces turned to each other. When they were almost past the doorway, Michel looked at them; his jaw fell and his blood froze. It was M. Konrad and M. Immermann. They went by without seeing him. For fully a minute Michel stood paralyzed with fear; then, beginning to tremble, his teeth chattering, he ran out into the street, rounded the corner and all but collided with a priest standing beside a parked car.

"Please, Father," he cried. "I'm lost!"

"Don't shout, for heaven's sake," the priest said in annoyance. "Quickly, now! Get in!"

Father Uscátegui arrived at the top of the stairs in time to see the Mesnard boy hurrying down the hall. "Here, what's this?" he demanded severely. "Where do you think you're going?"

"Dormitory, Father," the boy replied, disconcerted. "To fetch Luc Casella. He's not in study hall."

"Who sent you?"

"The prefect of studies, Father."

"Oh! Very well. Carry on."

Father Vincent came out of his quarters and approached with a questioning look. "He's been missed," the other priest said to him in a low voice. Father Vincent nodded. His face was drawn and haggard, and he looked sick. "He got out all right," he said. "I saw him go out the door. I hope to God—"

The Mesnard boy was coming back. The two men fell silent as he passed them. "The prefect will be out in a minute," Father Uscátegui said. "Let's not be seen with our heads together." Father Vincent agreed, watched the other go down the stairs, and turned to go to his room.

"Father!" The prefect of studies was calling him, alarm in his voice. He turned again and saw the lean figure hurrying toward him, lifting his cassock in his haste. It's begun, he thought, his heart sinking. *Ad majoram gloriam Dei.* "The rector," the prefect said. "I've got to— Do you know where he is?"

"Chapel," he said. "What is it, Father?"

"Boy missing. And do you know who? The Casella boy. Have you seen the papers? What I'm afraid of— The canon must be informed at once."

"He's saying mass," Father Vincent said. "Missing? He must be around somewhere. If you like—"

"Would you?" the prefect said gratefully. "I've got those boys in there. I'll say a word to them, and help you myself."

"Gladly, Father."

He hoped he had sounded properly casual about it. Not that it made any difference. In a little while he'd be called on the carpet, and heaven knew how he'd get out of it. But in the meantime he'd better carry out the farce to the end.

Within five minutes the entire school was in a state of alarm. Priests wandered through the building and about the school grounds, looking in every room and closet. Brother André, at the point of tears, stood in the doorway of the lodge, assuring all who passed that he had *not* let the boy out. And no one had come in either, only the externes. The boy must still be in the building.

It was an ancient rattletrap coupé, with a flat metal surface where the back seat would have been, and had a right-hand drive. Sitting to the left of the priest, bundled in his coat, which he had found on the seat, feeling the wind whistling across his face through the ill-fitting window, Michel stared ahead of him, his heart still thumping. He felt quite ill from the shock he had just undergone. It was incredible that they had not seen him. They had passed by so close to him that he could have touched them with his hand. A turn of the head, a casual glance, and—he shuddered to think of it. His stopping in the doorway had saved him. Otherwise, he would have run full tilt into them in rounding the corner. They couldn't have helped seeing him then, and would have recognized him in an instant. They didn't need any photograph. How that M. Konrad had stared at him at the trial! As if he would eat him up with his eyes!

The car wound its way down a long S-curve to the river and over the bridge. The houses had become sparser, and were interspersed with groves of trees, black against the snow-covered fields. The priest, who had been silent until now, began to speak. It was possible that they had been seen, he said. If so, he might have to come forward. He would tell the authorities that a boy had come to him on the street and said that he was lost. This was true. He had given the boy a lift to the edge of town. He had not asked the boy where he was going, and the boy hadn't told him. This was true, too. If they ever caught up with him, he was to remember to say the same thing. He didn't want to get people in trouble, did he?

"No, Father," Michel said.

"Do you know me? Have you ever seen me before?"

"No, Father."

The priest grunted. A moment later he pulled over to the side of the road. To the left, a dirt path meandered down a snowy slope amid trees, crossed a tiny rounded footbridge over a narrow stream, and came to an end at a country road over which a truck was making its way. Beyond the road was a gate by a small white house with a steep slate roof. The gate was open, and a figure dressed in black stood motionless, leaning against the post. The priest pointed, and Michel got out of the car.

"Good luck, child," the priest said. He was thin and wiry, and his face was bronzed. "Don't be discouraged. You have many friends who will help you." He nodded and drove off.

Michel stared down the slope. The figure had not moved, but Michel knew the man was watching him. Father, I am the boy you are waiting for, he repeated to himself. Was this the end of the trail? Or a new starting point? Would it ever end?

It was cold. Michel shivered and started down the path.

Konrad and Immermann arrived at the courthouse at quarter to eight. "A bit early," Konrad said doubtfully.

"Let's wait inside," Jules said. "I'm freezing."

The great double door under the portico of columns was locked, but the policeman on guard told them that the Parquet was open and could be reached directly by a door at the rear. They found the door without trouble, went up a flight of stairs, and found themselves in a small anteroom before a partition with several grilled openings in it. Before one of the openings a small, wiry man of indeterminate age, who wore a shabby corduroy jacket and faded black trousers tucked into rubber boots, was expostulating with someone whose hands could be seen through the wicket. Yes, his daughter. He had given her away to the man to be his wife, not his punching bag. A mass of bruises. The man was a brute. Let him have his fun elsewhere. He was her father, he had taken her away, and had come to swear out a warrant.

The man, who seemed to be a farmer, spoke in a controlled fury without moving. Beside him stood a plump girl of about eighteen, her face stolid and bovine, with an ugly purple mark on her cheek.

"What is it?" A man had appeared in the bend of the corridor. Konrad took in the handsome, somewhat puffy face with the fair mustache and the lock of sandy hair hanging over the forehead. Was this Fontanel? The farmer turned to him and began to repeat his story. His daughter. A mass of bruises. "Not here!" the newcomer snapped at him, looking at his watch. "Come into the office." He led the distressed father and daughter around the bend.

Konrad approached the wicket and asked for the procureur.

"Name and business?" the man within said tersely.

"Konrad. Louis Konrad. I was told—"

"Ah!" the man said, looking at him curiously. "He's been waiting for you. That was him." He nodded toward the bend in the corridor. "He'll be free in a minute. Just sit down and wait."

Konrad sat down on the wooden bench against the wall, and Jules sat down beside him.

"I wonder if Michel is here already," Jules muttered. Konrad glanced at him, saw that the great beaked face was tense and expectant, and shrugged. He himself felt oppressed and averse to talking. For the first time he wondered what he would say to the boy. Michel didn't know him, would no doubt be frightened. He was glad that Jules was along. Michel might remember him; but even if he did not, it wouldn't take Jules long to break the ice and inspire the child's confidence.

The waiting seemed very long to Konrad. Several times he caught a movement in one of the wickets in the partition, and had the impression that someone had bent forward to stare at him. At length there came a clumping of boots, and the couple appeared, the father speaking angrily, the daughter listening with the same wooden expression as before. They went down the stairs.

A man's head appeared above the partition and nodded at them. "Around the corner," he said. "The office at the end of the hall."

Konrad and Jules stood up and walked down the hall. The door at the end was open. Through it Konrad saw Fontanel seated behind a desk, writing busily. As they approached, the telephone rang. Fontanel picked it up with a grimace. "Yes?" he said. "Speaking." Konrad did not want to retreat, nor yet give the impression that he was eavesdropping. "Wait," he said in a low voice to Jules, and stood in the hall, his face averted.

"Who?" Fontanel said. "Well, it's after eight now. What's happened? What do you mean, a delay?" For a long moment there was silence. Konrad, glancing curiously through the open door, saw Fontanel's jaw slowly drop and a look of dismay come to his face. "You can't *what?*" he shouted, leaping to his feet. "If you can't find him, he's not there. You said he couldn't get out. And that means—why, damn it, man, he's been kidnaped, from right under your nose!"

With one accord Konrad and Jules turned and raced unceremoniously into the office, as Fontanel, stunned, let himself sink back into his chair.

"I'm Konrad," he snapped. *"Who*'s been kidnaped?"

Fontanel, still holding the receiver, his face suddenly drawn and pale, nodded in confirmation.

5

"Gentlemen," Bishop Reynaud said, leaning back in his seat and spreading his hands, "I am desolated at the news. It was only yesterday that I learned, quite by chance, that the boy was in my diocese. I assure you that he was brought here without my knowledge. And, incidentally, without the knowledge of the rector of St. Ignatius, who was shamelessly deceived in the matter of the boy's identity. And now you inform me that he has disappeared. I can hardly believe it. Surely a child cannot disappear just like that. And why do you say he was kidnaped? Isn't it more likely that he has run away?"

"No, Your Excellency," Fontanel replied. "Our investigation has eliminated that possibility entirely. We have questioned the prefect of studies at the school, and a number of the boy's fellow students. The Benedek boy was last seen falling into line at seven-twenty to go to study hall. He was wearing his school uniform, naturally without his overcoat, and was carrying his books, like all the children. But he never got to study hall. His absence was immediately noted, and a search begun. And that search turned up two interesting facts. One, the boy's books were found in the dormitory, not in his own cubicle, but in the cubicle next to his. And his overcoat was gone."

"Dear, dear," said the bishop. "And what do you deduce from that?"

"It was obviously a plot, Your Excellency," Fontanel said promptly. "The boy slipped down the stairs as the line of children passed it. He had to be carrying his books, or the monitors would have noticed it at once. At the moment of escaping, he either handed his books to an accomplice in the plot, or abandoned them on the stairs. It was someone who was trying to delay the discovery of his absence who returned the books to the dormitory. And it was another accomplice who was waiting outside, probably in an automobile, who had his overcoat ready for him."

"But really," the bishop said mildly, "why could not the child have left the line, slipped back to the dormitory, left his books, put on his coat, and gone out the door? There is nothing about your theory that precludes—"

"First," Fontanel said, "no student wearing an overcoat could have walked through the school during class hours without attracting attention. And second, his books were in another boy's cubicle. The person who returned them made a mistake, one that the boy himself would never have made."

The bishop pondered, then nodded. "Yes," he said. "I see your point. That is good reasoning." His face had become very grave. He turned to Canon Blevitz, who sat quietly to one side. "I believe you told me that the boy was being held incommunicado? That no one from outside was allowed to see him or speak to him?"

"That is correct, Monseigneur."

"Then there can be only one conclusion, I'm afraid." The bishop spoke decisively. "The boy was helped by someone within the school itself."

"That's the same conclusion we reached, Your Excellency," Fontanel said, nodding. "And that's why we have come to you."

"Whom do you suspect?"

Fontanel hesitated. "Our investigation is not completed yet," he said at length. "But, confidentially, we have our eye on Father Vincent."

"Vincent?" The bishop was astonished. "But my dear sir, Father Vincent is the least likely person one could think of to do such a thing. He just doesn't have the temperament for it. No, no, you're quite mistaken, I'm afraid."

Fontanel insisted respectfully. There were several things Vincent would have to explain before he could be cleared of complicity in the kidnaping. It was he who had brought the boy in the first place, or at least he in the company of his sister. Then yesterday afternoon he had received a mysterious telephone call from Biarritz, urging him to come at once to the Temple there; and it was known that the Dames of the Temple were Michel's correspondents. And finally, the gatekeeper at St. Ignatius swore that he had been vigilant at the door during the morning, that he had never taken his eyes from the entrance, except for a period of about five minutes, when Father Vincent had entered the lodge to speak to him. And that must have been the moment that the boy went out the door. He, Fontanel, didn't say that Father Vincent was necessarily implicated in the escape; but the priest certainly had some explaining to do. They would soon know his story. Right now Father Vincent was before the examining magistrate; all the other priests and brothers of the school were being had up as well. The mother superior of the Biarritz Temple had been cited, and efforts were being made to locate a woman who had appeared at the school yesterday afternoon with a bag of cookies for the boy. The gatekeeper said she had not been allowed in, she had left the cookies and gone on her way; but they were leaving no stone unturned, they were questioning everybody who could possibly have had any connection with the kidnaping. Even Canon Sombre. Everybody. And when all that mass of evidence was sifted, and their stories compared, they would no doubt have a pretty good idea who could have done it. But all this took time. And in the meanwhile, the boy—

Bishop Reynaud said, "I gather you have no idea where he might be."

"None, Your Excellency," Fontanel said. "He has simply disappeared. We have of course taken our precautions. Within a half-hour of his disappearance, we had road blocks mounted on every route out of Garonde, and every train that left here after seven-thirty has been searched at some point along its itinerary. We have found nothing."

"Why then," the bishop said, "the boy must be still in Garonde."

"That is our belief, Your Excellency. But where? We can't search every house in the city. We have issued bulletins over the radio, and the afternoon papers are carrying the boy's photograph, the entire police force is combing Garonde, area by area. But unless the child was observed in entering his hiding place, we are not likely to turn up anything. And those who kidnaped him will not be frightened by the hunt into giving him up. For that—"

"Yes?" the bishop prompted him.

"Your Excellency," Fontanel said, "there are priests involved. That is obvious. It seems to me that an appeal from you, their bishop — If you would issue a statement—"

Bishop Reynaud leaned back in his chair and said carefully, "I know very little of this affair. I have of course seen the notices in the newspapers, but these are unreliable at best. Last night, having just learned of the child's presence in my diocese, I communicated with Monsieur Fouquet-Quarles for an opinion on the legal implications of his stay in St. Ignatius. It was, you understand, purely a precautionary measure, and for my own information. And I learned that there may be some doubt over the authority of the law to seize him and turn him over to his family, in view of the appeal to the Court of Cassation. And it seems to me . . ."

Until now Konrad had sat quietly between Fontanel and Jules, his eyes fixed on the bishop's face during the colloquy with the procureur. He had noted every expression, every turn of phrase, of the prelate, whom he had despised at first sight. The man was too handsome, too smooth, too clever. Reynaud had complimented Fontanel on his reasoning, and the procureur had bridled with pleasure; but Konrad was sure that the bishop was leading the man on, letting him explain what had been obvious to him at the beginning. And the bishop of Garonde was not "desolated" at the news; it was the wrong word to have chosen, it smacked too much of the empty formulas of condolence. And now he had invented a new scruple, and set himself up as an interpreter of the law. Konrad was in no mood for this evasive treatment. He interrupted to say, "There can be no doubt whatsoever, Your Excellency. The law is clear. The child has been awarded to his family by an executory Appeals Court decision, with which all citizens must comply."

"That's so, Your Excellency," Fontanel in a placating voice, frowning a little at Konrad, who read in his looks a warning that he had been too emphatic.

"I do not pretend to a knowledge of the law," the bishop replied. "But that is precisely my point. This is a matter that the agents of the law must come to an agreement about before taking any irreversible action. Monsieur Fouquet-Quarles was of the opinion that a different interpretation is possible. He intends to ask an opinion of the Minister of Justice himself. You, have asked for my help, gentlemen, but I really fail to see what I can do to aid you. I do not know by what means the child was removed from the school. I do not know where he is. By this time he may be far away from my diocese. The law is doubtful, to say the least. And there is the problem of conscience."

"Conscience!" Konrad said, staring at him.

"Yes, Monsieur Konrad. The conscience of the boy, that of the priest, whoever he may have been, and my own. Has it ever occurred to you that the boy may not want to go to his family? You may be sure that he left the school willingly enough. He was certainly not removed by force. It would have been impossible to remove him kicking and screaming from the premises without attracting a great deal of attention. Then, what was the motive of the priest? We of the cloth are not men of violence. The person who helped this child to escape must have been impelled by an irresistible conviction that he was in the right. I am not sure that he would obey my order to give him up, even if I knew who he was, which I do not."

"I see," Konrad said thickly. "And your own?"

"The child is baptized."

He had known it was coming. In that instant he had the impulse to smash out at that smooth imperious face, which confronted him with the unquestionable conviction that its owner was the custodian of the only truth. How often had he come up against this hermetic blindness on the part of these—these brainwashed fanatics! Why couldn't they see what was obvious to the dullest understanding, yes, to the mule in the treadmill and the cur in the street, that a child belonged to his family? Knowing it was useless, almost stifled in his anger, repeating the gambit he had fallen into so many times that he could have said it in his sleep, he cried out, "But he was circumcised first! The baptism is invalid. It was done without the consent of his parents and without the knowledge of the Family Council responsible for him. And in any case, it does not give anybody the right to keep the boy from joining his family. Suppose it were the other way around? Suppose I took a baptized child, and had him circumcised? Does that mean the child belongs to me?"

The bishop said shortly, "I will not enter upon a discussion of our different faiths, Monsieur Konrad. I will say only that the baptism may have been irregular, but it is valid nonetheless. And this is a serious matter, very serious."

"Is this Christian charity?" Konrad said.

Fontanel said quickly, "Monsieur Konrad means—"

"Monsieur Konrad means what he says," Konrad snapped at him.

The bishop's eyes narrowed, and he reared back, looking at Konrad down the length of his nose. Konrad glared back at him. "Let me make my position very clear," the bishop said in a dangerous tone. "You have asked for my help in a matter which does not concern me. This controversial child was brought to St. Ignatius without my knowledge, and was removed without my knowledge. In the present state of affairs I cannot help you. But I am a law-abiding citizen like anyone else. I shall do my best to get to the bottom of this. When the facts are in my possession, I shall do what I conceive to be my duty, both to my cloth and the laws of my country. More I cannot say. And now, gentlemen, I think no useful purpose can be attained by prolonging this interview. Good day."

Konrad leaped to his feet and strode out of the bishop's office, down the stairs and into the street. Jules followed at his heels. It was several minutes later that Fontanel joined them, his face flushed and indignant. "You had no right to speak to him like that," he said.

Why had he stayed behind? To apologize for the disrespectful infidel? To smooth His Excellency's ruffled feathers? To kiss his ring and repeat his request for help?

"Monsieur le Procureur," Konrad said cuttingly, "you have had two days of this, and I have had five years. You must kindly allow me to be the judge of my words."

Fontanel's face became hurt and sullen. He was going back to his office, he announced stiffly. For his part, Konrad replied, he was going to get something to eat. It was four-thirty, and he had had nothing since an early breakfast.

"Very well," Fontanel said. "If there is any news, I will leave a message for you at the hotel." He touched the brim of his hat and marched down the darkening street.

"Puppy dog," Jules said, staring after him.

"What do you think?" Konrad asked.

Jules shook his head decidedly. "I don't see it. A real bishop. The genuine article, like in a book. But not the mastermind."

"Why not? You heard what he said. His conscience. His duty to his cloth."

"No. There are too many loose ends. And it's too contradictory. If the bishop knew the boy was coming, he'd have made better arrangements. Even if he tried to pull a fast one on the head of the school, he'd have certainly let his adjutant in on it. But no, the adjutant helps the rector report to the police. The bishop must have chewed him out on that one. But Old Smoothie didn't know about the boy in advance."

"Maybe not," Konrad agreed gloomily. "But he knows more than he's telling."

"That's how you get to be bishop. And you've got to have that look. You know, dignity."

"Damn it all!" Konrad said in exasperation. "Someone's got to be giving the orders here. It's not Mademoiselle Rose. She couldn't handle this from jail. Why, there's a whole chain involved. The Vincent woman gets him into the school. Somebody gets him out, ten minutes before the police come to take him to the procureur's office. If the bishop isn't behind this, who is?"

Jules suggested that they had better get something to eat. They walked in the direction of the hotel. After the meal, they decided, Konrad would go to the examining magistrate's office, to see what he had been able to turn up; and Jules would cover the procureur's office.

"Christian charity!" Bishop Reynaud mused.

"The man was wrought up," Canon Blevitz said. "It must have been quite a shock. I was in the procureur's office a quarter of an hour after he learned about it. He was smoldering. I thought he would have a heart attack."

"A singularly unpleasant man," the bishop said. "Canon, I want to talk to Father Vincent. But I don't want to single him out. Get on the telephone, and tell Sombre that I want his entire staff to come to the rectory, one at a time at fifteen-minute intervals, beginning at seven o'clock tonight. I must know what the examining magistrate got out of the man. We may have to move the boy on."

The office of Examining Magistrate Bessat was scarcely large enough for a desk, the recorder's tiny table forming an L with it, and a chair placed in the angle they made. On all four sides of the room were bookshelves filled to overflowing; books jammed every available inch of space, lay piled on the top shelf up to the ceiling, were stacked in piles on the floor. The venetian blind over the window was turned down and a heavy velvet curtain drawn over it. Only a pool of light from a lamp on the magistrate's desk and another on the recorder's table dispelled the murky gloom of the crowded quarters. It was stifling and unbearably hot. Konrad, shaking hands with Bessat and nodding at the recorder as he took the seat pointed out to him, had the impression that neither light nor air was ever allowed to penetrate this sanctum of the law. The image of a spider's web crossed his mind.

Bessat was pale and undersized, with a strangely bulging forehead and thick-lensed glasses that gleamed in the lamplight. He spoke in soft but decisive tones. He was glad that M. Konrad had dropped in, he said. The investigation was far from complete, but some interesting facts had been turned up. Did M. Konrad know a Sister Veronica, a nun of Touville? She was mother superior of the Temple Order there. Surprised, Konrad shook his head. What did she have to do with Michel?

"I've just been in communication with Touville and Marseilles," Bessat said. "Mademoiselle Vincent brought the boy here from Marseilles, where he had been attending school under the name of Jean Dupont. His correspondent there was the mother superior of the Temple community of that city. A Sister Celeste. She has been questioned, and admitted that the Benedek boy was brought to Marseilles by Sister Veronica and that together they placed him in the school Notre-Dame-de-Lis. This was on January eighth, which means that the boy was taken there immediately after the trial. Mademoiselle Vincent, who has been arrested, says that she picked the boy up in Marseilles and brought him here to Garonde, upon the orders of Sister Veronica. And the nuns of the Biarritz Temple, who acted as Michel's correspondents here, say they did so to oblige Sister Veronica. Wherever one touches this case, the name of this nun crops up. But that's not all. It seems— What's the matter? Monsieur Konrad? Are you ill?"

He had let out a groan and put his hands to his face. In that instant everything had fallen into place with such blinding certainty that his brain reeled with its force. Fool that he had been! The answer had been staring him in the face the entire five years he had dedicated himself to the Benedek affair! The very first person he had spoken to had given him the clue. She had taken Michel to the Nursery, Mme Quertsch had told him, but only after she had first tried to get him into the Touville Temple. The nuns there had given her Mlle Rose's name. The Temple! The order founded for the express purpose of converting Jews to the true religion! Why had it never occurred to him that they would not so easily give up the prey that had fallen like a ripe fruit into their hands? Corroborating details leaped to his mind. The nuns who invariably sat in on the trials, quietly observant in the back row. The two nuns that someone had seen accompanying a boy answering Michel's description in the railway station. The ease with which the boy had moved from one religious school to another, had his way paid, kept out of sight, secured the collaboration of the fanatic priest of Sep, the lying bishop of Touville, the conniving Cornelians of Strasbourg. He had thought it was all Mlle Rose's doing, had wondered at her amazing ingenuity and ability to strike where least expected. Even from prison, he had remarked to Procureur Jeanpré. And all the while—fool! And it had taken this magistrate of Garonde, who until today had been no more concerned with Michel Benedek than he was with Konrad himself, only a few hours to get to the bottom of it all!

He turned a haggard glance at Bessat, who had half risen in alarm, and said with difficulty, "I'm all right. Go on, please."

The magistrate's glasses flashed in the lamplight as he settled back. "The nuns of Touville have been questioned as well. Between them and the nuns of Biarritz, I have been able to make a rough timetable of Sister Veronica's movements the day before the kidnaping. She left Touville on the eight-thirty express Sunday night, and arrived at Biarritz—"

"Do you mean," Konrad said unsteadily, "that she was *here?*"

"Indeed she was," Bessat said, nodding, "and astonishingly active, it seems. She arrived at Biarritz at two-fifteen Monday afternoon, and immediately proceeded to the Temple." As the magistrate went on in his soft voice, Konrad sat still, trembling with repressed emotion as the pieces of the puzzle fell into place. Vincent's hurried visit to the Temple, summoned by the nun, who "gave him news of his sister." The conference in the bishop's rectory "to discuss the legality of the police quest." The telephone call that Vincent admitted having received that night "in reprimand for his deception of his superior." Coupled with his astonishment that all this had been happening while he himself was riding across France in that ridiculously slow and tortuous train, or taking his ease at the hotel, or strolling about the river before sunrise, was the mounting fury with which he said to himself that the Church had come out into the open at last. A nun, a priest, a bishop! There was no hiding their part in the deed, not any more! The Rose woman was in jail. So was Mlle Vincent. Now it was the turn of the other criminals, those who hid behind their cloth and lifted bland, self-righteous faces to questioning, and lied, lied, lied in the name of their twisted truth! All of them!

He was on his feet, towering over the magistrate, who took off his glasses and looked at him with raised eyebrows, and the recorder, who stopped writing and lifted his head. They were all to be arrested, he cried harshly. It was Vincent who had done the job, spurred on by the nun and the bishop. And perhaps with other priests as their accomplices. They were all to be locked up at once. Yes, the bishop too!

"You will please sit down, Monsieur Konrad," Bessat said with unexpected firmness. "And you will refrain from raising your voice. In the exercise of my official functions, I represent the law of France."

He had just passed the most wretched day of his life, and for a moment, under this reprimand, his self-control slipped away from him. "I know that law," he snapped. "It pretends that all are equal before it. I will believe it when I see these people behind bars. You will either give that order or admit that you dare not touch a bishop of your faith."

Bessat struck his desk a blow with his fist and stood up. For a moment the two stared at each other. Then Bessat pushed his chair aside and began to pace up and down behind it, taking three steps and wheeling to take three more, his hands behind his back. Konrad shrugged and sat down. He had gone too far and he knew it. He was angry enough not to care.

Finally the magistrate stopped walking and said to the recorder, "Tear it up. This gentleman never came here today. What I have to say is off the record. And what I have to say, Monsieur Konrad, is this. I don't know what encounters you may have had with representatives of the law before now. But in this office justice will be meted out insofar as the law provides. Neither you nor the bishop of Garonde is competent to tell me my duty, and neither is above arrest. And for your information, sir, my faith is not that of His Excellency. Nor yours. I am a Protestant. So much for your suspicions. And now," he said in a softer tone, sitting down again, "allow me to continue."

Konrad passed his hands over his eyes. "I beg your pardon," he said. "I have hardly slept for three nights. I am afraid I'm not myself."

Bessat put on his glasses. "Hear me out. Sister Veronica went from here to Paris. The police there were just too late to catch her, she had already taken the train to Touville. But the police of Touville will be waiting for her on her arrival. The order for her arrest has already been issued. Father Vincent has been questioned and released. That does not mean that he has cleared himself, merely that for the time being there is not enough evidence to do anything else. He has denied any part in the kidnaping. If proof to the contrary is forthcoming, he will be arrested. There is no need to be hasty. He will not escape. And as for the bishop, he too will be questioned. Not here. Out of respect for his rank, I will go myself to the rectory. But if he gave the order for the deed, you may be sure he will not admit it. Nor will Father Vincent. And until I have facts on which to go, I will not arrest him or anyone else. But be assured of this, Monsieur Konrad. The child will be found, and the truth will be known. And when it is, punishment according to the law will be meted out, regardless of where the blame falls."

Konrad said nothing.

"Let me give you a piece of advice, Monsieur Konrad," Bessat said. "Go home to Touville. There is nothing more you can do here. The law has been set in motion. A crime has been committed, a very grave crime. You have sworn out a complaint against X for kidnaping and murder. The law will not rest until that complaint is satisfied. Your efforts are no longer needed."

Konrad stood up. "For the moment," he said, "I will go to my hotel. I must rest and think. I ask you to forgive me for my outburst." He walked out, overcoming by an effort of the will the dizziness that came over him. He had reached the end of his energies. There was nothing to do but to let the law do for him what he had almost done for himself, but allowed through his blindness to fall once more from his fingers.

When he had gone, Examining Magistrate Bessat sighed, glanced at the recorder, and went to the window, lifting the curtain and parting the blind. The recorder joined him, and for a moment they stood in silence, watching the tall figure move slowly under the street lights.

"I wonder what it's like to be a Jew," the recorder said.

"A strange person," Bessat rejoined. "But admirable in his way."

6

THE GRANDFATHER CLOCK gave a faint whirring noise and struck a single soft musical note. Michel started apprehensively, and turned toward the tall slender shape looming at his side in the darkness. He had just closed the door of the back bedroom behind him, taking pains not to make any noise, and was standing motionless, holding his breath and listening, when that menacing sound broke on his tense nerves. It was nine-thirty. The clock was silent again. Michel swallowed hard, fighting back a wave of nausea, and stared at the kitchen doorway, which opened onto the hall a few feet ahead. Through the kitchen was Mme Larastazu's bedroom. Had she gone to bed? The presbytery was still, and there was no light except for the gleam at the far end of the hall, under the closed parlor door. The priest was probably still up, then. But the housekeeper might be still awake too, with her door shut, and might hear him in the bathroom.

Michel was wearing a long white flannel nightgown that came to the floor, and a pair of Father Nagorra's black woolen socks. He had been in bed, about to read the book Mme Larastazu had given him, when he heard that strange inhuman snarl just under his window. He had sat up abruptly. The single-burner hotplate, set sideways on the ledge of the gable, glowed redly against the dark curtains, like a huge eye glaring at him. He had the sudden unreasoning fear that that unearthly sound had been directed at him, and that someone or something was watching him from outside. But how could that be? The curtains were drawn. For a moment he was tempted to run to the door and call the housekeeper, until he remembered the contents of his dinner plate lying out in the snow. He had gotten up, pushed the hotplate aside, and peered fearfully out. The moonlight lay on the hillside behind the cottage, casting an eery spiderweb of shadows among the bare trees and brambles rising upwards. Far above, over the crest of the hill, clouds limned with pale light scudded across a thin slice of sky. And a few feet below him, standing just clear of the snow banked against the cottage wall, a cat stood arched and hissing, its metallic eyes fixed on something at the foot of the window. As Michel watched, the snarl came again, another cat leaped out into Michel's vision, its paw lashing, and the other turned tail and ran.

With Michel's relief came a tightening in his stomach, a sour taste in his throat, and the awareness that he was going to be sick.

Now he stood in the hall, listening for any sound from the housekeeper's room, fearful of the remedies she might force on him, yet more and more aware that whether she was awake or not, he could not delay any longer. Silent in his stocking feet, he glided past the kitchen, glancing in. Mme Larastazu's door was shut, and no light shone under it. He continued to the next door and, closing it quietly behind him, reached for the string dangling from the light. He could not find it in the dark. The next moment, struck by a sudden paroxysm, he hurled himself retching toward the toilet, just in time.

Five minutes later, empty, trembling both from the violence of his vomiting and the icy cold of the tiles, Michel sat weakly on the floor, leaning back against the wall. He felt miserable, and homesick as never before. Not even his first day at St. Louis Gonzaga, knowing he would not see his Maman Rose until Christmas, if then, had he missed her so keenly, or felt so lost and helpless. It was incredible that he should be here, among strangers in this far corner of France. It was incredible that his Maman Rose should be in prison, like a criminal. What had they done to deserve this? Waves of self-pity went over him, and he tried to imagine his Maman Rose in her prison cell. Was she thinking of him, and missing him, as he missed her? He cried softly, wiping away the tears with the sleeve of the nightgown.

After a while he felt better, although he was still abominably weak. He ought to be getting back to his room. But he felt such a disinclination to move that he let his head sink to his knees and stayed where he was. At least, he thought gratefully, Mme Larastazu had not heard him. She must be sound asleep. Exhausted. And no wonder, after the day she had had, mothering him.

That morning he had gone down the snowy slope, crossed the

little footbridge over the frozen brook, approached the motionless figure in black by the gate, and stammered, "Father, I'm the boy you're waiting for." "Did anyone see you?" the priest had demanded. "I don't think so, Father," he had replied. That was the extent of his conversation with Father Nagorra, who had led him into the cottage, where a white-haired lady had swooped upon him with little clucking cries of concern. She had shooed him into the narrow back bedroom with the slanted, beamed ceiling, and begun the fussing that had not stopped all day. How dreadfully thin he was! He must be starved, he must be frozen, his feet were wet, he would catch his death of cold! She had brought him a mug of hot tea, and when he had obediently gulped it down, she prepared him breakfast. That was the beginning of a series of meals and snacks that made Michel shudder to think of now. Well-nourished and plump herself, with round white dimpled hands and a soft, pouter-pigeon breast, she had a mania about food, that woman. Every two hours. At eleven, another cup of tea and a slice of bread and jam. With hot food inside you, you could throw off infections. At one, luncheon, brought to him on a tray, for he must not stir out of his room because of the drafts. He would be a different boy when he left St. Dominique du Val. At three, apple juice and a bun. Fruit juice helped your digestion. At five o'clock Michel tried to protest; she had brought him a sandwich and another cup of tea. Useless. Didn't he want sturdy bones? He had to eat, for she stood over him until he did. By dinner time Michel was in despair. The sandwich he had forced down against his will lay heavy on his stomach, and he felt bloated with all that tea. Fortunately, this time Mme Larastazu did not stay; she had to serve Father Nagorra, she said. Why was the priest so thin, Michel wondered. When she had gone, he opened the window quietly and, doubling over the sill, scraped a hollow in the crusted snow and emptied his plate into it, patting the crust back into place afterwards. By the time that snow melted he would be far away from this house.

Mme Larastazu had been in and out of his room all day. After clearing away the breakfast tray, she came in to have him kneel and offer up a prayer of thanks for his deliverance. She brought him a hotplate as an improvised heater, and popped in periodically to inspect it. After lunch she was back to say the rosary with him. She left the house in the early afternoon, but returned in a short while carrying a net bag filled with clothing, which she had picked up at the homes of various members of her family. Then came the fitting of the stiff black serge suit her sister had sent for him. It was too big, and required several trips back and forth between his room and hers, where the sewing machine was. Another visit, during which Michel had to pray for the welfare of the donors, whose outlandish names Mme Larastazu cued him with in a whisper. Another, to rub his chest with a vile-smelling yellowish embrocation, to keep his "passages" clear. Twice more, to ask how he felt. And finally, since he had professed ignorance about St. Dominique du Val, after whom the church up the hill was named, she brought him a book that had the saint's story in it, and stayed until he had said his evening prayers.

Michel heaved a sigh of relief when she left him for the last time, announcing that she was going to bed, but if he needed anything . . . He had been jumpy and low-spirited enough after his narrow escape that morning. The good lady's well-meant but excessive attentions, the lack of privacy, had rubbed his nerves raw, and he wondered in despair how much of this petting and cosseting he could take. How long would he stay at St. Dominique du Val? Not long, he hoped. But he had no idea. He had not seen Father Nagorra all day, except at his arrival.

In the dark bathroom Michel stirred finally and stood up. His legs felt rubbery under him, and his head ached. He was still shivering from the cold, which seemed to have penetrated to the bones. What was the matter with him? Was he going to be really sick? His nausea was gone, yet there was a heaviness about his heart. He could not get the image of Maman Rose out of his mind; he saw her as she had been in the courtroom, turning toward him as he walked by, a look of surprise on her face. He had hurt her, he knew; he longed for her forgiveness, and for her arms about him, and the sweet smell of her shoulder.

He had opened the bathroom door and stepped out into the hall before he saw that light was streaming from the open parlor door, and heard men's voices within. Who could it be at this hour? He had heard no one come in. Was it the police? His heart thumping, Michel was about to scurry to his room when Father Nagorra came out of the dark kitchen behind him, a bottle in his hand. Startled, the priest asked what he was doing, going about in the dark. He had been in the bathroom, Michel whispered, his teeth chattering. The priest touched his cheek, uttered an exclamation, and said, "Come to the parlor, there's a fire going."

It was not the police, then. Michel let himself be urged along. As he entered the parlor, he saw Father Vincent standing by the window; then he saw another man in a cassock sitting on the sofa. It was the thin priest who had brought him in the car that morning. Both looked grim and worried, especially Father Vincent, whose face was taut and tired. But as Michel looked at him timidly, the priest came forward, saying, "How are you, my boy?" Michel was at the point of blubbering; the kindness in the man's voice, the friendliness of that pat on the shoulder, brought a lump to his throat. "He's frozen," Father Nagorra said, leading him toward the fireplace and pushing a chair closer to the heap of glowing coals. "Here," he said, pouring a finger of amber liquid into a round-bellied glass he took from the mantelpiece. "Don't sip it, toss it down." Michel obeyed and choked; cool on the tongue, the liquid hit his chest like a burst of fire. He didn't know what had got into the old woman, Father Nagorra said in annoyance; he would speak to her tomorrow. Letting the child freeze! Michel, sinking into the chair, his face contorted and his eyes filled with tears of shock, gasped, "Oh no, Father!" The thought that tomorrow Mme Larastazu would be even more attentive sent panic through him.

"What?" Father Nagorra said, surprised.

The three priests were looking at him. Michel caught his breath and explained. It wasn't Mme Larastazu's fault, he said. She had taken good care of him. But something he had eaten had disagreed with him. He had spent too long a time in the bathroom, and had got chilled.

Father Nagorra stared at him, then, unexpectedly, grinned. "Has she been stuffing you?" he demanded.

The thin priest on the sofa whistled softly, getting up and coming forward. He and Father Nagorra exchanged knowing glances, both grinning. Michel hung his head without answering. He was certainly not going to complain of that good woman, who had done all she could that day on his behalf. If only she would do a little less! But he said nothing. The thin priest nudged him and said, "Fight back, my boy."

Then they let him alone. Michel sank gratefully into the soft chair, feeling the heat of the fire playing over his body and glowing on his face. The shock of the brandy was beginning to wear off, leaving him warm and relaxed. The priests were out of sight behind him. He listened to them speak, enjoying the sound of their voices, attentive because they were talking about him and the aftereffects of his escape. Father Vincent did most of the talking, his voice wry and amused at himself in the role of the man caught in the middle. He had had to face Canon Sombre, who had been fetched from the chapel, purple in the face, crying, "What's this? What's this?" What he had answered was the truth: at the seven-twenty study-hall bell he was in the gatekeeper's lodge, remonstrating with Brother André about the fumes from the stove. After that the rector had glared at him every time they passed each other. The police had come, and even that fellow Konrad, wandering morosely through the school, his hands in his pockets. He had been had up before an examining magistrate, and he had just come from the bishop's. Quite a day, in short. And tomorrow promised to be even worse. Konrad and the police were out for blood. They hadn't accepted the theory that the boy had run away on his own. They called it "kidnaping." Had they heard the radio bulletins? The police were combing the city, they had set up road blocks on every road leading out of town, and the latest report was that they were going to use bloodhounds.

The thin priest pooh-poohed this idea, but Michel stirred uneasily on his chair. To be hunted by dogs, like a wild animal! His feelings were not soothed by a dreadful story Father Nagorra told, about an orderly at the municipal hospital, who had run amuck with a razor, pouncing out on people from behind bushes and cutting their throats. This was in 1937, he said, during the height of the Spanish Civil War, and all sorts of wild rumors had gone about, including one that the killer was an Italian bombardier who had gone crazy and had vowed a one-man war against the Basques on both sides of the Pyrenees. For three days the city lived in horror, cowering in their houses, while the police and angry citizens' committees went about in a real jungle hunt. They finally tracked the fellow down with bloodhounds, and riddled him with bullets, since he wouldn't be taken alive. A wild west show, Father Nagorra said dreamily. Cowboys and Indians. Michel shuddered.

Let them, the thin priest said scornfully. Bloodhounds couldn't trace the boy in a car. And a good thing too, Lisiaga, Father Vincent said. So that was the thin priest's name, Michel thought. He was a Basque, then. Nagorra was also a Basque name. Yet they could not have been more different. Father Lisiaga was wiry and bronzed, with a high-ridged nose and keen, alert eyes. Like a hunter. Or an artist. And the other was round-faced and owlish, patient, soft-spoken, with a snub nose and worry-lines in his forehead. And both different from the stocky, square-jawed mountaineer type described in books. And Father Vincent? That was not a Basque name. No, Michel remembered, Mlle Vincent had told him her family was from Grenoble.

He hadn't known that about bloodhounds. He supposed it was because of the tires. He imagined himself back at St. Louis Gonzaga, among his friends, saying quietly, "Bloodhounds can't follow you in a car, you know." How did he know, they would clamor, even Kevin, who knew such odd things. And he would say, "Well, one time they sent bloodhounds after me in Garonde, down in the Basque country, and—" But what was he thinking of? He would never return to St. Louis, he had closed that door himself.

It was very pleasant by the fire. He was saturated with warmth now, and a little drowsy. The voices had faded into a vague background out of which came words and phrases that touched his hearing and died away. Now and then his curiosity was aroused, and he struggled back into wakefulness to listen. It was all right, he felt, they knew he was there and had told him to stay and get warm. But precisely during those exchanges that most interested him they adopted a guarded tone and left things half said and understood. About the bishop, for instance. He had been "very decent," Father Vincent said. Told him he was not to worry, he would be "taken care of." But for the moment, of course . . . The police suspected him. Nothing could be done about that. But if he kept certain things to himself— Michel imagined him making a gesture as he broke off, and had to guess at his meaning. Another time they spoke of a letter a "certain party" had brought; but here they lowered their voices, and Michel could not hear what they said, except Father Lisiaga's remark about an "open fight."

Michel must have dozed off, for his body gave a great start and he stared up to find Father Vincent looking down at him. There was a queer, one-sided smile on his lips. "I'm leaving now, Michel," he said. "Heaven knows if we'll ever see each other again. Remember me sometimes. I'm leaving you with Father Nagorra and Father Lisiaga. They'll do the best for you."

"Father," Michel stammered, and stopped, his throat constricted. "Thank you," he finally managed to whisper.

"God bless you, my boy," the priest said huskily, turning away.

At the door Father Vincent paused and said he wouldn't come back. It was too dangerous. It would be well for them to move quickly. The door closed behind him.

There was a long silence. Then Father Lisiaga said, "What do you think, Tom?"

"Is there any choice?"

"The old way, then?"

"Yes."

Again they were silent. Father Lisiaga chuckled. "It's been a long time. I thought those days were behind us—1944, remember?"

"How could I forget? By God, they came through here like a funnel. I was thinking of it just the other day, when I saw old Chamo in town. The old thief hasn't changed in the past forty years. The cocky walk of him! And what is it now? I asked him. Still sheep, Father, he said. But Saxons were better, eh Father? And to give the old devil his due, he got them out. One of the true stock."

"Well," Father Lisiaga said, "here we go again."

"There are no more Pyrenees," Father Nagorra said gravely.

Michel's memory stirred. Louis XIV had said that when he married the Infanta Maria Theresa of Spain. He had married her at the border, and he had made that remark that was in all the history books, which explained that now the border didn't exist any more. But the great king was wrong, because Spain didn't recognize his claim to the succession, and there was a great war over it. Why was Father Nagorra quoting that now?

"Then we're agreed? Vergara?"

"Yes."

"The boy doesn't have to cross. Not unless things get too hot on this side. I'll be in touch with the bishop, and can telephone Vergara if necessary. There's a phone in the café next to the church. And so we stay in control. I'll run over there tomorrow in the car, and have a talk with him. And check the road blocks on the way."

"Old times, Antoine," Father Nagorra said.

"Old times, Tom."

Father Nagorra appeared beside Michel's chair. "Run along to bed, youngster," he said. "You're warm as toast now."

"Yes, Father," Michel said meekly. He shook hands with both priests and went to his room.

There, sitting on his bed, he pondered over the strange conversation he had just heard. What was the "old way"? They had spoken so cryptically that much had escaped him. In 1944 the war had still been going on. And Saxons were Englishmen. But who was Chamo, the "old thief"? And Vergara, who was at a church and was probably a priest? And who was not in Garonde, since Father Lisiaga would have to pass the road blocks to see him.

How complicated everything had become! And how much trouble he was causing everyone!

He was wide awake now. In spite of the hotplate, the room was cold, and his drowsiness gone. It was late to have his light on. Mme Larastazu might awake and come to scold him. But he did not feel like going to sleep. His eye fell on the book the housekeeper had given him. St. Dominique du Val. It didn't sound Basque. She had been shocked to learn that he had never heard of the saint. There was a relic of his up at the church, she had said. Authentic. The saint's hand, in a perfect state of preservation, showing as plain as could be the two ugly holes where the nails had gone in.

Michel picked up the book. It was entitled *The Christian Year*. Opening it, he saw that it was the same type of book as the one that was required reading at St. Louis Gonzaga, which the boys called the *Book of Days*. It told the lives of the saints, one for each day of the year. But this one had been written by a Spanish monk and translated into French.

Where was his own *Book of Days?* He had left it behind him at St. Louis Gonzaga, having no inkling then that he was not coming back. What had happened to his things? No doubt they had cleared his cubicle for someone else. By now his secret was out, and had been discussed a thousand times. In his mind's eye he saw his classmates in their rare moments of leisure, their heads together, talking of him. Had they guessed about the crucifix? Had Kevin told them? How far away it all seemed! And yet, only two months had gone by since he stood on the platform at Cassarate and looked up at the high plateau where the school was, and Kevin came up behind him to tell him . . . How could he have told then that he would find himself here today, dodging M. Konrad and the police, and prey to the ferocious mother instinct of a Mme Larastazu?

He sighed, thinking of the day he had just passed. Then he settled back on his elbow, and opened the book.

St. Dominique du Val, he read, was born in Zaragoza, Spain, in the thirteenth century. His grandfather was French, a famous warrior who had fought with Alphonse the Battler at the siege of Zaragoza, in which the Moors were expelled from that city. As a reward, the king gave him extensive lands and titles of nobility, and the Sieur du Val settled down in the city he had helped to free from the infidel. There was born his son Sancho, who became a loyal vassal of James the Conqueror, and a notary famous for his uprightness and severe justice. And there too was born Sancho's son, Dominique, destined to become a saint and martyr.

Michel turned back to the previous page and looked at the heading. Dominique du Val had lived from 1237 to 1250. Michel stared at the dates. Why, he was only a boy, like Tarsicius! He had died at the age of thirteen. He flipped the page and read with renewed interest.

"One afternoon, as Dominique was returning home from his church school, he saw a boy shivering with cold near the Martyrs' Cross. Filled with compassion, he approached and said, 'Do you have parents?' 'Yes,' the unknown boy replied, 'but my father is in prison. A Jew sent him there, because my father owed him money for some work he did, and couldn't pay him. And my mother is sick in bed.' 'Poor little boy! Come to my home. My father may be able to do something for you.' Thus spoke the warmhearted child, taking the unfortunate one by the hand, as tears of sympathy flowed down his cheeks. As he saw it, nothing was impossible for his father. And certainly, because of his office, Sancho du Val was well acquainted with the snares of the Hebrews, and his sense of justice had led him to undo many of their intrigues and speculations. For this reason he was cordially hated in the Jewish quarter of the city. An entire section of Zaragoza belonged to that people without entrails."

People without entrails. Troubled, Michel lifted his eyes and stared ahead of him. Then he read on.

"Dominique was familiar with the streets of that area, where the clan of the circumcised hid themselves. He often went through them, returning from the cathedral to his home, because it was a shorter way. What most disturbed him about those people was the hatred they felt for the Cross. He often saw the Hebrews at their rites and ablutions, or listened to the guttural sound of their prayers, pronounced in a language unknown to him. Then his Christian sensitivity became irritated, and as a protest against them all he began to sing the songs he had been taught in the cathedral: antiphonies, motets, hymns to the Virgin and the saints. This might be construed as a challenge, and that was the way the inhabitants of the quarter took it. From the wretched, narrow windows came forth inflamed looks like arrows, menacing fists, cries of vengeance.

"One Saturday the Jews were celebrating their weekly rites under the vaults of the synagogue. The Grand Rabbi arose and made his commentary of the texts that had just been read. Perhaps in his discourse there was some allusion to the hated notary of St. Michel. Perhaps he spoke of the audacity of his son, who dared to disturb the streets of the ghetto with the liturgical hymns of the Christians. 'Besides,' he added gravely, 'we need Christian blood. If we celebrate the Paschal feast without it, Jehovah will blame us for our negligence.'

"This argument convinced the entire assembly. To maintain alive their hatred of the disciples of the Crucified One, the Jews used to knead their unleavened bread with the blood of a child stolen from the Christians. As it was not possible to find victims every day, they passed the blood about from synagogue to synagogue, for even though it might dry out in the bottles or flasks, it did not lose its force.

"And so it happened one afternoon, when Dominique was crossing the Hebrew quarter, that a linen cloth suddenly fell over his head; he heard a mocking guffaw, and felt himself dragged away by a brutal hand that clutched his throat. The aggressor was Mosé Albayucet, a usurer with an emaciated, waxen face, in which it was easy to see the reflection of cunning cruelty. His narrow eyes, hidden by enormous lashes, gave forth that pallid brilliance derived from the voluptuous contemplation of gold. His nose gave him the aspect of a bird of prey. His den was in a murky warren of the street that is today called St. Dominique du Val. He took the boy to his home and put him in a box, awaiting the opportune moment for the bloody rite. At first the boy wept like the child he was; then he thought of the cross he bore on his body and on his coat of arms, and generously offered up his life.

"That same night, under cover of the dark, Dominique was transferred to the home of one of the chief rabbis, a sumptuous edifice on that same street. There the princes of the synagogue were waiting: swollen bellies, yellow faces, hooked noses, long beards, wrinkled foreheads, hairless skulls, and eyes gleaming with cruel joy and malice. Dominique trembled, holding in his hands the crucifix that hung from his neck.

"A fawning voice said, 'Dear child, we do not wish to do you any harm; but if you want to leave this place alive, you must trample that Christ with your foot.'

" 'Never!' said Dominique with great energy. 'He is my God.'

" 'Then you will have to trample your God.'

" 'No, no, a thousand times no!'

"Meanwhile, those evil ones became impatient. 'Let us finish quickly,' they said, not without nervousness. And there began the tragic and sacrilegious parody. Someone handed over the hammer and nails; another circled the boy's temples with a crown of thorns; another held those soft hands, and Mosé Albayucet nailed them to the wall with four blows. Then others were given the task of opening the veins and receiving in flasks and cups the blood that emerged from that little body twitching in spasms of pain. Dominique prayed in a low voice. His life was escaping from him, his body remained without blood and without strength, his small blond head hung inert on his breast, like a cut rose. The containers were full. While the other executioners were washing their hands, Albayucet removed the body from the wall and mutilated it. He kept the head and the hands, and turned over the trunk to one of his companions. Quickly the bloody stains disappeared from the floor and the wall. It was twelve o'clock when the rabbis went quietly to their homes. Thus in the ghetto of Zaragoza the day of August 31 came to an end, and September 1 began. It was the year of grace 1250.

"During the nights that followed, there was weeping in the house of the notary, unrest in the city, lights on the riverbanks, and in the ghetto, near a deep well, a black dog that would not stop howling. It was the dog of the notary of St. Michel, the only one who could quiet him. The well was emptied, and at the bottom appeared two pierced little hands, a head crowned with thorns. Later, some fishermen came across the maimed trunk, bruised and cut by knives and daggers. All was discovered. With his confession Albayucet himself did no more than repeat what the man in the street had already guessed.

" 'Yes, I did it,' he cried, flinging himself about like an epileptic. 'Kill me, it doesn't matter. The eyes of the boy are following me, and sleep has fled from my own.'

"It was a persecution of love. The martyr had earned repentance for his murderer. Albayucet was baptized, and then climbed tranquilly to the gallows."

Michel was stricken with horror as he read this dreadful account. Was it possible? This book had been written by a man of God; it bore the *nihil obstat* on the inner cover; it had to be true. But that meant—His father. His aunt from Palestine. M. Konrad. M. Immermann. Those he knew were Jews, and those who passed him on the street or sat near him on trains who were of them without his knowing it—did they practice those macabre rites as well? Did Jehovah, the God of the Jews, still require it of them? Suppose M. Konrad caught up with him, and he were turned over to his family. Would they give him bread to eat mixed with Christian blood? But he was a Christian! He too wore a holy medal about his neck, stamped with the crucifix! Was that why they wanted him? Oh no! he cried to himself, his blood running cold at the thought.

That afternoon, as Mme Larastazu was rubbing him with the yellow ointment, she had commented, "Blue veins, that means royalty." Michel looked down at his chest and shuddered. His face was covered with sweat. He felt tiny and naked, as though he were a loathsome worm God was looking down at from the awful heights, before turning away in disgust. His great sin, which he had managed to bury under his more immediate fears, rose up before him in all its ugliness. He had still not cleansed himself through confession and penance. What was to become of him? How much better it would have been if he had never been born!

The next day Michel stayed in bed. He awoke in such listlessness that Mme Larastazu became alarmed and summoned Father Nagorra. He was just tired, he said. It was nothing, really, Father. And so they let him alone, although the housekeeper tiptoed in every now and then, her face solemn and worried. Michel pretended to be asleep. He did not want to talk to anyone, and in truth dozed a good part of the time.

He himself did not know what was the matter with him. He knew only that he felt miserable, he trembled at the slightest noise, tired tears welled to his eyes for no reason, and his thoughts were a gloomy morass that went on churning and churning even when he was half asleep, until they became so menacing that he started and sat up. Under his closed eyelids he saw a pale blond head hanging, like a cut rose. Or he himself was that bloodless body nailed to the wall, and a waxen, beaked face was looking at him with a terrible expression in its glittering eyes, heavy-lidded like those of M. Konrad. And once he saw himself staring at a crucifix on a door, and someone came and stood accusingly behind him, and it was Father Scala.

His thoughts seemed to have gotten away from him. His body lay stretched out on the bed, thin, fragile, helpless; his brain crouched over it, sluggish but constantly in squirming motion, like a feeding octopus. In protest he tried to think of pleasant things: the brief party at the Nursery, where Léah had imitated Mother Veronica; the policeman's face at the station in Marseilles; his friendship with Kevin. But before long he found himself staring blankly ahead, oppressed as ever, these images replaced by other, more gruesome ones.

Thus that long, weary day passed. At night, having eaten nothing all day, he managed to down a cup of tea laced with a spoonful of brandy, and a slice of toast. He had to get some strength in him, he told himself. The arrangements were made; he would be leaving on Friday, Father Nagorra had said. But how could he go anywhere in this condition?

". . . the facts are these. On January eighth little Michel Benedek walked out of the courtroom in Touville and disappeared. This was a Thursday. For ten days there was no news of him. Madame Lindner, the boy's aunt, who had come from Israel to attend the trial, was in despair. But on Sunday, January eighteenth, in the city of Marseilles, telephone lines hummed busily in the parish of Notre-Dame-des-Lis. A photograph of the Benedek boy had appeared on the cover of a Sunday magazine of national circulation, and the children of the parish school were certain that the boy in the picture was none other than a classmate of theirs, a newcomer to the school, whom they knew as Jean Dupont. They told their parents. Astonished, the adults telephoned each other, comparing the children's stories. There seemed to be little doubt. Jean Dupont was the controversial child over whom the indomitable Mademoiselle Rose of Touville and the family of Israel had been battling for years."

Michel sat in the parlor. He wore the suit Mme Larastazu had fitted for him. It was still too big, and bulged stiffly about his seated body. Under the jacket he wore a gray woolen sweater, which clung to him snugly and was warm. His overcoat lay over the back of the chair, and on the floor at his side was the small, battered traveling bag that had been dug up from somewhere for him. It gaped at the edges, and was held together by a strap around the middle.

He was better, but still weak. He felt shrunken and boneless, but he could walk. A doctor had come the day before, examined him, asked what he was frightened of, and had left a pungent green medicine for him that gave him a burning sensation in the pit of his stomach. Perhaps it was the medicine, or just plain exhaustion, but he slept well that night, dropping off dreamlessly into a welcome oblivion.

Now he was ready to go. Mme Larastazu stood by the window, peering out into the darkness. Father Nagorra sat on the sofa. The voice of the radio announcer, crackling with energy, filled the room. It was the six-o'clock news analysis.

"The next morning, Monday, the children of Notre-Dame-de-Lis went to school, eager to see the boy whose name had appeared in headlines during the previous weeks. More astonishment. Jean Dupont was no longer at the school. The elusive Michel Benedek, the mystery boy of France, had disappeared again. But his brief apparition, as well as his escape, remained a local secret. Outside the parish of Notre-Dame-de-Lis, nothing was known. No one went to the police. The parents of the schoolchildren kept their discovery to themselves, either in a deliberate conspiracy of silence, or because of a common fear of being involved in an affair that has aroused such bitter recriminations on both sides.

"The days passed. In Touville the Appeals Court announced its verdict: it declared itself incompetent, and ordered the procureur to prepare a new brief. Mademoiselle Rose was imprisoned. In effect, therefore, the original Appeals decision of the previous year remained in force, and the police redoubled their efforts to find the missing boy, acting on the charge of kidnaping and murder filed by Madame Lindner.

"Where was the boy? All France wondered. Only a handful of conspirators, and the boy himself, knew. Certainly here in Garonde, so far from Côte-des-Alpes, no one had any reason to suppose that our city would soon find itself the scene of the next act of this strange drama. But last Sunday, February first, two weeks after Michel Benedek's disappearance from Notre-Dame-de-Lis, the rector of St. Ignatius opened a newspaper, and saw staring at him the features of a child he had admitted to the school only two days before, under the name of Luc Casella. He went to the police, who notified Madame Lindner in Touville. That night the legal representative of the child's family, Monsieur Konrad, took the train for Garonde to receive the boy from the hands of the rector of St. Ignatius, Canon Sombre, into whose custody the child had been remanded, and in Touville Madame Lindner, too ill to accompany him, wept tears of joy.

"What happened then is still a mystery. Again the child disappeared, under the very noses of the school authorities and the police. Early Tuesday morning, a few minutes before the rector was to take him to the Parquet and Monsieur Konrad, little Michel was nowhere to be found. His books and his suitcase were still there; but not the boy or his overcoat. The conspirators, operating as if by magic, had struck again.

"But this time there was no cover-up. Things had gone too far for that. The name of the woman who had brought Michel Benedek, alias Luc Casella, to St. Ignatius was known: Mademoiselle Isolde Vincent, city councilor of Touville, heroine of the Resistance, sister of a priest who is a member of the teaching staff of the school here in Garonde. The name of another visitor to our city was also known: Sister Veronica, mother superior of the Temple Dames of Touville, who arrived here on Monday afternoon and left Monday night, having spent the intervening hours in various hurried conferences here and in Biarritz. Both women were arrested and interrogated. And the tale they told is an amazing one, reminiscent of Mademoiselle Vincent's own underground activities of a decade ago."

The announcer paused for effect. Michel listened, stunned. No one had told him. Mother Veronica in jail! The aristocratic Mother Veronica, so dedicated to God, so awe-inspiring, so saintly! A nun imprisoned, like an ordinary person! Wouldn't the Holy Father be dreadfully angry? Wouldn't he order her released? And she, along with Mlle Vincent, had gone to jail for him, Michel! He shrank into his chair, not daring to look at Father Nagorra.

"It was Mother Veronica," the announcer said dramatically, "who took Michel Benedek to Marseilles the night of the trial. It was she who got him into Notre-Dame-de-Lis under the name of Jean Dupont, paying the tuition fees out of her own pocket. And it was she who, picking up a magazine ten days later in Avignon, saw Michel's photograph and hurried back to Marseilles to withdraw him from the school before the children returned to classes the next day.

The boy left the school, but not Marseilles. Mother Veronica found a hiding place for him with a priest of that city, one Father Cancialotti, and returned to Touville. Her part was over, for the time being. She was waiting, biding her time. For what? For the verdict of the Appeals Court. If it turned out to be in favor of Mademoiselle Rose, no further secrecy was necessary; the boy could resume his real identity and return home.

"On January twenty-ninth the court made its pronouncement, and Mother Veronica's hopes were dashed. Now Mademoiselle Vincent enters the picture. That same night, armed with a false school identity card in the name of Luc Casella, prepared in advance, she obeyed the direction of Mother Veronica by appearing in Marseilles, picking up the boy, and taking the night train to Garonde. Moved by her eloquent invented tale of family disaster, the rector of St. Ignatius took the boy in. All was well, the conspirators thought; only a photograph linked Luc Casella with the missing Benedek child, and they had taken the precaution of disguising his appearance by cropping his hair and giving him glasses to wear. But they had reckoned without the retentive mind of Canon Sombre, rector of the school. In his own words, 'the boy looked vaguely familiar.' He compared photographs, and the game was up.

"The news flashed throughout the country. By that night . . ."

By the window Mme Larastazu made a frantic motion with her hand. "A car!" she announced. Father Nagorra sprang to his feet and turned off the radio. "No, it's a truck," the housekeeper said after a moment. The priest shrugged and flipped the switch again.

". . . curiosity. But before going on, let us return to Marseilles for the moment. Interrogated by the police, Father Moineau, Superior of Notre-Dame-de-Lis, admitted having signed the school identity card in the name of Luc Casella, although he understood the child's name was Jean Dupont. He did it 'to oblige a nun,' he said; but denied vehemently knowing the boy's true identity.

"Father Cancialotti, parish priest, knew the child only as Luc Casella, according to his testimony. He had taken the child in out of charity, he said, having been told a vague tale of a pending lawsuit. The Vincent woman had lied to him, he said angrily. He was willing to cooperate with the police. The Benedek boy was in Belfort; Mademoiselle Vincent had told him that was where he was taking him. In Touville, however, Mademoiselle Vincent, shown this sworn statement by the priest of Marseilles, expressed wonder at it, saying that she had bought two tickets to Garonde and that was where she had gone. In view of Canon Sombre's evidence that the child came to his school on Friday afternoon, and could not in fact have gone to Belfort in the intervening time, the police of Marseilles are continuing their interrogation of Father Cancialotti to determine whether this false clue is an attempt to obstruct justice.

"Only the mother superior of the Marseilles Temple has admitted knowing the boy's true identity. She aided Mother Veronica in placing him at the school in that city. She did so in full knowledge of the facts. The child is baptized, she said. The Appeals Court decision of last year she considers to be a miscarriage of justice; the final decision is still pending. This is Mother Veronica's argument as well and that of Mademoiselle Vincent. Both of these, it is to be noted, admit their participation in this chain of events, but only as far as St. Ignatius. They did not remove him from the school; they could not; both were far from Garonde at the time. They claim they do not know how the boy was kidnaped, or who did it, or the child's present whereabouts. And there the matter rests.

"Who removed Michel Benedek from St. Ignatius? 'Barbarians,' says Maître Hector Gens, famed Paris lawyer and academician who defended the interests of the family in the January trial. 'People who need instruction in canon law.' Maître Gens is of the opinion that His Eminence Cardinal Rapallo, apostolic delegate to France, should be requested to intervene. As a precaution, Maître Gens has urged the authorities to double the guards at the Spanish border, for fear that an attempt might be made to smuggle the boy over into the protection of Cardinal Segura."

Father Nagorra grunted, his face expressionless.

" 'Religious fanatics,' says Madame Lindner, Michel's aunt. She has sent a telegram to the Minister of Justice in Paris, asking for immediate action.

" 'Anti-Semites,' says Monsieur Konrad, agent for the family.

" 'The priests of St. Ignatius,' says Procureur Fontanel of Garonde. But, in his opinion, only a few of them. There can be no doubt, he says, that the majority of the staff had nothing to do with it. Some did not even know that the boy was in the school. But the most careful study of the premises and interrogation of the staff have not revealed the guilty ones.

" 'Persons unknown,' says Bishop Reynaud of our city. Perhaps there was a plot, perhaps not. In a press conference this afternoon,

His Excellency expressed amazement that none of the authorities involved seem to have taken in consideration the point of view of Michel Benedek himself. Is it not obvious, he asks, that this child, who is baptized, does not *want* to be turned over to his family? It is entirely possible that the driving force in all this is the boy himself. He may have simply walked out of the school on his own, realizing that he had been discovered. He may have enlisted help from sympathetic people about him. The truth will probably not be known until Michel Benedek is found. His Excellency expressed every confidence in the religious of St. Ignatius, whom he called 'representatives of the finest tradition of French clergy,' and deplored the anti-clerical sentiments expressed in certain newspapers, which have leaped to unjustifiable conclusions. Questioned about Mother Veronica's admitted visit to his rectory the night before the kidnaping, Bishop Reynaud stated readily that he had already volunteered this information to an examining magistrate. The nun had come to ask his advice about the legality of the family claim, since the Court of Cassation has not yet pronounced. He had referred the question to the Minister of Justice, through a highly placed intermediary, and had urged Mother Veronica to return to her community and allow the law to take its course. He knew nothing of her activities after that, other than the fact that she had been arrested, a shameful indignity, in his opinion.

"The statements of the bishop's adjutant, Canon Blevitz, Sister Marie-Candelaria, mother superior of the Biarritz Temple, and Sister Veronica herself—these being the ones who were present in the rectory at the time—bear out His Excellency's recollection of the interview.

"And so we are left with the question, Where is Michel Benedek? Where is this boy whose fate has gripped the imagination of all France? Where is this boy who has divided our country into two bodies of violently opposed opinion, like Alfred Dreyfus, innocent cause and victim of the great scandal that convulsed our political life a half-century ago, whose scars are still apparent in our society today? Is he in Belfort, after all? Did Father Cancialotti speak the truth, in spite of the contradiction of the timetable? The police, leaving no stone unturned, are pursuing their investigation in that city.

"Is he in Strasbourg? There is evidence to support this view. Yesterday a postcard was received at the Municipal Nursery of Touville, addressed to the directress, Mademoiselle Rose. This is what is written on the card: 'Dear Maman Rose, I miss you terribly, but otherwise I am well. How are you? Please do not worry about me. From my window I can see the river. It is beautiful. I send you millions of hugs and kisses. Your M.' This card, posted in Strasbourg and written in a childish hand, has aroused the greatest interest among the police of Touville, as might be imagined. This mysterious initial M—does it stand for Michel? Is the handwriting that of the Benedek boy? No one knows. The police of Strasbourg have been alerted, and are investigating.

"Is Michel Benedek in Avignon? What was Sister Veronica, who by her own admission had hidden the boy in Marseilles, doing in Avignon the Sunday of January eighteenth? Was it to find a new hiding place for him because of the photograph that appeared that same day? No, says Sister Veronica. It was not until she had already arrived at Avignon that she saw the magazine with the photograph. She went to Avignon to confer with the mother superior of the Temple there on community matters. The mother superior at Avignon confirms this statement.

"Is Michel Benedek, as most believe, still in Garonde? If so, his whereabouts have so far successfully eluded the most extensive manhunt in the history of our city. If so, it must be with the connivance of some of our citizens, who are either principals or accessories in this act which, however they may justify it to themselves, is qualified by law as the extremely grave crime of kidnaping. And what of Michel himself? Does he know the commotion he has caused, willingly or not? Is he quivering in fear? Is he amused? Again, no one knows but himself.

"And now, ladies and gentlemen, I close this news analysis with a special announcement from the police authorities. It is addressed to the child himself, wherever he may be, in the hope that he, like all Garonde and environs, is listening at this moment to this broadcast."

The speaker's voice swelled with a new emphasis.

"Michel, give yourself up! If you do, none of those who participated in your escape or kidnaping will be punished further. All charges will be dropped. All those imprisoned on your account will be released, including your Maman Rose, who now lies at the point of death in the Touville prison infirmary. Michel, pick up the nearest telephone, and—"

Michel did not hear any more. He was on his feet, gaping at Father Nagorra, who was staring at him in alarm. Then he was at the door, flailing his arms as the priest tried to hold him, screaming, "Maman Rose!" Didn't Father Nagorra understand? His Maman Rose was sick, was dying, and he had to go to her! This was what he thought he was saying as he struggled frantically with a strength that astonished the priest; but in reality he did no more than repeat the name over and over again. At the same time the priest was shouting too, and Mme Larastazu was hurrying up, her hands raised, and she too was saying something; the radio was blaring forth a marching song; all these combined into a roaring sound in Michel's ears, as though the entire world had suddenly burst into a nightmarish static.

Then Father Nagorra was shaking him, his face thrust forward, shouting, "Stop it! Stop it this instant! Turn that off, for God's sake!" This last was to the housekeeper. There was a snap, and the radio was suddenly silent. "Be reasonable, boy. She's in Touville. Do you understand? She's far away. You can't go to her." He held Michel by the shoulders, more gently now, saying the same things as Michel stared at him, his eyes burning and his heart thumping like mad. He hardly knew what the priest was saying; he knew only that he had to be going and this stranger would not let him and there was no way he could explain. He did not even hear the door open. There was a moment when he looked up and there were three faces looking down at him. Then he was lifted up bodily and placed on the sofa, and again a face was close to his, only now it was that of Father Lisiaga, who was kneeling on the floor in front of him.

Michel said to him piteously, "Maman Rose."

Father Lisiaga and Father Nagorra tried to explain it to him. Their voices were calm, insistent, reasonable, as though he were a pouting child. His Maman Rose was sick, yes, but not that sick. She was not going to die. The radio announcement was only a police trick, to get him to give himself up. Michel did not believe it. He stared at them, wondering why they were lying. He knew inside himself that she was dying. He had betrayed her and now she would die. Like his father. And everybody else.

Besides, they said, there was nothing he could do. He had to be grown up and understand. It took a whole day by train to get to Touville. And he couldn't even get to the train. They were looking for him everywhere, and especially at the station. The moment he stepped out of the house he would be picked up. And then they wouldn't take him to his Maman Rose. They would take him to his family across the sea, and he would be farther than ever from his mother. Then she might truly die, of heartbreak, knowing she had lost him forever.

The third priest stood in the middle of the parlor, a big burly man who said nothing. Listening to the others, Michel stared blankly a long time at this one before his eyes took in the unfamiliar face, the great shaggy fur jacket over the cassock, the keen blue eyes twinkling at him under the low-slung beret. Then the priests' urgent words sank in and he understood what they were trying to tell him, and he let himself slide, sobbing, prone on the sofa.

He did not know how long he lay there, full of wordless misery. The men spoke together in low voices. Someone shook him gently by the shoulder. He found himself sitting up. He had to leave, they said. They had come for him. The cars were outside, it was dangerous to delay any longer. Since he did not move, they lifted him to his feet and helped him into his coat. The cold outside struck him in the face like a blow. Then he was standing beside a car in which another man wearing a beret sat in the driver's seat. Someone opened the door and Michel got in the back seat. Father Nagorra handed in his bag. There was a long angry scratch on the priest's cheek. Had he done that? The strange priest got in and sat down beside him. He was so big that Michel had to squeeze into the corner, his knees drawn up uncomfortably because of the bag on the floor.

They were driving into the night. Michel shook himself as though from sleep and looked about him. The headlights of the car stabbed out onto the unlit road and picked out a familiar coupé ahead of them. Father Lisiaga's car. Where were they going? It didn't matter. If it wasn't home, nothing mattered. And who were these men? The one in front was short; only his beret and the back of his neck could be seen over the top of the seat. Was he a priest too? The other one, at his side, seemed enormous in the dark. The beret was pulled down toward Michel, covering most of his face. The broad profile that jutted out was rocklike. Michel turned away.

The road was unpaved and rutted with ice, and the car jounced heavily. Michel crouched in his corner, his heart sick, hearing again the impersonal voice of the radio saying those dreadful things. He felt numb and empty. If he could only have five minutes with his Maman Rose! He would accept whatever happened to him after that. Five minutes, to look at that dear face again, and whisper why he had done it, and receive her forgiveness and her blessing. Surely they would give him that much! Even a M. Konrad could not be such a monster as to deny such a request! But as that fearful name crossed his mind, the face of Mosé Albayucet rose up before him, its eyes full of hatred. Would those princes of the synagogue have even listened to Dominique du Val if he had asked to see his mother? They would have roared with laughter.

But the police. They were French, and Catholics, like himself. If he told them his story, wouldn't they let him see Maman Rose before turning him over to M. Konrad?

The cars had come to an intersection. They stopped, then turned left and continued on their way. The new road was broad and smoothly paved, and the cars picked up speed. The big priest at Michel's side was tossing something from hand to hand without looking at it. His head did not move; his craggy chin thrust out, his eyes fixed on the road over the driver's head, he threw the object back and forth in the dark with little smacking noises as it struck his palm. Was it a weapon of some kind? A knife? Michel shivered. It had suddenly sunk in that he was really being kidnaped, as the radio had said. Mother Veronica, Mlle Vincent, Father Vincent had helped him escape; there was no question of resistance, it was what he himself wanted. But at the cottage he had wanted to go back, and they hadn't let him. He had fallen into the hands of strangers who were carrying him off to an unknown destination against his will. He would never see his Maman Rose again.

The car slowed down. Ahead of them Father Lisiaga's car had come to a stop. The brake lights winked once, twice, three times. "Road block," the driver said briefly. He pulled over to the right and stopped, turning off his lights.

Michel's heart gave a great thump. Road block meant police. Ever since the priests' conversation Tuesday night he had wondered how road blocks worked. He had supposed that the police put some kind of barrier across the road, and looked into cars to make sure the person they were looking for was not in them. He had imagined that when it was their turn the people he was with—he had taken it for granted that it would be Father Nagorra and Father Lisiaga—would invent a new identity for him, as Mlle Vincent had, and they would get by. But if that was so, he realized now, what would prevent him from crying out to the police, "I'm Michel Benedek!" and begging them to take him to his Maman Rose?

Did he dare? He tried to see himself opening his window and shouting these words, and this huge, menacing priest reaching out to silence him. Who knew what the man might do? Was he really a priest? Michel had heard that during the Resistance the Maquisards sometimes used the cassock as a disguise. Perhaps these men would resist, fight it out, make a run for it in the car. Would the police shoot at them? He didn't know. He was only a little boy who had wandered into an adult world where his brief experience of life didn't mean anything and you couldn't tell what people would do. He couldn't even be sure but that they had told him the truth, that the police bulletin was a trick, and his Maman Rose was not dying after all. If they were right, he would be making a gigantic mistake, putting himself into the jaws of the wolf. And he had to decide within a few minutes. Maman Rose! he cried to himself. Tell me what to do!

In his agony of indecision he glanced at the priest at his side. The man had tossed the object into the air, caught it and put it in his pocket. It was nothing but a black rubber ball. The priest heaved himself up, got out of the car, and came around to Michel's side. "Let's go, Benedek," he said. It was the first time he had spoken. His voice was soft and cheerful. What were they going to do? There was no time to think about it. Michel got out of the car, and the priest reached in for his bag. The car shot forward at once; Father Lisiaga's car had already disappeared ahead of them. Michel and the priest were alone on the dark road.

"Follow me," the priest said. He turned and walked away from the road toward the dark woods hemmed by a white picket fence part way up the slope. Michel hesitated, then walked after him. His legs were stiff and wobbly, and his shoes struck the frozen ground with clattering sounds; once he stumbled. The priest turned his head and made lifting motions with his hand. Michel tried to obey. He walked more carefully, lifting his foot high at each step. But it was tiring, and he fell behind. The priest waited for him at the fence, by the open gate. "Come on," he said, and set out again. Now the going was easier. They were on a roughly paved road scarcely the width of a car, which curved to the right up a steepening slope. Trees surrounded them, bare and icy under the rising moon. Michel walked behind the priest, his breath beginning to labor. The fur of the man's thick jacket was black and curly; he cut a strange figure, like a bear with skirts.

They rounded the curve and came to a house perched on the crest. Michel had only the vaguest impression of a white façade of mortared stone and green shuttered windows before he was following that broad back up three steps to a wide balcony and a door beyond, which opened noiselessly as they approached. The priest shook hands briefly with the man who stood there, then beckoned to Michel and disappeared inside. The man made no move as Michel went by into the dark hallway. Then he was crossing a lighted room in which three or four men and women sat, their faces turned toward him, quiet and unblinking and unsurprised. Michel hurried behind the priest, who had simply raised his hand in greeting and gone through the doorway on the other side. Where were they going? And these people, had they been expecting them? How odd, that passing glimpse of family life within a stranger's home, caught in a blink of the eye like a camera's shutter, leaving him with an image he would carry with him the rest of his life!

Now they were outside again, in a flat terrain of spaced trees. Hurry! the priest gestured to him, half hidden amid the ghostly trunks. Michel went on. They came to a clearing, then another fence. The priest vaulted over it, bag and all, in one catlike motion; he reached over for Michel and lifted him effortlessly to the other side. High in the air, Michel saw the sky whirl about him; he saw an outcropping of rock etched against the moon; and caught a glimpse, far below, of a vast, dark expanse without limits. What could it be? It was not until he had followed the bulky figure down a steeply descending flight of steps hewn out of the rock and stumbled to his hands and knees on the narrow stone landing part way down that he realized that what he had seen was the sea. The man picked him up and sat him on the lowest step, where he caught his breath in shuddering gasps and stared out over the mysterious, white-flecked water stretching out before him, framed by V-shaped cliffs. The wind was keen on his face, and whistled in the brambles clinging to the outer edge of the landing; there was a subdued roaring below him. All Europe lay behind him; ahead, across half the world, was America; and he was hanging over the void on a narrow strip of rock, about to drop off.

The priest had kneeled down beside him. "Courage, son. Can you walk?"

Walk where? There was nowhere to go, they had reached the end of the world. Michel did not answer; he had run out of strength, and his legs were like cotton under him.

"We mustn't delay," the priest said, looking up at the sky.

"There's too much moon. We should have been here a half-hour ago. Come, there's no help for it." He picked Michel up under his arms, placed him upright two steps up, and squatted down on his heels, saying, "Grab hold." Michel climbed on his back, putting his arms over the man's shoulders and clutching the fur of the jacket under the man's chin. Enclosing Michel's legs with his arms, the priest picked up the bag, parted the brambles with his free hand, and dropped lightly two or three feet to a ledge below. And then they were off, moving by a half-hidden footpath across the steep face of the cliff that plunged down to the sea far beneath. The priest, like some sure-footed animal, walked, climbed, crawled, jumped across narrow gullies, clung to niches in the rock or rusty iron stanchions; he hummed as he went, now and then calling out softly in encouragement, "That's it, Benedek, hold tight."

Michel had lost all sense of direction. Sometimes he was staring at the moon, low on the horizon; sometimes at the white surf flung upwards from the gleaming black rocks at the sea's edge below. Or his face was turned toward the cliff, which inched by him, gray and seamed and cold. Fear gave him renewed strength; he gripped the fur with all his might and squeezed with his legs, feeling the man's muscles bunching under the fur. Dizzy with this wild, fragmented landscape, he closed his eyes and tried not to think what would happen to him if they fell.

It seemed hours before the priest stopped and grunted. Michel lifted his head and looked about him, then slid to the ground. They were standing on a flat stone surface in a wide crevice of the rock. The sea lay behind them; ahead, the beginning of a descending path through stunted shrubbery, ghostly in the moonlight. The priest was breathing hard. "Not as young as I was," he said, grinning. "But from here it's clear and downhill."

They set off down the path. "Mind the branches," the priest muttered. Michel put his hand before his face and warded off the branches that whipped behind the other. His feet were like lead, but he was ashamed to protest after what the man had done. He was still aghast from that fantastic crossing. If he had known what lay ahead of him, nothing would have induced him off that ledge. He stumbled along behind, his teeth clenched, keeping his head low and his hands raised. Now the path dropped rapidly, they entered a clearing, and the surface under Michel's feet became smooth and slippery. Looking down, he saw that they were walking on ice. Then they were on the path again, a dog was barking, and the priest had stopped, his head held high, listening. Michel's scalp prickled as he heard the sound approaching them, a full-throated baying now, and the crashing of a heavy body through underbrush. The priest's arm scooped out and gathered Michel behind him. "Don't move!" he warned. Then the dog was on them, a huge pale animal running low, lean and muscled in the moonlight, its jaws open. The priest crouched a little and barked a low command. The dog stopped, gave a high-pitched yelp, and leaped. Michel ducked his head and clung to the fur jacket. But what was this? The priest was holding the dog with both hands under the jaw, shaking him playfully, nuzzling him with his nose, and the dog was springing up and down on its hind legs, as tall as the man, whining and licking the man's face. Michel almost sobbed in his relief.

The priest was speaking in a hoarse whisper. The dog dropped to the ground and stood motionless, looking up. Again the priest spoke. The dog barked once, and trotted off and was lost to sight.

"The Irigoyens' dog," the priest said shortly. "Come on."

The car was waiting for them by the side of the road. Michel fell into his back corner. The bag bumped his legs, and he drew them up. Then the car was moving along the road as before. They passed a dark shape motionless to the right. Lights sprang out behind them, and a moment later Father Lisiaga passed them with a wave of the hand.

As if nothing had happened, Michel thought, shuddering. As if he had fallen asleep, had had a brief, frightening dream, and had awakened to find himself still in the car, moving smoothly through the night. So this was how the Basques passed a road block! Like mountain goats.

And the police? His chance was gone, and perhaps he would never have another. What would he have done if the passing had been as he had imagined? He still didn't know.

What would become of him?

The priest began to sing softly. His voice was a low, rich baritone, and the words, unintelligible to Michel, had a harsh, rubbery but not unmusical sound. The driver turned around, grinning, and muttered something. His face was pale and smooth, almost boyish; Michel could not guess his age. The priest broke off his song, laughing, and turned to Michel. "That's the old language, Benedek," he said. "I was singing about you. It's called—" And here he said some words that fell on Michel's ear without meaning. The priest spelled it out for him. C-H-A-. *Charinoak Kaiolu.* "It means 'The Captive Bird.' It goes like this." He sang again, waving his hand.

> *"The little bird in its cage*
> *Sings a sad song.*
> *It has enough to eat and drink,*
> *Yet it longs for the free air.*
> *Because*
> *Because*
> *Liberty is good.*
>
> *Another bird flies by.*
> *'Little bird flying free,*
> *Beware of the cage.*
> *If you can, keep free*
> *Because*
> *Because*
> *Liberty is good.'*"

He was the captive bird. He was the captive of these men wearing Basque berets, who were cheerful now that they had passed the road block. But evidently the priest did not mean it that way, as if Michel were free now that he had got away from the police.

They passed a road sign, momentarily lit up by their headlights. St.-Jean-de-Luz. Then they were in the city, which seemed sparkling with lights after the dark road. The priest's hand was on his arm. Obediently, Michel sank down in his seat below the level of the window. He could open the window and shout, he supposed. It would do him little good. Maman Rose, he thought longingly. How could he find out about her? Maybe, if there was a telephone where he was going— But there was! In the café next to the church, where that priest was. Vergara. He could call the Nursery and speak to Manon. But even as he thought it, he knew it was impossible. They wouldn't let him; and even if he sneaked away he didn't have a centime in his pocket for such a call.

They were in the country again. Michel straightened up and stared listlessly out the window. He had the faint recollection that St.-Jean-de-Luz was south of Garonde. Then they were driving toward the Spanish border, and farther away from Touville. Surely they would not cross the border! He remembered what the radio bulletin had said about Maître Gens and the doubling of the guards.

The landscape became an indistinguishable blur of dark shadows, broken by trees bordering the road and lights in the distance. They passed through a village, then another. Still they went on. Finally the car slowed down and began to descend a long gentle slope. About a hundred yards ahead Father Lisiaga's car was turning left. Now they too were at the turning. As the car swung into the narrow road banked high on both sides, Michel saw at the bottom of the slope to his right a broad paved area beyond which was a squat stone building flooded with lights, and behind it the arches of a bridge. Three or four men in uniform stood by the building, watching them as they turned off and drove away.

The frontier. Police guards. He had been that close.

The road climbed steadily amidst rocky, wooded terrain. At several points Michel saw the gleam of moonlight on water to his right. He watched the priest, whose broad head moved slowly from side to side as he looked out into the darkness, his eyes intent and narrowed.

Again Michel had to slide down in his seat. A little way farther, and the car shuddered and stopped. Father Lisiaga was standing outside their window, making gestures. The big priest opened the door, handed the bag out, and said softly, "Come on, son." Michel clambered out stiffly. No sooner had he set foot on the ground than he was hoisted over the fur jacket like a sack of potatoes. He caught a glimpse of the two cars, one behind the other, their lights out, facing a sheer black wall; a cluster of gray houses huddled side by side, with gleams of light showing through the chinks in closed shutters; the moon shining over a stubby church steeple; then he was being carried swiftly up a flight of stone stairs, beside a grimy stone wall that seemed to be the side of the church, through a graveyard whose slabs leaned crazily in all directions, up another stair. A door opened, and Michel was on his feet, reeling, in a rustic kitchen filled with the smell of cooking. No, he was sitting down on a wooden chair, and an old woman standing by the black stove was looking at him. So was a young girl with a broom in her hand in front of the fireplace. And the big priest was kneeling down in front of him, steadying him with a hand on his shoulder.

Michel stared at that broad, craggy, weather-beaten face as though he had never seen it before. Queer, how blue and twinkling those eyes were. And those strange lids, that folded downward at the outer corners. Everything was queer and floating and unconnected somehow. Even the chair he sat on. The priest was saying something. Michel made a great effort to understand. He was Father Vergara, the priest said. Welcome to Aitzmendi, Benedek.

Michel gave a great sigh, and pitched forward into blackness.

7

AND IN THE fourth watch of the night, he came to them walking upon the sea.

"And they seeing him walking upon the sea, were troubled, saying: It is an apparition. And they cried out for fear.

"And immediately Jesus spoke to them, saying: Be of good heart: it is I, fear ye not.

"And Peter making answer, said: Lord, if it be thou, bid me come to thee upon the waters.

"And he said: Come. And Peter going down out of the boat, walked upon the water to come to Jesus.

"But seeing the wind strong, he was afraid: and when he began to sink, he cried out, saying: Lord, save me.

"And immediately Jesus stretching forth his hand took hold of him, and said to him: O thou of little faith, why didst thou doubt?

"And when they were come up into the boat, the wind ceased.

"And they that were in the boat came and adored him, saying: Indeed thou art the Son of God."

Father Vergara smiled down upon the page. He had always loved this little incident within an incident, the story of Peter, almost comic in its human implications. Only Matthew had it. Mark and John had Christ walking on the water, but said nothing about Peter. And Luke omitted the miracle altogether. But then, neither Mark nor Luke had been there. They were not among the original twelve. And John, it was generally agreed, had written his gospel long after the Synoptics, and had been concerned not so much with the history of events as with combating heresy; indeed, he might have forgotten Peter's abortive attempt to emulate his Master.

Still, Father Vergara reasoned, Mark might well have included it.

He had got most of his information from Peter himself. Was it likely that Peter, relating to the follower he thought of as his "son" the wonder of Christ walking on the water, should have omitted the part that so closely concerned himself, and for which he had been rebuked by the Lord for his lack of faith? Of the authenticity of the incident Father Vergara had no doubt. Peter had tried to walk on the water; he had even managed to take a few steps, according to the account; it was only when the wind blew that fear entered into him, and he faltered and sank. The other apostles in the boat saw him. It was not the sort of thing anyone would invent.

Well then, whose character was revealed by the omission in Mark? Mark's or Peter's? Not Mark, he concluded. The faithful disciple, for all his adoration of the apostle he had followed to Rome, certainly showed no attempt to whitewash his human failings. On the contrary. Mark's account treated him more severely than the others did; for the Gospel according to Mark was really Peter's, and Peter was his own harshest critic. There was the incident in Caesarea Philippi, where Jesus called Peter "Satan" and ordered him out of his sight for not savoring "the things that are of God"; Jesus' vigil at Gethsemane, where he reproved Peter for sleeping; Peter's denial of the Lord in the court of the high priest. Mark had them all. Why not the walking on the water?

Sitting at his broad table covered with books and papers, Father Vergara stared dreamily at the pale flames of the candles in the menorah. His soul was at peace. This was the best time, the still hours of the night when he left the present behind him and walked with Peter through the days that changed the world. He had studied in Garonde, in Paris, in Rome; and those years of promise and saturation in learning had been good. He had returned to the Grand Seminary in Garonde as professor of moral theology, and that had been good too. But after his brief military service and at his own request, to go back to the earth and the humble people he loved, and to write his Life of Peter, he had been granted the parish of Aitzmendi; and this was the fulfillment of his search. He wanted no more of the cities of men. He did not seek preferment. During the day and sometimes into the night he was the priest among his flock, the Basque among Basques, the mountaineer among the hills from which he drew his strength. He performed his duties in the ancient stone church that dominated the village, married, baptized, shrived; walked in Aitzmendi and the surrounding farms, part of the life around him; drank coffee or applejack in kitchens, blessing the house as he left it; gossiped over farm fences about the price of pork and next year's crops; joked with the men at haying time, and even shouldered his way among them, answering their salty jests with saltier ones of his own, outdoing them at hoisting the heavy ricks onto the oxcart, as he did at wood-chopping and at handball—the big bull-like man of the soil, hard-boned, weatherworn, steadfast, humble yet inviolate like his race, superstitious like them, and gay as a child.

But at night, when the lights of the village had gone out and fires were banked on their hearths, Father Vergara retired to his study, which was also his bedroom, drew the curtains, and changed his worn cassock for a coarse woolen robe with a monklike hood. He built up the smoldering fire with the skill of long practice, trimmed the wicks of the candles in their seven-stemmed candelabrum—for he loved to work by the warm, living light of tallow candles—and when all was in order and the ritual of preparation had been completed, he let his great bulk sink into the massive oaken chair he had made himself, and sighed in pure contentment. Like Machiavelli, he thought sometimes, recalling the passage in the Vettori letter where the wily scholar had written, as if with him in mind: "The evening being come, I return home and go to my study; at the entrance I pull off my peasant clothes, covered with dust and dirt, and put on my noble court dress, and thus becomingly reclothed I pass into the ancient courts of the men of old, where, being lovingly received by them, I am fed with that food which is mine alone; where I do not hesitate to speak with them, and to ask for the reason of their actions, and they in their benignity answer me; and for four hours I feel no weariness, I forget every trouble, poverty does not dismay, death does not terrify me; I am possessed entirely by those great men."

That food which is mine alone. The man had had the true passion, Father Vergara reflected. No one who had not could have written these words.

Then, crossing himself, Father Vergara plunged into the books he had accumulated through a lifetime of economy. Where his own texts were lacking, he had the resources of the seminary library and his notes, laboriously gathered in the great libraries of Europe, for he read with ease Latin, Italian, Spanish, and of course the French he had learned as a child along with his native Basque; with sufficient fluency Hebrew and Greek, both ancient and modern; more haltingly, German.

But best of all he had had his *Wanderjahr,* in which he had followed the steps of the first of the apostles from Capernaum on the Sea of Galilee through the Holy Land to Jerusalem; and from there through the many stages of his travels, which led inevitably to Rome and martyrdom. It was then, under the different skies in whose light the fisherman had walked, that he felt for the first time that he had begun to understand this greatest of all the followers of the Christ. For the pure, brooding light, shimmering with tender incandescence, that lay on the simple, rude dwellings of Capernaum and the shore of the inland sea was not the harsh, raw canopy into which Jerusalem on its rocky hill thrust its guilty spires; nor the mystic translucence that enveloped the olive trees of Corinth; nor yet the majestic, melancholy, balmy sky that lay like a benediction over Rome. From the itinerary of the sun alone you could trace the development of the apostle: at first the unawakened man of his clime, burnt by sun and spray and wind, simple of understanding yet so brimming with faith that he could drop his nets at a look and the command, "Follow me"; son of Galilee, whose men were known for their love of independence, their courage, their rudeness tempered by generosity, their inconstancy; Peter the candid, impassioned, loyal, blindly impetuous, brusque, petulant, timid, and obstinate. It was he who dared say to the Master, "Behold, we have left all things, and have followed thee," in which could be understood what he had not quite dared to say, "What will you give us in exchange?" It was he who, after years at the Rabbi's side, could still ask, "Master, explain this parable to us"; who slept when he should have been awake, during the storm, on Mount Tabor, on Olivet; who at the prophecy of crucifixion cried out at the shattering of his dream of triumphant Messianism and drew God aside to remonstrate with Him; who protested that he would never deny his Lord, and denied Him only hours later. Yet it was this same Peter, Simeon, Cephas the thick-headed, who first recognized the Messiah in his leader, who drew his sword to defend him and used it too before he could be stopped, who was the only one of the apostles to wait amid the enemy during the mockery of a trial. This was the Peter whom Jesus snatched from his net-mending at Kefar-Nahum, the natural man, the man of action and faith, full of energy and unrest.

But the Peter of the Passion was already another man. Gone were his questionings, his vacillations of faith, his protests, his slowness of understanding. The Lord had taken this rough lump of Galilean clay, and tempered him into the rock He had foreseen in him, the rock on which His Church was to be founded. There were more brilliant men; but none better forged to be the undisputed leader of the small community of believers who lived quietly in Jerusalem, waiting, teaching, keeping the faith. It was enough, Father Vergara thought, to stand on the ramparts of the divided city and watch the sun sink below the hills to understand this other Peter.

And still another man under the sky of Greece: the teacher, the witness, he who cannot rest for what he has seen with his own eyes, and goes to bear the glad tidings; not with the frenetic fire of Paul, but with the unshakable conviction of the practical, unimaginative man who must be believed because he believes himself; whose words, though not those of a mystic, have become luminous with knowledge and faith.

And finally, at Rome, now old and grave, the theologian without a book, the vicar of God on earth. The remade man at his journey's end, with the tree of his faith now rooted in the new Babylonia and already shaken by storms. The author of the first of the encyclicals, his first apostolic letter, whose unemphatic terms are yet shot through with an unearthly light and show how far this transformed being had traveled from the fisherman who looked up from his nets to see God watching him.

Father Vergara leaned back in his chair and mused on the passage in Mark. The presumption of the man. "Lord, *if it be thou,* bid me come to thee upon the waters." The presumption and the faith. He might just as well have said, I have seen that you can do this wondrous thing. Do you have the power to make me do the same? Do I have the faith to try? He had quailed during the test, yet he had been the only one to attempt it. It was impossible that Peter could have forgotten it. He had forgotten nothing; every detail of the years in which he had walked with the Almighty was burned indelibly into his soul.

Father Vergara got up and poked up the fire, laying another stick on it. He stood brooding before it, watching the flames perk up and catch. Was it because it was the old man of Rome who had talked to Mark? He had told him of his every weakness but that one: his obduracy, his bewilderment, his lack of alertness, his feet of clay.

Was it because that ducking had its ludicrous side, and marred with laughter the awful image of God walking on the sea? How much sense of humor had the fisherman had? How much had remained to him in his last years?

He sighed and looked at the couch where the boy was sleeping.

He considered him gravely, weighing the problem he presented. It was not the keeping him hidden; that was easy, it was enough to keep him within bounds in the study, which no one from the outside entered. The old woman and the girl would not give the secret away. And it would not matter if they did. Father Vergara knew his people; the Benedek boy could have the freedom of the village, and no one would betray him. It was the boy's health, his hysteria, his unaccountable weakness that had made him faint and that had kept him dozing around the clock, with only fitful awakenings throughout the day. It was now Saturday night, and still the boy slept as though God's hand were on him. Something was very wrong. The boy had not wanted to go, they had had to carry him to the car, and there at the road block he had had the urge to run away. Father Vergara had looked over his shoulder as he started up the slope, and seen the boy's furtive glance around, the fixed, pale, staring face, the hesitation before he followed. He wanted to go to his Maman Rose. But that didn't explain his listlessness *before* the bulletin, which Nagorra had warned him about, and for which the doctor could find no physical cause. This boy had been crushed and frightened by something too big for him to grasp. It might be the hue and cry after him, the hunt throughout the country; but was that enough to account for the dazed look of him, the sense of a creature in shock; the *haunted* expression in those eyes?

Father Vergara had once confessed a convicted murderer an hour before the execution, and remembered with a vividness that nothing could efface the dreadful counterpoint of mumbled response and the repeated thud of guillotine being tested in the prison courtyard. The man had turned ashen pale. He had shuddered each time the vicious knife fell, yet he had continued to speak. In the circumstances it was inhuman to expect that tortured soul to concentrate on what he was saying, and without trying to make sense of the incoherent words Father Vergara had absolved the man quickly and gone to quarrel with the warden. He had thought of this scene this afternoon, when the boy had had one of his waking periods. Nila had brought him some soup, and fed him spoon by spoon; and as the priest straightened out his desk, pretending not to watch so as to leave the child at his ease, he had seen the boy's fearful eyes following him and yet not quite looking at him, as though some monstrous presence were distracting his attention. As though, he had thought at the time, the Angel of Death were also hovering about.

A bird. A tiny quivering bird held in the hand, its downy sides trembling with the rapidity of its heartbeat, paralyzed with fear. Looking at the back of that close-cropped golden head motionless on the pillow, Father Vergara felt tenderness invade him, as he did for all of God's hurt creatures. If only he knew the cause of the child's suffering! Too bad the good news had come so late. The boy would no doubt sleep until morning. He would tell him then, he thought, first thing.

He glanced at his watch. One o'clock. He ought to be asleep. But his problem intrigued him, minor though it was. He ought to have a look through some of the commentaries to see if any of them had struck upon the point. Guignebert, for example, the scoffer who demanded slide-rule evidence for everything, and so would confirm no more than that sometime around the beginning of the Christian era, somewhere in Palestine, had probably lived a man whose name was something like Jesus, who had caused some fuss or other and had been very likely put to death by somebody. All that learning, Father Vergara reflected cheerfully as he returned to his desk, dedicated to disproving the hurricane that had turned the world upside down, simply because those first battered by it had stammered out confused tales of what they had seen.

He winced as he sat down. He was tired, and the crick in his back had begun to act up again. Tomorrow he would have to see about having a cot brought in. Last night he had put the boy in his bed and had slept in the chair by the fire. Fifty-three. An age at which a man ought to slow down a bit, seek his little comforts, not do rash things like crawling across cliffs with a living load on his back. Would he live long enough to finish his life's work?

He picked up his pen and bent over the pad of cheap yellow foolscap. His stack of notes was already two feet high, carefully cross-indexed, almost complete. A few more months, and he would be ready to begin the writing. The drudgery was largely behind him. The rest would be a feast. He wrote for perhaps twenty minutes, absorbed in his task, until the candle flames flickered strangely and he looked up.

The door was ajar. He was mildly surprised. Could he have forgotten to close it when he came in? He had gotten up and taken a few steps toward the door before he looked at the couch and saw that it was empty.

He stared, frowning, more puzzled than alarmed. It was true that the candelabrum blocked his view of the couch; but why had he not heard him? Had the boy gone barefoot? Yes, there were his shoes on the floor, half hidden by the hanging blankets. Father Vergara thought of the icy stone steps and frozen flagstone path to the outhouse, and hurried out the door and down the short passageway to the kitchen. It was as he had thought, the outer door was wide open and moonlight streamed in. A chair was out of place. It had been taken from beside the table and set directly in front of the fireplace, where the banked coals gleamed redly under their coat of ashes. This was so strange that Father Vergara paused to consider it. He had been the last in the kitchen before retiring to his study and relieving the girl Nila; and he had certainly not left the chair in this awkward spot, where anyone entering in the dark would stumble over it. And Nila had gone straight to the room she shared with the old woman. Then it must have been the boy. Why?

Father Vergara found himself staring up at the chimney. It was bare, except for the two nails he himself had driven into the brick years ago, and the wires he had fastened to them. The wires hung loose now, bent and rusty. The crucifix was gone. A shock went through the priest's huge frame, as disbelief wrestled with the evidence of his eyes. Had the boy dared? What deviltry was this? Haunted, he thought; the boy's eyes were haunted. He shook himself angrily, and in two leaps plunged down the outer stairs, striding to the outhouse and flinging open the door.

It was empty. He had known that it would be.

Simon, sleepest thou? Couldst thou not watch one hour?

But he had been wide awake! And still the boy had given him the slip, under his very nose!

His mind raced. The boy could not have gone far. The flickering of the candles must have been caused by the opening of the back door. He must have gone the way he had come, through the cemetery, around the church, down the steps by the handball court and into the village. From the village there was only one possible way to go: the narrow road through the woods to the highway, and the border guards. If he was running away. But the priest's heart misgave him.

The boy was barefoot! He had not taken his shoes, when he might so easily have carried them in his hand. Nor his overcoat. That was in the closet, whose door creaked. Barefoot, in his nightgown—and with the crucifix! In this freezing February night!

Perspiration trickled down the priest's blanched face. The quickest way to head the boy off was to go through the house and out the front door, which would let him out on the plaza before the church. But as he turned on his heel he caught a glimpse of something white moving in the distance, down by the river. An instant later he was racing down the stony slope. If it was the boy, he couldn't go far. There was no road, no path by the Bidassoa. There was only the broad, shallow river, with thickets hanging over the banks to make passage difficult; beyond, the dark, forbidding mass of Mount Choltococagna blotting out the sky. If the boy tried to cross, the ice would bear him up; and even if he broke through, the water would come only to his knees. Yet Father Vergara ran with fear in his heart. The Bidassoa was the border between France and Spain. Every two hundred yards on the other side was an outpost with its sentry, who would shoot first and challenge afterward.

But when he arrived at the riverbank, the boy, if it was the boy, had disappeared. Perplexed and angry, the priest pulled back over his head the hood that had slipped down as he ran, and gazed up and down the river. The Bidassoa was calm in the moonlight, its slow current scarcely heard under the ice. There was no one in sight. Father Vergara whirled in his tracks and stared at the wooded incline to his right. If it had been one of the village boys he was after, he would not have hesitated an instant. But this boy was a stranger, he couldn't know of the track up to the tunnel mouth. Unless he had glimpsed the peristyle the village fathers had set back in the bushes, to keep the livestock out. Even as he wondered, he heard something moving up above. He opened his mouth to shout, then realized the danger. If the boy began to run!

In one motion he stripped off his heavy robe and stood in his shirt and trousers. Then he ran back some twenty yards over the route by which he had come, and plunged into the bushes. He was over the peristyle in his stride and bulling his way up the scarcely visible track that snaked its way up the hill, crashing through the brambles that pulled at him and ducking under the low-lying branches of the trees. Madness! he thought as he ran. Only a few minutes ago he had been lost in his biblical studies, comfortable and serene in his study; and now he was out in the night on this wild chase. He was not even sure it was the boy he had seen. The noise he had heard might have been anything. Yet he could not take the chance. If there was madness here, it was on the part of the boy, who must be completely out of his mind to come out all but naked as he had. And the crucifix! What in God's name had he wanted that for?

Thank God! he breathed to himself. He had burst into the clearing at the top, and there was the boy standing at the fence that circled the pit. Barefoot. In his nightgown. As he had supposed. And holding the crucifix in both hands thrust out before him.

Father Vergara's voice burst from him. "Benedek!"

The boy did not move. He gave no sign that he had heard, his eyes fixed on the little wooden cross, his face pale and pinched in the moonlight.

Blessed Peter, *the boy was asleep!*

Even as he realized it, the priest began to run; and at the same instant the boy slipped over the fence and took two paces forward. Father Vergara, hurdling the fence behind him, saw at the peak of his leap the boy raise the crucifix over his head and lean forward over the yawning blackness of the pit beneath his feet. He had already jumped as the priest hit the ground behind him, scooping the boy out of the air and hurling himself backward at the same time. He struck the ground heavily, the boy on top of him. The fall knocked the breath out of him, but he sat up, gasping, and seized the boy's arm. The boy's eyes were open. As the priest looked at them, they widened, a new light entered them, the boy twisted his head violently in one horrified look about him, and began to shriek.

The boy couldn't stop shivering. He sat on the edge of the couch, wrapped in blankets, a towel over his head and tucked under his chin. His face was blue with cold and his teeth chattered. Squatting on the floor in front of him, Father Vergara leaned aside to let the old woman pour more hot water from the sooty kettle into the basin, holding the poor bruised feet in one hand away from the vaporous stream. Behind him Nila laid stick after stick of firewood on the already blazing pile. Father Vergara wiped the sweat from the back of his neck with his shirt sleeve, and eased the boy's feet into the steaming water. Already they had begun to swell and become discolored; ugly jagged scratches crisscrossed the skin, and a lump had risen on one instep, where the thorn had gone in. Father Vergara studied them grimly. It would be at least a week before this boy would walk again.

He had been right, he told himself. If the Rose woman had died, and this child were so depressed and disconsolate that he tried to kill himself—that would be a frightful thing, but not unheard of. But for him to make the attempt, sleepwalking or not, when all he knew was that she was sick—no, that didn't make sense, there was more to it than that. Nothing made sense: the crucifix; the unerring bee-line the boy had made for the caved-in tunnel, the only spot for miles up and down the river where it was deep enough for his purpose, when he couldn't know it was there; the strange cry of "Vati!" he had let out at the first moment of his regained consciousness before he began to yell and struggle.

Some horrible secret lay locked within this boy's breast, some devil powerful and evil enough to seize hold of him when his waking guard was down and push him to self-destruction. It was not willful; the boy fought against it with his conscious mind, at what price could be seen in his wasted frame and sunken, distracted eyes. And from all appearances it did not date from yesterday, and would be stubbornly entrenched and rooted. He had to be careful, Father Vergara decided. The boy's life was in his hands. He uttered up a short, silent prayer and, his heart constricted, bent over the wounded feet.

After a while the shivering stopped, and the boy began to perspire. His legs were pink with the heat as far as the knees. The rent skin of the feet was raw-edged but clean, all but the lump whose center was an ugly blue puncture. It might have to be opened later, Father Vergara thought, but for now it would do. He thanked the old woman and the girl, and told them to go to bed. Wrapping the boy's feet in a towel, he began to talk in the low, soothing tone one uses to frightened animals. He was going to pour some medicine on the wounds, he said. It would hurt, but he was to bear with it because it would cure him. This was not any medicine you could buy in a store. If you went to a pharmacy and asked for arnica, you would get something like it; but this was better, this had been made right in their own kitchen from the arnica flower itself, which grew in these mountains. It was a bright yellow flower that the people hereabouts called "mountain tobacco." As he spoke he patted the feet dry and poured the infusion over them, holding the basin underneath. The boy stiffened slightly as the liquid hissed and frothed in the wounds, but he said nothing. Good lad, Father Vergara thought. Gently he wrapped the gauze in loose windings around the feet, then slid a pair of his own white woolen socks over them, still talking. The boy listened to him as though hypnotized. How much did he remember of his strange outing, the priest wondered. Why hadn't he asked any questions?

He had to find out. And better now than later. This child was going to make a complete confession. Everything. It was the only thing that could save him.

He began to ask questions, at first sitting on the couch alongside the boy; then, when he noticed that the boy shrank away from him, on a chair that he pulled up. Did he remember getting up from the bed? Why had he done so? Why had he left the house?

The boy shook his head, murmured something, did not want to answer. Father Vergara insisted gently. The boy squirmed, and said in a low voice that he did not remember having gotten up. He must have been walking in his sleep. Father Vergara asked if such a thing had ever happened before, and the boy, not meeting his gaze, admitted unhappily that it had. Had he ever told anyone? A doctor? A priest? The boy shook his head.

"Why did you take the crucifix?"

At this the boy looked up with such astonishment that the priest realized that he was telling the truth, that he was probably not aware of anything that had happened between the time he fell asleep on the couch and his awakening at the edge of the pit. And what a fearful experience that must have been! He did not want to torture the boy; he told him simply and without emphasis what he had witnessed, making a mental note of the strangely agitated look in the boy's eyes as he described how the chair had been placed before the fireplace and the wire twisted and broken off. Had that happened before too? he wondered. When he came to the last-second rescue, the boy cried out and buried his face in his hands. Could it be that he *still* did not know what he had tried to do? But he had awakened then; what did he think he was doing there? Father Vergara asked the question. The boy wouldn't answer. Father Vergara prodded, asked again, rephrased the question; surely he must have thought *something,* otherwise why had he yelled? The boy stammered that he didn't know. He had opened his eyes, seen him, seen the black void at his feet, and had thought— Now it was the priest's turn to be astonished.

"You thought that *I*—" he demanded incredulously. He began to laugh, and the boy, glancing at him sideways, gave a shamefaced grin.

"But you know now, don't you?" he said, his face grave again. "Be honest with yourself, Benedek. You tried to jump. You don't remember that, but I saw you. It was so close that I almost went in with you. The crucifix did, as a matter of fact. It fell from your hands as I pulled you back. You believe me, don't you? I have no reason to lie to you."

The boy made no answer. "Do you believe me?" Father Vergara said patiently.

The boy nodded, his face turned away.

"Why did you do it?"

He didn't expect an answer. How could this child know the buried motives that drove him in his sleep? If he was worried about his Maman Rose, Father Vergara went on, he needn't be, any more. Maman Rose was all right; that is, she was still sick, but not so seriously as the police bulletin had made out. She was certainly not going to die. He had the information direct from the Nursery at Touville, from a young woman named Manon. It was Father Lisiaga who had got it for him. Early that morning Father Lisiaga had driven to Bordeaux and called the Nursery. He had had a difficult time convincing the person who answered, Manon, that the call was bona fide, that he knew where Michel was and could get the message to him; especially since he had had to speak guardedly for fear the police were monitoring the Nursery phone. And in case the operator was listening. But finally Manon was convinced, and became all excited and begged for news of him. For Maman Rose's sake, she kept repeating; it would make her so happy! She was indignant at the news broadcast. It was a lie, she said. She had just spoken to their lawyer, who had been to visit Maman Rose in the prison infirmary. She said to tell Michel not to worry, that Maman Rose was better and was out of bed and walking about when the lawyer arrived, and that Michel was to stay hidden and not get caught.

Why was the boy so distrustful? At his first words the boy had straightened up in his sitting position on the couch and his eyes had opened wide. But at the end his face fell and he looked away.

Father Vergara said quickly, "Who is Léah?"

The boy muttered that she was a girl at the Nursery.

"Well, Manon said to remind you of something. A party at the

Nursery. When Léah made you laugh by imitating some Temple Dames."

Thank God it had occurred to Lisiaga! How well he had judged the boy's state of mind! He had asked Manon for some private bit of identification so that Michel would know he had really spoken to her. Watching the boy, Father Vergara saw the information go home. The boy stared, his eyes suddenly alive with memory; then he burst into tears.

Let him; the best thing he could do. Father Vergara got up and stood looking down at the boy. For an instant he let his hand rest on the boy's head, noting with a catch at the heart that this time he did not pull away, then went to his desk. It was three o'clock; he had to be up before dawn for early Sunday mass. He shrugged. It would not be the first time that he had worked through the night. But this time it was a living soul he was struggling with, and not the saint dead these two thousand years. The same family, he thought. This boy had sprung from the same hermetic race into which God had chosen to be born, and from which He had won his first apostles. All the Jews now spread about the world had descended from that nucleus, which had burst asunder under the pressures of history and scattered its seed. The amazing thing was that they had kept their identity; even that little pocket of Semites recently discovered in India, from some stage of the Diaspora. They were indistinguishable from their neighbors, they were dark-skinned and small-boned, oriental to all appearances; but they had conserved their religious practices, a primitive form of the Hebrew language, and a legend of their source. If it was a miracle for Christianity to have won out against the tremendous forces bent on its destruction, Father Vergara mused, it was just as much a miracle for Jewry to have survived in a Christian and pagan world.

It was while he was engaged in these reflections that the dreadful suspicion struck him that perhaps they had all been wrong. The nun Veronica, the Vincent woman, her brother; yes, Nagorra, Lisiaga and he himself. Even the bishop, who had told Lisiaga that he didn't want to know where the boy was, but that he had better be moved on. Had any of them asked the boy what *he* wanted? Hadn't they, on the contrary, assumed what he himself had assumed, that of course the boy didn't want to go to his family? Hadn't Mlle Rose said so? Hadn't the boy been baptized?

Even as his mind reeled at the thought, corroborative details came to him. The lawyer Gens, who at the Touville trial had spoken of a "violation of conscience"; the "I don't know" of the boy himself when asked if he wanted to be a priest, which the anti-clerical newspapers had made a great deal of; the fact, which he had witnessed himself, that the boy had not wanted to be moved on, and had even contemplated running away; the boy's haggard appearance, product of some inner torment; tonight's shocking episode, indicative of the death wish lurking within.

Not the illness of his foster mother. Nor his fear of getting caught. Nor madness. Suppose it was nothing more than the simplest, most likely thing of all, that the Benedek boy longed to be where a world at peace would have allowed him to be, with his natural family? And that he dared not say so?

Easy now. Easy, Vergara. If this was so, a terrible injustice had been done, and he was in a hell of a dilemma. He had the boy, yes; but this thing was way over his head. On the one hand, the bishop had already made his position clear; and the archbishop in Avignon, who had got the nun the letter from Rome; the Holy See itself; and canon law, which was categorical, in spite of Maître Gens's slanted interpretation. But on the other hand there was the agony of the boy himself. The right of the individual to be himself, to be free to choose his way of life according to his own conscience. Liberty, he said to himself with a silent groan. Liberty, which he as a Basque was ready to defend with his life for his nation and himself. He was one of that race which had successfully defied the Roman legions in its narrow mountain passes in an age which had seen these same legions crush Jerusalem like an eggshell; which had pulled the tail feathers from Charlemagne's mighty host, and laughed at Roland's horn; which had, alone in Europe, resisted the enslavement of feudalism and held its head high, vassals to no man. The Basques of the *fueros* and *fors*, which no king on either side of the Pyrenees had dared to disregard, so fierce was the Basque will to die rather than to have their blood-won rights of autonomy taken from them. The Basques, who refused to accept a stranger as one of themselves, but who had never yet betrayed a stranger to the enemy.

The enemy. *He* was the enemy. And that song he had sung to the boy in the car, to cheer him up. Captive bird, indeed. That must have hurt. No wonder the boy shrank from him, regarded him in fear.

Not so quick, he told himself. There was one way to find out. He had the opportunity to do what no one else had done, and that should have been done at the very beginning of this terrible mess. Be fair! he admonished himself. Give him every chance. No casual question and pat answer! And if the boy admitted it— God help me! he thought. Good-bye, tranquillity. Good-bye, the sweet, peaceful nights, the savor on his lips of the food that was his alone, the joy in his heart to be doing what he was born to do. Good-bye, Peter.

He turned slowly, and regarded the boy, who had stopped sobbing and was sitting there gravely watching him. For your life, boy, he said to himself. Because if I fail you now, you'll try it again, and this time you'll succeed. For your salvation, boy. God give me the wisdom to recognize the truth.

"Benedek," he said, "I need your help. You're the *only* one who can help me. I don't know what to do with you. It's as simple as that. I want to do what you want for yourself, but I don't know what it is. Forget I'm a priest, forget the police are looking for you. You're a guest in my house in Aitzmendi, and you're free. You can do what you want, except for one thing. For the time being you can't go to your Maman Rose. You understand that, don't you? If you tried, you'd be caught and taken away. If you want, you can stay here indefinitely, the rest of your life if you choose. We can have your hair dyed, put you with a family that would take care of you, and you can go to school here like any other village child. Or," he went on, noting the intent gaze the boy had fixed on him, "I can take you across the border into Spain. You'd be safe there, I'd find a sure place for you, and they'd never find you. If you were discovered, the French police would be powerless to take you. The Spanish government would be glad of a chance to pay back the French for the refugees that crossed the border during the civil war, that the French wouldn't turn over to Franco. If you don't like that idea, we can consider another hiding place for you. Elsewhere in France, although that's likely to be dangerous. Switzerland. Italy. North Africa. Everything is possible. Or if you prefer," he said in the same reasonable tone, "I can turn you over to your family."

"What?" the boy said uncertainly.

"Of course," he said. "If that's what you want. I promised, didn't I? I swear," he said. "You tell me what you want, what you *really* want, and I'll do it. Do you want to go to your aunt?"

"Oh no!" the boy breathed with such alarm that the priest felt a surge of relief. At the same time he was puzzled.

"Why not?" he insisted.

The boy stared at him incredulously, and began to explain. He had become articulate at last. Father Vergara listened with growing anger. They had filled this innocent child's head with lies, or at least distortions of the truth. "Excuse me, Benedek," he interrupted, "but that's all nonsense. I've been in Israel, and what you say just isn't true. Slavery? What slavery? It doesn't exist. On the contrary, the Jews in Israel are truly free for the first time in centuries. Because what they've had as unwelcome aliens in other countries wasn't freedom, it was subject to the whims and decrees of the authorities, or worse, of the common man who looked for a scapegoat for his own frustrations. I tell you, my visit to Israel was one of the most moving experiences of my life. There's a new race there, they're fighters and they're tough and they're revitalizing the country. They've liberated themselves at last from centuries of oppression, and they're going to stay free at any cost. And what you say about your aunt doesn't make sense. Use your head, child. She would be the last person in the world to sell you into slavery, if such a thing existed. Your own aunt? She'd smother you with kisses and cherish you like the apple of her eye. And how much do you think you're worth to this man Konrad? Ten thousand francs? A hundred thousand? Do you think Konrad would have been after you all these years for the profit he could make on you? He'd be a poor businessman if he had. Those trials must have cost him or somebody a fortune. Do you know why they want you so badly? I can't answer for Konrad's motives, because, frankly, I can't quite figure him out except that it isn't money, it can't be; but your aunt? She loves you, that's why. You're her nephew, part of the clan. I'd have done the same thing. If a nephew of mine had been taken away, I'd turn the world upside down to find him."

"But they eat Christian blood!" the boy exclaimed.

"Now, in God's name, where did you hear that?"

Father Vergara listened to the answer. Of course, he thought. The boy had been in the parish, and that well-meaning blunderer of a housekeeper had to put the book in his hands. A Jewish boy. His anger gave way to sadness, and he rose and walked to the fire. At length he sighed and turned. What he was going to say, he said, was difficult to understand, but Michel was an intelligent boy and could follow it. The Church was a living organism that existed in time, and was subject to history like any other living thing. Although the

Church was the repository and interpreter of God's eternal truth, not even the Church could know all truths and all facets of every truth because the Church was made up of men, however wise and saintly they might be, and because it was not given to men to know more of the divine than God wanted them to know. And so the truth, although in itself eternal and immutable, was in the awareness of man subject to history as well, that is, it evolved as men, through the exercise of reason and through later revelation, gradually grew to understand it. The concept of purgatory, for example. Purgatory was an accepted part of Christian dogma today, but it had not always been so. It had taken centuries of Church tradition to elaborate it from certain hints in Scripture that had not been properly understood at the time.

In the same way, Father Vergara went on, just as a number of unquestionable truths had been imperfectly known, a number of distortions of the truth and popular superstitions had been widely but temporarily accepted. The superstition about the Jews drinking Christian blood was one of these. It was only a superstition, it did not form part of Christian dogma, and had never been officially announced by the Church. It was a very natural superstition, for it sprang from the enmity and lack of mutual comprehension that had always existed between Jews and Christians since the crucifixion of the Saviour and the refusal of the Jews as a whole to follow the new convenant. He himself had no doubt but that the Jews had unsavory stories about Christian practices, which they swore to among themselves, but which were false nonetheless. Just as the tale of the Jews drinking or eating Christian blood was false. It just wasn't so. A Jew would no more think of defiling himself in such a way than he would by drinking the blood of a pig. Yet the superstition was widespread in the Middle Ages, like many others that have since been disproved, and many churchmen, since they were men, believed it. Some still believed it. It would take time for such hate-inspired tales to die away, but eventually they would. And perhaps the day was closer than one might think.

"There's a new spirit, a new ferment in the Church today," Father Vergara said. "I've watched it grow for some time. A new generation of high prelates who are dissatisfied with the divisions among men, who feel that the Church can do more than she has done to wipe them out and unite all under the one God and His law. For the moment this spirit of reform is kept in bounds by the traditionalist element within the Church, but eventually it will have its way. There will come the day in which a series of ecumenical councils will clear away certain old concepts and establish new ones. Church thinking about the Jews will be, must be, one of them. And you will see the account of St. Dominique du Val dropped from the liturgical year, or altered in line with the new understanding. No, Benedek," he concluded, "you may not want to go to your aunt, but you must have better reasons than these."

But he was French, the boy protested. French and Catholic. He had been baptized. He didn't *want* to be anything but French. And if he went with his family, they wouldn't let him practice his religion. Mother Veronica had said so herself.

"Probably not," Father Vergara agreed. "Those are good reasons. If that's what *you* want for yourself."

The boy nodded vigorously. Yes, Father, that was what he wanted.

He had been mistaken. His theory had crumpled like a house of cards. His dilemma had disappeared, only to be replaced by the original one.

Why had the boy tried to kill himself?

The ugly secret he had first suspected was there after all, and had to be pulled up by the roots. An immense pity welled up in him for the boy, and what he had to do to him. He strode to his desk and took up the handball that was always within reach. He stood musing a long moment, his eye fixed on the candelabrum with its seven flames. It was of crude earthenware, burnished with time and use, sand-colored except for the Star of David picked out in white under the central stem; a lovely thing in its very simplicity, but fragile. He had had to wrap it up in his spare soutane and carry his bag himself to protect it. It was not an article for the tourist trade. He had admired it in one of the fisher huts of Capernaum, and had reluctantly accepted it as a gift when the aged couple put it in his hands and backed away smiling, refusing his money. No doubt Peter himself had lit the Sabbath candles in a menorah such as this, and rejoiced in the holy day of rest. Moved by impulse, Father Vergara slipped off the tiny silver crucifix he wore on a chain around his neck, seized the menorah, and approached the couch. He sat down on the chair before the boy, set the menorah on the floor to one side, holding the crucifix in his left hand. *In his signīs,* he thought. Then, bouncing the ball on the floor and catching it again, he said grimly, "All right, Benedek, tell me about your Vati."

It was still dark. Father Vergara lit the light in the sacristy and walked through the cluttered room to the church, falling heavily to his knees at the altar. Although the gloomy nave was wrapped in a chill no less than outside, he wore nothing over his cassock; he did not feel the cold. He was numb, exhausted, aghast, haunted by the boy's face. Never in his experience had a confession come harder, or taken more out of him. For two hours he had ripped at the boy, probed, prodded, implacable in his search for the truth. Two cruel hours of soul surgery, which had sickened him as though he were dissecting a living being screaming under the knife and felt his own nerve ends curling under the pain. The boy had backed up on the couch against the wall, sweating; he had lied and denied, his eyes darting from one side to another like an animal trying to escape; taken refuge in muteness; cried out under a lucky stroke that penetrated his defenses; sobbed, writhed, gone into contortions; made tacit admissions, retracted them, admitted them again; and finally, realizing there was no way out, having already given away glimpses into his inner torment, he had shrieked out torrents of self-accusation in which the priest could understand at last the cancerous guilts and twisted emotions that had driven the boy to his desperate act.

Listening, Father Vergara cursed silently the blindness, the selfish loves, the egotism, the narrow dedication of those who had brought this child to the brink of self-destruction. To the brink, no; he had leaped; it was not because of any hesitation of his own, any resurgence of his life forces, that he was still alive. If not for the inscrutable will of God, who had placed a bumblingly stupid and complacent hulk of a priest at the right spot and given him the necessary ray of enlightenment, this shattered vessel of the spirit would be lying now empty and lifeless in the black waters of the Devil's Rump, beyond all remedy.

At that moment Father Vergara had prayed for the power to resuscitate the child's soul from death everlasting. Now, kneeling before the altar in the dark church, he renewed his prayer. His task still lay before him. There had been no time to begin it. Already lights had begun to blink on in the houses of Aitzmendi. It was the hour of the mass, and the priest could not stay with the boy any longer. He had given him a few words of encouragement, had told him there was hope; he had summoned the girl Nila and given her strict orders not to leave the boy's side a single instant while he himself was gone; he had locked the door in leaving, and gone to begin the daily sacrifice.

He had got the confession, but that was only the beginning. There was an obstinacy about this child that showed how deep the roots had gone. It would not be easy to give him the will to live again. Yet it was his task. Aitzmendi was the dead end for this boy, there was nowhere for him to go from here unless he were made whole again.

"Lord, grant me the wisdom. And Peter Evangelist, lend me the power of your words."

Thus he prayed, humbly; his eyes, he knew, were bloodshot, his chin bristly with stubble, he was unkempt. Like Jacob, he had wrestled all night with the angel, and had been left, if not lame, with a devil of a backache. May God forgive him his physical condition. There was so little time to do His work.

Father Vergara heaved himself painfully to his feet, genuflected with a grimace, and walked heavily up the aisle to the entrance. He slid the bolt and flung both doors open. The sky over Choltococagna was shot through with the first pale light of dawn. It was the hour. He unlocked the little door under the steeple, seized the rope, and sent peal after peal over Aitzmendi.

8

HE WAS IN THE NURSERY. He lay in his bed by the window, filled with well-being, pleasantly aware of the lethargic warmth that lay over his relaxed limbs. His body knew that it was not morning yet; it would be hours before the alarm whirred faintly in the distance and the stairs creaked as Manon went down to put on the coffee. Across the hall Maman Rose still slept. Good Maman Rose, whose presence filled the Nursery like a benediction. He did not have to get up for a long time still. Time enough when he heard the first creaking of the gate, and anticipation began to tingle in him to think that perhaps today was the day that his father was coming for him.

But his dreams were seldom so pleasant. More often he relived that horrible moment of anguish in which he was violently jerked in the air like a rag doll, and he opened his eyes to see everything swirling around him like a crazy wheel—black, icy woods in the night, the moon outlining a mountaintop, a man's face thrust up to his, a dark pit at his feet and the sound of water.

Or he lay dead on some river floor, his eyes vacant and unseeing, his hair moving gently in the cold current, beyond caring and beyond thought, at last; except that a voice was calling him.

Then he would start and wake up, staring about him in fright, taking in the dark, book-lined room, the desk with the spidery candle holder against the curtains of the window, the fireplace gleaming redly, the great bulk of the priest asleep on the cot a few feet away. Aitzmendi, he said to himself. He was in Aitzmendi, and alive. Everything came back to him, and his mind went over the fantastic series of escapes that had brought him here to the edge of France; and he thought about God, and why He had permitted so much misery and pain in the world.

He didn't want to die. He didn't know why he had done what he did. How could he, when he didn't remember any of it? He remembered waking up the last time, when the silent girl brought him a bowl of soup. He had eaten, still groggy with sleep, and dozed off again; and then he was screaming out in the woods, the world was upside down, and he was being carried through the night, slung over the priest's shoulder. It was as though he had another person inside him, another Michel, who was out to destroy him, who lay in wait like an evil thing to catch him off guard and set him to do crazy things. Was the rector of St. Louis Gonzaga right? Had Satan got hold of him?

No, Father Vergara said. His devil was called resentment. Rebellion against the will of God.

But how could that be? He had tried with all his strength and all his heart to be good. He had studied hard, had prayed and fasted and mortified his flesh, even more than was required of him by his spiritual director at school, who ought to know what was acceptable to God. He had *wanted* to obey God's will, and if he fell short sometimes it was because he was only a little boy, and he made up for it as he was supposed to, by being heartily sorry he had offended, and confessing, and—

Like with the crucifix you took from Father Scala's door?

But he hadn't taken it! Or at least, he didn't know he had. If he had, where was it? The door was locked, and they had searched—

You know.

No, Father, truly he didn't. If he did, he would have confessed it.

You know you're supposed to confess even your doubts. Why didn't you?

But they would have thrown him out of school! And it was the only place he was safe from M. Konrad.

You left the school anyway. You told the truth at the trial so you wouldn't have to go back. And it wasn't because you were afraid you were going to be expelled, it was resentment. The same resentment against God that made you take down the crucifix. Because you had realized, deep inside you, that you didn't want to enter the Seminary and become a priest. Isn't that true?

He didn't answer.

Benedek?

Voices. They were only voices inside him, remembered from his conversations with Father Vergara, which kept on going in his mind when his dreams woke him up. No matter where they started, they went in ever-narrowing circles that always ended at the same point. Then, frantic with fear at what was coming next, he tried to shut them off, turning his mind to other things, anything, to keep those merciless questions from digging where the pain was.

It seemed to him that he had been locked up in this room for ages. He had lost track of the passing of the days. He slept at odd hours. The curtain had been pinned together at the bottom so that no one could peek in and see him. In the morning the sun streamed through the gap in the curtain at the top, and lay on the fireplace in a column of light; as the day progressed, the light lengthened on the floor and inched toward him on the couch; then, when the sun went behind the mountain, the light became diffuse and gradually dimmed out until it was night. It was his clock; only sometimes he napped during the day, and woke up not sure that it was the same day, and that he had not slept through the night to the next. The bell of the church next door tolled and echoed in the room, making the books vibrate on their shelves. This happened every morning, while it was still dark; but several times it happened in the dark of early evening. He no longer left the room; ever since he had hurt his feet they had brought him a chamber pot, which was kept under the couch. On either the third or fourth day, he had soaked his bad foot in a basin of hot water into which a handful of crushed dried leaves had been tossed, and the abscess had opened up and discharged a quarter-inch of black thorn and a quantity of thick, ugly fluid; after that the wound began to heal. They fed him, they changed the bandage on his bad foot—the bandage on the other had been removed days ago—they came to empty the chamber pot. The silent girl they called Nila came and poked up the fire, or banked it at night, making the sign of the cross over it; she dusted the desk and shelves and swept the floor and brought him basins of water for him to wash. Occasionally the old bent woman could be heard grumbling in the kitchen or shuffling in the hall. And always, except for the hours he had to be away about his duties, Father Vergara was there, moving about the room; or seated at his desk amid his papers; or sleeping on the cot at his side; or talking to him, questioning, explaining, as he bounced his ball.

And the rabbit, Benedek. Why did you kill it?

He hadn't wanted to kill it. But it couldn't run, because of the smashed paw. It hadn't seemed fair. He had done it to end its suffering. Out of mercy.

Why didn't you take it back to the school? Since it came from there in the first place?

He knew why; the priest had explained it to him. But it was like a phonograph record that wouldn't stop. On it went within his mind, question and answer, a hundred times for the once Father Vergara had brought it up. *He* was the rabbit; he had seen himself in the rabbit's place, unable to run, and pursued on the one hand by M. Konrad, and on the other—well, the other was more complicated. The school authorities. The Seminary awaiting him. God. Deep down he hadn't wanted *them* to swallow him up any more than M. Konrad, only he hadn't dared admit it to himself. The rabbit was his first act of rebellion, and the crucifix the next. Rebellion against the God who had permitted his father—

It did no good to scream, Stop! I won't listen! Nobody was talking to him. Father Vergara lay like a tree trunk on his cot, his face a dim blur in the dark. It was only the ghost of his voice that kept after him, that never let up. He had to face it, the voice said. There was hope, but only after he had understood himself.

I've never met a boy like you, Benedek. So stubborn. So intense. You've fixed your mind on a mistaken idea, and you won't give it up. Do you know why? It's your justification. You're full of anger and bitterness, and at the same time you feel guilty about it. And so you cling to your idea. There *can't* be any hope. If there is, you've been wrong all the time, and you can't stand that, because it leaves you without any reason for the things you've done. We're going to change all that. We're going to bring everything out into the open. You're going to see you have no reason for resentment, you won't feel guilty any more, and you're going to stop walking in your sleep.

And so it went. On and on. His father. He had loved his father too much, and blamed him too much. Yes, *blamed*. He was all mixed up, his love being bound up with hate, just as it was for God. Foolishly, for his lack of understanding, his pride, his refusal to seek advice. He blamed his father for being a Jew, for having crucified Christ, for having been caught by the Nazis and abandoning him, for *not* abandoning him. Even when he thought of his father in hell, and suffered for it, he passed the blame on to his father. On the other hand, he had loved his father, and missed him dreadfully, had deified him and thus got his thoughts in such a mess that it was no wonder he had tried to bury them. But a rotten thing buried infected all about it. He had poisoned his mind with his thoughts. It was like the thorn in his foot. The longer it stayed in his flesh, the worse it got. It had to come out. The treatment had hurt, but now it was out and the foot was healing nicely. Did he want to die? Did he want to continue walking in his sleep until he made another attempt on his life, and this time there would be no one on hand to save him?

No, Father.

Try to understand, then.

But it was terribly hard. Patiently, the priest sat with him, explaining point by point, and Michel listened and thought. And when the priest let him alone, Michel went over what he had said in his mind. Usually this was at night, when all was still and there was nothing to distract him from the voice that hammered at him.

Benedek, what is baptism of desire?

He had known at once where Father Vergara was going. There had been a time when he had clutched at it as the possible answer, only to be dashed down again by the argument of invincible ignorance. But he answered obediently. Baptism of desire was that of the non-baptized who, under the influence of actual grace, emits an act of perfect contrition or of perfect love of God, which includes virtually or implicitly the desire of baptism.

Yes, he understood it, Father. Baptism didn't have to be by water, or administered by the Church. But that didn't apply to his father, because—

That was when Father Vergara told him to be silent and listen. It wasn't only his father. The problem was bigger than that, in fact it was one of the thorniest questions in all theology, one which had exercised the best minds of the Church in its two thousand years of existence, and was still open to question. What happened to the virtuous unbeliever? Unrepentant sinners were damned, whether Catholic or not. It was dogma that those who died within the Church in a state of grace were saved, after a time of purgation. But what of the others? Did he realize how many they were? Think, Benedek. Right now, of the more than two billions of those who made up the population of the world, perhaps four-fifths were unbelievers—apostates, heretics, schismatics, Jews, Moslems, heathens. What was going to happen to them? Could a God of love have excluded them absolutely from the Kingdom of Heaven? And that wasn't all—human beings in one stage or other of evolution had existed in the world for many, many thousands of years before the advent of the Saviour and the institution of baptism. More billions, who would have to be excluded by too strict an interpretation of dogma. And still more billions when one counted the centuries of the Christian era, and those who had rejected the new convenant, or never heard of it. And still more, countless more, if one imagined the future and supposed that the same proportion obtained then as now; if one supposed, that is, that 80 per cent of the world's population for thousands of years to come would not be Catholic, and were therefore doomed. These billions and billions he was talking about were not grains of sand or leaves in a forest—these were human souls, whose fate could not be ignored by a Church whose very name meant "universal" and which claimed to speak for all men.

Michel's brain reeled at these numbers, which he could not even imagine. He had never realized the extent of the problem.

Something to think about, Benedek. You've studied Latin. Translate this sentence. *Facienti quod in se est, Deus non denegat gratiam.*

He had been first in his Latin class. He came out with it at once: God does not deny His grace to those who do what good they can.

For hours afterward he repeated the Latin to himself. So many unbelievers! Enough to overflow the boundaries of hell. Was it possible? God does not deny . . . Was this the hope that Father Vergara had held out to him? A God of love. Among so many, perhaps his father . . . But no, he protested to himself, frightened even at hope, after so many disillusionments; that applied to those who had never had the chance to win the faith that saves. The Chinese peasant, buried in his village, hitched to his plow like a mule in a treadmill, untaught, unknowing. The Indian of the Americas, before Columbus. Those bound in invincible ignorance. But not those who lived among Christians, who knew of Jesus and his teaching, and who had rejected it. Not his father.

Still . . . God does not deny his grace . . .

Was it the way out? He would not let himself think so. Because if he had hope again, and again it was taken away from him, then— He didn't know what. How many times could you have your heart smashed, and survive?

Yet little by little the hope grew. For Father Vergara was not done with him. Every morning, every afternoon, every night he sat for a while by the couch and talked. Now Michel found it easier to admit what had been so hard before. He accepted everything—his fears, guilts, resentments; yes, he had taken the crucifix, he must have; he should have confessed it; the false communion was a mortal sin, which he would never commit again, no matter what the circumstances; his father was just a man, with a man's strengths and weaknesses. But please, Father, tell him more about salvation.

Father Vergara told him more. Baptism was necessary to salvation. So was faith. This was dogma, infallible, not open to question. But what was baptism? What was faith? What was necessity? It was here that Michel had been misled, had applied his own definitions to these difficult questions, and had come to the conclusion that had tortured him so much. It would take years of study before Michel began to understand their complexities; he could not hope to grasp in a twinkling, he, a little boy, what theologians argued about among themselves, each with his own shading of opinion. But so much was not needed, not at this stage. Forget about invincible ignorance. He was to remember only the infinite goodness of God, that man had brought suffering and death upon himself by his first disobedience, that we couldn't know God's purposes, that it was easier to pour the ocean into a thimble than to understand His ways. He had dared to judge God for having judged his father! Did he know better than God the state of his father's soul? Yes, and his mother's! No one knew what agony of conscience, what remorse, a suicide went through between the act and the yielding up of the soul. There was time, even if no more than a few seconds, to cry out God's name in a burst of repentance. There was hope for her too. Hope, Father Vergara said; not certainty, no one could give him that. But wasn't hope enough? Wasn't it for lack of hope that he had got himself into that dead end from which he had tried to escape by self-destruction? And all the while it was quite possible that the souls of his father and mother were trembling for him in purgatory, seeing how he had gone astray, and fearing to lose him forever. He was to pray for them. And in his spare time he was to read this book.

Michel was in a daze when Father Vergara had left him. It was early afternoon, more than a week after his arrival at Aitzmendi. He sat cross-legged on the couch, the blanket over his shoulders, dreaming over what he had heard. It was perhaps an hour later that he looked at the book the priest had left. It was in Italian, and bore the title *La Salvezza di Chi Non Ha Fede*. Salvation of those who do not have faith. Or, salvation of the unbeliever. A whole book of almost four hundred pages on what he had believed was his own, secret problem! The author was an Italian Jesuit priest, and the book bore the *nihil obstat* and the imprimatur. He ruffled through it, glancing at the chapter headings, until he came to the last page. The word "Conclusion" stared up at him. It was only a half-page, and he read it.

"Are adults who die unbelieving all equally damned?

"Yes, if by unbelieving we mean without any faith in God, but in this case the fault is always that of the unbelievers alone.

"No, if by unbelieving we only mean not believing explicitly what the Catholic Church teaches. In this case God will see whether a man has at least that faith which is practically possible for him in his actual circumstances.

"In any case, membership of the Church will be an immense advantage for every soul; hence the inestimable value of Catholic preaching.

"The practical result of the whole enquiry is the justification of the Church's attitude over two thousand years: An ardent and assiduous zeal for the conversion of unbelievers, without rest or stay, with prayers and tears and the sacrifice of all we are and have; total abandonment to Divine Providence, without discouragement, when faced with the mysterious phenomenon of persistent unbelief in so many souls!"

Michel read this passage again and again. He hardly dared to understand what the words said. But it could not be clearer. Those who had no faith at all were damned, Catholics or not. This he accepted. It was the next sentence, the one beginning with "No," that he wondered over, revolved in his mind, turned about to see whether more than one interpretation was possible. Unless words didn't mean what they meant, there was only one. No, you were *not* damned just because you were not a Catholic. It didn't say anything about invincible ignorance; it didn't say anything about knowing what the Church taught, and rejecting it; or about whether you were a Jew or anything else. It said "a man." "God will see whether a man . . ." That meant everybody. Catholic or not. Everybody who had *some* faith. What was "practically possible" for him in his "actual circumstances."

Michel thought of his mother. He had had a mother too, Father Vergara had reminded him. It was all right to love his Maman Rose, but he was not to forget his mother. How much faith would God require of her? The Nazis took everything away from her: her home, her country, her family, her husband. These were her actual circumstances. She could not have had much faith in anything if she committed suicide. Yet the newspapers had said that it was because of him that she . . . She had had faith in *him;* or rather, that God would save *him,* with her out of the way. If he were God, Michel thought, he would accept that. Just as He had accepted the widow's mite.

Hope, he thought. Hope, not certainty. But if a boy had hope . . .

Still he resisted. He did not know why himself. He had been wrong, he admitted; Father Vergara was a priest, and had said so; and the book had said the same thing, and its author was a priest too, a Jesuit, like those he had studied with. Then why was he so numb, why did the good news not stir more emotion in him? Perhaps it was because he could not pray. The penance Father Vergara had given him was to say the Lord's Prayer morning and night. A very light penance, he knew, for sins as heavy as his. It should have been easy, especially when he remembered with what fervor he had said this prayer years ago, when the world had no roof over it and his Vati and God the Father were one and the same thing. Was that why the priest had chosen this penance? To put his Vati in his place?

Two mornings and two nights he kneeled beside his couch and said the words aloud. They were only words; he had the feeling that they rose no higher than his head, that God had not accepted them. And he knew that he had said them without conviction, as if he had known in advance that they were not enough.

Another day passed. It was February twentieth. It was two weeks ago that he had come to Aitzmendi, carried on Father Vergara's shoulder like a sack of something. He had no cause to be afraid. His Maman Rose was much improved; Father Lisiaga had spoken to Manon again on the telephone, and Manon had told him that the news that Michel was well and safe had been like electricity to Mlle Rose. She sent him her love. And he *was* safe. The village of Aitzmendi continued to ignore his existence in their midst. Everybody was talking about him, Father Vergara said; but they had no inkling he was in the presbytery, in their very center. The newspapers and radio had not let his case drop either; their claims and counterclaims grew more extravagant every day.

Yet a strange restlessness had come over him. It wasn't the hunt, nor his being cooped up still in the room, now that his feet had healed and much of his strength had returned. It was something else, something inside him, like a pinpoint of flame that grew and grew as the day progressed and would not let him sit still. That evening, for the first time, he had dinner in the kitchen with Father Vergara; he hardly touched the food, although the old woman served them a *piperrade,* eggs scrambled with a purée of tomatoes and green peppers, which Michel had found delicious the previous Friday, the other meatless day he had spent at Aitzmendi. Father Vergara talked and joked the whole time, more than ever in a good humor. No nonsense about Basques, he said. A *piperrade* was meant to be whisked from the stove to the mouth still sizzling from the flame. By the time it got from the kitchen to the dining room it had lost half its savor. The presbytery didn't even *have* a dining room. What a silly idea it was to set aside a special room just to eat in! A man studied where his books were. Why not eat where the food was?

Michel had the vague feeling that the priest's mood was prompted by his presence in the kitchen, a sign of his recovery; and he was moved by the kindness of the man. At the same time he was so filled with his own thoughts that it was difficult for him to respond as he should. Something was going to happen, he decided; he had a sense of expectancy. Sometimes he caught himself listening to something far away, as if his name were being called just out of earshot.

Nevertheless, he laughed when Father Vergara told a joke. It was about God and the devil. It seems that God was very angry at Satan for having tempted Adam and Eve. He called a council of the angels, and asked them what was the hardest task on earth that He could put Satan to do, as punishment. "Let him learn Basque," the angels said unanimously. And so God sent Satan to the Basque country. He had to stay there until he had mastered the language. Poor Satan began to sweat. This was the worst thing that had happened to him since he had been cast out of heaven. And it was such a useless thing to do! What would he do with the language after he had learned it? Only Basques understood it, and it was ridiculous to try to talk to *them,* they wanted no part of him. But he had to try, or stay there forever. He went to work. At the end of seven years he had learned only two words—*bai,* meaning "yes," and *ez,* meaning "no." God relented. The punishment was too hard, even for Satan. God told the devil he could go home. No sooner had Satan crossed the bridge at Gastelondo than he found he had forgotten the two words.

There was a moment during the meal when Michel was startled out of his queer introspective mood. It had to do with Nila, who was serving the table. He had gotten used to her silence, and set it down to an incurable shyness. But as they were having their dessert, someone rapped at the kitchen door. Michel jumped; the door was only a few feet away, and the sound was loud and menacing in the small room. Yet Nila did not seem to notice. It was not until Father Vergara reached out and touched her arm, nodding at the door, that she turned to look at it. At the priest's signal, Michel hurriedly left the table and went to the study. Once he had shut the door behind him, he heard the kitchen door open and the sound of voices speaking. What was wrong with Nila? Was she deaf?

"Deaf and dumb," Father Vergara confirmed a little later, when Michel, troubled, asked him.

He told Michel her story. Nila was the granddaughter of the old woman in the kitchen. Her mother had died in childbirth; her father, a shepherd on the Spanish side of the Pyrenees, had abandoned the child when he learned of her condition. The girl had grown up wild, like an animal in the hills. At the age of eight or nine she had taken to disappearing for days at a time. She slept in barns, out in the woods, in caves. When she was hungry she appeared in farmhouses and was fed by the inhabitants, who regarded her as a creature of God. Her grandmother, who kept her own farm then, could do nothing with her. Father Vergara had caught glimpses of the girl at various times, and tried to approach her, but she ran away from him. But then the old woman had had to give up her farm, and had come to the presbytery as housekeeper. One day, a little more than a year ago, Father Vergara had entered the kitchen and found the girl there. Someone had beaten her; there was an ugly bruise on her cheek, scratches on her arms and legs, and her dress, little more than a rag anyway, was torn. There were other things too, the priest said, averting his eyes. Michel wondered at the infinite sadness in his voice. She had been here ever since, the priest said. It had been like taming a cat that had taken to the woods and gone wild. She already could read lips. He had taught her to read and write, and it was that, more than anything else, that had civilized her. Now she was tame, a good girl, industrious, and very helpful in the presbytery. She was twelve now. Incidentally, Nila was not her name. He called her that, short for Petronila, the legendary daughter of St. Peter.

"By the way, Benedek," Father Vergara said, "don't let on that you know about her condition. She's fooled you all this time, and she's very pleased about it. Just don't say anything to her when her back is turned. Otherwise speak normally."

Michel promised, his heart wrung by compassion. To think that he had never noticed! He remembered with what naturalness Father Vergara spoke to her, and her habit of fixing her eyes on his lips as he did so. What must it be like, he wondered, to live cut off from the world like that, in silence, unable to say the things that rose up in you? When Father Vergara sat down with his books, Michel stopped up his ears with his fingers and tried to imagine a lifetime of the terrible remoteness it produced in him. He dropped his hands hastily, close to tears. Poor girl! She was his age, and had already suffered more than he would in a lifetime. His father had loved him and protected him as long as he could, while Nila's had simply left her. And while he didn't remember his mother, she had cared for him in his first years, whereas Nila's . . . And he had had his Maman Rose. With all that he had been unhappy, concerned with himself, bitter, lonely, hurt, because heaven hadn't come down to earth for him, because he hadn't realized how well off he was, because he had taken all his gifts for granted and wanted more.

As the evening wore on, Michel's perturbation grew. He lay on the couch, pretending to read, but the words lay meaningless on the page. Several times he felt the priest's eyes on him, and was grateful that he did not speak. Did Father Vergara know what he was thinking? Did he know of the struggle that went on inside him, the falling of his last defenses, the longing to hurl himself headlong into the bosom of God, who had filled the world with pain but who had Life Everlasting to give him? Why? he demanded of himself; and answered in Father Vergara's voice, You are only a little boy. No one can know the purposes of God.

He would never know why things were the way they were, why some were born to happiness and grew tall and strong and certain of themselves, surrounded by love and comfort, and died in the fullness of age with the assurance of salvation in their hearts. And why others were outcasts, and died like vermin behind barbed wire, or on the street of poison they took themselves; or lived in a world of perpetual silence where they were beaten and couldn't even tell who had done it. These things were beyond human understanding.

Strangely, the realization filled him with joy. How dreadful it would be to know and not be able to do anything about it! Or worse yet, to know and have the power, and be responsible for the conduct of the world and the billions upon billions of souls in it! To let this one die young, to strike this one deaf and dumb, that one blind, knowing the necessity for it and yet having to suffer in silence the pain you had to inflict on your children. And the doubts and the bitterness of those you had created out of love and been forced to punish for their disobedience. No, it was better not to know, Michel decided. You could go raving mad with that kind of knowledge. It was better to leave that to God. And to help Him as much as you could. By acceptance. By prayer. Because prayer was nothing but love that you were returning to its source.

How lonely God must be!

A kind of peace entered into him. The beginnings of something he could call happiness. He gave up pretending to read; he lay back on the couch, staring up at the ceiling, imagining his vision penetrating the building and going up, up, up to where God was. The prodigal son, he thought; he was the prodigal son, who had been lost and was found again. For the first time he understood the parable. It wasn't only the son who was happy; it was the father. It didn't matter what the son had done. It was enough that he had come home.

When Nila came in to bank the fire for the night, he sat up and smiled at her. She looked surprised, and then confused. There was so much he wanted to tell her. But it was no use. You couldn't say things like that. He watched as she kneeled by the fire, skillfully massing it together and sprinkling a layer of ashes over it. She stood up, glancing shyly at him, made the sign of the cross over the heap of coals, and looked at Father Vergara.

"Thank you, Nila," he said gravely. "Good night."

As she turned to go, Michel also said, "Good night, Nila."

She gave a silent giggle, turned red, and ran from the room.

Father Vergara was smiling at him. It was Michel's turn to be confused. Why had she blushed? He had only said good night. Would the priest tease him? But Father Vergara said only, "Do you know any Spanish, Benedek?"

"No, Father."

"If Nila could speak, she'd have said a little prayer when she blessed the fire. A little verse in Spanish. It's the custom here. It goes like this." Father Vergara recited a few lines. He had Michel repeat it after him, correcting him until he had it down.

Si viene Dios
Que vea la luz
Si viene el diablo
Que vea la cruz.

"God and the devil," Father Vergara said. "It's said when you prepare the fire for the night. If God comes, let Him see the light, that is, let the fire still be burning. But if it's the devil who comes, let him see the cross I made over it, and go away."

Even Nila, Michel thought. Even she prayed to the God who had made her like this.

That night Michel lay awake, full of exultation. It was like music. Like angels singing, and you were caught up in that wonderful harmony and felt that you were part of a great net of sound that stretched up to the heavens. This was what he had been feeling all day, but now it was as though his whole being had caught fire and burnt away all that was evil and unworthy in him. All his sins of the past that had estranged him from God. He had no resentment left. It was total surrender, and he was waiting only for Father Vergara to be asleep to make his offering.

Finally he could wait no more. The priest's breathing came to him in the darkness, gentle and even. Michel stared at the prone figure, filled with thankfulness. To think that he had been afraid of this man, who had kept him from giving himself up, had saved his life, and opened the door to salvation! He eased himself out of the couch to his knees.

"Our Father, who art in heaven . . ." How sweet the words were to his own ears! For his father and mother in purgatory. For Maman Rose. For Nila. For all those who suffered and lost their way. Lastly, for himself, in humility, accepting in advance whatever lay in store for him, turning his will over to God. God had not failed him; he had failed God and His Church on earth. He had a lifetime before him to make up for his errors.

He did not feel the hard floor under his knees; he heard nothing, saw nothing, was aware only of the joy within him. He did not hear Father Vergara get out of bed. He was alone, and then he was not alone. Father Vergara was kneeling beside him, his great head bowed down, praying with him. The priest's face was shining, and tears streamed down his cheeks.

"Vati," Michel stammered. Then he was in the priest's arms, and both sobbing like little children.

Aitzmendi. A tiny handful of houses on a hill beside a river. So small and unimportant that you could look for it for hours on a map and never find it. In Touville, in Paris, in Cassarate, who knew where it was? Aitzmendi? Sounds Basque. Probably some wretched little village lost in the hills down there. Yes, Kevin—it had no importance, it was only the place where he had died and come to life again and was happy.

For two weeks Michel's world had been Father Vergara's study; now its boundaries had expanded to include the house and views of the village. He had the run of the presbytery, provided he was careful and didn't let himself be seen from outside. Peering through a crack in the curtain of the front parlor, you could see the small, sloping cobblestoned plaza that dropped away from the steps of the church, and the villagers going about their business. The men moved slowly, but with an air of purpose. They invariably wore the dark blue beret; some wore heavy, shapeless coats, others the same kind of black sheepskin jacket with the fur turned outward that Father Vergara had on when he came for him at St. Dominique du Val. There were few women. Occasionally an oxcart moved heavily across the square, its wooden disc wheels clattering on the cobblestones and protesting stridently against the axle. There were eighteen steps going up to the church door; they were worn and cracked and eaten black with time. So was the squat façade of the church, with its stubby steeple. Over the front door the bald round face of the clock shone whitely. It bore the inscription *Omniae vulnant, ultima occidit.* Each hour wounds, the last one kills. The amusing thing was that the clock had no hands, it had stopped heaven knew how long ago. And so the warning was useless, the last hour, by this clock anyway, would never come. It was fitting somehow, Michel felt. It was as though time itself had stopped for him, as though by stepping into Aitzmendi, which seemed to have been there forever, he had changed the pace of his life, had found a breathing time in which to heal and become himself again.

The sheer black wall that had puzzled him at his arrival was for playing handball. A *frontón,* Father Vergara called it. It stood at right angles to the church, on the far side, and on a lower level. In the early afternoon Michel could see men playing there, bounding with incredible agility, amid laughter and cries of triumph. Sometimes Father Vergara joined them, hiking up his cassock around his waist and smacking the ball with such force that the sound could be heard within the house. Michel winced to hear it; he had hit the ball once in the study, at the priest's urging, and his hand had stung for an hour afterward. Yet when Father Vergara hit it, it sounded like a pistol shot. A wonderful game, he had said, a Basque game. He would teach it to Michel sometime, when his case was settled and he could let himself be seen again. He had showed Michel his hand. The palm was like leather, and in the center there was a broad, rounded callus as hard and yellow as horn.

To look out the kitchen window you had to stand on a chair, for the single small pane of glass was set up high, near the ceiling. From there you could see the slanting roof of the café next door, tiled in red half-cylinders, the open terrace underneath, and the area before the entrance. At this time of year there was little you could see, for those who frequented the café sat indoors. Once, however, there were some visitors who seemed to have come from some other world. They came in a huge, glittering gray car that Michel recognized as a Rolls-Royce. It was driven by a chauffeur in uniform, with polished boots. A man and a woman got out, both tall and slim and elegant; the woman wore a very full wrap-around fur coat that reached to her ankles, the man a soft yellow cloth coat with a belt of the same material knotted carelessly in front. They stood for a moment before the café, while the man pointed in circling motions toward the mountains, speaking earnestly, and the woman nodded, smiling. Then they entered the café, and the chauffeur followed them with their bags. Michel wondered who they were. They seemed so incongruous in the village, with their lean, handsome, foreign faces, their blond hair and obvious wealth.

He wondered even more an hour later, when, from the front window this time, he saw them leave the café and head for the entrance of the presbytery. At their knock he scurried to the study. Father Vergara answered the door, and sat with the visitors an hour in the parlor. They were English, he told Michel later. Nine years ago the man was an aviator with the British Air Force; he had been shot down over Bordeaux, and the Maquisards had brought him to Aitzmendi. Father Vergara had helped him and two others cross the border into Spain. Now he had come back to show his wife the scene of his escape. Who would have thought it, Father Vergara said, pleased. At the time the man had been just another Britisher in uniform, one of many who had slipped through the village to the other side. Now it turned out that the man was an earl, and owned half of England, or thereabouts. He wanted to show his appreciation, he said. What could he do for Father Vergara? Nothing, Father Vergara said. He had everything he needed. Well then, the man said, he would have the clock in the church repaired. It had driven him half crazy while he was here, staring at the blank face and wondering what time it was. Strange people, the British, Father Vergara said laughing. Who needed a clock? It was time to eat when you were hungry, and time to go to work when the sun came up. But all right, he had told the earl; it would make him feel better to tell the House of Lords that he had helped modernize France.

From the kitchen doorway Michel often looked at the river and the mountain beyond. When it was cloudy the vista merged into a dull mass of gray; but on a clear day you could pick out an infinite variety of wintry colors, dappled in the sunlight, and even a mist of green high up on Choltocogagna, where the pines and fir trees grew. To the right was the wooded ridge like an inverted V at right angles to the river, dropping off at the edge in a steep bank. Michel no longer shuddered when he looked at it, yet his memory of the pit at the end was still fresh enough to be unpleasant. Sometimes he could hear the sound of a train and glimpse puffs of smoke rising above the bare apple trees across the river. Spain, he thought; how strange it was to be standing in France and yet be so close to another country that you could hear a train moving there! Then he dreamed of the wide world and its mysteries, and his heart swelled to think of the vastness of God's creation, and the opportunities he would have to explore it when he was grown up.

Other, more somber thoughts were his when he sat at the window in the priest's study, which overlooked a corner of the cemetery behind the church. *Memento mori,* Father Vergara had said, pointing it out to him. Yes, he had thought; how close he had come to occupying a place among those crazy, slanted tombstones! But that was behind him now. He was well again, eating ravenously and sleeping without dreams. Yet he would never forget. He often prayed at this window, glad to be alive, yet touched with a gentle melancholy to think of those whose lives were over and who were now resting in this bare plot of ground, at the world's end.

Incidentally, Father Vergara told him, these tombstones were interesting in their own right. No one knew how far back the oldest of them went, since time had worn the dates away. Some were simple slabs of stone, and some were pyramidal bases cradling rough, reddish-brown discs circled by a zigzag of linked W's. An archaeologist from Paris had gotten excited about them a few years ago, he said. He had photographed them, made sketches and line tracings, especially of the strange crosses in the middle of the discs. Father Vergara pointed them out to Michel. Some were like two crossed musical notes, others feathered at the four tips, and others were, astonishingly, swastikas. The archaeologist was writing a book tracing the spread of religion based on sun worship throughout the world, and he said that the swastika was invariably associated with the worship of Aryan sun-gods, from India and Persia through to Scandinavia. But he said that it was also found on monuments of the ancient Mexicans and Peruvians, and he had a theory that these were linked to the Basque country by the lost Atlantis. He hadn't tried to dissuade the man, Father Vergara said, but it was all nonsense. The Basques knew better. They hadn't come from anywhere; they had always been here, the original Iberians. It was probably some traveling Basque who had returned home and brought the tombstone design with him, and created a fad. The Basques were great travelers, did he know? They had discovered the fishing banks of Newfoundland before Columbus went to the new world, yes, and before Leif Ericson too. But they had kept the secret to themselves, and let the others get the credit.

Michel loved to hear these stories. Nothing was more pleasant than to sit on his couch at night, his legs drawn up under him, and listen to Father Vergara talk about his people. Did Michel know who it was who had established the principle of the freedom of the seas? The Basques, not surprisingly—they were the greatest fishermen of the world. They had established the principle in a maritime treaty with Edward III of England, in 1351. The farm and the fishing boat were the basis of Basque life. So important was the farmhouse, the center of family life, that younger sons and daughters voluntarily gave up the inheritance rights that had been granted them in France after the Revolution, so as to leave the house undivided to the eldest child, and thus ensure its continuity. And Basques took their patronymic from the house, not the family line. So old was their civilization that the Basque words for knife, plow, ax, were derivatives from the root *aiz,* meaning "stone." Aitzmendi? *Mendi* meant "hill." Aitzmendi, hill of stone. There were many such combinations: Abaiz, Mendigorri, Iturrimendi, Uhaitza.

Aitzmendi was terribly old, as old as the Christian era, or older. At one time the village must have been considerably larger, and served as a bastion of the French border. The English king, Richard Coeur de Lion, who laid claim through his mother Eleanor to the southwest corner of France, known as Aquitaine then, had built a castle here to defend it. The church, and this building next to it, were built on the site of the castle ruins, probably from the stones of which it had been constructed. These stones, Father Vergara said, patting the wall behind Michel. The king no doubt had been a brave man, but he was a cautious one too; the entire hill under the church was honeycombed by tunnels leading in all directions, in case of siege. As a matter of fact, the priest went on, glancing at Michel, that was what had created the pit at the river edge into which he had almost fallen. During a flood some years ago the river had backed into the mouth of one such tunnel, which followed the ridge, and it had collapsed far below the level of the riverbed. The other end of the tunnel lay under the church floor, but the entrance was blocked in now. The village fathers should have filled in the hole in the bank, because the water was deep there, and livestock had fallen in and drowned; but they had never got around to it. Instead, they put a fence around it, and a peristyle at the path leading up. But Basques were superstitious people, and the place had got an evil reputation because of the accidents that had already occurred, and a number of legends had grown up about it. Some said that at midnight on Corpus Christi Day you could hear the king's horses stamping and pawing the ground deep in the tunnel, eager to go off on the crusade. At flood time the river made odd gurgling noises as it entered the pit and swirled out, and people said it was the devil groaning at the weight of his chains. Those who went over the ridge and passed by on the land side were supposed to have bad luck unless they threw a stone in. If they heard it splash in the water, they were all right. But if not, they had to recite a little poem to keep the devil quiet. The poem went like this.

> *Take the stone*
> *And leave the soul.*
> *Close up tight*
> *You devil's rump.*

It rhymed in Basque, Father Vergara said, grinning. Devil's Rump. That's what the people around here called it.

Father Vergara had stories for all occasions. Once the fire gave a great sigh and settled, sending ashes flying. Michel jumped, and the priest told him not to be alarmed, it was only the *laminak*. Nila, who had entered the room at that moment with a bucket of coals, clapped her hands and nodded, laughing. She kneeled on the floor and watched the priest's lips as he told Michel about these fantastic ghost people.

The *laminak,* Father Vergara said, were as exclusively Basque as the *espadrille,* or, as it was known on the Spanish side, the *alpargata,* the rope slipper still worn by peasants. They were not pixies, or brownies, or poltergeists, or goblins, or djinns, or any other of the race of mischievous spirits that plagued other nations. What distinguished the *laminak* were their good intentions, their clumsiness, their grief at their failures. By day they hid in dark corners and spied on the human beings who lived in the house. Some people swore that they had seen one, and that in appearance they were small creatures, bumbling, not quite human. This was the cause of their grief. They wanted so much to be like the men and women they admired, and do the things they saw them do. All day they watched the inhabitants of the house or farm build fires, chop wood, sweep the floor, set the table for a meal; and at night, eager to help, they tried to imitate them. But they were simple-minded and clumsy, and there was no dexterity in their stumps of fingers. They dropped things, pushed them out of place, left disorder. Trying to rake the fire together, they more often scattered embers over the hearth. Trying to spin the wool prepared by the housewife, they left a mass of tangled knots. They spread dishes haphazardly over the table, and usually broke some. It was not mischief, everybody knew. They just wanted to help, but didn't have the skill. It was no use being angry at them. They realized themselves how badly they had failed and wept like children, as if their hearts were breaking. You could hear them crying, and couldn't help feeling sorry for them.

Father Vergara told this story in all seriousness, and Michel didn't know whether it was supposed to be true or not. But perhaps it was so. God had created angels and men in His image, and just as the angels were inferior to God, and men inferior to the angels, why couldn't there exist a race inferior to men but something like them? He tried to remember whether he had ever heard any strange sounds at night, like crying. He hadn't, but he would listen for them from now on, he decided, just in case.

So the time went by. A time of healing. Of happiness. It was good to be able to pray again, to lie on his couch thinking of the past, without pain; dreaming of the future, when he would be a man and make his own way. Would he be a priest? He didn't know. It seemed especially fine to him to be like Father Vergara, unlike other men of the cloth he had known; so robust, so rocklike in his strength, yet simple and gay. And yet, with all these human qualities, so serious and learned in the faith. At times it seemed to him the will of God that he should bury himself in some village like Aitzmendi, close to the earth and its people, a simple pastor amid his flock, and with the passing of the years gain sanctity. But it was lovely also to think of becoming a doctor, like his father. Could he be both? A doctor-priest? All in good time, he told himself. There was no hurry, it was so pleasant and peaceful here. During the day he wandered about the house, peeking out of windows and watching the life of the village around him, or read books out of the priest's vast library, or prayed, ate his meals, thought, daydreamed. At night he talked to Father Vergara, watched the fire, read, slept. His face had filled out, he was gaining weight, his mind was clear and sharp again. Far away, in the remote outside world that was not Aitzmendi, they were still looking for him, he knew. But that was the world of Michel Rose, Jean Dupont, Luc Casella; here he was Michel Benedek again, and safe.

9

✿

I N TOUVILLE a man was speaking. His voice pulsed through the
air of France and settled like a tired dove in homes, offices, cafés,
army barracks, automobiles, in barges and pleasure vessels moving
through the inland waterways or anchored in harbors—wherever
Frenchmen, alerted in the afternoon papers of the coming nationwide broadcast, turned on the radio and listened in wonder. Or joy.
Or fury. Or with a cynical shrug of the shoulders that said, What did
you expect? Something had to give.

It was an old man's voice, weighty, deliberate, precise and weary.
First had come a fanfare, then a chime and the information that it
was exactly 9 P.M. The announcer had stated gravely that the following brief address was in the public interest and emanated from Touville l'Abbaye, Côte-des-Alpes, and that the recorded performance
of the opera *Carmen* scheduled at this hour as part of the Friday
night series would follow immediately afterward.

"Ladies and gentlemen," the announcer continued after a pause.
"Monseigneur Rebenty, bishop of Touville."

"On this twenty-seventh day of February, 1953," the old man's
voice said, "I speak to you in my capacity as bishop of the Holy
Roman Catholic Apostolic Church, and with the ecclesiastical authority inherent in that charge. Lest any should think that what I
have to say applies to the diocese of Touville alone, I add that my
words have the sanction of His Eminence, Cardinal Loriol, archbishop of Avignon, Primate of France, and that it is at his instigation
that I speak. In the name of His Eminence, and my own, I address
this appeal to all individuals or groups, lay or religious, throughout
our country, or any lands whatsoever to which it may pertain. All
persons or groups of persons, whether professing the Catholic faith
or not, who may know the whereabouts of the child Michel Benedek

of this city, or who can furnish information leading to his discovery, are formally requested to come forward and make themselves known. If such persons prefer, they may act through an intermediary, or maintain their anonymity through a letter or telephone call. Whatever the means employed, they should address themselves to the judiciary authority. I repeat: It is my wish, and that of the highest authority of the Church of France, that anyone who can furnish information leading to the discovery of the child Michel Benedek should give this information to the police. No one who answers this appeal will be held accountable in any way for the part he may have played in the child's disappearance, or be required to implicate others."

After a long silence, the voice said, "Signed copies of these remarks have been sent to all the newspapers of Touville."

As the opening strains of the overture to *Carmen* burst forth, Louis Konrad reached out and turned off the radio. After the initial shock of surprise, he thought with grim pleasure, We've done it! We've forced them to their knees!

"But Louis," Rina said, bewildered. "What does it mean?"

He answered her in German, for Hannah's sake; she had already plucked at Rina's sleeve. "Mean? It means they've quit, that's all. They're backing out. They've finally decided they can't take any more, and they're ordering whoever has Michel to turn him in."

Hannah said harshly, "The *bishop* said that? I don't believe it."

"He said it," Konrad assured her. "And repeated it." Rina too turned to her and said that there was no question about what the bishop *said;* what she didn't understand—

No, no, said Hannah. What she had meant was that it was nonsense for the bishop to say "Whoever has the boy." What! He didn't know? Of course he knew. Those who had kidnaped Michel were priests and nuns. They wouldn't tell a bishop if he asked them?

The telephone rang. Judas, who had heard the broadcast, leaning against the doorway to the kitchen, answered it. "It's for you," he said briefly. He did not look at his father as he handed over the phone. Konrad took it, frowning; it was Jules.

"Did you hear it?" he asked in excitement.

"Yes," he said. He followed Judas with his eyes, still frowning; the boy stood in the living room, looking at his mother and the visitor, who were talking in German; then he drifted toward the kitchen and disappeared. Tall, like his father; wiry but smooth-skinned; fifteen, and already as strong as a man. It had taken a gang of them to beat him up.

"How do you like that?" Jules was marveling. "The archbishop too! They mean business. Did you know they were going to do it?"

"What?" he said. "No, I didn't. All the newspaper said—"

There was a grunting sound, and Lise's voice interrupted him. She took back all the names she had ever called him, she said. He was a genius. He had made the Church back down. She would like to see Odette's face now!

He had hardly hung up when the phone rang again. This time it was the pharmacist Arnauld, who bellowed, "By Christ, Konrad, you've got them on the run!" Konrad winced and held the receiver several inches from his ear. He hadn't seen Arnauld for several months. The last time had been near the pharmacy, where Konrad had stopped by on his way to Maître Paul's study. Arnauld wasn't in, but as Konrad crossed the street he had seen him, his face pink and quivering, his footing unsure, being led along the sidewalk by a boy. Taken to drink, Lévy said. Arnauld sounded a bit primed now, as if he had had one or two. His voice made the earpiece rattle.

Judas came out of the kitchen, his face sullen. He loitered a moment in the hall, then marched to the den, which he had been using as his bedroom ever since the arrival of Hannah. Oblivious to the voice squawking in his ear, Konrad stared after him. Should he follow him? Speak to him? What would he say? Sons, Konrad thought helplessly. Sons and fathers.

"Gypsy girls," Bishop Reynaud said. "Flowers in their pearly teeth and daggers in their belts. And music suitable for a bullfight. I have never liked *Carmen*. It is the most vulgar of the so-called great operas."

Canon Blevitz switched off the radio, his face thoughtful and worried.

Bishop Reynaud studied him for a moment, then turned to the priest who sat in the armchair facing him. "I do not know where the boy is," he said. "Contrary to the opinion hinted at in certain newspapers, it is the truth. I have thought it wiser not to know. However, you may inform the cardinal that means of communication exist with those who do know. I shall get in touch with them at once. Canon, would you be so kind as to put through the call? From your office, please."

Canon Blevitz hurried from the room. "Secrecy," the bishop said, amused. "It has become a game. Let a priest go out into the street, and all eyes follow him. What is he up to? Is he one of the conspiracy?"

"I know, Your Excellency," the priest said. "At the station—"

"Police," the bishop said, nodding. "They examined you up and down. Telephone wires are buzzing. They might even have followed you. Tomorrow reporters will call. Are there any new developments, Excellency? Bah! They are so obvious about it."

"It didn't occur to me—" the priest began apologetically, but the bishop waved his hand, saying, "It would have been worse to try to avoid them. Garonde is a hotbed of suspicion these days, Father Duplessis. One must go about one's duties in a normal fashion."

The telephone buzzed. Bishop Reynaud picked it up. "Yes?" he said. He listened for a moment, his face intent. Then he said, "That's what I wanted to talk to you about, Father. I am going to ask you to deliver a message for me to a certain party, who is in charge of that private matter we know about. Telephone him at once. And this is what you are to tell him . . ."

"Mon Dieu!" M. Farrade said plaintively. He waved his hand toward the bar, and Toine, catching the movement, turned the radio down. "Today if it's not loud it's no good," M. Farrade muttered. "Automobile horns, bicycles, the telephone, everything assaults the ear. Even music. Well, what did I tell you, Monsieur l'abbé? It had to come, eh? There are limits to everything." He put his elbows on the table and leaned closer to Father Vergara, thrusting forward his full, soft face. "You will not be offended at me, Monsieur l'abbé," he said confidentially. "I am no freethinker, I. The Church, very well. But in spiritual matters. It is not good for the religious to mix in the market place. Understand me, I am sorry for the boy, but that is a civil matter. What, a nun in prison! What next? The Church should be inviolable, within its own domain, of course. This bishop, what's his—"

"Rebenty," Father Vergara said.

"He is right," M. Farrade said with conviction. "It was time to withdraw. This quarrel does no good to anyone. Woe to him from whom the scandal comes! I too read the Bible, Monsieur l'abbé. I am a Godfearing man."

"I have always known it," Father Vergara said.

M. Farrade let his gaze wander around the café, then leaned closer, rapping his knuckles on his forehead in a significant gesture. "Hardheaded," he whispered. "Look at them, they are furious. I am Basque on my mother's side, but I can be reasonable. I am not tradition-bound. Do you know what they are saying? What? they say. Give up a fugitive to the law? A Catholic boy to the Jews? Never! We are Basques!"

Father Vergara knew all those in the café. Saralegui. Goytisolo. Iturrigorri, with his oldest boy. Three or four more. They had their heads together, discussing the radio message. Some glanced at him, curiously, then turned away. But he did not have to look at them to know what they were thinking. He knew his people. The pudgy proprietor of the café was right.

"Fortunately," M. Farrade pursued, lowering his voice still more, "it does not matter. The boy is not in France."

"Ah?" Father Vergara said with interest. "You have information, then?"

"I know what I know," the other returned mysteriously. "Toine!" he called, turning in his chair. "A small *fine*. You will join me, Monsieur l'abbé?"

Father Vergara held up his hand in polite refusal.

"To celebrate," M. Farrade insisted. "It is I who pay. It is not often that you set foot in my poor establishment."

"It is not good for the religious to mix in the market place."

M. Farrade stared; then he exploded with laughter. "*Touché!*" he sputtered, wiping his mustaches with the back of a fat finger. "But I insist! Toine! Make that two." He lowered his voice again. "The boy is in Algiers. How do I know? My wife's cousin—you have seen her, the one who squints—works in the telephone company in Biarritz. One day . . ."

Toine set down two glasses on the table. Father Vergara warmed his glass in his hand, listening to the story. Ten minutes more, he thought. He had no radio. It was natural for him to come hear the statement of the bishop announced in the newspapers. But it would not do to rush out.

"Rumors," he said indulgently, when the other had finished. "The boy might be anywhere. Garonde. Paris. Here in Aitzmendi."

"Quelle idée!" M. Farrade cried, laughing. "I tell you, Monsieur l'abbé . . ." He went over his argument again.

He let himself appear to be convinced. So much the better if it were so, he said. It was an unpleasant business at best. Let the Algerians worry over it. Then he sighed and drained off his glass. He had to be going, he said. M. Farrade urged him to drop in more often. After all, it was right next door. He was not to wait until there was another broadcast by the bishop. And no hard feelings, eh? Over what he had said?

Of course not, Father Vergara said. And he would be glad to visit more often. For each time that M. Farrade came to church, he would come to the café.

M. Farrade choked, coughed, whooped, cried out to the room at large: "Did you hear that, my friends? What a sense of humor! Do you know what he said? I said to him—"

Toine was at his side. "Telephone, Monsieur l'abbé."

"Who is it?"

"From Garonde. Father Lisiaga."

He glanced sideways at M. Farrade, who was shouting out his story amid laughter.

"Tell him I am not here."

He clapped M. Farrade on the shoulder and bade him good night. "Good night, lads," he called out cheerfully to the men by the bar. He walked out amid a chorus of replies. He thought, What in God's name am I to do?

The telephone would not stop ringing. Colbert called. Two reporters. André David from Paris.

Konrad had not seen Colbert since the fiasco of a hearing in June 1950, when Judge Minotard, after a wait of a year and a half, had annulled the Council decision making Hannah the guardian and thus forced them to start again from the beginning. But Jules had spoken to Colbert several times, and said that the man was obsessed by a sense of guilt for what had happened to the boy. And rightly so, Konrad had thought; like all the other members of the first Council. And Colbert had come damned close to letting himself be persuaded again, at the third Council. But he bore the man no grudge; they had all made mistakes. Colbert wanted to congratulate him. He said gruffly that perhaps he should have waited until the boy had actually been returned, but he wanted Konrad to know that he regarded the bishops' capitulation as a great victory for the family and its friends. It was the principle of the thing, he said. The Church had had to admit publicly that the unity of a family, *any* family, was more important than that baptism of theirs.

Konrad found this felicitously phrased, and used it with the reporters. To one of them, Pletzel of the *Touville Gazette,* who in the past had been particularly sympathetic to him and his cause, he spoke at some length. Bishop Rebenty had given no reason for his startling about-face, he said, but it was obvious enough. The Church dreaded scandal above all things. So long as their part in the affair remained hidden, and the Rose woman occupied the center of the stage in her role as tragedy queen, they had resisted the law with all the forces at their command. But once they were unmasked, the resulting public clamor had been too much for them. No, he didn't claim any credit for it himself. It was the flood of communications to the press that had done it. *This* was the real triumph, and vindicated his faith in the fundamental good sense and humanity of the nation. Bishop Reynaud of Garonde had loosed a whirlwind with his press conference, in which he had said, in effect, Let the boy himself choose. Professor Choudens' article, especially, had made short work of that point of view; and in the resulting controversy the Church had found itself under attack where it hurt the most: not so much for its part in the kidnaping which, after all, was a solitary incident that would be forgotten in time, as for its absolutist claim, even though it was unspoken, that it was a state within the state— worse, a state *above* the state. Pletzel asked him to elaborate this, and Konrad said that the issue had gone beyond the question of the boy. Surely Pletzel must have noted the tenor of the most recent publications. What people like Choudens, Werner, Fontaine, and others were doing was to strike at the very foundations of the Church by examining its role in society. That is, the question no longer was, To whom does the boy belong? but rather, What right does the Church think it has to do this? It was this, he said, that had worried Loriol and Rebenty into pulling in their horns. Yes, Pletzel could quote him. The more publicity given the announcement and its significance, the better.

André David was jubilant. Listening to his voice over the wire, Konrad remembered with grim amusement how unconvinced the man had been last fall on the occasion of Konrad's address to the delegates to the World Jewry symposium. He had followed Konrad to the vestibule, and had said bluntly, "Come now, admit you were exaggerating." Konrad had taken David to a café and talked to him for three hours, telling him all the things he had not had time to say in his speech—they had given him only twenty minutes—and in the end had won him over. Thank God! he thought now, gratefully. It was André David who had got the delegates to form their Benedek Committee, who had kept the matter alive in the Paris newspapers, and, most important of all, had got him Maître Gens for the trial. If the reactionary half of France hated Konrad's guts, he had made friends, too; a David was worth all the rest.

It was not only to congratulate him, however, that André David had called; he had got wind of something, he said. Cardinal Loriol had sent an emissary to Grand Rabbi Bendel in Paris. It was all very hush-hush. Bendel wasn't talking. But he had called a meeting of the Consistory. Had Konrad heard anything about it?

"No," Konrad said. "It's news to me. What's behind it, I wonder?"

"I don't know. I thought I'd ask you. Maybe Loriol wants Bendel to call off the dogs. But I'm only guessing."

"Very likely," Konrad said dryly. "But why Bendel? Why not me?"

David laughed. "He knows better than that."

"I'd be glad to call them off."

"Yes, when you have the boy."

Konrad was puzzled when this conversation came to an end. Throughout all these years, silence from the Primate in his palace in Avignon, when a word from him would have been enough to put that fanatic nun in her place. Watching, no doubt, to see how far the game could go without interference from him. At the cardinal's instigation, Rebenty had said. There was no reason to question this. It meant that Loriol had decided that the Church had suffered enough harm. But why the secret emissary to the Grand Rabbi, who had had no part in all this? Bendel, like Loriol, had wrapped himself in silence and refused to take a stand at a time when it might have done some good. It had taken the boy's disappearance from St. Ignatius and the sickening falsehoods of the Catholic press, which repeated all of the Rose woman's fables as if they had not been disproved a dozen times in court—yes, and invented some of their own—before Bendel had been moved to feeble protest. And what had he protested against? Not the flouting of the law, the high-handedness of these priests and nuns, sole interpreters of God's will; the arrogance of the Church; the pernicious canon on baptism, which blandly said, in effect, The world is mine; not against what counted, in short, but against the anti-Semitism the Benedek Affair had aroused. Dignified negotiation—that was the phrase the Consistory had used, Konrad recalled, when at their request he had sent them a copy of the facts in the case.

Was that why Loriol had approached Bendel? But there was nothing to negotiate, and in any case the Grand Rabbi was the wrong person. Or was it because a potentate like him couldn't talk to an ordinary mortal? The Primate of France to the Grand Rabbi of France. One Church to Another.

Konrad sighed and turned toward the living room, where Maître Paul was chatting with Rina. Unlike the others, who had telephoned their congratulations, the lawyer had appeared in person. He had two pieces of news about Mlle Rose, he had said. One was that Mayor Crisenoy had pushed an increase of salary through the city council for her, and had her decorated with the ribbon for Social Merit; and the other— But at this point André David had telephoned.

Standing in the hall, Konrad looked at Maître Paul, and thought, A true gentleman. Never once, in the years they had worked together, had the man so much as hinted at what the Benedek boy was costing him. It had been an accepted thing in the inner councils of the party that Barthélemy Paul would ride into the *mairie* on Crisenoy's coattails when the Boss decided to retire. Now there wasn't the slightest chance of it. Crisenoy had withdrawn his confidence, frozen him out. And Paul's name was anathema to a goodly segment of the city's voters. The "good" Catholics. Those who said, My Church, right or wrong.

There rose to Konrad's memory the torchlight procession of three nights ago, around the city jail. Placards of protest: "Anti-Christ Has No Place in France!" "Saintliness in Prison!" "Temple-Parents Association Protests Incarceration of Mother Superior!" "Is France a Christian Country?" Konrad and Paul had stood on the sidewalk watching, amid the throng of onlookers, noting the black clothing the marchers wore in sign of mourning, the flares they held high, the heavy wooden cross one of them had strapped to his back, their grim silence. Silence, that is, until a woman spotted Paul among the watchers and shouted, "Anti-Christ!" That had been the signal for a chorus of imprecations, screamed insults, and threatening gestures as the rest of the procession went by. The lawyer had remained impassive under the tirade; but in leaving he had remarked ruefully to Konrad that there was no help for it, he would have to remove his daughter from the Temple School. "Do you mean to say—?" Konrad had begun in astonishment. Yes, Paul had said. His daughter Marie was a day student at the Temple. He himself had often attended meetings of the Parents Association of the school. They knew him only too well, and blamed him for the imprisonment of the mother superior. But it wasn't fair to Marie to let her suffer for her father's doings. Lately there had been incidents . . . "But you never told me!" Konrad had said, and Paul had replied, "What difference does it make?"

He was about to enter the living room when Judas came out of the den, wearing his parka coat.

"Where are you going?"

"Out," Judas said briefly.

"It's late."

Judas waited, his eyes fixed on the door.

Don't you understand? Konrad wanted to cry out. Can't you see I'm doing this for you too? Instead he turned away, and Judas went out, slamming the door.

"Did you see his eye?" Rina said indignantly to Maître Paul. "They jumped him at school. Seven or eight bullies. Tell your father to send us to jail too, they said. And they rubbed a newspaper all over his face. When he came home I wanted to call the police, but Louis—"

"Rina," he said.

"Well, they didn't have the right. I know boys fight, but—"

The telephone rang. Konrad answered it, as Rina spoke on. It was Bira, calling from l'Argentière.

"Konrad? I've been trying to get you for two hours."

"So has everybody else," he said wearily.

"Oh? I kept getting the busy signal. You heard the broadcast? Well, don't pay any attention to it. It's a fake."

"What do you mean?"

"Of course," Bira said testily. "Do you think they'd back down now? Use your head, man. They just want to quiet the public clamor. Things have got too hot for them. Who's going to listen to the bishop of Touville?"

"But the Primate—" he began.

"Loriol has no authority over Reynaud. He's just *primus inter pares*. Reynaud's the little pope in Garonde, and that's where the boy is. Unless they've taken him over the border already. If Reynaud had made the announcement, it might have meant something. But do you think the priests down there are going to pay attention to Rebenty?"

What a labyrinthine mind the man had! To him nothing was what it seemed. Yet, Konrad thought uncomfortably, events had proved Bira right in the past. He did not argue.

"What do you advise?"

"Don't be taken in, that's all. Keep hammering at them. If the matter gets off the front pages at this stage, you're lost. You'll never be able to build it up again. And that's what they're counting on."

Hanging up, Konrad returned to the living room and said abruptly, "Bira thinks the announcement of the bishops is a fake."

He explained Bira's reasoning to them. Maître Paul disagreed. "What could they gain by it?" he demanded. "Suppose, as Bira says, it's just to stop the criticism. Who's going to know that? Sooner or later some good Catholic man-in-the-street, or old woman knitting by the window, or butcher's boy going around to the back door of somebody's home is going to catch a glimpse of Michel, and think he's obeying Church authority by going to the police. The risk is too great, and Loriol would know that, if Rebenty didn't. I don't say they're doing it cheerfully. The words must have stuck in the bishop's throat. But they're doing it, and that's enough. The announcement is its own guarantee."

Hannah was having her own discussion with Rina, who had summarized Paul's remarks for her. "Bishops!" she said; and there was a world of weary contempt in her voice.

Maître Paul got up to leave. Konrad accompanied him to the hall rack and helped him on with his coat. He asked what was the other piece of news about Mlle Rose.

"It's not important," Paul said. "It's just that we had a pretty stormy session at the city council today. Roustère made a motion that the council declare its lack of confidence in Mademoiselle Rose in regard to her fitness for her job. Right on the heels of the salary increase for her that the mayor sponsored. There was a near riot for a while, until Crisenoy ruled the motion out of order. He said it wasn't on the agenda. I tried to stop it, of course. Roustère approached me ahead of time and asked me to second his motion, and I advised him not to do it. All it would do, I told him, would be to win more sympathy for her. She's enough of a martyr already, I said. But I couldn't talk him out of it. Well, old man." They shook hands. Paul said, "We've had a good piece of news tonight."

"Yes," Konrad replied. "I'm waiting to see the reaction in the Catholic press."

"So am I."

They smiled at each other. One in a million, Konrad thought. He put his hand on the other's shoulder, moved by a sudden impulse. "Forgive my butting in, Konrad," Paul said, his face serious again. "If I were you, I'd pay some attention to Judas. It's not only the beating he got."

"I know."

"The boy's full of resentment. He sees himself pushed aside for this other boy, and it hurts him. He's still only—"

"What can I do?" Konrad demanded. "I've tried to explain it to him, but he doesn't want to listen. Short of dropping the whole thing—" He shrugged, as bitterness surged through him.

Paul regarded him curiously. "You can't. Not now. And neither can I. We both have some ground to recover when it's all over. But maybe it'll be soon now. After today I feel quite optimistic about it."

"So do I."

"Well, good night, old man."

"Good night."

He was pensive as he shut the door behind his visitor. Ground to recover? More than Paul knew. He thought of his driver Mornay, in the hospital with a smashed jaw, and his three trucks parked forlornly in the factory yard, and the vicious dents where the stones had struck. It was Mornay's misfortune to have opened the cabin window at the wrong moment. The other two drivers had threatened to quit rather than venture out. And before that his volume had already dropped off alarmingly, what with canceled orders and absenteeism. To change the brand name would be almost like starting over again. He would leave, he thought. When this was all over, he would set up his factory in another city. Lyons. Or Paris. If, he thought gloomily, there was anything left to set up.

Judas, he thought. What have I done to you?

In his mind there still echoed the bishop's flat, weary tones as they had come to him over the radio, and Bira's harsh, vibrant voice on the telephone. What was the truth of the matter? Was Bira right? If so, it was a contemptible trick. Contemptible either way, he thought. If the Church felt it was right in the position it had adopted in regard to the boy, then it should have stuck to that position even if it was destroyed in the attempt. And if it felt itself to be in the wrong, then it should not have backed up the Rose woman in the first place. But this paltering with yea and nay, this yielding to public opinion, this backing down when things got difficult, was the worst kind of hypocrisy. It was incredible to think how this monstrous excrescence had foisted itself on society, and still maintained its octopus-like hold on the spirits of men in the twentieth century. And the hierarchy itself —how could they believe in a God in whose name they broke all His commandments? They must know, he reasoned, they cannot be so stupid. Perhaps they admitted it among themselves, the higher-ups, of course. One front for the masses, another for themselves, who made God over in their own images each generation. Otherwise how could a sleek, oily fellow like Reynaud, a bishop no less, look you in the eye and tell you a deliberate, malicious whopper? How could any Catholic, for that matter, who really and truly believed all that rigmarole about sin and damnation, not live every moment of his life in constant horror and dread of an irritated God? Either you believed or you didn't; there was no halfway station. Of course, there was confession. There's where they had it over other religions. Sin all you damn please today, wipe it away tomorrow. Very convenient. Have your cake and eat it. Very, very nice. How surprised Rabbi Joshua would be to come back to earth and see what had become of his teachings!

"A remarkable woman," Father Duplessis said. "The cardinal first heard of her during the Occupation. She had set up a complete underground organization in Touville, to get children into Switzerland. It was linked to the Resistance group in Lyons established by Father Tellier, but the local *modus operandi* was her own. A fantastically daring method, because of its openness. But perhaps for that very reason it succeeded so well. She put the children in school buses and sent them through the heart of the city, singing at the top of their voices. Everybody smiled to see happy children going on a picnic, and the police stopped traffic to let them through. She explained it all to the cardinal. He was most impressed."

"And so was I," Bishop Reynaud said. "The mother general of the order told me of it."

"The cardinal summoned her after the Liberation, when she was decorated. He said to me afterwards, 'We shall hear more of this nun.' When the Benedek boy began to be talked about, the cardinal learned that it was Mother Veronica who had urged that the boy be baptized, and was his sponsor. It was Bishop Rebenty who told him. The bishop was under fire about it at the time. The man Konrad had attached himself to the case and was stirring up a fuss over the baptism. It seems he got after the local rabbi, put lawyers on it, got his Communist friends to protest, and so forth. The rabbi came to see him, Bishop Rebenty said, and wanted the baptism declared invalid and the priest who had administered it disciplined. The bishop was quite upset about it. The family was going to law over it, and Mademoiselle Rose was just as stubborn. The cardinal suggested that it might be well for the bishop to keep out of it. Leave it to the nun, he said. From what he knew of her she would manage the situation very well."

Bishop Reynaud nodded gravely, hiding his amusement. He could imagine with what relief Rebenty had received the suggestion. It needed only a five-minute conversation with the old gentleman to realize he was in his dotage, and wanted nothing so much as to be left in peace for his few remaining years. He said, "It was the cardinal who obtained the letter from the Holy See for her?" Seeing the priest's expression, he added, "I have seen the letter. In fact, she left it in my care, foreseeing that she would be arrested."

"The cardinal will be most pleased to hear that," Father Duplessis exclaimed. "He was sure that a person of her resourcefulness would not let it fall into improper hands. But the arrest was quite sudden. Yes, Your Excellency, you are quite right. I need not tell you that Cardinal Loriol is a man of extraordinary perceptivity in regard to public opinion. I have been with him for twelve years, and I am constantly astonished by his foreknowledge of coming events. From the very beginning of this painful case he has observed its ramifications carefully. He was convinced that there would be no easy solution. Trouble will come of this, he told me once. In September of last year, during his trip to Rome, he brought the matter before the Holy Office. He had anticipated the present situation, as you see. And so when Mother Veronica came to him—it was at the time of the trial, or shortly before—it was a simple matter for the cardinal to obtain for her the authority she needed. Fortunately, the letter was waiting for her when she appeared in Avignon some weeks ago. The boy's identity had already been discovered in Marseilles, and he had to be moved on."

"A pity," Bishop Reynaud remarked. "A matter of timing. No, not the Marseilles episode, that apparently couldn't be helped. I was referring to Canon Sombre. The rector of St. Ignatius. If Mother Veronica could have got to him first, all this would have been avoided. Not even she, however, can be everywhere at once."

He leaned back in his chair and consulted his watch. It was eleven-thirty. A frown momentarily crossed his fine features. Lisiaga had promised to make one last attempt and call him back. It was strange that this priest, whoever he was, should still be out of reach at this hour. An unforeseen complication. The cardinal might have given him more warning. Suppose the one who had the boy had heard the broadcast and immediately gone to the police? How was the fellow to know it was a blind? At best they were running a great risk with the announcement. Why add to it by failing to anticipate a possible slip-up in communications? He sighed and looked at the armchair by the window. Blevitz, scholarly soul, was sound asleep; he sat in a slump, his pale head drooped to one side, his glasses slightly awry. Lifting his wide-sleeved arm with care, Bishop Reynaud grasped the decanter and poured an inch of crystalline yellow cordial into two tiny glasses. He handed one to Father Duplessis, who took it murmuring his thanks.

"You must be tired after your journey," he said. "I do not think, however, that it will be long now. If you wish, you may retire. I see that Canon Blevitz has already done so, in a somewhat informal fashion. And tomorrow morning—"

"That is kind of you, your Excellency," the priest returned. "But my instructions—"

Bishop Reynaud nodded. "Very well. It is better so. And then we shall sleep with a clear mind. It was Shakespeare, I think, who said that the birth of an occasion is the best moment for dealing with it. Or so I construe rough Enobarbus' belligerent speech. The barbaric bard was sometimes lamentably baroque in his thundering line." He tapped the rim of the glass with a fingernail and listened with pleasure to the faint pinging sound. "You have read the Choudens letter?"

"Yes, Your Excellency."

"The dangers of a classical education. Remarkably well expressed. Pascal could not have done better."

"The cardinal said as much himself," Father Duplessis murmured.

"It smells of the École Normale. The purest tradition. And this delicate instrument, this rich yet simple subtlety that is the French language, to be a tool in the hands of a shopkeeper's son, who makes himself the spokesman for the ideas of Citizen Robespierre, and would grub out the Church root and branch! It is not," he said carefully, noting that Father Duplessis had blinked, "a question of snobbery. There is a nobility of spirit that has nothing to do with birth. Is it for the newly emancipated of 1789 to determine the role of the Church on earth? We whose mission was entrusted to us by the Saviour Himself, and which we have fulfilled these two millennia? 'Is it not time,' the learned professor inquires, 'to remember that the law is sole sovereign in France, that in our land no church can claim a legal power, that no sacrament has civil value?' As you see, I know this choice specimen by heart. I love the fellow's sarcasm: 'The Catholic family is sacred; the non-Catholic family is nothing, the sacrament of baptism pulverizes it at a touch.' And with what noble rhetoric he takes me to task! 'Let the boy himself choose!' he cries, the fine Ciceronian! 'What, after you have soaked him to the bone in your doctrine!' Now there," Bishop Reynaud said, wrinkling his nose in distaste, "is a truly elegant phrase. Soaked him to the bone. Like marinating a herring. *My* doctrine, if you please. I invented it. The cardinal is right, it is time to put an end to this nonsense. There is no telling how far it can go."

"We need a respite," Father Duplessis said. "In the present state of excitement—"

"Exactly. Let Monsieur Stalin return to the headlines for a bit. Or that other gentleman on the opposite side of the world, with the hardware name. Eisenhower. Iron-chopper. Hewer of steel. Did you know that Stalin means steel? Their very names show that war is inevitable. Let them quarrel over their spheres of influence and provide a circus for the people. Then perhaps—"

The telephone rang. Bishop Reynaud glanced at Blevitz, sighed, and rose to answer it himself.

"Your Excellency," Father Lisiaga's worried voice said in his ear, "I have been unable to reach the person in question. I have called a dozen times, and been told each time that he is not at home and it's not known when he will return."

"Then I'm very much afraid, Father," Bishop Reynaud said quietly, "that you'll have to go there in person. This is too important to wait until tomorrow. In fact, I regret that I did not advise you to do so at once. I thought we would save time, and as a result we have set ourselves back."

There was a long silence. Then Father Lisiaga's voice, strangely hesitant, said, "At this stage I'm not sure I could get through. The roads—"

"Get through?" the bishop snapped. "What the devil do you mean?"

"The plows won't be out until tomorrow. The roads will be—"

"Just a moment." He put down the receiver and went to the window, pulling the drape aside. The outer sill was heaped white. Enormous flakes of snow filled the air, falling like lead through the windless night, so thickly that the street lamp was nothing but a vague blur. When had it started? Less than an hour ago, for he had looked out then and all was clear. Yet already a heavy carpet of snow lay over everything. For a moment he admired the ghostly beauty of the scene, thinking of Ronsard and his last song. *"Méchantes nuits d'hiver, nuits filles de Cocyte . . ."* he murmured to himself. He returned to the telephone and said gently, "Father, I regret very much having to give you this order. But you must see that it is imperative. Snow or no snow, the man must be reached. You must go there. There is no other way."

Lisiaga was silent.

Bishop Reynaud waited, his eyes following Father Duplessis, who had moved to the window and was looking out.

"Very well, Monseigneur," Lisiaga said at last.

"Good luck, Father, and good night."

"Good night, Monseigneur."

Was there a trace of anger in the man's voice? If the place was far from Garonde, it was a cruel assignment. The bishop shrugged. Lisiaga would do as he was told. And he would get through.

Father Duplessis was staring at him, his face pale. Bishop Reynaud smiled back. "Timing," he mused. "If His Eminence had seen fit to communicate with me a day in advance— But rest assured, Father, the boy is safe. We are in Basque country. And a Basque priest would argue with the Almighty Himself before he would give the boy up."

He wished, he reflected, that he was as sure about it as he sounded. For the first time he wished he knew who the man was.

"In 1905," Chamo said, "I saw a storm like this. It came down in chunks. Like fists. For three days. Whole villages were buried. Some starved, some froze. I was a boy then, but strong. Fifteen. Sixteen. I helped bring the bodies out on sleds." He put his face to the window-pane, shielding his eyes with his veined hand. Under his tasseled nightcap the scar behind his ear was white through the grizzled hair. Was it a knife or a bullet? Father Vergara wondered. He had heard the tale both ways. Some said that the wily old smuggler had been am-bushed by the Spanish guards; others, that it was a fight with one of his own men, and that Chamo had left the body up a tree for the buzzards, as a warning to the rest.

"It will stop by morning," Chamo said, turning away.

Father Vergara stretched his feet closer to the fire. Steam curled from his boots, and his toes tingled. Twenty minutes ago he had stomped to Chamo's door like a walking snowman and pounded on it until he saw in the window the glimmer of a candle nearing, and Chamo, who went to bed with the sun, let him in. No surprise. The old man was not one to waste words or emotions. He had poked up the embers in the hearth, and waited woodenly to be told the purpose of this midnight visit. And asked no questions when he knew.

"If it does not," Father Vergara said, "we must go anyway. If necessary I can carry the boy."

"It will stop."

"The signals have not changed? It is still the blue above the red?"

Chamo nodded. "For a person, trousers."

"And socks for the hour. It is the same, then. What hour shall I say? Remember, he is a city boy."

"One o'clock. It will take longer. The *passeur* will wait."

On a clear day, Father Vergara reflected, it would be three hours, four at the outside. But with this snow . . . In a way, however, it was a blessing. No one would be idling about the mountain without good reason. Those who might would be just as interested in not attracting attention as he was. He looked at Chamo, who was gazing at the fire, his hard, lined face remote and still.

"How much?" he asked.

Chamo jerked his thumb toward the window. "Tomorrow it will be Santos. He will ask ten thousand."

"And you?"

"For me, nothing."

"I cannot accept that. You run the same risk. More. The crossing—"

"Understand," Chamo said almost angrily. "I do not do this for the boy. During the war, that was different. With the Saxons I understood. This I do not understand. You tell me, Do it. That is enough. But I do it for you."

Father Vergara inclined his head in thanks. "I will bring the money with me tomorrow." Iranzo would have to make the trip twice, he thought. It was either that or get a second car. Unless he himself crossed the border legally, it would be difficult to get back. It would be dark by then, and moonless. Not a time to be coming down Choltococagna after a blizzard.

There was nothing more to say. Chamo had agreed. He rose to his feet and bade the old man good night. The door clicked behind him and the bolt slid into place.

Father Vergara pulled his beret tightly on his head, lifted the collar of his fur jacket and plunged into the storm. Already the footprints he had made in coming were all but blurred out. Strange that there was no wind. The snow fell as though the heavens had opened and dumped it out. Like in 1905. He did not remember that storm, he was only five then. If Chamo was fifteen then, he was sixty-three now. And still as active as ever, as tough and gnarled as old hickory. There was none better, and he felt cheered at the thought that the old man would accompany them.

It took him a half-hour to reach the cemetery wall, although it was close enough to be visible from Chamo's farm, if not for the falling snow. He took his time. It was uphill, the snow was thick, and the ground under it treacherous with rocks and potholes. When he had arrived at his kitchen door, he took off his mittens and with his finger wiped away the snow that clung to his eyelashes. Then he removed his jacket and beret, and sent the snow on them flying with a snap of his wrists.

In the kitchen Nila was waiting for him. He interrogated her with his eyes, and she shook her head. Lisiaga had given up, then. Four times he had called. The last time it was Farrade himself who had come with the message, for the café was closed and Toine had gone. Fortunately, he was in the study, and Nila had obeyed orders. After the edifice of supposition that Farrade had reared from a chance remark overheard by his wife's cousin, there was no telling what he would do with the priest's refusal to answer a long-distance call. Lisi-aga would telephone again in the morning; or, if the snowplows were out early enough, he would drive down. By that time it wouldn't matter. At daybreak he and the boy would be gone.

He sent Nila off to bed and stood at the kitchen fireplace, warming his hands and staring up at the new crucifix he had fastened to the chimney. Some day, he thought, when the thaw came, he would lower himself into the Devil's Rump and try to recover the other one. The cross was of wood; perhaps it had floated. And he would send it to the boy, wherever he was, as a reminder. Not that he needed it. He was astonished at the quickness of the boy's recovery, the eagerness and depth of his religious feeling. What a loss, what a great tragedy it would have been if . . .

He put out the kitchen light and entered the study, shutting the door softly behind him. The boy was asleep; he lay on his back, one hand dangling over the edge of the couch. How often had he stood there and marveled at that face! A Da Vinci angel, wide-eyed, radiant-fleshed. The taut look was gone, the eyes no longer sunken, the skin fresh and pure. Was the boy dreaming? The lips were parted in a slight smile. He might have had a son like this, he thought. In these three weeks he had grown to love this child as though he were indeed flesh of his flesh. But no, such worldly ties were not for him. It was not for himself that he had saved the boy, remade him, re-stored his faith; it was for the boy, and for the God he craved for and could not accept. It was time to let go, not only for Michel's sake, but also for his own. But he would miss him; he had not realized how much until now. Moved, he silently blessed the child in his sleep, and stood in the dim light of the lamp, brooding.

For a long moment he relived the bitterness of spirit that had been his when he returned from the café. The bishop's statement was unequivocal; the Primate supported it; and that meant that Rome had capitulated and the letter was to be disregarded. The boy was to be returned. Their reasoning was obvious. He himself had been gravely concerned over the virulence of the attack in the press, and wondered where it would end. And so he had not been surprised. Rather, angry and rebellious. They didn't *know* this boy! They didn't know what he had been through. What the struggle had meant to him. What it would mean to be given up, now that he had found his way and was happy in his faith once more. After having come so close to destroying himself, this time there would be no saving him.

Murder, body and soul. He could have told them that, but now there wasn't time, the order was out.

Was this not, he reflected, what history had accused the Jews of doing? Of betraying the Man-God out of fear of Roman reprisals? It was a false argument to say that then the betrayed one was God, and this was a mere mortal. There was a little bit of God in all of us. And how did the Primate, or Rome itself for that matter, know that this or any other child was not the Saviour whose return the world was waiting for?

There was no use getting angry again. He had had his struggle between obedience and conscience several hours ago, and after long, earnest prayer and a harsh soul inquisition that had left him emotionally shattered but more determined than ever, his conscience had won. That's twice, he had told himself. Against the known wishes of Bishop Reynaud and the command from Rome, he had offered the boy the chance to go to his family, if that was what he wanted. He had been mistaken, but the rebellion had been there. Now, ironically, the situation was just the reverse. Now the Church had given the boy up, and again he had rebelled. God grant that was the end of it, and that there would never come a third time!

He put out the lamp and undressed swiftly in the dark. One-thirty. He would have little enough rest for the day ahead of him. And the boy—he would need every ounce of his newly regained strength to get through it. What should he tell him, by the way? The less said the better. Just that it was time to move on.

It was not the getting him away, it was what came afterward that would be difficult. He saw himself facing Bishop Reynaud with his explanation, the man's incredulous face darkening with anger, his biting words. And then what? The inevitable question: Where is he now? And the necessity of standing up to it, and refusing to tell. The consequences—but why think about that? There was really no choice. He prayed, commended his soul to God, lay down and was asleep.

10

❦

B EYOND THE KITCHEN STAIRS, down by the snow-covered bushes, a lantern gleamed in the dark. It was Nila who was holding it, high above her head. She stood motionless, the light outlining her raised arm and shining on the kerchief tied about her hair. Her face was a pale blur. The other figure, the bulky one partially hidden by the bushes, had to be Father Vergara. Why was he striking the bushes with a broom? From the study window Michel watched, intrigued, as the blows fell and the snow went flying. What a strange thing to do! The whole world was blanketed with snow. Why was it so important to clear these bushes that the priest had gone out in the dark to do it?

Father Vergara seemed satisfied. He had stepped back and nodded his head. The light was lowered suddenly as Nila stooped. She handed something to the priest, who shook it out and spread it carefully over the cleared branches. Michel could see that it was a shirt. From the basket at her feet Nila handed him articles of clothing, which Father Vergara placed on the bushes, using the broom to push them into place. It was incredible to Michel, but it looked for all the world as though Father Vergara and the girl were hanging out the laundry to dry. A priest! Michel said to himself.

No, he thought. There had to be some other explanation. He turned away from the window, looking up as he did so and noting that the sky over the mountain had paled. It would be daylight soon, and the great adventure would begin. He could still hardly believe it. Ever since Father Vergara had shaken him by the shoulder a little while ago, and he had listened sleepily to what the priest had to say, everything had been invested with a touch of unreality. Was it really true that he was moving on? Crossing the border into Spain? And in this snow, which hadn't been there the night before, but which had greeted his eyes like a magic apparition when he got up and looked out the window? Just like a smuggler, he thought. Evading the border guards. It was something out of a storybook. And yet here he was, awake and alert, dressed for the trip: woolen underwear and socks, two shirts for extra warmth, his sweater, and his suit over all; high-laced boots that the priest had found somewhere for him, a bit too big but better that than too small, and his feet would swell, he said; a real Basque beret that he would put on later, at the moment of leaving. It lay now on the couch with his coat and the knotted cloth containing his spare clothing.

Choltocoagna. He tried saying it as Father Vergara did, pronouncing the *Ch* softly, more like *Ty*. But he couldn't be sure how the rest of it went. Sometimes the priest stressed the next-to-the-last syllable, *ca;* sometimes the first; and once Michel's ear had distinctly heard the stress fall on the middle syllable, *co*. And the name of the river was also confusing. Usually it was Bi-das-só-a; but now and then Bi-dá-swa. What a strange language Basque was! It kept changing as you spoke it. No wonder the devil had given up. Yet at this moment Michel felt quite Basque himself. Dressed like one, he was going to slip through the border and climb a Pyrenee. He was too wide awake and tingling for it to be a dream; yet, watching the fantastic pantomime from the window, he had had a moment of doubt.

He was leaving, he repeated to himself. Another country, another life. Although the prospect frightened him a bit, he felt it fitting somehow. The old Michel was dead; he had buried that tormented soul in this very room. He was reborn, like a butterfly from a chrysalis. Reborn to the truth and the protection of his God, whom he had found again. Now he had to go ahead. For the moment there was no life for him in France. It was no life to be hidden in a room, not daring to show his face at the window. It was no life to be forced to stay out of school, when he should be studying and learning and preparing for the future. And he had a future now; Father Vergara had given him one again. Father Vergara was going with him; he would find a good place for him, where he could move about like an ordinary boy; provide for him, smooth his way; visit him often; get word to Maman Rose that he was well and safe in Spain. It was not forever. Some day he would return, and all would be as before. Better. There was nothing to be afraid of. Not with Father Vergara.

These thoughts passed through his mind as he listened to the sound of the back door opening, and the stamping of feet. A moment later Nila was in the doorway, beckoning to him. He followed her to the kitchen, where Father Vergara was already seated at the table.

"Eat hearty, Benedek," the priest said, gesturing toward a steaming platter of potatoes, ham, and eggs. His broad face was cheerful and glowing with the cold. Michel was too excited to be hungry, but he knew he would need all his energy for the climb, and he filled his plate, marveling in the meanwhile at Father Vergara's appetite. "More," the priest urged him.

After a while Father Vergara sighed and stretched. "Can't you finish that?" he asked Michel, who had laid down his fork. Michel shook his head. "In a couple of hours you'll wish you had." They arose from the table, and walked together to the study, the priest's arm around Michel's shoulder. Once in the room they kneeled and prayed. "Give us a safe crossing, O Lord," Father Vergara said devoutly. "We place ourselves under Thy protection, in this as in all things."

"Amen," Michel said. He added in his own heart, "And thank You for this kind, wonderful man."

Father Vergara rose and went to the window, where he gazed outward for a long time through a pair of binoculars. "It's still too dark," he said, turning away and putting the binoculars on his desk. "But we'd best be going. Nila will let us know."

Know what? Michel wondered; but he put on his coat and beret, and picked up his bundle of clothing. In the kitchen Father Vergara studied Michel, grinned suddenly, and pulled his beret down over his right ear. "Like that," he said. The old woman handed the priest a paper-wrapped parcel, which he tucked into his fur jacket. She said something in a low voice. Father Vergara nodded, and the woman turned to Michel and made the sign of the cross over his forehead. Where was Nila? He looked around and saw her standing in the semidarkness of the hallway. He approached her, and saw that her face was contorted as if with pain. "Good-bye, Nila," he said awkwardly. She stared at him, put her hand to her mouth and ran down the hall. He looked after her in astonishment.

Perhaps he should have kissed her, he thought in confusion.

Father Vergara spoke to him gruffly; he had opened the back door and was looking at him, waiting. Good-bye, house, Michel said to himself, suddenly quite moved. He would come back some day. He was certain of it. Clutching his bundle, he went through the door after the priest.

The world stretched out whitely before him in the first pale light of day. Below the steps and by the bushes the snow was broken by footprints; beyond, it was a smooth, unmarred blanket. Michel set out after Father Vergara, who had headed down the slope, bearing left toward the cemetery wall. Immediately Michel was in difficulties. The snow reached to his knees, and although he put his feet in the tracks made by the man, each step required the effort of lifting his knee almost up to his chest. By the time he had reached the wall he was breathing hard and filled with dismay. He had come only a stone's throw on his journey, and already the adventure had become somewhat grim. And all Choltococagna before him! He glanced back at the house, and saw Nila watching him from the study window. He forced himself to smile at her. Self-consciously she lifted binoculars and looked high above him, at the mountain. Michel suddenly understood, and looked at the clothing spread out on the bushes: several red shirts, two blue towels, a pair of trousers, and, to one side, a single white sock. It was a signal of some sort, and Nila was waiting for the answer from someone on the other side. She would let them know, Father Vergara had said—but how, if they were on their way?

The priest stood by the wall, gigantic in his shaggy jacket; he had hitched up his cassock and knotted it in front. "Let's go, Benedek," he said. "The village is up, and it's light enough for us to be seen. We can slow down later, but for now we have to get out of sight."

They set out again, skirting the wall and continuing on a tangent away from it. The terrain sloped downward toward the river, gray in the distance, fringed by black shrubs bending under their load of snow. Beyond lay the mountain, like a sleeping giant, so big that he could not take it all in without turning his head. He could not see its top, which was hidden by mist. It was incredible that he was going to climb it. How small and puny it made him feel! Nothing stirred in that vast panorama, except a solitary bird wheeling high above, and a thin plume of smoke coming from a farmhouse amid a clump of trees far ahead.

Michel followed the priest, who strode before him, probing into the deep snow with the heavy iron-tipped wooden staff he carried. "A boulder," he called back; or, "A log"; or, "Be careful, there's a hole here." Then Michel slowed down, feeling his way carefully, until he was over the obstacle. He had begun to breathe hard again, and found that he was perspiring, in spite of the cold. It had become lighter, and the snow took on a new gleam, touched with rosy reflections. The sky was clear and pale blue. He began to wish that Father Vergara would stop and let him rest, but was ashamed to speak. He slipped and fell once, and floundered about in the snow until the priest lifted him up. "We're almost there now," he said. "Just a little way more." Looking up, Michel saw that the farmhouse he had seen in the distance lay directly ahead. It was small and shabby, and its sloping roof was buried under snow, except for the area about the blackened chimney. Would they stop there? He hoped so. He brushed the snow from his arms and sides, and stumbled behind the priest until they had reached the door, which opened as they approached.

Minutes later, stripped of his overcoat, jacket and beret, Michel was sitting before the fireplace, perspiring and shivering at the same time. A gnarled hand appeared before him, bearing a wooden bowl of steaming porridge; it was the old man who was offering it to him. Dazzled by the snow, Michel had hardly distinguished the man's features upon entering. Now he saw a close-cropped, grizzled head, a hard, leathery face with deep lines that seemed to go down to the bone, remote, expressionless eyes like bits of black glass. He took the bowl in both hands, realized he still had his mittens on, set the bowl in his lap, pulled the mittens off with his teeth, and dipped the spoon into the porridge. It was delicious, and he was surprised to find that he was ravenously hungry. Yet he had breakfasted less than an hour ago.

Michel emptied the bowl as Father Vergara and the old man spoke together in low voices. He could not follow what they said, since they spoke in Basque. Or rather, it was the priest who did most of the talking; the other responded in monosyllables, or grunts. Once Father Vergara addressed the man by name, and Michel's memory took him back to another fireplace, the one in the parlor of St. Dominique du Val. Of course! he thought. Chamo! The one Father Nagorra had called an old thief. The one who took the Saxons out. This was a Basque smuggler then. The picture that Michel had formed in his mind of this race of men furnished them with fierce, mustached faces, colorful bandannas about their necks, pistols and knives in their belts. Like pirates. Yet Chamo, except for his hard features, seemed like the other villagers and farmers he had seen from the presbytery window; rather older, shorter, more bowed than most, and to all appearances quite harmless. Smugglers were like everybody else, he thought; and felt very worldly wise.

Chamo had disappeared into a back room. Father Vergara was by the window next to the door, his eyes narrowed, staring out. Michel got up and joined him. "How do you feel?" Father Vergara asked him. "Good, Father," Michel replied. And it was true; the rest, the warmth, the food had restored his energies, even his eagerness. The trip was an adventure again. If Kevin could see him now!

"There she is," Father Vergara said. Following his eyes, Michel saw the snowy slope down which he had come, and the gray cluster of buildings that was Aitzmendi on its hilltop. The back wall of the church was clear, and below it, the stone wall of the cemetery. And there, standing on it and waving something black, was a doll-like figure he recognized as Nila.

Father Vergara opened the door, removed his beret and waved it back and forth. "All clear," he reported to Chamo, who entered at that moment carrying in his hand what seemed to be a jumble of bits of wood and leather straps. Chamo said to Michel, "Stand still," and slid one of the objects over Michel's head and about his eyes, pulling at the straps until they were snug against his temples. It was a wooden eyeshield, with rounded cups for the eyes, each with a narrow horizontal slit to look through.

"For the snow," Father Vergara said. "With this sun you'd be blinded. It fits well enough. Leave it fastened, and push it up to your forehead." Michel did so, and saw Chamo hand a similar pair to Father Vergara, and slip one over his own head. The old man had put on a black sheepskin jacket like the one the priest wore, a beret and mittens. He wore knee-high rubber boots that seemed very heavy, and carried a staff like Father Vergara's. Michel hastily put on the clothes he had removed, and seized his bundle. They went out the door, which the old man closed carefully behind him.

They walked around the building to a shed at the back, where Chamo, unlocking the door with an ancient bronze key, pulled out a polished sheet of wood which he laid flat on the snow. Michel saw that the front end curled up and back, and that there were raised strips of black tubing at both sides. Why did they need a toboggan? He did not understand until they had cleared the house and reached the open field beyond. The toboggan was for him, Father Vergara said. The first leg of the journey was along relatively flat land skirting the river. There was no point in his tiring himself out before it couldn't be helped. In his newly regained confidence Michel was aware of a touch of resentment, but he did as he was told, squatting down on the smooth surface of the toboggan and grasping the tubing with his mittened hands, with his bundle under his legs. Then they were off, moving across the snow.

Michel pulled the snow goggles over his eyes, and found himself enjoying the ride. He felt sorry for Father Vergara, who was pulling him along, the rope cutting into the thick fur at his shoulder; but he knew the enormous strength of the man, and supposed, from the ease with which the toboggan slid forward, that he was not too great a burden. Ahead of the priest walked Chamo, breaking the trail, moving at a steady pace, his boots making clumping sounds in the snow.

They soon reached the river and moved parallel to it over slightly undulating ground amid shrubs half buried under white capes of snow. The Bidassoa seemed quite shallow; ice-encrusted rocks broke the surface of the water, which was frozen along both banks. In the center the water moved, leaden and sluggish, with a faint murmuring sound. On the other side was Spain, Michel realized. How easy it would be to cross over! Yet they made no move to do so, continuing along the bank; and he understood why when they passed a small rustic edifice perched on the opposite bank, and a man in uniform came out, a rifle slung over his back, and watched them go by. Michel could see him quite clearly; he was thin and dark, and wore his cap pulled low over his forehead. There was no expression in his face, but there was something unmistakably menacing in the man's attitude. Scarcely was the sentinel out of sight behind them than they saw another one. This one sat inside the hut, leaning on the sill of the open window, smoking a cigar. He too watched them pass with no sign. They passed a third and a fourth; at the next one Chamo turned slightly left and moved away from the river. This time the sentinel unslung his rifle from his shoulder, and Michel heard a sharp metallic click, as if the bolt had been shoved into place. Chamo spat into the snow with a sneer, and kept going. Michel could not resist a backward look. The sentinel stood with his rifle grasped in both hands, pointing up in the air. Michel knew it was ridiculous to suppose that the guard would shoot at them across the river, but the skin between his shoulders crawled nevertheless, and he was glad when they had left the river far behind them.

They were moving through open fields now, passing an occasional farmhouse on either side. They showed no sign of life except the smoke coming from the chimneys. At one, however, a man wearing a red-and-black checked shirt and baggy trousers was chopping wood underneath a high veranda. He paused to look at them, the ax gleaming in his hand. Chamo raised his arm in greeting, and the man waved back in recognition, and lifted his ax again. The thud of steel biting into wood followed them as they went by.

The valley in which they moved was like an immense, shallow bowl. To their left the snow, broken by trees and shrubs and now and then a fence or farmhouse, slanted gradually upwards to a low crest about a mile distant, topped by a feathery fringe of trees. The terrain was flatter to the right, until it reached the base of the mountain beyond the river; there the snow-clad slope leaped sharply skyward, out of sight. The valley was breathtakingly beautiful in the sunlight, silent, calm, and seemingly deserted. Though they were still at river level, and there were hills on both sides, it seemed to Michel that the sky, now an intense blue, was closer than he had ever noted it before. More even than at Cassarate, on its high plateau, the sky seemed to press down on him, as though, still on the ground, he were moving with his head in the heights. It gave him a giddy feeling, as well as a sense of grandeur. Was this why the Basques walked so proudly? he wondered.

After about an hour they stopped for a rest, in the shelter of a lean-to set up against an outcropping of black rock. By now the river was out of sight behind them, yet, oddly, the mountain seemed closer than before. He asked when they were going to cross the river. Chamo, who had squatted back on his heels and lit an evil-smelling pipe, said, "We do not cross."

"We're going around," Father Vergara said. "So far the Bidassoa has been the border. But a little way ahead the border moves north, and the Bidassoa enters the hills and becomes a Spanish river. The boundary line is up that mountain. That's where you'll cross."

"Spanish river," Chamo grunted. "No more Spanish than French." With his pipe he gestured vaguely over his shoulder. "We are near where I was born. On the other side. But I am not Spanish. Now I live on this side, but I am not French. I am Basque. They tell me, You cannot cross. There are laws. You must have a passport, pay duty. I do not accept this. The Bidassoa is in Euskualherria. Both sides are my home. I cross when I please." He spat sideways into the snow and put the pipe back in his mouth.

Father Vergara, reclining on his side, his snow goggles pushed up, winked at Michel and said to the old man, "You do not cross the Bidassoa in the daytime."

His tone was joking, but Chamo answered seriously, "I do not talk politics to a bullet. Up in the mountains is safer."

A few minutes later they were on their way again. The shrubs were thicker about them, and Michel noticed that the snow-covered ground no longer undulated but rose steadily upwards. Their pace was slower now, and the rope across the priest's shoulder cut deeper as he leaned forward against it. Still they went on. The sun had become quite hot, although the air was cold. Michel's face began to burn, and he pulled up his coat collar and buried his head forward as far as he could. For perhaps a half-hour more they continued in this way, until Chamo called a halt and Father Vergara let the rope fall with a sigh. He was breathing more heavily, although his expression was calm and cheerful. Where were they? Michel looked about him, and saw that they had stopped in a little pocket cut into the side of a hill. Ahead of them, at the deep end of the pocket, a boxlike stone house with a wide veranda thrust itself out of the hillside, its forepart resting on a low wall of mortared rock. The entire depression was in shadow, and seemed wild and uninviting.

At the priest's gesture Michel seized his bundle and got up from the toboggan, which Chamo slung over his shoulder and carried toward the house.

"From here on you'll have to walk, Benedek," Father Vergara said.

The mountain seemed to tower over them. Looking up, Michel saw tall trees rising in thick ranks up the slope, which for a little way was gradual in its rise, but then became perceptibly steeper. Up, up his eyes went over the mountain's flank, taking in the vast snow-covered contours, broken here and there by vertical patches of bare rock, and the forest like a growth of black hairs on the giant's thigh; far above there were no trees, and the mountain etched itself, bare of all but snow, against the bright, glittering sky. Still he could not see the peak; at that point the sky was milky, and Choltococagna rose into it until its outlines could no longer be distinguished. Michel let out a deep breath, as though he had been challenged and were about to do battle. He was going to climb this mountain, he told himself; and could not quite believe it.

Father Vergara seemed to sense his dismay. "We'll go slowly, Benedek. We're in no hurry now. So far we've made good time. The rendezvous isn't until one o'clock. We'll rest whenever you get tired."

"Rendezvous?" Michel said.

"We're meeting a Spanish *passeur*. He and Chamo will get you past the border and take you to an inn on the other side. Iranzo will be waiting for you there with his car. Do you remember Iranzo? He drove us to Aitzmendi from Garonde. He'll take you from the inn to a spot I've picked out for you."

"Oh," he said in a small voice. "Aren't you—?"

"It's only for a little while," Father Vergara said, glancing at him. "Once you're safely stowed away, Iranzo will come for me, and we'll go on together."

Chamo was back, without the toboggan. He looked up at the sun, shading his eyes with his hand, then grunted something and set off up the slope. "Let's go," Father Vergara said, seizing Michel's bundle of clothing and tucking it into his jacket. Michel followed him, full of protest. He had taken for granted that the priest would accompany him all the way. Now he realized that he was to be turned over to strangers. Chamo, whose face was a hard mask he could not read; a *passeur* he had never seen; the little man who had driven the car, whose features he scarcely remembered. He did not want to go with them alone, even for a little while.

But he had to concentrate on walking. The burly priest, with the trail already broken for him by Chamo, deliberately walked with sweeping movements of his great boots, clearing the way still more; but even so Michel found it hard going. In a few minutes he found the snow goggles an encumbrance. Though the narrow slits reduced the glare of sun on snow in the distance, they restricted his vision of what lay at his feet, making everything flat; besides, under the constant strain of climbing, his eye sockets filled with sweat that accumulated under the wooden cups. After lifting them several times and wiping his eyes, he let the goggles slide down under his chin and made his way with his head bent down and his eyes half shut.

They climbed steadily, zigzagging along a route among the trees and outcroppings of rock that Chamo picked out with no hesitation. To Michel it all looked the same, an even cascade of white out of which the tree trunks rose blackly, and which to his unpracticed eye offered no clue as to the best footing. Yet tirelessly the old man, with no apparent effort, tacked and wound his way, his arm rising and falling as his staff made muffled thumps in the snow; and from the smoothness of the ground beneath, Michel realized that they were climbing by a path of sorts that snaked its way upwards.

Once Father Vergara looked back and paused, and Michel saw that he had fallen behind. He struggled to catch up.

"Are you all right?" the priest said.

"Yes, Father," he panted.

He staggered on, his breath coming in wheezes, his chest burning with each intake of icy air. Would that terrible little man never stop? But after his comfortable toboggan ride for so many miles, it would be humiliating to ask for a respite. It seemed hours to him before Father Vergara's arm steadied him, and he looked up to see that they had come to a sort of shallow cave under an overhang, and that Chamo was already seated on the snow-free earth beneath. Leaning on Father Vergara's arm, Michel entered, stood still while the priest brushed away the snow from his body, then let himself sink to the ground. In the rocky cavern his breath sounded very loud, and he sensed that both men were looking at him.

After a while his breathing was easier, and he sat up and looked back along the way they had come. The snow seemed without perspective, but from the foreshortening of the trees beneath him he could see that they were perceptibly higher than before; yet, remembering how the mountain had looked from river level, he realized that they were not far along their climb.

An acrid whiff of smoke came to him. Chamo had his pipe going again, its bitten stem clamped in his yellowish teeth; he sat with his back to the stone, his forearms resting on his drawn-up knees, with no more sign of effort than if he had taken a hundred-yard stroll. Father Vergara, on the other hand, seemed flushed and warm. "Here," he said to Michel, taking from inside his jacket the paper-wrapped parcel the old woman had given him, and rolling it open. There was bread, a slab of cheese, chunky sausages, hard-boiled eggs. To his astonishment Michel found that he was hungry again. He accepted a piece of bread and a sausage, and as he bit into its tough, garlicky skin it seemed to him that he had never tasted anything so delicious. He chewed and swallowed, savoring each bite, feeling his stiff cheek muscles relaxing as he ate. Chamo refused Father Vergara's offer with a shake of his head, and the priest peeled an egg, took it in two bites, and washed it down with a mouthful of snow, which he scooped up at his side.

The other Father Vergara, Michel thought, and then wondered what he had meant by it. It depended on where they were, he decided finally. On the cliff over the Atlantic, on the handball court, here in the mountains, you forgot that Father Vergara was a priest, and saw only the trunklike legs, the shoulders bulging with muscle, the craggy, weather-beaten face of the athlete, the outdoorsman. It was in the study of the presbytery, however, that you saw the other side of him, the gentleness of the man, his compassion, his tolerance, his learning. The mountaineer and the man of God. He had needed both, Michel thought; without both he would have been lost, one way or the other. And now Father Vergara was going to leave him to other men. But it would not be long, he consoled himself. Father Vergara would join him again soon, he had promised.

Chamo knocked out his pipe on his heel and stood up, and Michel rose with a sigh. It was time to go again. Now, however, he was to walk in the middle, between the two of them, the priest told him. There were steep places ahead, and someone had to stay behind him for safety's sake.

For a while it was not as bad as Michel had expected. He seemed to have found a second wind that let him keep up behind Chamo, who moved remorselessly up and up without a backward glance. Before they had come to another halt, however, Michel was ready to collapse into the snow and give up. Only by a monstrous effort of the will did he keep his trembling legs going, lifting them up like dead weights and letting them drop with a jar that hurt the back of his head. It was Father Vergara who called the halt this time; and Michel, falling to his knees and sobbing for breath, knew that this break was for him alone, and that Chamo would have gone on. Father Vergara kneeled beside him and pulled him to a sitting position, cradling his head on his shoulder. Chamo had pushed his goggles up, and was regarding him with a speculative look in which Michel read disapproval; but the priest said, "Rest as long as you need."

Michel rested; got his wind back; wiggled his numb toes within his heavy boots, which were wet and leaden, until their tingling told him circulation had returned; and at length urged himself to his feet, dreading what lay ahead but knowing that it had to be faced. They went on, sometimes climbing straight up over paths covered by the snow, sometimes tacking to right or left around boulders or clumps of snow-laden trees and bushes; often the hidden path disappeared, and the ground became treacherous with buried obstacles. There were places, too, where Chamo scrambled somehow up steep rock faces and lowered his staff, bracing himself at the top as Michel, pushed from behind by Father Vergara, pulled himself up.

The view had become fantastically beautiful, but it was only with the edge of his consciousness that Michel was aware of it. He caught glimpses of the sky, pressing downward like a sparkling blue canopy; he was walking along snow-filled gorges, faintly bluish-green in their shadowy depths, like submarine grottoes; occasionally his eyes, watering from the effort and the cold, took in, still high above them and apparently no closer than before, the breathtaking sweeping rise of the mountain melting into the mist that obscured its peak; or, looking down, saw the black and mottled gray that was the Bidassoa cutting through the dunelike plain. From certain spots in their upward journey he could see Aitzmendi; but now it was a toy village, the hill on which it stood flattened out, its inhabitants invisible. And all about them, more clearly seen the higher they got, were other snowclad peaks stretching away interminably in the distance.

He saw these things, they etched themselves on his memory with the clarity of a picture postcard, and yet it was without any conscious act of vision on his part. His world had narrowed down to the trail Chamo left behind him, the imprints of his rubber boots, deep pockets in the snow, crumbling white at the rim but lit with rainbow blues and greens at the bottom. The world was snow, lying all about him, enclosing him in its clinging grip, clutching at his boots, which made little sighing sounds as he lifted them out of the wells that Chamo made. Snow, soft and cold and deep and terrible. He struggled in it, battered his way through it, wallowed in it, fell in it. It had become his malicious enemy, his nightmare, pulling at his feet and trying to drag him down. And always, ahead of him, the untiring black automaton that was Chamo, moving up through this pitiless white stuff as though it were his element, like a fish in water, a bird in the air, pausing only to glance up at the sun and shake his head in anger.

Michel couldn't help it. He knew they were stopping more often to rest than the old man had counted on. But he didn't stop because he was tired; he stopped when he fell and couldn't get up. Then Father Vergara would come up to him, kneel down so that Michel could lean on him, comfort him, telling him softly and gently to take a breather and that he was proud of him for doing so well. "He's been sick," the priest said once to Chamo who, standing on a rock before which Michel had collapsed, grunted and looked down at him, implacable as a bird of prey.

Sometimes, when the going was fairly level, and there was little danger of slipping, Father Vergara carried him as he had over the cliff, spread-eagled on his back and clutching with arms and legs. These were times of rest for Michel, in which he closed his eyes and let himself be lulled by the priest's lurching movement, and he looked forward to them and prayed that they would last. But he did not protest when he was set down again, for he could feel that mighty chest laboring under him, and knew how cruelly the man's strength was being tried.

The sun climbed steadily, reached its zenith, passed it; still they went on. Michel had lost all track of time. Time had frozen like the snow; Michel walked and fell, walked and fell, was carried, walked some more. His face ached as though an edge of fire lay against it; it was sunburn, as he realized when Father Vergara's face bent over him, and he saw that the priest's tan was overlaid with pink. The air was thin and without substance. He could not catch his breath, even when he was being carried.

Somewhere in their upward movement they stopped and ate some food. This time Chamo accepted some. Michel chewed on bread and cheese; it tasted like cotton to him, for even his throat was numb. At another point in their climb Chamo stopped and gazed across a gorge where a moving ripple had appeared in the snow. The ripple grew, slid slowly and ponderously downward, made a whispering sound that increased to a roar as the snow scooped up rocks and snapped off tree trunks, until it was a great avalanche that buried itself in the unseen depths with a thundering noise that made the air tremble. He had heard of avalanches, and thought of them as a mere sliding of the snow, soft and picturesque and harmless. Now for the first time he felt their great destructive power. They were lucky, he told himself. But he was too far gone to be frightened. He could not even respond to the note of triumph in the priest's voice, when, ages later, Father Vergara caught up to him and pounded him on the back, crying, "The ridge! The ridge!" He understood that they had reached the upward limit of their climb; but he knew that there was still some distance to go, that he couldn't make it, and that it would never, never end.

Had he fainted? He didn't know. He had no memory of any halt. He was walking through the snow, as he had since the world began, and then, without any transition, he was lying over the priest's shoulder, his head down over the man's back, his eyes were open and he was staring sideways down to his left with the same sense of unreality as though he had awakened on the moon and had opened his eyes to this delicate fairy landscape: a perfectly rounded, shell-like valley gouged out of the mountainside, its feathery white surface fixed in motionless ripples like an arrested sea. Michel closed his eyes again. Moon or earth, he didn't care. He was caught like a fly in a spider's web of snow, he would never get out, and it didn't matter, so long as he didn't have to struggle any more.

And so it came as a little shock to him when they stopped and Father Vergara set him down on a cushion of pine needles underneath a thatched roof, and said that they had arrived. It was the rendezvous, he said. Michel lay, half reclined, as he had been put down. It was too much of an effort to shift into a more comfortable position; he was utterly exhausted, and in a daze. A face was bending over him. Focusing his eyes with difficulty, he saw that it was Father Vergara's, and that it was red and streaming with perspiration. Then something was at his mouth, he was told to swallow and he did, and a slow bloom of fire crept down his throat and into his chest. He coughed feebly, lay back and closed his eyes.

Time passed, he did not know how much. He was terribly cold and stiff. His head lay on something soft. It was his bundle of clothing, which Father Vergara must have placed under him as he dozed. He turned, and stared up at the intertwined branches overhead, and listened to Chamo's voice. He could not make out the words, but gathered that the old man was swearing without emphasis in his own language. He struggled to a sitting position and saw the two men squatting on the ground, facing each other. Chamo was muttering his curses, monotonously, and the priest was staring down, his face set and worried. Father Vergara caught his movement, and turned to him, asking how he was.

"All right," Michel croaked.

"We have a problem, Benedek. The *passeur* isn't here. He was supposed to be here at one o'clock, and it's almost three now. It isn't that he waited and left. There are no tracks in the snow. He didn't show up at all."

Michel said nothing, looking from one to the other.

Chamo began to swear in French. He would cut the mangy dog's liver out. He would strangle him with his own bowels. His hunched shoulders made sharp, jerking movements, and Michel saw that he had a long, lean, wicked-looking knife in his hands, and was whit-tling away at a branch and making great slivers fly.

The problem was to cross the frontier without the *passeur,* Father Vergara said. It wasn't a question of knowing the way; Chamo knew it as well as the *passeur,* and it was only the code of the profession that made a man from the other side necessary. The problem was Michel's condition. It had been agreed that he, Father Vergara, would turn back at this point, so as to enter Spain legally at Hen-daye and pick Michel up as planned. But how could he turn back now, with still more than two miles to go to the inn and no *passeur* to help? It wasn't fair to Chamo to leave him with a boy whose strength had given out. Yet Chamo refused to budge another step unless he kept the agreement and turned back.

"You are a priest," Chamo said between bared teeth.

"And you are a stubborn mule," Father Vergara replied. "My father taught you these hills. He ran contraband before you were born. And his father before him. If I had not taken holy orders—"

"But you did," Chamo snarled back at him. "And if you are caught, what then? A priest *contrabandier!* I will have no part of it. I go alone with the boy, or I do not go."

"If you do not go, I will go with the boy myself."

"You will get caught."

"Then it will be your fault, and you could have prevented it."

"With you I do not move. That is my last word."

What had they given him to drink? It was rawer than brandy, and burned more. He felt his head swim. He shook himself, and listened to the men bickering. It was his fault, he told himself. They had arrived late because of him, and now it was because he could not walk that they could not agree on what to do.

"I can walk," he said, getting unsteadily to his feet and clutching one of the poles on which the roof rested.

The two men stared at him. "You see?" Chamo said in surly tri-umph.

It was a long time before Father Vergara gave in. To all his argu-ments the old man shook his head, his lips set in a grimace.

"Very well, then," Father Vergara said sadly. He insisted that Michel sit down again, and gave him what was left of the food. He waited until Michel had eaten it, then blessed him. It was only for a few hours, he said. Michel was not to be afraid. Chamo would get him through; he was a rock-headed old Basque, and not even the devil could catch him on Choltococagna. And Iranzo would take over from there.

Before going, he gave Michel a great embrace, then plunged abruptly down the hill.

Vati, Michel thought, watching him go. This man, who had given him life again, was like a second father to him.

He was alone with Chamo. "Come," the old man said, and stepped out into the snow.

It began again. For a while Michel kept up, driven by his proud boast and sheer desperation; but, inevitably, he began to lag. He did not feel his own body; he was nothing but a will that urged his legs up and down and watched them churn through the snow as if they belonged to someone else. A red mist gathered before his eyes, and still he went on. Once he bumped into Chamo, who had stopped and was waiting for him. He had seen him but could not stop. Another time Chamo got so far ahead that he was out of sight. Michel plodded over the tracks in the snow, sure that he had been abandoned and that he would die on this hellish mountain; or worse yet, go on and on forever. But Chamo came back for him, and carried him a little way.

Chamo had stopped. He stood still, gazing up and to his left like a dog that had caught the scent of game. Then he took off one mitten, put his finger to his lips, and made scampering motions in the air. He put on his mitten again, slid belly down into the snow and began to crawl. Michel understood that they were near the border guard. He lowered himself into the snow and crawled after Chamo. They were among stunted shrubs growing sparsely on uneven, slanted ground, beneath a shoulder of rock from which icicles hung. Michel inched along, trying to control his breath, which came in loud gasps. How near was the guard? It seemed to him that his breathing was very loud and could be heard at a great distance. Where were they going? Ahead of him rose a sheer slate-colored cliff that seemed so close that it occurred to him to wonder whether Chamo intended to climb it. Protest rose in his throat, but still he went on.

Michel's heart gave a great thump. Chamo had disappeared. One moment he had been crawling a few yards ahead of him, and now there was nothing but the furrow he had left and that came abruptly to an end. Michel raised his head and gazed wildly about him. What was this? Chamo's head lay on the snow, facing him; detached from its body, neckless, it lay on the furrow like a boulder, its eyes fixed intently on him. As Michel stared at it in horror, the head jerked sharply and the lips grimaced as if to say, Hurry! He had lost his mind, he thought; nevertheless, he crawled on, and saw that Chamo was standing in a narrow ravine that cut across their path at right angles, and that his chin was level with Michel's own.

Michel slid over the edge, and Chamo grabbed him, pulled him to his feet, signaled again for silence, and moved down the ravine, bent almost double. Michel had the almost uncontrollable impulse to look about for the guard; but he stifled it, and followed Chamo, bending down like him. The ravine narrowed, became deeper, passed under a spur of rock and became a short tunnel. Here there was no snow, and Chamo let him lie for a few minutes on the icy rock and catch his breath. Staring up in despair at the seamed rock roof, Michel knew that this time he could not get up again. But Chamo thrust his face close to him, and snarled softly, "Get up!" and somehow he found himself on his feet again, boneless and wobbly. They went on, emerging through the crevice at which the tunnel ended. Here the terrain sloped downward. There was a panorama of peaks before him, a snow-covered valley through which ran a river, and, in the center, far below, a gray patch of houses with a pall of smoke over them. Had they crossed to the other side? Were they in Spain? Michel did not know or care. He staggered on after Chamo, falling several times and getting up again.

Chamo said in his ear, "We are almost there." He did not open his eyes. He was lying down, the snow was like a soft pillow under his face, and there was no reason in the world to move. There was nothing so warm and delicious as this bed he lay on, and he would sleep awhile. Chamo's voice became a vague muttering, like a distant waterfall, and Michel drifted off into sleep.

He was awakened by a great thud. He opened his eyes and stared uncomprehendingly at something black and vertical a few inches from his face. Wood, wet and shining. A wooden step, with a glimmer of light on it. On it stood a pair of booted feet. It was a doorstep, he reasoned, and a man was standing on it, looking down at him. Then he was lying on the ground. But where in this wilderness of snow was there a doorstep? No, he was dreaming; he was about to close his eyes again when the boots moved. Another pair of boots took their place, then they too moved, and others came. Now he heard voices. Strong arms lifted him up and carried him into a smoky room. Behind him came two men, carrying a third, his body powdered with snow. Was it Chamo? Then Michel was lying on a blanket before a roaring fire, someone was loosening his boots and removing his beret and mittens; and he gave a great groan and curled up in the warmth that flowed like a benediction over his body.

It was a long time before he came to himself. He remembered collapsing in the snow and the glorious numbness that encased his limbs; he remembered the fall at the entrance to the inn; but the rest was a mass of bewildering sensations that only gradually entered his consciousness and formed a connected whole. There was the fire, which was warmth for his icy body and a dazzle in his eyes when he opened them to convince himself that he was not still in the white hell outside. There was a shoulder he was leaning against, and the gritty taste of hot soup in his mouth as he swallowed in response to a voice at his ear. Hands massaging his face and neck and stockinged feet. A face bending over him, that his eyes, opening and sinking wearily shut a number of times, puzzled over before the name Iranzo finally occurred to him. The smell of smoke in the air. A clinking of glass, the gurgle of water pouring, footsteps, voices murmuring. The realization that he was shivering violently and that his teeth made strange clicking noises. A painful tingling in his limbs. Images that his eyes took in and his mind tried drowsily to piece together: a man in a leather apron lifting a kettle from the fire; a dumpy, shapeless woman pouring water from a pitcher into a great wooden tub by the hearth, a few feet away from him; a dim ceiling crossed by warped, blackened beams from which strings of sausages hung down; a wooden counter, and behind it bottle-laden shelves against a cracked mirror; men dressed in sheepskin jackets standing about a table on which a man was lying.

His consciousness was like a voice heard at a great distance, for long moments slipping and fading away beyond recall, and then coming alive and urging him to awareness of the stir about him. Then the outer world was back again and pressing on him, and he told himself he was safe, that Chamo had saved him, that he was in Spain and his terrible journey was over, that he was at the inn that Father Vergara had told him about and that there were people here who were taking care of him.

He told himself these things, and little by little, as he recovered, the inn and the people in it took shape in his mind. He was in a taproom or bar of some sort, which was at the same time a shop. It was a dim cave of a room with only one shuttered window, and it was lit by kerosene lamps hanging against sagging shelves, stacked with food tins and cartons, that lined most of the wall space. There were rough, heavy tables and benches. A narrow staircase beyond the bar led upstairs; beneath it a trap door, its lid open and propped by the underside of the stair, gave access to the cellar. The man with the leather apron must be the owner, for it was he who shouted orders at the woman to bring more water, and snapped at the men to hurry up. Was the woman his wife? He called her María. She was quiet and submissive, with a broad face and mousy hair that straggled down over her forehead. The men by the table were massaging Chamo and talking to him; he answered them weakly, his voice hardly more than a whisper. They were hard-looking men, with dark, weather-beaten faces, and somber, slow-moving eyes. They all wore berets and boots. One had a knife thrust into his boot top, its handle wrapped in black tape.

The man at his side was Iranzo. He was younger than Michel remembered, but it was true that he had hardly seen the man's face the night he left Garonde for Aitzmendi. Iranzo was pale and fair-skinned, with light gray eyes and silken, almost colorless eyebrows. His lips were thin, almost sullen. It was he who had fed him the soup and massaged him. He sat on the blanket at Michel's side, his legs crossed under him, and in measure, as Michel was able to answer, asked questions. What had taken them so long? He had been waiting there ever since one o'clock, and it was after four when they arrived. Was it true that there were no tracks in the snow by the rendezvous? Chamo was furious with Santos, and the man had been sent for. How had Chamo hurt his leg?

At this Michel looked at Iranzo in surprise. Hurt his leg? Iranzo nodded, and said that the men had gone out and looked at Chamo's tracks in the snow, and seen that he had arrived dragging his left leg. It was paralyzed or frozen, or perhaps it was a severe sprain. He had fallen at the steps. How he had managed to carry Michel on his back in that condition no one could imagine. The men were massaging him, and they were preparing a hot tub to see if that would help.

Michel's mind was clearer now, and some of his strength had returned. He got to his knees, steadying himself on Iranzo's arm, and looked at the knot of men about the table where Chamo was lying. He would have liked to go to the old man, but decided that he would be in the way. The fire felt uncomfortably hot on his skin. Behind him was an empty table and bench; he moved to them and sat down, leaning forward on the table and watching the men strip off Chamo's upper garments. He caught a glimpse of Chamo's face as they sat him upright, and a chill went through him to see how drawn it was, and how the eyelids fluttered. How heavy his own head was! The scene he was looking at scarcely seemed real to him, as though it were happening far away.

There was a stamping of feet outside. A man entered, kicking the door shut behind him. He took in the room at a glance, and moved toward Chamo's table, waving his arms and shouting.

"Santos," Iranzo whispered; he had followed Michel to the table, and stood beside him.

The man spoke in Spanish, and Michel found that he could understand most of what he said. He *had* been at the rendezvous, he cried; it was Chamo who had failed to show up. They had said one o'clock. How long did they expect him to wait?

Chamo whispered something, and Santos started as though he had been struck. Then he flipped off the woolen knit cap he wore, and crouched, his feet far apart, his hand moving ominously to his hip under his jacket. The men about the table spoke sharply to him, and one of them stepped forward and pushed Santos back, speaking urgently in his ear. Santos let out a bellow, and shook his fist. Michel stared, his heart beating violently, as the man danced in rage. Why was he so angry? Had Chamo called him a liar? Santos was short and squat, with very wide shoulders made even bulkier by the sheepskin jacket that covered them, and his face, dark and malevolent, was disfigured by a broken nose, flattened and bent to one side. Michel had the impression that the man was drunk, and fear filled him for what he might do.

Santos was appealing to the men about the table. His voice was thick and hoarse as he demanded something of them, his hands clenched. *Justicia,* he said; and *palabra. Justicia* had to mean justice. Michel could not follow it. Was he asking the men to decide between him and Chamo? But Santos had lied! There were no tracks at the rendezvous. The men said nothing; they regarded Santos impassively, and the man became angrier, shouting and cursing.

Beside Michel, Iranzo suddenly hissed, and darted across the room. Santos broke off his harangue, peering at Iranzo with suspicion, as if seeing him for the first time. His glance traveled back to

Michel, who shrank as the man's narrowed eyes wondered at him. Then Iranzo was bending over the table, saying urgently, "Chamo? Chamo?"

After that everybody crowded around, somebody called out, "*Patrón!*" and the man in the leather apron, who had remained by the tub, watching the altercation with his arms crossed on his chest, hurried over. There were obscure movements, slapping noises, someone brought a glass of water, someone else set it down on the next table, where it teetered and toppled off, spilling the water on the floor and rolling forlornly against the wall.

Unbelieving, Michel watched as the men pulled off their berets and stood looking down at the table. He's dead, he said to himself in a daze. But it couldn't be! A moment ago Chamo had spoken; he had heard him himself! He had said something that had thrown Santos into a fury. How could he die like that, between one instant and the next, in a snap of the fingers? No! No! he all but cried out. He found that he had risen to his feet and moved forward. They were mistaken; the old man had fallen asleep; if he called his name, Chamo would awake and look at him.

The men stepped aside, making room for him; and Michel, seeing Chamo's face, felt his protest die on his lips. This stiff, alien flesh, so dreadfully still and empty, wasn't the Chamo who had skipped up the mountain, gazing at the sun and spitting in contempt into the snow. There was no use calling out. Chamo lay on his back, a blanket under him and doubled over his legs as far as the top of his trousers, which he still wore; his upper body was bare. Michel's eyes traveled unbelievingly over the white skin of the chest, bony and hairless, and the pale satiny scar that lay like a seam against the ribs; the abrupt line of demarcation at the neck, above which the skin was mahogany-dark; the lined face; the ashen hair, wet and matted down on his skull.

He had done this, he said to himself. It was the carrying him that had killed the old man. He might have left Michel in the snow and gone for help. He hadn't; he had carried him on his shoulder, and it was that that had paralyzed the leg and killed him.

The others were watching him. Standing by the table and looking down, Michel could feel their eyes on his back, and their silence. Were they blaming him? He wished he could say something; feel a stirring at his heart; cry; show Chamo and himself and these others that he was not devoid of feeling. But it was no good, there was nothing within him but a great numbness. He looked at that still, wooden face, and all he could think was, Another one. Another one who died because of me.

The silence was unbearable. He slipped down to his knees and began to pray.

Afterward he looked at Chamo's face again, trying to impress it into his memory, promising to remember him in his prayers always. He returned to his bench and sat down heavily.

Iranzo was beside him, thrusting his boots at him. "Put them on," he said in a low voice. "We'll be leaving now."

But Chamo's dead, he wanted to say. How could they leave with Chamo lying there?

"Hurry!" Iranzo urged. He seemed pale and frightened, and Michel took the boots from his hand. They had been by the fire, and though still damp were hot to the touch. Reluctantly, he put them on and began to lace them up, watching the man Santos, who was speaking softly to the other men across the room, and glancing now and then in their direction. He did not like the looks of the man, whose face was lowered and threatening. Michel began to hurry, feeling something ominous shaping itself in the murky room. He finished tying the boots, and slid into his jacket and coat. His beret and mittens were in the coat pockets. The mittens were sopping wet, and he put them back in the pocket. Iranzo had put on a leather windbreaker; he watched Michel as he dressed, his eyes urging speed.

"Hey, Frenchy!" It was Santos who spoke, stepping forward. "Where do you think you're going?" He spoke in French, strongly accented. Michel started, and Iranzo turned, staring.

"What about *him*, eh?" Santos shouted in sudden rage, thumbing toward Chamo, and leaping forward to strike the table with his fist. The man's face, thrust out, dark and menacing, was only a few feet away, and Michel could smell the liquor on his breath. "Are you going to leave him here?"

The man in the leather apron put his hand on Santos' arm, and spoke to him in Spanish. From his gestures and his tone, rather than from his words, Michel gathered that he was telling Santos to leave Iranzo alone, that they would manage somehow. Santos answered him surlily, waving his arms. They argued for some time, the landlord trying to calm the other, Santos shaking his head and talking in anger. Michel at length understood what the problem was. Chamo had crossed the border illegally, and had died on the Spanish side.

What were they to do with him? They would all be in trouble with the law if he were found here. And unless Michel had totally misunderstood what Santos was saying, the man wanted Iranzo to take the body back to France.

The landlord left Santos, came round the table, and spoke to Iranzo. He was a big man, but middle-aged and flabby; the skin was pouched beneath his eyes, which seemed tired. They had better leave, he said quietly to Iranzo. Santos was an ugly customer, and there was no telling what he would do. Iranzo replied angrily that he would like nothing better. He hadn't killed the old man, it was obviously a heart attack. What was *he* supposed to do with the corpse?

The landlord shushed him impatiently. He hadn't bargained to have a corpse on his hands either. But he would find a way out. Now he was concerned with not having another corpse around. Did Iranzo understand?

"Take him out on the mountain," Iranzo said with a curse. "Nobody has to know that he died here."

Suddenly heartsick, Michel looked at the body of the old man and back again at the two men. Surely they would not do that? The thought of Chamo lying out in the snow, perhaps for days or even weeks, until he was found, filled him with horror.

He was relieved when the landlord stared at Iranzo, his eyes suddenly cold, and said he didn't need advice. Especially of that sort. "Just take the boy," he said. "Wait until I distract his attention, and slip out the door."

Santos had edged closer. "Take him in your car."

Iranzo eyed the man with concern, but said nothing. Violence was coming, Michel felt. He wished fervently he were far away from there. Helpless, he watched and waited, ready to dash to the door. If only Father Vergara were here!

"I said to take him in your car. You've got a car outside."

"Don't answer," the landlord muttered.

But Iranzo cried out, "I can't do that. How can I get through the border with a body—"

He broke off and backed away as Santos made a dash for the table, grasping the edge with his hands, and feinting from one side to the other as Iranzo dodged in panic, trying to keep the table between them. The landlord shouted something. Michel shrank back, lost his balance on the bench and fell to the floor, but not before he had seen one of the other men seize Santos by the arm, and be flung off. The table creaked heavily over Michel's head as Santos hurdled it. Michel saw the man's bandy legs, wrapped in strips of gray felt over the boots, land on the floor, stumble and right themselves. There came the sound of a great slap, and Iranzo fell heavily to the floor and sat looking up, his eyes dazed. Then the men had Santos, and were dragging him back amid a string of curses.

A sudden silence fell. Michel, struggling to his feet, saw that all had turned and were looking at the woman called María. She was standing by the bench where Chamo's jacket had been thrown, holding up a fistful of money. While all watched, she thumbed through it and said something that Michel did not understand.

"Ten thousand," the landlord muttered.

Iranzo was up again, holding his hand to his jaw. "That was for you," he said spitefully to Santos. "If you had done your job. And if you had, he wouldn't be dead now."

Santos seemed stunned. He looked from Iranzo to the money in the woman's hand. Then slowly he reached out, took the banknotes, stared at them, scratched his head, and laid them down on Chamo's bare chest. "Masses for the peace of his soul," he said. He put his hand in his pocket and took out a worn wallet, from which he removed banknotes that he laid on the pile. One by one the other men reached for their pockets, handing money to Santos, who tossed it on the rest, crossing himself.

The landlord touched Michel's arm and made a meaningful motion with his head. Trembling with excitement, Michel moved noiselessly toward the door, which Iranzo was already opening. It was dark outside. A shout followed them, and voices raised in expostulation. Iranzo began to run, and Michel scurried through the snow behind him, fear striking at him. But no one came after them, and Iranzo, glancing back, slowed down, muttering to himself. Seeing his short figure and slight frame, Michel realized how little of a match he was for Santos, who might have killed him in his rage. Had he meant that, about putting Chamo out on the mountain, in the snow? The landlord had gotten angry at the suggestion. But what *would* they do with the body? And what would Father Vergara say? He would certainly blame himself for not having insisted more on accompanying them. But it was really Michel's fault, for being such a weakling.

He followed Iranzo along a snowy path trampled by many feet

until they reached a road from which the snow had been removed, pushed into huge piles along the edges. Iranzo's car was parked to one side, under some trees. He got in beside Iranzo, who started the motor and drove off in angry silence, staring straight ahead.

The next hour passed like a dream. He was still far weaker than he had realized. Only the fear of Santos had given him the energy to run behind Iranzo. But once in the car he sank into a dull apathy, which veiled his senses and made the next events seem remote and unconnected with him. He sat quietly as Iranzo drove. When the car stopped and the man motioned for him to get out, he did so mechanically and followed Iranzo up a snowy path to a farmhouse, where he shook hands with the elderly man who opened the door for them, and sat down in the chair that was pointed out to him. Iranzo left, saying he was going after Father Vergara. The farmer brought him a cup of warm milk laced with coffee, which he accepted gratefully; then the man disappeared, and Michel was left alone.

The room he sat in had a musty smell and was cluttered with heavy ancient chairs and rockers; otherwise it made no impression on him. He waited, sipping the milk and thinking about Chamo. He's dead, he said to himself over and over again. Only yesterday the old man was nothing but a name he had overheard. Yet today that stranger had given up his life for him. This great adventure, upon which he had set out so eagerly this morning, had cost a man's life. And he himself was a heartless wretch, to be thinking about it so calmly, with not a tear in his eye. But he was so tired!

He did not know how long he sat there, prey to his gloomy, accusing thoughts. Occasionally he found himself nodding, and wished he could lie down; but there was no couch in the room, and he did not dare lie down on the floor for fear that the farmer might think he was making himself too free. He was dozing in his chair, his head sunk uncomfortably on his shoulder, when he heard footsteps, and Father Vergara appeared, followed by Father Lisiaga, Iranzo, and the farmer. He uttered a low cry, and hurled himself into Father Vergara's arms, blubbering. The priest embraced him, then kneeled down to study his face. Through his tears Michel saw that he was pale and stern, and his blue eyes were not twinkling as usual but were full of a great sadness. He held Michel by the shoulders, and asked how he felt.

"Oh, Father!" Michel sobbed. "Ch-Chamo!"

Yes, Father Vergara said; he knew. He held Michel close, comforting him.

"But it was because of me," Michel cried.

"Don't think that for an instant. If it's anybody's fault, it's mine. I shouldn't have let myself be persuaded to turn back. But you saw how stubborn he was about it. Apparently his heart gave out under the strain. He may even have had attacks before, but he never let on to anybody. No one could have foreseen it. It's God's will, Benedek. We'll pray for him, you and I, and I'll say masses for the peace of his soul. And we'll do what we can to give him a decent burial. As soon as I've found a place for you, which we're going to do now, I'll make sure the body is brought back to France. He'll be buried in the churchyard. Now, pull yourself together. We have to be on our way, and it's late."

Michel could not resist glancing at Iranzo, who stood with his gaze averted. He had not noticed before how red and swollen the man's face was on one side. Santos must have hit him very hard.

All shook hands with the farmer, who patted Michel on the shoulder and wished him luck. Murmuring "Thank you, thank you," Michel went out the door with the three men. As they went down the walk, Father Vergara said that they would travel as they had the other time, Father Lisiaga going ahead in his car, and he and Iranzo and Benedek following him in the other.

"There won't be any road blocks this time," he said, "but we might as well be careful."

Father Lisiaga got into his car and started off with a wave of his hand. But Iranzo's car wouldn't start. Iranzo pumped the starter impatiently, grunting with annoyance. It was the carburetor, he said; it had been acting up lately. While he was grinding away with his foot, someone appeared at Michel's window, and he looked up, startled, to see a man in uniform peering in at them.

For an instant he froze, his eyes taking in the man's strange, cocked hat, the muzzle of a carbine rising over his shoulder, the figure of another uniformed man behind him; then he turned in fright to Father Vergara, who calmly reached across Michel and lowered the window. In the meanwhile Iranzo had turned in his seat, taken one panicky look, and started to open his door. The priest clamped his left hand on Iranzo's shoulder, forcing him down, at the same time that he spoke to the policeman, who had produced a flashlight and directed its beam on the ceiling of the car. The dim, reflected light shone on the faces at either side of Michel, only a few inches from his own, as the two men exchanged words in Spanish. The policeman glanced at Michel occasionally as he talked. He had a thin, pencil-line mustache, and fine white teeth that Michel looked at as if hypnotized. It suddenly occurred to Michel that they were in Spain, where Father Vergara had said that he would be safe. Then these policemen were not looking for him. Then why had Iranzo started to run? He wished he could understand what the men were saying; yet it could not be anything threatening, for Father Vergara smiled as he spoke, and once the policeman caught Michel's eye and gave him a slow, friendly wink.

Finally the policeman saluted, and to Michel's amazement he and the other man in uniform got behind the car and began to push. The car moved forward slowly, then gathered speed. Iranzo manipulated the gears, muttering fervently under his breath; the motor coughed, choked, caught, and with a jerk the car took off down the road, its motor roaring. Father Vergara opened his window, and leaned out, waving his hand. Looking back through the rear window, Michel saw the two policemen standing in the middle of the road, and saluting in reply. He sank back limply in his seat, stifling a hysterical giggle, as Father Vergara closed the window.

Iranzo let out his breath sharply, and said, "My God!"

"Guardia Civil," Father Vergara said to Michel. "Nice, pleasant young men. And very respectful. They wouldn't even let me get out to help them push. The one I talked to thought I was from Barcelona, because of my accent. God forgive me, I didn't deny it."

Iranzo said something over his shoulder.

"Yes," the priest replied. "They'll probably remember it later. But it can't be helped. We were lucky enough as it was."

Michel puzzled over this remark. Were they looking for him in Spain too? He asked the question, and Father Vergara said shortly that so near the border the Spaniards often tuned in on the French radio; but he seemed disinclined to pursue the subject, and instead began to talk about a priest named Father Hilarión. He had studied together with Father Hilarión at the seminary many years ago, he said, and had kept in touch with him ever since. A wonderful man, he said, with the warmest, gayest heart in the world. And a fine Latinist. Father Hilarión was the parish priest in the village of Berroain, about an hour's drive ahead. He would take Michel in, and provide for him, for the time being at least, until they had time to make more permanent arrangements.

In the meanwhile the car was speeding along the dark road, keeping a little distance behind Father Lisiaga's coupé. The farmhouse at which Michel had stopped was in a valley, but now they had left that behind them and were moving upwards, along a road that wound its way along the side of hills that grew steeper as they went. Michel looked out the window, watching the beam of their headlights as it swept around curves and threw grotesque shadows into the forest that lined the road on both sides. Berroain, he thought. He had never heard of it. Yet that was where he was going. What awaited him there? Whatever it was, he would not worry about it, Father Vergara was with him again and would take care of everything. He rubbed his eyes, yawned, and fell asleep.

Staring out at the dark snowbound forest flashing past, Father Vergara called himself all kinds of fool. If he had only answered the telephone the first time in the café! Ten steps across the floor, and Lisiaga would have gotten the message over to him. And none of this would have happened. Chamo would be in his cottage, alive; Lisiaga would not have spent that hellish night ramming his car through the unplowed roads; Iranzo would not have had his beating; and he and the boy would be seated at the table at home now, peacefully enjoying their dinner. Oh yes, there were all kinds of excuses he could give himself. The bishop's failure to get word to him before the broadcast instead of after it. The snowstorm. Santos' failure to show up. Chamo's stubbornness. None of this obscured the fact that he had swung into action too quickly, without verifying his information. That, in intention at least, he had needlessly defied his superiors in the Church. That he was headstrong and proud, and had set himself up as sole judge of another human being's destiny.

And to think that he had congratulated himself when, leaving the boy with Chamo at the rendezvous, he had plunged down the mountainside to Aitzmendi! They were a little late, that was all. And he would make up for it by taking the short way down. In a little over an hour he had plummeted the vertical distance the three of them had climbed with such painful roundabout slowness earlier in the day; and once at the riverbank opposite the village, taking advantage of the gathering darkness, he had slipped across the Bidassoa like a wraith, without even having to go to the trouble of distracting the sentinel, who was nodding at his post.

He had not been surprised to find Lisiaga waiting for him in his parlor. The surprise came later, at Lisiaga's explanation. What a face he must have presented to the other at hearing his words! He had sunk into a chair and stared at the man in such dismay that Lisiaga had guessed the truth. He had admitted it, of course, and Lisiaga, when it had sunk in, had jumped to his feet and began to walk up and down, grinning in his relief. He hadn't known what to think, he said. Neither the old woman nor the girl would tell him where Vergara was. He had even thought that Vergara had gone to turn the boy in. Now everything was all right. Vergara had jumped the gun, that was all. Sooner or later the boy would have had to be moved on. It was only after Lisiaga had got over his initial relief that the implications of the act came to him, and he became serious and regarded him with a thoughtful expression.

Lisiaga's tone was wry as he told of the night he had passed. It had been sheer hell, he said. His car had got stuck a half-dozen times on the way from Garonde. The last time was on the hill going up from the highway at the turn-off to Aitzmendi. He had given up, then, and slept in the car until daybreak. The noise of the snowplow awoke him. He started his car by drifting back downhill, and then followed the plow to the village. By then it was nine o'clock, and Vergara was gone.

Well, Father Vergara had thought, it's done. Let's make the best of it.

"Will you help?" he had asked bluntly. "The boy's at a farmhouse in Vera. Iranzo is coming for me. But it will save time if you drive me over."

Lisiaga had agreed, and they had set out, keeping a sharp lookout for Iranzo's car. By this time Father Vergara had recovered some of his equanimity. They had already crossed the border and were approaching the town of Vera when they flagged Iranzo down, and learned of Chamo's death. It was then that Father Vergara realized to the full the cost of what he had done. The trouble he was in with the bishop, the ordeal he had put the boy through, the difficulties he had caused for Lisiaga and Iranzo; all these faded away to nothingness compared to the loss of a human life. And it was all so unnecessary! The irony of it filled him with bitterness and self-accusation.

Why had Chamo died? Because one Father Vergara, proud to sinfulness, taking all on himself like a little god, had acted in disloyalty to his Church. Why had Chamo died? Because he had more respect for the cloth than the wearer of it did, and refused to let a priest run the risk of being arrested for what he himself had done all his life. Chamo had taught him a lesson of fidelity, and given up his life to do so.

Master, explain this parable to us.

Chamo's body would certainly have to be brought down the mountain to Aitzmendi. Time was the problem. It had to be tonight. But he had to settle young Benedek first; then return home through the border control at Hendaye; then go up the mountain again to the inn, and bring Chamo down. And be at the church for Sunday morning mass. Perhaps some of the men at the inn would help him, he thought. Santos surely owed Chamo that. He had manhandled Iranzo, but by now would be in a more reasonable frame of mind.

He sighed, thinking of what still lay ahead of him. But he deserved it, he told himself grimly. And much more.

Incidentally, what had got into Iranzo? His nerves must be pretty well shot. He had started to bolt when the police appeared by the car. Had no stomach for the job, that was obvious.

He turned to look at the boy, and saw that he was asleep, burrowed into the corner of the seat, swaying a little with the movement of the car. It was just as well. For a couple of days, at least, he would need all the rest he could get.

Well, his guardianship was all but over now. Another hour or two, and young Benedek would be safely installed, and life could go back to normal. The boy had been with him for three weeks, and during that time he had scarcely touched his life of Peter. There had been so much to do, to straighten out the lad's twisted thinking. What a mess Benedek had got himself into, through following a few mistaken ideas to their logical conclusion! Like himself, he thought with a wry grimace. On the other hand, it was astonishing how well the boy had responded, once the beginning was made. He had never met a boy with such capacities and depths to him. To have borne that hurt within him all that time, unable to adjust to it! His wounds didn't heal, but became deeper with age. The stuff of which saints are made.

Well, why not? This was no ordinary child. All you had to do was to look at him to see he was different. And once you had talked to him . . . An image came to his mind, that of the Christ child talking to the doctors in the Temple, while his parents were frantically looking for him. He was twelve then, like the Benedek boy, and already "all that heard him were astonished at his wisdom and his answers." Who could tell the ways of the Lord? That the boy had escaped so far the clutches of the law was in itself a kind of minor miracle. And it was another that those who came into contact with him fell under his spell, and did incredible things to save him. From Rome itself all the way down the scale to a surly old smuggler in the valley of the Bidassoa, who had more crimes on his conscience than any man ought to have and yet, dying himself, could not leave the child behind in the snow. And how could you explain that odd feeling you had when you looked at him, that stirring of the intellect, that sense of apprehension that there was more there than met the eye?

He himself had been content to live out his life in a tiny border village, putting whatever gifts he had to saving his humble flock and writing his book. Vergara, the priest of Aitzmendi, the author of *Peter*. The memory of the first of these would fade with the living generation, if indeed it lasted that long; the second, perhaps, would live a while longer. But who knew? These weeks with the boy, which he had been regarding as an interruption to his life's work, might in reality prove to be the true purpose of his existence, and give his life its meaningful direction. Like Chamo, who had lived for sixty-three years between his valley and his mountain, like a mule in the treadmill, and in one day met the Benedek boy, died saving him, and so perhaps earned his ticket to heaven. Like the thief crucified at Christ's side, who had saved himself by a moment of compassion. And as for himself, it might be through his brief association with the Benedek boy, whom chance or fate or Providence had thrown his way, that . . .

Bah! he said to himself in disgust. Dolt! Blockhead! Was he a priest, or a superstitious fishwife of Bilbao? And was he now concerned with perpetuating his stupid ego, which had got him into this awful tangle?

The truth was, he realized ruefully, the boy had upset him more than he cared to admit. He would miss him. And so would the girl. She was twelve, an impressionable age. An age for puppy love. Poor Nila! Her bursting into tears had been a giveaway. Things would be a bit gloomy around the presbytery for a while.

His voice sonorous, his full, precise lips caressing the rotund syllables, Father Hilarión said in Latin, "Nothing would have delighted me more. First, because it was you who asked me. Second, because when you spoke to me over the telephone, I guessed at once it was the Benedek boy, although you were naturally guarded in your speech. And then, I enjoy the company of youngsters. You know that all the instincts of my earthly being are toward the family life. If not for my vocation, I would have sunk into domesticity like a pig into mud. I would have married some fertile daughter of the lower middle class, and lived '*dans le vrai,*' as your Flaubert says in his corruption of the mother tongue, surrounded by my dozen or so apple-cheeked children, who would be exact copies of myself, fat and coarse and bursting with animal health. That is my nature. And so it would have been a pleasure to me to give this protégé of yours shelter."

Father Hilarión put up a thick, admonishing finger. "But consider the facts. You are in Berroain, a village of some six hundred souls. When a chariot from Gaul, flaunting its foreign markings, enters our humble precincts, it is an event that is discussed at every family hearth. Imagine the gossip if two such vehicles arrive, bearing Gallic priests and a strange boy, and only the priests depart. It would be guessed at once who the boy is. You must not think, because we are removed from the world in our mountain fastness, that our villagers are ignorant of what goes on outside. The Benedek affair is discussed in the cafés. The bishop's announcement was heard here, and commented upon. Unfavorably, I may say, and in great heat. The consensus is that the boy should not be given up, both for his salvation and for our Basque honor. But there is bound to be one righteous citizen, if not more, who would consider it his Christian duty to obey higher ecclesiastical authority. It was for this reason that I advised you to enter the village unobtrusively, and attract as little attention as possible. Alas, old friend, I had forgotten a simple fact: It is Saturday night. All Berroain and environs were in the streets, and saw you enter. At this moment, you may be sure, the village is buzzing with the great event."

Seated in the presbytery front parlor opposite the stout, rosy-cheeked priest, Father Vergara listened in silence. Everything that his friend was telling him he had said to himself during his short ride through Berroain. He should have known better. A village Saturday night was the same in Berroain as in Aitzmendi. The moment he had caught sight of the village, and recognized its humble festive air, he had foreseen exactly what would happen. Strollers in the plaza stopping to stare in open curiosity. Men in the cafés craning their necks, and commenting to each other. The half-dozen boys who gathered about the cars as they came to a halt before the presbytery, gaping at their cassocks and at young Benedek asleep in the back seat. The wait in the parlor, while a boy ran to the sacristy to summon the priest, and the news ran like an electric ripple over the icicled housetops.

He had had no choice, he told himself. He had not picked the day. But the damage was done, they could not stay in Berroain. He had already reached this conclusion when Father Hilarión appeared, panting with haste; he had remained only to greet his friend, and ask his advice.

"Understand," Father Hilarión concluded, "I do not refuse to stand by my commitment. I will do so if you still want me to. But now I would entertain the gravest doubts for the boy's safety."

"What do you suggest?" he asked; he too spoke in Latin, as was their tacit agreement during their rare meetings.

"Cántaras," Father Hilarión said promptly.

Father Vergara stared at him, his mind summoning up the little mountain village he had once visited, little more than a scattering of houses along a narrow road; yet there was a ducal palace there and, huddling in its shadow, a Benedictine monastery. The monastery at Cántaras! Yes, he thought, the perfect hiding place, with its boys' school into which young Benedek could disappear like one more swallow in a flock. But how—?

His friend had leaned forward; he tapped Father Vergara's knee and said, "Dom Pau is there."

"Ah!" he cried in satisfaction. "The very thing!"

Dom Pau! His former professor of theology, who must now be in his seventies. Dom Pau, Catalan, Benedictine, fiery man of justice, with his great eagle's head, his waxen skull gleaming through the uncombed remnants of his wild gray mane, and crammed with more knowledge than it was likely for any man to accumulate in a single lifetime. The explosive, unpredictable master who had quarreled with every living theologian of note, and would no doubt debate with the angels when the time came; who inspired love or hatred, but nothing in between; who would scold him for not having completed his *Peter* and six other books besides, and for having lost contact with the one who had taught him everything he knew; but who would take the boy in, and defend him against all comers, the devil included. If Dom Pau was at Cántaras, he was of course at the monastery. The combination was irresistible. Had he known the whereabouts of his old master, he would have looked no further.

Father Hilarión's round face beamed at him in delight at his reaction, and he returned the smile, his spirits suddenly cheered. "He is not the abbot?" he asked.

"Dom Pau?" the other said in shocked amusement. "Heaven forbid!"

He grinned back. No, that would be too much for any community.

Father Hilarión heaved his portly frame out of the chair. "If you agree, I will call him. It is best that he have notice of your arrival."

"It would be a great favor."

Left alone, Father Vergara remained musing for a moment. He had had a great stroke of luck. The trip to Berroain had not been wasted after all; it had led to something better. In any case, the boy could not have stayed with Hilarión indefinitely. A school was different; the boy had stayed for years in that school in Switzerland, and no one had suspected. If Dom Pau took the boy in. But of course he would! The old *enfant terrible* would crow with joy at the chance to challenge civil authority over such a tempting morsel as a child's soul. But time was pressing. It was eight-fifteen. The road to Cántaras was narrow, and likely to be full of potholes at this time of year. But it would be cleared of snow. Most of the way lay through the valley beyond Berroain, where they could make good time; only at the end would there be a stretch of climbing, to where the village nestled amid triple mountain peaks. Say nine-thirty. If only Dom Pau would let him go quickly! Allow a half-hour before he could plead urgency. That meant a mad race to the border. But with a little luck he could make it by midnight.

He heard Father Hilarión speaking on the telephone in the next room. He had gotten through, then. From the intonation he knew that his friend was speaking Latin. There was no danger of eavesdropping at the village switchboard.

He got up and went to the window. Looking out, he saw the two cars parked in the dimly lit street. The boys were still there, gathered about the coupé. Lisiaga had opened his door, and was sitting with his legs thrust out, talking and gesturing. The boys listened, staring at his face. In the other car Iranzo sat motionless, his body slumped down, his chin buried on his chest. Nothing stirred on the back seat. The boy was still asleep, then. Good.

"It's all settled," Father Hilarión said, entering the room. "Dom Pau will be waiting for you. He says to go around by the side way. You can park there off the street. He'll have someone waiting to let you in."

"Did you tell him who the boy is?"

"He guessed," Father Hilarión said, laughing. "He said to me, What are the last words sung by the assistants before the canon of the mass? Exactly, I said to him. And Matthew xxi, 9. Yes, he said, and don't forget Psalm 117, 26."

"Benedictus qui venit," Father Vergara said slowly. He nodded, pleased; Dom Pau had understood; his mind was razor-sharp still.

At their leave-taking they shook hands, and then, by a common impulse, embraced.

"How is Peter?" Father Hilarión asked.

He made a wry face. "He is not dead, but sleepeth."

"Be prepared," Father Hilarión said, still laughing. "It was the first thing Dom Pau asked me when I mentioned your name."

Iranzo's car would not start. As Father Vergara appeared on the step, accompanied by his friend, Iranzo had begun grinding away at the starter, to no avail. Lisiaga edged out his coupé, backed up, and pushed the other car down the street, as Iranzo shifted from gear to gear. It was useless. In the end, after wasting ten precious minutes, Lisiaga pushed the car to a garage that Hilarión recommended, where the owner, coming from his dinner with his napkin still tucked under his chin, said that he could repair it, but it would take at least an hour. Yes, it was the carburetor. Patience! Father Vergara said to himself, listening to the mechanic's explanation, unintelligible to him. There was still Lisiaga's coupé. They fished out young Benedek from the back seat, and transferred him, still asleep, to the flat shelf at the rear of the coupé, tucking a blanket around his body and under his legs. They would go ahead, Father Vergara told Iranzo; on their way back they would stop by the garage to see how the repair was going. If the car was repaired before they returned, Iranzo was to go back to France. Iranzo did not ask where they were going. He stood beside his disabled car, gloomy, his hands in his jacket pockets, staring after them as they drove off. The boys, who had followed the cars to the garage, waved after them, and Lisiaga waved back.

It was Dom Pau himself who was waiting for them at the side gate of the monastery garden. Scarcely had the car pulled up and stopped than Father Vergara saw the black-clad figure of his old master appear at the inside of the barred portal, thrown into relief by the car lights. The gate opened as Father Vergara sprang out. Dom Pau had changed little in the years he had not seen him; a bit more stooped; his mane, though unruly as ever, a little whiter; but the same proud bearing, the same fierce, impatient eyes and ruffled eagle profile.

"Where is the boy?" he demanded.

"In the car, *pater optime*," he replied, bending forward to kiss the old man's hand. Straightening up, he caught the gleam of tenderness that flitted across those veiled eyes before it disappeared.

"I have much to reproach you with," Dom Pau said. "But I am too angry now. Who is this?"

Lisiaga had got out of the car and was approaching. Father Vergara presented him to Dom Pau, who gave him a brief glance and asked what he did. Abashed, Lisiaga replied that he was in charge of the young Catholic workers' movement in Garonde.

"Doomed," Dom Pau grunted.

Lisiaga opened his mouth and closed it again, glancing at Father Vergara, who gave him a wink. "Angry, Dom Pau?" Father Vergara asked. "Not at me, I hope."

"I am punished in my old age," Dom Pau cried, waving his arms. "I have always been too proud. Now in my declining years the Lord has given me my cross to bear. But I say no more. Come, bring the boy, and I will take you to my abbot."

The abrupt transition was not lost on him. Staring, he asked, "Has he refused?"

It was the wrong word to have chosen. One did not "refuse" a Dom Pau. The old monk started, bristling. "He will not dare! I have not finished with him yet! The man is a child, a visionary. Outside of these walls he knows nothing, he has heard of nothing. But silence, or I will say too much. Come, you will see for yourself."

He thought, He *has* refused, then. Full of sudden misgivings, he went to the car. The boy was still asleep. Should he awake him? No, he decided. If he could sleep through the car-pushing episode at Berroain, and the awkward transfer from one car to the other, he must be utterly exhausted. He kneeled on the seat and, sliding his hands under the boy, lifted him up blanket and all, grunting as the strain wrenched at his back. Swinging his burden over the steering wheel, he eased his way through the door. Once on his feet, he hoisted the boy gently to his shoulder and returned to the gate.

Dom Pau led the way. They crossed a patch of orchard, whose trees were now bare and rimmed with ice; then an open space, roughly furrowed under snow. Beyond was an arcade of rounded arches, unlit and damply cold, through which they gained the unroofed cloister, overshadowed in the moonlight by the tower of the ducal palace that rose darkly beyond the monastery wall to the left. Once in the main building, Dom Pau stopped before a door, rapped, and entered, motioning for them to follow.

It was the abbot's study. In the light of a single bare bulb hanging from the ceiling, Father Vergara saw walls of rough, gray mortared stone, grim and dank as a prison, and a few pieces of shabby furniture lost in the gloom. A monk in Benedictine habit stood by an ancient cupboard, putting something away through the open door; the door creaked as he shut it and turned hesitantly to look at the intruders. The abbot, he thought. Across the room was a plain wooden bench against the wall by a bookcase. He walked to it and put the boy down, settling the bundle of clothing under his head. When he turned around, the abbot was ambling toward him, his chin raised and his face set in that peculiarly vacant expression Father Vergara had always associated with the blind.

Was it possible? he thought in wonder. No, the monk stopped by the bench and stood staring down at the sleeping boy.

For a long time he remained motionless, looking down. At his side Father Vergara was aware of a musty smell, like that of a cellar. Could it be the abbot himself? The man had a singularly unwashed appearance. His face was as gray and bloodless as the walls that surrounded him; he wore glasses filmed with dried perspiration; his habit was stained and mottled with food droppings and streaks of dust. In his harsh, ascetic features, his long, pinched nose, his remote eyes, his trancelike attitude, Father Vergara recognized the truth of Dom Pau's description. This was a visionary, a mystic, one of the simple, holy men of God, so caught up in his beatific vision that he had all but forgotten that he had a body. Why would he refuse? he reflected.

"A pretty child," the abbot observed at last, stirring and turning his head slowly.

Dom Pau stood in the middle of the room. Lisiaga had stopped by the door. Glancing up, Father Vergara saw the warning look the old man shot him, as if to say, Leave this to me.

In mild reproach, his voice hesitant and murmuring, the abbot said, "Dom Pau acted without my instructions. You must take the boy away again."

Father Vergara had the strange feeling that the monk did not really see him, although he had turned toward him in speaking; his eyes had swung past him and back again before they focused vaguely in his general direction. If he was not blind, he was very nearsighted. Or perhaps it was the glasses, which were dirty enough to impede his vision.

Dom Pau stepped forward and said sharply, "You cannot send him away."

"Cannot?" the abbot murmured with a faint smile.

Father Vergara moved unobtrusively to one side as Dom Pau began to argue. The abbot listened patiently, his head lowered, his eyes dreamy and crinkled with amusement. Dom Pau was quoting canon law; he had resumed his classroom manner, which Father Vergara recognized almost with nostalgia—his peripatetic delivery, the seminarists had called it, in a tone in which awe was mixed with laughter. The old theologian charged his ideas as though he were engaged in battle; he paced, head down, his hands clasped behind his back; he pranced, lifting his arms and stamping his feet; he tossed his head, his eyes gleaming, radiating energy and certainty; moved by the force of his own ideas, he raised his voice in abrupt shouts, then stopped dramatically and resumed his normal tone. Father Vergara remembered well how the sheer force and knowledge of the man affected students exposed to him for the first time; how they listened with held breath, pale, ill at ease, touched with shame both for their own abysmal ignorance and for the display of such raw emotion, as if the spectacle were slightly indecent. Out of the corner of his eye he saw Lisiaga staring, transfixed.

Father Vergara listened, marveling anew at Dom Pau's prodigious memory, that let him cite entire pages of the canons verbatim; but at the same time his mind was busy trying to understand the situation facing him. Was it possible that the abbot knew nothing of the Benedek boy? That was the impression he got from the manner of Dom

Pau's explanation; and he remembered the old man's earlier remark, "He knows nothing, he has heard of nothing." There were other impressions as well: that Dom Pau's argument was the continuation of a heated debate that had been going on ever since Hilarión's telephone call, and which his arrival had temporarily interrupted; and that the abbot, for all his unworldly ways, was deliberately baiting Dom Pau with his air of tolerant amusement, and enjoying it. Probably not the first run-in they had had, he thought, remembering Dom Pau's proverbial short temper and impatience with any discipline not his own.

"But it is unnecessary," the abbot said in the middle of a tirade. "The boy is baptized, is he not? Well, then." He moved slowly toward a U-shaped stool and sat down, wagging his head as though there were nothing more to be said.

Dom Pau spread his hands. "If he were not baptized he would not be here. If I understand you, Reverend Father—"

"What is there to understand? It is quite simple. The boy is a Catholic. No power on earth can change that."

"But they will take the boy to Israel and interrupt his Christian education," Dom Pau cried.

"Pooh!" said the abbot.

Dom Pau pulled up short and stared as though he had been struck. In that moment Father Vergara pitied him. He understood now the old man's remark about the cross he bore. But why was the abbot so hard to convince? Canon law was clear and explicit on this point, and Dom Pau had cited it unerringly. This was no Canon Sombre, so pathetically concerned to be at rights with the law. Was it only to spite the older man, the petty tyranny of the absolute ruler of a tiny domain? The abbot's remote smile made him uneasy; he thought of the bullfighter and his small precise arrogantly smooth movements making game of the ferocious animal plunging and snorting in his futile charges.

"Tell him about the letter," Lisiaga whispered in his ear.

"Wait," he whispered back, curious as to the abbot's reasoning.

Dom Pau had cast his eyes to heaven, as if begging for patience. In a smothered voice he said that the family, being Jews, would certainly force the boy to give up his religion and adopt theirs.

"As if God would let that happen!" the abbot said. He began to talk, his eyes roving restlessly about and alighting nowhere, his voice hesitant, his sentences unfinished. Why speak of the beliefs of the family as a religion? There was only one religion, and it was written that not all the wiles of the devil and his cohorts could prevail against it. He didn't see what all the fuss was about. Running and hiding, like children playing a game! Let the law do what it pleased. The boy was indelibly marked with the character of the sacrament, his soul was safe from all worldly harm except his own sin.

This was the gist of the abbot's argument, although because of his strange, broken delivery it was several minutes before Father Vergara understood it. When he had, he found it so incredible that he could only look helplessly at Dom Pau. The abbot might have objected on many grounds: the illegal entry; trouble with the law, both French and Spanish; classes had begun long ago; the irregular transfer from another school; etc., etc. But to come out with something as naïve, as unworldly, as this! Baptism was enough, the abbot was saying, if not in so many words, at least by implication. If he was serious—and there seemed to be no question about it—he was judging the world by the fire of his own ecstatic contemplation of the other realm; once the door was opened by the first sacrament, it was inconceivable to him that anyone who had caught a glimpse of the bliss beyond could yield to all the blandishments of the earth and the devil. And the other sacraments? A Christian education? The guidance, the wisdom, the comforts, the discipline of the Church? Unimportant, the abbot implied. And this was a monk! More, this was the superior of a teaching order into whose hands boys were entrusted for their religious education. The position of the abbot seemed to him to come dangerously close to heresy.

Apparently Dom Pau thought so too, for he inquired, with elaborate sarcasm, "Then, Reverend Father, the Church is unnecessary?"

The abbot raised his eyebrows and murmured that he had not said that. How did Dom Pau arrive at such an unwarranted conclusion? What else? Dom Pau rejoined. All that was needed was to baptize children and turn them loose into the world, with all its pitfalls. There was no danger. God would look after them, without any intermediaries. Calvin's God, of course, because the God whose Son had taken on Himself man's flesh and original sin had said . . . The abbot was vastly amused; his sides heaved in a dry chuckle as he whispered, *"Reductio ad absurdum."* Dom Pau returned to the attack, but Father Vergara had heard enough.

"If I may speak, Reverend Father?"

The abbot seemed surprised, as though he had forgotten his presence in the room, then he nodded.

"There is a letter from Rome concerning this case. It is a categorical order to all Catholics, lay or religious, to do whatever is necessary to keep the Benedek boy from falling into the hands of those who would interrupt his Christian education."

In mild wonder the abbot said, "You have seen this letter?"

It was not a moment for niceties of veracity. Vincent had seen the letter; he had told Lisiaga and Nagorra, and Lisiaga had told him. He could not have been surer if he had read it himself. But he was not going to lie about it.

"I have not seen it myself, but I have spoken to those who have."

He stiffened as he saw a look of doubt cross the abbot's face. A murderous itch communicated itself to the palms of his hands. Would the man dare?

It was Father Lisiaga who, unexpectedly, saved the day. Stepping forward, he handed the abbot a folded sheet of paper into which a seal had been stamped. Father Vergara's anger changed to stupefaction, then to monumental relief. The bishop! he thought. What irony! The bishop had given Lisiaga the letter to convince *him,* Vergara! As if he needed it! But because of that the letter was on hand at this critical moment, when—

The abbot gave in with the same mildness with which he had opposed Dom Pau. If it was an order . . . But the whole thing was silly, his amused smile told them. "You will take charge of this child," he said to Dom Pau, who looked at him in fury and strode from the room.

Father Vergara offered up a short prayer of thanks and, letting his breath out, looked at the boy on the bench. Good-bye, Benedek, he thought. God bless you and keep you. He would come back, see how the boy was doing, reassure him that he was not forgotten—but this was the real parting of the ways. In his mind he saw the boy awakening tomorrow morning in some quarter of this austere monastery, amid monks he had never seen before, and with no inkling as to how he had got there. He had been promised Berroain, and been given Cántaras, and Dom Pau. He would be disturbed, perhaps feel betrayed and abandoned. But the alternative would be to awaken him now and explain, and this he could not bring himself to do.

The abbot was watching him. Lisiaga had already made his farewell, and was putting the letter back into his pocket. He approached the abbot and, making an effort to keep the coldness out of his voice, thanked him for his kindness. The abbot sniffed, and murmured, "It is nothing. One more boy . . ."

Idiot! he thought. He bowed, and joined Dom Pau and Lisiaga in the hall.

"You have no idea," the old man said somberly. "There is nothing to be done with him. It is enough for me to make the most trivial decision—yet I am second in command here. I am surrounded by intrigue. Conspiracy. Factions. But I have sworn that I will not complain. Come, I will accompany you to your car, and you will tell me of your Peter."

Walking alongside Dom Pau, with Lisiaga coming behind, he replied that he expected to complete his research soon; then he would begin the writing. A year, perhaps, or a little more.

The fiery scholar clutched his arm and cried hoarsely, "Those of your generation are all alike, you think too much of the critics. A flock of sparrows!"

His generation or the critics? Father Vergara wondered. But he said nothing, and Dom Pau, his keen profile thrust forward like the prow of a ship, snorted. "Study and meditate, well and good. But I have always preferred to study and fight. Do you know why? Because I learn from my enemies. Nothing drives a little man like malice. Goad a man with criticism—merited criticism, mind you—and he will surpass himself in his research to find flaws in everything you publish. I am proud, yes, but toward men. Toward my work I am humble. I glean from everyone, even my detractors. Thus I make the whole world my collaborators, and the work prospers, to the greater glory of God."

"Flaws?" Father Vergara exclaimed. "In *your* writings?"

Those fierce hooded eyes glanced at him sharply; but Dom Pau seemed pleased. He did not mean publish at any cost and in haste, he went on more gently. No, a man worked in a circle. In his studies he came across a few details that did not fit accepted theories; these were "signposts"; they pointed to a new idea, a better interpretation, a revolutionary concept. With this hypothesis in mind, he broadened the field of his inquiry, looking for either rebuttal or corroboration. Concept, proof; proof, concept. Back and forth, in an ever-tightening circle, until he had established or disproved his thesis. This was the "philosopher's circle": that enveloping mental discipline whose proper application was the greatest test of intellectual integrity he knew of. When a man was sure, he published, and let the sparrows pick at it.

They had reached the gate. At another time Father Vergara would have liked nothing better than to discuss such ideas with his old master; but now he was in an agony to get away. He thought of the long road that lay ahead of him to the border; they would have to stop again in Berroain, to see if the mechanic had repaired Iranzo's car, and, if not, give Iranzo a lift into France; and all before midnight. And it was ten-thirty now. The obstinacy of the abbot had held them up; and now Dom Pau seemed disposed to chat.

He had looked at his watch. Dom Pau stopped, peered at him, and with unexpected generosity said, "But this is not the time. You are in a hurry. You will come back, and I will tell you about my new book. My last book," he said significantly. Father Vergara was about to protest, but the look he received stopped him. "A new *Summa*," Dom Pau said softly. "It will take at least ten years. And those years, I do not have them. But my pupils do." His veined hand rested lightly on Father Vergara's shoulder. "What I leave undone, they will finish for me. But we will talk of this later."

A biting wind had sprung up. Hatless as always, his hair whipping in the wind, Dom Pau embraced him and said, "Do not worry about the boy. The abbot has given in. He will not think about the boy again. Leave him to me. Ha!" he cried, in a sudden cackling laugh, "I will make a little theologian of him!"

Poor Benedek, he thought as he got into the car. An image crossed his mind: the Dom Pau of two decades ago, darting about the classroom, his fists clenched above his head, crying, "Fools! Fools!"; and the stricken seminarists cowering on their seats under the verbal lightning. Dom Pau and young Benedek. Heaven help the child!

Dom Pau remained by the gate, squinting in the wind. As the motor started and the car began to move, he shouted after them, "Finish! There are eleven more apostles!"

"I shall obey you, most excellent master," Father Vergara called back out the window. "Drive like hell," he said grimly to Lisiaga, who grunted and bent forward over the wheel.

It had taken them an hour and twelve minutes to reach Cántaras from Berroain. They made the return trip in fifty-three minutes. They found Iranzo in his car in front of the garage, starting and stopping his motor while the mechanic, who had put on a pair of greasy overalls, bent over it. Lisiaga skidded to a stop beside the car, and called out, "Is it repaired?"

"Yes," Iranzo called back. "It was the carburetor."

"Be ready in a minute," the mechanic said. "I'm giving it a last adjustment."

"Then you don't want a lift?"

"No, you go ahead," Iranzo said. "I'll catch up with you. Did you find a—?" He stopped, glancing at the mechanic, who had bent over the motor again.

"Everything is in order," Father Vergara replied.

With a wave of the hand, Father Lisiaga drove off. The village was dark and the streets deserted. At the highway, Lisiaga gunned his motor and picked up speed. Father Vergara looked at his watch, made a brief mental calculation, and settled back, closing his eyes. If Lisiaga drove as he had from Cántaras to Berroain, they would reach the border on time. But he preferred not to watch while he did it. He had had enough excitement for one day.

"Jews!" Iranzo thought savagely, as he raced down the highway. A good boot in the seat of the pants, that was what they wanted. Trouble wherever they went, and they went everywhere. Like gypsies. There was no satisfying them. Give them a hand, and they'd snatch the arm too. And argue with you about it.

He didn't pretend to know all the ins and outs of the affair. He left that to Father Vergara and the other priests—Lisiaga, Nagorra, Vincent. And all those behind them. The Church. He supposed they knew what they were doing. He did not want to know. The less he knew about it the better. He had helped out only because it was Vergara, the best priest Aitzmendi had ever had, who had asked him. You couldn't refuse a man like that. And what had he been asked to do? Drive a car, that was all. It wasn't like committing a crime, or anything like that.

But for his pains he had got a terrific smack in the face from that brute in the inn, and he still smarted to think of it. For what? For a Jew-boy, who was running away from his own people. And to read all that fuss in the newspapers, you'd think it was something important. He could just see himself riding about Spain with Chamo's corpse in his car, to cover up for them. They had their own country now, didn't they? Well, why didn't they go there, and leave decent Christians in peace? Hitler had knocked off a few of them, and now they felt that the world had to make it up to them.

That carburetor, now. If it had happened at home, he'd have fixed it himself; or gotten Maurice to help him. Maurice would have done it for a drink, a pack of cigarettes, a nothing! But no, it had to happen now, and he was out 800 francs for the job. Because a Jew-boy wanted to cross the mountain.

A wonder that fellow hadn't broken his jaw. If he had closed his fist, he would have. A good thing he was distracted by finding the money. Whose was it, he wondered. Probably Vergara's, it was just like him to do a thing like that. Well, the Church had plenty of money. But he had to work for his, and that 800 francs rankled. Maybe he could get the priest to foot the bill. It was for him that he had done it, after all. Certainly not for that snip of a boy, who hadn't ought to have aroused such a commotion in the first place.

He drove grimly, hunched over the wheel, racing against the clock on the dashboard, whose hands crept inexorably toward midnight. Several times he thought he had caught up with Lisiaga's car, glimps-ing lights ahead of him as he rounded the descending curves of the hills. Lisiaga was going like a demon, however, and he never closed the gap. Once he took a curve too widely, and he went off the road into the piled snow. It took him a precious pair of minutes to back out, swearing to himself.

When he finally approached the border check point, his clock marked five minutes to twelve. There was no sign of the English coupé, which must have got through. The lights were still on in the guard building, and as he drew to a stop at the lowered barrier, two guards carrying flashlights came to his car.

He had his passport ready. He handed it out the window to the nearer guard, who took it, yawning, and asked, "Anything to de-clare?"

He got out of the car to open his trunk, at the same time asking if a car with priests had passed by in the last few minutes.

"Two priests," the guard said, nodding. "They were just ahead of you."

"I suppose I'm the last for tonight," he said.

"Probably. We're closing now. You just made it."

He was about to re-enter his car, holding out his hand for his passport, when a voice called out from the lighted doorway of the building. The guard who had his passport snapped to attention, and marched over to the officer who stood there, his shadow monstrous before him. His hand on the car door, Iranzo saw the guard hand the passport to the other man, who turned toward the light to thumb through it.

Uneasiness darted through him. Don't be silly, he said to himself angrily. How could they know? He waited, eying the barrier in longing. How he wished he were on the other side of it, with all this nonsense behind him, and heading for his bed and a good night's sleep!

The guard was back, empty-handed. His attitude had changed. There was nothing sleepy or good-natured about him as he barked, "Come with me, please."

His heart sinking, Iranzo followed the man's heavy figure into the lighted doorway and into a tiny, cluttered office to the left. The officer he had seen from the car stood before a teletype machine that was chattering busily and thrusting out several thicknesses of rim-perforated paper with noisy jerks. The officer wore captain's insignia; his peaked cap was pushed back on his head, showing thick, black, glistening hair, and his collar was unfastened, as though he had been asleep before the teletype woke him up. Iranzo studied the man's profile, bent over the message he was reading. It was coarse and hard, and bore an expression of sleepy ill-temper. Iranzo let his eyes drop to the pistol butt peeping out of the holster at the man's hip, and noted its dull, worn look as if from much use.

I'll deny everything, he thought, already feeling fear crawling within him.

The captain lifted one booted leg and rested it heavily on a swivel-back chair, which slid under his weight and grated against the desk, as he scratched lazily at his groin. Then he nodded decisively, kicked the chair out of his way, and came up to the railing where Iranzo stood, the guard at his shoulders. His smoky eyes traveled up and down Iranzo and crinkled in an unmistakable sneer. Quailing under the look, which seemed to have hints of violence behind it, Iranzo fastened his eyes on the second button of the man's tunic, and waited.

"All right," the captain said. "Where's the boy?"

Santos! he thought. God help me!

"What boy?" he stammered.

The captain's hand came out and seized him by the front of the windbreaker, shoving him backwards to the guard, who grunted and grasped his shoulders.

"I'm going to ask you once more," the captain said in a bored, deadly voice. "Only once more. And this time you're going to answer." His hand tightened and twisted until Iranzo could feel the hard knuckles against his chest. "Where's the boy?"

"Let me go!" he cried in sudden hysteria. "I've done nothing. You have no right—"

The hand shoved him toward a chair and released him, so that he fell into it. Looking up, involuntary tears starting to his eyes, he saw the captain hitch his holster forward within reach and step toward him with grim purpose in his face. Was he mistaken, or was that pity written in the face of the guard behind him? What would they do to him?

"Don't you touch me!" he shrieked, cowering back. "I was only the driver."

He broke down and wept. Out of shame and humiliation. And rage. Why hadn't they left him out of it?

A Jew-boy!

Aitzmendi was ablaze with lights when the car pulled into the little plaza before the church, and came to a stop on the smooth floor of the handball court. Father Vergara had been dozing ever since the border-crossing; he sat up and rubbed his eyes, looking in wonder at the lights streaming from the windows of the houses. There's been a death, he thought; but whose? The odd thing was that there was not a soul to be seen in the plaza. It was decidedly awkward. They must have been looking for him, it was his duty to be there. And Chamo, up on the mountaintop?

"I'll have to put in an appearance," he said to Lisiaga. "Do you want to come with me? I can put you up at the presbytery afterwards."

Lisiaga shook his head. He had better get back to Garonde, he said; the bishop would be waiting for a report. He accepted Father Vergara's thanks with a nod of the head and a tired little smile; then backed out, turned, and headed down the dark road to the highway. Poor chap, Father Vergara thought, watching the lights disappear in the forest; he had had a rough time of it. Then he sighed, mounted the steps beside the church, and headed around it toward the cemetery. The old woman would tell him what it was all about.

But as he rounded the wall and glanced down the snowy plain dropping down to the river, he stopped short and stared at Chamo's cottage in the distance. The humble farmhouse, in which the old smuggler had lived alone, was lit up like the rest of Aitzmendi; but with a difference. Even at that distance, Father Vergara could see the thin shaft of light that shot upward from the slanting roof, where a hole had been worked into the thatch; and the crowd of shadowy figures moving behind the open door and about the grounds.

He had been right, it was a death. Chamo's. They had brought the old man's body down the mountain, then, and now the entire village was congregated there in mourning.

He set off down the slope. The going was easier than it had been earlier that day, for a path had been beaten by many feet in the snow.

As he approached the cottage, the men clustered in groups about the benches that had been set up outside stopped their conversation and stared at him. They know, he thought, seeing their faces. They came to meet him, their stiff black funeral capes hanging woodenly from their shoulders; they shook his hand silently, pressing hard to show that his secret was safe with them, and escorted him to the door.

The room was full. On one side were the women mourners, some sitting in the chairs that had been brought in to complement Chamo's scanty furniture, the rest standing; they wore the traditional hooded cloaks, their faces screened by heavy veils of lace. The men were on the other side. All turned toward the door as he entered. Those who were seated rose to their feet.

Chamo lay on the kitchen table, which had been brought in and covered with a fine linen mantle. Four candles burned at the corners of the table, casting a flickering light on the old man's face. Father Vergara crossed the room and stood looking down at the body.

The *chenhango,* the "neighbor," was at his side. It was he, bound by the solemn duties of friendship, who had made the hole in the roof, to allow Chamo's soul to escape to its heavenly rest; who, when Chamo's mortal remains crossed the threshold of his home for the last time, would light the handful of straw whose pale smoke, ascending, symbolized the setting free of the soul and whose pinch of ashes represented the dust that was left; who would make the collection for masses for the dead, and act as master of ceremonies at the funeral feast.

"Your blessing, Father," the *chenhango* said, holding out a candle. Solemnly, Father Vergara blessed it, and watched as the man lit it and held it over Chamo's bared breast. Seven drops of liquid wax dropped fatly on the cold flesh, forming a cross.

Rest in peace, old man, he thought.

The *chenhango* had stepped back. Behind him, in the crowd of men, Father Vergara saw Santos, his eyes bloodshot, his face haggard, staring at him. Their eyes met and held; then Santos looked away. Was it he who had brought Chamo down? It didn't matter. Chamo was home; the wheel had come full circle, their mission was accomplished.

It was with a strange sense of exultation that the priest lifted his eyes and in a voice that echoed in the hushed room began to chant the psalm, rich in allegory, so dear to the ancient Scholastics: *"In exitu Israel . . ."* For Chamo, who had passed from the Egypt that was the soul's enslavement to the body into the bliss beyond. For young Benedek, who had escaped from bondage, like his race of old. For his people, who surrounded him, humble sons of the earth who yet walked proudly, slaves to no man, and who would understand . . .

11

❦

THE MEN, dressed in their stiff, immemorial black, stood about the newly dug grave, staring gloomily at the casket that had been set down at its side on broad strips of canvas laid out in rows. According to the custom of Aitzmendi, the women had remained outside the cemetery wall; they wore the hooded cloaks that had been handed down to them through many generations, they bore small wicker baskets containing loaves of bread and lighted candles, and they chanted psalms in a high keening voice as Father Vergara, holding aloft a cross over the casket, offered up the funeral prayer.

Only part of the priest's mind was engaged in his pastoral duty, however. All Aitzmendi had turned out for the funeral; people had come from the far reaches of the Bidassoa valley, from the villages of Spain fronting the border, from French towns as far-flung as Ste. Engrâce, Mauléon, Garonde; Chamo's son, who had quarreled with his father twenty years ago and not seen him since, had come from Bilbao with two carloads of children, uncles, and aunts; even members of Chamo's dead wife's family, who had always referred to the old man as "that savage," were there. In short, everyone that could be expected for a *contrabandier* whose name was already a legend in the Basque country.

Except Iranzo.

Already the night before Father Vergara had wondered at his absence. Iranzo lived in nearby Béhobie. A number of the visitors had come from there to sit out the vigil where the old man lay in state; yet Iranzo had not presented himself at the cottage. Was he still sulking over the blow he had received? Or was it possible that he hadn't made the border on time? But even so, he would surely have crossed Sunday morning.

At suppertime, therefore, Father Vergara had gone to the café, and put through a call to the house of Iranzo's neighbor, for the man himself had no telephone. It was Iranzo's wife, however, who came to speak to him. The young woman, a soft-spoken, timid soul, was alarmed to learn that her husband was not with the priest. No, he had not been home since yesterday, Saturday, when he had left around noontime, saying he had some business to attend to with Father Vergara, and would probably be away until late at night. She had thought—Dear God! she cried in a sudden access of hysteria, what could have happened to him? Father Vergara had reassured her as best he could, but he had been far from easy in his mind when he hung up and returned to the presbytery.

It was now Monday morning, and still Iranzo had not appeared, and by now the priest was thoroughly alarmed. As he prayed he thought of the possibilities. Had Iranzo had an accident while racing for Hendaye and the customs control? Yet if this were so, the police would surely have notified his wife within a few hours. Unless the man had shot off the road at one of the curves over a gorge, and no one had noticed the signs of his fall. Would Saturday's adventure claim still another victim? He was being too gloomy, he decided. When the services were over, he would go to Béhobie. Iranzo would be there, and all would be well. If not—there was no help for it, he would have to go to the police.

The prayer was over. At Father Vergara's signal, the six pallbearers stepped forward, seized the ends of the canvas strips, and lowered the casket into the raw-edged pit. "Peace to your soul!" Father Vergara said, and, bending down, took up a handful of the reddish earth and threw it into the grave. At the dull sound it made, mournful like no other, a burst of lamentation came from the women beyond the cemetery wall. One by one the men stooped and flung handfuls of earth onto the casket.

A boy plucked Father Vergara by the sleeve; it was Pierre, the grocer's boy. His eyes, solemn and frightened, stared at him beseechingly.

"What is it, my boy?" he said, putting his arm around Pierre's shoulders.

For answer Pierre held out a folded piece of paper. Father Vergara opened it, read the few lines they contained, and nodded.

"Where are they?"

"At the edge of the village, Father. They said—"

"I know. Return at once and tell them I will come immediately.

Wait for me there, and say nothing of this to anyone until I come. It's all right, lad," he added in a kindlier tone, seeing the boy's expression. "There's nothing to worry about."

When Pierre had gone, slipping through the crowd, Father Vergara sighed, and circled the grave to Chamo's son, who was standing staring down at the casket, already partially covered by the spadefuls of earth that the gravediggers had begun to heave in. The man was about forty, taller and heavier than his father, but with the same close-cropped bullet head and expressionless black eyes.

"I have been called away," he said. "Don't wait for me for the funeral feast. I'll come later if I can."

The man nodded without taking his eyes from the casket. Father Vergara embraced him wordlessly, and went through the dispersing mourners to the presbytery.

Once in his study he changed quickly, putting over his cassock the thick black coat he saved for formal occasions. Into the pockets of the coat he put his handball and his breviary. Before leaving he surveyed himself for a moment in the mirror. A pair of blue eyes looked back at him, crinkling with amusement. "So clever," he murmured. Who could it have been? he wondered. His mind went back over Saturday's trip: Santos, or any of the others at the inn; the two policemen who had pushed the car in Vera; one of the villagers at Berroain. Someone at Cántaras. It might have been any one of these who had given him away. Or even one of his own villagers, who had caught a glimpse of him and the boy in the first light of day, heading for Chamo's cottage; and guessed the rest. He shrugged. It didn't really make any difference. And he would know soon enough.

He went out the front door, and was passing the café when M. Farrade called to him and came hurrying to the door, holding a newspaper in his hand.

"Monsieur l'abbé!" he cried, waving the paper. "Look at this! Who would have thought it?"

It was the *Garonde Éclair,* which had evidently just arrived. In bold black letters the headline bore the words: "BENEDEK BOY IN SPAIN!" Under it were two subheads: "Priests to Be Arrested" and "Iranzo Spills All." Father Vergara read through the story as M. Farrade sputtered at his ear. The stout innkeeper was excited, and waved his arms as he spoke. The boy had been in the area all the time! he cried. To think that *priests* would do such a thing! And what of the bishop's radio announcement, eh? M. l'abbé was not to think that he, Farrade, was anti-clerical, far from it, but this was a shocking business for men of the cloth to be engaged in. Where was law and order? Respect for the Code? The world they were living in!

The newspaper explained a great deal, but not all. Iranzo's disappearance was accounted for; he had been arrested at the border "as the result of information furnished the Spanish police." Questioned, he had implicated several priests, whose identity was being kept a secret by the police until warrants for their arrest had been issued. Most important of all, the boy's whereabouts were still unknown. Reading this statement, Father Vergara breathed a prayer of gratitude for the breakdown of Iranzo's car in Berroain. Iranzo had given everything away, apparently, but that one thing; and it was because he didn't know. Then it was not from Cántaras that the tip to the police had come, and the boy was safe.

He returned the newspaper to M. Farrade, saying gravely, "You are quite right, it is truly a shocking matter. And now, if you will excuse me—"

M. Farrade's eyes lingered on his coat. He asked guardedly, "You are going somewhere, Monsieur l'abbé?"

"To jail, I think," he replied, nodding and walking off. He crossed the plaza, returning the respectful greetings of the mourners, amused at the little incredulous shock that had leaped into the innkeeper's face as he turned away. In the middle of the plaza he stopped to light a cigarette. The two police officers were waiting by their car a few yards down the road to the highway; they stood unobtrusively behind the car, watching him approach. Father Vergara tossed the match aside, and sauntered toward them, his cigarette dangling from his lips. At the end of the plaza he passed under an open window, where several girls were leaning out, chattering and giggling. They put on serious expressions, and greeted him with a chorus of good mornings. He waved at them gaily, calling out, "Pray for me, *fillettes!*"

The police officers stepped out from behind the car as he came up. The taller of the two said, "Father Vergara?"

"Yes, my son," he replied. "You have a warrant for my arrest?"

The two spoke at once, in apologetic tones. They were only doing their duty. They had come during the funeral. But out of respect—

"I understand. Come, let us go."

They opened the door of the car for him, and he got into the back seat. One of the officers joined him, and the other got behind the wheel. Looking out the window, Father Vergara saw the boy Pierre, half hidden in a doorway, watching him. There were tears streaming down his face. Father Vergara looked over his shoulder. M. Farrade was still standing before the café, the newspaper in his hand, as if petrified. The people in the plaza had turned and were looking at the car, with consternation in their faces. A man let out a shout and shook his fist. Another began to run toward them as the car took off down the road.

12

🏵

MR. PRESIDENT!"
Thibaudet was on his feet. It was his resonant, baritone voice that had run through the vast hall. A faint rustle arose as the other deputies in the amphitheater turned to look at him. In the gallery the visitors leaned forward, staring downward, tense and expectant. Sitting in the front row, Konrad heard their expelled breath behind him, and sensed their hushed excitement. This was what they had come for.

At Konrad's side André David murmured, "At last!"

"The socialist deputy from the Côte-des-Alpes," the president said.

Thibaudet had a sheaf of papers in his hand. He waved them theatrically as he left his seat and walked down the aisle to the tribune, to which he mounted with firm rapid steps that echoed in the great chamber. The short, stocky figure bowed to the president, then turned to the semicircular rows of desks rising before him, and the hundreds of faces fixed on his.

"On Thursday of last week," he said, pushing the microphone aside in disdain, "or March twenty-sixth, to be exact, I made a protest before this venerable Assembly against the decision of the conference of presidents to exclude from the agenda a question that a number of my colleagues and I wished to put to the government. That question was this: 'What measures has the government taken, and what measures does the government contemplate taking, to find the Benedek child and return him to his family, in the shortest possible time?' My protest was not acted upon. The majority did not find it convenient to subject itself to the soul-searching implied in such a question. My demand was voted down."

"And rightly so!" a voice cried somewhere in the Right. Several deputies clapped their hands. From the Left a hiss arose.

Ignoring the interruption, Thibaudet said, "Respected colleagues, this question must be asked, and this debate must be held. I have in hand a document demanding that right, to which are affixed the fifty signatures required by our constitution. I invite the president to rule on the admissibility of my request."

A hum arose from the amphitheater. The president struck once with his gavel and stretched out his hand. Thibaudet handed the paper to the clerk, who gave it to the president. Thibaudet waited at the tribune.

"The chair finds," the president said, after conferring with his counselors, "that there are indeed fifty authentic signatures affixed to this request, and that therefore the constitutional requirement for forcing a debate has been met. The question must now be put before the Assembly as to the date on which this debate will be held. I shall ask for a vote in the usual procedure. All those who wish to fix a date for the discussion of Monsieur Thibaudet's question will please stand up."

At the scuffle of feet and the creaking of chairs that rose up to the visitors' gallery, Konrad leaned forward to the guardrail and looked down. André David did the same, muttering, "Now!" A number of deputies had risen and stood at their desks. Seeing how many they were, Konrad was astonished. After last week's fiasco, in which Thibaudet's demand was outvoted two to one, he had expected little response from the body of deputies; yet it seemed to him that now far more than half of those present were on their feet. Someone to the far Left was staring up at him. Konrad recognized the impassive features of Malletot, Communist deputy from Lyons. The memory of their quarrel came to him, the day he had torn up his card and left the Party. Solidarity! Malletot had shouted. And he had replied, Not with Germany, and walked out. Fourteen years. Malletot's face had got heavy since then. They stared at each other, neither giving any sign of recognition.

At the side of the hall clerks were making the count. They moved quickly. In less than a minute they were reporting to the chief clerk, who made a rapid calculation and handed a slip of paper to the president.

"Those opposed?"

Again the rustle of rising bodies, the count, the delivery of the paper.

"The vote is affirmative by a count of—" the president began; but the rest of his words were drowned out in a roar of jubilation that burst from the Left, followed by a vigorous applause that spread to the gallery, where ushers sprang into action with threatening gestures to enforce quiet. André David clutched Konrad's arm, saying with soft emphasis, "A victory!" The president pounded with his gavel. Thibaudet, chunky, black-haired, beetle-browed, waited calmly at the tribune.

André was right, Konrad thought, leaning back in his seat. The move had caught the Right and Center by surprise. It had been an open secret that Thibaudet was gathering the signatures; but none but the inner circle had known when he would spring it on the Assembly. Today the Socialists and Communists had turned out in full force. Gleefully, upon taking their seats in the gallery, André David had pointed out the many empty places in the Right and Center, and had predicted that Thibaudet's motion would pass.

"You may proceed, sir," the president said, when order had been restored.

"Thank you, sir. I propose that this debate be held the day after tomorrow, Thursday, April second, and—" he held up his hand as a murmur arose, and raised his voice—"and I wish to explain to the honorable ladies and gentlemen here assembled why it is that I insist on so early a date. This matter, which began as a dispute between individuals, a private affair, and then became a case for litigation, dragging itself for years through the courts of France, has now passed out of the field of the judiciary entirely. It is no longer simply a matter of enforcing a court decree. You who hear my voice, members of the highest deliberative and legislative body of our great nation, you who represent the will of our people, cannot fail to realize that the honor and prestige of France are at stake. The Benedek affair has become all things to all men. This child, innocent victim of the explosion of hatred that rocked the world a few short years ago, has become a political football, kicked at will in all directions by those who see in him a pretext to do battle for their own views. He has become a sign of the evil of our time, showing more clearly than anything else the dissensions that rack our country, the stubborn differences among us, our blind hatreds and passions, our mutual distrust. With the second kidnaping of the boy, and the subsequent arrest of the responsible priests and nuns, public opinion has been whipped to a frenzy. Throughout the country committees have sprung up: a committee 'For the Defense of the Faith'; a committee 'Against Excessive Use of Preventive Arrest'; a committee 'For the Protection of the Religious,' etc., etc. In Touville, Marseilles, Garonde, Bordeaux, citizens march in processions, bearing placards protesting the treatment of the clergy as common criminals. You of this Assembly, entering the Palais Bourbon a short while ago, saw on the Place de la Concorde two rival chains of picketers, jeering and taunting each other over the heads of harassed policemen. The peace of the forthcoming municipal elections is threatened; heads will roll when the returns are in. There are even threats of rioting at the polling places. In the Basque country the aroused populace has leaped to the defense of the kidnaping, and links the fate of the Benedek boy with the centuries-old Basque concept of individual liberties. Meetings, harangues from street corners, private conclaves, which begin with concern over a child and end with the shouting of the ancient cry of autonomy for the Basque nation, and the proud announcement of their most cherished principle: 'The individual is more important than the state.' Anarchy, if you please. Obscure threats and rumors fill the market place: certain anti-clerical newspapers will be bombed; the prisons of Touville and Garonde will be stormed and their inmates set free. In Bordeaux a certain ex-minister of Pétain's Vichy cabinet, booted out of public office at the Liberation as an anti-Semite and Nazi collaborationist and branded as ineligible for any government post, has plastered his city with posters, in which he weeps crocodile tears over the maternal sentiments of Mademoiselle Rose, and becomes hysterical over the imminent danger of Israel taking over the government in France; blatant demagoguery of the lowest sort, disguising a naked grab for power, whose purpose is to bring Hitlerism back to France. We are threatened, in brief, with civic violence and even civil war, and all thoughtful Frenchmen, shocked and disturbed, are eying the future with concern. In this alarming state of affairs the judiciary no longer has the power to act. It is the government itself which must take a hand. Awake, National Assembly! These words are scrawled on a poster carried by one of the picketers outside our hall. Yes, I thought, as I entered these august portals an hour ago, Awake, National Assembly! The eyes of all France, and indeed of all the world, are upon you. The situation is intolerable. The boy must be found and returned."

From the Left came a burst of applause, and Thibaudet fell silent, leaning on the podium, his thick shoulders hunched. As the hand-clapping began to die away, voices arose from the Right, dominated by one crying out, "Whose fault is it?" The president pounded for order, his reedy, colorless voice chirping over the microphone, "Gentlemen! Gentlemen!" Among the shouters an impressive figure stood up; a man of at least seventy, his face lean and cold, his brow contemptuous, his hair thick and white.

"Pisquet," André David murmured at his side. Konrad nodded; he had already recognized the shipping magnate of Le Havre.

"Will the honorable gentleman yield the floor?" Pisquet asked with icy politeness.

"No, sir," Thibaudet replied in the same tone. "I will not."

"I had hoped to save time by showing why the question the honorable gentleman wishes to put to the government is unnecessary."

"I too am interested in saving time," Thibaudet said. "It is for that reason that I cannot yield. I am already familiar with the arguments of the honorable gentleman from Le Havre. I have read them in his newspaper. But since I am not so fortunate as to own such a mouthpiece, I am forced to air my views here. And this I shall proceed to do."

Pisquet muttered something and sat down, amid a sudden burst of laughter in his immediate vicinity.

Konrad whispered, "What did he say?"

" 'Mountebank,' I think," André David replied.

The president said mildly that there would be no personalities, please.

Thibaudet stared at the group about Pisquet. "You laugh," he said, "and Rome is burning."

"Good for Thibaudet!" André David said with quiet emphasis, as applause arose from the Left.

"It is precisely of the honorable Monsieur Pisquet's argument that I wish to speak," Thibaudet went on. "But not only his, and that is the point. Throughout our country there are many newspapers like his, all devout, all conformist in their religious thought, all upholding the Catholic ethic. From the pages of these journals in the last days there has arisen the same cry. The words are different, but the sense is everywhere the same: The Catholic Church to the rescue! France, international Jewry, the baffled police—all may now rest easy and devote themselves to more pressing matters, for the hierarchy itself has undertaken to find the Benedek boy, and return him to the control of French justice. Yes, my respected colleagues, the hierarchy has spoken. It has no wish to obstruct justice; not only has it ordered all Catholics to turn in the boy, or to render information leading to his return, it has taken the initiative itself, it has undertaken the search with its own resources. This is what all these newspapers are shouting to the world, in a rare unanimity of voices that suggests a single source; that is, the Church itself."

"But isn't that what you want, Thibaudet? Where's the harm?" It was the deputy Passemain who spoke, rising among the desks of the Center waving a pair of horn-rimmed spectacles.

"Harm?" Thibaudet cried back passionately. "I will tell you where the harm is. I simply don't believe it, that's all. That offer was not made in good faith!"

Cries of protest immediately arose from the Center and Right.

"Sit down!"

"For shame!"

"How dare you, sir!"

"History teaches us," Thibaudet shouted into the turmoil, "that the Church is intransigent in her prerogatives. It teaches us to regard with suspicion any unwonted flexibility in her attitudes. When has the Church retreated from an established position without a struggle to the death? If she has done so here, we have a right to examine her motives. Alas! my friends, these are not always what she says they are! Mother Church, in her wisdom, sometimes moves in devious ways, knowing better than her faithful what is good for them. Let us look at this matter more closely." He held up an outthrust finger, like a schoolmaster. "On February twenty-seventh, Bishop Rebenty of Touville, speaking for himself and for the Primate of France, Cardinal Loriol, archbishop of Avignon, ordered all Catholics to turn the Benedek boy into the hands of the law. All France sighed in relief. The Church had reversed her position! After having supported Mademoiselle Rose in her long battle to keep the boy, the Church had chosen to yield to the law, and to all appearances an ugly struggle between civil and ecclesiastical authority was averted. But what was the result of this surrender? The very next day, the boy, who had been in hiding at the home of the parish priest of the border village Aitzmendi, was removed by this same priest, with the help of others of the cloth, and taken illegally into Spain. By priests, I insist; that is, by those who, more than others, should have been obedient to the dictates of their superiors. Where is good faith here?"

"That's talking!" someone cried to the Left.

"The priests, four of them, were arrested. While refusing to reveal their parts in this drama, they all insist on the same thing: Each one acted in accordance with his individual conscience, none of them had received instructions from their superiors. The bishops concerned, Their Excellencies Reynaud of Garonde, Loriol of Avignon, Rebenty of Touville, maintain the same; they are distressed; the act was contrary to their wishes. How strange, ladies and gentlemen! How strange that the priests of the Catholic Church, not without reason called the most disciplined army in the world, should be so obedient in some matters, so disobedient in others! Where is good faith here?"

"Atheist!" a voice boomed in the back.

"May God forgive you," Thibaudet said simply.

"The fellow is devilishly able," André David said with a grin, as a roar of laughter went up, in which even the Center and Right joined. Konrad nodded.

"These priests," Thibaudet resumed, "yes, and nuns too—these religious, who have acted in defiance of both civil and ecclesiastical authority and are now in prison—have they in reality served their Church so badly? You know who they are. Their numbers vary according to the sources of the report. They are not dozens, as some shocked complaints would have it believed. According to my count, they are eight: Mother Veronica of Touville and Mother Celeste of Marseilles, who hid the boy after the trial; Father Moineau of Marseilles, who signed the false identity card in the name of Luc Casella; Father Cancialotti, also of Marseilles, who obstructed justice by sending the police on a false trail; Father Vincent of St. Ignatius, who arranged the child's escape from the school; Father Nagorra of Garonde, who gave him shelter; and the priests Vergara and Lisiaga, who took him on the death march over the mountain into Spain. Not to mention a number of laymen, with whom we are not concerned at the moment.

"I repeat my question. In spite of the expressed disapproval of their superiors, have they served their Church so badly? Let us not concern ourselves with what is said, claimed, counterclaimed; let us look at the results. Have you not noticed a curious state of affairs in the public opinion of our country? Where before it was the anti-clerical forces who were attacking, and the Catholic newspapers on the defensive, now the opposite is true. For side by side with that other symphony, whose theme may be said to be 'Rest easy, Mother

Church will do the job!' we find another melody, becoming stronger every day, which goes like this: 'Let our religious go!' That this cry represents the opinion of a substantial part of our citizenry there can be no doubt. For our country, in spite of 1789, in spite of its reverence for the law, is basically *croyant*. Our anti-clericalism goes only so far. Up to the doors of the prison, yes, but not beyond. Priests and nuns in jail! the man in the street cries. What next, *mon Dieu!* That these religious have done a criminal act is to such a view beside the point. France is shocked, and the pressures have stalemated each other. And so these religious, these sacrificial goats languishing in their cells, have done their Church a good turn, by swinging the weight of opprobrium to the other side, which has gone too far."

Thibaudet paused and surveyed the sea of faces before him. His words fell like plummets of lead into the silence.

"I ask if this is not what the Church wanted. I ask if the true purpose of recent events was not to confuse the issues, to seek sympathy from the public, to strike dread into the hearts of observers over the extremes of anti-clericalism, and to gain time."

"A lie!" Pisquet was on his feet, brandishing a cane. "How dare you, sir? I refuse to sit here and hear my Church maligned. The Church has pledged herself. It is not for the likes of you—" A hubbub of voices drowned out the rest of his words.

Thibaudet had paled. "Take care, sir," he said in a strangled voice.

The president pounded with his gavel.

"No," Pisquet shouted, the spittle flying from his mouth. "Take care yourself! I need no advice from a godless person like you!"

"Gentlemen, gentlemen," the president cried into the microphone, still pounding with the gavel.

Thibaudet stepped from behind the podium, shaking his fist. "I warn you, sir," he shouted into the rising clamor, "you rely too much on your parliamentary immunity. I will not have my veracity questioned. You will either withdraw the lie, or deal with me!"

Against the background of the gavel and the president's chirping voice, other voices arose.

"For shame!"

"Disgraceful!"

"A duel! A duel!"

"Sergeant-at-arms!"

"To the field of honor!"

"Eat him up, Thibaudet!"

"Coal heaver!" Pisquet shouted back, beside himself. "And what will you use for a weapon, a shovel?"

"And you, what? Your cane?" Thibaudet cried, moving forward and shaking off the hand of the chief clerk, who had descended in alarm to the podium. But the clerk insisted, closing in and speaking in Thibaudet's ear. In the meanwhile, two men in uniform had converged on Pisquet, who turned, bristling, to the one on his right, his cane lifted; then, as the man stopped, sat down abruptly. Thibaudet shot his cuffs, smoothed down his hair, and, reassuring the clerk with a gesture, went back to the podium.

In the ensuing silence, the president, so angry that his voice cracked, warned both men that such behavior would not be tolerated. The next such breach of parliamentary procedure and elementary decorum would be met by an order of exclusion.

"But this is a farce!" Konrad exclaimed, aghast, to André David, who rolled his eyes mockingly sideways and whispered simply, "Legislators!"

At the president's curt nod, Thibaudet faced the audience, his hands outthrust in mute appeal. "I have been insulted and I have been warned," he said. "Very well, I turn the other cheek, godless though I be. What may be said about me I care not. It is not I who am in question here, but the Church."

"No, sir!" Pisquet shouted.

"Monsieur Pisquet," the president said ominously.

Pisquet arose and said, "Mr. President, a question of personal privilege. I am here to serve my God and my country. I refuse to believe that the two are incompatible. I will not sit here and listen to this kind of malice. Let that—that *person* speak of the Benedek affair, if he must. But let him not sully with insult what he is incapable of understanding. I state here and now, categorically, that each time he does so, I shall object."

"And I warn you, sir," the president said, as the tall, white-haired figure sank into his seat, "that any objections you may have must be expressed within the bounds of parliamentary procedure."

A sigh ran through the chamber. There was a tense expectancy in the air. What would happen now? Konrad stared curiously at Pisquet's lean, angry face, then turned to Thibaudet, who said in deliberate provocation, "I was speaking of the Church. And I repudiate with all the force at my command the suggestion that it is not my right to do so. Let the Church speak of paradise for the faithful; this is her province, I will not debate with her. But when the Church places herself in the midst of a human problem, one subject to ordinary experience and common sense, and assures us that black is white, that a thing is both so and not so—"

"I object!" Pisquet shouted, pointing his cane like an accusing finger at Thibaudet.

The president lost his temper. With a great bang of his gavel, he cried out, "You will either be silent, sir, *or take the consequences!*"

Pisquet sniffed audibly, but made no comment.

"The Church claims to be seeking the boy," Thibaudet said as if there had been no interruption, "but, ladies and gentlemen, I am not convinced. I watch the search going on in Spain, and I am not convinced. For what have been the results of this famous search? Has the boy been found? No, he has not. And yet, is it truly such a difficult task, for an authority as powerful, as universal, as awful as that of Mother Church? The boy was taken across the border on the last day of February. His itinerary is known up to the village of Berroain, whose parish priest, with an admirable respect for the law that his French counterparts would have done well to emulate, refused to take the boy in; after which the boy disappeared. Yet a modicum of reason must limit the area of possibility. The car with the boy left Berroain about eight-thirty at night, heading south; the kidnaping priests recrossed the border into France just before midnight, without the boy. Say about three hours of travel time, of which half must have been a retracing of their path. Perhaps less, but not more. Very well. Take a compass, place the point on Berroain, draw a circle at the extreme distance a car could travel on snowbound roads in an hour and a half. The boy is within that circle. These figures are not mine, my respected colleagues, they are those of the police, and accepted as logical by Cardinal Loriol himself. His Eminence announces that he will send a personal emissary to Spain to hunt for the boy. To appease the anti-clericals, who are naturally suspicious, seeing Mother Church's right hand attempting to undo the knot her left hand has tied—"

A snicker arose on the Left and spread to the Center, where it died away. Behind him Konrad heard someone laughing under his breath. In his seat on the floor Pisquet sat in stony disapproval, his thin lips curled.

"To appease the anti-clericals, I say, the cardinal sends, not a priest, but a layman, a Monsieur Lemoine, a social worker, a man of known integrity and training, with a wide investigative background. What happens? Monsieur Lemoine proceeds to the border, where he is beset by a host of reporters; he is photographed at the customs control, he is photographed with his back to France, facing the untracked jungle before him. The world waits. Monsieur Lemoine is at Vera; he is at San Sebastián; he is at Berroain; tirelessly questioning, interviewing, going from village to village within the marked circle. Four days later he is back at the border, where the reporters, who have mounted a permanent vigil there, pounce on him once more. Monsieur Lemoine is mysteriously secretive. He has not found the boy, but his mission was not a failure. He has come across certain clues. He knows that the boy is well taken care of, and is in good health. But there are difficulties. He is not at liberty to say more. He will report to the cardinal, and return to Spain. This time, he announces, he has no doubt but that his efforts will be crowned with success.

"To be brief," Thibaudet said, with a wave of his hand, "Monsieur Lemoine returns to Spain four times. Counting the first trip, five trips in all. As I speak to you, he is preparing to go back again. He is still sure of finding the boy, once certain as yet undefined obstacles are removed. But by now a whole month has gone by since the boy entered the hospitality of our great neighbor nation to the south, and Monsieur Lemoine's optimism now rings a little hollow. I pass over the question of how Monsieur Lemoine knows that the boy is in good health without having seen him, or at least seen those who are holding him, and ask the question that leaps to mind: Why is it taking so long?"

Thibaudet searched the amphitheater as if seeking the answer from the upturned faces.

"Look there," André David said softly in Konrad's ear. He followed his friend's nod, saw the figures slipping quietly into their seats, turned to David, puzzled; then suddenly understood.

"The call is out," André David whispered. "They've sent out the party whips. Ever since Thibaudet began they've been trickling into the hall. If it keeps up, they'll outvote the Socialist bloc."

"Why?" Thibaudet demanded. "Is this such an unreasonable question? Are we liars and godless because we wonder why the Church has not yet done what she herself has promised? What answer does Mother Church give us? Cardinal Loriol is silent; remote in his palace in Avignon, he does not deign to reply. It is the Catholic press that gives us the answer: 'Be patient, dear countrymen; Spain is not France; French law has no jurisdiction there, but can only request cooperation, as equal to equal; Cardinal Loriol cannot order Spanish priests to do anything, they have their own superiors. This is a time for negotiation, for diplomacy, for consultation of international law, etc., etc. In the meanwhile, the Spanish police are looking for the Benedek boy. Sooner or later they are sure to find him.'

"Patience!" Thibaudet said in scorn. "But France is the most patient country in the world. We are willing, no, we are eager to believe in the good faith of our authorities, civil as well as ecclesiastic. All we ask is that words be accompanied by action. We will even believe in Father Noël, provided we have our gifts on Christmas Day. But from Spain there come no gifts. Only promises. The Spanish police will surely find him. They are swarming over the country; they are leaving no stone unturned; they are pursuing hundreds of clues. It is only a question of time. This is what we are told, by a certain newspaper of Le Havre, and others of the same ilk. And we are expected to swallow this without question, and still the voice of conscience and the evidence of our own eyes.

"No, ladies and gentlemen," Thibaudet said thoughtfully, "I for one refuse to be silenced when the facts of the matter cry out for recognition. And the fact is that this supposed Spanish zeal to oblige wears a curiously lifeless aspect. It has no force of moral opinion behind it, it is apathetic and unproductive. The man in the street is indifferent, the Spanish newspapers scarcely mention the subject, and then only as a bizarre *fait divers* of French life; no Spanish priest thunders from the pulpit to denounce this crime against humanity; the authorities are strangely noncommittal, and do not even express indignation over the illegal entry. The bishop of San Sebastián, questioned by reporters, replies that he has absolutely no knowledge of the boy's whereabouts. The bishop of Toledo states categorically, 'The Benedek boy is not in my diocese.' The breadth of such a statement, I may say parenthetically, fills me with admiration; but then the Church is nothing if not absolute. But what of the civil authorities? Have they no weight in Spain? You have already guessed the answer. The governor of the province of Guipúzcoa knows 'nothing of this matter.' The Spanish Red Cross, contacted by the Red Cross of Geneva, reports that it 'has no information.' The Minister of Foreign Affairs in Madrid tells an indiscreet French visitor that he 'must await official French representation on the subject.' Sum total, nothing, *la gran nada*. Nobody knows anything, nobody offers to help, nobody takes sides, one way or the other. Only the police hunt goes on, without result. Alas, my friends, I find it hard to believe in this police hunt. Is it too much to speak of a conspiracy of silence? Is it too cynical to suggest that the word has gone out, from what source I will not allow myself to speculate on, not to search with too much zeal? To bustle about and find nothing? To hunt, in other words, everywhere but the right place?"

M. Labadie, Socialist, Lyons, called out, "Whisper 'Down with Franco!' and see if they'd find you!"

"Monsieur Lemoine," Thibaudet said, with an approving smile in Labadie's direction, "speaks of hidden difficulties. We are told that the Spanish clergy is independent of French ecclesiastical authority. But, my friends, the Church is not a kingdom, nor a federation of sovereign powers; it is an empire. Does the Church want the Benedek boy returned to the law and his family? Does she really and truly want this, without equivocation, conditions or reservations? I, the humblest and most erring of her sons, will tell her how to do this. Let the Holy Father speak! Let the Holy Father say, to Spain as well as to France, 'Give up the boy!' Can anyone have any doubt as to the result? I assure you that all these 'difficulties,' this willfulness of the Spanish clergy, would disappear like a snowflake in summer, and the boy would be returned within twenty-four hours. But no, not a sign, not a word from the Holy See! Rome is shrouded in impenetrable silence. Rome, like the authorities in Spain, knows nothing, has heard nothing, says nothing."

Someone to the Right began a heavy, insistent pounding on his desk. A clamor of protest arose from the Left.

"Order! Order!"

"Let him speak!"

"Exclusion, Mr. President!"

They were answered hotly from the Right, where several deputies had risen to their feet. Others rose on the Left, and traded insults, shaking their fists over the heads of those who had remained seated.

"Thibaudet! Thibaudet!" A chant arose on the Left, in time to the president's gavel.

"Mr. President! Mr. President! Point of order!" The voice came from the Center; it rose high above the others, and echoed in the gallery. Konrad tried to distinguish the speaker, but in the commotion below him could not until the man stepped out into the aisle, and he recognized the portly figure of Georges Romansch, former Resistance hero and one of Bidault's lieutenants in the founding of the MRP party. Romansch had removed his glasses, and held them high in the air, as he called out over and over, "Point of order!" But the Left had become obstreperous. At each of Romansch's demands, a chorus replied, "Thibaudet!"

The president's voice crackled over the loudspeakers, in vain.

"Point of order!"

"Thibaudet!"

It was Thibaudet himself who finally broke the impasse. Spreading his hands in mute appeal, and staring reproachfully at his allies, he succeeded in arousing a stream of hisses, which finally prevailed. The president tossed the gavel wearily to the table and shook his head. Konrad pitied him in that moment.

Romansch was smiling broadly. He had always been an admirer of the lucid rhetoric of the Socialist deputy from the Côtes-des-Alpes, he said; more, he had always admired the man, whom he was pleased to call his friend. He hoped the feeling was mutual.

Oh, but it was! Thibaudet assured him. More—he hoped that all present were his friends.

"Then the honorable gentleman from Touville will not misunderstand if I ask a question," Romansch said. "Is this the debate that Monsieur Thibaudet has demanded, or is it, as he announced, merely an explanation of the urgency of the debate?"

"Bravo!" someone cried. The Right burst into applause.

"Thibaudet!" the Left chanted.

The president spoke. He had been about to ask the same thing, he said. If M. Thibaudet—

"I will be brief," Thibaudet said.

"He had better be," André David whispered. Glancing at him, Konrad saw that his face was worried. He looked down at the floor, and saw that many of the empty seats had been filled.

"No, my *friend,*" Thibaudet said with sarcastic emphasis to Romansch, "this is not the debate. I am giving reasons why the debate should be held at the earliest possible moment, that is, at the next meeting of the Assembly, the day after tomorrow. In a moment I shall have done. There remains only to draw the conclusion from my previous remarks. And that conclusion is inescapable. We are not children, we are men of the world, we can recognize a double game when we see it. The Church is stalling for time. On the one hand, she makes a great public show of seeking the boy, all the while urging patience upon us; and on the other does not take the one step that would beyond question ensure the success of the quest. Why?" he demanded. "What is behind it all? The truth is simple, and I will tell it to you simply. It is this. The Church has absolutely no intention of returning the Benedek boy, now or ever. Ever!" he shouted into the murmur that arose. "This is her real position! All the rest is subterfuge to lull us asleep, to quiet our just indignation and our criticism. And I will give you my final bit of proof. To do so I must tell you a story. A brief little fable, both incredible and true, that constitutes an ironical footnote to the times in which we live."

Konrad exchanged a meaningful glance with André David. Here it comes, he thought, sliding down in his seat and resting his chin on his chest.

"My story," Thibaudet said, "begins a long time ago. In the year 1492. In that year the Catholic majesties of Spain, in their wisdom, expelled the Jews from Spain. In one small Spanish community called Villarcos, not far from the French border, the Jewish congregation, before setting out on their forced pilgrimage, exacted a promise from the village authorities to respect their graveyard in perpetuity. The promise was given and recorded in the village archives. The Jews left. Their immediate goal was Algiers, but they did not stay there. After a few years they embarked for the east, where they disappeared. In the meanwhile, Villarcos was growing. It engulfed the old Jewish cemetery, which formerly lay outside the village walls. Today that cemetery lies in the very heart of the city Villarcos has become; the headstones are all but obliterated, it is filled with weeds —but its integrity is still respected by the civic authorities, in accordance with the original promise.

"Strange, the Spanish sense of honor," Thibaudet went on. "Strange, and admirable. But what's to come is stranger still. In a recent meeting of the Villarcos city council, it was decided that the situation could no longer continue. Communications, traffic, progress were strangled by this blighted area in the city's center. Yet no one suggested that the city simply take over the land with no more ado. The promise was sacred. After much debate it was decided that only the Jews themselves could release Villarcos from the promise made more than four centuries before. But which Jews? Those of Villarcos had disappeared; if they left descendants, no one knew where they were. Well, then, the authorities concluded, let us ask the nearest Jewish community to release the cemetery in the name of all their brethren."

Thibaudet stopped. The vast hall was silent. The deputies sat unmoving, their faces intent. Like children, listening to a fairy tale, Konrad thought.

"Alas," Thibaudet said. "No such communities exist in Spain. The nearest Jewish congregation lies across the French border, in the city of Garonde. And that is why the tale of Villarcos enters the Benedek affair, and why I am telling it to you today. But I must be brief. The city council of Villarcos sent a delegation to Garonde, where the Jewish congregation met to hear their request. Release us from our promise, the council spokesman said, and the streets we shall build through the old cemetery will be named after the Jews of Villarcos sent into exile long ago. The leader of the congregation—Garonde has no rabbi at present—in turn asked for a week in which to consider the reply. The next day the Jewish congregation of Garonde sent a delegation of their own, not to Villarcos, but to Touville. And there they sought out a man known by name at least to all of you, the representative of the family of the Benedek boy, Monsieur Louis Konrad. They told him the story I have told you, and told him of their tentative decision. They would grant the permission requested by the authorities of Villarcos, they said, but they would ask a price for it. That price was to be the return of the Benedek boy. Did they have Monsieur Konrad's permission to offer to make the exchange?"

A gasp of comprehension ran through the hall, and a murmur arose. A number of faces in the fan-shaped body of delegates turned upwards, and fixed themselves on Konrad. Behind him there was a rustle of bodies, and he felt eyes on the back of his head. He had been spotted, he knew; even in entering the portals of the Palais Bourbon, and waiting in line to be admitted to the visitors' gallery, he had caught knowing glances of recognition among those about him. The newspapers, he thought ruefully. His ugly death's-head was familiar to all France. He slid still lower in his seat.

"Monsieur Konrad gave his permission," Thibaudet continued, "and the Jewish delegation from Garonde went to Villarcos. There they communicated their decision to the mayor of the city. The mayor was most disturbed; he had expected the permission to be granted as a matter of course. He too demanded a week, 'to take advice,' he said. A week later the delegation from Garonde was back in Villarcos. And there they were met by an adamant refusal from the mayor. In the course of their discussion, which grew quite heated, the mayor said some strange things. 'The Jews were ungrateful,' he said; they were 'stirring up all this fuss over a single boy,' while it was to the French Catholics, for the most part, that the French Jews who were still alive owed their existence. When one of the delegation asked in ill-humor whether the surviving Jews of the world should issue a public statement of thanks to all Christians for not having killed them too, the mayor shouted that it was not his business what they did, and that the Benedek boy was not his business either. He didn't know where the boy was, he said. And the authorities he had consulted had told him to keep his hands off it. There was nothing more to be said. The delegation, silent and angry, prepared to leave. In parting, the mayor said—and these, ladies and gentlemen, are his exact words, written down immediately after the meeting by the leader of the delegation—the mayor said, 'Come now, there must be some other basis for negotiation. But as for the boy' "—Thibaudet raised his voice to a shout, and punctuated each word with a jab of his finger—" *'but as for the boy, that is impossible, he will never be returned. I have it on the highest authority.'* "

A stunned silence greeted these words, broken by a great whack as Pisquet struck his desk with his cane and struggled to his feet, roaring. "A lie! A brazen invention! I demand that the members of that delegation be questioned under oath! And you, sir, are a scoundrel, knowing full well—"

"A lie, yes!" Thibaudet shouted back, surging forward and almost toppling the podium, "A lie by the Church!"

"Miserable wretch!" Pisquet screamed. "Worm! Get out of my sight, or by God—"

In an instant disorder swept over the amphitheater like a wave. A number of the deputies crowded around Pisquet, attempting to pacify him; while some of the deputies to the Left pushed their way into the Center and shook their fists at the knot of arguing and gesticulating men, calling out insults.

"Puppet of Rome!"

"Fanatic!"

"Nazi!"

Where the two circles met, pushing and shoving began. The whole Assembly was standing now, some bellowing arguments, and others, shocked, crying scandal. The roar arose like a great sea, echoing from the ceiling. Konrad, in vast astonishment, gazed at the surging mass of bodies below him until a movement of André David made him turn and look behind him. In the last row of the gallery an altercation had arisen; spectators, alarmed, were scrambling out of the way, while ushers pushed themselves among them to where a cluster of three or four men, on their feet and striking at each other, seemed at the point of toppling to the seats below. There was no telling what the fight was about. Their voices could not be heard over the general clamor. In an instant the ushers had pushed the entire group bodily into the aisle and out the door. Vaguely, over the sea of noise, Konrad could hear the hammering of the gavel, but he missed the order that must have been issued; for, turning around again and looking down, he saw that several men in uniform had closed in on Pisquet, who struck at one viciously with his cane and missed. Then the deputies surged forward, hiding the guards and Pisquet from view. For a few moments their bodies made indistinct swaying movements, as though impelled by some power outside themselves. The knot broke and scattered, and Konrad saw Pisquet's white shock of hair, considerably mussed, move up the aisle. Guards were carrying him, his elbows pinned to his sides.

Once Pisquet was put out, voices began to cry for order. Some of the deputies sat down, but the shouting continued. The president, pale and shaken, spoke into the microphone. Konrad caught only the word "exclusion," which aroused a great roar of anger from the Right. He gathered that Pisquet had been put out for the statutory fortnight. When the voices began to die away, the stamping of feet began. The president waved his arms, angrily scolding and pleading. Konrad thought his voice sounded hysterical. Thibaudet began to speak; those of the Right stamped harder than ever. Thibaudet grabbed his microphone and yelled into it. His voice, powerful enough to fill the hall without artificial aid, crashed through the loudspeakers, and set Konrad's eardrums to vibrating painfully. But his words came through, rising triumphantly over the thud of heels pounding in slow, insistent rhythm.

"The boy is still missing," Thibaudet yelled. "Our police are paralyzed. French law and justice have been defied and held up as a laughingstock throughout the world. Because of a crime committed by the Church, we must endure civil disorder and threats of violence, anarchy, and civil war. We are mocked by the very perpetrators of the crime, and made the victims of a deliberate and cynical hoax. Who is the aggressor? The Church! Who has lied and lied on every hand, forcing the lie down our throats through its fanatic press? The Church! Who is responsible for the rioting and violence? The Church! I say to you, to France, to the world, that it is time that we awaken and put a stop to this—this *blackmail!* This is an insidious grab for power. Who is it that governs our beloved country? Is it the people? Or the Church? I say to you, There is but one power in France: the power of the people, expressed in its law and civic principles. The Church has not learned its lesson from history! Then down with it! Down with the Church! The Church has no place in France, and France has no need of her!"

The rest of Thibaudet's words merged unintelligibly into the great yell of outrage that burst from the Right. Like a man speaking behind glass, Thibaudet continued for a few moments, his mouth wagging, his arms thrust over his head. His face had become purple with wrath and vehemence; the cords stood out on his bull-like neck. He seemed to be at the verge of an apoplectic stroke. Yet not a word could be heard. Finally, with a shake of his fist, and a jerky bow to the president, Thibaudet stepped down from the podium. The uproar increased in intensity as the entire Left arose and pushed forward. Dozens of arms reached for him, patting him on the back, embracing him, lifting him up; until Thibaudet, perspiring, protesting, was carried in triumph to his seat.

Konrad took a deep breath, and looked at André David, who shook his head and shouted in Konrad's ear that in all his life he had never witnessed a more disgraceful scene. So much the better, Konrad shouted back. France would have to sit up and take notice. This was not the man Konrad creating a disturbance; this was the National Assembly! Now, if the government would take up the question, the scandal would be even greater.

With Thibaudet out of the way, order was restored quickly. The president made himself heard. His voice hoarse and dispirited, he said that any further outbreak would be followed by the immediate adjournment of the session. When he had finished, a dozen deputies leaped to their feet. The president recognized M. Desclers, on behalf of the Ministry of Justice.

M. Desclers made his way to the podium, and waited until the Assembly was quiet. His face stern and impassive, he spoke in a dry tone. He congratulated the deputy from the Côte-des-Alpes for his moving appeal on behalf of the boy and his family. He too was moved, he said. Who would not be moved to contemplate the spectacle of human suffering involved in this struggle for the possession of a child? But the Ministry of Justice must limit itself to the juridical aspect of the case, and nothing else.

From the Left came a loud outcry. Desclers waited patiently until it had died away.

"I will not comment on the previous speaker's remarks on the Church," he said. "It is not my place to do so, nor that of the Ministry of Justice. The Keeper of the Seals is sworn to uphold and enforce the law. It is this that concerns him, and not what may or may not be in the minds of certain of the Church hierarchy. And the law is explicit. A decree has been handed down by an Appeals Court. That decree appoints the paternal aunt the child's guardian. We are in France. There is no other solution than to submit to a decision of justice."

This time the Left applauded, and someone cried, "That's better!"

"A woman who attempted to resist the court decree has been arrested. The child, who was located at a confessional school in Garonde, was removed and hidden by a group of priests acting in conspiracy; they too have been arrested. So has the mother superior of a certain conventual order, who seems to have been the moving spirit behind the act, and along with her a number of other nuns, priests, and laymen.

"I ask, therefore, who can reproach the police or the courts of law with failure to do their duty? Who can accuse them of laxness? Everything within their province that could be done has been done.

"Monsieur Thibaudet has spoken of civic disorder and threats of violence, in connection with the movement that has sprung up in our country, demanding release of the imprisoned religious on provisional liberty. I do not minimize the dangers inherent in this movement. It has even spread to other countries, and the Keeper of the Seals has received a number of opinions from foreign observers making the same demand. It is not too much to speak of an international scandal in this respect. In reply, let me say two things: First, any act of disorder or violence within our borders will be met by our agencies of law enforcement in accordance with our Codes; and second, the pressures for provisional liberty, both internal and external, will have no effect on the decision of the Ministry of Justice. The question of provisional liberty is a complex one, which the Ministry still has under advisement. If provisional liberty is granted to any or all of those involved in this crime, it will be done in strict accordance with the law and not as the result of any extralegal influence. Anything else is unthinkable.

"Finally, let me remind you that the legal process is not yet completed. The matter has been referred to the Court of Cassation, on two separate counts: one, the decision of the Appeals Court of July 1952, conferring guardianship upon the aunt; and two, the question of jurisdiction, arising from the claim of incompetence of the Appeals Court in January 1953. Yet it is proposed to question the government. It is a bad precedent to bring judicial matters before the tribune."

The Right applauded. Catcalls of protest came from the Left.

"In what way, I ask you," Desclers pursued, "could questioning the government modify the course of justice? We have here no political problem which pits one philosophical idea against another, but rather a matter which belongs exclusively to the judicial power. This Assembly should respect the separation of powers which is an inalienable part of our French heritage, and should vote to table Monsieur Thibaudet's demand indefinitely."

M. Desclers stepped down amid applause from the Right, and the cry, "Vote! Let's vote!"

With a sinking feeling Konrad noted that it was from the Right that the cry came, and that scarcely an empty desk could be seen.

"All those in favor . . ." the president began.

In a few minutes it was over. Thibaudet's motion was defeated by a vote of 390 to 227. The proposed debate was tabled *sine die*.

He had not really expected the motion to pass. But for a moment there, while Thibaudet was saying all the things that had lain like a stone on his heart for the past month, he had had an irrational surge of hope. That hope was gone. He looked down at his hands and thrust them into his pockets. What would he do now?

"Oh well," André David said, to cheer him up, "perhaps it's for the best. At least Thibaudet got his argument in before the motion was tabled. This way it'll get in the newspapers."

Konrad said nothing.

13

❧

THE CAPTION stared up at him. The newspaper was *Le Monde,* dated May 7, 1953, and the lead article bore over it the words "The Benedek Affair" in heavy black letters. The subheading read: "The Civil Chamber of the Court of Cassation, Rejecting the Appeal of Mlle Rose, Confirms the Decision of the Touville Appeals Court Making Mme Lindner the Child's Guardian."

The train had begun to move. Father Vergara was still breathless. Two months of prison had cut his wind; and he had had to run for it to make the station on time. Fortunately, Canon Blevitz had had his ticket for him, but even so he was the last through the gates, which clanged behind him as the whistle blew. But he had risked the few seconds necessary to pick up a newspaper at the station entrance. Now, as the train shunted its way through the maze of tracks of the Garonde yard, he let the paper fall to his knees and looked out the window. The compartment was full. The opposite bench was taken by a middle-aged couple, farmers by the look of them, and a sullen boy of about ten. On his own bench he sat by the door, next to a stolid peasant woman who had placed her hamper on the seat beside her and had reluctantly removed it on his arrival, setting it on the floor at her feet. An old woman sat dozing by the window. The train began to pick up speed. The last buildings of the city yielded to farmhouses set amid green fields and orchards, and then the rolling, wooded countryside heavy with the vegetation of late spring.

He had known that the case was coming up for trial. His lawyer had told him, during one of his visits to the prison. There had been a near riot at the National Assembly, Maître Irizarry had said; and because of that, and fearing civil violence, the Ministry of Justice had moved the Rose appeal up on the calendar. It had been heard yesterday. This was the decision, then. Mlle Rose had lost, finally, irrevocably lost.

He picked up the newspaper again and began to read. The text of the decision was couched in the multiple "whereases" and "therefores" of finicky legal jargon, but the sense was clear. Mlle Rose had attacked the Appeals Court judgment on various grounds: that her provisional guardianship, by virtue of the ordinance of April 20, 1945, could be ended only by the return of one or both of the parents, and not by a declaration of their decease; that the exclusion from the Family Council of December 1950, of M. Houdy, "repository of the last wishes of Dr. Benedek," tainted that Council with irregularity and fraud; and that the father had wanted his son to be French, and not to be sent to a foreign country. The Court of Cassation rejected all of these arguments, saying that the guardianship under the law of April 20, 1945, was expressly provisional, and must come to an end, whether by the parents' return or, in the absence of any ruling to the contrary, decease; that Mlle Rose herself had not included M. Houdy in the first two Councils, and that between February 1944, when the parents were arrested and the child entered the care of Mlle Rose, and February 1949, when M. Houdy for the first time became a member of one of the Councils, said M. Houdy had showed not the slightest sign of solicitude for the boy over whom he was now so belatedly concerned; and that if at the time of their arrest, the child's parents had not wanted him entrusted to Jews, this decision was obviously the outcome of the racial persecutions of the moment and was motivated by reasons of safety, and nothing in the behavior of Dr. Benedek or in his relations with his family could be construed as implying he did not want his son entrusted to his sister.

"Therefore," the Court of Cassation concluded, "Mlle Rose's appeal is rejected, and she is required to pay a fine of 7000 francs to the Public Treasury, an indemnity of 3000 francs to the defendant, and costs amounting to 5000 francs."

All very proper, Father Vergara decided. He had had little doubt that it would end like this, and was sure that the venerable and learned judges of the court had acted in the truest spirit of the law. So had Pontius Pilate.

But all of that was academic. Benedek was still in Spain, still safely hidden, and the courts could hand down all the judgments they wanted, they were meaningless unless the boy was in their power. And this was not likely to happen, Lisiaga had assured him one day in the prison courtyard, as they were taking their daily walk, and the attention of the guards was momentarily distracted. Canon Blevitz had crossed over to Spain, bearing a personal message from Bishop Reynaud to a certain bishop on the other side, Lisiaga had whispered; as a result, pressure had been brought to bear on a high civil authority, who in turn gave an order to the ranking police officer of the province. No, Benedek was safe in Cántaras, safer now than at the time of his arrival, when the news of the so-called death march burst upon the world, and any new boy in a school had to be the object of suspicion. The judgment of the Court of Cassation in itself meant nothing.

Yet Father Vergara frowned as he gazed out the window at the rich, green prospects of the land he loved, and his heart was heavy. In his mind one doubt had given way to another. The first had been this: Why had he been released from prison? There had been no general amnesty; no one else had been let go, not Mlle Rose, nor Mother Veronica, nor—more significantly—any of those who had been engaged with him in the same venture, Nagorra, Vincent, Lisiaga; why Vergara? The civil party—the aunt, the man Konrad, their battery of lawyers—had relented in his case alone, had granted him alone the provisional liberty all of them had been clamoring for these months past. It was a trap, he had decided: he was to be the pilot fish that led the shark to its prey. They would trail him, observe his contacts, tap M. Farrade's telephone, etc., etc. And did they really believe, he had wondered, that he would not see what they were up to? Or think they could follow him over Choltococagna if he decided to give them the slip and visit the boy?

This first suspicion had not lasted long; only up to the gate of the prison, where he had found Canon Blevitz waiting for him, with the urgent summons from Cardinal Loriol in Avignon. Even as they hurried to the station, Father Vergara was examining the implications of it. His release had been unexpected, without previous announcement, kept secret from the press and the public. Yet the cardinal had known of it. Had he perhaps been behind it in the first place? Then it was not a trap. But if not, what was it? A deal? Konrad and the cardinal? Impossible!

Yet the coincidence was too remarkable. Yesterday the Court of Cassation had pronounced; today he was released from prison.

There had to be some connection between the two. Had the cardinal decided to give up the boy? No, he said to himself, dismissing the thought; the Church could not do this. Benedek might be discovered, betrayed, stolen away from Cántaras; but the Church could not give him up. He had believed it once, at the time of the radio broadcast. He would not make that mistake again.

Then why had the cardinal summoned him?

To tranquilize his thoughts, he picked up the newspaper again. He found the entire third page dedicated to the repercussions aroused by the Cassation decision. Mlle Rose, one article informed him, had received the news very badly; she had suffered a relapse, and was now in a state of shock. Mother Veronica, on the other hand, was seemingly unaffected by it; the prison authorities, questioned, said that her daily routine, which included many hours devoted to prayer, had suffered no alteration. A reporter named Villein had interviewed M. Konrad, whose opinion, quoted in the caption, read, "No Alternative but Surrender." The court decision, M. Konrad said, placed the issue squarely before the conscience of France. The highest voice of justice had pronounced. It was up to France to decide. Church or State? The two colossi had met head-on, and one of the two had to back down. Which must it be? The Church, said M. Konrad. Another reporter had set up a microphone on the Champs-Elysées, and gathered opinions of the man in the street. Of twenty-three questioned, eight were in complete agreement with the court decision, six were against it, five had doubts (one of them suggesting facetiously that the boy be cut in half), three had bolted as soon as they realized what they were being asked (one of them muttering, "It's as much as my job is worth"); and one, a South African who had arrived in France only that day, had not heard of the case. Strangely, of those in favor of the decision, one was a priest, and of those against, one was a Jew, who had said cryptically, "That's all we need!"

Foreign opinion was still scant, but what there was of it was unanimous in approval. Already editorials had blossomed in newspapers in London, Stockholm, and Munich, expressing satisfaction and wondering why it had taken so long. An anonymous informant in Tel Aviv had telephoned a compatriot in Athens, saying that the announcement had been met in Israel by dancing in the street. The Congregation of New York State Rabbis had telegraphed congratulations to the First President of the Court of Cassation, thanking him in the name of "the Jews of America." The reporter who had gleaned these bits of information fully expected this trickle to become a flood in the next days, when world reaction had had time to express itself.

The most surprising article was one boxed in by lines at the bottom of the page, which stated that Father Vergara, the "ringleader of the kidnaping priests," had clutched the bars of his cell in rage on learning the news, and had cried out, "And this is justice!" Father Vergara stared at these words in mild astonishment. How true were the other reports? he wondered.

"The boy must be returned," Cardinal Loriol said.

Under the impact of these terrible words, Father Vergara felt the blood drain from his face. It was true, then. The premonition that had tormented him during the long ride to Avignon, which he had refused to recognize, and dismissed time and again, had not been unfounded. The Church was backing down, and the cardinal had summoned him to tell him so.

There had been no preliminaries. Upon arrival at the palace, Father Vergara had been taken directly to the Primate's study, where Loriol was waiting for him; he had kissed the ring, and taken the seat pointed out to him. Quietly, yet in a voice that admitted of no appeal, the cardinal had said the words that were still ringing in Father Vergara's ears.

"No," he said.

"There is no choice."

"No," he said again.

Cardinal Loriol sat in a massive black and gilt thronelike chair. He wore his full cardinal's regalia; in his long, blunt fingers he held the enameled cross that hung from a silver chain about his neck. The aura of authority rested on him like an accustomed mantle; yet the searching eyes that bored into the priest's were veined and weary, and the broad, once fleshly face had sunken in on itself, leaving it a gray, ravaged, bitter mask. He was large, and had been portly; now, though he sat in uncompromising rigidity, he seemed almost frail.

A long silence had shaped itself between them. "You are rebellious," the cardinal said at length. "Nor is this the first time. When you took the child over the mountain, you had already heard the radio broadcast. You chose to disregard it. At that stage you were right. I would have done the same myself. But now you are wrong."

Father Vergara said nothing. The cardinal's eyes bored into his.

He held the gaze steadily, his head high, waiting.

"Rebellious," the cardinal repeated. "And proud. I have watched you for a long time. The yoke is not easy for you. During the Occupation I thanked God for men like you, whose consciences could not bow under a vicious racial law, and who saved lives at the risk of their own. That was a time for rebellion. But there is also a time for obedience. Do not imagine, Father, that I will tolerate defiance. The decision is made. You must realize at what a cost it has come, yet you refuse to accept it. Why?"

"If your decision is made," Father Vergara retorted, "nothing I can say will matter. Yet surely you did not summon me from Garonde merely to tell me this."

"No. I have my reasons. You will soon learn them. But first I will listen to you." The cardinal leaned forward and spoke with quiet force. "I may be wrong, and you may speak from greater wisdom. It is not too late. Give me one reason, Father—one substantial reason why this boy should not be given up to his family—one reason I have not taken into account, and I will reconsider. I promise you this. Speak."

"Your Eminence," Father Vergara said, and stopped. Beyond the cardinal's chair, a window glowed with the bright light of late morning. A branch of oleander, with its lancelike leaves and pale rose blossoms, rubbed against the pane with a faint whispering sound. Spring, he thought. The forces of life had stirred deep in the earth, and had sprung into fruition in a riot of shoots and leaves and flowers reaching heavenward like a hymn of praise to their Creator. A time of promise, a time for living. And he had to find the words that would save a child from destruction. And not only the child, he realized at that moment in a flash of clarity. It was his own fate that was being decided as well. One depended on the other, for everything he lived for and hoped to be was bound up in this decision. He was committed, beyond his power to withdraw. And it was up to him to find the eloquence, the force, to sway a mind wilier, more experienced, farther-seeing than his. The Primate of France! Prince of the Church, who had arrayed himself in the scarlet vestments of his power in order to pronounce his death sentence. Father Vergara took pitiless stock of himself. God had given him his huge frame, his hard flesh pulsing with strength, the vital energies that coursed through his body, his mighty hands; all this was useless now. Take back Your gifts, he prayed, and give me instead the words I need.

He lifted his head and spoke. Yes, he said, he was too proud. All his life he had struggled against this sinful disposition in himself. Yet he had just spent more than two months in prison, which he had passed in prayer and meditation, ceaselessly questioning himself over his action with the boy, and he had come to the conviction that he could not have done otherwise. He was not a mystic, he said; he was a man of the soil, crude and earthly; yet at times, kneeling in his cell in the long, still hours of the night, it had seemed to him that the prison was flooded with a celestial radiance that dissolved the bars surrounding him and set his spirit free. Never had he been more convinced that he was doing God's work. Those two months had been the happiest time of his life. He would return to prison for the rest of his days with gladness in his heart, if by doing so he could persuade His Eminence to reverse his decision. He knew how difficult a decision it was to make, how everything had been taken into account. Everything but one thing, which His Eminence could not know. And that was the boy himself.

Without realizing it, he had risen to his feet and begun to pace up and down as he spoke.

He went back to the beginning. He had met young Benedek at Nagorra's presbytery, he said, and had found him in a state approaching hysteria, because of concern for his foster mother. He had tried to run away, and had had to be restrained by force. This was his first inkling that something was seriously wrong with the boy; that he was in a state of inner torment so great that his sanity was threatened. He told of the trip to Aitzmendi and the boy's collapse; his attempt at suicide while walking in his sleep; his reasons for it, the confession, the penance, the cure. He told everything, even his own first rebellion and his promise to give the boy up to his family, if that was what he wanted. How he had struggled for the boy's soul. How the boy had resisted him like a wild thing until the turning point was reached. How they had wept and prayed together the night the boy had finally and utterly accepted the hope he had held out to him, and pledged his soul to God and the Church. How eagerly and with what soul hunger the boy had drunk in his teaching in the days that followed, absorbing everything, meditating, healing himself with that knowledge. He had never known a child who had undergone a severer spiritual trial, or emerged from it more victoriously.

He talked on and on, speaking the thoughts that arose in his mind of their own volition. They presented themselves before him, clear and complete, needing only his tongue to give them expression. Pacing, lost in his narration, he had forgotten the deference due the rank of his listener. His voice rang through the still room.

"I will tell you my dream! This child has been chosen for a great destiny. He is marked. He is under the special protection of God. I have felt humble before him, as though I were instructing a strayed angel who knew things I could never hope to know. And this is the child that men would give up to forces that would destroy him! It is not for us to do this thing. I beg of you, with all the power at my command, to reconsider your decision."

Cardinal Loriol sat immobile, his head bowed slightly; only his eyes had moved during Father Vergara's appeal, fixed on his. They seemed sad, filled with an infinite pity. At times they had gleamed strangely.

Father Vergara stared at him. He had said everything. All but one thing. "Your Eminence," he said, his voice suddenly hoarse. "The Church will be judged by what she does with this boy. As the Jews were judged—"

He stopped abruptly and sat down. His fists were clenched. He looked at them wonderingly, and let his fingers open. These hands, he thought.

After a long time the cardinal stirred. "I do not dismiss your dream. I may tell you that Mother Veronica shares it. This may be a sign. But there are many paths to sainthood. If, having done all it is in our power to do to keep this child within the Church, we fail, are we not to understand that God meant us to fail, and that He has reserved some other way?"

He thought of the abbot of Cántaras, and his "Baptism is enough." It had taken the letter from Rome to win him over. But the letter was useless here. It was the cardinal himself who had obtained it, and had the authority to disregard it.

"Must we test God?" he asked. "Is it not we, rather, who are being tested?" And he quoted from Matthew: " 'The chief priests, with the scribes and ancients, said: "He saved others; himself he cannot save. If he be the king of Israel, let him now come down from the cross, and we will believe him." ' "

"You are impertinent with your parable, sir," the cardinal said sternly. "And you are bitter. You have suffered much for your conviction. But do you not think I have suffered too? For years now this unfortunate boy has been uppermost in my mind. My duty was clear, the boy had been baptized. Canon law and our tradition upheld me. He was indelibly marked with the character of the sacrament, he belonged to God. The law of the land did not provide for his safety. But our law is the law of God. He had to be saved, and only the Church could save him. I dedicated myself to that task. I prayed for guidance, I consulted the best minds among us, I took the matter to Rome. The Church could not take an official stand. We were caught between two irreconcilable positions: on the one hand, the exigencies of canon law, and on the other, a civil code that takes no account of spiritual matters. In France we have no legal existence, as we do in Spain. We are not the religion of the state, we are here on sufferance only, like all other faiths. We could not resist openly. Within these limits, what expedient have I left untried? My only recourse was to engage in delaying tactics, hoping that the family would tire of its pursuit, or that the law would eventually recognize Mademoiselle Rose's claim. I watched and waited, guiding Mother Veronica, yes, and guiding Mademoiselle Rose too, although she herself did not know it. It was I who got the boy into the Jesuit school at Cassarate, to keep him out of Konrad's clutches. It was I who located the child's other aunt, that poor disturbed woman, in an effort to postpone once more a final decision of the law. What can you tell me about this child that I do not know? Did you think his inner torment was unknown to me? I can tell you things about him that the boy himself does not know. That crucifix, for example, the one he took from the prefect's door. It has been found, over the crack in the rock where he buried the rabbit. A pathetic detail, a last futile gesture of the unconscious to turn away from the God who had brought that suffering on him. It was useless, as you yourself know. He is, as you say, in God's grip. And so, Father, are you."

This last was uttered with strange significance, as the cardinal leaned forward and stared at him. Father Vergara wanted to ask, What do you mean? But he kept silent, returning the stare.

"Watching," the cardinal went on. "Waiting. And all the while estimating the rising scandal, the damage to the Church, the loss of faith in the doubtful, the blasphemous voices that filled our public forums. But the man Konrad and his friends would not let the matter die. More than once I believed the limit had been reached, that Mother Church could no longer endure the attacks upon her. And still I waited. You took the boy to Spain, and were discovered, with all that followed. The arrests. The riots. The processions. The forces of anti-clericalism, which used the boy as a stalking horse to strike at the Church. Yet I waited. There was one hope left: Mademoiselle Rose's appeal to the Court of Cassation. We had to hold out until then. If the decision went in her favor, the law would be satisfied and would justify our position for all. That hope was dashed by the discussion of the case in the National Assembly. That scandalous session, even though it precluded executive intervention, shocked the public mind and aroused such a storm of protest that the Keeper of the Seals thought it prudent to move the case forward on the calendar. As you know, the case was heard and lost. In the lay mind we no longer have a shred of justification. And it comes at the very worst time, when passions on both sides are most inflamed. Today churches are being stoned, priests jeered at openly in the street. The Communists are making capital of our dilemma, and are winning new adherents every day. The Church has been harmed enough. We must save what is left. The decision was mine to make, and I have made it. You do not agree with it. I asked you for your reasons, and I listened while you spoke. With agony of spirit, praying all the while that God would enlighten you with the wisdom to find a way out that He had denied to me. Your answer was to point out what surrender would do to the child. Did you think I had not considered that? But what of the Church, and her God-given mission? We are forced to choose between a lesser and a greater evil. God knows I did not seek this terrible choice. On the contrary, for years I have done everything I could to avoid it. It can no longer be avoided. My duty is clear, and I must do it. And you, Father, if you sat in my place, and bore the weight of the charge God has laid on my shoulders, would do the same as I. There is no help for it. All that could be done has been done. We have failed. The boy must be returned."

Cardinal Loriol had leaned forward and spoken the last words with great force. The movement set the cross about his neck to swinging to and fro.

Father Vergara fixed his eyes on the small object. When he spoke, his own voice seemed far away to him, and leaden with despair.

"Not yet," he said.

"There is no choice."

"There must be a way."

"No. The Church can no longer resist the scandal."

"It will destroy the boy."

Cardinal Loriol said quietly, "Father, come to your senses. My patience will soon have an end. Remember the robe you wear. Would you endanger the Church of France for one boy?"

"Your Eminence—" He stopped. This drama was an old one. His eyes dwelt on the cardinal's outraged, authoritative face, which changed as he looked at it into a dark, alien visage of another land, another time. Where had he seen it before? Then the knowledge struck him, and he said the word before he could stop himself.

"Caiphas!"

Cardinal Loriol recoiled under the word as though from a blow. For an instant his eyes blazed and his hand rose, quivering with fury; then, mastering himself with a shudder, he grasped the cross and let his breath out with a deep sigh. In a voice suddenly weary he said, "May God forgive you for that undeserved insult. I shall pray for you."

Filled with a dry, helpless anger, Father Vergara did not trust himself to speak. And what was there to say? The hateful word had been uttered, it hung in the air between them, it was etched into the cardinal's brain. He could not withdraw it if he would. He studied the cardinal's drawn face, the nerve that throbbed over the cheekbone, the eyelids that the man had let droop over the pain. It was then that he realized the truth: this man was dying. It was with his last remaining bit of energy that he was attempting to wind up the long battle that had bled his Church so cruelly.

And he would die with this on his conscience.

Father Vergara's anger vanished, and pity flooded over him, and a vast sorrow for all mortals struggling blindly toward the light, for all those who suffered and caused suffering out of love of God, for the vain majesty of the figure before him, who was only a man in a scarlet robe.

And what of himself? The matter was out of his hands, closed, disposed of by an authority against which no further resistance was possible. What would happen to him now? Could he return to his presbytery and his ghost-ridden church with its handless clock, as if nothing had happened? In his mind's eye he saw himself, after his long absence, standing once again in his study, empty and forlorn, yet filled with the presence of the boy he had not been able to save. He saw his two-foot-high stack of notes on Peter, covered with dust on his cluttered table. Would he have the heart to finish his book now? Aitzmendi, on its moundlike hill under towering Choltococagna! Where in that little huddle of houses could he hide away from the terrible accusation in the soul of a betrayed child?

Misery! Misery! And was there nothing to be done? Nothing? Nothing at all? Why had the Primate sent for him? He asked the question, breaking the long silence, which had become oppressive. The cardinal stirred wearily, regarding him for a long time. "Not what you think," he said at last. "Not for you to tell me where the boy is. I knew that long ago. I have already got word to Dom Pau to have the boy in readiness for departure."

It had not occurred to Father Vergara that the cardinal did not know where Benedek was. He had assumed from the beginning that Lisiaga had told Bishop Reynaud, and this had been confirmed by Canon Blevitz' mission to Spain. The police authority would have had to be told where not to look. But he saw now that matters had gone further than he had suspected. His plea had been useless, discounted in advance; the cardinal had listened to him with a mind already closed. He could not restrain a grimace of anger as he rose to his feet.

If the cardinal saw it, he gave no sign. "A moment longer, Father, and I shall not detain you more. I must tell you of one last grace I have won for the boy. Some time ago I made overtures to the Grand Rabbi, in expectation of this day. He was powerless to make a commitment, and referred me to Monsieur Konrad. Upon the decision of the Court of Cassation, I sent an emissary to Konrad, asking for a concession. I asked that the boy be allowed to remain in France for several months after his return, to make the adjustment easier for him. And I asked that he be allowed to continue his Christian education, no matter where he might eventually be taken. Konrad is a hard man. To the first of my requests, he gave an outright no. He inquired sarcastically whether we had made allowance for the boy's adjustment in moving him from place to place. He said that the aunt has a husband who needs her. And he fears Mademoiselle Rose, who would try to see the boy, influence him, perhaps kidnap him again. Clean surgery was best, he said. As for the second point, he yielded readily, and so did the aunt. It was never a religious question with them, they said. The aunt said that there is a Franciscan monastery inhabited by French monks near her home in Israel, and that the boy would be allowed to attend services there, if he so desired. She would not prevent him, or force other teaching upon him. Perhaps you have your own opinion of Monsieur Konrad. I will tell you mine. He is a fanatic, an atheist, a Communist, a rabid anti-clerical, a Jew filled with bitterness over the treatment of his people by the world; but he is not a liar. It will be a comfort to you to know that in defeat we have gained a partial victory. The boy is not yet lost. There is still hope for him."

Father Vergara remembered Israel, its fierce nationalism, its proud, renascent Judaism, its revived language, its tough new hope. The boy would be drowned there. Smothered. If the cardinal was seeking comfort for himself . . . He shrugged.

The cardinal regarded him steadily. "You asked why I sent for you," he said, his voice taking on a new intensity. "I will tell you. Our claim has been that we did not know the hiding place of the boy. How are we to return him now? We could 'discover' him, of course, but there would always be doubt in the public mind. We must save what we can. Monsieur Konrad made a final concession. It was through his intervention that you were released from prison. Not the others. Just you."

"Oh God!" he groaned involuntarily, as the thought struck him. He raised his eyes swiftly to the cardinal's face. It was inflexible.

"It was you who took the boy into Spain," Cardinal Loriol said. "You will bring him back."

He was sitting on a stone bench under a tree in a little circular park, around which looped the cobblestoned street before returning upon itself. It was a quiet pocket in the old city, a dead end, whose ancient buildings faced the islet of trees in the center like memorials of the past. One of them was a hotel, before which a taxi was discharging passengers. He sat with his back to their gay chatter, gazing over the roofs of the houses before him at the immense bulk of the old papal palace, which rose in majesty high above, its pale walls gleaming in the sun. He thought of the so-called Babylonian Captivity, that long stretch of the fourteenth century when the popes, having been removed by force from Rome, were held in the massive pile before him like birds in a cage, at the pleasure of the arrogant French kings.

Behind him camera shutters clicked. The tourists were taking photographs of the palace. Perhaps one of these photographs, displayed triumphantly in America, would show the back of a burly priest sitting in the park. Local color.

He did not remember how he had arrived at this tranquil spot. There had been the moment when he had backed out of the cardinal's study, and pushed his way through the knot of priests waiting in the anteroom. Then there were streets, and shopwindows, and people eying him strangely as he strode among them, repeating in his mind the last exchanges of that incredible conversation. And then he was sitting here, the sweat running down his neck, wondering why his knee was hurting, until he recalled the bicycle toppling with a crash and the startled face of the young man who was clutching at him as he went over. He had helped the young man up, brushed him off, apologized; and yet, a little later, he could touch his knee in wonder.

But he knew what he had to do. The way out. The only salvation left. It had occurred to him in that instant in which he had stared up at the cardinal, and understood at last what lay before him, the final Judas role that had been assigned to him in the name of Christ and His Church. He would go to Cántaras, yes, as the cardinal had told him to do. Yes, he would remove Benedek from the school. And then—how simple it was! why had he not thought of this before?— they would run off together, he and the boy. They had done it twice before, they would do it again. But this time they would drop from the sight of everyone, the cardinal as well as Konrad. Anywhere! The world was wide enough.

He had said this to the dying man before him, whose ravaged face had creased in a smile of pity.

"You cannot. You have sworn obedience."

"You leave me no choice."

"On the contrary, the choice is there before you. It may interest you to know," the cardinal went on, observing him curiously, "that Monsieur Konrad's first reaction was the same as yours. What is to prevent him, he demanded, from running off again? My emissary assured him that it was impossible, that the first time you had acted on your own, but that now you would be under orders from your superior. But that is not truly the issue. You have shown that you are capable of defying your superiors. But you cannot defy God and God's Church. Run away? Yes, that is easy, you have only to use your legs. And then what? You would wither on the vine, and the boy with you. You cannot live without the Church, your habit is glued to your soul. There have been times in the past, I admit, when a single man has been given the grace to understand God's will more clearly than those in authority above him. Are you one of those? Are you ready to assume the awful responsibility of such a decision?"

The cardinal stared at him. Father Vergara made no answer.

He had until Sunday, the cardinal had continued. At four o'clock on that day M. Konrad and the aunt would be in the procureur's office in Garonde. He was to bring the boy to them there at that time, observing the greatest precautions to avoid publicity. How he did it was up to him. A car and a driver would be made available to him, if he wished. Once the boy was on the plane to Israel, he, Loriol, would make the official announcement.

He had tried to visualize himself handing the boy over to Konrad, and had shaken his head.

"Rebellious," Cardinal Loriol had said, while a gleam of unexpected tenderness came to his lips. "Rebellious and proud. God loves the meek, but He has, I think, a special corner in His heart for such as you. How little you know yourself! I leave my Church in your hands without a qualm. And I shall sleep tonight, for the first time in many nights."

That was when he had backed off, staring at the cardinal, who sat there, smiling, his hands playing with the crucifix about his neck.

Sunday. Would he sit here until then?

My Church, the Cardinal had said. Was it not his Church too?

He would run off. The alternative was unthinkable.

He sat there for a long time, he did not know how long. The tourists had entered the hotel and come out again, driving off in a cab, peering at him curiously through their sunglasses. A spot of sunlight had crept across the bench, had lain on his lap, passed over to the other side. Only the crests of the papal palace glittered; the lower part lay in deepening shadow. He had until Sunday. There was really no choice. But he had until Sunday. When he stood up at last, his knee had stiffened. He crossed the street, saw the concierge of the hotel staring at him, approached and humbly asked where the railroad station was. The man pointed wordlessly, still staring; then suddenly blurted out, "Bless me, Father!"

"In the name of—" He could not go on. He made the sign of the cross over the man's bowed head, and turned away. He felt the man's eyes following him as he walked off.

Sunday mornings, after mass and breakfast, Michel went to Dom Pau's cubicle, where the old monk, greeting him affectionately, sat with him at his vast worktable that stretched from wall to wall under the single window, and taught him his beloved science. This theology was far different from the watered-down stuff that was taught in class, suitable for twelve-year-olds. Dom Pau spared him nothing. "What you do not understand today, you will remember tomorrow," he was fond of saying. The sessions were hard, far harder than anything Michel had been subjected to before; and from Sunday to Sunday the thick tomes that he had to read and analyze took whatever time was left over from his routine studies. Yet Michel loved it. It was good to be studying again, after his long torment and enforced idleness, and he well knew the privilege he was being accorded in this intimate contact with a mind like that of Dom Pau. And the fiery old Catalan, considered an ogre by the boys, who quailed under his look, proved astonishingly patient with Michel, and even went so far as to grunt occasionally, "Not bad, not bad, we may make something of you yet."

Today, however, Dom Pau was sick. He had appeared at mass, but so pale, so feeble, that Michel, going up the stairs at the appointed time, expected to be turned away. But Dom Pau let him in; and, leaning on the back of a chair for support, his face grim, told him briefly to pack his bag and be ready to leave, Father Vergara was coming for him. It was so totally unexpected that only the priest's name entered Michel's consciousness. At last! he thought, full of joy. He had missed Father Vergara greatly, had asked after him, only to be told vaguely that Father Vergara was "busy." Then, understanding that he was leaving, but as yet without suspicion, he asked, "Where?" Dom Pau did not answer, but let himself sink on the edge of the couch, his face averted. Watching the old monk, Michel felt the smile freeze on his face.

Five minutes later Michel backed out of Dom Pau's cubicle, stumbled blindly down the stairs, and began to run. His boots echoed hollowly in the cloister; then he was outside, skirting the garden patch, racing across the playing field to the meadow beyond. There he tripped in the slippery long grass, and, sliding and rolling over at the same time, scrambled up and continued running, his eyes fixed unseeingly on the dark line of woods before him. It was not until he had crashed into the underbrush, and felt the branches and vines tugging at his body, slapping across his face and stinging his eyes, that he came to an abrupt stop and looked back, his breath loud in his ears. He felt stifled, choked, congealed with horror. Run! a voice inside him urged; and another pleaded, Not Father Vergara! But Dom Pau's voice was still in his ears. He was going to his aunt, it said. It couldn't be helped. Father Vergara had been in prison all this time, and now he had been released in order to come and get him and turn him over to . . . There was no mistaking the old monk's meaning, nor the shaking hand outstretched in a plea for understanding and forgiveness. Michel had said nothing, but backed away, as though Dom Pau had been converted before his eyes into a monstrous venomous insect reaching for him; and then, with no recollection of the path he had covered, he was in the woods, looking back at the still walls of the monastery.

Uttering a low moan, he began to run again. He did not know where he was going. He had to get away, anywhere, far from that face that was pursuing him, emaciated, waxen, with its narrow eyes and enormous lashes, and nose like a bird of prey. M. Konrad's face. The face of Mosé Albayucet. The two had become the same for him. But as fast as he ran, stumbling, gasping for breath, without heed of the branches catching at him, he seemed rooted to the same spot, as though it were the ground beneath him that was moving. Was he mad? Or was that laughter he heard? He was running in a cupped hand as big as the world itself, and a face as vast and blue as the sky was bending down over him, and it was all a huge cosmic joke at which the angels were splitting their sides with laughter, because that boy down there was not running at all but was sitting doubled up in a box, waiting for the princes of the synagogue to crucify him. He was staggering now, his body was drenched with sweat, and one eye was all but closed from a twig that had swiped viciously across his face; and yet he ran. It was not until he had tripped and fallen headlong, stunning himself with the impact, that he lay still and tears burst from his eyes.

The sun was high overhead by the time he had retraced his steps. Again he was at the edge of the forest. His chin cradled on his crossed arms, he lay on his stomach, his good eye fixed on the monastery. He was disheveled and streaked with sweat and dirt. His body ached all over, and blood dripped from a deep scratch along his chin, of which he was unaware until he saw the stain it made on his sleeve. He did not know why he had come back. Fences, his mind said; but he knew that wasn't so. The resolution had struck him with the same suddenness and force as his urge to escape. There had been no conscious change of intention. He had got to his feet after his fall, and to his own surprise had found himself heading back. Perhaps it was because the laughter had stopped, and an infinite, brooding sadness had taken its place. Had he wept for Michel Benedek there on the ground, clawing at the earth in his impotence? Hadn't it been, rather, for this wretched world, flawed while still fresh from the hand of God? Where love lost its way, turned against itself, festered and corrupted? It wasn't fences. Escape, where? Switzerland, France, Spain—and if he crossed the ocean, by whatever means, wouldn't other lands be shot through with the same curse, wouldn't he be the same Michel Benedek, causer of death and disaster to those who loved him? It had been his own laughter he had heard.

Yet he did not know why he had come back. The face was still there. It grinned at him like a chapfallen skull from the broken lines of the monastery walls glowing in the noon sunshine. It was as fearful as ever. Yet he could contemplate it. He lay still, the blood dripping from his chin, while through his mind marched the procession of those who had loved him, to no avail. His father, kneeling forever, in that fixed pose of grief that had followed him from his childhood and would never leave him; his mother, lying dead on a French street; Maman Rose, staring at him in surprise in the courtroom; all of them, one by one in an endless minuet, down to Chamo on the muddy table in the smoke-filled inn. Michel! Their voices whispered to him, broken with sorrow. Only one voice was missing; it lay in the future; all he had to do to hear it was to cross that meadow to where his newly refound Vati was waiting. To abandon him again.

He watched the monastery, while tired, burning tears ran down his cheeks and soaked his sleeve. Sooner or later they would come look for him. Father Vergara would come out and stand there, scanning the fields for the sight of him. And he would lie there watching, looking at that burly figure and familiar face, fixing them in his mind for the last time. And then he would go away. He tried to convince himself that this was why he had come back. What else could it be? This feeling he had, like a finger scratching at his heart, wasn't pity. Who was he to pity a Father Vergara? That was like pitying God Himself, who made His own choices, infinite in strength and wisdom. And love? Oh yes, Father Vergara loved him, he couldn't be mistaken about that. But then, how could he . . . ? This priest, this man of God, had joined the enemy, so as to get out of prison.

He was on his feet again, moved by an obscure impulse, walking within the wood but skirting its edge. Father Vergara or myself, he thought. If he comes back without me, they will put him in prison again. He moved warily among the trees, keeping his eye on the monastery, until the apple orchard across the meadow blotted it from sight. Then he crossed the meadow toward the back wall of the duke's garden. This was why he had come back, he told himself. To see if the angel was still there.

Even as he hoisted himself up the wall, he wondered at his body. He was moving like an automaton. He had only to think an action, and he was doing it, his limbs moving of their own volition. No, that wasn't it, the strange thing was that the volition seemed to be some-one else's. He had told his legs to run away, and here he was, still within sight of the monastery, hovering at the edge of discovery and disaster. Because he was sorry for Father Vergara. Because it couldn't go on. Because he couldn't keep seeking his own happiness at the expense of others. Each voice out of the past was like a chain linked to him, so that to keep on running he would have to drag the whole world with him. He had come back to see the angel, yes; but to say good-bye.

They were only men, like the rest. Not gods. Someone had to be sorry for them.

The garden stretched before him, much as he remembered it from that one view he had had of it, that Easter Sunday, when it had burst upon his dazzled sight like a magic place opening in his own heart. He had come from mass, where it was Dom Pau who had delivered the Easter sermon, entitled, "If the Seed Die Not." Dom Pau's impassioned cry still rang in his ears. " 'I am the Resurrection and the Life!' " Michel had been rapt out of himself. He had wandered about the orchard and the meadow beyond, murmuring these words to himself. And then, moved by curiosity to peek at the duke's estate, which lay alongside the monastery grounds, he had climbed the wall, as now, and he had seen—he had seen . . .

But the garden was deserted now, as he had half known it would be. The same maze of shrubbery and trees, somewhat more luxuriant now; the mound of mossy rocks, in whose crevices flowers grew, reds and blues and yellows; the tiny stream, opening into a pond drooping with languid grasses; the ancient sundial; far ahead, par-tially obscured by vegetation, the ducal palace, its windows hung with silvery drapes. But that wondrous figure, like an alabaster statue except that the breeze ruffled that cascade of golden hair and her breast rose gently to her breathing as she stared, pensive, into the water of the pond? Girl or angel, she was gone.

Michel wiped the tears from his eyes, and looked about him as though awakening from sleep. It was a glorious day; the sun shone like a blazing ball of gold in a clear sky, and the air was balmy and sweet with the fragrance of the orchards and meadows that surrounded him. In the apple orchard the blossoms were falling. They drifted down lazily from the laden branches, carpeting the black loam beneath. Across the duke's garden, over the other wall, he could see the bees swarming, drunk with nectar on that May morning, tiny specks of golden brown against the white and green.

He wanted to cry out. Why me? God, why me? He hadn't asked to be born. To bear the dreadful burden of love. To be responsible for others. But there was no rebellion left in him. He couldn't run any more, not with those chains. He had to accept it all, to swallow the world though he choked on it and begged to be let off, to be grateful for that glimpse of beauty that was the mysterious creature in the garden, girl or angel, and know that it was not for him to cherish more than her memory. Not himself. No, nor Father Vergara. God, and His will that you couldn't understand. God, and the resplendent world He had created, like the duke's garden; and then, for a single fault, had snatched away again, holding forth in its place this sorry caricature that was the reality of things, keeping that other for the afterlife, for those who had learned how to love, those who, like His own Son, had accepted the self-imposed chalice.

You could be sorry for God too.

He dropped off the wall, walked along the meadow to the apple orchard, and emerged from among the trees, facing the monastery. A heavy figure in black stood outlined against the arched passageway. The face, pale and stern, was turned toward him. Michel took two or three steps forward, then broke into a tired trot toward the waiting priest.

His back to the monastery, Father Vergara watched the boy as he ran.

It was now. Time had ended, and their lives had come to this: a boy running, a priest waiting, and God, silent, brooding over both. Both had been chosen; Father Vergara knew that now. For three days and nights of fasting and prayer, he had examined his soul as he had examined young Benedek's, stripping away the pretensions and justifications with which he had deceived himself. He, the priest of Aitzmendi, who had ripped into the boy for having tried to escape from God! And hadn't he tried to do the same thing himself? He too had given up. No, he had said to the cardinal again and again, like a self-willed child; until, his arguments answered at every turn, rendered mute by authority, in the despair that was the measure of his acceptance of defeat, he had hurled the spiteful epithet in the cardinal's face and washed his hands of the matter. You will die with this on *your* conscience, he had thought. And what of his own? Wasn't that the moment to decide to take the boy and run off with him? But no, *that* hadn't occurred to him until he had learned that it was he who would have to face young Benedek and speak the words that would shatter his spirit forever. There was no escaping the challenge. Two courses were open to him. He could turn the boy in to his family, or he could go into hiding with him. The third alternative, which was to bury himself in Aitzmendi and do nothing, was truly impossible.

He would not eat or sleep until he had chosen.

Three days and nights in his locked study, like a raging beast, until in the end he had known what he must do. There was only one choice after all. Either way the Church would survive and the boy would live. God's question lay not on them, but on him.

God had said, Abraham, Abraham. And Abraham had said, Here I am.

His eyes bloodshot, sweat matting his unshaven face, Father Vergara watched the boy run toward him.

Outside, beyond this shallow bowl of meadow warmed by the rich May sun, the world went about its business. Here, in this valley of decision, all life, all movement, had thickened and paused, so that even the boy, running, moved in languid arcs of slow motion. How far away and remote he suddenly seemed! Was it a trick of his senses, outraged beyond endurance? Or had time, drawing to its end, already begun to stretch itself into the eternity of God's mind? But it was still not too late! In this last instant, before Father Vergara opened his mouth to utter the words, the boy could turn and run away.

Run away, Benedek! Run away, Isaac, only-begotten child of my soul!

The boy ran toward him. Between each step and the next, Abraham said, Here I am, Peter dropped his nets, Christ said, Thy will be done, not mine.

How wise the old cardinal had been! Instrument of God himself, he had known that the tool does not move the hand that guides it. Dressed in his scarlet robes, his hand caressing the cross, his mission over, the cardinal sat in his thronelike chair, facing the Angel of the

Lord. His Church? He had left it in good hands. He had entrusted it to a poor parish priest, handball player, champion of liberty, biographer of saints, kidnaper of children; himself the Church he would resist. How could a Vergara assume that God cannot look after His own? Proud, rebellious, admitted. He would dare anything, except anticipate God.

He would take the boy to Konrad in Garonde. A holocaust did not require bound hands, an altar, a pile of wood, a lifted knife. And this pain that clutched his throat? But this was a feast! This was what he had been born to do!

Here I am, Father Vergara said, and stepped forward. No angel spoke. Then the boy was upon him, and the priest, incredulous, saw that streaked and suffering face full of love, the eyes brimming with tears, and the knowledge wrenched at him that the boy knew, and had still come to him; and he saw those arms opening for an embrace. Seizing the boy roughly, he thrust him back with a cry of shame. Again young Benedek tried to embrace him, and again he resisted. He said what he had to say, quickly, while he still had the strength. The boy gave no sign that he had heard, but reached out his arms again. Then Father Vergara's heart, not quite so tough as Abraham's, quailed and broke, and he turned aside and wept.